"What do I have to do to get rid of you?" Kelsey asked weakly.

Thomas laughed. "My company is that bad?"

"I just don't understand why you won't take no for an answer."

"Persuasion is part of my art." His tone was arch. "I've persuaded millions of people to buy products my face and body advertised, then had to persuade producers and directors that I wasn't just another bulging bicep above a deodorized armpit or a pair of tight buns in jockey shorts. I've persuaded television viewers to believe I'm the most clever, observant and incisively intelligent human being ever to grace the small screen as a mystery writer and murder solver, when I'm really not."

He paused significantly. "And I am going to persuade you to change your mind...."

Dear Reader,

Spellbinders! That's what we're striving for. The editors at Silhouette are determined to capture your imagination and win your heart with every single book we publish. Each month, six Special Editions are chosen with *you* in mind.

Our authors are our inspiration. Writers such as Nora Roberts, Tracy Sinclair, Kathleen Eagle, Carole Halston and Linda Howard—to name but a few—are masters at creating endearing characters and heartrending love stories. Their characters are everyday people—just like you and me—whose lives have been touched by love, whose dreams and desires suddenly come true!

So find a cozy, quiet place to read, and create your own special moment with a Silhouette Special Edition.

Sincerely,

The Editors
SILHOUETTE BOOKS

VICTORIA PADE
Breaking Every Rule

Silhouette Special Edition

Published by Silhouette Books New York

America's Publisher of Contemporary Romance

SILHOUETTE BOOKS
300 East 42nd St., New York, N.Y. 10017

Copyright © 1987 by Victoria Pade

ISBN: 0-373-09402-7

First Silhouette Books printing August 1987

America's Publisher of Contemporary Romance

Printed in the U.S.A.

VICTORIA PADE

is the mother of two energetic daughters, Cori and Erin. She laments that she has never traveled beyond Disneyland and instead has spent time plugging away at her computer. She takes breaks from her writing by indulging in her favorite hobby—eating chocolate. Her dog enjoys her fair share of candy bars, too, and they are both admitted chocoholics.

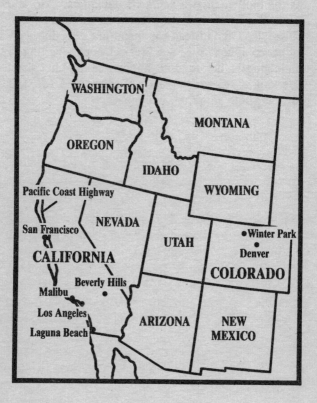

Chapter One

The jangle of the telephone summoned Kelsey and, laden with shampoo, conditioner, deodorant and bath powder, she emerged from the bathroom.

"I thought they were turning you off," she grumbled to the plain white wall phone as she rounded her Hide-A-Bed sofa and crossed the sparsely furnished studio apartment. Juggling bottles, she managed to lift the receiver and croak, "Hello?"

"Glad I caught you. I wasn't sure when you were leaving," her agent, Ali Robbins, said without preamble. "Lord, you sound awful."

"Laryngitis," Kelsey rasped. "Can you make this quick? I'm nearly late already. My bus leaves in half an hour."

"You're taking a bus to L.A.?" A strange note edged Ali's tone. "I was sure you'd be flying."

"I'm taking the Colorado Mountain Express into Denver to the airport. It's an oversize van. Winter Park isn't big enough to warrant a bus terminal," she explained with a tinge of impatience.

"His people approached me again."

Kelsey sighed but said nothing, knowing what was coming.

"He's upped the offer. One hundred thousand, Kelsey, for the screen rights alone." The agent crooned as if dangling a tempting lure. "Nothing to sneeze at, my dear. You could even afford a real apartment instead of that garret. Why not cash in on being a hot property?"

"I like my garret," Kelsey answered evenly, glancing out over the counter that sectioned off her kitchen space. The airiness of the place appealed to her. She had decorated it so lovingly, choosing calming, country shades of blue and cream for the matching chintz sofa and wing chair, the upholstered cushion of the bentwood rocker. Long hours had gone into refinishing the old ice chest angled in the corner, the single end table and the tall armoire with its flower-carved doors, each of which she'd scrounged from second-hand shops.

"It's an open space with a bathroom." Ali's description fit, too.

"Well, at least the bathroom is closed in." Kelsey pushed at a stray curl that caught on her eyelashes, unaffected by what had become almost a litany with her agent. "Tell him no, Ali." She stretched the phone cord so that she could reach her purse, which sat beside her typewriter on the claw-foot pedestal table. While Ali went on, Kelsey checked to be sure her tickets were there.

"I don't understand this."

"I know you don't." Kelsey could feel the argument coming, and she leaned against the wall to wait it out.

"You wrote a beautiful book which inexperience and lack of representation led you to practically give away for that crummy advance, and it'll still be a month or more before you even see a royalty check. I know damn well you can barely pay your bills, yet you turn down this kind of money and refuse the man of the decade the chance to make you famous by starring in it on the big screen. Are you sure you know what you're doing?"

"I'm sure." Kelsey imagined her agent shaking her precisely coiffed head and tapping an overly long ash from her ever-present cigarette.

"He wants to meet you. He thinks he can change your mind if you just hear him out."

"He's wrong."

"Oh, I don't know. The man didn't get where he is because of a shortage of charm."

"That book has already gotten me more publicity than I can handle."

"An occupational hazard, my naive friend. Resign yourself."

"Next book, maybe. But not this one. Not right now." Kelsey was quietly adamant.

"Kelsey, this kind of artistic temperament—the intrigue of the reclusive writer—is passé. This is the eighties. Mystery women have a short shelf life. The public wants to *see* who writes the books they love, get to know the author. They want glamour. And a deal with The Man would be a godsend in that department. So what are you hiding from?"

In the eighteen months since they had met at a writers' conference in Denver, Kelsey had never offered her agent any information about her personal life. She knew that Ali often had to play nursemaid to her other clients, hand-holding them through personal as well as professional problems. And she suspected that her own reticence left Ali with a burning curiosity about her. Recovering from a broken heart, her agent often guessed, though there was no basis for the supposition.

As always when anything threatened her well-guarded privacy, Kelsey treated Ali's latest questions as rhetorical and said nothing. The agent then cut the sales pitch and spoke as a friend. "He could do big, big things for you, Kelsey, and all on whatever terms you want."

"It's privacy I need, Ali, and you've just said yourself that that's exactly what I'll lose if I agree to this. Listen, if the man so much as buys gas, there's an article with pictures in every magazine and newspaper in the country. I can't handle that right now."

"I'd stick with you through every step. It wouldn't last long, anyway. Just a few pictures to go with the announcement, maybe an interview, and then you could fall back on the eccentric writer bit and be safely out of the limelight—with a very fat bank account as compensation."

Kelsey sighed. "The answer is no," she croaked. "I have to hang up. If I miss this bus, I'll be stuck up here."

The sound of Ali's long fingernails drumming on her desktop preceded a sigh of her own. "I really want you to think this over. If word gets out that you're afraid of publicity, it could be more costly than you realize." She let a weighty pause elapse. "Don't forget to call me the minute you get in. I may have news on the auction of the new book, and who knows when you might have to decide on an offer? A beach house, isn't it? It'll do your laryngitis good. Is it just in your throat, or are you all red-nosed and watery-eyed, too?"

"I look gorgeous," she deadpanned. "Now will you let me get off this phone?"

"Okay, okay."

"Goodbye, Ali."

"Kelsey..." More silence. "Oh, hell, never mind. Have a good trip."

The dial tone hummed in her ear, and Kelsey was relieved that she had been spared yet another of Ali's attempts to convince her. A glance at the Ben Franklin clock on the red brick wall of her living room sent her hurrying to the refrigerator without another thought.

The stocky white relic only reached the shoulder of her five-foot-four-inch frame. From the butter bin in the door she withdrew a plastic bag containing a foil-covered package. After peeling away the wrappings, she counted the stack of money there—twice—and then put it into a manila envelope, which she buried in the very bottom of her crescent-shaped leather purse.

For a moment she surrendered to tension, feeling it roil in her chest and shorten her breath as if she had just run a mile. She swallowed and dropped her head forward to ease the kink in her neck, letting her long, unruly hair drape down around her glasses. What she wouldn't give to stay secluded in the little mountain town of ski slopes, condominiums and shops disguised as Swiss chalets. The sparsely populated one-street village had been her refuge. But she couldn't hide forever. She was being pushed and prodded into the public eye, no matter how hard she fought it.

Kelsey snapped her head back up and shrugged her shoulders into a straight, strong line. "We're all responsible for our own actions," she lectured herself, "and sooner or later we answer for them."

After once again grabbing the toiletries she'd had in her hands when she answered the phone, she wedged them into the sides of a worn tapestry suitcase, zipped it closed, got a firm grip on it and tugged her purse strap up onto her shoulder. She took one last look around the apartment, then closed the door behind her and secured its three bolts. Then Kelsey McKenna made a mad dash to catch her bus.

Stepping through the hatch of the plane, Kelsey was so late that not even a flight attendant waited to check her ticket. Her seat—first class, front row, on the aisle—was easy enough to find, however, and she went straight to it. The expensive seat had cost her half the money she'd saved for March's rent, but if she had to fly, this was the only way her claustrophobia would allow.

Pulling her oversize gray cowl-necked sweater down over baggy blue jeans, Kelsey settled onto the bright orange cushion and fastened her seat belt tight. Next week at this time her ordeal would all be over.

She slid her big round reading glasses up her forehead to perch atop her wildly curly long auburn hair and leaned her head back. What a sore throat she had. A flat tire on the way had delayed the ski shuttle, leaving her no time to stop at the airport sundries store for cough drops. Instead, she had been forced to run down Stapleton's long corridors to concourse C, leaving her throat as dry as tree bark.

A pleasant-voiced flight attendant stopped beside her, asking to see her ticket. Afterward Kelsey let her head fall back again and closed her eyes. I'm really not up to this right now, she thought. But then there would never be a time when she was. She tucked her purse firmly between her thigh and the armrest.

Keeping her eyes closed, she tried to ignore the minor commotion surrounding the passenger who boarded just before the hatch closed. Then a slight jarring alerted Kelsey that the window seat beside her had been taken. Curiosity pried her long dark eyelashes open. First class was rarely so full that anyone sat in the very next seat.

Thomas Quinn-Patrick Sullivan!

If the hatch had still been open, she would have made a run for it.

She snapped her head forward before he looked up from securing his own seat belt. The panicked pounding of her heart in her ears was louder than the din of the jet engines starting up. From the corner of her eye she looked again to be sure he was who she thought he was, and then she craned her neck to peer at the rows of seats behind them. Empty, every one. Maybe it was paranoia, but she didn't believe his sitting next to her was a coincidence.

A monotonous roar filled the plane throughout the orchestrated instructions about seat belts, smoking and emergencies. Kelsey tried to calm herself with the thought that there was no way the actor could know who she was. She had allowed no publicity pictures. And how would he have known she'd be on this flight? But Ali's last-minute hesitation on the phone niggled at her composure.

The jolt of lift-off pressed Kelsey into her seat. Still she pretended not to notice the man beside her. But in her mind's eye the image of him was vivid. Six feet four inches of broad-shouldered masculine beauty. Five years ago, when his television series had first started, the mere sight of him on posters and magazine covers had made her stomach tighten. But now he was hounding her, agent to agent, for the screen rights to *A Second Season*.

Drawn to peek at him again from the corner of her eye, she saw that he was even better-looking in person, if that was possible. In silent awe she took in thick, wavy hair the color of summer wheat, the classic nose of Michelangelo's *David* above a full mustache that seemed to shimmer with reddish gold. His angular cheekbones and jaw kept his particular brand of beauty rugged.

Kelsey swallowed uneasily, assuring herself that the tightening in her stomach was what she got for skipping breakfast and lunch.

There was a dull ping, and the Fasten Seat Belts sign overhead darkened. Kelsey left hers on but, feeling suddenly constrained by it, loosened the tight cinch that usually made her feel more secure. Was he looking at her? She swallowed again, harder this time. You're no friend, Ali Robbins, she thought darkly.

"Can I get you something?" A stewardess appeared at her elbow, smiling warmly over Kelsey's head.

"Just coffee, thanks" came a low, gravelly voice richer than it sounded on television.

"And you?"

Kelsey heaved a sigh of resignation. "I'd perform unnatural acts for a throat lozenge, but I'll settle for a cup of tea."

The woman left, and Kelsey scanned the aisle uneasily. Thomas Quinn-Patrick Sullivan's voice eased around her, sounding smooth, confident and amused.

"Will a sour ball do?"

She had to look at him then. He was smiling, crinkling the laugh lines around sea-green eyes that seemed to sparkle with satisfaction. Without waiting for an answer, he reached for a flight bag beneath his seat. Kelsey's glance followed like a shadow. His khaki-clad thighs were spread to accommodate his long arms, one knee nearly touching hers. His wrists were bare beneath the pushed-up sleeves of a cream-colored nubby silk sweater, and honey-colored hair lightly dusted them and the backs of his hands. When his right hand came back up, he held one twisted end of a cellophane-wrapped candy between his thumb and long index finger as if it were bait. Again came that challenging grin. "What unnatural acts will you perform for it?"

"Lie on a bed of nails or walk barefoot over hot coals. They're my only tricks."

His expression was knowing as he handed her the candy. "How much time do we have to waste pretending we don't know each other?"

"We *don't* know each other."

His smile was smug. "We haven't met, but we know each other."

"My agent," she said in confirmation. "I can't believe she did this to me."

"Not easily, I assure you. It cost me a trip to New York, flowers, dinner and more persuasion than it takes to get terrorists to put down their guns. And all I got was a pretty vague hint that you were flying out of Denver this afternoon. I could have had an audience with the Queen of England more easily than getting to you."

Their coffee and tea arrived, allowing Kelsey a minute to gather her thoughts. When they were alone again, she turned her eyes squarely to his. "Look, Mr.—" Was it Sullivan alone or Quinn-Patrick Sullivan all together?

"Try Thomas," he suggested.

"You've been misled. I am not interested in selling the rights to *A Second Season*, no matter what the price. A personal appearance may have impressed my agent, but it won't get you anywhere with me." The strength of her tone weakened as the plane lunged through an air pocket, making her grip the arms of her seat.

"Afraid of flying?" Sympathy rumbled in his voice, but so did more of his amusement.

"No," she answered too quickly. In a more measured tone she added, "I am not afraid of flying. Only of crashing."

That made him laugh, but he immediately returned to his original subject. "After three months of bickering through agents for the screen rights to *A Second Season*, I decided it was time we hashed it out ourselves. But let's get one thing straight so I don't cause undeserved trouble: Ali Robbins didn't set this up, and she didn't give me any hope that I might be able to sway you. The only thing she said when I suggested that she arrange a meeting between us was that it was impossible because you were leaving town. My secretaries spent all last night checking airline reservations until they found your name. For all either of us knows, it could have been an unconscious slip of the tongue that gave me even that much information," he added in her agent's defense.

"Ali Robbins is not stupid."

"She's looking out for your best interests."

"Or yours."

He shook his head in denial. "I wanted a chance to explain it to you myself, bare my soul. What harm is there in that?"

What harm? He was so close that she could smell the airy scent of him and see every one of his thick eyelashes. Her gaze fell to the broad shoulders that stretched the silk weave of his sweater, and her memory supplied her with a vivid image of his bare, muscled chest and athlete's thighs, which were shown as often as contrivance would allow on his show every week. Kelsey had never felt so light-headed over the nearness of any man. What harm, indeed?

She tried to concentrate on his words again, only to find he had stopped speaking and was smiling patiently at what he read all too clearly in her dazed expression.

"You were saying?" She tried to cover up her distraction too quickly, and her voice came out in a husky whisper that sounded like a poor attempt at Mae West. His smile widened into a thoroughly entertained grin, and Kelsey wanted to melt and slither into an unobtrusive puddle beneath the seat. No doubt he was constantly surrounded by dumbstruck women, and now he must think her one of them.

Kelsey cleared her throat and tried to undo the image. "Then bare it and get it over with." Oh, no, it was getting worse! And he was enjoying it more. She closed her eyes tightly and spoke carefully. "Just give me your sales pitch so I can refuse it and be done with this."

She heard him chuckle, a low, throaty rumble that was almost his trademark. And then her eyes flew open as one of his knuckles feathered from the crest of her cheekbone to her jaw.

"Do you know how long it's been since I've seen a woman blush?" he murmured. "You're not what I expected, Kelsey McKenna." The tip of his thumb traced the underside of her jaw, and he smoothed a strand of her hair behind her shoulder.

Kelsey jerked her head away as if to flee the tingly sensation left in the wake of his fingers. "Business, remember?"

Apparently not. "I expected some hard-as-nails bitch who took pleasure in trying to make me sweat. Instead, I find a wild-haired bohemian who blushes and can't fill out her clothes," he teased.

"Should I be flattered?" Sarcasm was her defensive reaction to his description of her—and to the chills his penetrating gaze sent skittering over her skin.

He shrugged. "It was a compliment." Then he went on as if he were thinking aloud. "Lovely eyes. When you get angry, they turn nearly black."

Kelsey wondered if he'd said it just to see her face turn scarlet instead of pink, and it infuriated her that her cheeks obliged him. His glance alone seemed to reach for her, and she leaned away from him.

"What do I have to do to get rid of you?" It came out weakly and only made him laugh again.

"My company is that bad?"

"I just don't understand why you won't take no for an answer. The screen rights for *A Second Season* are not for sale. Not to you. Not to anyone."

"Ah, but persuasion is part of my art." His tone was arch but self-deprecating. "I've persuaded millions of people to buy products my face and body have advertised, then had to persuade producers and directors that I wasn't just another bulging bicep above a deodorized armpit or a pair of tight buns in jockey shorts. I've persuaded viewers to believe I'm the most clever, observant and incisively intelligent human being ever to grace the small screen as a mystery writer-murder solver, when I'm really not. And I am going to persuade you to change your mind."

Kelsey sipped her tea.

"Much as I hate to sound egotistical, I have to ask you something. Is Jonathan Martin me?"

The hero of *A Second Season*, Jonathan Martin, was the head of an immigrant family in the U.S. He fell deeply in love with an unattainable woman and vowed to have her at any cost. The novel traced ten long years of his life, chronicling his determination to bring himself and his family up through the social and financial ranks, as well as his continuing affair with Anna, until both Jonathan and love triumphed in the end.

"What makes you think you're Jonathan Martin?" Kelsey questioned noncommittally. The most attractive physical aspects of the character had indeed come from watching Thomas Quinn-Patrick Sullivan on television.

After all, he was a prime model for a romantic hero. But Kelsey wasn't about to admit it. Besides, there was much more to the character than a visual impression.

"I'll be honest with you." He was all business now, and Kelsey almost missed the teasing. "The book has all the right elements to be commercially successful—sex, glitz and glamour, triumph against all odds—everything. But Jonathan Martin touched something—some chord—deep inside me. It's hard to know whether what you wrote has such universal appeal that every man will find himself in it—in the sensitivity and vulnerability he camouflages so well—or whether the character was really based on things you saw in me with some—" he grimaced at his own mysticism "—some psychic perception or insight or something."

He sighed before continuing. "It's not as if much about me is left private, but you hit on things I make sure aren't open for public scrutiny. The truth is, that's not only intriguing but a little eerie, too. Still, it makes Jonathan Martin so three-dimensional that I know he's the perfect part to launch me into more serious work."

When he frowned, his eyebrows nearly met over eyes that darkened to the shade of a troubled sea. He went on, confidentially, intimately, lowering his head slightly to peer into her eyes. "I don't hear words from out of nowhere the way you must to write them. I wish I did. I can only interpret what someone else has created. It isn't fair for you to create something that does this to me and not let me use it. Don't you see that I can give your words voice?"

Several moments passed, and still he held her eyes with his as if to convey how serious he was. Kelsey couldn't help but wonder if his seeming sincerity was merely a beautiful performance by an accomplished actor. But it didn't really matter. Regardless of how genuine he seemed, there was more to her refusal than he realized. She simply couldn't reward his honesty—if that was what it was—with her own, any more than she could give him what he wanted from her. Instead, she offered him a little history to soften the refusal.

"Jonathan Martin is based on my grandfather's life. He came to the United States to escape the turmoil in Ireland and started his own liquor distribution business—at a time when it wasn't altogether legal. Over and over again I heard the story of how determined he was to win my grandmother, so it seemed natural to use that information as the basis of my novel. But the book was fiction. After Prohibition ended, my grandfather lived a relatively ordinary life and never aspired to anything beyond a small distributorship in Denver. But it was a very personal book to me. In a way, it gave me the courage to escape some turmoil of my own. I'm flattered that it made you feel so much, but I can't sell you *A Second Season*."

A small smile made his mustache quiver. His voice was as soft as hers, hypnotic, beckoning. "You can trust that I'll do it justice, that I'll use the same kind of care you put into the writing. This isn't just another project to me. It's as personal as a biography."

"Oh?" She had to break this spell he was weaving around her, and teasing seemed the safest route. "From what I read, you have a legion of Annas following you through life. That's nothing like poor Jonathan working so hard for one."

He frowned at first, but then he seemed to give in to her need to ease the mood. He winked. "I hate to shatter the image, but I feel as if I've been denied that one...so far."

"The libidinous Thomas Quinn-Patrick Sullivan? I can hardly believe that."

"Libidinous? I beg your pardon."

Kelsey laughed, and his handsome face moved in close again in mock surprise. "She does smile. I was beginning to doubt it. And with great teeth—no gaps, no caps, no fillings. Sign her up for the toothpaste commercial." He sat back in his seat, clasping his hands over his flat belly, his long legs out straight and crossed at the ankles. "What about you, Ms. McKenna? Are you attached to a husband? A live-in lover, perhaps?"

"If you're looking for someone to take hostage to force me to sell, you're barking up the wrong tree."

"Actually, it was a subtle way of finding out if I have any competition."

"For the book?" She was confused.

"For the writer."

Kelsey sidestepped that one. "What's wrong with your television show? Last I heard, it was the most highly rated series in the history of TV."

"Don't get me wrong. I appreciate everything TV has given me, made me, but I didn't dream my dreams in front of a television. I dreamed them sitting for hours and hours in a movie theater. If I never make it in films, I'll never feel as if I've really succeeded." Again his words rang with honesty. "Too many people, talented people, don't make the transition. I've been looking for just the right piece to launch me, and *A Second Season* is it. Every instinct tells me so. You made magic on the printed page, lady—magic I know will work *for* me because it's already worked *on* me."

Kelsey took a deep, steadying breath and wondered at how much he tempted her. This time it was with genuine regret that she answered him. "I'm sorry, but right now I can't let it happen. I have to say no."

"What's the biggest problem here? Tell me and I'll fix it."

Her laugh was tinged with minor hysteria at the thought. "The problem is something only I can fix, and any connection with you would complicate it disastrously." But he had touched her more deeply than he knew and her refusal wavered. "Maybe in a few months I can consider it, but not right now."

"Then just sell me the first option for it. We'll settle it all when you're ready."

She shook her head. "No. That would complicate things just as much as an outright sale would. I can't do it."

"This doesn't make sense. Give me a damn reason." His frustration sounded for the first time.

"I can't do that, either." She sighed, groping for a way to convince him she was serious. "People will be hurt by it. My answer has to be no."

"How could this possibly hurt anyone? I'll give you full creative control if that's what it takes."

"Control has nothing to do with it."

His handsome face was suddenly one tight, cynical frown. "Name your price."

The insinuation in his tone made Kelsey's face redden in anger. She spoke very slowly. "Nothing. No amount of money. No amount of persuasion. I will not sell the rights to *A Second Season* to you or to anyone else. If I decide to do it in a few months, you'll be the first to know."

His deep green eyes held her nearly black ones until another flight attendant appeared to remove their trays for landing. Kelsey seized the opportunity offered by the interruption, flipping her glasses down onto the bridge of her nose with a definite show of finality and grabbing a magazine from the seat's side pocket.

Thomas's low, exasperated exclamation claimed her attention. "Look, I don't want to tick you off. But neither do I want to lose this chance by sitting on my thumbs. In a week I wrap up the last show of this season. I want to spend my hiatus filming *A Second Season*. Your 'few months' would cost me another year before I could do it, and then we'd both lose the benefit of the publicity it's already generated by being the sleeper of the season that skyrocketed to the top of the bestseller lists. Tell me where you're staying in L.A., and we'll get together and talk this through.''

"There's nothing to talk through. My answer is no, and it will stay no for the time being.''

The Fasten Seat Belts sign pinged on, and the pilot's disembodied voice informed them they would be landing in L.A. in five minutes.

Thomas clicked his seat belt into place as Kelsey replaced the magazine and tugged hers tight. She slid her glasses onto the top of her head once more and clenched both armrests as if the pilot had announced a crash landing.

Thomas's anger seemed to dissipate, and he conceded to sympathy. "You know, there are thousands more automobile accidents every day than plane crashes a year. I'll bet you aren't afraid of getting into a car.''

"You'd lose your money," she said tightly.

Without asking or warning, he took her hand from the armrest and closed his much bigger, warmer one around it comfortingly. His touch was electric, and she yanked out of his grip. "Don't do that!" Her black eyes were wide.

"Didn't anyone ever tell you it helps to have human contact when facing your fears?''

"No.''

He pulled her hand back, holding it too firmly for her to escape him again. His elbow was cradled in the crook of her arm, settling them in close together for the landing. His "human contact" worked wonders. For the moment her pounding heart had nothing to do with fear.

"Where are you staying?" he repeated.

The jet lost altitude, and Kelsey's face lost color. But still she managed indignation. "None of your business."

Her senses were in overdrive. Fear put a buzz into her ears and dried her mouth. The light, clean scent of Thomas Quinn-Patrick Sullivan and the feel of his hand wrapped around hers sent her body temperature soaring and her skin into an all-over tickle. Dammit, the last thing she needed right now was to go into some sort of tizzy over a man.

The bouncing jolt of touchdown blanched Kelsey's face whiter still. Thomas squeezed her hand more tightly. "My Lord, your fingers are like ice. We're all right. Look outside. We're on the ground, just rolling up to the terminal. Take it easy."

The plane slowed, and Kelsey breathed more normally, letting her shoulders sag from the stiffness of tension. Sanity returned, leaving only the unwanted pleasure of his nearness. "I don't need this in my life right now." Her thought found voice.

He squeezed her hand and spoke in a barely audible tone that seemed to hint at more than just screen rights, "If you want to get rid of me, give me what I want."

Kelsey's only answer was to yank herself from his grip, flip her seat belt free and grab her purse with a vengeance. Thomas's hand snaked out to clasp her wrist and stop her from escaping as the hatch was slid open. "I'm not giving up," he warned.

A flight attendant blocked the passage that connected first class to coach, keeping the other passengers from realizing who occupied the front section. Another waited with a quizzical smile for them to disembark.

"I'll let you know if I ever decide to sell."

Still he held on to her, and Kelsey began to wonder if he was ever going to let her go. Then she had the unnerving thought that she wished he wouldn't. Fighting the feeling, she shot sparks with the voice of a frog. "You're keeping an entire planeful of people waiting."

His square jaw clenched. He glanced back at the press of people wanting to disembark and finally let go of her wrist. After pulling his flight bag from beneath the seat, he stood to his full towering height. "I'll find you, Kelsey McKenna. We aren't finished with this." And then his long legs took him quickly out of the plane.

Kelsey followed slowly behind, stepping from the ramp just in time to hear a question from one of the crowd of reporters that had surrounded Thomas Quinn-Patrick Sullivan within three feet of the gate.

"Is it true you're negotiating for rights to material for your first feature film?"

Her glance up was quick and startled, meeting those arresting green eyes above the group that had swallowed him. She saw him shake his head in denial but was unable to hear his answer. Held to the spot for a moment longer, Kelsey witnessed the approach of security guards forcing their way through to free a path for him to leave. All around her people stopped to gawk and crane their necks for a look at the man, for the sound of what he was saying.

To Kelsey the sight of so many intently watching eyes gave new strength to her determination not to be involved with this man in any way. It was just this public exposure that frightened her to death . . . and that her life could not bear.

Chapter Two

The lacquer-black Porsche streaked down Pacific Coast Highway just after midnight the following night. The early-March air was still, the sky clear of all but stars. Inside the car the soft strains of a jazz fusion tape were the only sounds as Kitridge Mason maneuvered through the relatively light traffic and Thomas Quinn-Patrick Sullivan stared out the side window.

"When do I get to know why we're headed to Laguna Beach in the middle of the night?" came the baritone voice of Hollywood's newest rising producer-director star as he reached to turn down the volume of the cassette player.

Thomas's head jerked around at the sound of his friend's voice. "Hmm—what?"

"Come in from the ozone, Thomas. As of four this afternoon, you're off the hook with that paternity suit, remember? There's no more reason to be so preoccupied."

"Paternity suit?" Thomas parroted dimly, his thoughts elsewhere. He rubbed his eyes as if to clear them. "Oh, yeah. I'm glad it's over. Nice baby, though. Funny. Lots of personality. I think he liked me."

Kit's brown eyes left the road long enough to take a good look at his passenger. "You sound sorry it wasn't yours."

Thomas shrugged, and because Kit was one of the few people in the world he numbered among his true friends, he admitted, "Maybe for a minute. Unfortunately, he came equipped with a barracuda for a mother."

"I think you're ready again, pal."

"Ready?"

"Marriage. Babies. It's not as if you're a kid. Thirty-five is a reasonable age for a second try. And you've certainly sewn enough wild oats. You've been making a lot of noises like you're ready, all right. After those pictures of you playing with that baby, it's a good thing the blood test cleared you, or they would have nailed you for sure. I thought you had hanged yourself. I was wondering if that might have been your intention," Kit pried.

"I told you, I never even met that woman before. The baby's blood type being different than hers or mine backed me up."

"Oh, I believed you. But kissing the kid looked incriminating as hell. Not to mention that it probably inspired a hundred other women to bring their little darlings to your attention. Next time the test might not be so conclusive."

"Don't worry, Kit. I've sworn off."

"Celibate? You?" Kit burst into disbelieving laughter. "Do I look like someone other than the man who arranged the blind date that rid you of your virginity, the man who has known most of the details of your sex life for the past twenty years?"

"Let's just say I'm reevaluating my life and what I want and need in it." Why did Kelsey McKenna's face pop back into his mind? That had been happening too often since he left her yesterday. It was like a song that played over and over in his thoughts whether he liked it or not.

"So, you still haven't told me why we're on this midnight jaunt," Kit reminded him, sending him a quick but probing glance.

Thomas didn't understand his own inclination toward secrecy in this matter. He and Kit had been working on a screenplay for *A Second Season* since they had first managed to get hold of the galleys. Of course, no one else knew about it. Until the rights were purchased, it wasn't theirs to do anything with. But Kit was as enthusiastic over the project as Thomas was. It would be a blockbuster, a career coup for them both, as well as a chance for them to work together. But for some reason Thomas suddenly found himself reluctant to let his friend in on Kelsey McKenna. It just didn't make sense.

"Kelsey McKenna is supposed to be at a beach house out here."

Kit's too-bushy red eyebrows arched in pleasant surprise, and excitement made his tone crisp. "Our old battle-axe is within reach?"

The joint possession rubbed him wrong, but Thomas hid it with a chuckle over one of their many unflattering predictions about the reluctant writer. Again she came to his mind's eye to taunt him with a reminder of what she was really like. Untidy long hair, a slight frame tantalizingly hidden beneath too-big clothes that dared him to wonder what they hid, peaches-and-cream skin that he was a total sucker for—a novelty among the carefully maintained suntans that surrounded him. He remembered all too clearly her wide coffee-colored eyes, her long, thin nose and the pale mouth that he had had an inordinate yen to kiss. He even liked her funny owlish spectacles—on her face and on top of her head. "She's not quite what our frustrations pictured," he finally responded.

The hesitation in that admission sparked Kit's curiosity, and his pale gaze rested on his friend for a moment too long. He had to hit the brakes hard to ease off a Volkswagen's tail. "Better or worse?"

"Better." It came without missing a beat.

"Are you going to let me in on this?"

Thomas was disgusted with himself. He knew it was unfair to leave Kit in the dark over anything to do with *A Second Season*. But, damn, these were strange feelings. It almost seemed like jealousy. To prove to himself that it wasn't, he relented. "To make a long story short, I finagled a meeting with her on a flight from Denver yesterday." He raised a palm to hold back his friend's enthusiasm. "I didn't get anywhere with her. She refused me all the way down the line."

"Oh?" Strong suspicion echoed in the black leather interior. "Are we talking about more than just the book here?"

Thomas rubbed the back of his neck. It had sounded like that, hadn't it? "I meant the book. Anyway, she wouldn't even tell me where she was staying. All I could get out of her was that she might make it available to us in a few months."

Kit groaned.

"I know. I explained what that would mean. I had every intention of finding out where she was and keeping at her."

"About the book," Kit goaded him.

"Yes, about the book, dammit. But before I had the time to pursue it, her agent called me."

"McKenna had a change of heart!"

"Not quite. She's disappeared again."

Kit's groan was deeper this time. "What's with that woman, anyway?"

"It may not be as bad as it sounds. She just failed to check in with Robbins the way she promised to. Could be she's mad at her agent for giving me the information to find her. She isn't answering her phone, so I tracked down the rental agent. He gave me the number of the people who live in the other half of the duplex, and I checked with them. She went in yesterday and hasn't come back out. If she doesn't answer the door, they have a key to let us in—just in case something has happened to her."

Kit glided the sleek little car around a motor home. "But you haven't alerted the FBI, the CIA or the Coast Guard?"

Thomas gave in to a smile at his friend's straight-man delivery. "Very funny. I suppose it wouldn't matter to you if this whole thing went up in smoke?"

"It would matter like hell. But all of a sudden that seems like nothing compared to what it means to you."

Thomas turned up the stereo.

Kit turned it back down.

"Something you're not telling me, Thomas?"

"Slow down or you're going to miss Laguna altogether."

In belated compliance with the decreased city speed limit, Kit eased up on the accelerator of his favorite toy, scratching his nose to hide a grin. "What's up, Sullivan?"

"God, you're nosy. Did anyone ever tell you that?"

"That serious, is it?"

Thomas sighed elaborately and rolled his window down a crack. The confines of the small car somehow seemed closer. "I met the woman and tried to persuade her to agree to sell the screen rights. She refused. I cajoled. She refused. I damn near begged. She refused. I confided. She refused. I told her to name her price. She refused. I got mad. She got mad. I tried to smooth things over. She still refused. That's it.''

''Sounds like you hit it off.''

''You better take it slower so I can read house numbers. From the address Ali Robbins gave me, it should be in the center of town—a duplex on the public beach.''

''Maybe I should take it from here, and you should stay out of sight. I don't want to lose this because you and the lady hate each other.'' Kit was teasing him.

''No,'' Thomas answered hastily, in so doing telling his friend all he needed to know. ''We don't hate each other.''

''I didn't think so.''

''She's just the most stubborn damn person I've ever met in my life. It should be up about two more blocks.''

Kit finally gave in to his friend's attempt to let the subject drop. But he could barely contain his excitement over meeting Ms. Kelsey McKenna.

Pacific Coast Highway had narrowed to Laguna's main street, which was jammed even at that late hour. The houses that lined it—a hodgepodge of styles, structures and colors—were all barely an arm's length apart, like new pups nudging for position at their mother's belly.

A surge of eagerness to see Kelsey again surprised Thomas. It was the book, he told himself. Only because of the book. ''There it is.'' He pointed to a pea-green clapboard house.

Kit swung into the center of the double driveway. ''Which side?''

''Left.''

''She must be home. Every light in the place is on, upstairs and down. Sure we aren't crashing a party?''

''I don't hear anything.''

"Maybe it's private."

Thomas ignored the remark and got out of the car, slamming the door.

"Not so hard," Kit berated him, closing his own more carefully before he followed, a much shorter shadow of his friend.

The house was a shabby little place crushed between a much nicer white stucco and a well-tended cedar. But that was the way of this last street before the beach: some houses were kept crisp and neat against sea-salt decay; others had owners more interested in the life out back on the sand.

Long, hurried strides took Thomas to the small slab of cement that was the front porch. The air was a chill, slightly salty tang, and from behind the wall of houses came the soft, rhythmic wash of waves against the beach. It was a lulling atmosphere, but it did nothing to soothe him.

Calm down, Sullivan. What's with you? You haven't been this anxious to see a woman since you were fifteen. What was there about Kelsey McKenna that drew him? Was it just the book, the thought that she had some sort of extra sensitivity to him, to the side of him he kept from public view? Could he be as fanciful as his own fans, intrigued by some image he had of her through her work? That would be an ironic twist when he himself was so fed up with just that kind of admiration.

But the feel of her hand was a memory so real that he had to rub his palm down his thigh to convince himself he didn't still have hold of her. Was the rest of her that soft? That smooth? That sweet? Would she mold that contained little body to him with as much abandon as did Anna, the woman she had created, the woman who had enraptured him on paper? Or would Kelsey McKenna be as reserved and guarded as she had seemed on the plane the day before? Ah, but the challenge of being the one to break down those barriers she had erected around herself, to be the one she finally let see what she hid so well—there was allure in that.

If he was to bet on it, he'd say there was fire smoldering there, waiting for a breath of air to feed the flames. It was there in the flash of those dark eyes, in the wildness of the auburn hair she left uncontrolled. It struck him suddenly that he wanted to be the one to find and feed that flame. God, how he wanted to be the one.

There was an empty hole in the metal plate where the doorbell should have been, so Thomas knocked and waited. Beside him, Kit peered over at the darkened windows of the neighbor's half of the house. Again Thomas pounded, harder this time, and again there was no answer.

When the third rap on the door still caused nothing to stir, Thomas rounded the garage to the other tenant's side. While he roused the neighbors, Kit tried futilely to see into the house. Back again, Thomas plied the key, turned the handle and tried to open the door, only to find it would not budge more than a hair's breadth. He put a shoulder to it and shoved, but the door was blocked from the inside.

"Kelsey! Are you in there?"

No answer.

"Kelsey, it's Thomas Sullivan."

Still no answer.

"What now?" Kit asked from his stance in the bushes, where he watched for signs of movement inside.

"Hell," Thomas answered irately. "They said next door that unless she snuck out in the middle of the night, she has to be in there." He tried calling again, with the same lack of response.

"Looks as if she's determined not to be bothered." Kit stepped back from the bushes and slid his hands into the back pockets of light blue corduroy pants. "Are you sure we aren't doing more damage by not respecting that?"

"And what if something's happened to her? With all the creeps who hang out on these public beaches, it's not as if it's safe around here."

With no further argument Thomas circled Kelsey's half of the house, checking for open windows. None on the lower level were open, but he spotted one on the second floor where the curtain was sucked up tight against the screen.

By the time Kit caught up with him, Thomas had pulled a ladder from where it rested against the half-painted side of the house next door, had set it just beneath the open window and was three rungs up.

"What the hell are you doing, Thomas?" Kit exclaimed in an urgent whisper.

"I'm getting into this house to see what's going on," the taller man called back as he climbed.

"Have you gone crazy? You'll get us arrested for breaking and entering—if you don't break your neck first."

"Just hold the ladder steady, will you?" At the top Thomas again called for Kelsey, but there was no response from that level, either. Ignoring Kit's reasoning, Thomas worked the screen loose.

"I'm going in," he called down to his friend. Then he shouted into the house, "Be warned, Kelsey McKenna: I'm coming in."

While Kit glanced around guiltily, Thomas turned the screen sideways and slid it through the curtain. The crash of glass screamed through the quiet of the night as the screen knocked into something on the other side of the ragged yellow drapes.

"What are you doing up there?" Kit demanded nervously.

Thomas ignored his friend and hoisted himself onto the ledge and over the sill, being careful to avoid what was now a pile of broken brown water tumblers on the bedroom's linoleum floor. For a moment he stayed put, getting his bearings and half expecting Kelsey to appear at any moment. The room was bare except for a twin bed made up in a ratty chenille spread. Kelsey's tapestry suitcase lay open on top of it. A second window faced the ocean, and pyramided in front of the mismatched orange curtains were six juice glasses.

When she didn't appear, he called, "Kelsey! Are you here?" But all remained quiet, still.

An empty bathroom was the only other room on the top floor. Thomas stopped at the head of the stairs, just short of kicking over a tower of clay coffee mugs. "What the hell is all this?" he muttered as he descended the steps. About halfway down his foot hit a tennis ball can and slid out from under him. Lightning reflexes kept him from falling as he clutched the banister and saw the can roll to the entrance below and bang into the metal leg of a vinyl kitchen chair whose back was shoved under the knob of the front door—the barricade that had prohibited a more conventional entry.

He made his way more carefully to the bottom of the stairway, dislodging the ugly red chair to open the door. Kit was nowhere in sight, so Thomas called to him and then left the door open as he explored further.

Again Thomas hollered for Kelsey as he passed through the kitchen at the front of the house. There he found four crude chimes, which were fashioned of spoons tied around the stems of wineglasses and hung from the rod within the folds of red-check curtains. From the dining area, its windows likewise rigged, Thomas headed through the arched entrance to the living room. He missed the length of kitchen twine stretched low across the doorway. His shin caught it, causing two barrel chairs to tumble with an enormous racket.

Up came Kelsey from amid a shroud of blankets on a brown couch against one wall, a wooden rolling pin held like a club in one hand, her wide eyes glazed.

"Don't come any closer!" she warned, waving the rolling pin, her ashen face pulled into a fierce frown.

Thomas's hands went out, palms first, to ward her off. "Take it easy, Kelsey. It's Thomas Sullivan, remember?"

Her brows arched high for a moment before she forced her eyes open as wide as an owl's. "Do you know me?" The words sounded so gravelly that they were nearly inaudible.

"I think that's supposed to be 'Do I know you,'" he amended, watching her closely and wondering what on earth was going on.

Still she held the rolling pin aloft, frowning with a confusion that seemed to weigh her down. "That's what I said. Do you?"

"Yes, I know you. Kelsey McKenna, writer. We met yesterday afternoon on the plane. Remember?"

She nodded slightly, still obviously mixed up. "Did Ali let you in here, too? I don't let men into my apartment. Oh, my word, there're two of you!" Higher went the rolling pin, wobbling weakly above her head.

Thomas glanced over his shoulder at Kit, who was coming through the door with his little-man swagger. "It's all right, Kelsey. He's a friend." But Thomas waved the other man away to a safe distance behind him.

"Whoa! This is one jumpy woman," Kit said, taking in the riggings all around the shabbily furnished place.

Thomas now noticed a Danish modern chair wedging the back doorknob, and a brown overstuffed chair pushed in front of it was an extra brace against entry. The only things left in normal position were an old console television, the sofa and a cluttered early-American coffee table with half wagon wheels as legs.

"What's going on, Thomas?" Kit whispered.

"I wish I knew."

"Something's not right here, man. She alone?"

"There's no sign of anyone else."

"Something scared her pretty bad, by the looks of this place." Kit glanced again at the rolling pin and Kelsey's glazed expression. She didn't seem to quite register their conversation. "It's a good bet she didn't get this scared from nothing."

"Kelsey, did somebody hurt you?" Thomas asked gently.

Kelsey blinked rapidly and thought it over. "I'm having a little trouble with dry eyeballs," she informed him matter-of-factly.

"Will you put the rolling pin down? I won't hurt you. I came to help."

"With my eyeballs?" she asked as if he were out of his mind. But she let her makeshift club rest in her lap as if it had become too heavy to hold up.

Taking her movement as encouragement, Thomas very carefully moved nearer. Pushing aside a chipped mug, a glass of water, a bottle of aspirin and the distinctive gold foil box of Godiva chocolates, he sat on the coffee table directly in front of her.

"I don't need help," she claimed as her wide, upraised eyes watched his tall body descend.

"Do you remember who I am now?" Thomas tried.

"A pest," she answered decisively.

Kit laughed from a distance.

"Won't let me alone," she went on to herself. "Keeps making that damn phone ring and ring. I thought they were turning it off, and I wish they'd hurry up so it would be quiet." She swallowed with obvious pain and trembled with a chill. "Turn the heat up."

"Do you know where you are, Kelsey?"

"Don't you?"

Thomas picked up her mug and sniffed.

"It's a toddy," she offered. "Tea, lemon, honey and a little brandy."

"More like a drop of tea in your brandy."

"It's so cold here," she defended herself. Then, as if that remark ended the conversation, she closed her eyes and let her head fall to the back of the dingy sofa.

Thomas reached to press his palm to her forehead, and Kelsey sighed comfortably at his touch. "Nice."

"She's burning up," he said to Kit.

Still sitting on the coffee table, Thomas moved very carefully nearer, clamped her legs between his knees and leaned forward to pinch the edges of the thermal blanket that had fallen open to expose her flannel-clad shoulders. That brought the rolling pin up again with amazing speed.

He caught her wrist before she could break his skull. "Kelsey, try to concentrate. You're very ill. I want to help you."

Her eyes attempted to focus, squinting and widening in turn, but failed.

"I'm going to take you back to my house and get a doctor."

"Mmm. No. I can't leave here. Business to take care of. Have to talk to Gordon and Gary. No doctor. Just let me sleep."

"I can't do that, Kelsey. You have a high fever."

"You could take her to a hospital," Kit suggested from behind him.

"Yeah, I could. But I'm not. I want her where I can keep an eye on her—make sure whoever scared her doesn't get a second chance," he added hastily.

"The woman is out of her head, Thomas. Do you think it's wise to play John Wayne and whisk her off? She's liable to come out of this and accuse you of kidnapping."

"I'll risk it." Seeing that Kelsey's eyes were again closed, Thomas very slowly pulled the rolling pin from her hand and once more tried to tuck the fallen ends of the blanket closer around her.

"Pervert." She came awake with a jolt and weakly slapped at his hands. "Who are you, anyway?" she asked as though she had never seen him before. Then, as if the effort of waiting for an answer was more than she could manage, she fell asleep again.

Thomas heard Kit's chuckle. "Not exactly hot for you, is she?"

"Drunk and delirious" was the explanation.

"You hope," Kit taunted, watching his friend carefully smooth back a stray strand of the woman's wild auburn hair.

In her sleep Kelsey swallowed with difficulty, but rather than fighting Thomas's ministrations, she nestled into them.

Thomas stood then, needing to tear himself away from her. "Do me a favor, Kit. Go upstairs and pack everything you can find that looks as if it belongs to her. There only seems to be one suitcase, and I saw it on the bed."

"Everything? Won't she be coming back here?"

"To a place that's scared the hell out of her?" he shot back impatiently.

"Okay," Kit agreed, his suspicions weighting the single word. "Everything goes." Seeing that Kelsey was oblivious to her company, Kit reached for the box of candy first. "Good taste in chocolate, lousy taste in beach houses. Funny woman." When he left, Thomas was setting the place in order and searching for the key to return to the neighbors.

Once Kelsey's belongings were ready to go, Kit again stood in the doorway of the shoddy living room while Thomas tried to rouse the author.

"Wake up, Kelsey. Can you do that?" he tried. But she only groaned her refusal. "I'm going to pick you up, Kelsey. Don't be afraid." He bent over her and effortlessly lifted her, blankets and all, in his arms. From somewhere within the cocoon of bedding, her purse fell out, and it was that that jerked her awake again.

"She sleeps with her purse?" Kit observed with disbelief, but he came to the rescue, handing it back to her before she nearly tumbled from Thomas's arms trying to retrieve it.

Kelsey rewarded the smaller man with a smile as warm and friendly as if they were longtime friends. Then she glanced suspiciously up at Thomas Quinn-Patrick Sullivan and said to Kit, "Do you know this man?"

A full laugh bellowed from the short, wiry producer. "Yeah, I know him. He'll take good care of you."

"It's cold in here," she decreed in amazement. "Aren't you cold?"

Kit breathed another laugh, sympathetically this time, and brushed her hair away from her mouth as she slumped into Thomas's broad chest. But before he could reassure her of his own comfort, her head jerked upright with alertness.

"Oh, no! Where's my candy?"

Kit showed her the gold box. "Right here, right here. It's all yours."

She took it from him and cradled it and her purse against her chest like a schoolgirl holding her books. Then, satisfied, she laid her head back against Thomas's shoulder, mumbling, "Fortifies courage. You can have one, but don't eat the crowns. I save those for last."

"Let's get her out of here." Thomas headed for the door.

"Okay. But I don't know how the two of you are going to fit in my car."

It wasn't easy. But Thomas didn't mind—until Kelsey began to wiggle into him for the warmest and most comfortable spot. Then his discomfort had nothing to do with close quarters. His breath caught in his throat, he swallowed with nearly as much difficulty as she did and sudden heat flushed his face. He closed his eyes, fighting down the quick rush of desire for her. The sensation was as fierce and strong as the second time he'd made love and known what was coming and how good it would feel. Where the hell had that thought come from?

Kit cleared his throat. "You going to make it, Thomas?" he asked dubiously.

"Just drive." His voice was hoarse.

Kelsey nestled in closer, sighed as if everything was perfect and informed Kit almost lucidly, "He thinks he's my hero."

"Yeah, I'd say it looks that way."

"Jonathan Martin was an inch shorter. No comparison."

Kit only laughed and set the car in motion.

It was six in the morning, New York time, when Thomas finally called Ali Robbins. But the agent's voice was clear and full of worry.

"I've been up all night, for heaven's sake. What's going on out there?" she demanded of Thomas.

"Kelsey is with me, at my house. I found her barricaded in that beach house, out of her head with a fever. The doctor just left. She has a severe throat infection and a temperature of a hundred and three. My housekeeper is bathing her down, but we can't give her anything until her toddy is out of her system. Do you know if she's allergic to any medication?"

"Good God," Ali breathed when he had finished. "She said it was just laryngitis. Is she going to be all right?"

"She will be as soon as she's on antibiotics."

"I don't know if she's allergic to anything or not. Did you check her purse for some sort of medical alert?"

"That's my next move. I just thought I'd ask, in case you knew." Thomas paused. "She keeps saying she has to take care of business with Gordon and Gary. Do you know anything about that?" Suspicion laced his voice.

"Never heard of them," Ali responded without a thought.

"So you don't know if there's someone out here I should contact? Some appointment I should break?" he tested further.

"No, I don't. I know she seemed nervous about this trip, and she kept denying that it was a vacation, but beyond that I don't have any idea why she's there."

For a moment Thomas wondered if there was something going on with *A Second Season* that they didn't want him to know about. But if that were the case, why would Ali Robbins have helped him hook up with Kelsey in the first place? Besides, the agent sounded as baffled as he felt.

"Well, she's being taken care of. Whoever Gordon and Gary are, they'll have to fend for themselves. I'll keep you posted."

In the guest room Sasha had finished the alcohol rub-down the doctor had recommended and left Kelsey asleep with only a dim bedside lamp burning. Thomas's shadow broke the golden glow glimmering across her features as he touched her forehead to see if the fever was down. She was still a furnace, not even moving now at his touch. His eyes stayed on her face. She wasn't beautiful, but she was so pleasing to him all the same ... so appealing.

Just the tips of his fingers traced her high cheekbone, around and down to stop on that mouth that seemed to draw his own even as she slept, her lips slightly parted, her breath warm against his skin. For just a moment he gave in to the desire to press the backs of his fingers against the too-warm skin at the side of her neck, then he forced his hand away.

The slightly rumpled sheet and blanket exposed the deep hollow of her collarbone, a starkly angular ridge beneath pale skin that smoothed into the curve of her shoulder. His gaze stuck there, and he felt like a randy teenager. He couldn't believe how much he wanted to see the rest of her.

God, she's right, Sullivan. You *are* a pervert. The woman is sick, and you want to play Peeping Tom. Clean up your act, man...or at least wait until she's well enough to participate.

He very carefully pulled the sheet up to her throat and tucked it around her. Then he took her purse from the walnut nightstand.

The contents held no warning of any allergies, but what he did find was a manila envelope containing seven thousand dollars in cash. Staring down at her peacefully sleeping profile, Thomas couldn't help but wonder about her.

"What's going on with you, Kelsey McKenna?" he asked very softly so as not to wake her. "Why rent a cut-rate shanty when you're carrying seven grand in your purse? Did someone scare you, or is it the money that made you surround yourself with booby traps? And why the hell are you carting around that kind of cash in the first place?"

Chapter Three

Lying naked in a strange bed in a room she didn't recognize was not a way in which Kelsey was accustomed to awakening. It was not a way in which Kelsey had *ever* woken.

Moving only her head, as if more activity might draw attention to herself, she saw that she was alone in a spacious bedroom of tan and russet. There was a tall, starkly modern walnut dresser against a far wall, and a lower matching one with a rectangular mirror attached to it on an opposite wall. The lamp bases were fat-bellied bean pots in natural clay, and at the foot of her bed was a Dakota sunburst soft sculpture in browns and bright oranges and yellows. Tasteful. Attractive. Obviously very expensive. And definitely unfamiliar.

Recent memory was elusive, and Kelsey had the unnerving sensation that a good deal of time had passed. She remembered arriving at the beach house in Laguna—this room was certainly not part of *that* shabby, misrepresented rental—and after resigning herself to staying because she had felt too miserable to protest, she had set herself up on the couch to rest. From then on everything was a blur.

But as she lay there, flashes of memory came. Thomas Quinn-Patrick Sullivan taking her from the beach house...a paunchy, stethoscoped man poking needles into her rear end...an enormous, exotic-looking black woman saying "Remember, I'm Sasha" each time Kelsey was startled by the unfamiliar face. Thomas Quinn-Patrick Sullivan over and over again, his hand pressed gently against her forehead...smoothing her hair...that deep voice telling her everything was fine, to just rest and get well...

So what she had thought was a strange, convoluted dream was the real thing. Was it possible that this place belonged to the man himself? Oh, Lord.

Her mouth was dry, but she managed to swallow to test her throat. It felt much, much better—a little scratchy, but nothing a glass of water wouldn't help. It was time to get a grip on what was going on.

As Kelsey swung her legs off the bed, clutching the sheet to her front, stiff muscles told her she had been inactive for a long time. With a moment's regret for tearing apart the perfectly made bed, she tugged the sheet free of its hospital corners and wrapped it toga-fashion around herself to search for her things, or at least for something to wear.

Her brush, lotion and perfume were on the low dresser, so she tried there first. Whoever had moved her in had done it efficiently; her underwear and pajamas were all folded and placed in the drawers as if she were a permanent resident.

As she gathered fresh underthings, Kelsey caught sight of herself in the mirror. If she had felt as bad as she looked, someone should have buried her by then. Her hair was a dingy mop of tangles, her face a pale, sunken mess. Had he really seen her like that? She cringed at the thought and hoped there was a bathroom she could slip into before another living soul had to be submitted to the sight of her.

Kelsey discovered her clothes hung up in a huge walk-in closet beside a connecting bathroom. It was her own shampoo and soap she found on an immaculate porcelain shelf within the ceramic-tiled shower, and she put both to good use.

Being clean was rejuvenating. Kelsey emerged feeling slightly spent but ultimately much better. Once she had managed to tug a brush through her hair and applied enough makeup to take away the scarecrow look, she pulled on pale blue twill pants that hung even looser than usual and a white V-necked sweater.

But then procrastination set in. She decided to tidy the room before facing whatever it was that lay beyond it. She replaced the sheet and made the bed, then searched futilely for her suitcase, having every intention of packing it for a hasty retreat after thanking her caretakers. It was then that she remembered her purse and the money in it and realized her handbag was missing. Now she knew she could put off going out no longer. She pulled the floor-length beige drapes open in a rush, but before turning away from the window, her attention was snagged and thoughts of the money fled.

The window was a huge multipaned square that looked out onto a redwood deck. Despite some white wicker furniture and an outdoor umbrella, she had a direct view into a glass-walled workout room in a parallel wing of the house.

The gym was brightly lit; floor-to-ceiling windows were open to catch the evening breeze. It was well equipped with an array of shiny metal and leather exercise apparatus, but the only thing she could put a name to was a slant board...and Thomas Quinn-Patrick Sullivan as he entered.

Kelsey told herself to move. She had to find that money. But the pull of him was stronger. She stayed put.

He wore bright blue nylon gym trunks that seemed almost fluorescent against his even, swarthy tan. His broad, hairy chest was bare, as were his muscled legs and long, attractive feet. It almost seemed unreal to her, as if she were watching him on her television screen, but the impact he was having on her pulse told her this was no staged fantasy. His weekly program had allowed her this vision of him many times before, but always posed as he waded into or out of a body of water, or as he left a steamy shower or a rumpled bed. Never had she seen him as she now did, at work, each muscle swelling beneath his skin, hardening, bulging, stretching the golden flesh taut. Fascination and a long-buried desire glued her to the spot.

He stretched, his big hands splayed out against the wall as if putting all his strength into moving it. First one knee bent and he pulsed forward, then the next as Kelsey's gaze ran the length of bulges and valleys that made up his long, lean body.

With his muscles loosened, he sat facing Kelsey, though across the distance he seemed unaware that she watched. His legs were spread wide, his feet braced on the tweedy carpet, calves and thighs like rocks while his hands curved around grips that he pulled forward, lifting weighted pulleys. His torso was straight as well-defined pectorals tensed to the task. Kelsey's gaze drank in the broad shoulders, moving up the sharp collarbone to his neck, corded with the force of exertion, to his remarkable face, tautened with each thrust of his arms, his perfect white teeth bared and then eased with the release.

Her stomach muscles contracted with his as he did sit-ups on the slant board, his head low, feet higher, hands behind his neck. Kelsey rubbed her palms with her fingertips to ease the tingling urge to smooth the narrow tightness of his sides all the way up that rib cage to the deep hollows of his armpits and across his chest as it rose into the curl and then relaxed again.

So this was what years of celibacy did to a person, she thought. It made you a voyeur.

She was lost in each swell, each hollow, each dimple of his back as he did push-ups, swallowing thickly as her gaze ran to his firm buttocks pressed against the blue shorts. How could just the sight of a man cause this reaction? Never in her life had she felt like this—hot and cold, nearly aching with desire. Her skin seemed to yearn for his touch—that touch she remembered too vividly from the plane, that intoxicating nearness. Never had she felt at once so out of touch with herself and yet as if every sense were heightened. It was almost a spell cast not only by perfect masculine beauty, but by something else about the man that she could not quite grasp.

Snap out of this, she warned herself. Move away.

But still she watched his profile as powerful arms pulled his body up until his face peered past the chinning bar. Sweat glistened in a light sheen, darkening the waistband of his shorts and dampening his wavy wheaten hair into dark curls that clung to his head. His skin would be so warm to the touch, slippery and silky, she thought. How would the earthy odor of perspiration mingle with that clean, airy scent she remembered so well?

When at last he finished, shook his long limbs and reached for a towel to pat his chest and shoulders dry, Kelsey found her own breath coming heavily, and she knew she had allowed her imagination to go too far.

The mixture of this man and her own newly discovered vulnerability to his sexuality was pure trouble. Topping that combination with any sort of professional connection with him would be nothing short of catastrophic. And right now the last thing she needed was any more of either trouble or catastrophe.

Kelsey turned from the window and took a deep breath. Pull yourself together and get out of here! she ordered herself.

The house was so quiet it seemed deserted, though with the thickness of the cream-colored carpet, Kelsey supposed the footsteps of a herd of elephants would be silenced. She crossed a slate-tiled entry and stepped down into a sunken living room crowned by skylights. Dusk was falling like a shadow over the domed windows.

Two long off-white couches faced each other opposite a low, perfectly square oak coffee table. Directly across from her was a ceiling-high stone fireplace. On either side of the fireplace were sliding glass doors that opened onto that same deck over which she had just played Peeping Tom. A long stretch of beach beyond eased into ocean, and that, in turn, blended into horizon.

For a moment Kelsey stood staring at the panorama, trying to control the overwhelming awkwardness she felt. Then a loud squawk rent the silence, and a flash of bright red and green swooped from nowhere. Kelsey shrieked and dropped behind one of the sofas, covering her head with her arms as if a dive-bomber had flown into the living room.

"Kelsey?" The distinctive black-velvet voice that matched the perfect body came in amazement from a double doorway that opened into the dining room. "Is that you huddling behind the couch?"

Much as she didn't want to appear the fool, fright wouldn't let her budge from her hiding place. "Was that a bird?" she demanded, her voice muffled in her lap.

"It's Sasha's macaw," Thomas Quinn-Patrick Sullivan answered quizzically. "He's harmless."

"Could you please get it out of here?" she asked, still not coming up for air.

"He won't hurt you."

"I don't like birds," she understated reluctantly.

Kelsey wasn't aware of the smooth, silent glide of the black woman as she removed the bird. When it was done, Thomas reassured her, "You're safe now. He's gone."

She breathed a sigh that was part relief, part embarrassment. Her head came up first, her wide eyes peeking above the couch to be sure the bird was indeed gone. Then, trying for as much grace as was possible under the circumstances, she got to her feet. An elaborate attempt to brush nonexistent wrinkles from her pants kept her eyes from rising to meet those of her host. Awkwardness was mild next to what she felt then. Wasn't it bad enough to find herself in this bizarre situation without humiliating herself on top of it? Sometimes the Fates were unkind in entertaining themselves.

"You're afraid of birds?" Disbelief and amusement mingled in his voice.

"Petrified," she confessed quietly.

"Just big ones?"

She shook her head. "Even sparrows."

"I see." He was trying not to laugh but couldn't resist teasing. "Have anything to do with the Hitchcock movie?"

Again she shook her head, automatically securing her glasses atop the unruly curls that cascaded around her face. "As a kid I was scared to death of the stuffed chickens in my Easter basket."

He stood only a few feet away, dressed just as she had seen him in the gym. A towel was draped around his neck, and his hair was damp with sweat. Kelsey's equilibrium suddenly went off kilter. She leaned against the sofa, desperately hoping her move looked nonchalant. Pulling her eyes back to his too handsome face took some doing.

"I'm not remembering things clearly." She hoped that crack in her voice would be attributed to her recent throat ailment.

"It's no wonder. For the past two days you've been completely out of it, with a high fever from a bad throat infection. Ben—he's the doctor who's been treating you—told me this morning that your temperature was down and he thought you'd be back to normal in no time. But I didn't expect to find you cured, dressed and dodging birds in my living room quite this soon."

"I've been here two days?"

"As of three tomorrow morning. When you didn't answer your phone, your agent called me. I found you in that beach house, delirious and sick as a dog, so I brought you here. Are you sure you should be up?"

"I'm fine." But still a little confused, she added mentally. How could so much time have passed?

Thomas saw her mental calculations and wondered if her business with Gordon and Gary had been affected. But there would be time to get into that. So he ignored her preoccupation and went on chatting as if her being there was a run-of-the-mill occurrence. "I'm on my way to the shower. I'll have Sasha fix you something to drink, and we can talk and have dinner when I'm finished. Are you up to it?"

"Oh, uh, no, thanks. I'll just be on my way." She grimaced at how inane that sounded. Surely there must be a graceful way out of this predicament. What *was* the proper protocol in such an absurd situation?

"Just relax, okay?" He acted as if she were deranged and he wasn't sure what she might do next. Kelsey took offense.

"I'm not nervous." Oh, you liar you. "I appreciate everything you've apparently done for me, but I'd rather get back to my beach house." Why did he keep looking at her as if she were out of her mind?

His big palms nudged the air to stall her. "I'll only be fifteen minutes. I want to talk to you, and the beach house is one of the things I want to talk about. Just sit tight." And he was gone.

There didn't seem to be anything else she could do. With a quick scan to make sure no more birds lurked in the rafters, Kelsey crossed to one set of sliding doors open just enough for the faint whisper of a breeze to drift in from the ocean and ruffle her hair. The sunset was pale gray and wispy white, and for a moment she stopped thinking about where she was and with whom and some of her tension eased. Until a melodious voice startled her from behind.

"I brought you tea."

Kelsey spun to see the tall black woman from her vague memories bending to set a silver tray on the coffee table.

"I'm Sasha, remember? Tommy's housekeeper."

Kelsey didn't remember much, but she smiled as if she did, anyway. Squarely built, Sasha was an exotic-looking beauty of perhaps forty. She had extremely prominent

cheekbones above deeply hollowed cheeks, a long, aristo-
cratically thin nose and a high forehead that curved like a
grapefruit before coarse black hair cupped her head like a
skullcap. Dressed in skintight leather pants and an equally
tight T-shirt with Twisted Sister emblazoned across an
ample bust, Kelsey judged her to be at least six feet tall.

"You've been taking care of me."

Sasha smiled, showing large white teeth. "You said you
liked tea, but I couldn't get you to stay awake long enough
to find out if you take cream or sugar in it."

"Just plain, thank you. If you'll tell me where my purse
and suitcase are, I'll pack and be out of your way."

The smile broadened, and a husky laugh filled the room,
"You've been worried about that purse of yours the whole
time. Tommy locked it up in the safe just after he brought
you home. I don't know where he put your suitcase."

"I see. Well, I suppose I'll have to ask him, then. I can't
impose any longer."

"I don't think he looks at you as an imposition." Sasha
laughed again at what seemed to be a private joke. "Have
your tea. Dinner will be a little while yet." The large
woman left, hips swinging, humming "Smoke Gets in
Your Eyes."

Kelsey moved from the sliding door to take up the
earthenware mug. But when she saw the lights in the gym
wing go on again, she was drawn back. However, it was
Sasha who had entered the workout room this time to
straighten it and close the windows.

In her mind the picture of Thomas Quinn-Patrick Sullivan in that room was almost more vivid than what she
was actually seeing. Once more her senses seemed electri-
fied. Too many feelings crowded up in Kelsey, and she
could think only that she needed to escape this place and
this man to put herself back on an even keel.

"Do you work out?" Thomas's voice startled her as he crossed the room, seeing the direction of her gaze. He was rolling the long sleeves of a pale yellow cotton shirt to expose thick wrists and forearms sprinkled with wheat-colored hair.

Kelsey took a sip of her tea to moisten her throat and buy herself a moment of composure. Then she forced herself to answer the glass door rather than stare at the man himself. "As in exercise?" Not bad, almost smooth. "I drive a car with a clutch."

He laughed. "You'll die young."

"But happy," she countered.

"Don't take this wrong, but can I feel your forehead?"

She knew that he was standing close—his clean scent drifted around her—but Kelsey misjudged just how near he was. When she turned to face him, she found herself barely a breath away, without any space in which to back up. She swallowed thickly and forced her tone to sound normal. "I really am fine now. I've always been a fast healer."

"Humor me."

His palm pressed to her brow was warm and smooth. And she felt ridiculous. "See?" But his hand stayed there, slipping slowly down to trace fingertips along her temple, down to her jaw. Kelsey's eyes shot to his, shaded and searching. She jerked away too quickly and then wished she had found more aplomb.

"Just checking to be sure you haven't wandered out here in feverish delirium," he teased before leaving her for one of the low couches. "Come and sit down so we can talk."

When he had moved away, Kelsey felt her lungs deflate from a breath she hadn't realized she was holding. She took a seat on the opposite couch so that they were well separated by the coffee table and hoped the distance would let her gather her resistance.

He wore a pair of faded blue jeans that were obviously old friends. They hugged him in just the right places without being too tight. His shirt had a short stand-up collar left open only to the second button, which she found sexier than if he had left it gaping to his navel. He looked freshly scrubbed, his slightly long hair shining in the faintly orange glow of a single lamp that Sasha had lit on her way out. His mustache was precisely groomed, cheeks and chin shaved smooth.

"You've given me two days of killing curiosity, Kelsey McKenna."

"I can't imagine why," she said carefully, wondering how much more than concern for her purse she might have babbled about.

"For starters, what scared you?"

"Scared me?" In honest confusion she parroted him.

His dark green eyes watched her with an intensity that did little to help her composure. "You don't remember the glasses at the windows, chairs wedged under doorknobs, booby-trapped stairs, a trip rope and the rolling pin?"

"Oh, that." Kelsey looked past him at the enormous American Indian abstract on the far wall. Was she to be left no secrets? "Simple safety precautions."

"Like the ocean is a little puddle. A locked door is a simple safety precaution. You were gunning for bear."

"It's just something I do."

"Come on. I was the rescuer, remember? Doesn't that earn me at least an explanation of what I saved you from?"

"Honestly, it's just my alarm system. Rustic, I'll admit, but effective enough."

"You don't expect me to believe that you always sleep with your purse and a rolling pin?"

She fidgeted, uncomfortable beneath his scrutiny, and searched for a way to explain one of her quirks without seeming totally eccentric.

Thomas watched her intently. What had her so jittery? The fever was gone. She looked good—too good. He remembered the feel of that hair, soft and silky despite the frizzy curls. He wanted handfuls of it pressed to his face, to smother himself in that fresh flower fragrance.

Kelsey sighed as she settled back and met his stare. Enough of being star struck. Her sleeping habits and alarm system were none of his damn business. "It was just a matter of being in unfamiliar surroundings and wanting to keep all my...traveler's checks and things safe. I'll bet you have a security system here," she said pointedly.

His handsome face broke into a grin. "An elaborate one. It came with the house."

"You see? It's no different, except that I have to bring my own. That's all there was to it. No drama. Okay?"

He shrugged those wide shoulders, stretching his arms out along the back of the couch. "If you say so. Ah, there's Sasha giving me the high sign. She makes a mean poached salmon that we wouldn't want to get cold." He stood and rounded the coffee table, holding his hand out to her.

Kelsey looked at it as if it were the apple being offered in the Garden of Eden. But in the end she took it because not to seemed to make too much of it. But he pulled harder than she expected, and she ended up colliding with his chest, her hand still caught in his between them. His dark green eyes pinned her like searchlights for a moment before he stepped back and led her into the connecting dining room.

A large space, it was dominated by an oval glass-and-chrome table surrounded by high-backed wing chairs upholstered in stark black velvet. Thomas didn't release her hand until he had taken her to one of the chairs, waiting until she sat to push it back in.

Kelsey barely noticed the black-rimmed china place settings, the smoky water goblets or the perfectly arranged meal that waited before her. "I really do appreciate your taking care of me, but if you'll get my suitcase, I'll pack and be out of your way tonight," she tried again as he took his own seat just around the upper curve of the table.

"To the beach house?" He stalled, taking a bite of steamed broccoli first, and then one of salad. When his mouth was free again, he went on casually. "You can't do that. I turned in your key and told them you wouldn't be back."

"You're joking, right?" Kelsey's appetite was absent.

Again he shrugged. "Afraid not. I thought something had happened to scare you and I was saving the day."

"I paid for that place in advance. Did they return my money?"

He had the good grace to look slightly uncomfortable, smoothing down his mustache with his thumb and forefinger before he applied the linen napkin to the corner of his mouth. "We haven't been able to get anything but soup into you since you got here. You'll retard your progress if you don't eat—not to mention that you'll insult Sasha."

Since it seemed she wasn't going to get an answer until she obliged him, Kelsey tasted the salmon. "I paid them four hundred dollars," she prompted.

"Yeah, well, they told me it was nonrefundable, but at the time I figured it didn't matter—it was worth anything to get you out of there. I had visions of lunatic beach bums harassing you. I even gave permission to relet the place when the next-door neighbor said she had a friend who wanted to take it over.''

Kelsey's fork dangled limply. How did you react when a person saved your life and put you in a terrible predicament all at the same time? She didn't have another penny to her name that could be spent on a place to stay, but anger didn't seem quite appropriate. A flat "Oh" was all she managed as the little color that had come back into her cheeks drained away.

"I'm sorry," he said, even though he wasn't. "I really thought I was doing what was best for you." Then he smiled smugly. "It looks as if I owe you my hospitality." Silently he added, *And let's see you try to sell that book out from under my nose that way.*

"I can't . . ." What options did she have? "I can't impose." But what else was there to do? At least for that night, at least until she had contacted Gordon. And what if his reception of her was not warm enough to include an offer of a place to stay? Could she get everything done within a few hours so that she could go back home right away? Lord, what a mess. And after such careful planning.

"Don't drift away on me, Kelsey. Did you hear what I said?"

She hadn't. But her attention came back as he leaned toward her, bracing his forearms on the table between them.

"I'm to blame for your losing the beach house and the money. I should have just brought you here and let you deal with whatever had gone on there when you were up to it. But you're already set up in a better room than you'll find in any hotel—a damn sight better than what you were staying in—and it will give us a chance to talk more about the book. I was planning a full attack on that score, anyway, so even if you leave, you won't be free of me. And if you stay, maybe we can work out something sooner than a few months from now."

"Are you sure you didn't plan this?" she accused ungraciously.

His grin was lopsided, lifting only half his mouth. "Not until after I'd gotten you moved in. Since then I've come to think of it as one hell of a stroke of luck." He paused, then planted his next words with a careful eye on her. "Unless you've been leading me on."

Had she missed something? "Leading you on?"

"You did promise me first crack at the film rights. Or are you in L.A. to let someone else talk you into selling them? You wouldn't be doing that, would you?"

"Not very trusting, are you?" she countered curtly.

"Not when it comes to business, to my future. Want to tell me who Gordon and Gary are?"

She went cold, and he saw it. So she *had* done some talking. How much? "They're just some people I came here to see." She watched him as intently as he had her. "What did I say about them?" She could only hope he didn't notice the softness of her voice.

"You said you had business with them. Is it about *A Second Season*?" Thomas's frown brought his eyebrows close together, emphasizing his suspicion.

Kelsey took a sip of water to help swallow the fear that she had said more. "It isn't the book. I gave you my word that if I sold the rights, you would be the one to get them. I don't have to tell you anything else."

"No, I don't suppose you do. So if the book doesn't have anything to do with why you're in L.A., you might as well stay with me. You can meet old friends just as easily from here, and we can talk over our agreement." Still he tested.

Kelsey stared up at the chandelier over the table's center, brass and glass lanterns balanced on five inverted arches. Thomas Quinn-Patrick Sullivan was definitely a complication she didn't need right then. Bad for her situation. Worse for her concentration and self-control. But for the moment she didn't seem to have a choice—not and keep that seven thousand dollars intact, which she positively had to do.

She lowered threatening black eyes back to him. "Look, you've put me into a position where I have to accept your hospitality. But if I stay, I don't want you to get the idea that it's for any reason other than necessity."

"I don't care what your reasons are, as long as I get the chance to use my hard sell." The sudden intensity of his mood lifted, and his eyes took on a devilish sparkle as he went back to his meal.

"It won't be for long," she warned, playing with her food.

"I'll take what I can get. Now eat your dinner and tell me if you're afraid of anything else that might be lurking around here."

Kelsey took a small bite of potato and thought it over. There was no need for him to know about her fear of left turns, that she became a quivering mass of mush at the prospect of a dental appointment or that at home the part of the rolling pin was played by a baseball bat. She had progressed beyond the days when she felt the need to alert the world ahead of time about her myriad quirks. They were just there, her own private set of eccentricities. And as long as they didn't interfere with day-to-day living, they were nobody's business but her own. "There isn't anything else," she lied and then thought again. "You don't keep snakes or rats as pets, do you?"

"Just the macaw, and he belongs to Sasha. She won't bring him here again."

His grin was broad, and he looked tremendously amused without making fun. Kelsey's heart gave a lurch. Dinner suddenly engrossed her.

"Was there someone besides Ali Robbins who would have missed you? I asked her if I should notify anyone else, but she seems to think you're the most disconnected person she knows."

"There isn't anyone. What about you? Am I intruding here?" If he could fish, so could she.

"I'm the only one who lives here, if that's what you mean. Sasha and her husband, Jake, live farther up the beach. Jake is my bodyguard."

He had managed to tell her as little about himself as she had about herself. Irritating. "I'll call my...friends in the morning and try to meet them tomorrow. If all goes well, I'll take a flight back to Denver tomorrow night."

"Then I hope all doesn't go well with your...friends. If you leave here before I've had my chance, I'm going to track you down and camp on your doorstep. I have an entire campaign planned." He gave an exaggerated wink that summoned an impromptu laugh from her. "I just want to live up to your opinion of me as a pest."

"Did I say that?" Kelsey felt her face heat.

"Among other things."

She didn't want to know what other things. "Sasha seems like an unlikely housekeeper."

"It's just a disguise. She's really a singer. Great voice. She's recording her first album, and I think she has a shot at the top. In fact, if we don't get out of here so she can clean up this mess before she goes to the studio for her rehearsal, she's liable to bring Henry back to scare us out. How about tea in the living room?"

"Thanks, but I'm about done in, and I want to get an early start tomorrow."

Thomas was behind her chair before she could move it, linking his arm through hers as she stood. Kelsey wished he would stop touching her. His effect was too heady, like guzzling champagne. But he kept her close to his side all the way to her bedroom door, as if she wouldn't have been able to find her way otherwise. Once there, instead of just letting her go, he turned her to face him.

"I really am glad you're staying, Kelsey." He said it simply, yet the words seemed to mean something far more personal than anything to do with her book. He raised his other hand to smooth the back of his fingers along her cheek, pushing her hair away from one small earlobe.

Sparks seemed to shoot from the contact point, and Kelsey's eyes widened. "It won't be for long," she repeated as if it would save her from his apparent pursuit. But her voice was so soft that it lost all power.

Thomas only smiled lazily down at her. "Maybe I can change your mind."

Did he mean about the book or about staying longer? She could only think that she wished he wouldn't try on either count. It was unnerving—and ultimately very, very dangerous—to find herself so susceptible to this man.

"Promise me you won't leave without giving me my chance?"

"It won't matter. If I sell the rights, it won't be for months. I'm adamant."

"'I'm adamant, *Thomas*.' Say my name, Kelsey." His tone was rich cream, intimate and stirring.

Kelsey swallowed hard and wondered if the house had suddenly gotten much warmer. But she complied with a small smile. "Thomas. I am adamant, Thomas," she teased.

"And I am more determined than you are adamant, Kelsey," he teased back.

Then, while she was still smiling at his imitation of her, his head lowered. He paused barely a second before his mouth found hers, his lips slightly parted. Kelsey's breath caught with a little gasp, but that was the beginning and end of her resistance. His lips were soft, and he tasted slightly of the orange that had been in the fruit cup for dessert. Warm and tangy. His mustache tickled but in a nice way. His arms encircled her gently, pulling her up against him enough for her to feel the tautness of her nipples as they brushed the hardness of his chest. And Kelsey wanted badly not to like it so much.

Stop this, she told herself.

How long had it been since she had even been kissed? So, so long. And this was so, so nice. Better than she had ever imagined as she had watched him kiss women on-screen. Better than her imaginings had been since she had met him and been so drawn to him.

And even though she knew it shouldn't be so, when it ended, she was sorry. She opened her eyes to his smile, bathing her like the warmth of sunshine, and knew she was in deep trouble.

Kelsey drew away from him, blinking as if to clear her eyes of sleep and focus on reality, staring into his shirt rather than into his sea-green eyes. "I might be contagious," she said, hoping her comment hid how shaken she was by a simple kiss.

"It was worth the risk," he answered in a hoarse whisper. "Get some sleep. If you need anything, just holler."

What she needed was to get out of there. But for the moment she was doing well just to shake her head, thank him and escape into her room.

Chapter Four

It was noon by the time Kelsey awoke the next day. Though she had meant to get an early start, she felt so much more like herself that she decided the extra sleep had been worth it.

After a quick shower she combed her hair and dressed in baggy jeans and an oversize baby-blue cotton sweater with the sleeves pushed up. Then she left her room to get on with what she had come to L.A. for in the first place.

The sound of voices from the kitchen drew her. Sasha stood above a mountainous bearded man sitting on a stool. His gargantuan shoulders were cloaked in a towel, his head half covered with lather that seemed blue-white against the ebony skin of the half she had already shaved bald with a straight razor.

"Tea's on the stove, Kelsey, honey. Help yourself," Sasha said. "This is my Jake. Tommy left him to take you around town today if you want."

At close range Jake was the most ominous-looking man she had ever seen. He stared up from beneath the heavy overhang of his brow, and Kelsey knew without a doubt that that glare alone could scare off King Kong. But then he smiled at her, his lips stretching the precisely trimmed Vandyke beard to show the gap between his two front teeth. It softened the fierceness of the bodyguard.

"Morning" was all he said, so slow and deep it sounded as if it came through a filter.

"Can I pour for anyone else?" Kelsey offered as she took up the red teakettle.

"Me, thanks" came the bass drum again. "Four sugars."

"That's so bad for you," Sasha berated, and Kelsey wondered at her courage. "Give him two," she instructed over her shoulder. To Jake she barked, "And hold still, or I'm going to nick you good."

"Ouch!" The slow-motion voice picked up speed.

"I told you. Kelsey, honey, will you come and stand right in front of this man so he can get a good look at you without wiggling around?"

Kelsey obliged, handing Jake his tea—with three sugars as a compromise.

"Scared of Henry, huh?" Jake grinned at her.

Kelsey shrugged and grinned back. "Fierce bird," she deadpanned.

"Henry's more chicken than macaw. One of these days I'm going to roast him—you're invited."

Sasha rolled her eyes. "Henry thinks Jake's head is a perch."

"And my new leather jacket is birdie litter."

"Henry has uncanny aim," she agreed. "Never misses something of Jake's. They don't like each other."

"Damn bird," Jake confirmed. Then he winked at Kelsey. "Good tea."

"Want breakfast?" Sasha finished the last of Jake's shaving and pulled the towel up around him like a hood. When she stepped from behind her husband, Kelsey saw that she wore dark brown leather pants and a matching vest that laced up the middle over bare skin almost the same shade.

Kelsey tried not to stare. "No, thanks. I have some calls to make."

The den Sasha had directed her to was a paneled haven with a large oak table for a desk. Low leather barrel chairs stood in front of it and a high-backed suede one behind it. Kelsey closed the door securely and set herself up in the suede recliner.

First on the agenda was a call to Ali Robbins, but the stall tactic failed when Ali's assistant informed her that the agent was out for the day. Before she could make the next call, Kelsey sat back with her teacup between both hands and stared at the phone cradled in a leather-bound box.

Her head felt light, and her breath seemed to knife through a constricted windpipe. The last sip of tea left her mouth still dry, but Kelsey reached for the receiver, anyway. Get it over with, she urged herself.

She dialed the number from memory, pausing only once, and that was more from tension than forgetfulness. After two rings an unfamiliar female voice recited, "Anderson, Bailey, Bardwick, McConnel and Olsen."

Kelsey cleared her throat. "I'd like to speak to Gordon, please." She surprised herself with an audible voice.

"I'm sorry, but Mr. McConnel is out of town until Thursday."

A wave of heat came up her back. The hand that held the receiver lowered in weak response. He had to be there!

She had to see him first! Kelsey took a deep breath and fought panic. Plunge in, she told herself. Get it over with.

"May I..." She had to clear her throat again. "May I speak to Gary, then."

"I'm sorry, but Mr. Olsen is away at a seminar and won't be back until the end of the week. If this is a legal matter, Mr. Olsen isn't accepting any new clients at the moment, anyway. He's getting married on Sunday and will be out of the office for three weeks afterward."

Kelsey's silence was long and hollow. Gary was getting married? She had never expected to come back to that. A shiver took her. "I'm..." She seized Thomas's description. "I'm an old friend. I thought Gary *was* married." She treaded a bit breathlessly.

"Oh, he was. But he's divorced now" came the chummy response. "I'm sorry, but I'm new here, and I don't recognize your voice."

Kelsey almost didn't hear her. Gary was divorced. She felt an odd mixture of relief, regret...and resentment. Resentment? She had no right to that. It shouldn't matter, anyway, she told herself.

"Are you there?" The secretary's voice finally recalled Kelsey from her own thoughts.

"I hope he'll be very happy," she said weakly and meant it, even though there was a tightening in the pit of her stomach.

"May I take your name and have Mr. McConnel get back to you, then?" The young voice tried again.

"No, that won't be necessary. I'll call back on Thursday for Gordon. Thank you."

She made the grip of her stiff, icy fingers on the phone relax. It fell within the circle of her hand to rest limply against her shoulder. For a long minute Kelsey stared vacantly. Then she replaced the phone in its box and snapped the lid closed. She sank back in the suede chair, sucked in a big breath and wondered how she really did feel about Gary's marriage. Sometimes it seemed so strange that there was change in things left behind, that they moved on even without her.

But she had come this far, and she had to see it through before she could go back ... go on. It didn't matter what was happening there, in either Gary's or Gordon's life. It only mattered that she accomplished what she had set out to.

Then it struck her that the delay left her in need of extending Thomas's hospitality. And just the thought of him somehow put everything into a better perspective.

It was a location shoot just north of Marineland. Thomas stood with the love interest of the week, explaining that her brother had murdered her stepmother by pushing her off the cliff at the foot of a classic white lighthouse with a thatched red roof. This was the last scene in the last episode of "Murder By The Book." The first scene had yet to be filmed, but Thomas had arranged to do all his work first so that he would be free to pursue other interests. Not that sequence mattered, anyway. This was big business, and filming was scheduled according to economics, not storyline.

The craggy cliff was blocked off by trailers and rope tied to pieces of equipment to keep onlookers at bay. Cameras, cameramen, the director, makeup artists, hairdressers, gaffers, idle cast members, script girls, writers and a number of other bodies connected with the show formed a semicircle around Thomas Quinn-Patrick Sullivan and Heather Halloway as the actress flubbed her lines for the fifth time.

"Cut!" the director shouted.

Thomas cringed and stepped out of the staged embrace that was meant to comfort the female character. It was through clenched teeth that he spoke to his director, out of the guest star's earshot. "I'm wrapping this up today, Pat. If you don't want us all to be embarrassed with the finished product, you'd better do something to get those lines to sink into her coke-fried brain."

"Lunch!" hollered the director. Then he turned to placate Thomas. "I'll see what I can do."

Thomas was not surprised to find Kit waiting with lunch when he climbed the three steps into the trailer that was his private dressing room. Having raided the lunch wagon, the smaller man had brought cold sandwiches, chips, pickles and iced tea. Hardly gourmet fare, but after nine grueling hours of taping, it didn't matter that lunch tasted like cardboard with mustard.

"If they don't stop hiring airheads with Dolly Parton chests instead of talent, I'm going to spit."

Kit drew back his head as if to avoid a slap. "Whoa. We are not in a great mood today, are we?"

"I'm trying to get the hell out of here, and that pea brain can't do three lines in a row."

"So what else is new? It never bothered you before." Kit popped a cherry tomato into his mouth.

Thomas dropped into a captain's chair and nearly guzzled his tea. "End-of-season impatience," he said, writing off his temper. "And what are you doing here?"

"Three guesses. What's going on with our writer friend?"

"She didn't come to until last night. I spent the evening explaining that I had forfeited her money on that beach house—for which she was not grateful—and trying to pump information out of her about what business she has with the Gordon and Gary of her mumblings."

"And? Are they competition?"

"She says no. But she's still holding on to that 'in a few months' routine." He finger-combed his hair back and sighed wearily. "Anyway, she doesn't like the idea of staying with me, and she was going to try getting out of here tonight. I conveniently kept her suitcase hidden. Let's hope that buys me some time."

"Why didn't you call me? I could have gone over today and tried to sell her."

Thomas looked away from his friend. "I left Jake with her. He's supposed to call if she makes a move."

"And can Jake talk her into selling?" Kit said snidely, clearly wondering why Thomas was trying to keep him away from Kelsey and none too happy about it whatever the reason.

"Get off my back, will you, Kit? The lady has been sick. I didn't want to start pushing the minute she got out of bed. I want to ease into it."

"Ease into it, my foot. We don't have time for that, especially not if she has someone else interested."

"Just give me a couple of days with her."

"Business or pleasure?"

"Both."

"I want to show her the screenplay."

"Lousy timing. Not yet."

A knock on the door forestalled Kit's argument, and a voice called, "Message for you, Mr. Sullivan."

"Come on in," Thomas called as he took up his sandwich.

The tinny door flew open and in bounded a man, camera in front of his face, flashes bursting with the rapid clicks of his Hasselblad.

"What the hell is this?" Thomas demanded.

The camera came away from the disappointed but unrepentant face of Bud Mitchell, a particularly unethical reporter from a scandal sheet for which Thomas steadfastly refused interviews.

"Where's McKenna?" the scrawny, birdlike man shot back. "Sources say you carried her off in the middle of the night, but your publicity people are being more closemouthed than usual. I had a tip that a *good friend* was waiting for you in here—thought it was her."

"Get out," Thomas snarled.

"I did my research," the man retorted snidely. Then he persisted fearlessly, "She wrote some big bestseller. Is it true you've offered a million-three for the rights?"

"Out!" Thomas unfolded his full height in a slow warning. Being nearer, Kit jumped up before his friend could reach the reporter.

"It's been a long day around here, Mitchell. If there's anything to tell, you'll be the first to know. Now shove off."

"Yeah, sure." With his camera clutched tightly he shook off Kit's hand and stomped from the trailer.

Kit locked the door after him and went back to his lunch. "Don't take this wrong, Thomas. I'm as against dealing with sleeze balls like that as you are. But what if we leak the possibility of your doing *A Second Season* to the right press? Maybe a little publicity would help pressure our girl."

"No way. She's liable to bolt for good. Besides, I don't want to go at her like that."

Both of Kit's bushy eyebrows arched high. "Protective of her, aren't we?"

"I like this woman, Kit. And I want to film her book. I don't want to jeopardize either of those things with some grandstand play."

"Appeals to the latent hippie in you, is that it?"

Thomas stretched out, propping his feet on the countertop across from him, leaning his head back and closing his eyes. Did anyone know what it was about another person that appealed to him or her? At least beyond the obvious, outward attraction? "That must be it," he answered facetiously.

"Just don't muck it up with romance, huh, Thomas?" Taking his friend's discarded pickle, Kit stood to leave. "I'll let you rest. Let me know when I can talk to the lady."

When Kit had gone, Thomas slumped low in the leather captain's chair. But it was impossible to really rest when he was so antsy to get the show finished so that he could concentrate his energy on Ms. Kelsey McKenna.

There was a strange frustration in him, as if he couldn't get enough of her. It left him with a drive to get back to her, to be with her, to get to know her so well that it would be like absorbing a part of her to carry around with him even when he couldn't have the real thing. Now that was crazy. But hadn't he exhibited a touch of insanity over her even before then? He had toted her book around even after he was finished reading it, as if just having it near gave him a connection with its creator.

You've been working too hard, Sullivan. You're going off the deep end.

But still her pull was there, understood or not. And Thomas didn't understand it. God only knew he had had his share of women. As lovers. As friends. As sparring partners. Even one as a wife. But never had he felt this . . . this need to know every detail about her, what was important to her, what made her laugh, cry, what made her happy or hurt . . . what would make her want him as much as he wanted her.

Did she want him? he wondered. The kiss had been good—no, great. But who could tell from just a kiss? She wasn't leaping at his offer for the book—something that would keep them connected. She wasn't even eager to spend a little time with him in negotiations.

Was that it? Was it the challenge of an uninterested woman? No, there was more to it. She was unique. Some might say strange—he preferred unique. She fascinated him. That had begun with watching her thought processes unfold in *A Second Season* and had only deepened with meeting her. She intrigued him. Turned him on.

Thomas heard his name being called to return to work. He stood, shaking his head at his own thoughts.

Dammit, he just wanted her.

It was well past midnight by the time Thomas got home. The house was dark and quiet, and he was disappointed. The first thing he did was check the guest room, relieved to find the door shut, meaning Kelsey was still there. For a moment he considered waking her, so much did he want to see her, talk to her. Instead, he took a bottle of beer from the refrigerator and went out onto the deck, tired but too wired to sleep.

The breeze that blew in from the sea was cold but not biting, the salt of the air slightly stinging as he breathed it in. Moonlight soaked the sand to a tan fluorescence. Waves crested, swallowed white moonglow and then shattered like glass against the beach in a restless rhythm of roar and swoosh and whispering retreat.

Rubbing the back of his neck, Thomas let his head fall forward and pinched his eyes shut against the burn of fatigue. When he opened them again, his peripheral vision caught sight of the pale cream of light behind the beige curtains of Kelsey's room. But just as his hopes rose like a helium balloon, the light went off. Thomas sighed and took a pull of his beer. The light went back on. Then off again. Curiosity moved him.

The Muse had a tendency to inspire Kelsey late at night when she was trying hardest to sleep. Scenes and dialogue began to play themselves out in her mind. She would turn the bedside lamp off, only to have a particularly satisfying part of her next book unveil itself to her. On went the light for her to jot it down on the small tablet she had learned to keep with her; then she would douse the light, lie back and hope for sleep, only to have the process begin again. Large portions of her books were written this way, nearly forcing themselves on her.

The knock on her door barely broke her attention, and without thinking, she mumbled, "Yeah, come in," her concentration uninterrupted.

Thomas pushed the door open wide. Engrossed in scribbling on a notepad, Kelsey leaned on one elbow in bed, her wild hair falling over half her face. She was so intent that Thomas thought he could move away again and she would never realize he had been there at all.

"Is everything all right?" He tried to gain her attention.

Only Kelsey's free hand rose, a sign that she knew he was there but couldn't stop right at that moment.

Thomas waited. When she finally finished writing frantically, Kelsey pulled off her owlish spectacles, swept her hair back with an unconscious whisk of her forearm and raised wide cocoa eyes to him, eyes glistening with the excitement these odd spurts of ideas always aroused.

"I'm sorry. What did you say?"

Her lack of artifice made him smile in spite of himself. "I saw your light going on and off and thought there might be something wrong."

"A nocturnal visitation of the Muse. I'm sorry if I disturbed you." She set her tablet on the nightstand and for the first time remembered herself, tugging the sheet to make sure it securely covered her men's nylon V-necked pajama top. You're a classless act, Kelsey, she groaned inwardly.

If he noticed her less than enchanting attire, it didn't show. "Can I lure you out of here? I'm in the mood for some company."

She dropped a dubious glance down at herself. "Sure. Just give me a minute."

When Kelsey had tied a heavy terry-cloth robe over her pajamas, she found Thomas waiting in the living room. He was stretched out, his feet propped on the coffee table and crossed at the ankles, his beer between both hands on his stomach.

"I poured you a brandy. You do drink it even when you're healthy, don't you?" He smiled appreciatively at the sight of her, so guileless and natural. He wished she would curl up in his arms. Instead, Kelsey took the snifter from the table and sat across from him much as she had the day before, tucking her bare feet up underneath her for warmth.

"I wanted to be out of here by tonight," she began, her eyes on her glass. "But Gordon and Gary are both out of town until later in the week." The subject was uncomfortable for her.

"Good." The one word was rich with satisfaction. "I was counting on your staying. I take it they weren't expecting you?"

Kelsey watched him grimace and shove off his shoes. "No, they weren't. But it's very important that I stay and see them," she answered hesitantly. Then she changed the subject. "Long day. Were you working this whole time?" Did it sound as if she were prying?

"Mmm," he groaned in answer, a throaty, sexy sound. "I was a bastard to my guest star because she couldn't remember her lines. She threw a fit this afternoon and refused to finish the scene until I did some bowing, scraping and halfhearted complimenting. I meant to be here early to fix dinner, spend the evening with you. But my impatience ended up costing me more time than it saved. Tell me you missed me, and I'll feel better," he teased.

Kelsey's face broke into a pleased grin, but she gave no quarter. "I wasn't bored. Jake barbecued hot dogs."

"His specialty," Thomas offered with a laugh.

Mischief sparkled in her dark eyes. "And Sasha tried out a song she's thinking of putting on her album. But to tell you the truth, I wondered if there was a message in her music. She said it was an a capella rhythm and blues piece done by Rory Block with the Persuasions." Kelsey cleared her throat and sang a little off-key,

God's gift to women,
That's what they think they are.
God's gift to women,
Just like a movie star.

Just because they want you
That doesn't mean it's good.
I'd rather have a plain man
Who'll love me like he should.

Thomas roared with laughter. "I'll kill her."

"Jake wasn't too thrilled with being considered a 'plain man,' either. She assured us it was just a song." Kelsey took a deep swallow of her brandy and buried her free hand in the folds of her robe.

"Why don't you come sit over here, and I'll keep you warm?"

"I'm fine, thanks. The brandy is working." And it's much safer, she added silently.

Thomas hid his disappointment. "What were you writing in bed?"

"I was hearing the voices of my new characters, as you so aptly put it. They were going at each other pretty hot and heavy."

"The book that's being auctioned now? Should I put in my bid for the screen rights?"

She laughed. "Actually, there are two books up for auction—one I've finished and another that's in the beginning stages. But they're both women's stories. Unless you want to do them in drag, I don't think they'll interest you."

He liked the sound of her laughter, a pleasant rumble devoid of giddiness. "Tell me about yourself."

Kelsey shrugged. "There isn't anything to tell."

"Family?"

"I'm alone."

"Have you always been?"

"My parents were killed in a car accident when I was fifteen. What about you? Can I have the inside scoop?"

He shrugged those wide shoulders beneath a pale cashmere sweater. "There isn't much to know. And what there is has been beaten into the ground with telling and retelling. Summed up more briefly than it ever has been before, I was born and raised in L.A. My folks live in Florida now. I was married once, for less than a year. No kids and no regrets that it didn't last."

That surprised her. Interviews with his ex-wife portrayed her as his closest friend, confidante and occasional lover. "You like being single," she guessed.

"Not really. As a matter of fact, it gets damn lonely." His deep green eyes scanned the room. "But the first time around was a hard lesson on being wanted for some reason other than me."

He took a long swallow of his beer and changed what was obviously an unpleasant subject for him. "What turmoil did writing *A Second Season* give you courage to escape?"

Kelsey sobered. Then she shrugged to make less of something she couldn't talk about. "It was just sort of the beginning of a catharsis for me—though at the time I didn't realize it. I was nearly finished with the rough draft when I hit a particularly low point in my life, and it struck me that I needed to start over again and rebuild the way my grandfather had."

She hadn't answered his question, but Thomas took her evasion to mean she didn't want to. He lightened the tone again. "Isn't there just a little of me in Jonathan Martin?"

Kelsey smiled. "I guess if you identify so much with him, there must be."

His eyes narrowed, but he grinned slyly at her. "Where did you learn so much about what makes men tick, anyway? The story may have been family history, but the insights had to be yours."

"Maybe it's just that I tried to make him human, to leave out any macho nonsense."

"Is he the man of your dreams?"

Kelsey averted her eyes to the reflection of the dimly lit room in the sliding glass doors. "I suppose in some ways he is."

"Then I definitely want to be Jonathan Martin."

A long moment passed in silence as Kelsey forced herself to look him in the eye and study his handsome face. "What are we doing here? Are you trying to buy my book with a come-on now?"

"Oh, I'm coming on to you—make no mistake about it. But not to get you to sell me *A Second Season*."

"Why, then?"

"Why not?"

"There aren't many men who fall over dead with desire when I stroll past—let alone superstud stars."

"Ouch! Be a little kinder. We triple-S men have delicate egos." But still he smiled, watching her as intently as she did him. "As for why the come-on, if there haven't been hundreds before me, it must prove that I'm one of a brilliant few. You think something's wrong with me because I want you?"

"I don't know what it means—except that it can't be safe or good for me."

All the teasing went out of his tone. "It means you're not like anyone I've ever met, and I'm pulled to you in a way I've never felt before."

"How many beers have you had?"

He toasted her with the bottle in his hand. "About half of one. Is what I'm saying so hard to believe?"

She nodded. "I am having a little difficulty with it, yes."

"I've been wondering—sometimes even fantasizing— about the author of *A Second Season* since I read the first chapter. Then I met you, and you hit me like a ton of bricks, lady. You're strange and lovely, and I feel as if I've just climbed the Alps and broken free of the dark, damp forest into a mountaintop of sunshine, wildflowers and perfectly clear air. I'm light-headed and lighthearted and desperate all at the same time for fear that you're not going to let me stay and bask in what seems like the cleanest place I've been in a long, long time."

Guilt was an arctic wind that froze Kelsey solid. "I'm none of those things," she said softly when she could thaw out her voice.

"You may not think so, but from where I'm sitting you are. I live in a world of fakes and forgeries and conniving and angling and manipulating. A place where people are too selfish, self-centered and self-absorbed to care if they hurt other people by using them to get what they want. Believe me, in my life, to be only what you are—fears, phobias and flaws flaring—is something special."

"I'm . . . not . . . as perfect as you seem to think. A long, long way from it, in fact."

"Perfection is just what I don't want. Perfect hair. Perfect face. Perfect body. Perfect dialogue. I think it's the imperfections you let me see that intrigue me."

His feet went to the floor, the beer to the coffee table and Thomas around it to sit beside her with the easy-jointed grace of a dancer. His arm came loosely across the couch back, fingering stray curls that fell there. He was so near. He lowered his head enough to peer directly into her eyes. She could smell the trace of beer on his breath when he spoke, and she could hear delight in his tone.

"There isn't another woman I know who drops to all fours when a bird swoops into the room."

She tried to make light of what was unnervingly not. "You're a sucker for functional phobics?"

"Thomas—say my name, Kelsey. Does it taste bad in your mouth?" His long index finger outlined her lips.

Kelsey swallowed thickly. "It isn't that." It's that I can't seem to say it without making it sound like a caress, she added silently.

The side of his finger smoothed the satiny curve of her cheek as his eyes pinned her back. Kelsey finished her brandy in one gulp.

Thomas took the glass from her hand and placed it on the table, settling himself in even closer when he sat back. His voice was soft and smoky, his long index finger back again to push the hair away from her temple. "What I'd like more than anything right now is to take you to bed and make long, slow love to you for the rest of the night."

Kelsey's heart gave a hard pound, her blood beat a drum rhythm in her ears and a chill ran the length of her spine. But she ignored the answer her body gave and forced common sense to prevail. Keep it light, keep it light. "Monday is take-a-loon-to-bed night?"

"God, you're hard on yourself. You don't really think of yourself as a loon, do you?"

"There was a time...." The way she said it left him wondering.

He raised her chin with one finger and touched his lips to hers in a light kiss. "I'm serious, Kelsey. I want you." Again his mouth covered hers, open just slightly, warm, moist, so tempting.

"Just like that—that simple?" She meant to be curt, but instead, her own voice was low and husky between kisses.

"Does it have to be more complicated?"

"It *is* more complicated. At least for me."

"Tell me why." He pressed a gentle kiss on the indentation of her temple, his mustache lightly tickling her. Just when she thought he was relenting, he took her lips again, his tongue teasing them open. She pulled away, feeling way too vulnerable.

"I just can't do this. It's not in me...." Kelsey stumbled. Her teeth caught against the dryness of her lower lip, and she ducked her chin to escape his kisses, speaking into the small gap between their bodies where her own breath filled the space with brandied heat. "It's something I can't do just as a night's entertainment. I know that sounds archaic, but that's how it is."

He smiled into her hair. "You're more than a one-night stand, lady. So tell me what it takes."

She shrugged, feeling silly and inadequate. How had she escaped modern sexuality? "There has to be more—feelings, caring, compassion—not just an urge. I have to at least feel comfortable with you," she ended with a desperate breath.

He chuckled softly, his exhalation gently ruffling her hair. His thumb traced the ridge of tendon down the side of her neck while his hand cupped the nape. "Will you give me the time for all of that, then?"

She looked up at him dubiously. His handsome face was only inches away, a slight stubble of beard beginning to shadow his chiseled jaw. It would have been so much easier if she didn't want him, if every sense didn't come alive just at the sight of him, if she didn't already care so much for the man. Kelsey had a sudden understanding of how a woman could settle for just one night. But she sighed and stuck to her guns. "We're not in the same league, Thomas, and I have the awful feeling that I don't understand the rules of yours."

"No rules. We just do what feels good." Again he raised her chin, only now it was to search her eyes with his own. "I would never do anything to hurt you, Kelsey."

"Then don't back me into a corner."

Minutes stretched by, and still he stared into her eyes, memorizing every feature and working hard to control his desire for her. Then he leaned back, holding his arms spread wide to free her. "No corners, then. But I'm not giving up."

Kelsey's initial reaction to her release was terrible disappointment. She knew she had to run or be lost. She stood and took two steps away, in the direction of the bedroom. "I think I liked it better when it was just the book you were after."

"I have news, lady," he said to her departing back. "From the minute I set eyes on you, I've been after more than the book."

Chapter Five

Finding a note on the pillow beside you may not be an odd occurrence when you sleep with someone. Finding a note on the pillow beside you when you sleep alone means that someone you did not choose to sleep with has snuck in and—contrary to the kind of fiction that portrays all women as Sleeping Beauties—watched you snore, drool and look like something the cat wouldn't bother to drag in.

Kelsey was not thrilled to find a note from Thomas Quinn-Patrick Sullivan on the pillow beside her when she awoke.

Kelsey,
Best-laid plans have been shot to hell again. Somebody screwed up half the film we shot yesterday, and I have to redo it today. How about coming out to the site? Actually, this is a rhetorical question—I have already arranged for the one and only Kitridge Ma-

son to pick you up and bring you out. Be patient with
him; he wants to do your book as much as I do and
has been ragging me to let him have a go at persuad-
ing you. See you this afternoon.

                                                    T.

P.S. Did you know you sleep with your mouth wide
open?

"Thank you so much for telling me," she grumbled as
she got up.

Today when she called her agent, Ali Robbins's assistant put her right through. "Great minds" came the
agent's voice a bit tentatively. "I was just about to call you.
Shall I brace myself to catch hell?"

"You're safe this time."

"How are you?" There was an unmistakable note of
self-satisfaction in her voice.

"Fine now."

"From what I hear, it's a good thing I got you hooked
up with The Man, or you would've been in real trouble out
there in La La land."

"Don't push your luck, Ali," Kelsey teased.

"So how's it going?" Insinuation was thick.

"Just fine." The wide grin of retribution wasn't evident in Kelsey's voice.

"Just fine," Ali mimicked. "You're going to leave me
dying of curiosity, aren't you?"

"There's nothing to tell." Kelsey was all innocence now.

"Nothing to tell, she says. America's heartthrob whisks
her off to his hideaway, and she has nothing to tell. Are
you going to see him again?"

"This afternoon. I'm going to watch him shoot some
scenes for his show."

"And what about *A Second Season*?"

"Nothing. I can't sell him the rights. That hasn't changed."

"Don't play too hard to get, huh, Kelsey?"

"Heard anything on the new one?"

"Things are heating up. It's generated serious interest—to the point of three different houses making me promise not to sell without giving them prior warning—and the offers are still gathering. Give me the number of that beach house so I can get hold of you."

Kelsey cleared her throat and savored the reaction her words would garner. "I'm not staying at the beach house. I'm at Thomas's."

"You dog! You saved that little tidbit to drop like a bomb, didn't you?"

"Uh-huh."

"I hope you enjoyed it."

"Uh-huh."

"What's going on, Kelsey?"

"Nothing. I'm just accepting his hospitality. Nice man."

"The queen of understatement. Are you going to let me in on what's happening with you and The Man?"

"We're getting to know each other."

"Intimately?"

"Platonically."

"You're out of your mind, my dear."

"So I've been told. Let me know if you hear anything."

"Let me know if you *do* anything."

"Not on your life. Bye, Ali."

Kitridge Mason's face was not as widely published as Thomas's, but since he was being touted as the next Steven Spielberg, it was not altogether unknown. He was waiting for her when Kelsey came out of the den.

At five feet eight inches he wasn't that much taller than she, his build spare and wiry. His red hair—thick, coarse and unruly—seemed to cry out to be described as a thatch. Freckles sprinkled his face, his neck, even his ears, and his smile was infectious.

He greeted her with the offering of a distinctive gold foil box. "I come bearing bribery. One full pound of Godiva milk chocolate crowns."

Kelsey laughed and accepted it. "How did you know?"

"You warned me the night we took you from the beach house that you saved them for last because they were your favorites. I commend your taste in candy."

Kelsey untied the gold cord that secured the box and offered it back to him. Without hesitation, he took two and popped them into his mouth.

"Shame on you. I can see you need tutelage in the art of eating fine chocolates. Hershey bars can be scarfed up. Godivas must be savored."

He extended his hand for shaking this time. "Kit Mason. Did Thomas warn you I was playing chauffeur today while Jake sits in on Sasha's recording session?"

"I knew about the chauffeuring part. I wondered where Jake and Sasha were."

"Now you know. All set?"

"Just let me grab my purse."

As Kit set the house alarm, Kelsey got into the sleek black car she had no memory of. When he slid into the driver's seat, she was busy settling herself. He cast a disparaging glance at the seat belt she pulled across her shoulder, tugged on, repeatedly tested and tightened, as if it were a comment on his ability as a driver. But Kit said nothing. The lady was spooked. So what?

"Were you also warned that I'd make a bid for the film rights to *A Second Season*?" he asked as smoothly as he guided the Porsche onto the highway.

"Thomas mentioned something I didn't quite understand about your wanting to do it as much as he does."

"Produce and direct. It would be the first movie Thomas and I do together. I was almost as crazy about your book as he was."

"I hope he explained that I won't sell the rights—at least not now." Kelsey freed her hair from the shoulder harness of the seat belt, hoping it didn't seem like what it was—the fidgeting of discomfort.

"He told me you wouldn't agree to it. Even he doesn't understand why not."

"Personal reasons."

Kit's brown eyes left the road to level on her. "Do you know what this means to Tom—to us both?"

"A great deal. But it can't change my mind."

He made a rueful clucking noise. "We're willing to pay premium price."

"I know that, too. It doesn't matter."

Kit Mason sighed, then spoke hesitantly. "Thomas would shoot me for telling you this, but he and I have already begun a screenplay."

Now it was Kelsey's turn to look askance at him, one eyebrow raised. "Oh?"

"Don't get mad. Nobody in the world has seen it but the two of us. I know it's an infringement, it's jumping the gun, we don't have any right, we're out of line, it's rotten and presumptuous and unethical and you could probably have our heads on a platter for it. Think of it as an academic exercise that can't possibly come to anything without your go-ahead. I'm telling you this because maybe if you read it, you'll see how sincere we are about turning your book into a movie masterpiece. We followed it religiously, and I think we've done it justice. Will you take a look at it?''

For a time Kelsey stared out her window at palm trees and the crispness of blue sky burned free of morning smog. She felt threatened. Not because they had been working on this project of theirs behind her back, but because it was evidence of how far-reaching this whole thing could be. If Kitridge Mason was not only in on it but also as enthusiastic as Thomas, who else might have been told how much they wanted the rights? And from there the incumbent publicity she was so desperately trying to avoid could be just a single step.

''Mad?'' Kit asked softly when she said nothing.

''Not exactly.''

''What, then? Peeved? Put out? Thinking of how soon you can get in touch with your lawyer and see if you have grounds to sue?''

''How many people know about this?'' Her voice was very controlled.

''I told you, no one but Thomas and me.''

''No, you said only the two of you had seen the screenplay you've written. Who else knows that you're going after my book and what you intend?''

Kit frowned over at her. His tone was sincere. ''Neither of us has told another soul.'' He judiciously failed to tell her that the rumor mill had put two and two together, anyway. ''Whatever the hang-up is, we'll take care of it. I promise you.''

He hesitated. ''I don't know what's gone on between you and Thomas—my guess is that you don't know much about the way he feels about you. He's learned the hard way to proceed with caution where women are concerned. But I've known him since we were kids, and I've been with him through the best and the worst of... affairs of the heart. He's got it bad for you—maybe even more than he knows. I haven't ever seen him as—I don't know—as involved, as obsessed, with any other woman. He takes care of the people who are important to him, and I have a feeling you're more important to him than anybody he's ever let in. Even if you don't trust me—although I give you my word I wouldn't do this any way you didn't want—you can trust Thomas. Completely. Implicitly. Not only is that the way he is, but also I've already seen how protective he is of you."

Protective? In what way? Why? What need had there been? Kelsey wondered. She chose her words carefully. "This book has turned too many eyes my way as it is. Any connection with Thomas Quinn-Patrick Sullivan and *A Second Season* can only complicate things even more. He can't circumvent that... and I can't allow it."

Again Kit remained silent in the face of the naiveté that fooled her into thinking her connection with Thomas hadn't already done that. "Will you just read the script?"

"It won't change anything."

He groaned through gritted teeth and squeezed her shoulder in a playful shake. "Are you always this stubborn? Who ever heard of turning down fame and fortune?"

Kelsey felt relieved that he wasn't pushing anymore. "Oh, I'd take the fortune, if only it came without the fame."

Discounting the phenomenal array of equipment, the scene itself seemed somehow smaller and sillier in real life than it did when filtered through and framed on a television screen. Kit had led the way through security guards posted every few feet around barriers keeping the mob of curious onlookers at bay. As they watched the scene being shot, he stayed by Kelsey's side.

Kelsey gained a new respect for Thomas's professionalism and talent. He made his job look so easy. It was beyond her how anyone could work without being distracted by so many watching eyes. He not only managed to ignore it, but his acting was superbly believable. She had read comparisons of Thomas's style with that of Spencer Tracy's—so smooth and complete that the character seemed to be the man and the man the character without delineation.

As she watched, she couldn't help but think of the things Kit had said about Thomas's feelings for her. It was a warm thrill, satisfying, flattering and exciting. But more, it was an odd reassurance, alerting her to her own rapidly growing feelings for him. When had she gone past being impressed with who and what he was? When had the star-struck admiration of the image become appreciation of the man himself?

It was the strangest thing—this feeling of his public image being removed from what he was to her, as if his job were merely a background addendum and not an integral part of what they had begun to share.

Oh, dangerous thoughts. More dangerous feelings. Could she handle them now? After so long and so serious a failure? And what *would* an emotional entanglement with him mean, anyway? Would it mean commitment? Could she deal with it if it did? She had spent so much of the past three years dissecting and analyzing the past. Without a man in her life, without those feelings that were coming out stronger than they ever had, she had not considered the future or even whether she was strong enough to enter another relationship.

Was now the time to consider it? It felt as if it were. Frightening. Unnerving. Elating. Nice—to feel things she hadn't felt in so long and have them be better than before.

For the third time Heather Halloway, the pouty, constantly preening guest star stopped the action because she felt that her lip gloss needed freshening. The director called for a break to set up the last take, so openly disgusted with the actress that he made no bones about apologizing to Thomas for the delays.

As if the crew had been standing stock-still for a portrait, when the word came, they all relaxed and dispersed, their voices no longer hushed whispers, their movements no longer inhibited. From beyond the rope border Thomas's name came in a chorus. Kelsey watched him amble over to the crowd with that athlete's loose-limbed grace, smiling congenially and accepting outstretched hands and accolades with friendly aplomb. Never did he react to the sometimes gushing admiration with less than the respect he might have shown a studio head. It was an impressive humility.

"I don't think he realizes yet that we're here. Let's wait for him in his trailer," Kit suggested, and he draped a brotherly arm across her shoulders to steer the way.

In minutes Thomas came in to the mobile home, delight illuminating his face at the sight of Kelsey. "I'm so glad you're here. I was beginning to think you weren't coming. Late again, huh, Kit?" he berated his friend over her head as he sat close beside her on the small built-in couch, his arm going possessively around her.

"I took the long way so Kelsey could have plenty of time to turn me down."

"She's a hard woman."

"Good thing, since I have to fend off attacks from all sides by persistent men." Surprised at herself for curving so naturally into him, she felt as if electric currents flowed from his arm through her body. Strange situation, she reasoned, and Thomas was merely the most familiar person in it.

Kit laughed. "Notice how it's 'persistent' now. When she was half crocked, we were just plain pests."

Color rose to a warm pink in her cheeks. "Half crocked? I thought I was delirious with fever."

"And a little drunk. Hot toddy was your medical explanation," Thomas offered.

"Think she might sell if we offer her the part of Anna?" Kit grinned at his friend, prolonging their teasing. "She was pretty interested in the acting that was going on out there."

"Research," she countered, ignoring the increased heat in her face. "Who knows when I'll need to write a scene about making a TV show?"

"I don't know." Kit was merciless. "I thought I saw some real appreciation for old Thomas here. I had the feeling you wanted to change places with heavenly Heather."

"Give her a break, Mason," Thomas chided, his pleasure at his friend's words crinkling the lines around his eyes. "The woman knows true art when she's watching it." Then to Kelsey he said in a soft aside, "My friend here moonlights as a matchmaker. Forgive his lack of tact. When are you leaving, Kit?"

"Use me and throw me away. Is that all I'm good for?"

"It is today."

"How do you know Kelsey isn't dying to spend more time with me? I'm not totally without charm, you know."

"Well, here it is, Kelsey. I have one more scene to finish up, and then I thought we could have dinner at a little Italian place that hides me so I can enjoy an uninterrupted meal out. We'll have a whole patio to ourselves, candlelight, a little wine, and I promise not to say a word about those film rights. Or we could have Kit horn in on us and listen to him plead. I leave it entirely up to you."

"Thanks, pal."

Kelsey pretended to consider it. "Sorry, Kit. No book talk is an offer I can't refuse."

"All right, all right. I can take a hint." Kit shot out of his captain's chair and headed for the door. "You will think about what I said before, won't you, Kelsey?"

"I'll think about it." She knew he meant reading the screenplay. She also knew she wasn't likely not to think about all the other things he had said, either.

"Beat it, Kit."

The slight man opened the tinny door and then turned back with a mischievous grin. "Tough luck, Thomas. They're ready for you again. No late-afternoon tryst in the trailer for you."

The decor of The Bistro was far from the usual red-checked tablecloths and candles in Chianti bottles that Kelsey had been expecting. It was all beveled glass, stained oak, cut crystal, Wedgwood china and white linen. A tuxedoed waiter served their pasta primavera outside on a patio surrounded by an eight-foot, surgically manicured hedge. Dressed in khaki pants and a peacock-green camp shirt, Kelsey was glad they were not mingling with the other more formally garbed patrons. In tan corduroys and a cream shirt, Thomas didn't seem to care how underdressed they were.

The night air was still and only slightly cool, rich with the scents of garlic, yeasty bread and the earthy pungency of dense shrubbery. After a brief visit from the owner, a man Thomas knew well, they were left to enjoy their meal in peace.

"Have you ever been married, Kelsey?"

The question took her by surprise. Her fork lay idle on her plate, and her hand tightened around the water goblet with a white-knuckled grip. Should she lie? It would be so easy to say no and keep her past the secret she wanted it to be. But in the end she opted for limited honesty. "I was, yes. Once."

The signals were clear to Thomas. It had been painful for her, was painful for her even in memory. "You don't want to talk about it?"

She stared off at the tall hedge, her voice tight. "I'd really rather not."

"Did it leave you soured on marriage forever?"

She wondered the same thing. "It was all very complicated. I'm not really sure. Did yours?"

His eyes caught and held hers, his mouth a slight smile beneath the full, perfectly trimmed mustache. "I thought so up until lately."

Her heart was racing, her skin alive, and every warning system blaring. Change the subject, she told herself. "Is this season finished for you now?" She seized on the parting goodbyes on the set, the crew wishing him a nice vacation.

Reluctantly Thomas let the original subject drop. "For the most part. I'll have to go in once more in a week or so when the editors have reviewed the film, decided where the sound track is weak and needs to be dubbed over. Then I'll go to the sound studio for a day or so and redo the lines in sync with the film."

"And then?"

"Then I wanted to begin work on *A Second Season*. But I promised not to talk about that tonight, didn't I? It's getting cold out here. What do you say to heading home?"

As Kelsey stood, one of her arms hit the spoon balanced on the edge of her saucer and flipped it to the floor. She bent to retrieve it, catching sight of a bright flash from behind as someone popped over the top of the hedge.

"What was that?" she asked urgently as she straightened.

"A camera flash, I'm afraid."

"Someone took a picture?" Her urgency grew.

Thomas watched her, concerned and confused by her response. "It was probably just a fan. He's gone now, Kelsey. It's okay."

"It's not okay! Can you get that film?"

His frown made his brows a shelf over troubled green eyes. "Honey, there's no way. Does it matter so much?"

"It does to me. That picture can't be seen."

"Fear of photographs?" He tried to make light of it.

"I can't have my face splashed over magazines and newspapers," she insisted, not relenting.

"You're safe. You bent over just as he took the picture. The only thing he got was a snapshot of your back. Lovely though it is, I don't think it's revealing enough for anyone to publish. It happens all the time. It'll end up in someone's drawer with the rest of 'my trip to California' pictures."

"You're sure?"

"Reasonably. Even if it did see print, there isn't a soul in the world who would recognize you, if that's what worries you." But why would it? he asked himself.

Kelsey's glance stayed on the spot the sneak photographer had vacated, fearful and worried just the same. "I hope you're right,'' she said ominously as he took her arm to leave.

The drive home was silent. Kelsey stared solemnly at the wood-grained dashboard of Thomas's silver Jaguar, lost in thoughts she would not or could not share with him.

Thomas watched her surreptitiously. Was this just another of her eccentricities, or was there more to it than that? Why would she be so concerned about a snapshot? Was she hiding from something? The law?

Come on, Sullivan, cut the melodrama. But he couldn't help thinking of all that money in her purse. Never had she let him know it was there, not even to keep it in the safe where it belonged. Instead, she just kept a silent vigil over the crescent-shaped leather bag.

God, how he wished he knew what was going on with her. His feelings for her were strong. Stronger than he had ever felt in his life. He wanted her—no doubt about that. But there was so much more to it than sex. It was as if he had found his pot of gold at the end of the rainbow. Nothing that had come before, in her life or his, mattered. But how could he let her know that when she hid whatever it was that caused her so much pain?

The circular driveway to Thomas's elaborate Spanish-style house was blocked by heavy iron gates in a six-foot brick wall that surrounded the grounds. It was an impressive estate, Kelsey thought once again as Thomas stopped the car near the carved double front doors.

Just two more days, she thought. She had to have complete anonymity for just two more days.

Thomas's arm rode her tense shoulders as he punched in the code that turned off the alarm before his key opened the door. All was quiet, dimly lit by one lamp in the living room directly in front of the slate-tiled entrance. Sasha and Jake had already left for their own house down the beach.

Thomas tossed his keys onto a marble-topped sideboard, still holding Kelsey. His hand moved to grasp the back of her neck, his long fingers digging into the tight cords there. "What you need right now is a long soak in the hot tub to relax you," he suggested gently.

Snap out of it, she ordered herself. There's nothing to do now but hope it was just some fan looking for a souvenir. She smiled up at him, touched by the concern that creased his handsome face and tugged at the corners of his mustache. "I should have known you'd have one of those."

"Standard issue. It's off the gym."

"I don't have a swimming suit."

"Great. Clothes just suds it up, anyway."

"I'll pass." She laughed at his overeagerness.

"I can't let you do that. You really need it. You're tight as a drum. It'll do wonders to strip down and sink into that warm water."

"For which one of us?"

"It wouldn't do me any harm." His grin was crooked and devilish.

"Not a chance, Sullivan, you lecher."

"I liked libidinous better."

"Same difference."

He sighed elaborately. "Okay, then, lady of steel, how about a pair of my cutoffs—you'll have to hold them up—and a T-shirt?"

"Ah, the old wet T-shirt routine."

"It'll start out dry." Lascivious relish sparkled in his eyes. "Besides, with that many clothes in the thing, it'll foam up like a bubble bath and you'll be camouflaged." He winked broadly. "And I won't look, anyway."

How easy it was to forget what she didn't want to think about and let her mind and senses be filled with him. And why not? she asked herself. Wasn't it time a little fun came back into her life? Hadn't she earned it a hundred times over? She felt carefree with him, almost as if he were there to share her burdens even when he didn't know what they were. So why not let loose?

Kelsey took a deep breath. It was as if she were coming to life again after a long hibernation. It felt good, and she decided to let herself go.

"Hollywood hot tubbing," she teased. "The depths of debauchery and depravity."

"I can hardly wait," he moaned in mock ecstasy.

The hot tub was built into a redwood deck enclosed in glass. Thriving ferns and philodendrons hung in green resplendence from heavy macramé ropes like leafy curtains.

"Daisy Mae goes a-dunking" was how she described her attire. On top she wore one of Sasha's T-shirts, emblazoned with a Mick Jagger snarl. The lower half of her ensemble was a pair of Thomas's frayed cutoffs, dipping to her knees and only staying up with the aid of a large safety pin pinching at least six inches of excess fabric at her narrow waist. Ludicrous it might have been, but Kelsey preferred this getup to a revealing, contour-cupping suit.

Thomas's eyes ran slowly from her bare feet up what he could see of shapely legs to the nearly obscured swell of her breasts behind Mick's forehead. "Sometimes I wonder if I'm every going to know what you're hiding under there."

"A variation on a common theme." And in she went to be further camouflaged by the gurgling water. Once there Kelsey was not opposed to feasting her eyes on Thomas's perfect body slowly descending into the bubbling cauldron, regretting the fact that he, too, was hidden by the water with only his broad shoulders revealed above the surface.

He leaned back, his head propped against the wooden rim, his eyes never leaving Kelsey's face. She felt his long legs stretch through the water until a big foot rested on either side of her, braced on the inner ledge that served as a seat. Slow mists of steam drifted around them, giving a hazy, dreamlike quality to their quiet late-night tryst.

"I shouldn't ask this when I've lured you in here to forget it, but maybe if I tell you that it's only because I care about you and want to help, you'll understand. Are you in some kind of trouble?"

Kelsey had the urge to run her fingertips over the sheen of his shoulders. Instead, she drew her arms through the water in a wide fan and sighed. For this answer she could look him in the eye and be honest.

"I'm not in any trouble. But I'd rather not talk about what I am in."

She let her head fall back, closing her eyes. For now the rest of the world could dry up and blow away and she wouldn't care.

Thomas watched her. Curiosity wafted away on clouds of steam and left him wanting her so much that it was an ache the hot tub couldn't soothe. His heart seemed to swell with feelings for her, desire for her, and rise into his throat. She was so beautiful to him, like something quietly wild— one of a kind, the completion of a part of himself that had always been left dangling.

Kelsey felt his foot float to her side. One ankle ran lightly from her waist to the side of her breast, plastered tight with the wet knit shirt, and down again.

"Are there sharks in your hot tub, Thomas?" she teased in a voice that was soft and rich. A faint smile curved her lips, her head still back, her eyes closed dreamily.

"Only guppies." His own voice was rough, a husky timbre.

She didn't realize he had moved from across the tub until he knelt in front of her. Kelsey drew her head up slowly, opening her eyes equally slowly, to find his face level and very close to hers.

Thomas watched her eyes widen to black orbs, but surprise and resistance were absent, and only serene pleasure shone there. She raised her hand slowly to his cheekbone, her fingertips brushing a soft wave of his damp hair back, only to return to the high crest of his chiseled face.

Somewhere in the back of her mind rang a feeble warning, but she quieted it. There sprang to life within her a need of her own—to be held by him, kissed by him, touched by him.

Thomas's face eased toward her with infinite care, offering her the time to change her mind, to push him away and refuse. Instead, Kelsey leaned forward a bit, tilting her head in anticipation. His kiss was so light that it was barely a brush against her waiting mouth. He gently tugged her bottom lip between his, then her upper lip, in the softest, most tentative caress, not wanting to rush her. But Kelsey met the short kisses, her eyes drifting heavily closed as she savored the warm, tender touch of his lips.

She raised a hand to his shoulder, her fingertips making feathery circles and then gliding to the deep hollow of his collarbone to stop at the side of his neck.

A sigh escaped Thomas with her acceptance. His hand rose to the base of her scalp, cradling it as his mouth covered hers fully. His mustache was like down against her skin. She parted her lips, allowing his searching, teasing tongue entry, matching the thrust for thrust in an intimate parry and then following the trail he led around her mouth, testing the texture of its roof, the sensitive inside of her cheeks, the tips of her smooth white teeth.

Kelsey felt his free hand slide up under the clinging T-shirt, and she curved her arm around the broad expanse of his back to free the way. The warm water gushed like hot silk against her bare skin in a divinely sensual way. No bathwater had ever felt like this, Kelsey thought. She ached for his palm to enclose her breast, to press against the hard nipple. Instead, it rested against her side, just below her breast, once again offering her a moment to think about it, to decide if this was where she wanted him to stop. His mouth still caressed hers hungrily, possessively.

She arched toward him instinctively, and at last his hand slid forward to knead her breast, to tantalize the hard nub with his thumb. As he circled the outer edge of her nipple, she thought she might cry out. Then his touch turned to a gentle pinch just before cupping the turgid mound, as if the urgency she felt were alive in him, as well.

His mouth left hers to rain impassioned kisses down the column of her throat as his hand slipped from her head to lift her higher out of the water, to free her breast of the warm liquid and pull her between his thighs. His rigid desire, barely contained in tight nylon trunks and pressed so demandingly against her, spoke of his own need, as if he could not get her close enough.

At last his mouth reached her, his tongue hot against her hard nipple. Kelsey's spine nearly snapped back, and her head fell to the rim of the tub. Her mouth opened in a deep sigh as her hands raced to the waves of his hair, holding him nearer. His fingers toyed with her inner thigh underneath the baggy leg of the cutoffs.

Without warning a shrieking alarm sounded, and every outside light flared to life, illuminating the grounds as brightly as sunshine.

Kelsey gasped, her eyes flew open and her head shot up as if she had been electrocuted, pulling her body away from Thomas. "My Lord, what is it?"

"Dammit to hell!" he gritted out, his voice husky and harsh with passion. "It's the burglar alarm. Something—or someone—has set it off. The police will be here in three minutes. Jake's probably already out." He wrapped his arms around her, ducking his head to look into her face. "You okay?"

As okay as anyone could be when the proverbial bucket of cold water has been thrown over her, she decided. "I'll be fine. You'd better see what it is."

"Dammit. I don't believe this." He stepped out of the hot tub, grabbing a towel and bounding from the room.

Once he had gone, Kelsey didn't wait another second before leaving the water, wrapping a Swedish bath towel fully around herself and retreating from the display of the glass room to the seclusion of her own bedroom. The Fates, she was sure, were rolling with laughter.

It was over an hour before things died down and Thomas knocked on Kelsey's door. She hadn't dared to set foot outside her room. Just the thought of sauntering out into the commotion as the star's squeeze-of-the-week made her cringe.

He had hastily pulled on jeans and a sweatshirt and now leaned casually against her doorframe, his arms crossed over his chest, each hand under the opposite armpit with only his thumbs jutting out.

"It was a damn reporter for *The Inquisitor*, Bud Mitchell. He's been hounding me for a story and thought he'd do a little peeking."

Kelsey's face blanched. "Did he make it to the window?"

"Jake had him by the scruff of the neck six feet inside the wall. I'd press charges of trespassing, but it would only draw more attention to him. It's better to evict creeps like that and forget it."

He scanned her tightly cinched terry-cloth robe and smoothly brushed hair as she sat in a tan chintz chair in the corner, her hands hidden in her pockets. "I don't suppose we can take up where we left off."

Kelsey smiled ruefully. "It's moving too fast for me, Thomas. I...got carried away. I'd rather it be a sane choice—without regrets in the morning."

"I know, no one-night stands. Does that mean that after this—which is one night—when it happens again it qualifies as a relationship?" His crooked grin let her off easy.

"I don't know if I'd go quite that far. But we may be headed in the right direction."

"No maybe about it, lady. We are definitely headed in the right direction." He shoved himself away from the doorjamb and crossed to her with long, determined strides to stop directly in front of her. Bending at the waist, his hands on the armrests on either side of her, his nose nearly touching hers, he said, "I want you, Kelsey McKenna, every way you can think of. And I'm not giving up until I get you."

He kissed the tip of her nose and was gone, leaving her a little disappointed that they hadn't taken up where they'd left off.

Chapter Six

The next afternoon was dark, rainy and gloomy. Thick clouds drifted low over the ocean like gray mists wafting from the murky water. Rain drizzled steadily, leaving the sand a darker brown seen through windows awash with a curtain of water. All was quiet, tranquil, soft, as if the world were wrapped in a cocoon of downy gray flannel.

Kelsey loved the feeling. Dressed in jeans and a turtle-neck sweater, the sleeves pushed up to her elbows, she stood at the sliding doors in the living room. Unaware that Thomas had finished his morning workout, had showered and was now watching her, she stared out at the weather, a hint of a smile curving her lips.

"Did you order this weather?"

"Mmm. If I could have, I would have."

"You really like this stuff?"

"Second only to snowstorms. I love it when everything is draped in shades of gray and white, as if color doesn't exist and you're living in an Ansel Adams photograph. It never seems depressing to me—just cozy.''

He looked over her shoulder at the ocean churning and cresting, the clouds hanging like heavy pillows of steam. "And how do you spend these days?"

"Baking brownies and watching old movies."

"The perfect answer—just what I had planned." He rested his arms across her shoulders, his chin propped on top of her head. "But I have to have popcorn."

"Horrible stuff."

"So you make brownies, and I'll make popcorn and supply the movie. Sasha and Jake are gone for the day, but there must be a cookbook around here someplace."

"You need a cookbook for popcorn?" She smiled back at him.

"Don't you need one for brownies?"

She shook her head smugly.

"You do brownies by heart?"

"Brownies, fudge and chocolate mousse. I only need cookbooks for hard things, like boiling eggs."

"You really are a crazy lady, you know that?" The pleasure he found in that fact was evident in the lines that fanned out from his eyes.

"What's the movie?"

"Ah, the classic example of why it's important to have good material. *Passion's Pawn*."

"Sounds as if there's method to your madness. Is this by any chance something too obscene to sit through?"

"I'm giving you a rare treat—a private screening of a movie seen only by the poor suckers involved in making it. It was my first try at a film. Low budget, thank God. As it was, I had to sell the shirt off my back and mortgage myself to the hilt to buy it and keep it from ever being seen."

"Is it some horribly filthy thing made in someone's back bedroom?"

"Give me a break. I do have some shame. It's a regular movie, just one that was so bad it would have ruined me before I began."

The screening room was a large, windowless space with six rows of oversize recliners lined up in front of an enormous screen.

Kelsey settled in with a plate of warm brownies and a pot of tea on the tablelike arm to her left while Thomas set up the movie. He dashed back to sit as near her as the narrow armrest between them allowed, pulling his popcorn bowl into his lap and reaching for her hand to twine their fingers together and pull her snugly to his side.

The credits began to roll.

"I did this the year after *The Graduate* came out. It's a good thing it was never released, or somebody would've been sued for plagiarism—that's how close a copy it is."

"Why did you do it?"

He shrugged. "I thought it was my big break. Starvation makes it tough to be choosy."

After a half-dozen names appeared on the screen, none of which Kelsey recognized, big, bold letters appeared: And Introducing Thomas Q.-P. Sullivan.

Kelsey laughed irreverently. "Q.-P.?"

"I know. The first time I saw it, it hit me that I sounded like a Kewpie doll. At the time I was afraid the whole thing was too long."

"Why not just Thomas Sullivan?"

"No flash! I had to stand out." He laughed at himself.

The movie was worse than bad. Thomas had the Dustin Hoffman role, though it took Kelsey a second glance to recognize him. He was clean-shaven, his hair so short he looked as if he were about to be inducted into the army. Without his mustache his face was almost boyish. Even his body was less developed, more gangly, certainly a long way from the well-muscled, powerful man he was now. Beyond the physical differences, his acting was appalling.

"This is the worst," Kelsey teased during the initial seduction banter with a woman whose sex appeal was dubious at best.

"Now don't make fun." He feigned injury, his lopsided grin giving him away.

Her eyes returned to the screen, where the young Thomas stood backed into a corner, his hands held like the proverbial fig leaf over brief swimming trunks.

"Wait for this next line—it's a beauty," he advised.

"I want your respect, Mrs. Rogers, and I know if I go to bed with you, I'll never have it."

Thomas roared at himself and the cardboard delivery. His head fell back, and his whole body shook with mirth beside her. Kelsey was enjoying herself every bit as much. The movie could have passed for high camp, and she liked the fact that Thomas didn't take it seriously. On it went, one bad scene giving way to another more horrendous and hilarious. There were poor angles, fuzzy focus and times when the music drowned out the dialogue. She had seen home movies look more professional.

The aging actress on-screen began to undress Thomas in earnest, and suddenly Kelsey's own amusement dropped like a rock into a pool of discomfort. The woman's hands slid up his chest beneath his open shirtfront as she raised pouting lips slowly to his.

Kelsey fidgeted. The scenes she had watched him film with Heather Halloway had been strictly dialogue. No touching. No kissing. Still, it wasn't as if she hadn't watched him at this sort of thing a hundred times before—he got the woman on every show every week. But somewhere, somehow, her involvement with him had changed her own feelings about witnessing it.

Thomas's mouth moved to her ear, whispering, "Jealous?"

Kelsey turned haughtily his way, coincidentally averting her eyes from the screen. "Me?" Innocence foamed over the single syllable.

Again his laughter was deep and booming. "It's okay. They fade to waves crashing against the rocks before it goes too far." Then his sympathy intervened. "Let me taste one of those decadent things."

Gratefully Kelsey held up a brownie. Instead of taking it with his hand, he bit off a corner very near her fingers.

"Not bad." He smiled as he chewed. "Now you try my popcorn—I make the best in the movie business." He insisted on feeding her a kernel from his fingertips.

Kelsey played along, easing the tension that had grown with the sex scene. "Yuck!" she groaned.

"No taste," he complained.

"Want the rest of your brownie?"

"My nutritionist would shoot me." He ran a finger up her ribs. "Where do you put those things?"

"They all go to my feet." Kelsey kicked one up into view. "Size nine. It means I have a good understanding."

"Of what?"

"Of how I get more for my shoe dollar than the size fives."

Thomas laughed and leaned in close to whisper, "It's safe to watch the movie again."

Kelsey wasn't too sure she wanted to see the rest of the film, but there didn't seem to be an alternative.

Once more Thomas's comical narrative helped. "Here she comes . . . The Daughter. Played by Mary Dowel."

The young actress in the role of Thomas's contemporary love interest had a vaguely familiar face. Kelsey remembered seeing her pictured with Thomas in a magazine article. An article on his personal life.

Sensing her thoughts, Thomas offered some information. "Mary was my first lesson in how the press can misconstrue things. They had us linked as lovers from a simple business lunch we shared with the producer, the director and two of the set designers."

"You weren't?" Kelsey cleared her throat, knowing the crack in her voice was telling.

"No, we weren't. We were friends for a while, until she dropped out."

"Dropped out?"

"She slept around too much, got to be known for that instead of her work—and taken advantage of for it. Last I heard, she had gone back to Minnesota and married a dentist."

A not too explicit love scene of Thomas and Mary Dowel filled the screen. "I don't know. Looks to me as if you're enjoying that." She tried teasing to ease her own discomfort.

Thomas chuckled. "Then it's the only part of this movie that has decent acting in it. I'm never comfortable, let alone aroused, doing those scenes. It's a good thing nothing below the waist shows, or my image would be as shriveled as my anatomy."

The scene changed. Now it was a strobe-lit disco with miniskirted women and paisley-shirted men writhing to the blaring sounds of The Monkees. Thomas's on-screen actions were forced, robotlike in their stiffness.

"Okay, so I was a little tense." He headed off her comment, nearly drowned out by several "nobody would ever actually say that" lines from the movie. Thomas cringed.

"Now you know how important good dialogue is. Yours in *A Second Season* is some of the best I've ever read. For the most part we could use it as is, without having to re-write it."

Kelsey refrained from saying he knew that well since he had already worked up a screenplay. But somehow it didn't matter as much that day as it had the day before. Maybe because the longer she spent with Thomas, the more she believed Kit's assurances that she needn't fear anything from this man.

He was so different from any of her preconceived ideas. She spotted no ego, no self-absorption, no phoniness. She was drawn to his easy intimacy with her, as if they had been together forever. It left her feeling comfortable with him, free to be herself.

She could feel his warm breath on her cheek as he leaned close to gain her attention. "Are you still with me?"

She was now. "Mmm," she murmured, keeping her eyes on the screen.

"Now comes the big confrontation: 'How can I marry someone who has slept with my mother?'" He feigned a high falsetto, repeating the lines verbatim. "'At least Howard is a decent, upstanding man! You're some kind of...of maniac!'" Thomas laughed again. "What great stuff." His sarcasm was playful. "Wait for it—here's the big finish: 'You can't go through with the wedding. You know it's me you love.' But no! She flings her flowers in his face and has him thrown out of the church. Fade to desolation as he walks out into the sea. The end. Clap, clap, clap."

He stopped the tape and turned on the lights, returning to sit beside her. "Is that the best movie you've ever seen or what?"

"Or what."

"How did it do in convincing you why I need *A Second Season* before I can try again?" He slipped her hair behind her shoulder with such familiarity that he might have been doing it for years.

"I didn't need convincing. But I still can't be had." Kelsey grimaced at the Freudian slip.

Thomas laughed again, this time with a low, sexy timbre. "Don't crush all my hopes at one time." He checked his watch. "I hate to disappear on you, but I have about an hour's worth of phone calls to make."

"That's fine. I have some things rumbling around in my head that I'd like to get down on paper, anyway."

"You mean that piece of tripe inspired you?"

"It comes from the oddest places."

"We'll meet in the kitchen in an hour, then. I'm going to wow you with my culinary expertise for dinner." His handsome face came in close, and her pulse raced. "And then I'm going to see what I can do about having you."

Thomas hung up the phone and sat back, the conversation with his attorney still playing in his mind.

"You're off the hook, Thomas. I have a copy of Jean's marriage certificate sitting right in front of me. No more alimony. She actually married that old guy. He's backing a sitcom for next season with her as the star. She gets all she wanted—money and fame—in one short, bald package."

Six years, Thomas thought. After only eight months of marriage, he had been dealing with Jean's demands for six long years. It was a relief to finally have it over with. No more of her attempts to get him to pull strings for a part she knew she was right for. No more of her needling him to raise her alimony. For the first time Thomas truly felt free of her.

The attorney had closed with what seemed like a premonition. "You ever tie the knot again, get a prenuptial agreement and avoid having to support an ex-wife into eternity. You're just lucky someone else finally picked up her tab."

What lousy advice to have to give: enter a marriage as if it were a business merger, protect yourself when the inevitable divorce comes. But then his lawyer had been through it four times himself and earned his living from the dissolution of other marriages. What else could he think?

Just how open are your eyes, Sullivan? Thomas asked himself. He had attributed the monumental mistake of marrying Jean to youth and ignorance. She was at least a good enough actress to have fooled him into thinking she really did love him, when in fact it had been only a career move for her.

Kelsey was so totally different. He couldn't imagine the need for a legal agreement to keep her from swindling him as Jean had. Her elaborate con game had netted her plenty over the years, even if it hadn't helped her career. But were his feelings for Kelsey clouding his vision again?

It seemed ridiculous even to compare the two of them. But once bitten, twice shy—wasn't that the saying? Except that he wasn't really feeling shy. Well, all right, maybe a little leery—it was second nature by now. But his circumspection was more curiosity about what secrets she was keeping and how they might affect what was growing between them. He didn't feel the need to protect himself from her—quite the opposite, in fact. He felt as if he could confide anything in her, that she would accept him as he was. But she must not feel the same way about him or she'd open up about Gary and Gordon and that seven thousand dollars.

Give her some time, Sullivan. What's the rush?

But there it was, anyway. Rushing was just what he wanted to do, to tear down every barrier between them and be forever bound to her in every way. She was the one. He had found her, and he knew it, in his gut, in his heart, in his head. More surely than he had ever felt about Jean. And once he caught Kelsey McKenna, he'd be damned if he'd let her go, so legalities were unnecessary. Maybe he was just being blind again, but he knew he could trust Kelsey, and that was more important than anything any lawyer could devise.

Sunset was a descending haze of charcoal as Kelsey stood at her bedroom window, her tablet and pen discarded with only the glimmer of an idea that had struck during the day spent with Thomas. But even away from him he absorbed her thoughts.

She had such powerful physical reactions to being anywhere near him, even to thinking about being near him. High hormones. It was as if he had turned something on in her that she couldn't turn off again. Something that ached to come fully alive and be satisfied before it would be content to recede again.

It wasn't as if she didn't recognize the part of it that was just plain desire. But there was more to it, and that was what frightened her. She had done so well alone. Were her feelings a rebirth of the need to be connected with people again? To end the seclusion that had nurtured her these past months? Or was it just Thomas and the need to be intimately involved with him alone—mentally, physically, emotionally?

Was it love?

Kelsey shivered at the thought.

And if it was, could she keep a grasp on herself, or would she lose everything to it? What it all boiled down to was, could she trust herself? She only wished she knew the answer to that.

Chapter Seven

An hour and a half passed before Kelsey emerged from her preoccupation, no more sure of herself than she had been before. She brushed her hair and pulled the entire mass into a knot at the crown of her head, a loose Gibson girl style with a few wild tendrils straying to curl down her neck.

The sound of pans clattering in the kitchen greeted her as she stood just outside the tall arched doorway. Thomas was at the sink, slicing mushrooms. He was intent, his brows pulled together, his upper lip lost beneath his mustache. A soft wave of wheaten hair fell onto his forehead. His big body dwarfed the black tile countertop. The paring knife was small in his hand but wielded confidently, his long fingers deft and clearly experienced at the task.

He had changed his clothes, replacing his sweatshirt with a knit shirt that hugged his broad shoulders and molded the hard rise of his chest, the short sleeves stretched wide over tanned, powerful biceps. Kelsey's gaze wandered to the curve of his tight rear end in well-washed blue jeans, down hard thighs pushing against the time-softened fabric to big bare feet. She fought against the urge to cross to him, slide her arms around his waist and turn her face into the valley of his spine. Instead, she drew her shoulders back and moved into the kitchen, which was warm with the scent of steaks broiling and butter melting.

Thomas turned to Kelsey, his exquisitely handsome face erupting into a delighted grin at the sight of her, which caused her heart to pound. "You're late, McKenna. I was beginning to think I'd have to wait for the Muse to leave again." He paused in carrying the cutting board, piled high with mushroom slices, to the stove to bend and kiss her forehead.

Shivers sluiced down her back and held her immobile for a moment as she watched him sauté the mushrooms, gently turning them in the butter and then adding wine at just the right second.

"You seem to know what you're doing," she observed, trying to hide his effect on her.

"It's from my dues-paying days as a waiter and cook," he explained. "I thought we'd eat in here at the butcher block. How about making yourself useful and setting it? Then you can toss the salad."

"I heard you were an overnight success." Small talk was so safe.

"Right. Overnight in seven years. Why do you think so many entertainers end up owning restaurants? It's because most of us have as much experience in the food industry as we do in the business. At least that used to be true."

"And now?" Kelsey kept her eyes on dressing the salad.

"Now they start out as male strippers. Hard to fall back on that when a paunch and wrinkles put you out of work. I'm all set here. Sit down, and I'll be right over."

Kelsey had no appetite as she waited for him on one of two high stools, silently lecturing herself on getting control of thoughts ruled by emotions. Why was it so hard to cool off that night?

"Wine, root beer, milk or soda water?" Thomas's voice interrupted her confusion.

"Root beer?" Distaste rang in the words.

"Sasha. How about wine?"

"Soda water sounds good." And safer, she thought. The last thing she needed was to lower her inhibitions.

Thomas filled two glasses with the fizzy beverage and ice and joined her. One bite of steak sent him into mock ecstasy. "My compliments to the chef."

Kelsey laughed, his levity helping to calm her raging senses. "I'm surprised you allow Sasha into your kitchen."

"I only cook for very special people." He winked at her, a devilish quirk that tugged on her heart and made it race. "But you'll never know how good I am unless you eat it."

Easier said than done. The last thing on her mind was food. She picked at it, anyway.

"I like this." His voice came softly, sensuously. "I can't think of anything I'd rather be doing than sitting here alone with you on a rainy night."

His eyes held hers, his mouth stretched into a lazy smile. Kelsey felt tingly, as if every nerve had surfaced in response to him, attuned to just his nearness.

"So." She cleared her throat. "Did you finish all your calls?"

"I did. I've put off dubbing this last episode until later so I can concentrate on you."

"I won't be here that long," she reminded him, thinking that what she had come to L.A. to do seemed far removed from the reality of being there alone with this man who churned up so many things inside her.

"I've been thinking about you and me."

"Oh?"

"I was thinking how good things could be between us. Professionally, but even more, personally."

Kelsey played nervously with her food. "You realize that you're giving me severe indigestion."

"The chef in me would take offense if you were eating anything. As it is, I think you have other things on your mind. Want to talk about it...or act on it?" The insinuation that he knew just what was going on inside her was clear.

Kelsey closed her eyes and breathed deeply as those other things swelled within her. Thomas's gaze dropped to watch her small breasts rise and fall beneath her sweater. When her eyes opened, it was to find his glance there, rising in heavy-lidded languor only after her nipples had hardened against the knit, speaking for themselves when Kelsey would deny that she ached to have him touch her.

"What's on your mind, strange lady?" he asked again, his voice a throaty answer to what was unspoken between them.

What if...she just...let herself go...?

Then a thought she had been suppressing poked its uninvited head into her mind and demanded to be dealt with before she could let herself go—if she ever could. "Maybe this is a little late—" or maybe I just didn't want to know, she added silently "—but from what I read, there always seems to be a woman in your life. Are you hiding her in the broom closet?" Or just keeping her out of sight while you woo the writer into selling you what you want? Too defensive, Kelsey—a bad sign, she told herself. "I don't want to be an interloper."

"I'm going to take this as an encouraging sign and give it to you straight, okay? I don't want anything coming between us."

Kelsey nodded, unsure and at the same time certain that she had to know what he was going to tell her. Naive one— had she really expected him to say there was no one else in his life?

"I've been seeing a woman pretty regularly for the past year or so. We're friends, sometimes lovers. Don't go pale on me—I'm trying my damnedest to be honest with you, when it would be so much easier to lie. As far as it goes— caring about each other, wanting the best—there is a commitment, the kind that means we'll always be there for each other. But the relationship qualifies squarely as friendship—nothing more on either side."

Did people who were just friends have sex? Kelsey's ears buzzed, and she wished the sensation would stop. His hand closed around hers, warm and comforting and electric all at once.

"Not something you understand—I can see it in your face, and I read it in your book. There's only sex with great passion, with solid commitment ... with love. Right?"

"Something like that," she barely managed.

"Want to know what I feel about you? What I see for the future?"

Could she handle it? Why wouldn't that last bite of food go down? The room seemed suddenly close, and surging fear washed through her like the fiercest tidal wave. She stood abruptly, spurred by an attack of the purest panic. Her words came out in a gush. "I need some air!"

She reached the kitchen doorway and fled through the house and out onto the deck to calm the short, shallow breaths that threatened to choke her. Long minutes passed as she fought to think of anything but Thomas or of how much she wanted him and how afraid she was of that desire.

The rain had stopped, leaving the air cool and moist and clearing the sky enough for a full moon to glimmer down and reflect in a pale stream on the water's surface. Kelsey stood at the deck's edge, gulping air and wishing she were anything but what she was. She leaned slightly forward, both hands braced on the iron railing.

By the time Thomas found her there, bringing two glasses of wine, she was at least breathing steadily. He handed her a goblet and propped one thigh on the railing, facing Kelsey, though she only stared out into the night. One warm hand closed gently around her stiff wrist, but he looked away from her, sensing that his glance unnerved her.

His voice was a soft breeze in the dark. "This is a little like living in my own private Woody Allen movie." He tried teasing her, but when it had no effect, sincerity filled his tone. "I'd never do anything to hurt you, Kelsey."

"Don't talk about it," she whispered, embarrassed.

"Tell me what you're afraid of."

"No." How could she tell him she was scared silly of how much she felt for him, wanted him?

Thomas let silence reign for a while, comforting her with his hand at her wrist, his thumb rubbing light circles around the bone that protruded there. After a time he said, "We're going to freeze our buns off out here."

His lightness reached her at last. Kelsey inhaled as much air as her lungs would take and held it. When she let it go, she felt sanity settle over her again. She finally sipped her wine.

"Some people like the sun. I like the cold." She discounted his complaint and then tried a little levity of her own. "I suppose I play the Woody Allen role."

Thomas saw her control taking hold, saw that she had won whatever private battles she had just waged, and tried to ignore his own erupting goose bumps. "Should I have lied?"

"It wasn't you. It's me—my own problem. It's passed now." She turned to him, her smile faint. "Call it stage fright."

But Thomas's glance was serious. "I want you in my life, Kelsey."

"You're not going to let me off the hook tonight, are you?"

"I want it clear that there's nothing to be afraid of here."

"Fear isn't rational, Thomas. You're talking to a person who is scared of sparrows."

He took her glass and set it with his on the table, then reached to smooth her hair away from her face in that way he had. "I think I'm falling in love with you, Kelsey. And I know I want to make love to you."

He tilted her chin to look into her moon-paled face. "Make that distinction, oh, lady of letters. I had sex with Karen. I want to make love to you."

Still he held her captive with his eyes. "How many men before me, Kelsey? Shall I guess? Just one—the husband you don't want to talk about. And you're afraid you'll end up as just another statistic in my autobiography. But that's not what I want. It isn't the first or those that come after that count—it's only being the last one that matters. And that's what I want you to be…that's what I want to be for you."

Kelsey swallowed the renewed rise of fear. "I only know that I feel too much for you."

The corners of his mustache lifted with the hint of a smile. "It's not possible to feel too much."

He leaned forward until his mouth pressed hers softly, his lips parted. His hand left her chin to cup her head and hold her to his kiss, a warm, sweet delight that was the final spark to the embers lying in wait in Kelsey.

A voice somewhere in the back of her mind rang a warning, but it lost its power as her senses filled to the brim with Thomas, moving her a long, long way from the silliness of rational thought right smack dab into the center of what she really wanted.

His lips deserted hers, but he pulled her to stand between his spread thighs, his hands reaching around her to clasp and rest on just the beginning swell of her rump. He leaned to stare into her face, taking her breath away with the gentle warmth in his handsome features. "What caused..."

"The panic attack?" She named it for him.

"Mmm."

Kelsey laughed a little, wondering how to put it. "I suppose it was the possibility that you were trying to seduce me."

"If I admit it was more than a possibility, are you going to run?"

"I don't think so."

"Does that mean it was working before and isn't now?"

She hesitated. Should she admit it? In the end her own needs ruled. "It's still working."

"What would happen if I just took you in to bed right now?"

Kelsey swallowed hard. Her voice was soft. "I'd go with you."

A slow grin spread his mustache. Thomas stood and took her hand, leading her silently through the house and into his room, which was lit only by moonlight filtered through the French doors. He released her hand and moved to the bed to pull back a wine-colored spread and blanket. Then, turning back to her, he reached to the bottom of his shirt with his arms crossed over his flat belly, curling it up and over his head in one motion. The night's silver glow threaded through his wheat-colored hair and touched only the tops of his broad shoulders, leaving his face shadowed as he neared Kelsey again, slowly, as if not to scare her off.

She waited and watched, swallowing a rise of fear in the odd mixture of desire and awkwardness she felt. But still she wanted him.

He stopped so close that she had to tilt her head back or have her nose pressed to his chest. His hands rose to curve on either side of her jaw, his little fingers guiding her head to where he wanted it while his thumbs gently smoothed over her cheeks. He lowered his face to a scant inch above hers and paused for a moment before he kissed her, short, chaste minglings of his parted lips with hers, inviting, slowly drawing her nearer.

Tension fled from her shoulders with each caress of his lips. She matched the fluid drifting of his mouth to and from hers. Her lips parted, accepting his invitation. Her arms wrapped around his waist, her palms flat against his lowest ribs, feeling the hard smoothness as they glided up his back to his shoulder blades, pressing more firmly to draw herself farther up into him.

Thomas braced himself on one bare foot as the other coursed a slow path from her ankle to her knee. The inner bulge of his thigh slid along the outside of hers, easing her against his body and the solid ridge straining from inside his jeans. His breathing grew heavy, and he raised his head as if to draw in air and slow himself down. Then his nose touched her in a slow trail from her forehead around to her earlobe, where his hot breath drifted from slackened lips, the bristles of his mustache tickling.

Hooking his thumbs in the back of her jeans, his fingertips rode the small rise of her derriere. The insides of his arms held her possessively as the breadth of his shoulders curved around her. "I'm going to make love to you, Kelsey. Long, slow love." He kissed her again, lingering, his slippery tongue running along the insides of her upper lip, then her lower.

One hand rose from her waist to stretch the full span of her shoulders; the other reached to the backs of her thighs to lift her effortlessly, his mouth still at hers. He laid her carefully on the cold sheets and himself beside her, half his body pressed over half of hers. His mustache feathered a path along her arched throat to the hollow of her collarbone.

"It's been a long time for me, Thomas," she whispered when she was more inclined to moan.

"No," he deadpanned. Then he said, "It's nice."

Kelsey felt the cool roughness of his cheek rub hers. He smelled fresh and clean and spicy. "Thomas..." she breathed.

"Hmm?" His concentration was on the silkiness of her skin. He loved her light fragrance, the smell of spring flowers and bluegrass that drifted faintly around her. The sweetness of her lip gloss clung to his mouth, and he liked tasting her even when their lips were apart.

"I'm..." A breathy moan stalled the words. "I just wanted you to know... this is safe."

A low, raspy chuckle rolled from his throat. "I wouldn't care if it wasn't." He nipped gently at her shoulder. "This is only the beginning for us, lady. I want us connected in every way... for all time."

Lost in the feelings he was raising on her skin, Kelsey decided they were just warmly voiced love words that washed through her mind without leaving an indelible mark.

Thomas knelt and pulled her up with him so that deft hands could slip beneath her sweater, easing it off, kissing each inch of her flat stomach as it was exposed. As the light cotton passed over her head, it took with it the few pins in her hair, leaving the wild mass to fall around her bare skin, concealing her as he unhooked her lacy bra and freed her breasts to the coolness of the room. Tingling shivers awakened her body to a heightened sensitivity.

His mouth found hers again, claiming it, easing her back to the pillows. One heavy thigh leisurely crossed over her, and his hands rose to fill themselves with her hair, playing in the silken frenzy of curls.

The first press of her tightened nipples into the springy hair that covered his chest sent a fresh surge of excitement through Kelsey, setting off a live wire inside her. Her tongue met his, even grew bold enough to follow his retreat and test the inside of his mouth, all velvet and wet smoothness. She found it a heady, provocative thought that a part of her had entered him.

Kelsey was barely aware that Thomas had unfastened her jeans until his fingers ventured to the nylon-encased swell just below. A throaty laugh sounded from her, and she decided to even the score. The first touch of the backs of her fingers against his belly drew a surprised gasp that turned instantly into a deep groan as she popped the snap above his fly. She explored his navel, nestling amid a vertical line of hair that disappeared below.

"Are you trying to drive me crazy?" His voice rumbled in a whisper against her neck.

She was unprepared for his hand pushing hers down inside his jeans just enough to spread his zipper and discover he wore nothing beneath. Then it was his turn to laugh, deep in his throat, before he slid from her side to peel them away.

She peered up at the body that had titillated her imagination for so long. He was magnificent, sleek, beautiful.

Thomas agilely removed her last barrier, as well, coarse blue jeans and frilly panties sliding off slowly. He paused to allow himself the sensuous delight of seeing her small, pale body dusted in moonlight.

Her hands reached to his hard, rippled stomach, fingers splayed, palms sliding upward until she reached the small nubs of his aroused nipples, following each soft bump around and over, feeling it grow harder still. Her back arched to him with no thought but that he was too far away and she needed the feel of him more than the sight. He moaned softly as her mouth sought his, her tongue tracing his upper lip beneath the mustache. His body rode hers again, and his thigh slid over to rest against the slight swell between her legs.

She felt his fingers glide up her side, the anticipation building in her until his palm took her breast at last, kneading, easing, rolling her own taut bud between thumb and forefinger as if learning the texture of a prized marble. His mouth lowered, and his tongue teased circles around her nipple. Kelsey's shoulders drew back, thrusting herself farther into his suckling mouth, pulling, drawing, nipping in gentle bites. Her hands entwined in the waves of his hair, and she was intoxicated by the wet feel of his lips, his tongue, his teeth.

NOW THAT THE DOOR IS OPEN . . .
Peel off the bouquet and send it on the postpaid order card to receive:

4 FREE BOOKS
from

An attractive burgundy umbrella FREE! And a mystery gift as an EXTRA BONUS!

PLUS

MONEY-SAVING HOME DELIVERY!
Once you receive your 4 FREE books and gifts, you'll be able to open your door to more great romance reading month after month. Enjoy the convenience of previewing 6 brand-new books every month delivered right to your home months before they appear in stores. Each book is yours for only $2.25—.50¢ less than the retail price, with no additional charges for home delivery.

SPECIAL EXTRAS—FREE!
You'll also receive the Silhouette Books Newsletter FREE with every book shipment. Every issue is filled with interviews, news about upcoming books and more! And as a valued reader, we'll be sending you additional free gifts from time to time—as a token of our appreciation.

NO-RISK GUARANTEE!
—There's no obligation to buy—and the free books and gifts are yours to keep forever.
—You pay the lowest price possible and receive books months before they appear in stores.
—You may end your subscription anytime—just write and let us know.

RETURN THE POSTPAID ORDER CARD TODAY AND OPEN YOUR DOOR TO THESE 4 EXCITING LOVE-FILLED NOVELS. THEY ARE YOURS ABSOLUTELY FREE ALONG WITH YOUR FOLDING UMBRELLA AND MYSTERY GIFT.

She needed to know him as intimately by touch as he knew her. His skin was taut and slippery, corded and bulging, roughened with coarse hair and satin smooth over rigid muscle. Her hands slid to his firm derriere, down hard thighs and then forward, hesitating for only a moment before sliding upward again until she found the shaft of solid, hot silk. Her first featherlight grasp brought a sharp gasp from him, and then a rumbling groan of pleasure.

He chuckled low, as if accepting a sensual challenge to match the flames she had ignited in him. She felt his hand run lightly down her side and each inch of her body curl upward as he left it, like a lazy cat's spine undulates against a caressing hand. He found her legs just barely parted, and his teasing fingers carefully made their way between.

"I want to be inside you, Kelsey." He breathed the words into her hair as his finger did just that. "Is your head as ready as your body?"

Her response was a soft moan of assent as she raised her hips against the heel of his hand. Her fingers trailed a telling path down his back to press him to her. "Yes, Thomas, yes."

She thought she might burst if he didn't complete what he had begun in her. She felt his arousal insistent against her side before his body covered hers. A slight discomfort stiffened her involuntarily as he pushed into her softness. Thomas stopped the moment he felt her reaction but the incompletion was far worse, and Kelsey arched up against him to finish his entry, needing desperately to feel him fully within her.

"Please, Thomas, now."

Knowing that he wasn't hurting her was all he needed to send his body into the urgent thrusts they both craved, driving deeply within her, filling and easing, taking her step by taut step to climb higher and higher until she reached an explosive peak unlike any she had ever known. Then he, too, found a culmination unmatched by any other.

"Are you all right?" He kissed her damp brow and ran his index finger along her hairline and down the side of her face.

Her exhalation was replete with satisfaction. "A little better than all right. You?"

He laughed, his voice still thick with passion. "A lot better. I want to stay here forever."

Her words, too, came slowly, huskily. "I don't think that's humanly possible, but it's a nice thought."

He rose on his forearms and lowered his head for three soft, lingering kisses that tasted of salt. His sigh was satisfied and resigned as he left her and rolled to his back. "Will you come and lie with me?"

Willingly Kelsey curved into his side, her head in the hollow of his shoulder.

Thomas's arm curled around her, and his hand played with a tangled strand of her hair as he turned his face into the top of her head. "I have a confession to make."

"Don't tell me this was all made possible through the wonders of surgery in Sweden?"

"You're a terrible smart ass sometimes, do you know that?"

"Now the criticism starts." She smiled languidly, feeling more wonderful than she could ever remember.

"I haven't been driven to a frenzy just from reading a sex scene in a book since I was fourteen. But *A Second Season* did it to me all over again. I've been damn near bursting at the seams, waiting for this to happen."

"I'm glad you didn't tell me before. I didn't know I needed to live up to some grand expectation. Not many things are more panic inducing than that."

"Especially to somebody who would wear armor-plated underwear if it wouldn't chafe. I just wanted you to know—" his tone was conspiratorial "—that you lived up to your work."

"Have I?"

"Mmm. Did I inspire it?"

"I beg your pardon?"

"I think I had something to do with the inspiration of Jonathan Martin. But all of a sudden that isn't enough. I want to have been the source for the fantasies that led to the sex scenes, too."

"The ego rises. I have never said you inspired Jonathan Martin."

"I did, though. I know it."

"What conceit."

"Admit it." His fingers did a tickling dance at her side. Kelsey squirmed. "Not a chance."

He held her tightly, captive to what was now the torment of his fingers on her bare, vulnerable skin. "Say it, or suffer the consequences."

"I don't like to be tickled," she ground out through gritted teeth.

"There's a way to avoid it."

"A knee in the groin?"

"Ah, the woman turns vicious. The truth will work better."

"You're out of luck, Sullivan. It's Clark Gable—Jonathan Martin was modeled after Clark Gable."

He let her have it, ten full fingers of torture, reducing Kelsey to a wiggling, screeching mass as every avenue of defense failed. She fought wildly, and Thomas loved it, ending up with her lying on top of him, her arms pinned to her sides so that she couldn't get back at him.

"When you least expect it," she warned with narrowed eyes and one raised brow.

"Revenge is not sweet."

She only smiled evilly and let her thigh drop between his. "I'll tell you when I've had a taste."

"You wouldn't."

She bent her knee, bringing it closer to his most vulnerable spot.

His smile was devilish. "You'd ruin the rest of the night. And I had such plans."

"It might be worth it."

"I'll make it more worth it if you don't."

"Think you're up to it?"

His hips arched into her. "Definitely."

And he was as good as his word.

The first haze of daylight found Kelsey snuggled in Thomas's arms, listening to the steady beat of his heart mixed with his deep, slumberous breathing. She stared at her hand resting on his chest, his much larger one pressed on top of it, his fingers curving beneath, holding it in his sleep.

How nice it would be to lie there forever.

Her heart constricted with the thought of what damage would be wrought to that tenuous beginning with Thomas if he ever learned exactly what she was hiding—for the day that was dawning was Thursday. And Kelsey had to face what she had gone to L.A. for in the beginning. The past and present had to crash head-on.

Chapter Eight

Anderson, Bailey, Bardwick, McConnel and Olsen" came the same young voice Kelsey had talked to on Monday.

"I'd like…" She had to clear a frog from her throat and take a deep breath. "I'd like to speak to Gordon, please."

"May I say who's calling?"

Gordon was back, then. No more reprieves. Kelsey's heart was in her mouth. "Tell him," she said softly, "that it's his sister."

"One minute, please."

Muted instrumental music took the place of the secretary's voice. The strains of "Moon River" grated on Kelsey's taut nerves. She felt as if the top of her head were about to blow off. Staring at the glowing reflection of midafternoon sun on the sandy beach beyond the window of Thomas's den, she tried to relax. And failed.

Waking up with Thomas and sharing a late brunch had forestalled this call. But he'd had to go out for an hour—to tie up some loose ends, he'd said—and Kelsey couldn't put the call off any longer. She had loose ends of her own.

A clatter broke the song, as if the receiver had been fumbled before it reached her brother's ear. His voice conveyed a fearful urgency. "Kay? My God, is that really you?"

For one blind second Kelsey nearly hung up. She took a deep breath and heard her own voice sound the way it had when she'd been seventeen and Gordon her guardian. "It's me," she confirmed.

"My God. Where are you?" he demanded in a way that left her unsure what his reaction was.

"I'm in Malibu right now. Can we meet?"

"When? Where?" Shock seemed to have left him nearly speechless.

"In an hour in that coffee shop around the corner from your office."

"I'll be there." He paused. "Are you okay?"

"Yes."

"An hour, then."

He was waiting in a booth in the back, staring out the window at nothing, when Kelsey arrived. The first thing she noticed was the horseshoe of scalp that reached into his auburn hairline above each of his temples. That hadn't been there before. He would probably end up with only the fringe of hair that their grandfather had had.

He looked good, fit, if a bit heavier than she remembered him. She wished she could stand there and just stare at him awhile, relearn his every idiosyncrasy, like that way he rubbed the side of his index finger over his top lip when he was nervous.

Did I get it, Gordy? Did I? Her own voice as a child came into her head from nowhere, as vivid as if she were only now rushing out of bed on that predawn Christmas morning of long ago.

How would Santa get somethin' like that down the chimney?

You said there was no Santa! I'm gonna go see!

Isn't there.

Is so.

Is not. Whatcha want with a dumb ol' dollhouse, anyway?

Kelsey watched her brother loosen his tie a notch and unfasten the button beneath. Did his hand shake just a little as he raised his coffee cup to his mouth?

It's okay. Don't cry so hard. I'm here. We still have each other, don't we? I'll take care of you. The child's voice was not quite hidden behind that of the man. So clear, that past voice, full of his own tears and fears and doubts on the day of their parents' funeral. *I'm a man now, Kay. I can do it.*

And he had, too. He had taken good care of her, put his own life on hold to make sure he was there for her. He had even refused a scholarship at Harvard Law School so that she could finish high school with her friends.

But it isn't fair, Gordy. You should be able to go.

I don't want to go. We need to stick together. We're so alone. And it had been her turn to comfort.

So alone. Don't hate me, Gordy. Please, please, don't hate me. I had to do it. You'll never understand, but I had to.

Lord, how sorry she was to have hurt him. She knew, without knowing any of the facts, that he would have felt responsible, taken the blame, that the whole mess she had left behind would have ended up in his lap. How could it not have, with his being married to Gary's sister? In fact, it had been at Gordon and Phyllis's wedding that she had met Gary. And all those complicated connections—law school together, partnership in the firm, brothers-in-law.

I'm so sorry, Gordy, she thought, feeling a lump form in her throat. Her nose tingled with tears she refused to allow into her eyes. So sorry. But you were as much a part of what I had to leave behind as Gary was.

He checked the time on the antique pocket watch handed down by that same grandfather from whom he had inherited his hairline. Responsible Gordon. He always knew what had to be done and did it. That simply. But it wasn't always, was it? We're different, you and I, Gordy. And I just couldn't be what you are.

Kelsey's eyes never left him as she walked to his table. Dressed in an Italian three-piece pin-striped suit, he looked prosperous, if a little stuffy. Monogrammed French cuffs peeked out above his stubby-fingered hands, and she saw his wedding band still in place. One of her worries was put to rest. At least she hadn't damaged his marriage.

"Hi," she said quietly as she slipped into the tufted red vinyl booth, the most common of greetings feeling awkward.

Gordon's round-cheeked face turned to her with a start, a sign of just how preoccupied he had been. A frown wrinkled his extended forehead as if he were as confused and uncertain of how to act as she. Kelsey endured his assessing stare, waiting for him to take her in the way she already had him.

"You look good," he said at last. "Different, but good. You let your hair grow and stopped straightening it. I like it."

"Thanks." She readjusted her glasses on top of her head, even though they didn't need it. "You look good, too. Successful."

"I'm doing okay."

"And Phyllis? How is she?"

"Fine. We have a two-month-old daughter, so she's really busy with new motherhood."

Kelsey's dry lips cracked into a smile. "You had another baby? I'm so glad. Congratulations." How odd it seemed to be talking like two mere acquaintances meeting on the street.

"I have a picture." He took his wallet from an inside breast pocket as the waitress came for their order. "I'll just have more coffee. Are you hungry, Kay?"

"No. No. Just tea, please, the same as always." But her mind seemed to shout *Nothing is the same. He's so uncomfortable with me. I'm so uncomfortable with him.*

She took the snapshot he held out. The baby was being bathed, her mouth open in a wide O of lament. "She's beautiful. What's her name?"

"Alice. We have matching bald spots."

So it bothered him. "It's kind of hard to tell from this if there's a resemblance."

"She looks more like Phyllis."

The waitress brought Kelsey's tea and refilled Gordon's coffee cup. But when she had gone, the silence that had descended didn't leave with her. Gordon looked out at the street again while Kelsey studied the mountain scene photograph behind him. There was so much to say. And so much they wanted to avoid saying.

Then they both spoke at once.

"You first," Gordon urged.

"I was just going to ask if you were happy... if everybody was healthy."

"Everything is fine," he repeated and then showed remarkable interest in sweetening his coffee and stirring it thoroughly.

"I'm sorry this is so awkward." Kelsey sighed. "If I knew a way to make it easier, I would."

When his brown eyes rose to her, they glistened with moisture, with emotion. His face was full of pain, and worry lines bracketed the bridge of his nose. "My God, what you did..." he said more to himself than to her.

The simply spoken words cut her more deeply than she would ever let him know. She deserved the wound. Brave it—the way an older child is told she's now too big to cry. Why must punishment be taken stoically? she wondered fleetingly. But all she said was "I know."

"Why didn't you call, write, let me know you were okay? No, don't answer that. I spent this last hour talking to myself—no recriminations. And no explanations. I won't ask why you did it, what went on between you and Gary. It's none of my business. Things have really just been repaired between us in the last six months. He thought I might have been in on it, as if I knew things about him too personal for anyone to know."

Gordon pinched the center corners of his eyes with his thumb and index finger, then cupped his forehead and pulled his hand down over his face. "I'm just so damn relieved that you're all right."

"Speaking of Gary..." How inane that sounded.

"He got a divorce." It seemed defensive.

"I know. Your secretary told me when I called earlier this week. I expected him to figure out a way to free himself eventually."

"I didn't know you had called before."

"I didn't leave a message. I didn't think I should call you at home."

"No, you were right not to. You know Phyllis." He took a breath that elevated his chest and then deflated it.

"I understand Gary's getting married on Sunday."

Surprise registered. "I suppose Liz told you that, too. Our secretary is pretty proud of it, since she introduced them. He's marrying a woman named Linda Harris. Do you want to know about her?" He obviously didn't want to tell her.

"Of course I'm curious. But I have too much to deal with right now to add that to it."

"Only curious? You don't care?"

"I care."

"Did you expect him to..."

"Wait? No, I didn't. Part of me is glad he didn't."

"And what about you? What's your life like now?"

"That's why I'm here. I live in a small ski town in Colorado—Winter Park. My name is Kelsey McKenna now— legally. I wrote a book called *A Second Season* and, its success has made anonymity difficult. I didn't want you...and Gary...to find out about it publicly."

He looked at her, visibly stunned, as if he were talking with someone he had suddenly realized he didn't know. And then, as if to conceal it, he rambled, "Phyllis bought that book. She loved it. She kept saying all the while she read it that it was like Grandpa O'Kelsey's life, but I never guessed..."

He frowned. "But what about your painting? I thought you'd be doing that."

"I gave it up." Kelsey looked away from his pained expression.

"You didn't really."

"I lost the joy in it. It..." She hesitated, hating to speak of the past. "It was too much a part of what I had put behind me. Even before I left, I had begun to write. It was an escape at first—like daydreaming on paper—and then it became something more. It turned into a way to work my problems out. I don't suppose this is making sense."

"I didn't know you were writing." It was almost an accusation.

"Gary..." She swallowed. "Gary didn't approve. He said he had sunk enough money into my painting supplies, and all I wanted to do was go off on some other tangent. I was hiding the writing. No one knew."

"I can't believe you aren't painting anymore. It was the only thing that ever made you happy." He didn't seem to have heard her explanation.

"Writing makes me happy now," she reiterated and then relented. "It isn't important, Gordon. It's just that the book has caused a stir. There are people after the movie rights, and I didn't want you to find out through some article that Kelsey McKenna is me." She finished in a voice that dwindled to a mere whisper. "Besides, I decided it was time to face up to what I'd done."

Again silence was a palpable thing between them, only now his eyes seemed to bore into her as if trying to learn who she was.

"Why didn't you come to me with your problems?" His tone was full of a hurt she couldn't bear. Kelsey sucked her cheeks into deep hollows and spoke to her teacup.

"I knew you would do this—blame yourself. But it was my problem, Gordon, not yours."

"I would have done anything for you, Kay. You had to know that."

"I did. You would have sacrificed your whole life for me. I couldn't have had that on my shoulders, too. Phyllis had just lost the baby, and things were bad for you. Besides, I just couldn't talk about it. I wouldn't have known what to say. I'd have just been another burden for you. And there was the family connection—Phyllis has always had such strong loyalties to Gary. As it is, I've worried and worried that I might have broken up your marriage. I didn't want that. I had enough problems without causing a whole pile of them for you."

His memory seemed sparked, and his voice hardened. "I won't say it wasn't difficult. She thinks the sun rises and sets on her brother. But it's over now. We're fine."

That deadly silence again.

Kelsey took another deep breath and forged on. "Your secretary said Gary was out of town until the end of the week. When he gets back, I want to see him."

"Oh, Kay, I don't think that's a good idea."

"That bad, huh?" She tried on a smile that didn't fit. "I have to see him, Gordon, no matter what. I thought maybe if you eased the way, told him I'm here, set something up..."

"I really don't know that it's the best thing to do."

"Please?"

"You have to know it won't be nice."

"I don't expect it to be."

His reluctance was almost a tangible thing. "I'll talk to him. Where are you staying? I'd ask you to come and stay with me, but, well, you understand how things are."

Kelsey fidgeted. "I'm not at a hotel. Oh, dammit, it's a long story, but I'm staying at Thomas Quinn-Patrick Sullivan's house."

Shock registered once more. "The actor?" Gordon asked dimly.

"It's a long story." She said it with a note of warning that she didn't want to go into it. She wrote the phone number on a napkin and slid it across to her brother. "I'll be waiting to hear from you."

Suspicion replaced shock. "Strange circle to have found you in. Was this... *actor*... the reason..."

"No. No. I just met him. He's the one who wants the screen rights to the book."

Her brother's brows pulled down over confused brown eyes. "You're so different."

"I know."

"So much . . . I don't know . . . more comfortable with yourself. Are you happy, really, Kay?"

He seemed desperate for reassurance. Her hand started for his, hesitated and then went all the way, squeezing tightly for emphasis. "I really, really am, Gordy. I'm all right."

He smiled at the familiarity only she had ever used. "I hope so. Can we see each other now, talk, write?"

"I'd like that." His eyes filled again, and Kelsey squeezed his hand harder. "Let's just get past Gary, and then we can go on from there, okay?"

He nodded his head in agreement and upturned his hand to hold hers. She watched his Adam's apple bob above his crisp white shirt collar. When he spoke again, it was with his old confident big-brother voice. "It will be all right. Maybe a little rough, but we'll get through it."

"I'm not afraid."

"But I don't think I can call you anything but Kay. Do you mind?"

Funny how the old name just didn't seem to be her. But what could she say? "Not at all. Go ahead. You'll let me know when you've arranged a meeting with Gary?"

"First thing." He looked at his watch again, more at ease now. "I have an appointment—ten minutes ago. You're sure you'll be at this number?"

"Positive."

"Then I'll be in touch." He stood, taking the check with him but suddenly reluctant to leave her. "Things are good with me now, Kay. If you need anything, even just to talk, promise you'll call me? I'll get the fireworks over with at home tonight, so you can even call there if you want."

"I'll remember."

He watched her for a moment longer before shaking his head at her. "Different. You're just so different."

From the open sliding door Thomas watched Kelsey sitting cross-legged in the sand, intent on the very last of the sunset. Unconsciously she took fistfuls of the grainy stuff and let it sift back out into miniature dunes in front of her, her narrow back straight. Strength, it said to him, and determination. Not hunched and beaten by whatever burden it was that she carried. He liked that.

Then his glance fell to the newspaper he held in one hand. Filthy rag. Two candid photographs stared back at him, one of him and Kelsey leaving The Bistro, the other of them getting out of the Jaguar in front of the house. In both Kelsey's face was in full, clear view, and the publicity she so feared was accomplished without her consent.

Damn. Again Thomas looked out at Kelsey, watching the breeze ruffle her wild hair. Sasha had picked up the paper at the grocery store checkout. She and Jake had purposely waited before leaving for Sasha's recording session to slip it to him without Kelsey's knowing.

Should he show it to her now? "She's real quiet and kind of sad-looking," Sasha had warned him. Whatever she had gone out to do had apparently not been pleasant. Why make her day any worse? Maybe she'd never have to see the damn thing.

Selfish reasons, Sullivan, and you know it.

Sure they were. He wanted her too much to have her scared off by garbage like those photographs. No matter what the reason for her being camera shy, it was shot to hell now, anyway, and there wasn't a thing to be done about it. So why rock the boat over it?

Thomas moved to the kitchen, tossed the newspaper into the trash and went out to Kelsey.

Sky and sea were a distant black curtain dappled with the silver glitter of stars and their reflections below. Kelsey's head tilted up at the sound of his approach, a quiet smile greeting him.

Thomas dropped down beside her, sitting on one knee, the other bent up behind her so that he surrounded her with the L of his legs. He brushed a strand of her hair from her cheek. "What's up, pretty lady?"

"Nothing. I was just waiting for you. All your loose ends tied?"

He sighed in mock exasperation. "For now. Every time I think I'm home free, something else comes up. How about you? Sasha said you went out while I was gone."

She turned back to staring into the distance. "You know, I had forgotten how good it is just to stare at the ocean. It kind of wraps around you, makes you feel calm, all your problems insignificant. That must be the draw."

Thomas overlooked her evasion and tried a different tack. "Sounds as if you've been here before."

"A long, long time ago. In another life."

"How many have you lived?" he teased, but somehow he knew she was serious.

"Only two," she answered practically.

A cool wind whooshed in off the water, whipping her hair back. Thomas shivered and pulled her closer, leaving his arm draped across her shoulders, his hand dangling near her breast. She wore an ice-blue cable-knit sweater big enough to fit him, and he had the thought that he would like nothing better than to climb into it with her.

"We're going to have to do something about this little difference—I'm colder than hell out here."

Kelsey smiled over at him again. "Sissy."

He stood up and pulled her with him, heading toward Sasha and Jake's house. Thomas's private section of beach stretched a half mile of flat, clean sand easing into the water. As they walked, not speaking, content to listen to the soft, lulling wash of the waves, his arm around her back kept them close together.

The small white clapboard house seemed to drink moonglow and shine with it. Outside was a huge hammock, swinging idly as if ghosts lounged in it. Thomas picked up an old army blanket and held it out for Kelsey to see. "A compromise."

Who could resist the appeal of a hammock? Kelsey got in, her back to the center so that she could continue to stare out at the sea. Thomas curved in behind her and pulled the blanket over them both.

"That's better," he breathed into her hair.

"Mmm," she agreed with a laugh, snuggling into him.

It seemed impossible to penetrate her preoccupation that night, so Thomas opted for silence for a while. One of his hands toyed with a stray curl; the other slid up under her sweater and around to her flat stomach to keep her up tight against his front. His thigh across hers held her pinioned just right. Her fresh bluegrass scent mingled with the crisp tang of seawater.

From behind, Thomas watched her profile limned in moonlight, and his heart swelled with a love for her that seemed to have blossomed like a rose in time-lapse photography—none the less real or strong for the speed with which it had grown. It seemed too right to question, as if instinct quelled any doubts.

"I have things and things and things to say to you, talk to you about. But now isn't the time, is it?"

"I'm sorry. There's a lot on my mind right now."

"I'm here, you know. I'd like to help."

"You are helping. I just need to be held. Funny how that is sometimes. The press of human flesh. For now that does more for me than you'll ever know," she said in a cloudy voice that dwindled to a whisper.

"I meant what I said last night."

"Did you say something last night?" she teased him, honestly not remembering too much of their love chatter.

"I said it was only a beginning for us, that I wanted us permanently connected."

It felt so good to have his big body cupping hers, cradling hers so completely as they swung gently in the night air. The day had been so full of emotion for her that she was left drained, too emotionally spent to deal with any more.

"Right now even the thought of the future—even as far as tomorrow—is a mountain my brain can't climb. Please let's just have now and forget the rest."

"Open up to me, Kelsey," he whispered, a warm breath in her hair.

"And the past is a sheer cliff I'm in the middle of scaling—don't make me look down when I haven't rested from today's climb yet."

His laugh was soft. "Metaphors? Are you ever going to tell me what's going on with you?"

"I don't know. Not tonight, that's for sure."

Thomas thought of the newspaper he had just thrown out. Maybe tonight was a night to let all secrets sleep.

"You're frustrating the holy hell out of me, Mc-Kenna—do you know that?" he teased.

"I don't mean to."

He pushed down on her shoulders, laying her back, his mouth finding hers softly, sweetly. His lips parted ever so slightly, and his mustache was a soft brush against her skin.

"You know," she said, lazy as a cat, "I think I could get to liking you almost as much as chocolate."

"That's high praise. Shall I try for winning out over it altogether?" His tone was a seductive insinuation as he nuzzled her temple with his nose. "No," he answered his own question. "Somehow I don't think you want that tonight, either, do you? That's okay. This is too nice to complain about."

He kissed her again, and Kelsey touched his cashmere-clad chest, comforted by the hard mound of muscle there. So many things were alive in her—fear, worry, a primitive need for comfort, to be touched and held and soothed in that special way she had forgotten until the night before in his arms. It seemed natural and right for Thomas to be the one she turned to, and for the first time she believed in a chemistry between two people. Somehow this man she barely knew answered all the needs in her, spoken and unspoken.

He kissed the tip of her nose, her eyebrows, the high crest of each cheek, and then pushed her back the way she had been before, cradled close against him, facing the ocean.

"I love you, Kelsey," he said softly to the sea. "You don't need to say anything, or even think anything tonight while you're climbing cliffs in your head. Just know how I feel about you."

Tears filled her eyes, hot and stinging and more powerful than any that had threatened that day. She couldn't speak past the tightness in her throat.

"Shhh." He hushed her thoughts. "Not a word. Not a word."

His lips pressed to the crest of her head, and then he settled his chin there and breathed a contented sigh.

I should tell him, she thought. He deserves to know. But she realized in a sudden wash of feeling that love was what she felt for him, too. Much, much too fiercely to risk the truth at that moment. Instead, she surrendered to the silent comfort he offered and let the balm of his body soothe her back into the state of limbo the sea had accomplished before.

Maybe tomorrow.

The hammock swayed like a warm cocoon. Kelsey's eyelids grew leaden and finally closed.

The lull before the storm.

Chapter Nine

Sasha was waiting with steaming tea when Kelsey came out of her bedroom the following morning. "You're up early. I heard your bathwater running when I came in, so I made tea. Tommy still asleep?"

"I didn't hear any sounds coming from his room." Kelsey accepted the tea and sank onto the couch across from where Sasha dusted. She hadn't slept for more than three hours, and morning not being her best time, anyway, she was dragging. She sat cross-legged to keep her stockinged feet warm beneath her baggy jean legs, spread the sweater she had tied around her turtleneck-clad shoulders for a more shawllike warmth and cradled both hands around the cup. "How's your record coming?"

"Wooo, girl, hot licks! Why don't you come listen sometime? Maybe it'd inspire you to immortalize me in your next book. 'Housekeeper rises to the top of the charts in a cloud of dust.'"

Kelsey laughed. "Somehow I don't think you're America's idea of a housekeeper, Sasha. Hazel never wore leather."

The front doorbell rang just then, surprising both women. Sasha headed that way. "Jake has the power off so he can fix where that reporter came over the wall. Somebody must've gotten through the gate."

From her spot on the couch Kelsey could not see the doorway. But she could hear perfectly. The man's voice pulled her heart to a pounding clot in her throat.

"I want to see Kay—no, that's not right—what did he say? Kelsey. I want to see Kelsey," he demanded, spitting out the name.

"Gary?" Kelsey managed to say, coming up behind Sasha as she tried to wrest his name from the irate man. "It's okay, Sasha. Let him come in."

Tension and an anger that seemed on the verge of erupting clearly made the housekeeper leery. But after a moment she stepped away from the door to allow him to enter. Instead of rushing past her, he stayed where he was, staring across the entry at Kelsey, whose face had paled.

"I didn't want to believe it was true," he said through clenched teeth, waving a newspaper in his white-knuckled fist. "But it is, isn't it? The hair is different, but it's you, all right." His tone was full of contempt, brittle, tightly reined. And still he stood on the doorstep, as if crossing it would unleash something violent in him.

"I wanted to see you. Did Gordon tell you?" she tried feebly.

"He didn't tell me anything but your new name and where the hell I could find you."

Kelsey doubted Gordon had had the chance for anything more. She took a deep breath, aware of Sasha's curious eyes. "Come in. We can talk."

"Talk? Talk? *Now* you want to talk. Isn't it a little late for that, Kay?" His tone was rapier sharp.

He was tall and lanky, with curly blond hair and a hawkish nose that became more pointy in anger. It could have been a spear as he started toward her, one slow, angry step per word. "Do you think I want to hear anything you might have to say?"

Instinct pushed Kelsey back a half step for each of his. "I wanted to explain. To—"

"Explain?" he shouted. "God Almighty, do you think you can? Do you think I want to hear any of your damn explanations after all this time? Now—when my life is finally on track again? What is it with you? Some damn need you have to torture me? Isn't what you did enough? Did you have to make me a laughingstock, too, with your damn face staring out at me from a lousy checkout counter gossip rag?"

"Gary, I don't know what you're talking about."

The back of her knees touched one of the couches, stopping her retreat just as he threw the newspaper at her feet. Kelsey looked down to see the front page of *The Inquisitor* with its blown-up pictures of her and Thomas. She pressed her eyes closed with her fingertips. All her efforts had been for nothing. She had gone there to avoid anything like that happening.

"I'm sorry," she said lamely to the pictures at her feet. "I didn't know.... I wanted to see you, talk to you, before anything like this happened."

"Is that so? You know what I think? I think you're a lying bitch!"

"Jake!" Sasha's voice barely registered with Kelsey as the woman ran to get her husband.

Gary took two more purposeful steps toward Kelsey, grabbing her shoulders fiercely, angrily, and shaking her so hard that her head wobbled. "You bitch! Is this where you've been for the past three years? Is this why you did it? To be with your lover? I could kill you! I swear I've never hated anyone the way I hate you!"

"What the hell!" Thomas's deep voice boomed from behind. He yanked the enraged man away from Kelsey just as Sasha returned. Jake pushed past her, taking over from Thomas to pull Gary's arms behind his back.

A string of the foulest epithets spewed from Gary's mouth as Jake dragged him out the front door. Kelsey could only stare dumbly, her head still spinning.

"Are you all right?" Thomas asked urgently, his own hands replacing Gary's on her shoulders, only gently now, steadying her. No one had even noticed that he wore only brown boxer shorts.

Kelsey took a big gulp of air and shook her head. "I'm okay."

"Shall I call the police?" His thumbs rubbed circles on her collarbone.

"No! No. Don't let Jake hurt him. He had good reason to be mad."

Thomas looked up at Sasha watching them. He nodded toward the front door. "Tell Jake to let him go—just to get him off the grounds."

When the housekeeper was gone, Thomas ducked his head to see into her dazed eyes. "Hey, are you sure he didn't hurt you?"

She shook her head, finally coming back to herself at the sight of those dark green depths full of worry. "I'm sorry about all this."

Very slowly Thomas took his hands from her shoulders, straightened and drew a deep breath. "I'm going to put some pants on, and when I come back, I think it's about time you let me in on what's happening here. Don't shake your head at me. I want to know what the hell is going on with you, and you're going to tell me. No discussion.''

Five minutes later he was back. Kelsey stood at one of the sliding glass doors, staring blindly out, her hands clenched around the trailing arms of the sweater around her neck.

"Talk to me, Kelsey," Thomas commanded, his voice both tender and relentless.

Silence.

Kelsey felt numb. Tired. Cold from the inside out. It was futile to try to keep a secret that wasn't one anymore. "I don't know if I *can* tell it. I never have before. Never...not to a soul."

"Just start at the beginning, and take me through whatever it is the way it happened."

She drew a deep breath again, raising and stiffening her shoulders. But her voice was soft. "I have the dubious distinction of being a statistic." Once more silence fell and sat like a living thing in the room between them as Kelsey struggled to continue.

"Come on. A statistic for what?"

She swallowed audibly. "I'm a runaway wife."

He didn't know what to say to that, and for a long time Kelsey couldn't follow it up, either. The words just hung in midair until finally Thomas said, "Tell me what happened."

Her voice was barely audible, a remorseful whisper. "It's not an easy thing to explain...it wasn't an easy thing to do. How can I make you understand? How can I explain how ashamed I am of it? Or how I still can't see any other thing I could have done?"

She couldn't face him, so she continued speaking to the glass door in front of her. "I was so...so unhappy. Lord, that's an understatement." She dropped her forehead to the cold glass, trying hard to find the right words.

"I don't know when it started. Maybe it was when my parents died. He never said it, but I knew I was a burden to Gordon—Gordon is my brother. Who wants to be stuck at twenty-two with a fifteen-year-old sister to raise? I didn't want it to be any harder on him than it had to be. That sounds so selfless. It really wasn't. The truth is, I was just a scared kid—scared sick that he'd leave me, too. He had just graduated from college and had plans to begin law school. I was afraid that if I wasn't perfect and didn't make it easy for him, he would just go away."

She took a deep breath as if storing strength to get through the rest. "It's insidious, though, trying to be perfect, to please everyone. And what I was—am—was so far from perfect. I knew how strange I was—being afraid of weird things and never quite fitting into the mainstream— so I had to work really hard to hide that. I don't know if this makes any sense to you."

Thomas watched her, knowing it was difficult for her to tell her story but hoping it would help her to talk about it, to get it all out in the open. "Just let me have it all, Kelsey."

"Every gory detail, huh?" She tried to make light of it, but the quaver in her voice betrayed her. Her head fell back, as if staring at the ceiling would hold the tears in her eyes.

"Every one," he demanded quietly, waiting expectantly as Kelsey searched for a way to put it all into words.

He watched her silent struggle, wanting to go to her, take her into his arms. But he knew by the way she avoided even looking at him that she needed distance to do this. He plunged his hands into the pockets of his low-slung jeans to keep from reaching out to her.

When she finally began again, her speech was stilted, as if she chose each word carefully.

"Somewhere along the way, being perfect became my life's work. Everything had to be just right. *I* had to be just right, just what everyone wanted me to be. I married Gary when I was nineteen, and the whole thing seemed to avalanche. The need to constantly please him and his family buried me alive. I played so many different roles that after a while I lost touch with myself."

"It got so I couldn't do anything without worrying if a dozen different people would approve—or how to hide it from or make excuses to those who didn't. Do you know what it's like to be a basket case from worrying that people might find out how many times you made your poor hardworking husband eat out? Or from agonizing over the cost of a pair of shoes? I was always bowing and scraping and apologizing and worrying and explaining."

She paused briefly. "Somewhere in all of that I lost sight of even what my own tastes were, what I really wanted or didn't want. Every decision, every act was based on how acceptable it was to everyone around me. And I went quietly crazy," she finished softly.

"There isn't an outline for these things, like one, two, three, this is what happened. I only know that nothing made me happy. I couldn't sleep. I was afraid of everything...everything..."

Again she fell silent for a moment. Then she continued in a monotone. "I was sick all the time—stomach trouble, female problems, headaches. I couldn't eat, and if I did, the food didn't stay down. I felt so isolated, so lonely, as if even when I was with people, I was invisible to them. And the tears. Lord, the tears. Crying became a way of life."

Thomas could see her arms wrapped protectively around her ribs, and he ached for her. "Didn't you talk to anyone about how you were feeling? Not even your husband?"

She laughed mirthlessly. "I tried—I really did. Gary wouldn't listen, no matter how I put it. 'What do you have to be depressed about?' he'd say. And then he'd tell me how good I had it, that I should just *do* something with myself, that he didn't have the time to bother with anything so stupid. He was busy and happy with his life, you see, as long as I kept quiet.

"And other people don't want to hear your troubles—especially nebulous ones. It sounds like whining. I considered seeing a psychiatrist or a counselor, but Gary didn't believe in that—the witch doctors would bleed him dry and make me think I really was crazy, he said. My doctor wouldn't look me in the eye. He'd just say it was hormones and scribble out Valium prescriptions. And poor Gordon was involved with his own life and problems. His wife had just had a stillborn baby. I couldn't go to him."

She began to remember it all. "The longer it went on, the better other women began looking to Gary. I don't know for sure whether he actually did anything, though there were several times when I was pretty sure he did—nights when he didn't come home at all. He started talking about how much fun so-and-so was, or how easy it was to be around another woman, or how attractive, witty, bright he found someone and why couldn't I be more like that, why did I have to be so negative? I was trying so hard to be what I thought he wanted, and there he was, upping the expectations. I wanted to scream that I was already dancing as fast as I could."

"So you took off," Thomas prompted.

"Not just like that." She turned to face him, her back straight, head high, looking him in the eye. "One morning I woke up and couldn't make myself get out of bed. I had slept twelve hours, and still I felt tired. So tired. I thought of the day ahead of me, of all the different masks I would have to wear just to get by—different ones for my mother-in-law, my sister-in-law, for a friend I was supposed to see, for my brother, for Gary...."

She took another deep breath as if she had just finished a race, her pace slowing. "And I just couldn't do it. Any of it. And I knew it would never change. And I knew I would never be happy."

Her voice quavered and dropped to a whisper again. "And I was so, so tired." She stopped and drew a breath filled with resolution and acceptance.

"I had thought of a solution before that, thought out all the details. It was just a matter of going out to the garage." Her voice was slow, calm, resigned. "I remember that I was numb and really cold, even though it was hot outside. 'A good airtight car,' Gary had said when he bought the BMW. I figured it was finally going to matter. I stuck one end of the hose into the exhaust pipe.... No, you don't need to hear that part."

Kelsey pressed her fingertips over her eyes, breathing so hard that her nostrils flared. And when she spoke again, her throat was so full of tears she could only whisper, "I wondered if it hurt to die." Then she raised her eyes to him once more. They were glistening and full, yet her voice was slightly triumphant.

"I had forgotten the keys." She gave a small ironic smile. "I couldn't even do that right." She sucked in her cheeks for a moment. "But then I realized I didn't really want to die. I just wanted—needed—to be free."

She sighed and squared her shoulders, and Thomas not only heard but also saw the transformation in her.

"I had started writing *A Second Season*—it had begun as an escape from reality, I guess. But the more I worked on it, the more sense I came to see in my grandfather's leaving behind what was intolerable and building a new life. That day, out in the car, the only options I saw for myself were to die or to run away." She drew another deep breath. "Suddenly I had the courage, and I ran away. But you see, when you run from something, it trails behind you like a tail. You're never *really* free of it, even when you convince yourself it's far behind you.

"It took me a long time to get to know myself again, as if every mask had been a layer of subterfuge I was buried under and I had to peel them off one at a time to find myself again. It took even longer to learn to accept what I found and be comfortable with it. I had to live in a cocoon for a while until I was strong again and mentally healthy. And then I knew I had to come back and own up to what I'd done. I had to do it before I hurt them any further by having my picture slap them in the face in connection with selling you the rights to *A Second Season*. Guess I blew that."

She searched his face, fearful of finding contempt there. But all she found was a mirror of her own pain and, if not understanding, then acceptance without judgment.

"Then you're still married to him?" Thomas asked reluctantly.

"No. He got a divorce. On grounds of desertion, I'm sure. In fact, as I understand it, he's getting married again on Sunday. Brave man."

"How do you feel about that?" He tested her carefully.

"It hurts a little." Her brown eyes met his squarely. "But I didn't come back here to reconcile with him, if that's what you mean. And I never would have made love with you if I hadn't known I was free."

He hesitated before asking, "Did you have kids?"

"No. Heavens, no. I wasn't totally stupid. I knew enough to know I couldn't handle parenthood on top of everything else. So. There's the skeleton in my closet. An ugly old bag of bones. I'm sorry you got mixed up in it. I'll make sure I finish it on Gary's territory instead of yours." She tried feebly to lighten the mood and hide the tension that still radiated from her.

But Thomas wasn't having any of that. Eyes the color of a sea in turmoil pierced her. "You can't mean you're going anywhere near that guy again. He's totally out of control. It's not safe."

"He'll calm down. It'll be all right. I know him." But did she? Kelsey had never seen Gary behave the way he had that morning. What if she didn't know him any better than he had known her? Still, she had come this far. The rest of the way had to be traveled. "I have to see him, Thomas, and get the whole thing over with."

The house on Bryant Street seemed larger than Kelsey remembered it, a red-brick ranch with a steep, shake-shingled roof that made it look like a huge, lounging turtle. The shutters that framed every window were freshly whitewashed, the shrubs beneath precisely trimmed. All spruced up for its new mistress, she couldn't help but think.

"You're sure you want to do this?" Thomas asked from beside her when the Jaguar had been parked at the curb for a full five minutes and she still hadn't gotten out.

"Gordon said Gary had calmed down some. He's agreed to see me. I'm sure that means he'll be more in control." It wasn't so much a fear of facing her ex-husband that kept Kelsey in the car as it was of entering the house they had shared for seven years.

Thomas reached to the nape of her neck, digging beneath the turtleneck and the sweater draped there to find her muscles tightly corded. "Remember, if he's civil and you don't want me in on this, just give me the high sign and I'll wait outside."

Kelsey's glance went to the two-story house next door. Wouldn't Betsy, the block busybody, love *that*. Thomas Quinn-Patrick Sullivan waiting on the Olsen porch would give her gossip material for a month.

"I don't think you should have come at all." She fell back on the argument they had had just before leaving his house. Thomas had insisted he accompany her for safety's sake if nothing else.

His hand rode the small of her back up the long sidewalk to the shadowy front porch. The baby's breath she had planted below the railing had overgrown to fill twice the space she had originally blocked out for it. She remembered the lady in the seed shop not understanding why she wanted to grow the stuff if she wasn't going to use it for bridal bouquets and Gary's complaint that it would take over the whole yard. But she liked the explosion of tiny white flowers, liked having an abundance of it to pick for accents in nearly every room of the house. So she had cultivated it, anyway, and withstood the criticisms.

How strange seemed the sound of the doorbell from outside. A muted memory. Gary flung open the heavy oak panel, snarling that he was on the phone in his office and leaving them to let themselves in through the glass storm door.

Inside nothing had changed, and that was disconcerting. The sturdy plaid davenport was still under the picture window, and Kelsey still hated it. She had wanted a navy-blue chintz camelback sofa, but Gary had overruled it as impractical. The only difference in the living room was in the pictures on the walls; artsy photographs now hung where once her oil paintings had been.

Lost in thoughts and feelings, Kelsey wandered, running a hand across the carved mantel, unconsciously checking the corner tile of the interior border to see if it was still loose. It was.

For a moment she was again responsible for the place, picking a string off the matching La-Z-Boy, brushing a speck of dust from the low end table, straightening the pleated shade on the brass lamp.

She crossed into the dining room, spending a minute at the tall china closet that displayed the silver-leaf pattern they had chosen just after they had become engaged, along with the crystal goblets and silver trays that had been wedding gifts. They all seemed to belong to someone else now.

Missing from atop the highboy was the big basket she had kept filled with fragile baby's breath. But then she noticed the absence of her favorite flowers from all the places she had kept them before. A few flowers. A few paintings. Had they been the only things that had reminded him of her?

Still wandering, she entered the kitchen. Her kitchen. The yellow flowered wallpaper she had put up herself was still there, not even faded. And the odd assortment of china molds, tin plates and spoons still decorated it just as she had arranged them. Would his new wife change it when she came to live here next week? Kelsey wondered.

All through her explorations Kelsey felt bittersweet pangs as she came across items she had chosen with love, those same things that had become symbols of the domesticated person she had been trying so desperately to be and was not—then or now.

For a moment she stood at the kitchen sink, feeling the heat of afternoon sunshine through the window beneath the ruffled swag valance and scalloped shade. She had stood in that same spot for a full half hour on that day three years ago. So afraid that she had been sick, hating herself so much that it had brought bile to her throat, and yet knowing she couldn't stay—not and survive. She had left her wedding band on the marbled windowsill.

"Kelsey? Are you all right?"

It was Thomas's voice from the doorway behind her, warmer than the sunshine on her face. Had he followed her down that maudlin memory lane? She turned to him, leaning back against the kitchen counter, her expression calmer than he had expected. She nodded in silent answer to his question before pushing away with her hips and returning to the living room.

They nearly collided with Gary as he came out of his office, and the time for reverie was past.

"Let's get this over with," he said with a sneer. "I don't know why you feel you have to push it."

"I wanted to try to make you understand what had happened."

Gary's blue eyes narrowed at Thomas. "He's what happened."

"No, he isn't. We only met last week."

Thomas chose the arm of the davenport as a seat, and Kelsey saw Gary bristle. The cushions were for sitting, not the arms, she remembered him lecturing. But now he only turned his head, pretending Thomas was not there at all.

Kelsey hid her hands in her jean pockets. Where to start?

"I've had months and months to realize I didn't handle this well, that I should have tried to work it out and at least be honest with you. But I made the mistake, and that can't be undone. All I can do now is try to make amends, apologize, and I know that must seem feeble to you.''

"You'll never know," he snarled.

Thomas watched her throat move convulsively as she began telling the story much as she had to him. His arms were crossed over his chest, each hand clasped under the opposite armpit to keep them from clenching in anger. His heart broke for Kelsey, and he wanted to wring the other man's neck for the snide comments he slung at her, for rejecting all she was trying to explain to him, for condemning her as crazy—always was, always would be, she should be locked up. . . .

"You want to know what it was like for me?" Gary shouted, red-faced, bending forward as if to pin Kelsey back. "First I was scared to death that something had happened to you, that you'd been kidnapped or had an accident. I called the police before I checked your closet. Now there was a mistake."

Self-disgust at the very thought whirled him around, and he began pacing as he railed at her. "Do you know how embarrassing it was to discover everything gone with a smirking cop standing behind me? God. No sympathy from the authorities—too much from relatives and friends. Do you know what it's like to watch the news and wonder if every gruesome crime could make your wife turn up as the victim? I even got to go to the city morgue once to see if a half-decomposed body was you," he spat sarcastically. "I can guarantee that's a once-in-a-lifetime experience.

"Sometimes I was so worried about you that I'd find myself in a cold sweat. Other times I was so mad that I couldn't breathe. How could she do something like that? I would ask myself a hundred times a day. What did I do wrong? Didn't I give you everything you wanted? Didn't I work hard to provide? And what did I get for it? Do you know what it's like to be whispered about? To face pity from people who used to respect you? Do you know how I felt about myself, the doubts? My God, I was impotent for months, thanks to you.''

He stopped short, staring up at nothing, his nostrils flaring with shallow breaths of rage. ''And then, even when I thought it was over and I'd try to start fresh, I'd have to face explaining to a new woman why I wasn't quite free. Then I'd see her wondering what I was hiding that had driven my wife to do such a thing.

''Not even a note, for God's sake, nothing to even say why. And in all that time not a word. You didn't even give me the option of a divorce. No, I had to present a declaration of search in court—stand in front of a judge and admit you had run out on me and no one could find you. Then the court signed the order allowing me to run notices in the papers once a week for a month. It constitutes serving a summons—it also lets the whole damn world know what's happening in your life. When the ads go unanswered, it's just a matter of signing default papers. By then the humiliation was complete, and I had started to wish you were dead.''

Kelsey took it all silently, as if understanding his need and granting him his due. Thomas didn't feel that he could be the one to stop the flow of words, but hearing it all ate him alive. What it must be doing to her, he thought. But never did she waver or flinch or cower. The only signs of her guilt were the ashen pallor of her face, the white lines around her lips and the fierce grip of her fists on those dangling sweater sleeves.

And when Gary stopped at last, pouring himself a full two inches of Scotch from a corner wet bar, Kelsey didn't insult him with a mere apology. Instead, she reached into her purse for the envelope of money that Thomas had been wondering about for so long.

"Nothing will ever make what I did right, Gary. I know that. I've thought of the money I took from our savings account as a loan all this time, and I want you to have it back."

He spun around with a look of disbelief pulling his otherwise handsome features into an ugly sneer. "Is that why you came back? Well, you can keep the money! It would have been worth it to me never to have to see you again."

She placed the envelope on the wet bar's tiled counter, carefully distant from where he leaned his hips as if he needed the support. "No matter what you say, I'm returning it," she informed him softly.

Thomas watched the other man pick up the envelope and take the money out, fanning it like a hand of cards as he stared down at it. Before anyone realized it was coming, he had flung it into her face.

Startled, Kelsey lurched backward, her eyes wide. Thomas lunged from his perch, blocking any further attack Gary might have had in mind. "Now wait a minute!" he boomed. "She doesn't deserve that!"

"You don't think so?" Gary spat at the taller man. "Well, have at it, pal. You want her? You really want to risk it? Be my guest. She's all yours. Now why don't the two of you get the hell out of my house."

Kelsey stepped to Thomas's side, wishing there was something she could say or do. "Please, Gary, I—"

"Just shut up, Kay. Just shut up. There's nothing else you can say that I want to hear, and I can't stand the sight of you." Then to Thomas he sneered, "Get her the hell out of here before I lose what control I have and break her neck."

Thomas clasped Kelsey's tension-taut arm, steering the way. They hadn't even moved off the front porch when the sound of Gary's glass crashed into the closed portal behind them. Kelsey jumped as if it had hit her squarely in the back and froze in her tracks for a split second before taking a deep breath and moving on to the car.

Chapter Ten

It was a full twenty minutes after Thomas and Kelsey had left the house on Bryant Street before either of them spoke. Then Thomas broke the heavy silence.

"How're you doing over there, lady?" he asked with a sidelong glance.

"I'm okay" came Kelsey's response, stronger than he had expected.

"Want to talk?"

"No."

"Want me to talk?"

"I'd rather you wouldn't, if you don't mind. There really isn't any more to be said about this whole mess, anyway."

And that was that.

Throughout the evening Kelsey stayed in her own room with the door closed, writing as if she were possessed.

Outside Thomas paced and worried that now that she had taken care of what she had come for, she would disappear from his life like smoke in the wind.

How exactly did she feel about him? She had never said. It was understandable that she had been absorbed in her own problems. Still, he couldn't help wondering if her feelings for him came anywhere near what his were for her.

Thomas threw back a last swallow of brandy as he made the circuit past Kelsey's bedroom door for the fifth time. Would her past affect their relationship? Was she afraid of the commitment? She had, after all, not let herself be involved with anyone for the past three years.

But that isn't all you're worried about, is it, Sullivan? Be honest with yourself. What's eating you?

The picture she'd painted of the woman she was when she ran away didn't seem to be the same Kelsey he knew. Her lack of convention was part of what appealed to him. But was she really so different?

He hated the doubt, but there it was, a nagging, anxious feeling in the pit of his stomach. What if, when he least expected it and loved her the most, she disappeared? How could he stand losing her that way? Or *any* way, for that matter? Could something like that be guarded against? Would honesty do it? Would love? He didn't want her to be anything but what she was, the slightly off-center woman he had begun falling in love with in the pages of her book. But did she know that?

Once more he paced outside her door. What is this? he thought. Insecurity, for heaven's sake? Don't be a jerk, Sullivan. She wouldn't do it again. Look at the agony she's gone through over it. She's no fool. What's passed is passed. History doesn't necessarily repeat itself. Didn't it take strength and stability and mental health to go back there and do what she did today? Sure it did. Not many people could have faced up to a mistake the way she had.

It had just thrown him off, that was all. There wasn't anything to worry about. Everything would be fine. Of course it would. Everything would be just fine.

When, by about midnight, Kelsey had poured the day's feelings out onto paper within the context of her next story and her hand ached and was gnarled with writer's cramp, she finally emerged. She found Thomas on one of the off-white living room couches in front of a big-screen television set that, when closed up, appeared to be only another oak cabinet. Sunk low in the overstuffed sofa, his feet propped on the coffee table, his head fallen back against the cushions, he was sound asleep.

Kelsey clicked off the old Andy Hardy movie and gave in to the urge to study him. He didn't look peaceful. His brows were pulled into a frown, and she wondered what dreams caused it. His full lower lip had disappeared beneath his mustache, pulling his chin up into a slight tilt.

His feet and bony ankles were bare below jeans whose hems had worn to a feathery fray. One hand lay flat against his firm belly; in the other hand a brandy snifter teetered, braced against the next cushion.

Kelsey took the glass from his limp fingers and set it on the coffee table. How could she have come to feel so much for him in such a short time and amid so much emotional turmoil? But she had, and leaving him the next day was not going to be easy.

What else could she do, though? She had accomplished what she'd set out to do. She couldn't just become a professional houseguest now.

What *did* one do in these circumstances? she wondered. Surely long-range commitment didn't come from a week's acquaintance and a night of making love. So it must be one-night stands or vacation flings and then back to the real world. What an unsavory proposition. Were other people simply more resilient, smart enough not to let their hearts get entangled the way hers was? Did that make the inevitable parting easier?

It didn't really matter, did it? Because it was already too late. And this parting wasn't going to be easy for her in any way.

But at the moment, thinking about it made it all the more painful, and she had had more than her share of pain for one day. She wanted to curl up beside Thomas and be taken into his arms for this last night with him. Did that make it casual sex? No, there was nothing casual about it. Not to her. Not even if this was the last time she ever saw him. But if she couldn't have a long-term relationship, she could at least have now.

Still, she was new at this game, so when he stirred, stretching his neck and blinking his thick-lashed eyelids beneath his wheaten brows, Kelsey settled for rounding the couch and clasping only his shoulder. "Why didn't you go to bed?"

Thomas yawned broadly. "I was hoping I wouldn't have to go alone." He pressed the inside corners of his eyes with his thumbs and then dropped his head back again to look up at her. Her features were calm, her small smile serene, and he couldn't believe he had thought the thoughts he had earlier that night. His heart was safe with her.

"Thanks for giving me some space tonight."

"S'okay. I figured you had to come out eventually." He covered her hand with his. "What the hell were you doing in there, anyway?"

"Working."

"You're kidding."

"What did you think I was doing? Sulking?"

His shoulder shrugged in her hand. "Tough day."

"Mmm. I'm glad it's over."

"Is it?"

She took a deep, revitalizing breath. "Yeah, it is."

"Good" was all he said, reaching up to the back of her head to pull her mouth down to his in a kiss that made Kelsey wonder if his dream had been more erotic than troubling. But it was something she needed, too, and she yielded to the angled invasion of his tongue.

"This isn't an easy thing to do standing on my head," she said, laughing, when she came up for air.

"Then come down here and find a better way." He kept hold of her hand as she moved around the couch, pulling her down on top of him. His arms encircled her, molding her to him before he settled his chin against the top of her head, which rested snugly in the hollow of his shoulder. "Here's what I think. We've spent one hell of a day dealing with the past, and tomorrow is time enough for taking care of the future. So how about if we spend tonight just making love until we drop?"

"*Just* making love? Is that all?" she teased, reveling in the feel of being wrapped in his arms, his leg across her hip holding her tightly. It all felt too good, and she needed the comfort of him too much to disrupt it just then with news of her plans.

"Are you up to it?" he asked more seriously.

But the past two days had saturated Kelsey with seriousness, and she wasn't having any. "I thought it was you who had to be up for it."

"Let me know I'm not pushing too soon, and I think it can be arranged."

"You mean just admit I'm interested instead of waiting to be swept off my feet with the overwhelming urges of spontaneous passion? I don't know. Premeditation is tough on my outdated morality."

"Valentino it is, then." He laughed lasciviously and then frowned with the intensity of The Sheik and ravaged her mouth in part parody, part passion. "How am I doing?"

"At what?" She feigned innocence, batting her eyelashes.

"So the lady wants to play games, huh?" He lunged to his feet, yanking her with him and up over his shoulder like a sack of meal, swatting her soundly on the small rise of her rump. "Now I know where all those brownies and Godiva chocolates went."

"Funny man. I hope you get a hernia," she said to his back.

He kicked the bedroom door wide and crossed the room in three strides to fling her down on the Chianti-colored bedspread. Then he stood over her, straddling her legs. "We'd both be sorry if I did."

"Not me. I'd love to see you writhe in misery."

"Forget the misery. I'll writhe for you, anyway." He bent over her, his hands on either side of her head as his mouth lowered to tease her unmercifully with short kisses and mustache ticklings all over her face. Then he sucked on her earlobe as one hand slid under her sweater. "Ah . . . you drive me wild, lady."

She only smiled her pleasure, arching her breast into his hand and yielding to the shivers he sent up her spine. "Want to know which part of Jonathan Martin is you?" she teased.

"All of him," he answered confidently.

"The back of his knees and his buns." The last word eased into a moan of pleasure as he pushed her sweater up and his suckling mouth tormented the hard point of her nipple.

Thomas laughed, drawing away from her to pull her sweater all the way off and then tug at her jeans, only to find that this time *she* wore no underwear.

"And which character were you?" he said in a voice so husky that it was nearly inaudible as he shed his own clothes and lay beside her, pulling her into his arms.

"I get to be a little of all of them, or all of them get to be a little of me—whichever you'd prefer." She couldn't get enough of the feel of his skin, smooth and warm over hard muscles.

Now it was Thomas's turn to arch into her hands, flexing his back as she traced it with her palms.

"What I'd prefer—" he said trailing kisses back down to her breast and smoothing a heated path with his hand down her stomach to her thighs and then between "—is to be *inside* you." And his fingers accomplished it.

Words were lost then in the building waves of passion as they moved together like well-rehearsed dancers, responding instinctively to the needs of the other. They made long, slow love, and even though Kelsey had not spoken the words, the feelings flowed freely and left her without a doubt about what it was she felt for Thomas.

But when each had found the perfect peak only the other could give and Thomas rolled them onto their sides, still joined, and whispered into her hair, "I love you, Kelsey," she kept her own feelings to herself. They were too new and unexplored yet to expose.

His words made it all the harder to tell him what she had put off before. But as dawn came in a rosy blush across their entwined arms and legs, she knew it had to be done.

Her voice was soft, and though she tried not to sound hesitant, she couldn't help it. "I've made reservations on a two o'clock flight back to Denver today."

For a minute she didn't think he had heard her.

"You can't do that," he said finally, firmly.

"It's all right. I also called Ali and told her to work up the sale of the screen rights to *A Second Season*. There's no reason not to let you have them now. I don't think either Gordon or Gary could be any more hurt than they have been already. And you were right: there's more of you in Jonathan Martin than I realized even when I was writing him. You should play him."

"Uh-uh. You can't leave. No way. Not a chance. I'm not letting you go."

Kelsey laughed a little at that. "Too bad you're undecided."

He pulled away, staring down at her angrily, hating the renewal this turn of events gave to his earlier doubts about her. "I can't believe you're even thinking about it. What the hell was this tonight? The farewell performance? We make love like this, and then you drop the bomb?"

"I know how it seems. But I can't just hang around here forever. I've taken care of what I came for. I have to go home now."

Thomas studied her. Was that all there was to it?

Then his anger and doubts receded behind his usual confident, teasing manner and the quirk of a lopsided smile. "I see. The lady isn't sure where we stand, now that the necessity for her being here is past. Well, here it is, love. I'll repeat what I said before: I want you in my life in every way."

He pressed his fingertips to her lips to forestall her refusal. "I know, too soon. So let's put it into safe, easy terms. You can't leave. I need you here to pick your brain about Jonathan Martin, and I have a thousand questions about how to do justice to converting *A Second Season* to the screen. So if you can't stay just to be with me, you can consider it a professional courtesy and stay for that."

"But, Thomas—"

"No 'but, Thomases.' You're not getting out of here, lady, I need your input, and you owe it to yourself and to your book to make sure it's done right."

"I have work—"

"You bet you do—right here. You're between books until the other one sells. Why sit on your thumbs in Winter Park while I butcher your baby in L.A.? I need your guidance to make Jonathan Martin perfect, and after these past couple of days, you owe me."

"Dirty pool, Sullivan."

"You bet."

How could she fight to leave him when all she wanted was to stay? "Okay, but just for a while, just to talk you through the character, even though I know you don't really need it."

He reached for the bedside phone, punched out a number and waited. "Kit? Open your eyes and listen. Kelsey is selling us the rights. I need you to get your butt out of bed, get Bernice on the phone to Ali Robbins in New York and get the lawyers drawing everything up. I want Kelsey on the payroll as story consultant. She'll be with us all the way."

Story consultant? With them all the way? That was news to her. What happened to just having her brains picked to do justice to Jonathan Martin and her book? Could it be only a matter of terminology—Thomas legitimizing her contribution to his efforts? But fear niggled at Kelsey. Did he expect more of her than she had just agreed to? Or was she being paranoid? She decided on paranoia. His approach simply meant more time with him—that was all.

Thomas rolled back and settled her into his side to sleep at last. "All set. With you as my personal guide to old Jonathan, we can't go wrong."

The feel of his big body cradling her banished all doubts. It felt so right. *She* felt so right. They were in tune with each other. He didn't expect more of her than she could give. If nothing else, after all they had been through, he knew well that part of her that needed complete honesty in what was expected of her.

There was nothing to worry about. Story consultant was just a title that meant she would tell Thomas some of her thoughts about the character and book that might not have been overtly apparent, small things that would help his performance and the transition of *A Second Season* from the printed page to the screen. That was all. It was really just a guise to give them more time to explore their feelings and where they might be able to go from there. Nothing to worry about.

She hoped.

Chapter Eleven

The park was crowded, even for a Friday afternoon. Mothers read or chatted with each other as rambunctious children crawled like uncoordinated monkeys on a jungle gym that looked like a Daniel Boone fort, two white-haired gentlemen played checkers on a picnic table and exhibitionist teenagers rushed the season dressed in nothing but running shorts to sail a chartreuse Frisbee through the air.

Kelsey sat atop a weathered picnic table, her feet on the bench below, her arms hugging her knees. She watched her brother approach, pushing a stroller, and wondered if he had remembered and chosen this particular park for its lack of trees and therefore shortage of birds.

High silver-gray clouds blocked the sun. The bare breath of a breeze ruffled the wild curls of her hair, which was held back by her glasses. She smiled broadly at the sight of Gordon behind the pink-flowered baby carriage. It seemed so odd to see him there. But he looked at home, glancing down at his passenger often to make sure she was all right. He wore a maroon-and-white sweat suit, had a yellow-checked diaper bag slung over his shoulder and a blanket grasped under his arm, and still he managed to look every bit as staid as he had in pinstripes.

"Hi, kiddo!" He parked the stroller beside her and leaned to kiss her cheek.

Like old times, Kelsey thought gratefully as she watched him spread the blanket, set the diaper bag on it and unstrap the massively swathed baby to get her out of the stroller.

Kelsey hadn't been too sure of his attitude when they had spoken on the phone. Thomas had voiced the desire to meet Gordon but said he would cause too much commotion in a public park and had suggested they have their afternoon together at his house. But Gordon had vetoed that idea vehemently. Now he seemed fine.

"Can I hold her?" Kelsey asked as she hopped down from the picnic table to sit cross-legged on the blanket.

"Sure. Just let me change her diaper first."

The whole scene delighted Kelsey's sense of humor, but she refrained from teasing. Still too soon. He might take offense.

Dry diaper accomplished, Gordon handed his daughter over.

"She looks just like Mama! I can't believe it. Hello, little Alice McConnel. What pretty brown eyes you have." Kelsey kissed the tiny, faintly feathered head, and her niece responded with a wail. "Uh-oh. Looks like we're not fast friends."

Instinct made Gordon reach for the baby, setting her on the blanket between them. The wails ceased. "She's not much for being handled. Don't feel bad."

Kelsey offered the wee fist her finger and settled for that. "I was surprised you called. Glad, but surprised."

"I wasn't sure if I should—call you *there*, I mean."

" 'There?' At Thomas's? Why not?"

He shrugged and looked away. "It just seemed... strange. I don't know. I feel funny about him."

"He wanted to meet you."

"So you said. I didn't... wasn't ready to meet him."

Resentment? It didn't make sense. "You do believe that Thomas had nothing to do with my leaving, don't you?"

"Yeah, sure. It just doesn't seem right. Anyway, Phyllis was going to be gone for a couple of hours—getting her hair cut for the wedding on Sunday—and I thought you'd like to see the baby."

"I'm glad you called. I wanted to see you again, too. How did Phyllis take all this?"

"You know Phyllis. Baby brother never could do any wrong, and you never could do anything right."

Kelsey was surprised he had noticed. At the time it had seemed as if only she recognized the unspoken criticism. "It isn't hurting your relationship with her, is it?"

"She blows a lot of steam, but that's all. There's no problem."

But Kelsey couldn't help remembering that this meeting had had to take place away from Gordon's home ground. He obviously didn't want to get into whatever conflicts he was having with his wife. "And what about Gary? How is he doing?" she asked instead.

"He got plastered last night, put the money in an account for Alice this morning and said he didn't ever want to hear your name mentioned again. I think there's a lot of show to it at this point. No matter what he says, he's relieved to know you're all right. Now he can get on with his life. If anything, you seem to have dispelled any guilt he had about it. Now you're just the Big Bad Bitch who did him wrong for no good reason. Case closed. On to the woman who appreciates him as he deserves." Gordon tucked a loose corner of the baby blanket under his daughter's side. "What about you? How're you doing?"

That day she could answer with a genuine smile. "I feel as if it's all finally over with, too. I hadn't realized how much it was weighing me down until it was all taken care of. Life really does go on—over the hurdles and on to the next lap."

Kelsey watched Gordon's face settle into an unconscious frown. His chin pointed to the baby between them, who was rooting toward Kelsey's finger. "I keep thinking that if only you had stuck it out, worked through your problems, you could still be with Gary, have a baby of your own."

"Look how rotten I've done with yours," she said, trying to make light of his words. "She can't even stand for me to hold her. What would have happened with one of my own?"

"That's not like you," he chastised. "You'd be a good mother. Don't you want kids?"

"Maybe someday. It just wouldn't have been right then, with Gary." Patience, she advised herself. "I know it's hard for you to understand, Gordy, but I did what was best. I suppose that in a different frame of mind I could have gone about it better, but the end result needed to be the same."

A disapproving silence fell before he changed the subject. "Have you been painting at all?"

"Not in the last year and a half, no."

"You couldn't have just given it up. It was your whole life."

"But I did. A lot of what was my whole life before was wrong for me."

"Not painting. You were born an artist, Kay. It's a gift. You shouldn't deny it in yourself."

"Gordon..." Her tone was too curt, and she amended it. "Gordy, it's the creativity that's a gift. I haven't abandoned that. I've just rechanneled it into writing. Try to understand. Painting became painful—too much of a connection with things better forgotten. Writing is very healing to me."

"You used to love to paint. I can't imagine your not painting."

Kelsey sighed in frustration. "That's just how it is, okay? Can we talk about something else?"

Apparently not, for silence fell between them again. The baby began to cry, and Gordon took a bottle from the diaper bag.

"Can I try?" Her niece allowed Kelsey a necessary diversion. This time the baby quieted in her arms.

"Are you ever sorry, Kay?"

She glanced up at him from beneath arched eyebrows. "Sometimes," she admitted. "I missed you—a lot. There were times when I missed Gary. The marriage wasn't all bad. But leaving was something I had to do, Gordy. I needed to be on my own, away from both you and Gary, to grow into myself. You know me. I spent a lot of time scared stiff. And sometimes I was so lonely. I guess writing kept me company during those times."

"I still think you should be painting."

Back to that. Just as surprising as what he did realize was what he still refused to recognize. She knew he didn't mean to be as critical as he sounded, that he was trying hard to fit her into what his memory of her was. Maybe it felt safer to him, more comfortable. But it was no easier now than it had been three years ago to feel as if what she really was was being overlooked in spite of her efforts at honesty.

Should she battle it out, force him to see past the mask she had worn before? Or leave him to his illusions? She really didn't know. In the end she settled for not lying to him, not pretending, but simply being herself with a quiet determination and hoping he would come to realize on his own that she wasn't the same person he thought he had known before.

Gordon took the baby to burp her, seeming to know he was handling things badly and yet not understanding why. Another change in subject seemed in order. "How long will you be here?"

"I don't really know. I'm going to work with Thomas on developing the character he'll play. But if my new book idea sells, I'll go back to Winter Park to write." She seized Thomas's term to help dispel the judgment she read in her brother's face. "Staying here awhile is a professional courtesy."

"But you're living with him."

"It isn't a permanent situation. I'm a houseguest."

"And that's all there is to it? Just business, nothing personal?"

"You sound so hopeful. Thomas isn't a Mafia boss, for crying out loud. He's a very nice man."

"He's an actor." He said it as if being a Mafia boss were preferable. "It's not like you to do something like this, Kay, to get carried away. What if this doesn't mean the same thing to him that it does to you? You could be just a little light entertainment to him. This can't have been an easy trip for you. You're vulnerable. Maybe you aren't seeing things clearly. Men like him—"

"You don't even know him, Gordon. You can't judge what kind of man he is."

"Can you? I'm only playing devil's advocate, Kay."

"Come on, Gordy. Don't be like this. I don't want to fight."

He sighed, shaking his head as he looked off at the old men playing checkers. "It's none of my business, I know. I'm just worried about you, kiddo. If he really is someone you just met, you can't know him all that well yourself. I'm so afraid you're jumping into another big mistake."

"Hey." She reached for his arm. "I'm okay now."

"Are you really? First you desert your husband, and now you turn up living with a television star. It's just not like you. I'm afraid you've gone off the deep end, and this is just more evidence of it. And then, before I know what's happened, you'll disappear, and I'll go back to wondering if you're dead or alive or safe or hurt or... or even sane."

Kelsey took a deep breath, telling herself his reaction was nothing more than she should have expected but being hurt by it all the same. When she spoke, it was very, very slowly.

"It's probably hard for you to see it, but leaving Gary was the first sane act I performed in a long time. I've changed, Gordon. You said it yourself the other day. But it isn't that I've changed *into* a crazy person—I've changed *out* of one. I'm with Thomas for two reasons right now. For business and because I care more for him than I have for any person except you. I'd like you to accept that and feel confident in my decisions, but I know it's tough for you. So if we can't talk rationally about him, we'd better not talk about him at all."

"I only want what's best for you."

"I know you do. I appreciate that and love you for it." She paused, then once again tried to make him understand. "Look, big brother, we're both different people than we were three years ago. You aren't responsible for me anymore. We're just two people who have to find a way to come together as individuals, as friends. It's hard, I know, but that's how it is."

He searched her face for a long moment, still unsure. "Will you promise me that no matter what problems you ever have, you'll at least let me know what's going on with you? That you'll never leave like that again?"

"Sure," she answered easily enough. "I'll call and gripe at you if the butcher so much as threatens to give me less than lean hamburger."

"I'm serious, Kay. It hurt that you cut me off that way. We're family, and I want to know everything that's bothering you. If you can't come to me, who can you turn to?"

"Okay, okay, you have my word."

"I hope you're telling me the truth and you are all right now," he said dubiously.

Kelsey reached out and gave him a hug, hoping it reassured him. "I am, Gordy. I honestly am."

"I expected you back earlier than this." Thomas met her at the door, his handsome brow creased with worry.

"I'm sorry. I didn't realize it mattered."

He pulled her into his arms as if needing the feel of her. Odd, she thought. "Is everything all right?" she asked.

He laughed, and her confusion at his response disappeared. "I doubt if you'll think so. You have about half an hour to get ready." He let her go, stepped back and took her hand, bowing over it to gallantly kiss it. "Congratulations. As of late this afternoon, you're one hundred thousand dollars richer. Kit is surprising us with a celebration party. Sasha just warned me."

"No!" Kelsey blanched, panic edging her tone. "I'm no good at parties, Thomas. Being around a lot of people is one of my phobias."

He winked at her and tucked her into his side by twining their arms together. "You'll do fine. These aren't barracudas coming to dinner. They're mostly friends in the form of possible backers, studio people, promoters, distributors and only the good guys of the press. It will double or triple your sale of paperback rights as a movie tie-in. Big business, love. Movie-making is a collective endeavor," he said, heading for the bedroom. "Come along, my shy little lass. I've had Sasha move all your things into my room."

"But I'm not a collective endeavorer," she protested on the way. "I'm at my worst at things like this. I clam up, freeze. My brain clogs, and I can't think of my own name," she said in a rush. "I'll leave and come back later."

Kelsey veered the other way, but Thomas wasn't having any, and he held their course down the hall. "No way. You're in this the same as I am. If I'm stuck, so are you," he said. "Just stick close. I'll handle everything."

"I can't, Thomas. I really can't. You don't know." She stopped cold, pulling back like a mule on a bit before crossing the bedroom's threshold.

Thomas faced her, bracing his forearms on her shoulders and dipping his face to look into her eyes. "Hey, I'm sorry to spring this on you without warning. I know it sounds overwhelming, and the truth is, I'm no more thrilled about these things than you are. They're just sort of a necessary evil. But I'll be right here for you all the way. It won't be so bad. You'll see. It's simply part of a game we need to play to get this project under way. No big deal—I promise."

"You don't know," she repeated, her face ashen. "I'll dribble my drink and babble and say all the wrong things. I'm a hider, Thomas."

He pulled her into his arms, close and comforting. "You don't have to do anything but sit beside me and smile, if that's what you want. I give you my word that it will not be a big deal. These are all nice folks."

But to Kelsey it was more than a big deal. All things considered, she would rather spend the evening in the aviary at the zoo.

Within an hour the house was packed with every size, shape, texture and tone of California body. Kelsey, between the protective arms of Thomas on her right and Kit on her left, was being ushered to the screening room for an interview with half a dozen reporters. The noise of music and voices receded behind the closed door, and the assault of questions began.

"Is *A Second Season* your first book?"

"What did you do before you became a writer?"

"How long have you known Mr. Sullivan?"

"How did you meet?"

"Mr. Mason says the book was tailor-made for Mr. Sullivan. Did you write it for him?"

"Did he inspire it?"

"Have you ever been married, Ms. McKenna?"

"How old are you?"

"Where were you born?"

"Is it true you're living together?"

Microphones and tape recorders were thrust at her. Minicams and flashes blinded her and made her feel naked before their recording lenses. And for all the personal interest, she felt dehumanized and invaded.

At first Kelsey did well, fending off the too personal questions and managing a quip here and there. But the longer the interview went on, the more it ground her down, the more inadequate she felt, the more bumpkinish. She began to worry about how she must appear to them, thought that she should have hidden her glasses, should have tried to tame her hair, should have worn less baggy clothing and tried to look more like the precisely put-together women who occupied the rest of the house. Critics seemed to be sizing her up behind notepads and microphones.

Rapid-fire questions were shot at her as if the mass of reporters couldn't learn about her fast enough. The only thing they didn't seem to want to know was her shoe size, and Kelsey wondered how six reporters could seem like sixty.

Thomas felt her grow more and more tense beside him, heard her voice become softer, brittle. He sensed her feelings of being cornered, knew panic was welling up in her.

"Enough, guys, enough," he broke in. "We're all here for a celebration—work is over for the night."

Kit jumped in then, offering to prolong the session and answer any and all questions about the movie as Thomas led Kelsey out. But within half an hour the press conference dispersed and the reporters rejoined the party, all with a single goal: getting a private chat with the author and new woman in Thomas Quinn-Patrick Sullivan's life.

Everywhere Kelsey turned, another reporter followed with a casually prying question over a catered canapé or a phony interest in replenishing her drink. Thomas tried to steer them away from her with a clever comment or a funny rebuff, but it seemed nearly a conspiracy as he was separated from her, cornered by the same friendly disguises and just as doggedly pursued when he made attempts to return to her.

Kelsey felt cornered and was surprised at how inept she had become at putting on the mask she had worn so often for Gary's business dinners and parties. Her body was stiff with tension, her voice barely audible and two octaves higher than normal. Perspiration dripped from beneath her arms and ran down her sides, and she could feel her hair sticking to the back of her neck.

"Buck up, darling," Kit whispered as he passed her. "I know it's a drag, but it will help get us off on the right foot."

Kelsey could only nod as yet another reporter entwined his arm with hers as if they were old friends and began what was coming to seem like an interrogation.

"What? I'm sorry, I've lost track of your questions," she said for the hundredth time. She felt the muscles in her cheeks twitch as they atrophied into the smile she had forced for hours.

The room was hazy with smoke that stung her eyes and made every breath she took feel thick. The voices were a buzzing din that closed her in, and she suddenly realized that if she didn't get out, she was going to hyperventilate.

"You'll have to excuse me," she nearly shouted at the overly interested man still waiting for the answer to his repeated question. Kelsey yanked her arm free and made a beeline for the bathroom, locking the door and falling back against it to catch her breath.

This must be how hunted animals feel, she thought. And suddenly it's open season on me.

Kelsey hated parties, but this one made all the others she had been to before seem like picnics. She knew that the minute she set foot outside the bathroom, another reporter would be waiting, and then another and another. And there was no way she could face it.

Salvation beamed at her in the form of the frosted glass window over the bathtub. Sliding it wide, Kelsey pushed the screen out and climbed through, dropping farther than she had expected to the sand below.

Now you really are crazy, Kelsey, she thought fleetingly.

The sense of freedom and the fresh chill of night air made her feel giddy. Keeping safely to the shadows, she moved down the beach toward Sasha and Jake's place. The roar of the party dimmed, and the farther she retreated the better Kelsey felt. She slid the pushed-up sleeves of her V-necked sweater back down to her wrists and headed for the hammock that still swung outside. Sitting in it, she emptied sand from her Loafers and eased back, and for the second time that day she wished to be back in Winter Park.

Homesickness hadn't struck until that day. But during the worst of Gordon's "it's not like you" insistence and again during the party, a renewed yearning for seclusion had cropped up in her. It was so much like before: the need for flight. And Kelsey wondered if the person she had been three years ago was really so remote from who she was now. Had she progressed, healed, if the first confrontations with what she had run from made her feel the need to run again? Could it be that she wasn't as strong as she had thought?

"There you are. You all right, girl?" Sasha's voice came from a little way up the beach as she neared. "Tommy's frantic and worried sick about what's happened to you, but he couldn't come looking himself without bringing the whole party after him. He was about ready to throw everybody out when I said I'd find you. Somebody do something wrong back there?"

The tall woman blended with the night sky as she stood over the hammock, hugging her arms around her midriff, which was only scantily covered by a partially laced leather vest.

Kelsey couldn't manage another smile, but her tone was friendly. "I just couldn't take any more. I'm no good with a lot of people. Oh, hell, who am I trying to kid? I'm antisocial. Reclusive sounds better, but it all means the same thing. I do all right with one or two people, but too many for too long makes me crazy."

"Well, tonight ought to send you right up the wall. I've never seen a bash like this in this house in all the time I've been with Tommy. I know he gets stuck going to these things off and on, but he never has them here. Can I tell him you're coming back?"

"No!" Kelsey took a breath. "I didn't mean to jump down your throat. And I'm sorry if it looks rude, but I can't stand any more of it back there. Just let Thomas know everything is all right and I'll be back when it's died down. And whatever you do, don't let anyone else know where I am."

Sasha left Kelsey to drift back to her self-doubts. She sat on the hammock, watching the moon move higher in a cloudless sky and wondering why she couldn't function the way other people did. But the fact was that she just couldn't, and if she tried, it was a sure road to self-destruction. She hadn't expected to ever be so at odds with herself again, and yet there she was, feeling inadequate and hating herself for what she couldn't be.

So what was she going to do? Should she leave Thomas and go back into hiding? The thought turned around and around in her head, wrenching her stomach and leaving her unaware of time or sound or anything but the misery of a quandary she had already suffered once in her life.

But then there he was, and all it took was the sound of his low voice, teasing and sweet, the sight of that chiseled face and mustache quirking with a concerned smile as he appeared from out of the night shadows to sit beside her in the hammock, to make her feel better. His warm hand taking hers gently, pulling her up close to his side, was the clincher, and Kelsey knew he wasn't someone she wanted to leave. The need for flight became the silly fancy of a weak moment.

"That was a pretty good disappearing act. I had my eyes on you every minute and didn't see you go."

For the first time Kelsey realized she must have been sitting out there for a long time. No more sounds drifted from the big house, and her fingers were nearly numb with cold. "I climbed out the bathroom window."

He laughed. "That's a novel solution to a Hollywood party. I'll have to remember it."

"Is it over now?"

"Kit managed to move it to his place," he said. "I was worried about you. This was one hell of an initiation into the publicity you've worked so hard to avoid." He leaned to have a full view of her face. "I, uh, was worried you had run away."

It was Kelsey's turn to laugh, ruefully. "I've been out here worrying about the urge to do just that."

"You were seriously thinking about leaving?" His tone was cautious and his heartbeat too fast.

"Today and certainly tonight, my garret in Winter Park was looking pretty appealing."

"It was that bad for you tonight?"

"I told you—party phobia. I hate this stuff."

"I'm sorry it was so hard on you, Kelsey. I should have taken your protests more seriously. Why didn't you slug me in the jaw or kick me in the shins and refuse it cold?"

"I tried. Okay, maybe not hard enough. I didn't want to disappoint you."

"Hey, I'm in love with you, lady. I can handle a little disappointment. I couldn't handle losing you. Everything calmed down now?"

"I think so."

"No more thoughts of going on the lam again?"

"They stopped when you came out here. Strange effect you have on me." And then the words came on their own with her sudden knowledge of how true they were. "I love you, Thomas."

He didn't say anything at all for a minute, and then he cleared his throat. "Well, it's about time, lady. I was beginning to wonder if you were playing around with me." He pulled her head into the side of his neck, turning his face into her hair. She felt the warm gush of his breath in a sigh.

"General consensus has it that it's you playing around with me."

"Your brother being general consensus. I hope you set him straight—my intentions are definitely honorable." All teasing aside, his voice grew soft and solemn. "Marry me, Kelsey."

"The man is never satisfied," she teased. Then she added more seriously, "Let's not talk about that right now. Let me get used to the feelings first, to your life, and see if I can handle it. Then maybe."

"You know this party thing doesn't happen that often."

Should she tell him she didn't know if she could stand for it *ever* to happen? Instead, she said, "Sasha told me."

"I'll do whatever you want, whatever makes you feel comfortable—even build you an escape hatch in the bathroom. You don't know what you do to me, love. It can be any way you want it."

"I want it slower, Thomas. I can't commit to a relationship again until I'm sure of myself."

"But no more thoughts of running. I want your solemn vow that if it even crops up in that wild head of yours, you'll let me know and we can talk it through."

An underlying note of urgency in his tone brought Kelsey's head away from him to look curiously up at him. His frown confirmed her fears. "Do you think I would do it again—on some whim?"

"I never worry about your being whimsical, McKenna."

"But you are worried about my running again," she persisted.

"What I'm worried about is your keeping things bottled up instead of confiding in me. We can work through anything, Kelsey, if only you let me know what's bothering you. Trust me enough for that, and I know I won't have anything to worry about." But even though the words weren't a question, there was a hint of fishing in his tone.

Kelsey stared into his shadowed eyes for a long moment. First Gordon and now Thomas. It was like being labeled a thief—once a thief, always a thief. Once a runaway, always a runaway?

But then, she had been thinking about it, hadn't she? Denial and injured pride were lost in the face of fact. So instead of arguing, she reassured him, "I do trust you, Thomas. I've been more honest with you than with anyone in my life, and even though the thought might strike, it isn't a viable possibility. I don't think it's really any different than anyone's thinking of getting away when things get tough."

He pulled her back tightly into his arms, belying the lightness in his voice. "Hey, I'm all for getting away. We could start with a honeymoon."

"Give me a break, Sullivan."

"Only if you say you'll think it over."

"I'll think, I'll think!"

But even as she said it, she knew it was going to take more than thought. It was going to take time and experience to convince Kelsey she could handle it.

Chapter Twelve

The sound of the radio alarm blaring at six on Monday morning was like the starting shot of the Kentucky Derby.

Kelsey and Thomas were the first to arrive at Kit Mason's office in downtown L.A.—a three-room suite complete with a bright-eyed secretary in the outer reception area, Kit's private office and a fair-sized conference room where they waited.

Kelsey paced a slow path around the huge oblong table that took up nearly the entire space, running a hand over the tops of each of fourteen gray leather chairs. She avoided Thomas as he stood at the wall of carpet-to-ceiling windows that framed the jagged skyline and the twenty-one-floor drop to the pavement below.

"Tell me what happens," Kelsey said, not having actually thought about the process before. She had assumed her part would involve only simple conversations between her and Thomas and occasionally Kit. Now she had the feeling she had been naive.

"Meetings mostly," he answered easily enough. "First thing this morning we're talking with two of the best screenwriters in the business and a script consultant they always use."

"I thought you and Kit had written a script."

"So he did tell you about it. I thought he might have. Actually what we did was a broad outline—a rough draft of a screenplay. It's just basically transferring the book to film-script form. Now we'll all work together—you, me, Kit, the screenwriters, the script consultant, the production manager, the cinematographer, the art director and several secretaries and stenographers to keep track of all our ramblings. We'll rearrange, cut what needs to be cut, integrate locations to tell the story as succinctly as possible, decide camera angles, actors, dialogue—"

"Enough! Stop! I don't know anything about any of that."

Thomas came up behind her, his arms circling her shoulders, to kiss her earlobe. "Don't worry about it. You don't have to know any of this stuff. You're here for me and to play watchdog over your baby. You can answer any questions that might come up about motivation or keep us from forgetting something important."

But a sudden wave of apprehension swept over Kelsey. And it was well-founded.

What began on Monday was a week of juggling budget meetings, technical meetings, creative meetings, organizational meetings, consultations, conferences, cooperations, collaborations, discussions, disagreements and debates. People. People. People. Never in her life had Kelsey spent so much time with so many people. Preproduction was a harsh introduction to the constant, never-ending social encounters that went into putting a movie together.

And none of it was easy for her. It made her uncomfortable to hear her words read, dissected and often discarded or so rearranged that the meaning was distorted. It was hard to hear her favorite scene ruthlessly discarded because it would cost too much to film, or her favorite lines of dialogue scrapped because "even though they speak well, it's too long—we'll bore our audience to death." But never did she voice her objections or her displeasure, never did she disagree. In fact, her greatest contribution came in pouring coffee.

A Second Season was no longer "her baby," as Thomas liked to call it. In this form it was *his* baby, and Kelsey was merely an observer. She was out of place and fast losing all desire to foster the illusion that she was involved. The week that passed was the longest she had spent in her life, each day an agony of its own.

As much as she loved Thomas—and that was considerable—she desperately missed her own work and the solitude of it. This was Thomas's world. And Kelsey knew with glaring clarity that she did not fit in—not even when the project was based on her writing.

Why was she there? she wondered a thousand times a day. Try as he did, even Thomas had to abandon his efforts to draw her into conferences on subjects of which she had even less knowledge than the stenographers had.

"What's more important in this shot?" it would go. "The fact that she's more interested in her food than in Jonathan? Or that she's using the food as a distraction to keep from pouncing on him? Or that she wants him to *think* she's more interested in the food when she really can't keep her eyes off him when he isn't looking? We have to decide before we can determine how to shoot the scene."

Tracking shots.

Medium long shots.

Dissolves.

Pulling focus.

Kelsey was lost in a sea of technical jargon that could have been Greek for all she understood it. They all seemed to have a mental picture of how scenes would appear on the screen, an ability she lacked even had she grasped what they were talking about.

By Friday afternoon she was totally saturated with the sight of faces too numerous and constantly changing to put names to, with the persistent drone of eager voices, with the smell of coffee and cigarettes and with the mask that had grown to hide her true feelings about the very things that Thomas thrived on.

Kit, Thomas and a cast of six were so intent on their argument that Kelsey doubted they would miss her, and she desperately needed a little time out of the loud, smoke-clouded room. But her hand had barely closed around the doorknob when Thomas's voice rose above the others.

"Kelsey? Where are you going?"

She stopped, feeling the urge to lean her forehead against the door in defeat. Giving a peeved sigh, she said, "The bathroom." She immediately regretted her tone and amended it. "I'll only be a minute."

"I could use a break myself. I'll go with you." He stood quickly to follow.

"Geez, Thomas" came Kit's impatient voice. "It's just down the hall. She can make it on her own, can't she? We're right in the middle of this."

"He's right," she said. "Just go on with what you're doing."

"Give her some breathing room, man. What's with you lately? I've never seen you so possessive," Kit persisted.

But Thomas leveled his friend with a glare. "We can all use a break." He didn't hesitate another minute before taking Kelsey's arm and leading the way.

If he noticed Kelsey bristling with embarrassment, he didn't show it. Unable to ignore Kit's disgusted sigh and the rumblings that followed them out, she felt her face heat. This couldn't go on. She was a fish out of water, and everyone knew it. Feelings of inadequacy were running rampant, her claustrophobia was raging and it all just couldn't go on. *She* couldn't go on.

In the ladies' room she splashed cold water on her face again and again. What was this but playing another role? Pretending she was involved, interested, when really all she could think about was how not to look like a fool? She didn't know what she was doing and didn't care to. She liked working alone—thrived on it.

Some people were good at collaborating; they liked the social contact. But for Kelsey it was inhibiting, over-whelming, miserable. No more! she wanted to shout. Just leave me alone. But already the disguise was in place, and instead, she plastered on yet another smile to face Thomas, who waited just outside.

As they returned to Kit's office, he talked about the argument in progress. Kelsey nodded, Kelsey mumbled her agreement, Kelsey laughed when she was supposed to. And Kelsey didn't hear a word of what Thomas said.

"I need a shower," Kelsey announced as they entered Thomas's house after nine that night. She thought that if she didn't get the reek of cigarette smoke out of her hair, she would be sick.

"Mmm, sounds great." He flipped through the mail and messages Sasha had left on the coffee table. "There's a note here for you to call Ali Robbins. It says no matter what time you get in.''

Kelsey groaned. "Are you sure? Maybe she didn't realize it would be this late—it's past midnight in New York.''

Thomas handed her the slip of paper. "Sasha always marks the time of incoming calls. This one was just two hours ago. I'd say she really means no matter what time you get in.''

"Okay.'' Kelsey sighed disgustedly. "First the call, then the shower.''

For a long time Kelsey stood with the beating spray of dual shower heads directly on the back of her neck, her head hanging forward. She let the miracle of the warm water be the only thought in her mind, savoring the feel of each tight muscle relaxing in turn, the soft, steady drone. That night, for once, she didn't even have to keep her eyes trained on the space above the shower door to stave off claustrophobia.

By the time Thomas opened the glass panel to join her, she was too calm, too lulled even to be startled. She only turned her head without lifting it and barely opened her eyes to see the glory of his naked body parting the steam.

Here it was—here *he* was—the ending to every hectic, loathsome day, the reason she had hidden the tumult of her true feelings. Lord, how she loved him. Maybe that was her fatal flaw. But when they were back home, alone, and they came together each night in love, it dissolved every miserable thing she felt during the day like a drop of dye in a vat of water. And even though she knew that wasn't going to happen completely that night, she needed it to happen for just a little while.

So Kelsey turned in his slippery wet arms and let him raise her face to his with the curved knuckle of one finger beneath her chin. And when his mouth lowered to hers, softly, gently seeking, she sighed away even the ragged edges of thought and slid her hands up his hard chest to encircle his neck.

Neither of them spoke, the verbiage of the past week making more words an intrusion on what they were sharing now. Their lips met and parted, teased and grew serious. Their tongues played and chased and licked water droplets, hers from his shoulders, his from the tip of her nose. Palms did a sliding massage, his down her arms, down her thighs and back up again to her breasts, hers down his back to the tight mounds of the most perfect derriere.

Only when they had let all the hot water run out did Thomas pull Kelsey from the shower and wrap them both in a Turkish towel. For a while they stood in their white cocoon, kissing hungrily now, passionately, urgently. Then the towel fell away, and in silent consensus they went to his oversize bed.

This time when they made love, there was a desperation in Kelsey. If the other aspects of their relationship had become strained that week, this had not. Their desire and need for each other was stronger than ever, an explosive, fulfilling passion. They came together in perfect harmony, sensing each other's needs, knowing instinctively how to please and excite and sate.

But that night when it was over, Kelsey found no respite in Thomas's arms. Lovemaking had only temporarily soothed her sore spirits by keeping reality at bay. Once past, she knew all the more certainly what she had to do.

She rolled away from him to lie on her back and stare up at the ceiling, her arms clasping the sheet tightly across her breasts.

"Kelsey?" Thomas's deep, passion-hushed voice sounded confused. "What's up, McKenna? Talk to me."

She swallowed hard and sighed, grateful for the darkness. "I'm going home, Thomas." She said it so firmly, so finally that he knew the difference between this and the last time she had voiced her intent. It hit him like a wrecking ball.

"You're supposed to be thinking about marrying me, not leaving me, remember? Whatever it is, we can work it out."

"I've accepted an offer for the book that's finished and the one I've just begun. I'll be working under a deadline for the first time, so I can't put it off. And even if I could, I don't want to. I need to write."

"You can write here."

"I'm going home."

"The truth, Kelsey. I want the plain truth. You could write as easily here as in Winter Park. Is it just my asking you to stay that you want? Shall we set up a formal living agreement not based on smoke-screen motives like business and professional courtesy? Because you know how I feel: I want you here, with me, as my wife. And barring that, then at least committed to living with me to test our compatibility before we actually do get married. But the bottom line is that I want you here, in this house—not in some damn garret in Winter Park—because I love you."

"I can't," she said softly into the night.

Thomas flicked on the bedside lamp, ripped the sheet away from his lower half and pulled on his jeans. Then he crossed to his closet and tossed his robe at Kelsey. "Get up. We're going to have this out face-to-face."

As she shrugged into the heavy French terry robe, she said, "I think we both need some time to think things over—away from each other. I don't know if I can handle your life and the quantity of people in it."

"Where the hell did that come from?" he demanded in outrage. "Everything's been fine this week—great, in fact—and now you come up with this?"

"Everything's been fine?" she shot back angrily, a week's worth of frustration surfacing. "Maybe for you it has. But I've been pretending, Thomas. Pretending to enjoy your work when I hated every minute of it, pretending to be interested, to understand it, to care. Pretending, pretending, pretending! And I can't go back to that! Not even for you."

He raked his fingers through his hair. "Did I ask you to go back to it? To ever be anything but what you are?"

"It doesn't have to be a written request. I thought I was supposed to advise you on the character, but instead, I found myself in the middle of all your technical conferences. What did I look like but just another hot-pants hanger-on? There was no good reason for me to be there. You pushed me into situations that forced me to pretend. You expected things of me that I couldn't give. Do you really think that's any different than anything Gary or Gordon or anybody else ever did?"

"Is it the same, Kelsey? You tell me! Is what I know about you, love about you, all some damn mask you've put on for the occasion?"

"No, dammit! You've seen the worst of me. But that doesn't mean it can't start all over again—it has this past week."

"You said it was all behind you, that you're stronger, healthier now," he accused.

"I am when I don't feel responsible for pleasing someone else. But commitment to you means being thrown to the lions around here, and I can't handle it. I fell back into old patterns, hiding what I really felt to please you, trying to be what it seemed you wanted. I can't risk going back to all that.''

She spun away from him because the sight of him tugged too strongly on her heart. She loved him, wanted him, but she knew it couldn't work for her.

''Spell it out for me. Are we talking about the conferences this week? The party last week? The photographers? The pictures in scandal sheets? The fifty phone calls every night even after putting in twelve-hour days? The open-door policy for Kit and his cohorts? What?''

''All of it!''

''I'll adjust it. You can forego movie-making and avoid parties and we'll take the phone off the hook after eleven. As for the publicity, we can do the bunny hop every time we're off the grounds so no one can see your face. Not such big things.''

''And not enough for me and inhibiting to you and your career even at that. You're talking about restructuring your entire life, alienating yourself from your friends and work associates. You can't do that, and I can't handle it the way it is. Your life would be overwhelming for a person who could stand being in the limelight all the time. I'm a long way from being that person.''

''What's the alternative?'' He was too intuitive, too in tune with what went on inside her head even after so short a time together. His words stung. ''Avoiding the risk by spending your whole life hiding? Is that what you want? I have news for you, lady. You've already taken the risk. You're already committed to me whether you like it or not. Feelings commit you to another person a hell of a lot more than words or papers or laws. And the one thing you can't pretend is that you don't feel anything for me.''

He crossed to her, and his hands on her shoulders turned her to face him. Kelsey looked up into green eyes that reflected a maelstrom of anger and pain. "You know what it looks like to me? It looks as if you think that telling me you're going means you're not running away. But that's just what you're doing, isn't it? Instead of saying 'Hey, I don't want to do this' and working it through, you hightail it back to Winter Park. Great solution. Are we adults here, or are you a dumb kid who can't ever see your way through any problems that come up?"

Kelsey's nostrils flared with rage. "You want to talk problems? I have one for you. Let's talk about you, Thomas. What about your doubts? The problem here isn't only me. Look at the way it's been between us since you found out about my past. Every time I leave a room, I see you wondering if I'm coming back. You're afraid that if you lose sight of me, I'll be gone. Tell me how either of us can live that way."

"That's a damn lie," he lied.

"You wanted honesty. Let's have it all the way down the line." Her voice quavered, speaking things neither of them wanted to acknowledge. "When you found out I had deserted my husband, something happened to the way you see me, didn't it? All of a sudden I didn't seem to be the same person. It became dangerous business to entrust me with your heart. What if I ran out on you, too? Today you couldn't even let me go to the bathroom alone. My God, what kind of a life can we possibly have together if you worry every time I go to the bathroom?"

She knew she had struck home when he turned away from her, walked across the room and pressed a palm against the wall to lean on one outstretched arm. His head dropped forward and hung there.

"All right, maybe just for a minute I wondered. But that's all, dammit. A moment's doubt. It's only human, and that's all there was to it."

"Is it? Come on, we're doing truth here, remember?"

He raised his head and spoke at the wall. "The truth is that you told me yourself after last Friday's party that you were thinking about running again."

"It started before that. You sent Sasha out looking for me five minutes after I had left the room."

"We can work it out." It was as close to an admission as he would go.

"Can we? How? By chaining me to your side?"

"Better that than your running away. Your leaving isn't going to change how many people it takes in my life to do my job. It isn't going to teach you how to deal with that."

"And changing the subject isn't going to wipe out your doubts—and I'm not running away, dammit! I need time to regather my wits. To think about what being with you means. To decide if I can ever handle it. And you need time to decide whether you can believe in me."

He turned and fell back against the wall, crossing his arms over his bare chest. For a long while he stared down at the thick shag carpeting. Then he pushed himself away from the wall and came to stand directly in front of her, frowning down at her, the corners of his mustache pulled down fiercely. His hands bracketed his narrow waist, riding the unfastened waistband of his jeans.

"Separation isn't the answer, Kelsey," he insisted.

Now it was her turn to move from the spot. She paced the floor at the foot of the mussed bed, hiding her hands in the arms of his robe. "It's the only answer for me. This whole thing has gone too fast, swept us both off our feet...."

"Only because it's good between us, right between us."

Fear and anger made her unfair. "Is it? Or is it only good and right between us if I pretend to be what you want and you can keep me on a short leash?"

"You know better than that."

"No, I don't," she said in a voice so small that it was barely audible. She didn't want to believe her words, but she wasn't sure she did know better.

"Do you want me to say I'll give up everything for you? That we can buy an island and spend the rest of our days playing Robinson Crusoe? I'm willing, if that's what it takes."

Her hands shot up in the air and sliced back down. "Oh, good. Then you could pretend for me. Wouldn't that be grand? How long do you think you could stand me for taking away what you've worked for, what's as integral a part of your life as my phobias are of mine?"

"You'd be surprised, lady."

"I'd be surprised if we lasted a year."

Thomas grabbed her and swung her roughly into his arms, squeezing tight. "This hurts too much to be the right way."

Kelsey's eyes filled, but she locked her jaw and fought the tears back. She couldn't afford to be weak now, so she left her own arms dangling at her sides.

"You can't tell me that doing this feels good to you," he said into her hair.

"I have to do it. No matter how it feels."

"Dammit, you don't have to." But he knew she was going to, anyway. After a long while holding her, he let out a ragged sigh. "Give me some idea of how you mean for this to go."

Kelsey swallowed hard and shrugged, at last giving in to the need to hold him, letting her arms encircle his waist. "I don't really know. Except that I don't want to see or talk to you for a while. If I do, it's too easy for me to think that maybe all the pretending is worth it.''

The words to say he would make it worth it to her were right there in his mouth. But he knew how much harm saying them would ultimately do. He wanted her, but it was her lack of artifice that had been the strongest initial attraction—what he had fallen in love with in the first place. Without that neither of them could be happy.

"I hate this," he ground out.

"It's something we both need, Thomas. Maybe it's something I'll always need, something you'll have to accept if we can ever have a future together." She pulled away from him because staying in his arms was weakening her resolve. "I'll call the airport and see if I can get a flight out tomorrow."

"So that's how it's going to be? Back to our separate corners—you to decide how to handle the public side of my life, me to do some soul-searching—whether I like it or not?"

"I guess so."

Thomas saw her waver and decided to take the whole matter less seriously. So she needed a little time to get used to his life, their relationship. It wasn't really so critical, was it? He gave her a half grin and teased, "Okay, lady, so I give you a week of being left absolutely alone to think and regather your wits. How long do you suppose it will take after that for me to convince you we were meant to be together?"

"This isn't a game, Thomas." She faced his forced lightness with a grave frown.

"Give me credit for a little faith in you, huh?"

"Is that what it is, or do you just think this is another panic attack that I'll get over with a few breaths of mountain air?"

"You don't think there's anything of a panic attack to your reaction?" he challenged.

"I think that if you write this off as a panic attack and think it's going to take care of itself, you're amazingly shortsighted." Kelsey's temper was reignited. Her eyes were the shiny black of sealskin, and she spoke through clenched teeth. "This is the second time in recent memory that what I've said has been disregarded on the basis of possible insanity. I didn't like it from Gordon, but I decided he had reason. You don't."

Again Thomas finger-combed his wheaten hair, dropping his head back to stare at the ceiling as if seeking guidance. "I didn't say you were crazy."

"No, you just decided to humor me. Do you know how patronizing that is?"

"Do you know how frustrating this is?" he shouted now, leveling stormy green eyes at her again. Then he sighed and shook his head, rubbing the back of his neck. "All right, dammit. No humoring, no patronizing, no shortsightedness. You need time, and you're taking it. There's not a hell of a lot I can do about it, is there? You just want me to stand here and watch you go." He flung his arms out wide, "So. I'm standing here and watching. Go."

She did.

Chapter Thirteen

April in Winter Park had never been so gloomy. Or was it just ugly and gray through her eyes? Kelsey wondered as she waited in the corner phone booth for Ali to accept the collect charges.

Never had her apartment seemed so empty, the silence so silent, the nights so slow. Catch-22. She couldn't stand to live Thomas's highly populated life, she couldn't stand living her reclusive one without him. Damn. She wished she had never met him. Love was complicated enough when lives meshed. But put the celebrity with the recluse, and what you had was catastrophe. And after all she'd gone through to rid her life of calamity! How the Fates liked to toy with us, she thought.

"I just called to tell you to send all the contracts to Winter Park. I'm back," she said to Ali Robbins when the usual how-are-yous were over.

"Oh" was all the agent answered, a pause elapsing while Ali inwardly debated. Curiosity won. "I thought you were in for an extended stay in L.A. From the sounds of you, coming home wasn't the result of a happy parting."

"In this case 'happy parting' is a contradiction in terms," she admitted, feeling too rotten even to try for a lilt in her voice.

"Want to talk about it?" Ali asked cautiously, sensing there was no room for teasing this time.

"Not particularly. How long before I can expect some money?" Kelsey had spent her first hours back evaluating her financial predicament. Last week she had agreed to sales of over two hundred thousand dollars between the screen rights and the new books. But she had only thirty-one dollars and fifty-three cents to her name.

"Royalties on *A Second Season* are due anytime now, but I wouldn't expect much on this statement—it hasn't been out that long. As for the other book and the screen rights, it will be at least a month, maybe six weeks. You know how things are—contracts have to be checked by lawyers, read, signed, sent to be signed on the other end and all that before any money changes hands. I'm doing what I can, but I'd say at least a month."

Kelsey closed her eyes to the snow blowing outside the glass booth. She hadn't paid the last half of March's rent; now she wouldn't be able to pay April's. Thank God the Jorgensons were compassionate souls and the electricity was paid up. All she faced was a month of macaroni and cheese and watching how many squares of toilet paper she used at a time. Wasn't success grand?

After the prolonged pause Ali asked, "Kelsey? Are you there?"

"Yeah. I'm here." Pride kept her from letting her agent know just how bad things were. "Listen, something's wrong with my phone, so if you need to reach me, use that number I gave you before. The Jorgensons will give me the message, and I'll call you back.''

"Are you all alone there? Maybe you should get yourself some company and talk for once, Kelsey. You don't sound so good."

"Hey," she chided, "I'm tough as nails. Besides, you know how we artists feed off misery—ups our productivity like crazy."

"Are you working already?"

"Sure. Nothing like a little heartache for attracting the Muse. She's a sadist, you know—loves to visit us, the bravely suffering."

A sand truck rolled past just then, drowning out Ali's response with its loud engine, its snow-crunching tires and the creak of its latch opening to spread sand over snow-covered streets. Twenty to twenty-five inches of snowfall had been predicted. For the first time since she had come to the mountain ski resort, Kelsey thought what a long way it was from April in Paris—or even April in L.A.

"You'll have to say it again, Ali. I couldn't hear you."

"I said, you can make all the wisecracks you want, but I think there's a lot of truth to them. Are you sure you're all right?"

"Except for freezing my tail off at the moment, I'm fine."

"Are you going to see him again?"

"I don't know. I needed a little space, a little time. Who knows?"

"I was going to put in a plug for advance publicity—recommend you use the relationship to your advantage. Not such a good idea now, huh?"

"No, and not a unique one. I came home to half a dozen letters and telegrams wanting exclusive interviews. I have to go now. Just do what you can to speed up the money, okay?''

"Sure. Take care of yourself.''

Kelsey tugged her wool stocking cap back down over her ear, replaced her mitten, pulled her muffler up over her nose and mouth, ducked her head, plunged her hands into her pockets and trudged home—a vision of dejection.

It had only been a day and a half since she had left California. So how come it seemed like years? And how come she felt as if someone other than herself had made the decision to leave? She kept having to remind herself that this whole thing had been her choice, not anyone else's. She could still be there, with him.

Then she thought of where he was and remembered that being with him meant being with a man who didn't trust her to go to the bathroom alone. It meant being with a horde of other people who made her feel as bad as she had being Gary's perfect wife and Gordon's perfect sister. And she knew why she had to be plodding through six inches of crystalline snowflakes.

What would happen at Thomas's with her gone? Kelsey tortured herself with the thought at least once an hour. Images of the other women at that party tormented her. Perfect bodies. Gorgeous hair. Gleaming smiles. And eyes that said "Take me, I'm yours" every time they looked up at him.

And what about his "friend" Karen? Would he go back to her? They would always be there for each other—wasn't that how he had explained it? Uncomplicated sex with a friend. Oh, Lord.

Kelsey snuck up the back stairs to her attic apartment and slipped in. She would have to face the Jorgensons with a request that they wait for the rent money, but she just couldn't do it yet. Instead, she had kept a low profile so that no one would know she was back.

Once inside again, she clicked all three locks into place and shed her winter gear. Her typewriter stood waiting, beckoning with the invitation of escape. And Kelsey took it, grateful for the release.

The headquarters of Kitridge Mason Productions was quiet, a single desk lamp shining in the private office where Kit poured yet another glass of Scotch for his friend and partner late on this Tuesday evening.

Thomas sat slumped in a modern chrome-and-leather chair in front of the table that served as Kit's desk, his tennis-shod feet crossed at his sockless ankles and propped on the glass top. "I can't believe she took off," he said to the wall of windows beyond which L.A.'s night lights sparkled like sedate fireworks.

"So you've said." Kit handed him the glass and sat like an elf on top of his desk. "You know, your moping around has cost us a bundle these past two days. We've been unproductive as hell."

"Don't go overboard on the sympathy, Kit," he growled, watching the amber liquid swirl in his glass.

"I don't have to. You're feeling sorry enough for yourself. Come on, man, snap out of it. It isn't the end of the world—just a little vacation. You'll work something out with her."

"She thinks I don't trust her."

"She's right. And don't give me that look as if you want to punch me in the face. I told you I had never seen you that way with a woman before. You don't trust her. Not that I don't understand it—after all, she did split on one relationship. That's heavy stuff. I just think you're looking at it in the wrong perspective."

"Is that so?" Thomas said snidely.

"Want my amateur-shrink opinion?"

"I don't know. Are you analyzing me or Kelsey?"

Kit shrugged and came out with it, anyway. "At first I'll admit I thought the lady was out of her skull. I mean, I've known a lot of women to sleep with a lot of weird things, but never a rolling pin. Then I thought, she has some fears, so what? We all do. Some people call them superstitions—the mysticism makes them romantic, and that we can all understand. But Kelsey's aren't quite so mainstream. They're off center, like she is. That doesn't make her crazy. Crazy would be if they incapacitated her, but they don't. She faces them, deals with them, goes on with her life. She's not crazy."

Kit took a swallow of his own drink and then began again. "Now I'll grant you she made one hell of a socially unacceptable blunder by deserting her husband. And you're worried it was a major craziness that could crop up again at any time. But I see even that as ultimately pretty healthy. She was in a situation she couldn't tolerate, and she bailed herself out." He held up his hand to stop Thomas's comment on the understatement. "I said it was socially unacceptable. Tell me, Thomas, if she had been starving and stolen a couple of apples from a fruit stand, would you condemn her as a compulsive thief?"

"Come on. That's damn silly."

"It's stealing, and that's socially unacceptable behavior. What I'm getting at, my friend, is that sometimes we have to break the rules and hurt people to save ourselves. That's what she did. Then she went out and set herself up in a life that made her happy. She made the best of it. Dealt with her problems. And then turned around and took care of the business she had left behind. This is a strong lady, Thomas. And she didn't run away from you. She gave you a chance to decide for yourself if you can accept what she is, what she's done in the past. If you can't, then you'd better stay the hell away from her. If you can, then you can work through the rest of it. Build her an ivory tower where no one can get to her when we all overstep the bounds of your privacy, if that's what it takes. Get to be a bastard. We'll all live through it.''

Thomas sighed heavily, dropping his head back and closing his eyes. "It all sounds great, but it doesn't change the feeling in my gut."

"Then I don't know what to tell you, pal. Except that maybe she's worth having for whatever time she gives you, and if she takes off..." Kit shrugged again. "Then you deal with it when it happens and figure that being with her for any amount of time is better than none at all."

Thomas pulled his head up slowly, leveling troubled green eyes on his friend. "Could you live like that...be satisfied with that?"

Kit thought about it for a long time. "I don't know, man. Maybe if I loved her enough. But maybe if I loved her that much, it would only make it worse. I'm just the advice giver here. I'm glad it isn't my problem."

He watched Thomas throw back a measure of Scotch that his friend normally would have nursed for an entire evening. "All I do know is that you'd better do something to get your head straight. Just call her or something—anything to get your mind back to what we're working on. We can't go on much longer wasting time like this."

The heel of Thomas's right hand pounded unconsciously on the armrest of his plane seat. When he realized what a blatant show of tension it was, he stopped. And then his left leg began to bounce up and down.

He felt as if this was the longest damn flight he had ever been on. The pilot must be taking the long way to Denver.

So this was what it was like, he thought. She says she's going one place, and you find out she isn't there. No word, no clue. You don't have any idea where the hell she is, what's happened to her, if she's all right, dead, alive. It was every bit as bad as her ex-husband had said.

Thomas's stomach was a hard knot. He could feel a muscle twitch in his temple. What if he had waited to contact her as she had asked? The trail would have been stone-cold before he found out. Dammit! Had she been planning this flight all along? Was it all a lie to buy herself time to get back to Winter Park and collect her things before disappearing again? He couldn't believe it, couldn't believe she would do that to him.

Well, by God, he wouldn't give her three years before she faced him. He'd find her, no matter what it took, and shake her silly. First Winter Park. She had to leave a trail of some kind—a forwarding address, something. If he tore the town apart and still couldn't find anything, he'd head for New York and Ali Robbins again. If he had to park himself in her office for a year, he was going to find Ms. Kelsey McKenna!

I 70 and U.S. 40 hadn't been bad, but Berthoud Pass had been a little tricky even for the four-wheel Jimmy that Thomas had rented in Denver. It took him until ten Wednesday morning to get to Winter Park. Once in the sleepy village, he stopped for directions and found the old converted three-and-a-half-story Swiss chalet-style house without a problem.

Feeling as if enough time had been wasted, Thomas went directly to the manager, a frail-looking white-haired man with one eye in a perpetual pinch. When Thomas told the old fellow that Kelsey had come back late Sunday night, concern creased Mr. Jorgenson's lined face even more, and his eye closed completely.

"We haven't seen her," he fretted as he led the way up three flights of stairs at a pace almost as slow as his speech. "But then we try to mind our own business round here. Still, Kelsey usually comes on down to see us. Good girl, Kelsey—pleasure to have her rent with us. Takes real good care of her little place, never complains even though it can get real chilly up in that attic. Not sure about letting you in, but what with being a famous personality and all, s'pose it's all right. So you're going to make her little book into a movie? Wait till I tell Marge. Here we are. Let's knock first, just in case."

Thomas's hands clenched and unclenched as the little man beat a weak fist on the door. Not a sound came from the other side.

"Guess we'll have to use the keys after all," Mr. Jorgenson drawled. "Surely do hope nothing has happened to our Kelsey."

It took some fumbling with three keys for the old man to finally open the door as Thomas fidgeted behind him. Once accomplished, the solid panel moved only an inch ajar.

The brief explanation of her previous suicide attempt played itself out in Thomas's mind as if it were spoken through a bullhorn. Sweat erupted on his forehead, and his heart beat so loudly he could hear it. Had she been that upset?

"Move aside!" he shouted at the old man.

Mr. Jorgenson stared up at him, dumbfounded. Thomas pushed him out of the way and backed up a step. With one big booted foot he kicked the door. Wood splintered, the doorknob broke off, a ladder-back chair on the other side cracked and fell, and still a chain and bolt held tight to dangle a chunk of broken frame from the door's edge.

Heedless of the damage, Thomas shoved his way past the rubble and into the apartment just as Kelsey came bounding out. Buck naked, she held a towel in front of her breasts with one hand, with the other grabbing a baseball bat propped beside the rumpled Hide-A-Bed to wield it high over her head while soapsuds dripped from sopping hair into her squinted eyes. She blinked twice against the sting of shampoo and the unbelievable sight of Thomas Quinn-Patrick Sullivan, Mr. Jorgenson's openmouthed astonishment and the shambles of her door. "Oh, my God!" she shouted and spun around to dash back to the bathroom, not realizing she allowed her spectators a full view of a damp, curvaceous backside.

"Mr. Sullivan!" Mr. Jorgenson exclaimed in disbelief of all his old eyes had witnessed.

Before he could say more, Thomas turned his efforts to pacifying the elderly man, assuring him that if he would call a carpenter to repair the damage immediately, Thomas would pay for everything.

"Is it all right to leave you here alone with this guy?" Mr. Jorgenson hollered to Kelsey before he would go. But Kelsey was rinsing herself off and didn't answer, so he had to settle for sternly advising Thomas that he'd be back.

With a sigh and a disbelieving shake of his head, Thomas pushed odd pieces of the door and frame back into place so that it almost closed and gathered the sections of the chair he had broken. He only realized Kelsey had returned, wrapped in her robe, her hair turbaned in a towel, when her angry voice sounded from behind.

"Damn you, Thomas. Look what you've done to my door, to my chair! And now not only has my landlord seen me in nothing but soapsuds and a towel, but he knows I'm a spook! What are you doing here?''

He turned to her, shrugging out of the sheepskin coat that made him look as if all those muscles beneath his hunter-green ski sweater had been honed from a rustic mountain life. ''I was worried about you,'' he tried simply.

''Oh?'' Her tone was full of insinuation. ''And why would you be worried about me?''

''Is this the whole place?'' One hand swept the room.

''Except for the bathroom. Don't change the subject.''

Thomas took a turn around the tiny apartment, stopping at the big round claw-footed table scattered with crumpled papers—notes scribbled on everything from torn magazine pages to scraps of paper towel to sheets from notepads. ''You really have been here working, then,'' he said half to himself.

''Two lousy days, and what did you think? That I had come back here, packed everything and headed for parts unknown?''

''I couldn't stand it. I tried to call, and when I heard that your phone was disconnected, I got worried.'' He made it sound so reasonable, hoping his words disguised all he had really been thinking.

It didn't. Not to Kelsey. She crossed to her bed and with angry punches, shoves and tucks began making it up and folding it back into a sofa. ''I suppose you still want to deny that you don't trust me? That you aren't a bit worried I might just disappear? All you've done is confirmed that you're more doubting than I ever suspected.''

He had been leaning over the counter to peek into her kitchen, and he spun to face her, angry himself now. ''What the hell was I supposed to think? Your phone was disconnected! Phones only get turned off if you've moved.''

"Or failed to pay the bill," she shot back.

His hands bracketed his narrow waist, and his thick-lashed eyelids narrowed so that only slits of stormy green showed. "Come on, Kelsey. You don't strike me as someone who doesn't pay her bills."

She threw first one blue-and-white-flowered cushion into place and then the other, speaking through gritted teeth. "When I have the money, they're all paid right on time."

"You just shelled out seven grand to your ex. Don't tell me you couldn't pay your phone bill."

"Not that it's any of your damn business, but the only way I could scrape that money together was to renege on several bills—the phone bill being first. If I could have afforded it, don't you think I would have gone to a hotel rather than stay with you in L.A.?"

"And what about Jorgenson? He swore he hadn't seen you, that you weren't back yet. It sounded to me as if you'd snuck in and out so no one would know where you'd gone."

"The second half of last month's rent bought my plane fare, and I can't pay him this month's rent, either. He's good about it, but I wasn't up to asking for the extension just yet. If you were so sure I had run away, what are you doing here?"

Thomas raked his hair back. "I came to see if I could find any clues to where you had gone. When Jorgenson opened the door and it was rigged with one of your booby traps and he said he hadn't seen you, I was afraid you might have done something rash."

Kelsey dropped wearily onto the chintz sofa she had just made up, her hands pressed between her knees. She shook her head, staring at nothing in particular on the oval braided rug. "My God," she breathed. "So that's what you think of me. If you let me out of your sight, I'll either run away or kill myself. That leaves us in one hell of a fine mess, doesn't it? Worse than I ever thought."

"It was just a series of dumb misunderstandings. Don't blow it out of proportion." He stood with his back to her, staring out the alcove window at the ski slopes.

"And that's one big load of bull you're hoping I'll swallow so I don't see how really bad things are in your head."

Just then old Mr. Jorgenson called from the hallway. "You all right in there, Kelsey?"

"I'm fine," she answered in a falsely bright voice.

"Okay to leave you alone with that guy?"

"It's okay."

"Carpenter'll be here in half an hour to fix your door."

"Thank you," she called back.

The silence was broken only by the sound of the elderly man's shuffling steps back down the stairs. When even that noise was gone, Kelsey and Thomas remained as they were, she staring down at the floor wondering how it could ever work out between them, he staring out the window wondering how he could ever overcome this desperate feeling that if he didn't bind her to him and keep constant tabs on her, he would lose her.

Finally, Kelsey stood, said she needed to get dressed and dry her hair before the workman came and disappeared back into the bathroom.

For a long while Thomas stayed where he was, a muscle in his jaw working fiercely. Who was he angry at? Himself? Her? Life and love?

He turned slowly back to the room, taking it all in. He hadn't realized her touch in Gary's house, but now, seeing it all around him there, he recognized her quiet, tasteful hand in both places. Yet there was also a difference in the two. Where the other had been overly bright and cheerful, this place was calm and cozy and comfortable.

Wondering just how short of funds she was, he rounded the small counter and checked the ancient refrigerator, which was so low he had to bend to peer in. One stick of butter, two eggs, half a lemon—dry and withered—and a single potato. The cupboards weren't any better. Tea, one can of tuna, a box of macaroni and cheese and three chocolate bars. Still searching, he discovered her trash, tellingly empty of all save used tea bags, a few paper towels, two chocolate bar wrappers and the large gold foil Godiva candy box that Kit had given her.

"Haven't you eaten anything but tea and chocolate in two days?" he called to her.

Kelsey came out then, baggy jeans and oversize sweater in place, her hair a wild mass of shining curls held back with those big owly glasses, the rest left to fall eratically around her shoulders.

"Playing detective?" she asked coolly.

"Why the hell didn't you tell me you needed money?"

"I don't," she lied.

"Are you going to have heat for much longer, or is that going, too?"

"All paid up. Mind your own business."

Thomas sighed in the face of the darkest frown he had ever seen distort her beautiful features. "Look, I blew it, and I'm sorry. Let me put my mind at rest that you at least have food and won't get kicked out of here, and then I'll go back to L.A., we can start our separation all over again—your terms—and go from there. How about it?"

He couldn't bear the look of profound disappointment in her dark eyes, as if some dearly held belief had been irreparably shattered. When she just stood there looking at him like that, he knew honesty was all that was left to him. Again he raked his hair back, sighed and stared at the ceiling.

"I'm only human, Kelsey," he began, his tone raw and ragged and the first she had heard lately that she knew was the man speaking and not the actor. "I'm in love with you. The feelings I have for you haven't ever been in me before for another living soul. I don't want not to trust you."

His head lowered, but still he didn't meet her eyes. "God, how I don't want not to trust you," he said to himself. "But you're right. The suspicion is there, and it makes me act like a jackass. But it doesn't change how much I love you, how much I want you. We *have* to find a way to work it out."

Kelsey watched him. She knew she should be grateful that he was finally being honest with her. But it hurt too much.

"I could check in with you every hour on the hour for the next thirty years, Thomas, but the first time an hour and a half went by, you'd figure I had left. I think..." She swallowed the strangling emotions in her throat. "I think that *we* can't find a way for you to trust me. *You* have to find a way, all by yourself, to believe in me. Just the way I have to find a way to deal with being a part of the life you live—all by myself—or not do it at all."

His green eyes met and held her black ones, both of them feeling so much, wanting so much, and yet so far apart.

When the sound of Mr. Jorgenson's voice and a second pair of heavy footsteps intruded, Thomas held out a hand to her. "Then I guess we both go at it according to your plan. But I'm not leaving here until I know you're taken care of. Clear?"

Kelsey could only nod, too frazzled and hurt for pride to deny him this. She ventured a small smile, took his hand and made a try for levity that was too quiet and too sad to work. "I'll show you Winter Park's latest attraction—a Safeway. But make sure anything you spend is deducted from the money you pay for the rights to *A Second Season*."

When they returned two hours later, Kelsey's door was fixed, complete with three new locks, a new bolt and chain and Mr. Jorgenson waiting with the keys. While Kelsey went in with the groceries, Thomas settled up the damages and her rent with the still suspicious landlord.

Knowing he should leave but not wanting to, Thomas once more strolled through Kelsey's apartment while she packed her cupboards and refrigerator. For the first time his eyes caught a stack of canvases propped behind a wing chair that matched the sofa. Without asking permission he pulled them out, a dozen paintings all about two feet wide and three feet high. Glancing quickly through them, he saw that they were all paintings of women, not just head-and-shoulders portraits, but full body paintings, some nude, posed so that each position and posture was as important as the facial expressions.

"Some of these are beautiful," Thomas said over his shoulder to Kelsey.

Kelsey stopped to glance his way and see what he was talking about. Then she went on with her chore. "I suppose some of them are passable. None of them is beautiful." There remained a solemnity between them still, a tension.

"Why are they stuffed back here?"

"Van Gogh."

"He didn't like them?" Thomas said in his own small attempt at lessening the strain he knew would stay until things were resolved.

Kelsey was still busy in the kitchen, but in the small open space she could be heard without raising her voice. "Mental state has a way of influencing what we create even when we aren't conscious of it. Van Gogh's paintings got progressively harsher in color, line, content the wackier he got. With me it was the reverse. The earliest of them—when I was the most depressed and lonely—are the darkest, most maudlin-looking. By the time they perk up, I was better. I don't particularly want mementos of that time hanging on my walls. But they're too big for my storage closet, and I haven't had the heart to pitch them into the trash, either."

"I'd like to have them."

"No, you wouldn't. They're sad, ugly paintings, most of them."

He flipped through them again. There was also something about them that Thomas felt drawn to, felt the need to study. "You said you didn't want to look at them. Let me take them and keep them for you. They'll be out of your way, and if you ever want to see them or have them back, you'll know where they are. I won't even show them to anyone if you don't want me to."

Kelsey stopped in the middle of refolding a grocery sack to stare over the counter at him. "How would you get them back to L.A. with you?"

"I'll have them crated in Denver. Can I take them?"

She shrugged. "I guess so, but they're liable to give you nightmares."

"I doubt it. Don't you paint anymore?"

"Now you sound like my brother." Kelsey came to lean one hip against the table, far enough away from Thomas to avoid his magnetic pull. "For a while I did a few sketches here and there, but every time I picked up a brush, it was like stepping back in time." She watched him going through the paintings again, and it made her uncomfortable. "You'd better get going, Thomas, or you won't make it down the pass before the roads freeze for the night."

He put the canvases against the arm of the couch. "I could stay just tonight, go back in the morning."

"Don't make it harder than it is. Please."

"I'm going to pay your phone bill before I leave. If you need anything . . . want anything . . . you'll call me?"

"Sure," she whispered around the lump that clogged her throat.

"I still hate this, McKenna."

"I know" was all she could manage.

Two long strides took him to her. He crushed her into his arms. "I love you, Kelsey. So much. There are ways out of these damn hang-ups of ours. We just have to find them. Agreed?"

She nodded her head against his chest, hearing the rapid beat of his heart. "Go now," she said softly.

All at once he let go of her, pulled the canvases under one arm, swiped up his coat and slammed out the door.

And for the first time in three years, Kelsey gave in to tears.

Chapter Fourteen

It was actually the paintings that gave Thomas the idea. He studied them, rearranged them until he was satisfied that he had their order just right, and then he spent every waking hour at home looking at them from every angle, in every light, as whole compositions, in parts, as separate paintings and as a series.

They were all Kelsey, he realized, though some of them didn't even resemble her. Some seemed young and frightened, others old and worn. There was shame and humiliation and even one grotesque of a woman in a clown's costume carrying a boar's head mask under one arm, a jester's under the other and a devil's face half on, half off her own disfigured features. One feeling ruled all but the last of them, drawing Thomas in as if he were living it—such profound pain and sadness that there were times when he couldn't bear to look at them.

Only the last three showed something different, easier to view, more pleasing to the eye. The colors paled; the lines eased and finally flowed smoothly. Each of these women seemed at peace, calm, quiet, peering out from the canvases first unabashedly, then challengingly, then with a serenity and confidence that said she could handle whatever came her way. This last was the Kelsey Thomas knew, the one among them all that made him smile with familiarity and long to have her back with him all the more.

The longer he studied the paintings, the more he began to feel that they were, indeed, visual evidence of the stages of change she had gone through. Like photographs in a family album, they chronicled her growth. Thomas began to believe that the woman who had begun these paintings was not the same one who had emerged—just as the adult in the family album is so far from the child pictured.

And when, in the end, he knew every detail of each painting by heart, he took what he was sure were the first and the last and put away all the others to compare only the beginning and the end.

And then he went to see her brother.

Within a week of Thomas's visit, temperatures hit the mid-seventies and spring came to even the mountains of Colorado. Winter Park's annual Spring Fling frolics turned the small town into a mini Fort Lauderdale during spring break. Crowds were drawn by the antics of ski jump contests over enormous puddles of melted snow at the slope basins and outlandish races where bikinis and Hawaiian-print shorts replaced long underwear and ski togs. Beer was consumed by the barrel, and revelry abounded everywhere but in Kelsey McKenna's garret.

Unlike three years ago, the longer Kelsey spent alone in her apartment, working and brooding, the more miserable she felt. Writing was only a temporary escape, the pleasure of which began to wane as her imagination wandered more and more to Thomas when it should have been scouring the streets of eighteenth-century England as a young pickpocket.

Yet as luck would have it, she was absorbed in the first real bit of inspiration she had had in a week when Thomas chose to call.

"What time is it?" she asked him distractedly, glancing at the night sky beyond her windows.

"Two in the morning here. Don't tell me you were working," he said, a bit peeved. "I purposely waited to call now, figuring I would rather have you sleepy than thinking of your next paragraph."

"Sorry," she mumbled, stretching the phone cord to the table so she could scribble a catch phrase of the next paragraph.

"I need your attention here, lady." Thomas's low voice was a slow drawl, and Kelsey wondered whether he was tired or drunk.

"You have it," she said honestly, leaning against the wall and closing her eyes. Then she spoke before gauging her words. "It's good to hear your voice."

"That's a step in the right direction. How are you?"

"You know," she hedged. "How are you?"

"I've been busy."

Kelsey's heart sank a little. Too busy to miss her? she wondered. "How's the movie coming?"

"Great, from all accounts. I haven't been busy with that. I've been busy working out my half of our problem."

Kelsey's pulse drummed in her throat. "Oh?" was all she could manage. Was he calling to tell her the solution was never to see her again? She should never have left.

Stupid. Don't give up on me, Thomas, she wanted to say, but she knew she couldn't. It had been her choice, and she hadn't resolved her part of the dilemma yet. All of a sudden she didn't want to hear what he had worked out. "Are you all right?" she asked cautiously. "You sound a little ... strange."

The rumble of an easy laugh lightened her heart immensely. "I am so damn tired that I can't see straight. Revelation isn't a simple thing to come by."

"Oh?" she repeated, afraid of the relief she was feeling.

"I went to see your brother today."

Silence.

Relief turned to trepidation. "Why?" Her voice was soft.

"I wanted to know you three years ago."

"Are you deliberately torturing me?"

Again he laughed. "I don't mean to torture you at all."

"Then tell me what's going on," she demanded, still not understanding his slow pace.

"I formed this theory. Maybe it was insight. I don't know. I've spent a week with your paintings. It came to me that the Kelsey McKenna I know—and was worried might leave me in the lurch—was not the same Kelsey McKenna of three years ago. So I went to see your brother. He doesn't like me."

"I think you're just the scapegoat." So many emotions were running rampant in her that Kelsey didn't know what she was feeling. Hope. Fear. Dread. Love.

"Scapegoat sounds about right. Anyway, after a while he gave up on some of his resentment and told me all about his little sister. He doesn't know you very well, does he?"

"Where is this headed, Thomas?"

"I love you, Kelsey." There was a teasing lilt to his tone now, and an underlying serenity. "I called to tell you that I love you. And that my part is taken care of."

"Just like that?"

"Did you happen to tell me anywhere through this whole thing that you really aren't the same person who ran away three years ago? I can't remember. It probably wouldn't have sunk in, anyway. But those paintings told me a lot about you, lady. More, I'm sorry to say, than I ever would have believed if you did just say it. So I went to see your brother. He told me all about the way you were. Happy. Content. The perfect homemaker. You could have been Donna Reed. Painting was a spare-time thing that rounded you out, and he doesn't know where this writing stuff came from, but it's bound to die out as soon as you find yourself a *good* man again—like Gary. Then you'll quit wearing those funny clothes that don't fit and do something with that wild hair and go back to painting and have babies."

Kelsey clamped her eyes shut tight and said nothing.

"Do you want to have babies, Kelsey? I never asked."

"I don't know. Maybe someday," she said softly, saddened to think that she had failed so utterly to show her brother what she was really like now.

"I'd like to have a baby with you, Kelsey."

"Are you drunk, Thomas?"

"Not in the least. What you are hearing, my lovely lady of letters, is utter peace. Trust, if you prefer. You know what I discovered, Kelsey? That I know you better than I thought. You didn't change before my eyes the way it seemed. The person I met, the person I fell in love with, just isn't the same one you were three years ago. And better still, what we have together is different than what you had then. Think about that one, McKenna. Think about what we have together—all by ourselves—regardless of how much the world intrudes. I don't believe you and old Gary came anywhere near it. I think there wasn't a time—not even alone with your husband or your brother—when you weren't pretending.''

"I think you're right, and if you lived a normal, quiet life, I might do just fine. But that isn't so.''

"Okay, so you fell into some heavy-duty role playing to get along in my life. But it wasn't ever there when we were alone, was it? Think about it, Kelsey. You won't be working with me—that cuts out one hell of a lot of it. I can keep my work out of the house, and I think you can handle the few of my friends I let in. As for the damn publicity, I can only promise to protect you as much as possible. It comes in waves, anyway. If you wait it out, someone else always becomes a better story eventually. Our whole life won't be lived in a fishbowl, just certain parts of it. I think you're strong enough to handle it, and I think the bad stuff is made up for by what we have together.''

Tempting. It was so tempting. But was she strong enough? Or did it just seem as if she could handle it because she was removed from it now, because she wanted so badly for it to be true? Too badly. There was danger in wanting something so much that she was tempted to mold herself to fit it. That frightened her. And fear spoke.

"Or is it that you're such a prize catch that it's worth it for me to sacrifice my sanity? No, thank you. I've already been in one relationship in my life where my needs always came second.''

He didn't say anything for a long time. When he did, his voice was edged with anger. "If you really believe that, lady, then we've just wasted a hell of a lot of time and pain for nothing.''

Silence came again as Kelsey listened to her heart pound its way into her throat. Take back the words, she told herself. You know you didn't mean that. But she couldn't speak, could only stand frozen and afraid.

"I'll tell you what," he said finally, coldly. "I've done my part, purged my demons. Now it's all up to you. Do me a favor—tell the Muse to take a hike, and give me and our future some concentrated thought for a change. You're using writing as a painkiller to keep your feelings away from the surface. This time jump in with both feet and muck around in them until you find a way to deal with your half of this thing. If you manage it, let me know."

The receiver went dead in her hand. Kelsey hung it back in the cradle and let her forehead fall to the wall beside it. He thought it was so easy. But he didn't know.

For two days Kelsey didn't eat or sleep or write or even think about her work. Thomas hadn't given her an ultimatum in so many words, but that was how he had left it just the same. He could honestly say he trusted her and assure her he would do his best to keep the public side of his life removed from their private life. Compromise. That's what it came down to. He had done his part, would do more. Either she came the rest of the way or...

Kelsey couldn't think of that or.

He was right about their relationship. There was never any pretending when she was alone with him—and that could not have been said of her marriage to Gary. Alone with Thomas it was easy to be herself. And maybe that was all that really mattered.

But was it? When the life he lived was *so* public and *so* full of other people and Kelsey found it nearly impossible to be herself with any of it? Wouldn't she lose herself again? Wouldn't the pretending take its toll, put such a strain on her that she would lose everything she had gained in leaving Gary and Gordon behind? Wouldn't she come to resent Thomas for drawing her back into it? Wouldn't he come to hate her?

The ringing of the phone interrupted her panic. Kelsey jumped a foot, raced to it and then couldn't bring herself to lift the receiver. What if it was Thomas? What could she say? What if she made things worse the way she had when they last talked? What if it wasn't Thomas? Lord, how she needed to hear his voice, she realized suddenly.

She picked up the phone. It was Ali Robbins. Kelsey's heart sank to her heels.

"Money's on the way. Royalties came in—not too shabby. I cut you a check and mailed it today. How're you doing?" The agent's voice was bright and cheery, and Kelsey cringed at the sound of it.

All on its own everything came pouring out then, as if Kelsey's head and heart were too full of all she had been agonizing over. She needed to talk, and Ali was a safe listener. Only when Kelsey had finished her woeful tale did the agent say anything.

"Christmas dinner," she said calmly. "I've been married for fourteen years. My mother-in-law is German. My father-in-law is Spanish. Every year Christmas dinner is knockwurst and tortillas smothered with green chili hot enough to remove car paint. I eat about four bites, run for the bathroom and it all comes back up. Every year. I hate it. I dread it. Every year for a week before Christmas I gag just in anticipation. But I love the guy. So I do it. I hate it. But I do it. Nothing changes in me. By the next day I eat everything in sight." Ali paused after her little story, letting Kelsey think about it.

Kelsey thought about it. And then she burst out laughing. "Knockwurst and tortillas?"

"Smothered in green chili. I don't mean to belittle your fears, Kelsey. But have you thought that maybe you're taking this all a little too seriously? I can see how your past would make you worry, and I can hear absolute terror in your voice, but maybe, just maybe, it's clouding your thinking a little. After all, it's the man you'd be spending your life with. The rest . . . well, every relationship comes with built-in irritations. Loony in-laws, grasping exes, snotty stepkids—something. I know you're allergic to people, but sometimes you just have to grin and bear things. For me, it's Christmas dinner. Why not try looking at the whole thing with a little humor? Maybe it'll help."

It was remarkable how much better Kelsey felt when she hung up. She fixed herself a peanut butter sandwich and ate it at the window, watching the dots that were skiers moving down the slopes in the distance.

Okay, so what do we have here? she asked herself. You're scared silly of flying, but you do it, right? A couple of hours and it's over. You're scared silly of the dentist, but you go, right? Well, not for seven years, but you will when you have the money, right? A few hours and it's over. Can you look at Thomas's public life that way? A few hours of misery, of forcing smiles and conversation, of breathing funny smoke and feeling inadequate and grotesquely pale—isn't it worth it?

What about the parade of people and the incessant phone calls? You could hide and unplug the telephone.

Publicity? Reporters jumping out at you, asking personal questions? Being royal pains in the neck? You'll hate it. You'll cringe. You'll clam up. You'll look like a scared rabbit ducking behind the nearest potted palm. No help there.

And what about the fact that you'll always be Thomas's oddball lady? Inferiority complex. That old trap of conformity. But he likes you the way you are. You like you the way you are. Can't you say to hell with everybody else?

Reduced to sarcasm, it all seemed less formidable. The good outweighed the bad. But realistically, could she handle it? Was she strong enough?

There had been so much vacillating between the past and present when she was in L.A. Facing the havoc she had wreaked, walking a fine line between the person Gordon thought her to be and who she actually was had put such a stress on the progress she had made. Thomas's life on top of it had been just too much. But with the past taken care of, and all the bad aspects of a future with Thomas taken one at a time or curbed and avoided whenever possible, would it all seem so overwhelming? Hadn't he learned, too, what she could and couldn't handle? Wouldn't he keep from pushing her into those situations if he could?

But *was* she strong enough? That was what it all boiled down to. Was she strong enough to bounce back from those times and things that couldn't be changed?

She would have to be was the decision Kelsey reached at last. Because she knew she couldn't handle the alternative.

Was she too late? Kelsey worried all the way down the mountain, sitting in the cramped back seat of the Jorgensons' Volvo. She had put in a call to Thomas, only to have a reluctant Sasha inform her that he was scouting location sites in Denver. Without time to do anything but grab her purse, Kelsey had bummed a ride with her landlords, who were headed to the city and Mrs. Jorgenson's podiatrist.

But on the way worry had set in. He had been in Denver for two days. Why hadn't he called or tried to see her?

One minute Kelsey told herself it was an irrational fear—hadn't she been the one to insist on being left alone to sort through her feelings? But the next minute she remembered the anger in his voice the last time they had spoken. What if going to see him was a mistake? What if she had pushed too far and Thomas didn't want to see her?

Seventeenth and Welton on a late Thursday afternoon was crowded with men and women in business suits, the usual array of shoppers, lanky teenage boys toting twenty-pound ghetto blasters on their shoulders and an aged black man in a wheelchair playing jazz on a saxophone. The plush red velvet lobby of the Fairmont was dimly lit by three crystal chandeliers, the piano bar in the center only beginning to fill with the cocktail crowd.

Thomas, Jake, Kit, the art director and the cinematographer had all taken suites on the twenty-sixth floor, Sasha had told her. So Kelsey headed for the elevators. One glance in the smoky mirror once the elevator doors had closed did not buoy Kelsey's confidence. Her hair was a wild mass of tangles from the early April wind, her eyes were fearfully wide and her skin pale except for the bright pink cold spots high on her cheekbones. And her clothes! Why hadn't she stopped to change? A white T-shirt tucked into baggy jeans and covered with an overly large chambray shirt, the sleeves rolled up to her elbows, was her chic ensemble. No wonder the bellman had looked askance at her.

The only help for it now was to run a quick brush through her hair, an act she was caught in the middle of when the elevator doors opened to two people waiting on the top floor. Kelsey finished the task without the aid of the mirror and then turned to find the Denver Suite. But she rounded the corner a mere two feet before coming up against a towering side of beef in a polyester suit, his badge proclaiming him a security guard.

"May I help you?" he asked imperiously, glaring down at Kelsey with enough suspicion to make her feel guilty of anything.

She drew a breath and stretched to her full height. "I'm looking for the Denver Suite," she answered as if she had every right to be there.

It didn't matter.

"I'm sorry, but these rooms are off-limits."

She tried a little lie. "I have an appointment to meet Thomas Quinn-Patrick Sullivan."

The beefy guard nearly cracked a smile. His fish eyes appraised her, beginning with her black leather tennis shoes and stopping at a few strands of windblown hair she had missed, bunched at the top of her head. "I'm sorry. No one gets past here without prior notification. I was not told to let anyone in today."

"Look, I'm a personal friend," she tried feebly.

"Aren't they all?" he mumbled to himself. "Not even personal friends get by me without prior notification. Sorry."

"What if I give you my name and you just ask him if he'll see me?"

"I can't do that."

Stubborn, pigheaded baboon. "I have to see him." What did one do in a situation like this one? "I have twenty-two dollars. Will you do it for that?"

Now he merely sneered. "Lose my job for twenty-two dollars? Sorry. If you don't get off this floor, I'll have you removed."

Desperation struck. "Thomas!" Kelsey screamed, "It's me, Thomas!"

The security guard's stubby hand closed around her arm just as Kit's voice came from behind. "What's going on here?"

"Kit!" Kelsey breathed in relief. "I need to see Thomas. Will you tell this man I'm not some deranged fan?"

One bushy red brow arched as his snide tone knifed through the tension in the hallway. "I'm not too sure you aren't." Then he spoke to the guard. "It's all right. She can come back."

The beefy man eyed her up and down once more dubiously, but he stepped aside when Kit confirmed it by taking her elbow.

"First my room and then Thomas's. We can talk while I make sure everything's set—he's coming back here for an interview with a few locals."

At that news Kelsey balked instinctively, but Kit held her arm tightly, pinching it with his grip. Couldn't she even do *this* in private? "I'll come back later."

"Not a chance. We're going to talk," Kit decreed, keeping hold of her even after he had unlocked his door, grabbed a bottle of Maalox and left again.

Thomas's room was across the hall, a spacious suite of mauve and dusty-gray elegance. It wasn't until the door was closed firmly behind them that Kit let go of Kelsey. Nervously she rounded the room, pacing past velvet wing chairs and a floral sofa, circling the oak dining table surrounded by eight high-backed chairs, peeking into the small room that held a wet bar and refrigerator, avoiding glancing through the open double doors that led to the bedroom.

"Sit down and relax, why don't you?" Kit suggested as she passed him.

"I can't," she confessed, plunging her hands into the pockets of her jeans beneath the floppy shirt she wore.

"Suit yourself." He uncapped the bottle of Maalox and toasted her with it. "Cheers. I'd offer you a swig, but you've put me in need of the whole bottle myself."

Kelsey frowned at the comment as he threw back a long gulp of the chalky stuff, but it wasn't in her nature to invite a confrontation. "I don't want to be here if anyone but Thomas is coming. Can't I wait in your room?"

"That'd be good. Then word could leak that we share you."

Still she didn't want to face the sarcasm in his tone. "Then I'll hide in the bedroom until they leave."

"And what if someone wanders in there and finds you? Make a hell of a juicy discovery. Why not just face them honestly and let Thomas handle it? He's good with the press. Or did you come here to stir up dirt?"

Why was he treating her this way? He had always been so friendly before. Was it a sneak preview of what was to come from Thomas? Kelsey screwed up her courage. "If I'm not welcome here, then I'd rather you told me now so I can get out before he comes back."

"This is Thomas's room. You've come to see him. It isn't my place to tell you whether or not you're welcome. But if you had come to me, it might be a different story." He took another swallow of Maalox. "You know, I was on your side in this. Up until this last part. Thomas had himself together again before he put in that late-night call to you. But was it enough? No, you had to shoot him down all over again, didn't you? What the hell do you want from the man? Blood? You knew what his life was like before you got involved. If it freaked you out so much, why'd you let it go this far?"

Kelsey took her glasses from the top of her head and then pushed her hair back with them again. She looked away from the small redhead. "It wasn't something that I planned," she said softly.

"You know what he's been like to work with? Not like the Thomas I know, I can tell you that. He's like a wounded bear. Holdups and griping and nothing pleases him. This little fiasco of yours is costing us an arm and a leg in delays. We shouldn't even be here looking for locations yet, but every story conference was like locking up a caged animal. He bit our heads off or stormed out of every damn meeting until I figured I'd better get him the hell away from closed spaces."

Kit slammed his medicine bottle into a drawer of the credenza. "Look, if you've come to make him a happy man, I'm all for this foray. But if you're looking to cause more problems or end it with him, then I wish you'd have a little mercy on us all and get the hell out of here."

Kelsey swallowed hard. No virtual stranger had ever spoken to her so harshly. Her face burned, and her eyes felt as if they bulged from her head. Her first inclination was to deny his accusations, but that would have been a lie in the face of Thomas's obvious confidences. Her second was to fall over herself explaining and apologizing. But it was her third inclination that ruled. Too many emotions, too much pressure, too much stress, too much of everything. Kelsey snapped. She leveled raging black eyes on Kit.

"Who the bloody hell do you think you are, Kitridge Mason? Just because Thomas told you what was going on between us doesn't give you the right to light into me like that. I'm sorry if he's been crabby and slowed down your work, but it hasn't been a picnic for me, either. And playing confidant doesn't make it your business. Even if I'm here to wreak holy hell, it isn't any of your business. So drink your damn Maalox and get off my case."

For a long moment they just stood staring at each other, nose to nose. Then Kit gave a mirthless chuckle. "Well, I guess you told me."

"Well, I guess I did. I've been through hell in the last month—and worse in the last couple of weeks—trying to work this out. I don't need you dumping your load on top of it. Friend or not, you can just climb down off my back."

"Okay, okay. Geez, when you decide to quit playing Mary Sunshine, you go all the way." His elfin face broke into a genuinely amused grin. "What was it you were worried about again? Hiding your real feelings behind a pliable, friendly face? I think you've overcome it, darling. You're home free."

Kelsey's eyes grew round and her jaw slack with shock over her own words, her own audacity. Gordon would have had to set up an hour-long chant of "that's not like you" for this one.

"Relax," Kit said, seeing her reaction. "I had it coming. I'll live to insult you another day. And big news—I don't think any less of you. So, how'd it feel to put me in my place? Is the world still turning? The sun still shining? My God, it is. You may make it after all, darling. Now go comb your hair and cool off. From the sounds down the hall, I'd say you're about to meet the press again."

Chapter Fifteen

Kelsey took a dozen deep breaths. She had rushed into the bathroom off the living-dining area and now wished she had chosen the one off the bedroom. At least then she could have eased slowly into the room, maybe stood in the bedroom doorway until Thomas noticed her. As it was, she could hardly stand and wait with the toilet as a backdrop. Oh, Lord, couldn't she do anything right?

Her heart was pounding so hard and so fast that she thought it was going to race out of her chest. Her head felt light, her ears buzzed and she wished she had stayed in Winter Park and just called.

She could hear the friendly banter as Kit offered drinks, cameramen asked Thomas where he wanted to sit and reporters shot him a few friendly preparatory questions.

Oh, Lord. How could she just burst out of the bathroom into that? What would they all think?

She heard Kit ask to speak to Thomas for a minute.

Oh, no. What if he didn't want her? What if her showing up like this only made him angry? He had every right to be. What had she said? Maybe he just thought he was such a prize catch that it was worth her sanity? Oh, Lord. What if he asked her to leave? Wouldn't the press have a field day with that?

When a knock sounded on the bathroom door, Kelsey jumped a foot. Her first instinct was to scan the space for a window to climb out. Of course there were no windows.

"Kelsey?" It was Thomas's voice, soft, soothing. All chatter in the background stopped as his eager guests eavesdropped. Kelsey cringed and held her breath. Maybe if she passed out, she wouldn't have to face them.

"Can I open the door?" Thomas asked when she didn't answer.

If there had been a shower, she would have hidden in it. As it was, she opened the door just a crack and stood behind it. She could see Thomas in the mirror.

"Why don't you let me in?" he asked again, as if he were gentling a skittish colt.

Kelsey thought of all those people watching and listening. Oh, Lord. What must they think? Some loon had locked herself in the bathroom in order to get an audience with The Man. She took another deep breath. Nothing to do about it now. Still hiding behind the door, she opened it enough to admit him.

"I tried, Thomas. I really did try," she whispered so no one would overhear once the door was locked behind him. Too embarrassed to look at him, she stared at the center of his blue cashmere-clad chest. "I thought I could do it, but I just can't walk out of the bathroom into a press conference."

Only concern showed on his handsome features. "It's all right, Kelsey. You don't have to."

"It was a dumb mistake. Kit said to use the bathroom in your room, but I didn't think about a hotel room having two baths, and so I just came in here, and then I didn't know how to get out without looking like an idiot," she explained in a rush.

"It's okay," he reassured her, wondering and worrying about how much damage this situation would do to what he hoped was her coming to reconcile with him. He smoothed her hair behind her shoulder and then raised her head with the caressing pressure of his hand at the nape of her neck. "Why are you here, Kelsey?" he asked.

"Kit told me to comb my hair and cool off after I got all heated up reading him the riot act," she answered, too befuddled to think his question had a broader sense.

"Not in the bathroom. Why are you here to see me?"

"Oh." She sighed deeply, swallowed and rubbed her fingertips nervously across the tip of her nose. Her gaze moved about the small space. "I can't talk about it in here."

"Then just tell me this," he said softly, sadly. "Are you here to say goodbye?"

The pain in his voice stabbed her, dissolving the doubt renewed by this incident. "No," she whispered into the face she loved so dearly. "I didn't come to say goodbye."

His full lower lip disappeared beneath his mustache in a slow smile. "Sit tight" was all he said, and he was gone, standing just outside the bathroom door where his voice carried as clearly to her as to the roomful of press people.

"Folks, we're going to have to put this off for another time. I have a lady in this bathroom who has come to propose to me, and if I make her wait, she's liable to not make an honest man of me after all."

A wave of chuckles responded, but no one moved. Walk out on a juicy scoop? Never.

"I'll make it worth your while tomorrow," Thomas insisted. "Take care of this, will you, Kit?" And he slipped back into the bathroom, leaning against the door that muffled the sounds of Kit doing what he could to clear the room.

Thomas grabbed Kelsey's shirtfront and pulled her close. "You *did* come to propose to me, didn't you?" he teased.

"I don't know," she blurted out. "I thought I could handle some of this, but look where we are. And I can't promise it will get any better. And there's always the chance that I'll hug the wall and become a zombie at parties, and people will begin to think you've married one of the FBI's ten most wanted women, the way I always hide my face from photographers, and I'll never have a tan, and I can't stand tight clothes and sequins and—"

"Okay, forget it. You really are too flawed." He laughed. "Did you come to tell me what you can't do or what you're going to do?"

She closed her eyes and took another deep, fortifying breath. "I came to tell you I'll try."

He kissed each of her closed eyelids and pulled her into his arms, pressing her cheek against his chest and lowering his chin to the top of her head. "So you told Kit off, huh?" he said raggedly.

"Something fierce," she admitted.

"Good for you. He's been grouchy as hell lately."

Kelsey smiled at that, soothed by the steady drumming of his heart. "I love you, Thomas."

She felt the heat of his breath as he turned his face into her hair, kissing her head. "No," he deadpanned and then leaned away so that when she looked up at him in question, his mouth lowered to hers in a deep joining.

Kelsey's arms went up around his neck, pulling herse
higher in his embrace as his arms tightened around her. B
relief and reaffirmation turned rapidly to passion's flame
His tongue played at the inside of her lips and then we
deeper to meet hers. His hands went up under her chan
bray shirt and then found their way beneath her T-shirt
the bareness of her back.

Kelsey drew away from him then. "I don't think w
should do this. What if Kit or somebody is still out there?"

"Kit? You still out there?" Thomas called loudly.

"Yeah," Kit called back.

"Anybody else?"

"Just me."

"Well, get the hell out."

The ripple of Kit's laughter was cut short by the closin
of the outside door as he left. Thomas made a great sho
of peeking through a crack before throwing the bathroom
door wide.

"All clear." He again took a fistful of her shirtfront an
pulled her across the living room and into the bedroom.

"I wish you wouldn't do that," she groaned. "I didn'
bring anything else to wear, and I already look like a lad
construction worker without your adding wrinkles."

They stopped beside the bed before Thomas turned t
face her. "Right. Don't wrinkle the clothes. Get rid o
them." He slipped his hands inside her shirt and slid i
from her shoulders. "And you don't look like a lady con
struction worker. You look like a hippie," he teased, kiss
ing his way up her stomach after the T-shirt as he raised i
and pulled it off, taking her glasses with it.

"Shouldn't we talk, Thomas?" Kelsey breathed th
words out heavily.

"Mmm. Lots. Later." His mouth reached hers once more to plunder with the warm, wet point of his tongue. "I need you too much right now to be coherent."

Kelsey understood the feeling well. Without another word she found the edge of his sweater and rolled it up his hard, flat belly, past the broad expanse of his muscular chest and shoulders and up off his head, leaving his wheat-colored hair mussed in a way that made him look all the sexier.

Next to go was her bra, freeing them to come together, warm flesh on warm flesh, in a perfect meeting. Their kisses became more urgent then, their hands less teasing, more searching, exciting, until neither could stand the barrier of pants and those, too, were shed.

Wrapping her tightly in his arms, Thomas laid them both on the bed, his mouth leaving hers to find the hardened crest of her breast, circling it with his tongue, suckling and teasing the tautness of it.

Kelsey filled her hands with him, as if starved for the feel of firm muscle and the stretch of sinewy tendon, roaming his well-defined back and sides and cupping the hard flatness of his divine derriere.

When neither could wait another second, Thomas joined their bodies into the exquisite union no one else in the world could offer either of them. Together they climbed until each found an ecstasy that celebrated their love and confirmed that all obstacles were nothing compared to what they shared.

Thomas rolled to his back, pulling Kelsey with him to lie nestled against his side, snug and perfect, her thigh resting over his, his arms circling her completely. He sighed, replete, content, happy. "Okay. Now talk."

"I forgot what I was going to say."

"You were going to say you love me more than anything in the world, there isn't a problem we can't deal with together, and you can't wait to marry me."

"I was?"

He frowned down at her. "Weren't you? Fair warning—if the answer isn't yes, I'll sue for breach of promise."

"I didn't make any promises."

"Your body just did. It will never let anybody else near it."

"Egotist."

"Sure," he agreed, kissing her forehead. "You're a hot property, lady, and I'm not letting you go."

"You got what you wanted."

A slow, sensuous grin stretched his lips as his hand cupped her breast in reminder. "Yeah, I did, didn't I?"

"I meant *A Second Season*." But the huskiness in her tone told him his reminder was working.

"That's a hot property, too. But you're hotter." A gentle pinch of her nipple arched her back and elicited a slight moan of pleasure.

"Don't torture me, Thomas," she invited.

"Never, love, never," he said sincerely, releasing her breast to wrap her close to his long, hard length once more. "I'll do whatever it takes to make it all easier for you, Kelsey. One whisper in my ear and I'll get you away from anything that bothers you. Good enough?"

"We'll be okay," she agreed calmly, surely.

"We really will be, you know. I love you too much to ever let anything separate us."

"No more worries about my running away?" she tested quietly.

Thomas laughed lightly. "None."

"Good. Because I wouldn't ever do it again." She craned her head back to look into his eyes. "It's probably shameful to say it, but I love you more than I ever did Gary. He was Gordon's choice. You're mine."

"Gordon won't like that. Somewhere along the line he's gotten the impression I'm disreputable."

She smiled up at him. "He's right. Look what you're doing to his sister."

"Let's do more." His hand found her breast again in a playful squeeze before he rolled her to her back and pinned her to the bed. His sea-green eyes gleamed as he searched her face, and his mustache quirked with a smile that made Kelsey feel full of sunshine. "I love you, lady, so damn much."

And then he did.

* * * * *

It was a misunderstanding that could cost a young woman her
virtue, and a notorious rake his heart.

THE BARGAIN

When Ashleigh Sinclair
arrives at Ravensford, she thinks
she's been hired as a governess,
but Lord Brett Westmont has other ideas....

VERONICA SATTLER

Silhouette Special Edition

COMING NEXT MONTH

#403 SANTIAGO HEAT—Linda Shaw
When Deidre Miles crash-landed in steamy Santiago, powerful Francis MacIntire saved her from the clutches of a treacherous military. But what could save her from Francis himself, his tumultuous life and flaming desire?

#404 SOMETIMES A MIRACLE—Jennifer West
Bodyguard Cassandra Burke wistfully dreamed of shining knights on white chargers. Cynical ex-rodeo star Alex Montana had long since turned in his steed. As they braved murder and mayhem together, just who would protect whom?

#405 CONQUER THE MEMORIES—Sandra Dewar
For social worker Carla Foster it was time to face the music. In an adoption dispute, Drake Lanning recognized her for the singer she used to be, and he vowed to learn why she hid her talent . . . and her heart.

#406 INTO THE SUNSET—Jessica Barkley
Lindsay Jordan wasn't just another city slicker playing cowgirl, no matter what ornery stable manager Nick Leighton said. And despite his sensual persuasion, she wasn't greenhorn enough to think of riding off into the sunset with him!

#407 LONELY AT THE TOP—Bevlyn Marshall
Corporate climber Keely LaRoux wasn't about to let maverick photographer Chuck Dickens impede her progress up the ladder. But traveling together on assignment, the unlikely pair found that business could fast become a dangerously addictive pleasure.

#408 A FAMILY OF TWO—Jude O'Neill
Hotshot producer Gable McCrea wanted newcomer Annabel Porter to direct his latest movie. But what inner demons prompted him to sabotage her work . . . and her growing love for him?

AVAILABLE THIS MONTH:

Silhouette Desire

**Available
August 1987**

ONE TOUGH HOMBRE

Visit with characters introduced
in the acclaimed Desire trilogy
by Joan Hohl!

The *Hombre* is back!
J. B. Barnet—first introduced in *Texas Gold*—
has returned and make no mistake,
J.B. *is* one tough hombre . . . but
Nicole Vanzant finds the gentle,
tender side of the former
Texas Ranger.

Don't miss *One Tough Hombre*—
J.B. and Nicole's story.
And coming soon from Desire is
Falcon's Flight—the story of Flint Falcon
and Leslie Fairfield.

D372-1R

NO SAFE PLACE

By Richard North Patterson
Published by Ballantine Books:

THE LASKO TANGENT
THE OUTSIDE MAN
ESCAPE THE NIGHT
PRIVATE SCREENING
DEGREE OF GUILT
EYES OF A CHILD
THE FINAL JUDGMENT
SILENT WITNESS
NO SAFE PLACE

NO SAFE PLACE

PLACE

Richard North Patterson

BALLANTINE BOOKS • NEW YORK

A Ballantine Book
Published by The Ballantine Publishing Group
Copyright © 1998 by Richard North Patterson

All rights reserved under International and Pan-American Copyright Conventions. Published in the United States by The Ballantine Publishing Group, a division of Random House, Inc., New York, and simultaneously in Canada by Random House of Canada Limited, Toronto.

www.randomhouse.com/BB/

Library of Congress Catalog Card Number: 98-96410

ISBN 0-345-42902-8

This edition published by arrangement with Alfred A. Knopf, Inc.

Manufactured in the United States of America

First Ballantine Books International Edition: December 1998

10   9   8   7   6   5   4   3   2   1

For Chase
Our youngest son

NO SAFE PLACE

PROLOGUE

The Campaign

April, the Year 2000

ONE

At eight in the morning of his last day in Boston, Sean Burke paced out tight circles on the corner of Kenmore Square, waiting for the abortionist, a nine-millimeter semiautomatic handgun hidden in the inside pocket of his army jacket.

Sean knew his enemy from the demonstrations—a slight man with brown wisps of hair and hollow cheekbones, gray soulless eyes that ignored the pickets even when they cried out, *"Don't kill me, Mommy and Daddy,"* in the imagined voice of a fetus. Part of Sean prayed for him to come; that other part, frightened and irresolute, hoped he would not. He encouraged himself by imagining the faces of the children he would save.

He passed forty minutes this way. With each moment, Sean felt more anxious.

And then the man was there, emerging from the subway.

The abortionist's hands were in his coat pockets. His eyes focused on the sidewalk, and his breaths became thin puffs in the surprising chill of a bright April day. He did not notice Sean.

Sean swallowed. His throat was dry, his mouth sour, the pit of his stomach clenched and raw. Clumsily, he reached a gloved hand into his left pocket and popped the last antacid pill into his mouth, teeth grinding it to chalk.

Dr. Bowe disappeared inside the building.

It was an old brownstone hotel, converted to offices for doctors, dentists, milliners, discount jewelers; passing through the double glass doors, a pregnant woman could be shopping for a necklace, not seeking an accomplice to help murder her unborn child. Sean knew only that the offices were on the first floor: because of a court order, pickets were required to stay outside and keep the walkway clear. The red carpet, their leader, Paul Terris, had named it. But neither Paul's exhortations nor all their protests had stopped the flow of blood.

Yet Sean stood there, still afraid. The chalk in his mouth tasted bitter.

If Sean acted, he would have to leave all he knew behind: the comfort of the church where he served as caretaker; the room above the parish offices, his home for three years now; the compassion of Father Brian Shaw, who praised his work and worried, in his soft-voiced way, about Sean's "intensity." In the newspapers and on television, in the streets and the bars of Charlestown, they would call Sean a murderer.

Let God be his judge, then. God and the children.

But Sean stood frozen, a slender man, with lank black hair and pale-blue eyes. Alone, as he had felt almost all his life, Sean watched the random pageant of the city pass him by: tardy workers rushing from the subway; cars honking; students heading for Boston University; an Asian nanny with a plaid wool scarf at her throat, pushing a baby in a blue carriage. They did not notice him and would not have understood had they known.

Then he saw her—a young woman in a wool coat, knit cap pulled tight over her curly red hair, her face more Irish than Sean's own. He could imagine her sitting next to him in school.

Pausing on the sidewalk, she gazed at the double glass doors beneath the letters that spelled "Kenmore Building." Sean could feel her reluctance as intensely as he felt his own.

She was there for the abortionist, Sean was certain. Her back to Sean, she seemed barely to move. In his mind they were coupled: if she did not enter, perhaps Sean would grant the clinic a reprieve. Just for today.

Please, he murmured, *save your baby.* He prayed she was not one of them.

With a shrug, so small that Sean perhaps imagined it, the young woman walked toward the door.

Sean felt the anger come. If she was not worthy of the life she bore, then *he* must be.

Oblivious to traffic, Sean crossed the street. As he touched it, the gun in his pocket reassured him.

On the Saturday before last, he had driven to New Hampshire and bought the weapon at a package store: the same model, the owner informed him, that the Turkish guy had used to shoot the Pope—small, light, easy to conceal. Sean stifled his dislike. "God bless the Holy Father," he said simply.

In the woods nearby, Sean had practiced.

Aiming the gun, he had imagined looking into his victim's face, blocking out all doubt, all fears. His aim had been good—first trees, then rocks, then a careless squirrel which had almost vanished in a single shot. But now Sean's hand shook.

He was five feet from the door, then four feet. Each step felt leaden.

He must remember the lessons of history, Sean told himself. If he could have murdered Hitler, the Nazis would have called him a criminal, reviled the name Sean Burke. Perhaps Göring and the others would have hung him on a meat hook. And, perhaps, millions of others would have lived—Jews and Slavs, Gypsies and children . . .

Damp with sweat, Sean paused in front of the door, taking a last deep breath of morning air.

He walked into the dim hallway, looking to both sides. He saw a travel agency, an accountant's office. And then he found it.

A green laminate door with metal letters: "The Boston Women's Clinic." Since the demonstrations had failed, the abortionists in their arrogance no longer had a guard there.

Sean took the wool cap from his inside pocket and pulled it over his head.

For a last moment, his left hand rested on the doorknob. He made himself imagine the red-haired girl, nervously waiting for the abortionist to put a plastic tube between her legs and suck the life from her womb.

Sean murmured a final prayer and opened the door.

The girl was there. She gazed up at him from behind her magazine, as if surprised. With her cap off, her hair was a riot of red curls.

"Yes?" the receptionist asked.

Sean turned to her—a vulpine older woman with hair dyed a frightening black and lipstick as red as blood.

Softly, he said, "I'm here for Dr. Bowe."

The skin of her face was pale as parchment. She stared up at him from her swivel chair, still but for her left hand. There was a panic button beneath her desk, someone had told him; the day the others had occupied the waiting room, she had used it to call security.

"Don't." Sean's voice was harsh now. The red-haired girl dropped her magazine.

The receptionist's throat moved in a convulsive swallow, choking her words. "What do you want?"

Sean took out his gun. "To stop you," he answered, and pulled the trigger.

It was a kind of magic. As her head snapped back, a hole opened in her forehead. There was a soft concussive sound, like a melon hitting cement, almost lost in the red-haired girl's cry.

Sean stared in stupefaction as the woman died in front of him, blood trickling from her forehead. Only when she hit the carpet did Sean turn to the girl.

"Don't move." His voice came out panicky, too high. Gun in hand, he stumbled down the hallway.

The abortionist was in the room where he did his work, bent over a metal cabinet in the corner. Sean stared at him, then at the table covered in white paper, the altar where women sacrificed the innocent. His hand trembled as he raised the gun.

Dr. Bowe barely had time to peer sideways before Sean shot at his temple.

The red stain appeared. Sean watched in near astonishment as the abortionist fell to his knees, face pitching forward into the files of his victims. Only then did Sean register the melon sound again.

With a rush of anger, Sean lifted Bowe's warm twitching body and threw him onto the table, wrenching his legs open in the spraddle of all the women whose children he had murdered. The abortionist's eyes were glazed, his mouth agape, as if protesting this indignity.

Sean heard a gasp behind him.

A nurse stood in the door, a stethoscope around her neck, mouth forming words that would not come. Sean did not want to kill her; she was a tool, like the receptionist. But he had no choice.

"I'm sorry," he murmured, and shot her in the chest. The nurse crumpled in the doorway, then was still.

Sean stepped across her body, looking down at her. At least her family, if she had one, could gaze into her face without flinching. Sean walked down the hallway in a trance.

The red-haired young woman shivered on the couch, staring at the dead receptionist, too frightened to move. Tears streamed down her face. Sean could not bring himself to kill the life inside her.

Sean knelt in front of her, giving comfort, seeking it. "I had to stop him. Your sympathy should be with your baby, the life I came to save."

Comprehension filled her eyes. "I'm not pregnant," she stammered.

Sean felt the blood rush to his face. He stood, humiliated and confused, blood pounding like a trip-hammer in his temples. His finger squeezed the trigger.

"*Please.* I only came here for an IUD . . ."

Sean dropped his gun and ran from the building.

There was a subway station at the corner.

Sean rushed down the stairs and through the turnstile. Some vestige of discipline made him find the men's room, leave his jacket, gloves, and wool cap in a stall, and walk to the platform with a numb unhurried stride, a young man in a Holy Cross sweatshirt.

Take the green line to Court Street, then transfer to blue. He recited this like a rosary as the subway stopped and he boarded the half-empty car. No one looked at him.

She was lying. Sean had saved her baby, and she had lied to save herself, believing he would think it less damning to thwart life with a piece of plastic. Perhaps Sean had taught her better.

Dazed, he imagined the sirens screaming as the cars arrived at Kenmore Square.

At Court Street, the subway doors hissed open. Arms folded, head bowed, Sean walked out and waited in the dingy tunnel, a portrait of urban anonymity.

He had asked Father Brian if he could take a week's vacation in New Hampshire. "Surely," the priest had answered in his mild way, "but is early April a good time? The mud season, they call it in New England."

Within minutes, the subway for Logan Airport came.

Sean's suitcase was in a locker at the airport.

He pulled it out. If his plan worked, the last trace of him found in Boston would be the jacket, the hat, the gloves. Remorse mingled with relief now at the lifting of his burden: he no longer stood watch, armed only with signs and slogans, while children died.

Face pinched, he went through security at Gateway C.

No one stopped him. He headed for the gate with his scuffed black suitcase, surrounded by vacationers, students on spring break, commercial travelers leaving their homes. But the only person in line was a black woman with glasses and a briefcase. Uncomfortable, Sean hung back until she was finished.

The blond ticket agent raised her eyebrows. "Next?"

There was a hint of challenge, Sean thought. This might be the end: the red-haired woman could describe him, and he was certain that the police kept files on Operation Life.

"Next?" she repeated, impatient now, studying his face.

Sean pulled the ticket from his back pocket and placed it on the counter.

She flipped it open. "Mr. Burke," she said. "Photo ID, please."

Sean took out his wallet. To his own eyes, the photo on his driver's license looked furtive. For a long moment, the ticket agent looked from Sean to his photo and back again.

One call, he thought. The airport swarmed with cops and blue-uniformed security officers. His palms felt moist.

"Did you pack your luggage yourself?" she asked.

"Yes."

"One bag?"

"Yes."

"Did someone you did not know give you anything to carry?"

Sean drew a breath. "I wouldn't do that," he said.

The ticket agent hesitated, watching him. "Zone C," she told him. "Seat twenty-five B. They board about one-fifteen."

Once on the plane, Sean realized, he would be trapped. He did not board until the final call.

At two o'clock, the plane had not taken off.

A mechanical problem, the pilot explained in his John Wayne voice—a systems light that won't come on, probably just an electrical short. Sit tight and I'll keep you posted.

Sean bowed his head. They were holding him, Sean thought. At any moment, they would evacuate the plane and clap handcuffs on his wrists. The feeling came to him again: he was a small and lonely boy, terrified of his father, despairing for his mother's blank indifference. There was no safe place for him.

Sean stood abruptly. He reeled to the rear bathroom, past the other passengers, their faces weary, trapped, indifferent.

His own face in the mirror was white. When the retching started, racking his body, all he saw in the basin was saliva and traces of blood. The bathroom felt like a closet.

Sean opened the door, gulping for breath.

Slowly, he returned to his seat. He kept his eyes averted from the woman sitting next to him.

Ten minutes later, the pilot made his final announcement. Then the plane lifted into the air, vibrating with power, and Sean Burke left Boston forever.

TWO

Raising the Mauser, the gunman stepped from backstage, bracing his wrist with his left hand.

His target turned to smile at the woman beside him, sharing his applause with her.

"Kil-can-non," the crowd chanted, and then Senator James Kilcannon saw the assassin. Kilcannon's mouth fell open . . .

"Gun," someone cried out. Two Secret Service agents leaped onto the stage, as the cheers of five thousand people turned to screams.

The gunman took one last step forward, and fired.

The hair on James Kilcannon's crown seemed to rise. He crumpled, falling on his side, then his back. There was a pool of blood beneath his head.

Kilcannon's lips parted, struggling to speak . . .

"Kerry . . ."

Kerry Kilcannon snapped awake, staring at Clayton Slade.

The hotel bedroom was dark around them. "Kerry," Clayton repeated. His voice was quiet now, but his full black face was intent. "What is it?"

Kerry realized he had bolted upright, gripped by fear. But Clayton was more than his campaign manager. He was Kerry's closest friend; there were no lies between them.

"My brother," Kerry answered. "It's the same, always . . ."

Clayton puffed his cheeks, exhaling softly. Amidst the deep disorientation of his dream, Kerry could hear voices coming from the television in the other room. They were in a hotel suite in Portland, he remembered—another room in a four-month trail of hotels and motels, towns and cities.

Clayton braced Kerry's shoulders. "You've won, Kerry. We think Mason's conceding any minute."

Kerry gave himself a moment to recover. Rising, he walked into the sitting room in boxer shorts.

"Make way," he said to no one in particular, "for the future leader of the new world order."

There were three others in the sitting room, gazing at the television: Kit Pace, Kerry's press secretary, who in her intelligence and directness was an ideal reflection of his campaign; Frank Wells, the graying, elegant professional who was media adviser; and Kevin Loughery, Kerry's personal assistant—a gangly young man from the fading Irish section of Newark where Kerry had been born—still a little in awe of his role as witness to history. Turning, Kit gave Kerry's lean frame a sardonic once-over. "Not bad for forty-two," she said. "Heading for California, Dick Mason retains the lead in body fat."

Kerry raised both hands, like a boxer, in a mock gesture of triumph. "What have we got here?" he asked.

From over his shoulder, Clayton said, "CNN has just projected you the winner. NBC, CBS, and ABC already have. All we're waiting for is Dick to fall on his sword."

On the television, a pert newswoman stood in a ballroom, filled with Kerry's supporters, trying to speak over the cheers, excitement, laughter. "This is more than another victory," the woman began. "Twelve years after the assassination of James Kilcannon on the eve of the California primary, only that same primary would seem to stand between Senator Kerry Kilcannon and his late brother's goal—the Democratic nomination for President of the United States . . ."

Frank Wells turned to Kerry. "Congratulations, Kerry."

Kerry shook his head. "Seven days yet," he murmured, and turned back to the television.

"It's been a remarkable insurgent candidacy," the newswoman was saying. "A few short weeks ago, the conventional wisdom was that Kerry Kilcannon could not overtake a sitting Vice President. But Kilcannon has managed to persuade more and more voters to hold Dick Mason responsible for the President's recent misfortunes—a near recession; the collapse of welfare reform; a thousand-point drop in the Dow; recurring allegations of adulterous affairs, one involving the President's principal economic adviser and the breakup of her marriage; and a series of revelations arising from apparently illegal contributions made to the Democratic Party within the last year, which have underscored Kilcannon's attack on the current system of campaign finance.

"Dick Mason has been Vice President for eight years, Kilcannon hammers home in speech after speech, and in that time their party has 'lost its majority, then its identity, and finally its soul . . .'"

"So we should lose the White House too?" Kit murmured.

On the television, Kerry heard a new voice, the anchorman's. "What can we expect in California, Kate?"

"Seven more days with no holds barred," the newswoman answered. "So far, Kerry Kilcannon hasn't missed a single opportunity. You'll remember just last week, when it was revealed that Dick Mason worked behind the scenes to amend last year's budget bill to protect tobacco growers from his home state of Connecticut. Within hours Senator Kilcannon countered with a proposal for a new tobacco tax for programs to 'help our children read instead of die.'"

Frank Wells laughed aloud. "I still wish I'd thought of that," he said—the new member of the team, flattering the candidate.

Feeling Frank's need, Kerry smiled a little. "I hope it was succinct enough."

"The base which Kerry Kilcannon has assembled," the reporter went on, "has elements of the party's old coalition— particularly minorities—as well as a clear majority among women attracted by his proposals on education, day care, job training, and crime . . ."

No, Clayton thought to himself. It was far more than that.

Standing to Kerry's right, he watched him in the dim light of the television. After their fifteen years of friendship, Kerry's profile was as familiar to Clayton as the profiles of his wife and his daughters, as the painful memory of the younger son Clayton and Carlie had lost. Kerry's thin Irish face, at once boyish and angular, reminded Clayton of the young lawyer he had first met, scarcely more than an impulsive kid. The wavy ginger hair was also much the same and, as always, Kerry's blue-green eyes reflected the quicksilver surfaces of his moods—sometimes cold, at other times remote and almost absent, at still others deeply empathic or crinkled in amusement or outright laughter. But the man who had emerged from the cross-country gauntlet of primaries was changing as Clayton watched.

Kerry's hypercompetitiveness was the least surprising: his astonishing ability to get up every morning in a strange town; to give the same speech six or seven times, making it seem fresh, until falling into bed again; to give dozens of important local politicians private time in his limousine; to fight the fatigue of mind and body and spirit that running for President imposed; to set aside all doubt that he could beat Dick Mason. Clayton had seen elements of this molten single-mindedness—sometimes ruthless and close to angry—since Kerry had prosecuted his first big case. To Clayton, it was still the least attractive, most troubling, and now perhaps most necessary aspect of his friend's persona.

No, the key was that Kerry could touch people in ways Clayton had never seen—not from anyone else or even, before this, from Kerry himself.

It had first struck Clayton at the end of a long day in New Hampshire. Kerry was speaking to a small gathering at a senior center. His voice was hoarse, his form a little off; realizing this, he had cut himself short and asked for questions from his audience. This feeling of contact, Clayton knew, made Kerry come alive.

An old woman stood, her legs like sticks, so thin that Clayton found it painful to look at her. She was poor, she said, voice quavering with shame and desperation. At the end of every month, she had to choose between food and medicine.

Her voice broke and she began sobbing, unable to continue. The only sound in the deadly silence was her keening, muffled by the hands over her face.

An attendant started coming for her. But Kerry had stepped from behind the podium. He put his arms around the old woman, his own eyes shut now, seemingly oblivious to those around them, whispering words no one could hear. He did not appear to know or care that his speech was at an end.

Afterward, Kerry had declined to repeat what he had said to her. It was the old woman who had told CBS. "I won't let that happen to you," Kerry had murmured. "I promise."

It was instinct, Clayton was sure—somehow Kerry had learned at forty-two to reach into his past, the fears of his own childhood, until he could feel what it was to be someone else. But the promise he made was almost breathtaking in its assurance; the clip of Kerry comforting an old woman ran on all three networks . . .

"Kilcannon's barely unspoken message," Clayton heard the CNN reporter summarize, "is that Dick Mason is too weak, too compromised, too mortgaged to special interests to improve the lives of those who need it most. Not even yesterday's slip of the tongue, in which Senator Kilcannon opined that an unborn fetus was a 'life,' seems to have affected his support among Oregon women . . ."

Kerry leaned back in his chair, closing his eyes.

He had been tired, he knew. Yesterday was one of those mornings, ever more frequent now, when his bones ached and a kind of sickening fatigue seized his entire body. His right hand was scratched and swollen from the grasping of a thousand other hands. Shaking hands along the rope line, Kerry had felt himself wince.

Cornered by a pro-life activist in a local TV audience, Kerry had told the truth as he knew it: As a matter of policy, he was emphatically pro-choice. But it was also his personal belief, as a Roman Catholic, that a fetus was the beginning of life, and that to claim that life did not exist until three months, or six months, was splitting moral hairs.

Watching the television, Frank Wells murmured, "You just can't say that. Women are too frightened."

Kerry opened his eyes. For an unguarded moment, the sight of Frank annoyed him. With his smooth gray hair, his diplomat's face and manner, Frank sometimes seemed to have slipped into the campaign from a drawing room in Georgetown. But he had done inspired work for virtually every prominent Democrat in the last twenty years, including James Kilcannon. Kerry felt Clayton watching him.

"I was tired," he said mildly. "Telling the truth is my own funny way of diverting Dick's attention."

Kit Pace leaned forward, all blunt-cut hair and snub features, her stocky frame radiating the intensity of her concern. "Most of it wasn't so bad, Kerry. But, please, eliminate the word 'life' from your vocabulary, so we can keep this thing a one-day story. The idea that women are taking a 'life' will inflame the hard-core pro-choicers and arouse the press—as you damned well know. Especially with that Boston thing this morning."

Slowly, Kerry nodded. "Insane," he murmured. "Three dead people, their families. Who would do that?"

"God knows." Kit paused, signaling her transition to the professional. "I got out a statement right away—sympathy for the families, the appropriate measure of outrage and disbelief. That should help a little." Her tone became dry. "You were quite eloquent, in fact."

Kerry gave her a quizzical smile. "Did I use the word 'life'?" he asked, and then Dick Mason appeared on the screen.

The Vice President was flanked by Jeannie Mason and their three children—a girl and two boys, all young adults, their faces as clean and unthreatening as their father's. But the children lacked Dick Mason's shrewdness or his actor's gifts. Their faces were contorted in smiles so spurious they seemed like open wounds, while Mason's smile for the crowd was broad, his chin tilted at a Rooseveltian angle of confidence and challenge. Imagining the emptiness in Dick Mason's stomach, the terrible, almost inconceivable prospect that a lifetime of striving might come to nothing, Kerry saw in his opponent's smile an act of will that was close to bravery. He wondered if what helped sustain Dick Mason was lingering disbelief . . .

"You can't win," the President had said to Kerry. "Dick won't let you."

It had been less than five months ago, a bitter-cold December day. The President had kept him waiting in the reception area of the West Wing. Idly, Kerry had studied the oil paintings of historic scenes, a gilt-framed clock, an ornate brass chandelier. He was being made to hang out with the donors and the lobbyists, Kerry thought with humor, and commenced watching the children of a pudgy man who must have contributed money to the President or Dick wheedle boxes of presidential M&M's from the somewhat starchy receptionist. That no one seemed to recognize Kerry only heightened his amusement.

At length, the President's assistant, Georgia Heckler, appeared and led Kerry to the Oval Office.

The President looked gaunt, more tired than Kerry had seen him, his graying hair more sparse than even the month before. Wondering if the rumors about the President's health were true, Kerry imagined Dick Mason watching this man for signs. A lonely job, they always said.

Georgia shut the door behind them.

The President gave Kerry a thin smile. "So you think you want this chair," he said without preface.

Kerry appreciated the opening; the President knew how much Kerry despised the political politesse that the President himself called "the dance of the cranes and the swallows."

"I plan to run," Kerry answered with equal directness. "I know you support Dick. But I hope you'll withhold a formal endorsement until we see how the primaries shake out."

"Stay neutral, you mean? Just as you did when the press was falsely accusing me of destroying a long-dead marriage, and Dick stepped forward to defend me." The President folded his hands, tone softening. "In a very real way, Kerry, you'll be running against me. To run against Dick, you'll have to. And Dick's been loyal *and* effective."

Kerry watched his face. "Loyal, I'll accept. Do you want the price of loyalty to be a Republican Congress *and* President?"

"Oh, I don't think it's as bad as all that." Above his smile, the President's eyes were keen. "You've got the virus, don't you. You looked around and decided you were better than anyone in sight. Including Dick and me."

Kerry shrugged and smiled, waiting him out; as a child, he had learned the gift of watchful silence.

"That's only the first step," the President said at length. "The easiest and the most deluded. Later you find out that the demands of a presidential campaign are much greater than you imagined, that the fishbowl you've entered is far more degrading, that the sheer enormity of what it takes to run for President—let alone the chance that you might win—threatens to overwhelm you.

"The few men who become President refuse to acknowledge any of the realities that would stop anyone else: that they're giving up all hope of privacy; that their life is run by strangers and semifriends who want what only a President can give them; that they're probably *not* qualified—by temperament or intellect or sheer strength of will—to be President after all." The President paused, then finished softly. "It's not enough that Jamie wanted it. For the first time in your career, Kerry, it all has to come from you."

Kerry felt himself flush with anger. "Maybe I can borrow it. Whatever 'it' is."

The President raised a hand. "That wasn't meant as an insult. What I'm saying is that you've yet to face the total humiliation of starting an underdog campaign from scratch. It's not just begging people you loathe for money and trying to look happy doing it. It's things like the afternoon I wasted in New Hampshire hunting for a fucking ceramic poodle because a woman I wanted to be a delegate in Iowa collected them and she was torn between me and three other guys who were leading me in the polls."

Kerry made himself smile at this, though his voice retained a hint of challenge. "You've just given me a slogan, Mr. President. 'No fucking ceramic dogs.'"

The President did not smile back. "Dick Mason understands, because he's been Vice President for eight years. You don't. Because you can't. And Dick's the only one of you that's been through the moral X ray our media friends reserve for someone on the national ticket, and survived it. You join this club at your peril, Kerry." He paused again, moderating his tone. "You asked for my neutrality, not my advice. But advice is all I can offer you, Senator. That and the old saw 'Beware of what you wish for . . .'"

On the eve of the New Hampshire primary, with perfect timing, the President had endorsed Dick Mason.

It had cost Kerry the primary. Underfunded and understaffed, his campaign verged on collapse.

But Kerry and Clayton would not give up. And then the surprises started—narrow losses in the South, a startling breakthrough in Florida, a split in Illinois and Ohio, an outpouring of small contributions in response to Kerry's new pledge not to take more than two hundred dollars from anyone. Then came wins in Michigan, Pennsylvania, Nebraska, and now Oregon. Aided by a series of events beyond Dick Mason's control, they had fought the opposition—a sitting Vice President, an incumbent President, the countless party leaders who gorged on the flattery and favors and just plain pork that only the President and Dick could provide—to a draw.

Dick Mason had always meant California, their final stop, to be his firewall. He had visited the state thirty-three times in less than four years; Kerry could not seem to read his newspaper clippings from California without encountering a photo of Dick Mason dispensing computers to schoolkids, or funds for earth-quake relief. Now California would decide things; in the latest poll, Dick Mason still led by three percent.

But there was one historic fact that Dick could not avoid and no one else would ever forget: Kerry's brother had died there.

Ah, Jamie, Kerry thought to himself. He was certain that James Kilcannon would have savored this irony, one far richer than Dick Mason could ever know. But then Jamie no longer laughed, or awakened at night from dreams.

Buttoning his shirt, Kerry watched Dick Mason quiet his supporters.

"When you see Dick Mason," Kerry asked Clayton, "do you think President?"

Still watching the screen, Clayton studied Mason with his accustomed look of keen intelligence. "When I see Dick," he answered at length, "I think android. But *Dick* thinks President—he never thinks about anything else, and no one's ever wanted it more. Don't start underrating him *now*, when he's cornered."

It was true, Kerry knew. Dick Mason rarely made mistakes, never courted controversy that didn't serve his interest, clung to the bread-and-butter issues—Social Security, job security, Medicare—with the tenacity of a terrier. He was everyone's fa-vorite neighbor: friendly, a little overweight, always pleased to help, with an easy laugh and a look of total sincerity. Dick could campaign for hours and his gaze would never waver, his grip never weaken, his voice never crack—the Energizer bunny, Kerry had called him. But that dismissive shorthand omitted Dick's magical ability to summon in a heartbeat just the right emotion, whether beaming approval, quiet indignation, or the misty-eyed sentiment of the sensitized man. Dick Mason was hell at funerals.

Dick's face was solemn now. "Before I congratulate Senator Kilcannon"—there were boos, and Dick raised a placatory hand—"or say anything on behalf of this campaign, I'd like to request a moment of silence for the three victims of the brutal act of terrorism committed this morning at the Boston Women's Clinic."

There was a murmur of affirmation. Then the Vice President bowed his head, and silence fell. When Dick looked up again, his mouth was a thin line of determination.

"I want to assure the victims' families that we will never rest until the perpetrator of this cowardly act is brought to justice. And I want to assure everyone—whether they support or oppose us—that we are unequivocal in our defense of every woman's right to choose, unmolested and unafraid. The time for ambiguity has long since passed . . ."

Frank Wells frowned at the screen. "Then you might mention gun control, asshole."

Clayton turned to him. "I want to add a question to tomorrow's tracking poll. Something like 'Which candidate will better protect the safety of women who pursue their right to an abortion?'"

Frank walked to a corner of the room and picked up the phone. Kerry barely registered this; he had stopped knotting his tie and was watching Dick Mason. "These Boston murders were made for him," Kerry murmured.

"This is a contest," the Vice President was saying, "between two very different kinds of leadership for the Democratic Party. One rests on experience, tested leadership, and a vision—unfettered by extremism—in which every American shares in the expanding opportunities of a new century . . ."

"Controversial," Kit Pace said in tones of awe. "Even revolutionary."

"The other . . ." Here, Dick Mason paused for emphasis. "The other rests on impulse, inexperience, and a taste for the expensive and extreme."

"But which one is *me*?" Kerry asked.

Clayton emitted a short laugh, still watching the Vice President. On the screen, Mason raised his head, his hair a shiny silver blond beneath the television lights. "To Senator Kilcannon," he continued, "I say two things.

"First, Kerry, congratulations on a hard-fought victory.

"Second, I challenge you to a final debate in California about

the future of our party and our nation—anytime, anywhere."
Pausing, Dick Mason grinned, and then he shouted above the
cheers of his supporters: "You may be running, Kerry, but you
can't hide."

"What *is* this bullshit?" Kit Pace asked. "You won the only
debate he'd sit still for, and he's ducked you ever since."

Frank Wells had put down the telephone. "It's Dick's version
of the Hail Mary," he said. But what Kerry registered now was
Clayton's thoughtful silence.

Kerry sat next to his friend, watching Dick and Jeannie and
the kids wave to the crowd as the CNN reporter spoke over
them. But only the picture seemed to interest Clayton.

"Look at them," he said to Kerry. "When everyone else in
high school was trying to get dates, Dick was auditioning First
Ladies. He'll be running for President from beyond the grave."

Kerry kept watching. The petty part of him, he knew, wanted
to think that a monomaniac like Dick Mason deserved awful
kids who hated him and sniffed airplane glue at rock concerts.
But these kids had done well, appeared to be genuinely nice,
worked hard for their father, and seemed to love and respect
him. And Jeannie Mason was terrific.

It was far more than that she was pretty—though with her
slender frame, her short blond hair, and her lively blue eyes,
Jeannie was surely that. It was her humor, a recognition that
much of the political pageant was really quite absurd: even her
attempt at a political spouse's robotic gaze of admiration was
leavened with amusement. Jeannie tended the home front with
brisk efficiency and, when she could, campaigned for her husband tirelessly; whatever bargain life had handed Jeannie
Mason, she was clearly determined to make the most of it.
Kerry had always liked her tremendously.

They had first met at the dinner party of a doyenne of
Washington politics, the widow of a wealthy former statesman
whose millions she had used to amass considerable influence as
a fund-raiser. Patricia Hartman's invitation had signaled, if not
her favor, at least that Kerry's arrival in Washington was a
matter of great interest; that the interest had derived from the
related facts of his brother's murder, and his own prior ano-

nymity, would have discomfited Kerry even had he not seldom seen such opulence, so carefully displayed.

"That's a Matisse," Hartman had noted as he stopped to study an oil painting, her voice suggesting both satisfaction and the confidence that Kerry required an explanation. Kerry simply nodded—to remark on the painting would have seemed foolish, and he was already bedeviled by the thought that, at dinner, he might pick up the wrong fork.

"Will your wife be moving here soon?" his hostess asked. "I'm so very anxious to meet her."

This was a probe, Kerry knew; he was being cross-examined, his weaknesses assessed. But to dissemble would have made him feel more awkward. "Not soon," he answered. "And maybe not at all."

The bluntness of his response, combined with his disinclination to explain, seemed to surprise her; despite her bright-red hair, she was well into her seventies, and her face was so immobilized by plastic surgery that it dramatized the widening of her eyes. "Oh," she told him firmly, "she *must*. A serious career in politics demands a total commitment." She moved closer, her tone becoming intimate. "I adored Jamie, God rest his soul. But I always thought the absence of a wife hurt him."

Not as much as getting shot in the head, Kerry wanted to answer—the knowing, proprietary tone with which she mentioned his brother annoyed him. He made do by saying mildly, "I suppose Jamie thought there was time."

This seemed to give her pause. Turning to the dinner table, Hartman said, "Well, I've seated you next to Jeannie Mason, Governor Mason's wife. Ask her for advice—she's such a help to him. They were here for several years when Dick was in Congress, you know."

Two more hours of condescension, Kerry thought. With the joyless affect of a death row inmate, he shuffled to the dinner table.

Seated next to him, the fresh-faced blonde with amused blue eyes introduced herself as Jeannie Mason. With quiet humor, she added, "I saw Patricia walking you through orientation. Have you memorized the rules yet?"

Her irony surprised him. "Just one," he answered. "That

Meg should quit her job and move here. Patricia says I should ask you for advice."

The blue eyes narrowed slightly. "Because I'm a credit to my gender?" she murmured, and then the smile flickered. "I just hope she didn't call me an 'asset.' It makes our marriage sound like my husband's personal balance sheet."

She seemed comfortable in this hall of mirrors, Kerry thought, and yet a detached observer. "I think that's what Meg's afraid of," he ventured. "But less of being an asset than a wholly owned subsidiary."

Jeannie gave him a sudden, reflective glance. "She's right to be." She paused, as if appraising both Kerry and how much she should say. "I've made my own decisions," she said finally, "based on what was best for *us*. But sometimes it's not easy. How much harder it would be if your partner's a draftee." She smiled again. "As long as you're reelected, Patricia will manage to forgive your wife. She always needs an extra man at dinner."

Kerry felt himself relax. There was something inherently kind about her, and honest; perhaps for that reason, Kerry thought, he did not feel the need for self-protection. It was only at the end of the dinner that he identified another reason: Jeannie Mason did not feel required—or perhaps was too perceptive—to say anything about his brother.

As the dinner broke up, he turned to her again. "I've really enjoyed this," he said. "Sometimes I feel like Dorothy in *The Wizard of Oz*: 'We're not in Kansas anymore.' "

His light comment had an undertone—betraying, Kerry feared, how at sea he often felt. As if sensing that, Jeannie gave his hand a brief sisterly touch. "Welcome to Emerald City," she said. "And now you have two friends in town. At least whenever we're here."

On the evidence of his wife, Kerry had reflected, Dick Mason must surely be worth knowing . . .

Twelve years later, Kerry thought, Jeannie and the kids still made him consider that there might be more to Dick than he had come to believe. And, Kerry had to concede, he felt something else he did not wish to feel: envy of Dick Mason, and not just because his family was an electoral asset—a change from the

President's tattered marriage, a reflection of the ideal most people still seemed to want.

"Jeannie Mason," Kerry murmured, "is a truly great woman."

Clayton grunted. "Win in California, and you can offer Jeannie Dick's job."

Kerry read this for what it was: a grudging reference to a handicap that Patricia Hartman had first identified and that no campaign manager could fix—Kerry's lack of children or even an ostensibly adoring wife. But even before their divorce, Meg had considered Kerry's first run for the Senate a betrayal tantamount to adultery. She would not have come here happily.

Abruptly, Clayton stood. "Let's go, young Lochinvar," he said to Kerry. "It's showtime."

THREE

They took the freight elevator to the ballroom with two agents from Kerry's Secret Service detail, Joe Morton and Dan Biasi. Kerry chatted with them easily. With all the selfishness, Clayton thought, the tunnel vision that running for President required and with which Kerry was fully equipped, Kerry still saw the people around him. He did not need help to remember their spouses, their children, their hobbies, the things they were proud of, the favors they had done for him.

Some of Kerry's secret was that he genuinely liked people—except, Clayton added wryly to himself, when Kerry *didn't* like them. That, and the fact that Kerry never lied to them, was part of why so many of his colleagues in the Senate had supported him despite the political risks. And it was one of the clues to what kind of President Kerry Kilcannon might become.

"You still working out?" Kerry asked Joe Morton.

Joe nodded. "Got to keep up with you, Senator."

"Great." Kerry grinned. "How about San Diego tomorrow, say about five a.m. I'm sure the hotel will open its gym early to accommodate our great crusade."

Joe grinned back; he had loved Kerry, Clayton knew, from the day—in a teasing gibe at Joe's sober garb, bland even for the Service—that Kerry had sent out Kevin Loughery to find Joe a set of love beads and a Nehru jacket so garish that the Partridge family would not have worn it. "If you're that crazy," Joe said now to the prospective President of the United States, "I guess I am."

"Don't you need sleep?" Clayton asked Kerry.

Kerry turned to him, no longer smiling. "There's a very long list of things I need, pal. But I'm putting adrenaline ahead of sleep."

Clayton caught the look in Kerry's cool blue-green eyes, the silent reference no one else would have understood. And where would *she* have fit, Clayton wondered, if the world were as Kerry Kilcannon wished.

The ballroom was jammed. Glancing about, Clayton saw that everything was in order: the signs were painted on both sides, the better to be seen on television; there were young people rather than local officeholders on the platform, to underscore Kerry as the candidate of tomorrow; two more members of the Service detail stood at the base of the platform, between the press pool and the Minicams. Noticing the Service was a habit Clayton had formed weeks earlier. "Somewhere there's some nut out there," he had said to Peter Lake, the special agent in charge, "oiling up his gun so he can go for the doubleheader."

Kerry walked to the podium. When the crowd quieted for him, he thanked his principal supporters by name and uttered a few pleasantries about Dick Mason. Then he began the part of the speech which was truly his—that of the outsider, the reluctant hero, called upon to tell his fellow citizens how things are and how they should be.

Kerry had no notes. Twelve years before, in his first speeches, he had awkwardly read words written by others, feeling like an impostor. But he had learned. Now the sea of faces in front of him—college kids, professionals, old people, more minorities than Oregon was known for—were the source of strength, a quiet elation.

"Kerry . . . ," they began chanting.

Kerry smiled. "That's me."

There were laughter and cheers, and then Kerry held up a hand. "There's still a lot to do," he said, and the crowd was quiet again.

"There's still a lot to do," he repeated, "when people believe that their government has been bought by special interests, when they watch those running for office barter their integrity—dollar by dollar, donation by donation, cocktail party by cocktail party—in a system of quasi-legal bribery . . ."

The crowd cheered; this allusion to Dick Mason's recent problems with the tobacco lobby had not been missed. Pausing, Kerry did what he always did: began to focus on a few faces in the crowd—a young Asian girl, a middle-aged man in a union jacket—until he felt he could almost touch them.

"There's a lot to do," he said, "and, together, we will do it.

"We will train mothers and fathers for meaningful work, help educate their children instead of standing idly by while their children's futures go up in smoke.

"We will protect our right to choose in the deepest and broadest sense. For it is not just *women* who deserve a choice; it is everyone who chooses to work for a better job and a brighter future . . ."

Watch it, Kerry warned himself. But the crowd seemed almost giddy now.

He paused again, and then found the words he wanted. "It is every mother, father, son, or daughter who refuses to lose one more person they love to a coward with a gun . . ."

The crowd erupted.

Minutes later, Kerry was at last able to finish, with his signature line: "Give me your help and your vote, and together we'll build a new democracy."

Clayton Slade watched from one side of the platform. *Don't do it,* he silently instructed Kerry. But, of course, Kerry did:

stepping from behind the podium, he went down the steps from the platform and plunged into the crowd. As they fought their way beside him, the phalanx of Secret Service agents wore harried, tight expressions.

Damn you, Clayton thought.

The energy of a thousand people cut through Kerry's fatigue. He took each hand, each face, a moment at a time, looking into the eyes of the person in front of him. "Thank you," he kept repeating. "Thank you." To the Asian girl he said, "We'll make it, I think"; finding the man in the union jacket, he touched his arm and said, "Thanks for staying up with me." Next to him, the Service and the camera people and Kevin Loughery jockeyed for position.

"Senator," a young NBC correspondent called out, pushing a microphone between two well-wishers. "Will Dick Mason's new emphasis on abortion rights cause trouble for you in California?"

Intent on his supporters, Kerry ignored him.

"Senator," the newsman tried again. He twisted his body to thrust the microphone at Kerry and then, quite suddenly, fell.

Kerry felt an involuntary rush of fear. The crowd rippled with confusion; instinctively, Dan Biasi pulled Kerry away, shielding his body.

"It's Mike Devore from NBC," Kerry managed to say. "I think something's wrong with him."

Joe Morton positioned himself at Kerry's back. Kerry could see the newsman on the floor; his head twisted back and forth, and his face was contorted in pain.

Kerry saw the swarm of agents look around them, refusing to be diverted. "I didn't hear shots," he heard Joe murmur.

Dan Biasi pushed the onlookers aside and bent over the fallen man. Dan felt the man's leg and foot and then came back to Joe and Kerry. "Looks like he tripped," Dan said. "I don't know how, but he may have broken his ankle."

"Get someone," Kerry said. "Use the ambulance outside." He did not need to add the rest: *the one you keep for me.*

Dan shook his head. "I'm sorry, Senator. We can't do that." He pulled out his cell phone to call 911.

The paramedics were there in ten minutes, carrying a stretcher. They took the reporter away. Kerry resumed shaking hands, suddenly feeling tired and mechanical.

Clayton Slade appeared behind him. "Ready to roll," he said crisply, and the Service convoyed them to Kerry's limousine. Clayton did not mention the incident.

Lights flashing in darkness, the motorcade of black Lincolns rolled toward the airport. Kerry's car was flanked by cops on motorcycles. There were two Secret Service agents in the front seat; Clayton and Kerry sat in back, staring into the formless night of a city that could have been anywhere.

Back in the bubble, Kerry thought. Once more he marveled at the vortex he had created, of which the motorcade had become a symbol: a force that swept up thousands of people—politicians, volunteers, the press, the countless strangers who felt they loved him—in the hope he would serve their dreams, their aspirations, their cold ambitions. It was a world unto itself, sealed off from any other reality; Kerry had stepped into the crowd out of more than the need to prove to himself what he could never prove—that he was not afraid. He also needed to meet people one at a time, as he had in Iowa and New Hampshire, when far fewer of them seemed to care. The age of innocence, Kerry thought.

He turned from the window. "This debate," he said. "What's Dick up to?"

Clayton's gold-rimmed glasses reflected the swirling red of flashing lights. His index finger grazed his salt-and-pepper mustache.

"I'm trying to work that one out," he answered. It was all he said; it had become their shared trait to use no more words than necessary.

Kerry fell silent. "Ellen Penn called today," Clayton said at last.

"What did she want?"

"To ask if you've lost your mind."

Clayton did not need to elaborate. Ellen Penn was the feisty junior senator from California, the chairman of Kerry's campaign there. Her support of abortion rights was as fervent as her barely concealed dislike for California's senior senator, Betsy Shapiro, a preeminent politician who supported Mason. Ellen Penn had risked supporting Kerry from a complex mix of motives, all unspoken: idealism; a desire to best Senator Shapiro; the hope of becoming Kerry's Vice President. In the new environment—a strengthening of pro-life forces in Congress, the continuing and corrosive war over partial-birth abortion, a surprising Supreme Court majority that threatened to cut back on abortion rights and thrust the issue to the forefront—Ellen Penn would see Kerry's comments as worse than an embarrassment. And now there was Boston.

Kerry slumped back in the leather seat. It was nearly midnight; the flight to San Diego would take three hours. He hoped he could sleep.

In the lead press bus of the motorcade, Nate Cutler allowed himself to wonder what he was doing with his life.

He had been with the Kilcannon campaign since January. In three months on the road, he had seen his apartment in Washington only twice; headed for California, he still had his wardrobe from Iowa and New Hampshire, had not had a haircut for six weeks, and was down to his last set of clean underwear. Even by the standards of presidential candidates, Kerry Kilcannon was hyperactive; sometimes Nate thought his own greatest skill was finding Laundromats in burgs too small to have a hotel with laundry service.

Nate looked around the bus. At thirty-nine, he was small, dark, wiry, and resilient, and this last was a good thing; his peer group in the national press was an energetic bunch, predominantly female and sometimes a decade younger. They were usually quite voluble, joking or exchanging gibes or information. Now, shrouded in darkness at the end of a long day, they seemed depleted by the effort of filing yet another story. They looked like rows of ghostly heads: some talked, keeping their voices low; others tried to sleep; still others stared into the darkness.

"Kilcannon was *on* tonight," someone said behind him— Ann Rush of the *Times*, Nate was pretty sure.

"He always is when he believes it." The voice belonged to Ed

Foster of the *Globe*. "I think Mason pissed him off with the abortion thing. Kilcannon already thinks the guy's a whore."

Ann laughed. "Mason just cares about my reproductive rights."

"We *all* do," Ed answered. "But Kilcannon cares about your soul."

That was what Nate was doing with his life, he admitted to himself—chronicling the only interesting politician in the race.

For Nate and his colleagues, Kerry Kilcannon was a relief. The last years of the nineties had not been a heroic time—not for politicians and not for the press. The politics were small-bore, he often thought: petty men taking small chances for selfish reasons, trying to manipulate just enough of a cynical public to keep themselves in office. The depressing result for journalists was that they, too, had become less important, reduced to covering politics as if it were a horse race, their thought pieces demoted from the front page to a place well behind the coverage of the latest celebrity murder trial. And just as damaging for all concerned was the competition to report on personal scandal, warmed to a white heat by the tabloids and Internet gossip columns, which seemed to have diminished both the standards of reporting and the standing of politicians generally. So that both reporters and the politicians they reported on seemed smaller than their ambitions—except, perhaps, for Kerry Kilcannon.

Nate did not think that Kilcannon's "lapse" the day before was a slip of the tongue at all; it was something Kilcannon needed to say, an act of rebellion against being packaged, a blow for his own authenticity. This element of surprise was what kept Nate sharp through the mind-numbing repetition, the sense that he and his colleagues had been hijacked by a process meant to ruin their lives and make them crazy. There might be a campaign book in Kerry Kilcannon, and if he won, Nate Cutler figured to be the next White House correspondent for *Newsworld*.

Like most of his colleagues, he viewed Kerry Kilcannon with a mixture of journalistic detachment and personal regard. In his dealings with the press—the professional adversary of any politician—Kilcannon was honest, accessible, and often humorous, leaving the impression that he liked reporters and accepted their role. And Nate credited Kilcannon, more than most politicians, with the sincerity of his beliefs, a willingness to take risks.

Of course, Nate did not flatter himself that he *knew* Kerry Kilcannon; perhaps no one but Clayton Slade did. Kilcannon gave off a sense of inner complexity that was unusual in a politician. This was enhanced by his refusal to indulge in contrived self-revelations about personal traumas and familial tragedies; in fact, the biggest mistake a reporter could make was to press Kerry Kilcannon about his brother. The answer to what drove Kilcannon the man remained a puzzle.

Nate started. There was a vibration in the pocket of his sport coat. Tired as he was, it took him a moment to remember that he had put his pager there.

He took out his cell phone and called the sky-page center. The message was terse: Call Katherine Jones ASAP, at a San Diego number.

Nate sat back, curious. The only Katherine Jones he knew of was the executive director of Anthony's Legions, a group named after Susan B. Anthony and devoted to raising money for pro-choice women candidates. Nate had never met her; her call could only relate to the campaign.

Glancing around at his colleagues, Nate decided not to return the call until they reached the landing strip.

Kilcannon's chartered plane was on the runway, a shadowy silver and black. The bus dropped them near the rear of the plane; a Secret Service agent stood by the metal ramp, ready to inspect the ID tags the press wore around their necks and to check their names against the security list. From experience, Nate knew that this process would give him the time he needed.

He walked out on the darkened tarmac so that no one could hear him and dialed the number he had been given.

It was the Meridian Hotel in La Jolla. Nate asked for Katherine Jones; after a moment, a brusque woman's voice answered.

"This is Nate Cutler," he told her.

"Good. I want to meet with you tomorrow morning, early. In confidence."

Perhaps because of the hour, Nate found that her peremptory phone manner annoyed him. "On what subject?" he asked.

There was the briefest hesitation, and then the woman answered, "Kerry Kilcannon."

Kerry Kilcannon's voice rose. "We will protect our right to choose in the deepest and broadest sense. For it is not just *women* who deserve a choice; it is everyone who chooses to work for a better job and a brighter future . . ."

Rising from the edge of the bed, Sean Burke turned up the volume. His fingers felt awkward.

Now Kilcannon seemed to look straight at Sean. "It is every mother, father, son, or daughter who refuses to lose one more person they love to a coward with a gun . . ."

Sean's hands began to shake. Abruptly, Kilcannon vanished from the screen, replaced by a woman reporter.

"Senator Kilcannon's speech," she began, "was an effort to confront the Vice President and put the choice issue behind him. But Kilcannon finds himself criticized by leading members of his church for his pro-choice stance, and now some pro-choice leaders question yesterday's remarks on when 'life' begins. This poses an uncomfortable dilemma for Kerry Kilcannon as he heads for California, where, in his party's primary four years ago, women accounted for fifty-eight percent of the vote.

"In this increasingly volatile campaign, suddenly refocused on the issue of choice by today's anti-abortion violence in Boston, a portion of the women's vote may become volatile as well . . ."

He was not violent by nature, Sean told himself. He had never killed before today; he had not wished to shoot the nurse or the receptionist. But the lesson of history was that soldiers must kill aggressors and their tools so that the innocent might live . . .

The motel room seemed to close in on him, making Sean feel trapped and smothered, the two sensations he feared most. He got up and turned on both bedside lamps, the ceiling light, and the fluorescent tube in the bathroom. His stomach hurt again.

When he turned back to the television, Sean saw a body on a stretcher.

He flinched. Paramedics were hauling the body through the same glass doors Sean had entered that morning, now three thousand miles away. Staring at the stretcher, Sean wondered whether it was the receptionist, the nurse, or the abortionist; covered by the white sheet, the body could be any one of them.

Another newswoman was speaking. "The sole witness, a twenty-two-year-old woman who had come for birth control advice, told police that the unidentified assailant was slender, about six feet tall, with dark hair and blue eyes."

Closing his eyes, Sean prayed that they would not find him.

"The Boston police are asking anyone with potential information about this crime to call 1-800-JUSTICE." Sean returned to the bathroom, spat blood into the sink, and swallowed two antacid pills.

The television, he realized, was eroding his resolve, making him weak. He forced himself to turn it off.

Sitting on the edge of the bed, Sean began listening for sounds.

He had done this when he was a small boy, covers pulled over his head, waiting for the echoes of his father's rage—an angry voice, a slammed door, his mother's cries. Now the only sounds he could hear were the hum of car tires, the deep motor sounds of ponderous trucks, the unearthly whir of air-conditioning in a cheap motel room—strange noises in an alien city. Sean felt both scared and angry, a pygmy bent on his final, enormous task.

He could not stay inside this room.

He opened the door and stepped out into the parking lot facing Lombard Street. Breathing deeply, Sean tried to absorb his new surroundings—the slow night traffic, the chill air, the fog swirling around him, misting the neon sign of the gas station across the street. He had never been to San Francisco: he had not known it would be so cold.

Shivering, Sean promised himself that he would begin tomorrow. Seven days was not much time.

FOUR

At four in the morning, when the Washington bureau chief called, Lara Costello had been awake for the last five hours.

She had returned from Africa three weeks earlier, after nearly two years in the Middle East, Bosnia, Rwanda—anywhere there was an election, a conference, a famine, a war. Three weeks was plenty of time to readjust sleeping patterns. What was happening to Lara was different.

She was not burned out, Lara told herself; she was having trouble making the transition. Her memories seemed indelible: drunken parties in Sarajevo while mortars fell all around them; mutilated bodies with their genitals missing; her translator Mira, who, when the fighting broke out again, disappeared in the rubble of her own apartment; dying children with distended stomachs; tortured prisoners. She could not accept that they were suddenly irrelevant to her life, her work.

After several hours of this, she had walked to the bedroom window of her rented town house and gazed out at the quiet Georgetown street, imagining her neighbors resting up for tomorrow's bureaucratic turf wars, a meeting on the Hill, a gallant effort to make some client safe from the scourge of FDA regulation. Washington was a true company town, she thought; everyone worked for the government or wanted something from it, and, at least in Georgetown, the company was keeping all of them nicely fed. This would become her reality, she knew—just as she had learned to make a good restaurant in London her reality for a night when she was fresh from Africa and starvation. It would just take time.

Time. In her three weeks back, Lara had come to realize that two years could be a long time when you were thirty-one. While she was overseas she had force-fed herself new cultures, made new friends, developed new skills and new defenses—in short, learned how to survive. Those two years had filled a void; to leave all that behind, even for a major promotion, hurt. Perhaps it was melodramatic, but the best analogy Lara could find was tearing a fishhook out of her own stomach. Even the worst things were part of her.

There was no explaining this. To old friends and family, her most intense experiences were distant and abstract, Bosnia or Africa places on the map, a half-remembered headline. But to Lara they were people whom her broadcasts had sometimes helped, perhaps by shaming a warring faction into allowing shipments of food to pass, or by pressuring her own government to try to relieve hunger or stop the systematic slaughter of one group by another. Sometimes she had been able, at the margins, to influence a small piece of foreign policy. It was difficult to have worked so hard, and cared so deeply, and then to leave. But Lara's work had made her a public figure, and the network wanted her home.

She understood how this had happened: the image of a young woman broadcasting from harsh conditions was compelling, and overseas there had been far less competition. And, the president of the news division had observed with irony, she had a quality as important as her gender or her Latina mother: high cheekbones. Lara had black hair, intense dark eyes, a sculpted face, and pale flawless skin. Though it had never mattered to her much, she was a pretty woman, and in television that counted. Especially if one's next assignment was on what a colleague had labeled "the star track": anchorwoman for the weekend news and a prime-time weekly news show.

Lara had turned from the window, gazing at her bedroom. She would rebuild her life in the city she once had wanted desperately to leave. Then, she told herself sardonically, somehow she could bear the burdens of celebrity, a million dollars a year, and a job most of her colleagues would kill for. She did not expect sympathy from anyone. Less than two years earlier, Lara had been an underpaid reporter for the *New York Times*, one of those semianonymous print journalists who combed Capitol

Hill for news and nuance. The only people who would understand her restiveness were overseas: journalists in sub-Saharan Africa, diplomats, AIDS workers, human rights activists . . .

He would have gotten it, she suddenly knew; at times she had believed that he could grasp what it was like to be an old woman, or a small child. But the thought of him deepened her sense of solitude.

"We go through life alone," he had said to her once, "and then we die." It was said wryly, as though he did not truly believe it; he had a gentle way of making fun of anyone who inflated their own difficulties. She would remember that in the weeks ahead.

That was what she was thinking when the telephone rang.

It was the bureau chief, Hal Leavitt. He did not apologize for the lateness of the hour.

"We've got a problem," he said without preface. "Mike Devore's broken his ankle. There's no one to cover Kilcannon in California."

Lara felt stunned. She sat on the edge of the bed, trying to collect herself.

"Are you there?" Hal asked.

"Yeah. Just waking up."

"Look, I know you've got another week's vacation, but I thought of you right away. This primary's the tie-breaker, you're from California, you started your career in San Francisco, and you know Kilcannon from covering the Hill."

Lara drew a breath. "And if that's not reason enough, I've been overseas for two years, haven't followed the primaries, don't know the issues, and am open to charges of bias—every other month or so, the President's or Mason's people complained that I was picking on them. Or have you forgotten?" She paused. "You must have been out late, Hal, drinking with the boys. It's the worst idea I've ever heard."

Hal's voice was level. "It's only seven days, Lara. I'll take the heat from Mason. If there is any."

"That's one thing. But I've always thought that ignorance was a problem for a reporter. It makes *me* uncomfortable, anyhow."

For the first time, Hal sounded annoyed. "We'll have a clippings file ready. You can read it on the plane. When you land in Los Angeles, call Mike Devore from the limo. He'll get you up to speed." His voice became crisp. "We'll make this as easy as possible—limousines, prepaid ticket, anything you need. The car's coming at nine."

Desperate, Lara searched for excuses. "There's something else," she said more evenly.

"What's that?"

"I have my own biases here." She paused, choosing her words with care. "When I first came to the Hill, Kerry Kilcannon helped me get oriented and gave me a little credibility. I liked him, and I came to respect him as a senator. I *don't* admire Dick Mason: to me, he's one of those politicians who view everything, including dead African babies, in terms of their career. Unless Kilcannon's completely changed, I know who *I'd* vote for. I worry about my own professionalism here."

There was a moment's silence, and then Hal responded in a voice of strained patience. "*All* reporters have personal feelings, Lara. We *all* vote for someone."

Lara felt sick at heart. She could go over his head to the president of NBC News, but what could she say? Only the truth would get her off this assignment. And the truth could destroy not just her career, but his.

"Seven days," she said at length.

"That's right."

Mechanically, Lara walked to her desk and picked up a pen. "Give me some names—campaign manager, communications director, press secretary, press travel person."

He did that. Lara found herself staring at the name Clayton Slade.

"Do you have their schedule tomorrow? Where they start, where they'll have been by the time I catch up?"

"Sure. I'll fax it to you."

Lara thanked him, and got off.

She was still sitting at her desk, hands over her face, when the fax came through.

She picked it up. The Kilcannon campaign was overnighting

at the Hyatt in downtown San Diego. With the three-hour time difference, it was roughly one-thirty.

Lara waited until eight forty-five, just before the limousine came, to place the call.

At six o'clock, when the Secret Service escorted Kerry back to his room, Clayton was waiting. He had already brewed the pot of coffee provided by the hotel.

Kerry wiped the sweat off his forehead. "Good workout?" Clayton asked.

Kerry stopped to look at him; if Clayton had a weakness, it was his discomfort with confronting Kerry in personal matters. Clayton had that look now—narrow-eyed and pained, like a man with an unaccustomed hangover. His bulky form slumped in the chair.

"What is it?" Kerry asked.

Clayton sat back, watching his friend's face. "Lara Costello just called me."

Kerry felt himself become still.

"She's replacing Mike Devore." Clayton's voice was quiet, unhappy. "She clearly doesn't know if *I* know, but she figures I probably do."

It was hard for Kerry to respond. "What did she say? Exactly."

"It was very understated, professional. She's joining us today in Los Angeles. She'll be gone after Tuesday. There was no one else to take Mike's place." Clayton folded his hands. "What she was telling me, between the lines, is that she couldn't get out of it. I think she wanted you to be prepared but didn't feel it was right to call you. I certainly agree with that."

Kerry tried to absorb this. "How did she sound?"

"Like I said, professional." Clayton's voice softened. "I don't know her, Kerry. It just seems like I do."

Kerry stood, arms crossed, head down.

"I'm sorry," Clayton said. "It's bad timing. A few hours isn't long to get used to this."

Kerry rubbed the bridge of his nose. After a time, he murmured, "I'll be all right."

"You'll have to be." Clayton rose from his chair. "There's a speech that goes with this, pal, and it's my bad luck to have to give it. Remember how we always used to know who was screwing who at the prosecutor's office? The only clueless ones were the couple themselves—somehow they always thought they were invisible.

"You're a candidate for President of the United States. The reporters who follow you around are trained observers, at the top of their game, out of their minds half the time with too fucking little to think about. Start giving Lara Costello meaningful glances across the tarmac, and somebody will wonder why."

Kerry gave him a resentful stare. "I'm not stupid, Clayton. And she's not interested."

Clayton's eyes were steady. "There are a lot of people, Kerry, who have a lot invested in this. Not just you, but everyone who's sacrificed career and money and time with their family to make this work. A campaign manager who *wasn't* your friend would say, 'It's a choice between this woman and your candidacy. If you choose her, fine, but I walk. If you choose the presidency, don't go near her.'"

Kerry gazed around the sterile room. "No one knows," he finally said.

Clayton frowned. "At least *three* people know—her, you, and me, because you told me."

"I was a mess . . ."

"And *she* wasn't?"

Kerry shook his head. "At the end, she wouldn't see me. I can only guess how she was."

He felt Clayton's hand on his shoulder. "I'm sorry, pal. I really am. I know how you feel." He waited a moment. "But I also know *you*, and you're the best candidate in the race. You won't let yourself lose that too."

Kerry studied him. "So what else do you recommend, exactly? Besides me pretending she doesn't exist."

Clayton paused. "I may need to see her, Kerry. Right now, we don't know who *else* knows. With her on the campaign—"

"If anyone talks to her," Kerry cut in, "it'll be *me*. What happened was between us, not you."

Clayton's face was hard. "That makes me the one, doesn't it?

If you're seen with her and some reporter catches on to this, *our* campaign and *your* future won't be all that you'd be trashing. She'll go down with you."

Slowly, Kerry felt his anger die.

Turning from Clayton, Kerry walked to the window. For some moments, he stared out at San Diego Harbor, watching the first shimmer of sunshine turn the water light gray.

How did I get here? he wondered. Forty-two years of living, he supposed: the first thirty before Jamie's death, and then the twelve very different years of which Lara had become a part. But the skein of circumstances was so long, so tangled, that there was no simple answer.

Newark

1964–1976

ONE

Kerry Kilcannon's clearest memory of early childhood was of his father bleeding.

It began as many other nights had begun—with the sound of a slammed door, Michael Kilcannon coming home drunk. He would teeter up the stairs to the second floor, talking to himself or to someone he resented, pausing for balance or to take deep, wheezing breaths. Kerry would lie very still; until this night, Michael would stumble past Kerry's and Jamie's rooms to the bedroom at the end of the hall, and the beatings would begin. Through his tears, Kerry would imagine his mother's face at breakfast—a bruised eye, a swollen lip. No one spoke of it.

But on this night, Kerry's door flew open.

Michael Kilcannon flicked on the wall light. The six-year-old Kerry blinked at the sudden brightness, afraid to move or speak.

His father walked toward him and then stood at the foot of his bed. Blood spurted from his forearm.

Terrified, Kerry watched red droplets forming on his sheets.

Michael glared at Kerry, his handsome, somewhat fleshy face suffused with drink and anger. "Look," he barked. "*Look* at what you've done."

Kerry stared at the bloodstains, stupefied.

"Your *wagon*, you pissant. You left your fooking wagon on the path . . ."

Kerry shook his head reflexively. "I'm sorry, Da," he tried. Then he began to cry, trying hard to stop.

Mary Kilcannon appeared in the doorway.

Her long black hair was disarranged, her skin pale in the light. Kerry was too afraid to run to her.

Entering, she gave him a look of deep compassion, then placed a tentative hand on her husband's shoulder. Softly, she asked, "What is it, Michael?"

Throat working, Kerry watched his father's angry face.

"The wagon." Michael gazed down at the sheets with a kind of wonder. "Sharp edges . . ."

Eyes never leaving her son, his mother kissed Michael on the side of his face.

"That'll need tending, Michael." Still trembling, Kerry watched his mother take his father by the hand. "We should go to the hospital."

Slowly, his father let Mary Kilcannon lead him from the room.

Kerry could hardly breathe. Turning, Mary Kilcannon looked back at him. "Don't worry about your father . . ."

Somehow Kerry understood that she meant he was safe tonight. But he did not get up until he heard the front door close.

His eighteen-year-old brother, Jamie—tall and handsome, the family's jewel—was standing in the door of his bedroom. "Well," Jamie said softly, to no one, "they cut quite a figure, don't they?"

Kerry hated him for it.

It started then—the thing between Kerry and his father.

Two days later, the stitches still in his arm, Michael Kilcannon, with two tickets a fellow patrolman could not use, took Kerry to a Mets game. Michael knew little of baseball—he had emigrated from County Roscommon in his teens. But he was a strapping, handsome man in his red-haired, florid way and, when sober, a dad Kerry was desperately proud of: a policeman, a kind of hero, possessed of a ready laugh and a reputation for reckless courage. Michael bought Kerry popcorn and a hot dog and enjoyed the game with self-conscious exuberance; Kerry knew that this was his apology for what no one would ever mention. When the Mets won in the ninth inning, Michael hugged him.

His father felt large and warm. "I love you, Da," Kerry murmured.

That night, Michael Kilcannon went to Lynch's Ark Bar, a neighborhood mainstay. But Kerry felt safe, the glow of his day with him still.

His bedroom door's opening awakened him.

Rubbing his eyes, Kerry looked at his father across the room, half glad, half afraid.

Michael staggered toward him and sat at the edge of the bed. Kerry kept quiet; his father was breathing hard. "Bastards." Michael's voice was hostile, threatening.

Kerry's heart pounded. Maybe if he said something, showed his father sympathy . . .

"What is it, Da?"

His father shook his head, as if to himself. "Mulroy . . ."

Kerry did not understand. All he could do was wait.

"I'm as good a man—better," Michael said abruptly. "But *he* makes sergeant, not me. They give it only to the kiss-ass boys . . ."

As she had two nights before, Mary Kilcannon appeared. "Michael," she said in the same soft voice.

Kerry's father did not turn. "Shut up," he said harshly. "We're talking . . ."

Fearful again, Kerry looked at his mother. Her words had an edge her son had never heard before. "Leave the boy alone."

Michael Kilcannon shrugged his heavy shoulders and rose. With a slap so lazy yet so powerful it reminded Kerry of a big cat, he struck Mary Kilcannon across the mouth.

She reeled backward, blood trickling from her lip. Tears stung Kerry's eyes; watching Mary Kilcannon cover her face, he was sickened by his own fear and helplessness.

"We were *talking*." Michael's voice suggested the patience of a reasonable man stretched to the breaking point. "Go to bed."

Gazing at Kerry, she backed into the hallway.

Michael turned from her and sat at the edge of his bed. He did not seem to notice that Kerry was crying.

"Mulroy," he repeated.

Kerry did not know how long his father stayed, mumbling resentful fragments. Kerry dared not fall asleep.

After this, Kerry never knew when it would happen. On some nights his father would come home and beat his mother. On others he would open Kerry's door and pour out his wounds and angers. Kerry learned to make some sound or comment so that Michael thought he was listening, to fight sleep or any sign of inattention that might set his father off. Michael never touched him.

As long as Kerry listened, he knew that his father would not beat Mary Kilcannon.

As deeply as Michael Kilcannon terrified him, so Kerry loved his mother.

She, too, was from County Roscommon. At twenty-one, she had given birth to James Joseph; Kerry Francis had not been born until she was thirty-three. Between, there was a string of miscarriages.

Mary retained a faded prettiness, like a rose preserved in the pages of a book. But what Kerry adored was her laughing green eyes, like crescents. The mere sight of Kerry seemed to make her smile.

They lived in the Vailsburg section of Newark, populated by Irish and a scattering of Italians. Vailsburg began with the leafy expanse of Vailsburg Park, a rolling tract of land with several ball fields; it ended with Ivy Hill Park and the grander homes of South Orange, where the snobs lived. The streets were tree-lined and quiet, with neat two-story wooden houses populated by the families of policemen and firemen, civil servants and small-businessmen, the odd lawyer or accountant. Children ran free, playing games in the streets, protected by mothers like Mary, who shouted at drivers who went too fast. There were several playgrounds with basketball hoops, and in the winter, the fire department flooded a section of Ivy Hill Park and turned it into a skating rink.

Mary Kilcannon taught Kerry to skate there, laughing as he flailed his arms, clapping with pleasure as his efforts became stronger and surer. She made him forget what was already clear—that he would never be as tall as Jamie, or as fast and agile at sports. She was the one person on earth Kerry was certain loved him as he was.

Without speaking, Kerry and his mother became conspirators. What Michael Kilcannon imposed on them at night was a shameful secret, never to be discussed. Kerry knew that his mother could not ask the police for help. Michael Kilcannon *was* the police; to tell his friends would shame him, perhaps make him even more brutal. Within the tight community of Vailsburg, where a quiet word from a policeman was enough to nip trouble in the bud, Michael treasured his reputation.

Every morning, Mary Kilcannon prayed at Sacred Heart.

In the half-lit vastness of the church, Kerry would watch her rapt profile. Kerry, too, found the church consoling—its hush, its seventy-foot ceilings and beautiful stained-glass windows, its marble altar, framed by a fresco of Jesus ascending. Sometimes they stayed for an hour.

One snowy winter morning, they wended their way home. They made a game of it, Kerry trying to walk in his mother's bigger footprints without making footprints of his own.

His prize was a cup of hot chocolate. As they sat at the kitchen table, his mother smiling at him, Kerry felt he would burst with love. But it was she who said, "I love you more than words can tell, Kerry Francis."

Tears came to his eyes. As if reading his mind, Mary Kilcannon said, "Your father's a good man when he's sober. He takes good care of us. He's only frustrated, afraid he won't succeed as he deserves."

The words were meant as comfort. But what Kerry heard was that they were trapped: from the long nights with his father, he sensed that the reasons for Michael's failure to rise were the same as for his abusiveness, and that this would never end until someone ended it.

Kerry squeezed his mother's hand.

But outside their home, Kerry knew, Mary Kilcannon would always be known as James's mother.

It began with how much Jamie favored her, so closely that only his maleness made him handsome instead of beautiful. By seventeen, Jamie was six feet one, with an easy grace and with hazel eyes that seemed to take in everything around him. Vailsburg thought Jamie close to perfect: he was student body president of Seton Hall Prep; captain of its football team; second in his class. Jamie's clothes were always neat and pressed, nothing out of place. Girls adored him. Like most obvious expressions of emotion, this seemed to amuse Jamie and, perhaps, to frighten him.

This was Jamie's secret—his ability to withdraw. To Kerry, his brother seemed driven by a silent contempt for both parents, the need to be nothing like them. From an early age, Jamie was too successful for Michael Kilcannon to disparage. Because of Jamie's size and his attainments, the father came to observe a sort of resentful truce with his older son: Michael received praise in public, was reminded in private of his own inadequacy. But Jamie did not raise his hand, or his voice, to help his mother.

When Jamie left for Princeton on a full scholarship, he would not let his parents drive him there.

Jamie did well at college, played defensive halfback on the football team, became involved in campus politics. His much younger brother dimly imagined classmates thinking that Jamie did this easily. But Kerry knew that as he fearfully waited for his father to climb the stairs, he would sometimes hear his brother, through the thin wall between their bedrooms, practicing his speeches, testing phrases, pauses . . .

Kerry never forgot the Christmas vacation of Jamie's second year away.

Jamie was running for something. He practiced a speech late into the night; sleepless, Kerry listened to his brother's muffled voice.

Michael Kilcannon came home.

Hearing his father's footsteps, Kerry wondered whether Michael would open the door or go to his mother's bedroom. He sat up in bed, expectant, as Michael's footsteps passed.

A moment later, Mary Kilcannon cried out in pain.

The only sign that Jamie had heard was the silence on the other side of the wall. Tears ran down Kerry's face.

No, he would never be his brother James.

TWO

He did not have to worry: at Sacred Heart School, no one mistook him for Jamie.

Kerry was short, slight, and a recalcitrant student. Reluctantly, he submitted to such rudimentary discipline as learning to walk in a straight line, to keep silent between classes, to respond to the hand bell that ended recess. Once, he smashed a bee with a ruler; instantly, Sister Mary Catherine swatted the back of his head. "That was one of God's helpless creatures," she rebuked him.

Ears ringing, Kerry wanted to say, *So am I.* But the nun's words stayed with him: though he fought often, it was never against anyone weaker than he was.

His rage seemed close to suicidal; Kerry Kilcannon challenged only boys who were bigger, older, and without mercy. All it took was some offense to Kerry or another smaller boy, and Kerry would throw a punch. More often than not, he would absorb a beating that did not end until someone stopped it—Kerry was awkward, unskilled, and to quit felt like death to him. By the time he was twelve, his fistfights were so frequent, so violent, that he hovered on the edge of expulsion.

Then he fought the bully Johnny Quinn.

Johnny had "borrowed" the prized new bike of Timmy Scanlon, a nine-year-old Kerry liked. Laughing, Johnny returned the bike, covered with mud.

When Timmy began crying, Kerry punched Johnny Quinn in the nose.

The fight went on for an hour, cheered by avid boys. Kerry took a savage beating. Blind with pain, blood pouring from his nose and mouth and a cut at the edge of his eye, Kerry passed out at last.

When he awoke, the first thing Kerry saw was his mother, crying. "Why?" she kept saying. "Why?" Even if he could have spoken, there was nothing Kerry could tell her.

He had suffered a chipped tooth and a broken nose, and the two stitches at the corner of his eye left a scar.

Michael Kilcannon took a rough pride in his son's combativeness; Kerry had distinguished himself at little else.

In desperation, Mary turned to Kerry's godfather.

When Father Roarke, the principal, called Kerry to his office, Liam Dunn was there.

The two men looked at each other, then at Kerry. "Hello, Kerry," said Liam.

Kerry was surprised. Though Liam always asked after him and never forgot his birthday or his name day, his selection as Kerry's godfather had been more for the prestige it conferred. Liam had long ceased to be his father's partner on patrol. He was now councilman for the West Ward, into which Vailsburg fell, an intimate of Monsignor Conroy of Sacred Heart. Even at twelve, Kerry knew that the green line that marked the route of the Saint Patrick's Day parade ended at Dunn's Tavern because Liam wished it; that immigrants looking for work could find help from Liam Dunn, with his friends in the labor unions, the police, the fire department; that the Dunn Association, Liam's own charity, supported Vailsburg causes generously; that when Frankie Burns, the idiot son of impoverished parents, had been killed by a car, it was Liam who paid for the funeral. Liam never spoke of any of these things; others did.

Liam turned to Father Roarke, his voice and manner deferential. "May I take Kerry for a walk, Father?"

The priest nodded. "Surely."

Gently, Liam Dunn touched Kerry's elbow and steered him from the room.

It was the first chill of fall. Kerry wore a lined jacket, Liam a wool coat and a muffler. Their breaths made thin smoke.

Liam did not say where they were going. For block after block of Vailsburg they simply walked, occasionally making small talk, Liam sometimes gazing into the distance. Oddly, Kerry was not nervous; Liam seemed a man comfortable with silence.

They stopped at Ivy Hill Park.

"Why don't we sit awhile," Liam said.

They found a green wooden bench. For a time, Liam was quiet, content to watch the park. Kerry studied him: he supposed Liam was in his mid-forties, like his father, and, like Michael, big. But although Liam was fleshier, the bulk seemed to serve him, to be part of who he was. His short hair was quite red; his seamed face soft only in the chin; his ridged nose more Castilian than Irish; his eyelids were so heavy that they seemed half closed. But when he turned to Kerry, his eyes were clear, penetrating.

"I hear you fight, Kerry."

Kerry could only nod; the evidence was on his face.

"It seems not well enough," Liam said softly. "Tell me, do you know *why* you fight?"

Kerry did not want to answer. But this was Liam Dunn.

"I hate bullies."

It hurt to say this, Kerry found. Something seemed to move in Liam's eyes. "Your mother . . ."

Kerry's stomach clenched like a fist. "Your mother," Liam repeated, "is afraid for you. Do you want that?"

Kerry could not look at him. He felt Liam's large hand on his shoulder. "If you want to fight, Kerry, then you need to learn how. There's a place for that, a man who can teach you boxing."

Slowly, Kerry turned.

Liam's eyes met his. "What do you say?"

Kerry nodded. It was as if Liam Dunn had willed it.

"There's a condition," Liam said.

Kerry felt himself stiffen. "What is it?"

"That until you learn, there'll be no fighting. For your mother's sake." Liam smiled now. "Not to mention your own."

As Kerry gazed at him, Liam stuck out his hand.

Kerry took it. "Good," Liam said. "We've made an arrangement."

He stood.

Kerry knew that this was a signal—Liam Dunn had other

things to do. They walked in silence to the school, Liam seemingly preoccupied.

Liam stopped at the edge of the playground. "I've been thinking," he said. "There's a favor you can do for me."

Kerry was surprised. "What?"

"On Sundays, after Mass, I visit the bars to chat a little, see people who may want to see me. Some Sundays I may need you to help me remember things."

Kerry doubted this, and, had it been true, Liam had four sons of his own, helpers to do his bidding.

"What about my father?" Kerry asked.

Liam's eyes grew hooded. "It'll be fine with Michael," he said. "I'm sure of it."

Every Tuesday and Friday afternoon, Kerry Kilcannon went to the CYO gym to box.

It was a half-lit rabbit warren of rooms with pictures of forgotten Golden Glovers on the walls. Kerry felt small and out of place; when his coach, Jack Burns, asked him to hit the heavy bag, a fifty-pound leather sack hanging from the ceiling, Kerry uncorked a series of angry left-hand haymakers. At length, he missed entirely and the heavy bag, swinging toward him, knocked the ninety-five-pound twelve-year-old to the floor.

"I guess you're left-handed," Jack said.

Jack was large, gray-haired, and patient, with the tonsure of a monk and a placid expression to match. After three lessons, Kerry decided that a man who never raised his voice or lost his temper could know nothing about fighting. Only his promise to Liam kept Kerry there.

It was hard. For the first three weeks, Jack tried to teach Kerry to fight as left-handers did: using the weaker arm, his right, to lead with a jab, then following with the left. But to Kerry, the left hand was his only strength; all he wanted to do was throw a wild left hook and try to decimate whatever stood in his way.

Finally, Jack put Kerry in with another twelve-year-old, Terrence McCaw, a bit more experienced and far more disciplined. Kerry's wild left never landed; the equally slight Terrence simply stepped inside and peppered Kerry's face with jabs.

Only the use of oversized gloves kept this humiliation from causing damage.

Jack stepped in and took Kerry aside. "Getting powdered, aren't you. Just like out in the world."

Kerry stared at the canvas.

"Thing is," Jack added, "you can do much better, especially with the left. But that would take practice, using your brain. So how do you want to go through life—as good as you can be, or as bad as you are now? Besides me, *you'll* be the only one to know what you decide."

This stung Kerry. "I want to be better."

Jack nodded. "Then there's a way. If you've the patience for it."

He began teaching Kerry to box like a right-hander.

This meant that Kerry's stance caused him to use the left hand not as a power punch but as a jab. Hour after hour, Jack stood Kerry in front of the heavy bag, while Kerry learned to fire short left hands, just to keep the swinging bag from hitting him.

"One," Jack would say. "One, two."

Whack, whack, whack.

Kerry's left jab became more like a piston—stiffer, stronger, quicker. Kerry felt his anger surge through each punch. Suddenly the rage he did not understand became his friend, his servant. He was tireless.

This routine went on for months. One day, Kerry realized that he loved the smell, the feeling of his own sweat, of fighting through fatigue. He imagined Johnny Quinn in front of him.

"I want to fight now," Kerry told his coach.

"Soon enough," Jack told him. "First you need to do something with the right."

The something was simple. After throwing left jabs, moving right to keep away from his imagined opponent's power punch, Kerry would step straight inside and deliver a right hand to the face. His right was weak, but Jack assured him that it would come.

Finally, Jack let him go another round with Terrence McCaw. "You don't hate him," Jack said. "You want to win, is all."

The first time Terrence hit him, Kerry swung with a looping left hand. Terrence hit Kerry again and knocked him down.

Tears of anger came to Kerry's eyes. "Which Kerry is it?" he heard Jack ask.

Kerry got up.

As Terrence came in, eyes alight with the vision of another knockdown, Kerry made himself see not a boy but the heavy bag.

Three straight left jabs—*whack, whack, whack.*

Terrence blinked, off balance, and then Kerry threw his right.

It was weak, a powder puff. But Terrence was so astonished that his feet tangled and he fell to the canvas.

Kerry felt triumph and pride surge through him. He couldn't wait for Terrence to get up.

Jack Burns stepped between them. "Touch gloves, boys," he said. "You've both learned something." Pausing, he said to the bewildered Terrence, "Next time, you'll have to watch for Kerry's right. It's coming on."

Kerry's heartbeat slowed. He no longer wished to pummel Terrence McCaw. He wanted to practice his right.

On his way home, Kerry realized that, outside the gym, he had not been in a fight for perhaps six months. He was keeping his word to Liam Dunn.

His other new activity was with Liam himself—going to the bars on Sundays.

Kerry's mother hated drink for what it did to Michael. To Kerry, bars were a dark mystery—the place where his moody father became the devil who seemed more furious every night he held Kerry hostage or, as his helpless son listened in mute agony, beat Mary Kilcannon.

"The Irish disease," Liam said of drunkenness. "But there's more to the bars than that."

There was.

After Mass on Sunday, they would be jammed by one o'clock. Liam called this the spiritual yielding to the temporal. The taverns served as community center, employment service, political intelligence system, and meeting place for single men and women. A politician who didn't know the bars, Liam said, was a fool waiting to discover himself.

So they would go to the bars, Liam and Kerry, sometimes with one or more of Liam's sons—up and down and around South Orange Street, the main drag of Vailsburg, to Higgins' Tavern; Lenihan & O'Grady's; Cryan's Tavern; Malloy's Tavern; Lynch's Ark Bar, run by a widow from Ireland; Paul's Tavern; McGuinness' Bar. Liam taught Kerry to remember names: in six months, he came to know twenty-five to thirty Irish tavern owners in Newark.

"The Irish," Liam explained to Kerry, "ran politics in Newark from the 1920s till just a few years ago, when the Italians elected Mayor Addonizio." He paused, adding mildly, "The Italians won't have quite so long a run."

It took Kerry a few more months to see what Liam meant.

Kerry came to like the bars for their gregariousness, their Celtic memorabilia, their dark wood, the smell of beer, the sound of men and women laughing, the Makem Brothers on the jukebox, the large "family rooms" filled with tables, where Liam or other politicians would sometimes stand a party. Kerry listened, and he learned.

Liam Dunn would join the crowd, let people have a private word if they wished. They often did, about sewer problems, the hope of a job for themselves or a cousin on the way from Ireland, the need of money for a promising boy at Seton Hall or a daughter whose leukemia had drained the family coffers. Liam never lied: he said only that he'd do what he could, then usually did more than he implied was possible. Liam remembered not only names and special days—he had a book for that—but the central themes and details of people's lives and the lives they held dear, for which there was no book.

Liam, Kerry decided, truly cared what became of people who needed help—people like Kerry. Kerry could never imagine Liam Dunn practicing his speeches like Jamie, though Liam could introduce a fellow politician as if the man was Bishop Sheen and, when he wished to, capture a room for himself. Once, when Kerry asked why Jamie was not here learning politics, Liam said only, "He's a gifted boy, doing it his own way. He may go far, that one."

"But shouldn't he be working with you?" Kerry asked.

This made Liam smile. "Last thing Jamie needs or wants, Kerry. In many ways this is a bit *small* for the lad, and more power to him. Perhaps he can build us a highway or two."

Kerry puzzled over the meaning of this. But Liam Dunn was much quieter in private than in public, and what he said was sometimes elliptical. It was as if he had learned politics a person at a time.

One day, walking home from Lynch's Ark, Liam tried to explain.

"People," he said, "mostly worry about themselves and their own—money, health, what have you. But if they feel safe about that, then they'll see ways they can help others. Including me.

"That's why this neighborhood of ours is such a fine thing, of which my job as councilman is a small part. Vailsburg's a seamless web: the family, the church, the schools, clubs, sports—all the ways we know each other and have things in common. No one will ever starve; widows will have the slack taken up and their kids' way paid. It all has little to do with me or anything in government. People are *glad* to help, because they know if their turn comes round they'll be taken care of." They stopped in front of Kerry's white frame house. "Of course, it helps that we're all Irish. Or Italian."

Kerry nodded. Something in Liam's tone reminded him of his comment about the Italians: that their day would be short.

"So," Liam asked abruptly, "you've been with me all these months. What are people most worried about?"

Suddenly Kerry saw it—the problem people muttered about after their third beer, the way his father spewed hatred at the foot of Kerry's bed—and knew that Liam believed everything would change.

"Black people," Kerry said.

Liam nodded. "Blacks. And it's a fool who thinks there's anything for it. Or should be."

Kerry was quiet. "Da hates them," he said at last.

For a time, Liam said nothing. Then he asked, "Would you like to stay the night with us? Mrs. Dunn would be glad of your company."

Kerry's heart rose. He looked at Liam's ruddy face with a

kind of love. Then he thought of his mother, alone in the darkened house, waiting for his father to come home. He could not leave her there; his father seemed worse each month.

Kerry did not know how to say this. He stared at a crack in the sidewalk.

He felt Liam watch him, then touch his shoulder. "Sure," Liam said. "Things to do."

He did not ask again.

Michael Kilcannon emitted a breath so deep and shuddering that Kerry could smell the whiskey even as he felt the hatred—as clearly as he knew that, even more than usual, something was terribly wrong.

"Niggers," Michael repeated. "They came near to ruining this city in the riots, and now one of the fooking monkeys wants to be *mayor.* So they'll burn the city again, use it to do barbe-cue. And then they'll barbecue *me.*"

Kerry did not understand what his father meant about himself. But he could remember the riots, by smell and sound. He had been nine. The riots began with an incident between police and blacks in the West Ward: through the open screen of his bedroom window, Kerry could smell the smoke, hear the sirens. An older boy, nearer South Orange Avenue, swore to Kerry the next day that he had seen flames dance against the night sky and thought the city would burn to the ground.

For the next five nights, Kerry listened in his bed to the wail of sirens, the repeated popping that was surely gunshots. Though untouched, Vailsburg felt eerie, besieged: the bars were closed; the doors were locked; and the patrol cars were everywhere, packed with three or four cops, their shotguns sticking out open rear windows, reminding Kerry of an aircraft carrier. And then one morning all was silent again, and Newark was never the same.

A few days later, his father took Kerry for a ride in his squad car. There were still groups of blacks loitering near looted, burned-out shops. The majestic city hall—its steps flanked by fierce gold eagles, its airy mass topped by a glistening gold dome—was a focus of city history and civic pride, the prize contended for by warring factions of ethnic whites. Kerry was shocked to see some lots around it reduced to charred shells.

"This is what these animals do," Michael said. "And they'll do it again unless we stop them."

Kerry could see, clear enough. It made him angry.

"But you *will* stop them?" he asked his father.

Michael Kilcannon's face had been a grim line . . .

"You see," he told Kerry now, "two nights ago, I shot one— robbing a store. Nineteen years old, and a blessing he died before killing someone worthwhile. The friends of this Gibson man, the nigger who would be king—it's not enough they want their own to skip over whites and make sergeant before they can *read*." Suddenly Michael leaned across the bed and jerked Kerry by the T-shirt until his face was inches away. "They're saying your father's a *murderer* . . ."

Kerry felt himself shiver. He could imagine his father and his closemouthed partner, a bottle of whiskey in the back of their patrol car, finding a black man in an empty store. Even now, his father's eyes were like gray-blue bullets.

"They're saying your father's a murderer," Michael repeated, "and your fooking friend Liam won't touch it . . ."

When Liam Dunn decided to support the black mayoral candidate, Kenneth Gibson, against Hugh Addonizio, Kerry could not understand.

There were murmurs in the bars, hard faces, threats on Liam's telephone to murder his sons and give his daughter to a gang of blacks. Liam went about his affairs, taking no overt notice of the fact that business at Dunn's Tavern was off, that fewer people spoke to him, that a popular ward leader, Paul Slattery, was making the Sunday rounds to talk of running against Liam when his council seat came up.

To Kerry, the bars felt like a gauntlet. But he stuck by his godfather out of loyalty and anger at how some people shunned him. Kerry would apologize to no one.

At the end of one tense Sunday, Liam took Kerry to the same bench in Ivy Hill Park.

"I hear the boxing goes better," Liam said. "School, too—no more Ds, and not a fight to your name." He patted Kerry roughly on the shoulder. "All that, and you begin to understand politics as well. No telling how well you can do."

Thinking of Jamie, and then the hostile faces in the bars, Kerry clenched his fists. "I'll never run for anything."

"No need to," Liam answered. "You'll find the thing that's right for you." He paused for a moment. "But, about me, don't think that what you're seeing is all there is. It's just something that people *need* me to go through."

"What do you mean?"

"I mean they're scared, so they're angry, and they want me to tell them it will all go away—the blacks slowly moving into Vailsburg as friends talk about leaving, the crime they feel spreading, the loss of their own power, which began well before they noticed. But it would be stupid to tell them that hating blacks is an answer. Let alone a program." He turned to Kerry. "Telling the truth when it's hard is what political capital is for. Unless you want to be an errand boy."

But how can blacks be worth it? Kerry thought. Finally, he said, "It seems like people hate you."

Liam looked at him. "You don't hate me, do you?"

Firmly, Kerry shook his head.

As Liam stood, restless, Kerry sensed the pressure beneath his godfather's air of calm. "Do the right thing, Kerry, and things tend to come out right in the end. But the first is the only part you control. And sometimes going to bed square with yourself is a day-to-day kind of thing." For the first time, Liam smiled. "Of course, some of these fools can't count. Like Slattery."

"What do you mean?"

"That I may need black votes going forward, but blacks also need some of mine. And that the victory margin Paul Slattery thinks he's tallying is moving to the suburbs." Liam's eyes were distant, sad. "Don't know there's any man can stop it—me included. Your brother James is well out of this. But then I wonder if he didn't see it coming."

"What?"

"The end of things, this life we have in Vailsburg. Slow but sure." He paused again. "Not a burden Jamie should have on his mind, running for state senate in Princeton. A nice, safe, liberal place like that."

Suddenly Kerry had the sense that Liam had talked to James, and recently. In the next instant, he understood that a policeman father found to have murdered a black youth not only would make life terrible for Kerry and his mother but could do Jamie's career great harm. And then the last piece fell into place. To his father's arrogant pleasure, the most vocal members of the black community had suddenly dropped their demand for his indictment. Liam's new allies . . .

Kerry clutched Liam by the sleeve of his coat. "Did *you* save my father?"

For a time, Liam appraised Kerry with what, beneath the heavy lids, seemed a very intense interest.

"It's as I said," he finally answered. "Do the right thing, and things tend to come out right in the end. That applies to Michael too."

The night James Kilcannon won election to the New Jersey State Senate, he barely acknowledged either parent. It was in keeping with how he had gotten there—going away to Princeton; becoming a leader of anti-Vietnam demonstrations; casting his lot with the reform wing of the party. To his supporters he was attractive, articulate, and the antithesis of machine politics. They did not know or care about his family.

Nonetheless, Michael and Mary Kilcannon drove to attend Jamie's victory celebration. Jamie was plainly uncomfortable at this; his most extended mention of family was of Kerry. Remarking on his brother's age, the victorious candidate grinned and said, "You're next, Kerry—if you can get your grades up a little." The clip was notable enough to show on TV: the handsome new state senator was himself only twenty-four.

Watching Jamie on television, Kerry scowled; it had been weeks since Jamie had spoken to him, and he saw himself as a prop. Kerry was much more concerned with the race between Gibson and Addonizio for mayor of Newark, on which Liam Dunn's future rested.

* * *

The night of the election, Liam's house was guarded by police. The week before, someone had lit a brick doused in gasoline and thrown it through a window.

Liam had been reluctant to have Kerry stay with them, let alone go out with him that night. But Kerry insisted. "You say this is history. I want to see it." So he went with Liam in the back of a squad car driven by a tight-lipped policeman to the victory celebration for Kenneth Gibson.

The exultant crowd—some white, mostly black—was filled with a sense of unleashed energy; though black voters were now the majority in Newark, no black man had ever been elected mayor. Watching with Liam as Gibson declared victory, Kerry felt an answering sympathy that surprised him; the powerlessness of these people had been taken for granted, and now they would have their day. The streets near City Hall were filled with celebrants.

"You'll never again see a white mayor of Newark," Liam murmured on their way home. When they arrived, Liam's house was quite safe; Vailsburg was quiet as a tomb. Liam said hardly a word.

The next month, with the mayor-elect's support, Councilman Liam Dunn became chairman of the Essex County Democratic Party. Liam's adversary, Paul Slattery, never ran for anything.

THREE

At sixteen, Kerry Kilcannon fought in the Golden Gloves.

Jack Burns had held him back as long as he was able. But Kerry had grown to one hundred forty-five pounds stretched over five feet ten inches; he had fought in exhibitions, trained tirelessly. This was the only way he could know how good he was.

His father and mother came to Kerry's first match, part of a crowd numbering a few hundred—Michael somewhat contemptuous of his slender son's chances, Kerry's mother unsure if she could watch. Perhaps, Kerry thought bleakly, it reminded her too much of home.

His first opponent was an Italian boy, Joey Giusti. Shorter and barrel-chested, Joey tried to push Kerry against the ropes and batter him; through the earholes in his head protector, Kerry heard the cheers of Italians as Joey threw punch after punch. Kerry simply burrowed into a crouch and took them—on the arms, the shoulders, the top of his head, everywhere but the chin—as Joey's partisans roared and Kerry's father shouted, "Fight, dammit, fight."

At the end of round one, Kerry had thrown three punches.

Sitting on his bench, Kerry made himself ignore his father's disgust and the puzzlement of the crowd. "Okay," Jack said. "I think he's punched himself out now, and he's taking you lightly. This is your round."

The bell rang, and Joey almost ran across the ring. Kerry could read the contempt in his eyes, the eagerness of a bully.

As Joey uncorked his first left hook, Kerry ducked. The left hand, a little slower now, sailed over his head, then Kerry hit the Italian boy with a left jab to the nose.

Whack.

Joey blinked, stunned, and Kerry hit him with three more. Blood began dribbling from Joey's nose.

Whack, whack, whack.

When Joey covered his face with his gloves, Kerry started on his ribs.

Left, right, left. Sweat flew off Kerry's face as he drove punch after punch into Joey's midsection. The boy gulped, swallowing hard, and his weary arms came lower.

Kerry shot a left jab to the nose again. The shock ran through Kerry's arm. There was a fresh spurt of blood, and suddenly the referee was between them.

In the next three fights, Kerry never had to use his right hand to the jaw.

He and Jack were saving that. The lesson Kerry had begun learning was that training counted, discipline mattered, and strategy paid off—he must last however long a fight had to last. It occurred to Kerry how different he was from the twelve-year-old brawler, not just in skills but in attitude. The pride he felt was new, and he carried it quietly.

Not so his father. "You're finally good for something," Michael said with heavy-handed jocularity.

When it turned out that Kerry's opponent in the finals was a black boy, Marcus Lytton, Michael was full of interest and advice. "I've been watching this kid," he told Kerry. "Flashy, with no guts. Hit him hard, and he'll fold up like a cardboard box." For encouragement, Michael Kilcannon put two hundred dollars on his younger son and made sure that Kerry knew it.

When Kerry entered the ring that night, the gym was filled with blacks and Irish.

A small fight broke out, and the cops dragged away two drunken adults, one white and one black. Kerry could feel the city's tension simmering in the ring. He told himself to concentrate on Marcus Lytton.

Kerry was as prepared as he could be. When Lytton threw his right, Jack had advised, he left himself open for a split second—enough time for Kerry's own right to do real damage. But the main thing was to keep the left jab working, keep Marcus off him, pick up points.

When they introduced Kerry, the Irish began cheering.

For a moment, everything stopped. Kerry could feel himself and Marcus in the ring, spotlighted in the darkness, the focal point of passions far bigger than they. Then the excitement became part of him: his heart pounded, blood sounded in his temples, his slender frame filled with an energy that waited to be used. He stared at Marcus's smooth body, close-cropped hair, serene, almost sweet face, black impenetrable eyes. The bell rang.

Before Kerry reached the center of the ring, Marcus hit him with a three-punch combination.

Kerry's head snapped back. He had never seen hands this fast, had no time to think. Marcus was all over him now—left to the head, right to the stomach, a quick sideways step, then a right to the jaw. Each punch was stiff and had a purpose: Marcus Lytton was not going to punch himself out.

The Irish had stopped cheering.

Marcus hit Kerry in the stomach and followed with a punch to his left eye.

Reeling backward, Kerry knew at once that the eye would close. Marcus came forward.

Kerry ducked a left hook and shot a jab to Lytton's mouthpiece, and the round ended.

He walked back to his corner, the cheers resounding for Marcus, and sat on the bench. Jack squirted water on his head. "You're going to have to get off first," Jack said. "Jabs in his face, then look for the right. You can't lose another round."

As soon as the bell rang, Kerry was across the ring. He jabbed Marcus once, then twice more. Marcus looked startled, and then Kerry staggered him with a right to the forehead; lower, Kerry realized, and the black boy might have gone down. Then they were at each other—punch after punch, ducking, punching again, blocking, Marcus clipping Kerry's face, Kerry banging the other boy's ribs. The round ended with the blacks and the Irish on their feet, fists raised in the air.

Kerry had never felt so tired; it was as if they had fought the last thirty seconds underwater. The pummeling to his forearms, used to block punches, was making them stiff and heavy. His ribs ached.

"Good job," Jack said soothingly. "You took that round, so this is the clincher. Keep him off you, and look for the right."

When Kerry stood, the Irish stood with him and began chanting.

"Kerry, Kerry, Kerry . . ."

"Kill him." Suddenly Kerry felt the hopes, the hatred, the frustration of a city and an era his neighbors thought was dying. There was a sourness in his stomach.

Marcus hit him with a short right hand.

Kerry stepped back, to the elated screams of Newark blacks, righted himself, and hit Marcus coming in. As Marcus's head snapped, Kerry felt the Irish stand again.

"Kill him," the voice yelled once again, and Kerry recog-

nized it as his father's. Kerry's lip was bleeding, his left eye almost shut. Blind will kept him going.

Marcus bore in with a murderous glare and hit Kerry with a three-punch combination. It had become personal: somewhere in the next terrible minute and a half, weathering a rain of punches with his head ringing and his legs unsteady, Kerry learned who was better.

"One more minute," Jack called to him. "Knock him out."

Kerry ducked a punch, pivoted, and hit Marcus in the stomach with everything he had.

Marcus's eyes widened in astonishment and pain, and then the mouthpiece flew from his gaping mouth.

The whites screamed with frenzy. For a brief moment, Kerry saw the punch he had to throw—the right, directly to the black boy's exposed mouth. The fight could end there . . .

"Bring the right," his father bellowed.

Kerry's right hand froze. The punch, when it came, was a moment late, bouncing off Marcus's upraised forearm.

The crowd moaned.

For Kerry, the rest was slow motion. Marcus pedaling backward with wounded eyes. Kerry pursuing with leaden arms and legs, an instant too slow, as if the messages from his brain were taking detours. The final bell. The referee raising Marcus's hand in victory. Blacks standing. Whites quiet in their seats.

The ride home was quiet too—a few words of consolation from his mother, relief that it was over. From his disgusted father came one weary question: "Why are you so afraid to bring the right?"

Kerry said nothing.

He never fought in the ring again. But for several weeks, Kerry went to the gym and punished the heavy bag until his arms gave out.

FOUR

At seventeen, Kerry was as big as he would ever get: five feet ten, one hundred fifty-five pounds. He was a full three inches shorter than his handsome brother, the state senator, that much shorter and sixty pounds lighter than his father, the policeman. Beyond boxing there were not many sports for a boy who was neither big nor fast of foot nor a natural leader, let alone one who still lost his temper in frustration at his own lack of talent.

Finally, Kerry made himself a serviceable soccer goalie. "Serviceable" captured Kerry's senior-year Bs and Cs, no honors won, a slot the next year at Seton Hall University, a few blocks from his home. For the longer range, Michael suggested that Kerry go into the police department. "It's enough for a lot of us," he said, "and no point worrying about why you're not your brother. After all, who is?"

Kerry did not respond. His father's failure was etched in the deepening creases of his face, the bleary eyes, and the only relief he found beyond drink was abusing his wife and belittling his son. Kerry's mother seemed almost broken. Perhaps, Kerry thought, his father's women had been the final degradation.

Michael still sat at the foot of Kerry's bed, but often now he talked of the women he met in bars or on the job, so much younger, so much more admiring. Quietly disgusted, inexperienced himself, Kerry simply hoped that this diversion would help Mary Kilcannon. But the beatings Michael gave her grew worse, especially after his second citation for police brutality: the time Michael had beaten a black man into a concussive state for trying to "escape." It brought him a reprimand, a month's suspension, and a dangerous self-hatred; the night after this happened, Mary Kilcannon needed two stitches on her upper lip.

Kerry drove her to the hospital, despair and hatred warring in his heart. When she came out of the emergency room and into the night, Kerry simply held her, cradling her face against his shoulder.

"Leave him, Mom," he murmured. "Please. It can't be God's will that you should stay."

"It's only the drink." Mary closed her eyes. "Divorce is a sin, Kerry. And what would I do?"

The look in her once-pretty face, now so pale and thin, pierced him. When they came home, Michael Kilcannon lay passed out on his bed. Kerry wondered how it would feel to kill his father in his sleep.

Mary watched her son's face. "I'll call the priest," she said. "I'll call Father Joe."

Far better to call Liam, Kerry thought. Surely there were policemen who cared nothing for his father, prosecutors who owed Liam Dunn a favor. But the priest was his mother's wish.

"Yes," Kerry said. "Call Father Joe."

The next Saturday, the slender, balding priest came to the Kilcannons' home and spoke quietly to Kerry's father. His mother stayed in her room. For several hours, his father sat still and silent, and then, before dinner, he left.

He returned after midnight.

Kerry heard his feet on the stairs—heavy, decisive—then the ponderous breathing as Michael reached the top. He did not stop at Kerry's room.

Kerry's mouth was dry. He lay on his bed, dressed only in boxer shorts, listening for sounds.

His mother screamed with pain too deep for Kerry to bear.

For a moment, Kerry's eyes shut. Then he stood without thinking and went to his parents' room.

His mother lay in a corner, dressing gown ripped. Blood came from her broken nose. Her husband stood over her, staring down as if stunned, for once, by what he had done.

Kerry stood behind him. He felt so much hatred that he barely registered his mother's fear as she saw him.

The look on her face made Michael turn, startled. "You," he said in surprise.

Kerry hit him with a left jab.

Blood spurted from his father's nose. "You little *fuck*," his father cried out.

Kerry hit him three more times, and Michael's nose was as broken as his wife's. All that Kerry wanted was to kill him; what his father might do to him no longer mattered.

Kerry moved forward. . . .

"*No,*" his mother screamed, and Michael Kilcannon threw a savage punch.

It crashed into Kerry's shoulder; he winced with pain as Michael lunged forward to grab him.

Kerry ducked beneath his father's grip and hit him in the midsection.

The soft flesh quivered. Michael grunted in pain but kept coming, eyes focused with implacable anger. Arms blocking Kerry's next punch, he enveloped him in a murderous bear hug.

Helpless, Kerry felt his ribs ache, his lungs empty. His father's whiskey-maddened face was obscured by black spots, then flashes of light. Kerry sensed himself losing consciousness. With a last spasmodic effort, he jammed his knee up into Michael's groin.

Kerry felt his father stiffen. His eyes were great with surprise. Panting for air, Kerry lowered his head and butted his father's chin.

Michael's grip loosened. Kerry writhed free, almost vomiting, then stumbled to his right and sent a flailing left hook to his father's groin.

His father let out a moan of agony, his eyes glazing over. His mother stood, coming between them. "*No,* Kerry, *no.*"

Still breathing hard, Kerry took her in his arms and pushed her to the bed with fearful gentleness. "Stay," he commanded. "Let *me* finish this."

She did not move again.

In the dim bedroom, Kerry turned to his father.

Michael struggled to raise his fists. Kerry moved forward. *Whack, whack, whack.*

His father's eyes were bleeding at the corners. Kerry hit him in the stomach.

His father reeled back, mouth open. Suddenly Kerry thought of Marcus Lytton.

Just as Michael once had ordered, Kerry brought the right.

It smashed into his father's mouth. Kerry felt teeth break, slashing his own hand. His father fell in a heap.

Kerry stood over him, sucking air in ragged breaths, sick with rage and shock and astonishment. His eyes half shut, Michael spat tooth fragments from his bloody mouth.

Kerry knelt in front of him. "Touch her again, Da, and I'll kill you. Unless you kill me in my sleep." He paused for breath, then finished: "I wouldn't count on doing that. I'm too used to waiting up for you."

After that night, Michael Kilcannon never hit his wife again. His younger son never hit anyone.

The next year, at the age of thirty, Kerry's brother James was elected a United States senator.

The Campaign

Day One

ONE

When the telephone rang, Kerry let Clayton Slade answer.

He continued gazing at San Diego Harbor, faintly aware of Clayton's voice, oblivious to the morning sunlight spreading on the water.

Sometime today, he would see her again.

"Kerry?"

Turning, Kerry sensed that his friend had been waiting for some moments; Clayton had the unflinching look that went with reading Kerry's thoughts.

"What is it?" Kerry asked.

"Mason." Pausing, Clayton seemed to watch for his reaction. "He's canceled his campaign appearances."

Kerry felt surprise pull him back into the present. "He can't be withdrawing."

"No way."

Kerry looked at his watch. It was six-thirty. He had a half hour before the strategy meeting, then sixteen hours of speeches, interviews, shaking hands.

"Then he's trying something new," Kerry said, and headed for the shower.

Sitting alone on the patio of the Meridian, Nate Cutler took in the palm trees, the soft ocean breeze, and the curious subtropic light he associated with California when seeking out a metaphor: a dream state; perhaps a film set; or maybe a used-car lot in pastels.

He knew better—California was a complex place. But Nate was a child of the East: a boyhood in Manhattan; college at

Dartmouth; journalism school at Columbia; a career spent in Washington. He found it strange that the next President of the United States might be selected by the thin-blooded citizens of this underzoned shopping mall, most of whom got their political education from watching thirty-second spots on television. Nate liked smoky bars, Scotch, and the snap of autumn; the bite of real political argument among people who knew the issues; the crowded, ethnic urban jangle of Manhattan; the monomania of Washington. In a way that Nate saw as Darwinian, Washington evolved the most perceptive and resourceful journalists; the most tenacious bureaucrats; the most dedicated, intelligent, and ruthless politicians; the most sophisticated and self-aggrandizing professional class that any urban center had to offer; and, in seeming contradiction, the most cynical and incompetent city administration in America, partly because it was the one organ of government that few of these strivers gave a damn about. And then there was that sad by-product of obsessive self-promotion, the used-to-bes: ex-congressmen or appointed officials who, once forcibly retired, discovered that they had focused so intensely on becoming who they formerly were that there was no one left inside.

To Nate, the ecosystem of Washington had an awful, endlessly fascinating ability to seduce and destroy. He had long since faced that his own self-image depended on the conceit that he was too smart and too ambitious to fail. That he would shrink from reporting what he had just learned was strange to him.

For the last few minutes, Nate had been holding the Democratic nomination in his hands.

When he first read the document, Nate had been quiet for a moment, stunned.

"How did you get this?" he had asked.

Katherine Jones lit a cigarette. "All that matters," she said finally, "is whether this document is authentic. And whether the counselor's story checks out."

Nate appraised her. Though her short hair was the color of straw, Katherine Jones reminded him of a Buddha figure without the compassion: gimlet-eyed, heavy-lipped, self-satisfied.

Her skin was flecked with the pink subcutaneous bursts of a heavy smoker.

"Not quite *all*, Katherine. You came to *me*."

Jones drew on her cigarette. Nate sensed that she was trying to appear unperturbed. "Based on what he's said, Kilcannon is *not* a reliable friend to pro-choice women. This document exposes him as an adulterer and an opportunist—"

"If that's true," Nate cut in, "so are any number of congressmen who support your position. Is *that* fair game?"

"If *this* is true," she replied at once, "Kilcannon's also a hypocrite."

"Perhaps."

Jones stubbed the half-smoked cigarette. "Just say you're uncomfortable," she said abruptly, "and we can go to the *Times* or the *Post*."

No, you couldn't, Nate thought. You know that the *Times* still dislikes this kind of story, and that the *Post* would have its own reservations. You chose me because the weekly newsmagazines are struggling to compete with TV and the dailies and because, if we're satisfied this is true, we'll make sure that everyone reads *Newsworld* when it hits the stands on Tuesday. You can imagine me hyping our story on *CNN Weekend* as clearly as you can envision Kilcannon on the cover . . .

You, or whoever is using you for camouflage.

"If my editors decide it's news," Nate answered in an even tone, "we'll print it. But they'll also ask me how my source got a confidential counseling document, whether you've spoken to this counselor, and who put you in touch with her."

Jones paused, then responded with weary patience. "The person I got it from has never met or spoken to the woman who wrote this memorandum. *I've* never met or spoken to her—"

"And this lady won't talk on the record, correct? As you understand it."

Jones shrugged. "Maybe you or your colleagues can persuade her to go public. As it was explained to me, she's come to doubt the morality of her work."

Suddenly Nate grinned. "Politics really *does* make strange domestic partners, doesn't it?"

Jones arranged her mouth in a perfunctory show of amusement. "Sometimes women don't get to choose," she said, then pointed at the document. "You *knew* her, right? When you worked at the *Times*?"

Nate's smile turned sour. "As an old editor of mine used to say, 'we're equal opportunity destroyers.'"

"You *could* be." Jones touched the document with her forefinger. "Because if you run this story, it will bury both Kerry Kilcannon and Costello. No matter who put this conscience-ridden counselor on our radar screen. Or yours."

That was true, Nate guessed. Looking across the table at Jones, he felt very tough and very cold. "You're willing to do all that," he asked, "but you're not endorsing Mason?"

Jones's face closed. "Anthony's Legions endorses pro-choice women, period. But sometimes we're forced to defend reproductive rights the best we can. When fanatics commit murder to force women to have babies, that means stopping 'pro-choice' hypocrites like Kilcannon who wring their hands about abortion so they can siphon votes from either side." Jones lit another cigarette, briskly shaking the match. "But we're not just passing documents to the press. Keep an eye on Kilcannon's Los Angeles event this afternoon . . ."

After she left, Nate reread the counselor's notes.

His job was not a simple one. Fairly often, some politician had accused him of betrayal; in one case, through no fault of Nate's, his source, a legislative aide, had been fired by the offended congressman. But he could not easily imagine ending someone's chance to be President, let alone that of a man he still believed essentially decent. Far less had Nate conceived of destroying a friend for something that, however ethically complex, was at its heart as private as, judging from this document, it was shattering. But what unsettled Nate most was not his personal reservations but another of those unavoidable truths—his own rush of excitement at the start of what could be the political story of almost any journalist's career.

It was seven o'clock. He had roughly an hour to get back to the hotel and catch Kerry Kilcannon's motorcade.

Nate went inside to call his editor.

TWO

Clayton Slade sat at the long wooden table of a meeting room in the San Diego Hyatt, preparing to preside at the morning strategy meeting. With seven days to go, he appeared calm, good-humored; a moment earlier, he had opined to Kerry's California campaign manager, a onetime entertainment lawyer, that politics was "show business for ugly people." Preoccupied as he was, Kerry joined the laughter.

Clayton, Kerry thought once more, was indispensable.

To start, Clayton's equanimity was a godsend. If a campaign was hours of boredom punctuated by panic, the next seven days would be hysteria at warp speed. No one would sleep much; everyone would be on the move; nerves would unravel; tempers would fray; people who had worked together for months would discover with blinding clarity how stupid most of their colleagues were. But Kerry could also feel the adrenaline high of sheer excitement: the men and women in this room had the candidate's total attention, and seven days to win or lose.

Clayton was their center of gravity. He was the person whose authority to speak for Kerry was beyond challenge; who asked the right questions; who made decisions on the spot; who never lost his judgment or his nerve; who could make people do what he asked without raising his voice. While Kerry flew from city to city, Clayton would read the nightly tracking polls; decide what ads to run; soothe major supporters; approve each day's campaign schedule; monitor press coverage; keep an eye on Mason; watch Kerry at key campaign events; help design the daily "spin" that Kit Pace would feed the press; sort out good advice from bad; resolve disputes before they festered; fire anyone who became a problem; and tell the candidate the truth without worrying about his own position.

Kerry would no more have picked another manager than he wanted to be President without Clayton as his chief of staff; though he knew Clayton aspired to be the first black attorney general, that would have to wait. Kerry was not eager to tell him so; sipping the bitter hotel coffee, he reflected wryly that he would never have to if he lost. But that meant losing to Dick Mason, and it was Clayton himself who had formulated Slade's Rule of Order: "The candidate comes first."

"Let's get rolling," Clayton said. "Kerry's got one hour."

Clayton looked around the table. He had made sure that the California working group was big enough for diverse opinion, yet small enough to make decisions and, with luck, minimize leaks.

The five consultants had been picked by both Kerry and himself. The first three decisions had been easy enough. They had chosen Kit Pace, the quick-tongued press secretary, in part because a visible woman aide would help a candidate who had no wife; Frank Wells, the gifted media consultant, because the fact that no one wanted him working for Dick Mason outweighed his reputation for self-aggrandizement; and the campaign pollster Jack Sleeper, young and bearded and cocky, because Kerry liked people who defied conventional wisdom.

The last two advisers were Nat Schlesinger, the wealthy public relations executive, whose personal signature was the bow tie and whose rich experience in presidential politics had begun with James Kilcannon; and Mick Lasker, the sharp-featured California campaign manager, a Los Angeles lawyer in his fifties who had run California for Kerry's brother until the night James was killed. Kerry had understood that using his brother's people provided his insurgent campaign with a built-in network; his chief reluctance had been whether they confused him with James Kilcannon or simply saw him as a second chance for reflected power. The two men were different in manner and appearance: Nat Schlesinger was round and gray and outwardly placid; Mick Lasker a somewhat frenetic man whose assertiveness seemed to mask a certain insecurity. But neither Nat nor Mick was a fool; Clayton had noticed how seldom they mentioned Kerry's brother.

"Let's start with Kerry's schedule," Clayton said to Mick.

"Okay," Mick said in his clipped lawyer's voice. "First, we all know that California's a media state. This isn't New Hampshire—no way Kerry shakes hands with twenty-five million people. The biggest question every day from now till Tuesday is who's won the airwaves for that day: who's running the best ads, whether Kerry's campaign events get the first thirty seconds on the local news and, to a lesser extent, the most column inches above the fold in the next day's paper.

"Our schedule's designed for that. Every day, Kerry will have events in at least three of the five big TV markets: Los Angeles; San Diego; Orange County; the San Francisco Bay Area; and Sacramento and the Central Valley. Roughly ninety percent of the votes."

Mick looked around the table and then focused on Kerry. "Normally, you'd expect to get major coverage only in the markets you've visited that day. But we've worked out 'theme days'—instead of Kerry giving the same speech day after day, he'll have a new emphasis each day, driving home his positions on a major issue our polls and focus groups say works for him. It all makes the case we need people to get: that Kerry's the candidate of change, not a shill for special interests—the one candidate honest enough and brave enough to actually work for *us*."

Pausing, Mick permitted himself a fleeting smile. "By a fortuity of timing, today is women's day—the day Kerry reminds Dick Mason that California women are more than wombs who vote. We start with school loans in San Diego; emphasize day care in Sacramento; talk about expanding family leave in Oakland; and, in Los Angeles, visit a battered women's shelter." He turned to the pollster, Jack Sleeper. "Every poll Jack takes says that combating domestic violence resonates with women across economic lines. And, psychologically, it feeds on the shooting in Boston."

Jack Sleeper nodded. "In our tracking poll last night, Kerry, abortion rights was the number one concern of nine percent of white females most likely to vote. That's a five percent jump, and we think it's mostly a reaction to the killings."

"Be sure to mention the shooting at your event in San Diego," Mick Lasker said to Kerry. "Chances are that's what the local stations will go with. Don't let Mason stay out in front."

As was his custom, Clayton noted, Kerry had let others speak before he did. "And Thursday?" he asked Mick. "Once I've gotten over the shock of Boston?"

"You don't get over it. Tomorrow you highlight your anti-crime positions: using the coast guard to interdict drugs; the equitable application of the death penalty. The major event is a speech to victims' families about gun control." He paused and then finished, "There's no way Dick Mason trumps that one, Kerry."

Kerry stared at him. For a moment, the room was silent; tomorrow was the twelfth anniversary of James's assassination. "I'll want to see that speech," Kerry said softly. "In advance."

Clayton made a note. In a bland voice, as if nothing had happened, he said to Mick, "Let's move on to Friday."

Mick fidgeted with his glasses, seemingly grateful to be rescued. "As of now, that's urban day. An event on job creation and encouraging the high-tech industry and trade with Asia. A brief meeting with black and Hispanic leaders who are for us—"

" 'Brief'?" Kerry asked. "Haven't any of them been shot?"

Mick seemed to wince; the quiet comment reminded Clayton of how mean Kerry could be when someone had crossed the line with him. "What the candidate meant," Clayton said with gentle irony, "is that he *likes* African Americans."

Now Kerry smiled. "Some of them." Turning to Mick, he said in an even tone, "I understand you're being practical, Mick. But I won't treat minorities like a dirty secret."

Mick leaned forward. "Kerry," he said with new intensity, "we *all* wish it were 1968, when people cared about civil rights and Bobby Kennedy carried the California primary because blacks and Latinos voted for him. *I* worked in that campaign, and I marched in Selma my sophomore year in college. I *care* about those things."

Kerry nodded. "I know you do—"

"Then hear me out, please." In mute appeal, Mick turned to Clayton, then went on. "In the last decade, this state passed initiatives against affirmative action and providing health benefits and education to the children of illegal immigrants. Both of which you opposed—"

"Because they were so mindless," Kerry interjected. "You and I will never live to see the day that being a white guy isn't a better deal. And you have illegals in California partly because whites want cheap labor. Why create a generation of disease-ridden juvenile delinquents—"

"*You* know that, Kerry, and a lot of minority leaders admire you for it. But you already have them." Mick nodded toward Jack Sleeper. "Jack can tell you. It doesn't matter that most Californians are now nonwhite: they don't fucking vote in primaries. In the last primary, the nonwhite vote was twenty-three percent, and some of them will vote for Mason no matter what you say. That leaves seventy-seven percent white folks, who'll decide whether you'll be the party's nominee for President. A lot of whom may wonder if you care about them as much as blacks or Latinos."

For the first time, Frank Wells spoke. "I disagree, to some extent. To win, you need to turn out nonwhite voters, and I think you can. What you can't do is alienate suburban whites by spending your precious thirty seconds of airtime surrounded by urban blacks, unless you're in a church and one of their children *has* been shot." Frank's tone was calm and somewhat world-weary. "No one likes it. But first we get you elected, *then* you do what's right. The smart way to turn out black and Hispanic voters is with mailers and phone banks and ads on ethnic radio—things that no one sees on television."

Clayton watched Kerry's gaze grow cool. "I value all of your thoughts," he said politely. "Sometimes hearing out an argument makes things clearer. And this is pretty clear to me. On Friday I'm going to the Latino section of San Francisco and then to South Central Los Angeles. Period."

There was another brief silence, then Mick spread his hands in an expression of despair, half serious and half joking. "I'm just sorry Friday's not Cinco de Mayo."

Everyone laughed.

"I've got twenty minutes," Kerry said. "What other lousy decisions can I make?"

Mick's smile was more relaxed. "A candidate should make speeches, Kerry, not decisions. Decisions are too important."

Defusing tension with self-mockery, Clayton thought again, was a gift that Kerry had. But Mick's rejoinder was more than a joke; because Kerry resisted following his advisers' blueprint by rote, he drew their admiration and frustration in roughly equal measure.

"What about the economy?" Kerry asked. "With all these issues, the whole idea is we're not leaving anyone out. I need to emphasize job security."

"The economy is critical," Mick answered. "You should hit that closer to election day, like Saturday and Sunday, and with ads. But Clayton says you may need to squeeze in a debate."

Kerry nodded. "So Dick Mason told all America last night. I don't think I could duck it if I wanted to."

Mick paused for a moment. "That brings up one more problem, Kerry. Abortion. Mason means to stick it to you."

Kerry raised his eyebrows. Softly, he said, "If you want me to endorse fetal-tissue research, I've already done it."

Jack Sleeper put down his coffee cup. "Dammit, Kerry, the vote in the last primary ran about fifty-eight percent women. It's women who reelected Ellen Penn, she keeps reminding me, partly because she's so pro-choice."

"I know that." Kerry's voice was so patient that Clayton could hear the effort this took. "But Dick Mason's wasting his time. Even with all that's happened, abortion's about the fourteenth issue most people care about; no one ever won just by being pro-choice unless the alternative is some born-again who runs around waving photographs of aborted babies." Kerry's tone took on an edge of irony. "Voters seem to find that in bad taste. Anyhow, what I said the other day about 'life' isn't all that new—people are just listening closer. And it didn't hurt me in Iowa and New Hampshire."

"Kerry's right," Nat Schlesinger put in. The others turned; Nat spoke seldom, and when he did, they listened. "Anguish isn't such a bad position," he went on, "as long as the candidate's unequivocally pro-choice and uses words like 'painful' instead of the word 'life.' Who in their right mind loves abortion?"

"Anthony's Legions," Mick replied. "And any other pro-choice group that believes words like 'painful' grease the slippery slope to back-alley abortions."

Clayton saw Kerry's eyes harden. "Three percent," Kerry said. "If that. I'm pro-choice too, remember? All I've ever said is that an abortion isn't like an appendectomy."

Jack Sleeper frowned. "Before these Boston shootings, Kerry, you were right about the three percent. Maybe four percent in the Bay Area—well-educated white women who see choice as a litmus test.

"Dick Mason's not a fool, and he can read polls as well as anyone. My tracking poll last night has him winning by two percent. Okay, who really knows? But your base in California is women—fifty percent, steady for the last five weeks—and you're losing among men. All Dick wants to do is steal enough of that three percent to win."

"And your advice?"

"Have a 'pro-choice' position you could write on the inside of a matchbook, then run on *your* issues. And *don't* let yourself get drawn into a debate about abortion, for God's sake. Otherwise the media will turn your thirty seconds into guerrilla theater starring the scariest pro-choice women they can shove in front of a Minicam." Jack shook his head, as though in wonderment that he needed to explain this. "You're home free, Kerry. Maybe if there were some character issue Dick could hang this on, like you screwing other people's wives, Dick could use what you've already said to make you look like a phony moralist. But he's got nothing, so he can't. Unless you continue to help him."

For the first time, Clayton saw Kerry's face close, his thoughts drift. Kerry looked at his watch and then around the sterile conference room: art from Sears; artificial flowers; light-cream wallpaper.

"Doesn't someone else have this room reserved?" Kerry asked. "Maybe for an Amway meeting?"

"Anthony's Legions," Kit Pace said dryly.

Clayton shrugged. "We've got another half hour, Kerry,

reviewing Frank's greatest hits. Thirty-second spots of you at your most adorable."

"Hate to miss it," Kerry said, standing. "But I've got *Good Morning San Diego*. A whole fifteen minutes, and it's free. I don't even have to watch myself."

The telephone rang. Clayton rose to answer, listened for a moment, and then signaled Kerry to stay.

"What is it?" Kerry asked.

Clayton took a moment to answer. "Dick Mason just landed in Boston. He's speaking in front of the abortion clinic in an hour."

We should have guessed, Kerry thought. "New federal legislation," he said at once. "Unleash the resources of the FBI. Anything this President can do for him."

The room was quiet again. Then Nat Schlesinger shrugged. "It's still a one-day story."

Frank Wells looked up at Kerry. "Maybe you should go to one of the funerals. Preferably a woman's—the nurse or the receptionist."

"No," Clayton said crisply. "Kerry will call the families. But he won't follow Dick Mason around like a little dog, trying to be more like him. This campaign will be won in California, and we've already got a plan."

He had made himself sound quite confident, Clayton thought. But the look on Kerry's face as he left, pensive and preoccupied, mirrored his own questions.

THREE

At eight o'clock, when Nate Cutler returned to the Hyatt, the press assembly area buzzed with nervous activity.

Some of his colleagues had picked up their laundry—"Turn in by 9:30 p.m., back by 8:00 a.m.," the hand-lettered sign said—and were leaving their suitcases on the stretch of sidewalk designated by the Secret Service. A Secret Service agent and two San Diego cops with a metal detector and a dog trained to sniff out explosives were going through their luggage, which the Service would not return until they reached that night's hotel. No one complained about the security: everyone knew that John Hinckley Jr. had shot Ronald Reagan while standing amidst the press corps; everyone remembered that the last presidential candidate to be murdered was Kerry Kilcannon's brother, shot by an assassin who had insinuated himself among the stage crew. Nate put his Secret Service ID tag around his neck and went to the private dining room reserved for Kilcannon's entourage.

In the opinion of the press corps's resident epicures, the dining experience provided by Kilcannon's people was better than Mason's but worse than Bob Dole's—which, according to campaign lore, had set the modern standard for fine dining. Nate had been too distracted by Katherine Jones to eat, so he scooped up some scrambled eggs and sat with Lee McAlpine from *Time* and Sara Sax from *Newsday*. Lee was small, dark, and feisty; Sara was willowy and sometimes so fey in manner that Nate was still astonished that her reporting was crisp, smart, and to the point. They would provide him with some distraction, Nate hoped; he had been forced to leave his editor a somewhat cryptic message, and the notes folded in the pocket of his sport coat still unsettled him quite badly.

"What's up?" Nate asked Lee.

She shrugged. "You've seen the schedule. This is the day that Kerry Kilcannon reveals the answer to the age-old question 'What do women want?'"

Nate grinned. "What *do* women want? My ex-wife forgot to tell me."

Lee gave Sara a slightly wicked look. "I can only vouch for what Sara wants." She nodded toward Dan Biasi of the Secret Service, dark and slender and earnestly handsome, eating at a table by himself. "Sara spotted him in Portland last night, protecting the candidate from TV reporters who trip over their own feet. Now she wants to fuck him—"

"Lee," Sara protested. *"Jesus."*

Nate turned to her. "Is that true, Sara? You're a Secret Service groupie?"

Sara rolled her eyes toward the ceiling. "He looks nice, okay? I'm thirty, I'm horny, and I haven't been laid in three months."

"Who has?" Nate inquired, and put an avuncular hand on Sara's shoulder. "But, Sara, *we* can help. Look around you— you've got friends here. Why go to an outsider?" Pausing, Nate had a brief ironic thought, then added, "I don't think that's even ethical."

Sara raised her eyebrows and made a show of surveying each table for prospects among the press. Nate and Lee followed her gaze; it stopped abruptly at three burly camera guys from the networks—in attitude and outlook, the blue-collar contingent of the press corps, variously featuring a ponytail, a Dallas Cowboys cap, and a Marine Corps tattoo. When Mr. Tattoo produced a cigar, Lee burst out laughing.

"I rest my case," said Sara.

"What?" Nate asked her. "You were wanting *foreplay*?"

"I thought so," Sara responded. "And not from little red bugs, either."

"The Cowboys hat is the tip-off," Lee observed.

Nate smiled. "Sometimes a hat is only a hat. But a cigar always smells."

Lee gave him a droll look. "We are so clever, aren't we? And it's early yet."

"Nate has an advantage," Sara put in. "He filed his story last night, he doesn't look hungover, and somehow he got a haircut—"

"*I* did the haircut," Lee said.

Nate nodded gravely. "We were going to have sex, but we were both too tired. So I buffed her nails instead."

Abruptly, Lee seemed bored with banter. "What do you two make of what Mason's doing?" she asked. "This Boston trip."

Nate chose not to answer; what he might know made him closemouthed. "You try," he said to Sara. "I've got no idea."

Sara thought for a moment. "I can imagine Mason lying awake thinking, *California killed this guy's brother, and now they'll think they owe him.* It's not just the abortion issue; Mason's looking to borrow a little sympathy, especially from women, remind them of what a feeling guy he is. I mean, Boston's not Oklahoma City, but it's the only tragedy we've got. At least until some airplane crashes."

Lee nodded, then turned to Nate. "No theory at all? You've usually got two or three."

Never forget, Nate told himself, *how perceptive these women are.* "Not a one," he answered, and then his pager beeped.

Edgy, Nate checked the message, then stood. "Better run," he said. "Bus leaves in fifteen minutes."

Lee gave him a probing look. "What is it?" she asked. "The Pulitzer Prize Committee?"

Nate smiled. "Yeah. They're calling to apologize."

He went quickly to find a pay phone—something with a hard connection, where no one could overhear.

Nate hunched inside the open phone booth. Next to him, a pompous businessman was talking about computer chips; Nate's editor, Jane Booth, spoke as loudly as she could. Her office door was shut, she had assured him, and no one else would hear.

"It's a killer story," she said, "with two big questions: 'Can we source it?' and if we can, 'Will we decide to print it?'"

Nate could already imagine an agonized series of editorial

meetings—the political editor, the managing editor, the executive editor, and even the publisher would have to approve every step their reporters took, and the decision as to whether *Newsworld* should change the course of this campaign would be weighed with care. Substance was important, and so was appearance: the press's fascination with itself was such that if *Newsworld* printed the story, their competitors would follow with ten other stories, detailing how the decision was made to end a presidential candidacy and, in all likelihood, the career of a now-famous woman journalist.

"What do you think?" Nate asked. "If it's true, will we print it?"

"We damned well *should.*" Jane's tone was combative, as if she was preparing for argument with her male colleagues; Nate could imagine her, gray-haired and gaunt and more than a little intense, pacing as she spoke. "To me, the first thing that makes this story a legitimate public issue is that it sheds real light on who Kilcannon is. People should know what drives him."

Nate glanced at the man next to him. "The idea that we're *explaining* him ignores the fact that we'd be *eliminating* him. Were we just explaining Gary Hart? Or was there a serious question of judgment there?"

"There's one *here* too," Jane snapped. "Kilcannon was sleeping with a reporter who covered him. That's not like fucking some model for No Excuses jeans."

"So pull up what she wrote about him," Nate replied. "Maybe she gave him a break, maybe she didn't."

"Do you think *we* should give *her* a break, Nate?"

The question had an edge and more than one dimension—whether Nate would push the story; whether he was soft on Lara Costello; whether he'd gone native after three months of covering Kilcannon; whether he really wanted some competitor to beat them. "No," he said in a lower voice. "But I've got a confidential counseling document which describes a woman in emotional extremity—one who only felt comfortable talking to a stranger who was ethically bound to protect her secrets. I remember some of the things I told my marriage counselor—"

"Nobody cares about your little kinks," Jane cut in, "and no one should. You're not running for President."

"Believe me, I never would. But I understand your point."

Mollified, Jane spoke in a practical tone. "The real problem is sourcing it. Our rule is still two sources, even now, and you say this woman doesn't want to speak on the record."

"The *real* problem," Nate answered, "is proving it. In theory, any nut job with a political ax to grind could put any fiction in a document and swear to God it's true."

"You believe Costello was a patient, don't you? Would this counselor make that up too?"

"Probably not, and we can probably prove it, even if *that's* supposed to be confidential." Nate checked his watch. "Look, Jane, only two people in the world know the truth. At some point we're going to have to ask them, even if all we get is lies. I need to know when and how to approach Kilcannon."

There was a thoughtful pause. "Wait on that, okay? Costello's here in Washington and easier to get to. I'll ask someone who knows her to invite her out to lunch."

Imagining Lara's feelings, Nate became queasy at the thought of such an ambush. He knew the pressures *Newsworld* could put on her, the implicit threats to check with neighbors or ex-colleagues should Lara deny an affair. He remembered an incident during the last campaign, when several second-tier papers tracked a bogus rumor that a conservative presidential candidate had contracted AIDS. The supposed source had been a nurse at a private clinic. One reporter had threatened her; another sent her roses; still another arrived at her home with toys for her cat; several more descended on her neighbors and then her employer. Finally, the woman had quit her job and moved.

"If someone saw Lara leave his apartment at five in the morning," Nate said at last, "that looks like an affair. An affair makes this counselor's story a lot more credible. And if Lara claims she never saw Kilcannon except in public, and *that* looks like a lie, then she's a lot less credible about everything. The catch is that once we start visiting friends and neighbors, our competition is likely to find out."

"True," Jane answered. "What I'm recommending is that

this afternoon we send someone to knock on this counselor's door, at the address you gave me in Maryland."

"Be sure to ask her who she gave this memo to. If I understand this woman's motivation, I can't imagine her calling Anthony's Legions. Even Katherine Jones swears the lady never talked to them."

"So where *do* you think this is coming from?"

"I've been trying to figure that out." Glancing at the adjacent booth, Nate saw that the businessman was gone. "My thought is the GOP. Maybe they think Dick Mason will be easier to beat."

"Wouldn't they wait until Kilcannon was nominated," Jane said promptly, "*then* let this out? That way they'd win in a walk."

That made sense, Nate admitted to himself. "Suppose they think the counselor's shaky?" Nate responded. "If it's Mason, wouldn't one of his people go to whatever reporter he's closest to and say, 'I've got the story of a lifetime, and the deal is it didn't come from us'? Why so elliptical, unless it's the Republicans and they don't want to get caught picking the Democratic nominee?"

"Maybe. Anyhow, we'll try to trace how the memo got to Katherine Jones." Jane's tone became thoughtful. "The timing of this argues for Dick Mason, you know. He's the one who needs this out before Tuesday."

Already, Nate thought, they had focused on the campaign—who was doing what to whom. Lara Costello was beginning to seem like the victim of a drive-by shooting, or maybe one of the three dead people in Boston Dick Mason was using for fodder. But Jane had reminded him of a central fact: whoever had planted the story, *Newsworld* did not control it, and the leaker's desire to see it printed would be as keen as the instincts of Nate's rivals.

"If you're right about Mason," he said, "his campaign may slip it to someone else unless we move by the weekend. Even to the Net or the *National Enquirer*, if Mason's desperate enough. He'll hope that some paper in the mainstream press will report what the *Enquirer*'s reporting and that the rest of us will fall into line. With great reluctance, of course."

Jane laughed softly. "As someone once said, 'Politics ain't beanbag.' Neither is journalism."

"Well," Nate said, "better run. Tell me when to approach Kilcannon's press secretary. And leave a message on voice mail to let me know what's happening."

"Will do."

"Oh, and one more thing. Send someone over to my apartment, and FedEx me some lightweight clothes I can wear in paradise. This wool sport coat is feeling like chain mail."

Jane laughed again. "I'll have them send your Hawaiian shirts," she promised.

Nate got to the press buses with about a minute to go.

There were a couple of seats left in the third bus. Nate walked with his briefcase to the back and found himself sitting next to the cameraman from NBC, he of the Dallas Cowboys cap. The man nodded curtly; Nate generally did not condescend to talk to him, and now felt somewhat elitist about using him for sport this morning.

"So," Nate asked, "how's Mike Devore doing?"

The man shrugged. "Pissed, mostly. He's spending the next month in an ankle cast."

"If you talk to him, say hi. Tell him for me that he's gone to a better place."

The cameraman laughed. Encouraged, Nate asked, "So who's replacing him?"

This brought a genuine smile. "With all respect to Mike, we've gotten an upgrade. It's Lara Costello."

Nate sat back. "*Lara,*" he said at length. "Yeah, it'll be nice to see her."

FOUR

A few minutes after Kerry left the meeting, Kit Pace had checked her watch.

"I've got to get downstairs," she said. "Start telling our friends in the press what we'll be accomplishing at every stop. They get so anxious when they're not plugged in."

Clayton smiled; Kit had proved expert at roving through the back of the plane, feeding tidbits to the media and telling them what to think. "I guess by the end of the day," he said dryly, "Kerry will have overachieved again."

Kit smiled back. "He's astonishing that way. Thing is, some of our press pals are so lazy that they're grateful for my help. Not the best ones, of course, but even *they* respond to kindness."

Mick Lasker was refilling his cup at the coffee urn. Over his shoulder, he asked, "What kind of access are you giving them?"

Kit stood. "I don't see why we change now, Mick. Every so often, Kerry goes back to the press section, says hello, answers questions—"

"Because"—Mick turned to her now—"he's a little bit of a freelancer, and now the stakes are too high for any fuck-ups. Maybe you should rein him in some."

A shadow of annoyance crossed Kit's face. "I don't know what his brother was like, but Kerry won't be handled. And shouldn't be. Kerry's funny, charming when he cares to be, and the press knows he doesn't bullshit them." Kit folded her arms. "I've been watching this for three months now. As much as they can let themselves, our reporters have started rooting for him. I'm not going to tell Kerry Kilcannon to start hiding in the john."

Clayton turned to Mick. "Kit's got a problem, Mick. The candidate thinks *he* actually won those primaries. It's the damnedest thing."

Clayton watched Mick measure the gulf between them: Clayton the friend of the candidate, who was there because he believed in Kerry; Mick the professional adviser, who, but for his association with James Kilcannon, might have worked for Mason. "At least," Mick said at last, "Kit ought to prioritize access. For the next seven days, the national press matters a whole lot less than the local TV stations and the major California papers—the *L.A. Times*, the *Chronicle*, the *Mercury News*, the *Sacramento Bee*. *They* should get any formal interviews."

"You agree?" Clayton asked Kit.

She nodded; once again, Clayton was grateful that he never had to prod her to make the right judgment. "Yeah," she said. "That much makes sense. Even the bigfoot reporters will understand why we're doing that."

"Okay," Clayton said. "Thanks."

Hastily, Kit headed out the door.

"The big decision," Frank Wells said at once, "is how much we spend in advertising."

Clayton nodded. "Right now, we've got about four million until we hit the federal spending cap. After that, we can't spend money until we win the nomination. California's a black hole; you spend two million just to lose. Shoot all our cash now, and Kerry's living off the land."

"*Don't* shoot all your money now," Frank retorted, "and there's no nomination to worry about."

"You think that's right?" Clayton asked Jack Sleeper.

The pollster stared at the table. "It's close," he said at last. "The biggest difference will be advertising, no question."

"Let's see the ads," Clayton ordered.

Frank Wells walked to the video monitor. "The basic idea," he began, "is compare and contrast."

"In terms of guts, Kerry kicks Mason's ass. Dick's got the passion of a Norwegian dairy farmer and the spine of a mollusk. Mention any interest group—the AFL-CIO, the wrinklies, the teachers unions, Anthony's Legions—and Dick drops his pants and starts bending over. He's the ultimate pander bear."

"People know that," Jack Sleeper told Clayton. "Poll Californians on 'independence' and 'integrity,' and Kerry runs ahead. The problem is, compared to a known quantity like Mason, Kerry feels like a risk. Passion and spontaneity can be a little unsettling in a President."

"These ads make a virtue of that," Frank explained. "Plus the fact that Kerry's young, good-looking, smart, and the fastest-rising politician since his brother. For a lot of upwardly mobile voters, boomers especially, he's an idealized version of who *they* want to be." Frank paused a moment. "The only problem, Clayton, is he's got no family except a mother he won't let us use and an ex-wife he won't let us ask for help."

"Don't ever try," Clayton said sharply. "You leave Meg right where she is, teaching school in New Jersey."

Frank looked defensive. "I was hoping to remind people that Kerry isn't gay. That's out there, you know."

Clayton gave him a cold smile. "It's good for ten percent in San Francisco. Let it be, Frank."

"Why not his mother?" Jack Sleeper said. "Doesn't he like *her*?"

Beneath the frustrated question, Clayton knew, was something deeper: the sense that Kerry was an enigma, too private for a politician, and that only Clayton could crack the code. "That's just it," Clayton said. "Kerry likes his mother very much.

"For my part, I think people want a President, not a group-therapy facilitator. Some mystery is not so bad, and voters like it that Kerry has an idea of himself that's separate from politics." He turned to Frank. "Show me the positive ads first."

Frank put in a cassette and pushed the button. "You should know," Jack Sleeper put in, "that we've tested Frank's ads with focus groups. These are the ones that rated highest."

The first ad was from campaign footage, Kerry with a group of multiracial kids at an inner-city school, talking about education. "I guess minority children are less threatening to white folks than their parents," Clayton commented. "Smaller, anyhow."

"Yup," Frank answered crisply, and put on the next ad; Kerry in a living room with fertile-looking young adults, talking about gun control. As was his habit, Kerry had loosened his tie and rolled up his shirtsleeves, and his hair was slightly mussed. It was easy to imagine him white-water rafting.

"Killing people," Kerry was saying, *"is the only point of an assault weapon. It's time we held the gun lobby and gun traffickers responsible for these kinds of murders . . ."*

"Good," Clayton remarked.

Frank kept watching the screen. "Mason's against assault weapons," he said, "but can you imagine him taking on the gun lobby? Listen to him, and you'd think all these gun nuts found their AK-forty-sevens under cabbage leaves."

"At least until Boston," Clayton rejoined. "Now we'll see . . ."

"Kilcannon," the ad's voice-over finished. *"The truth, for a change."*

"What about Social Security?" Mick Lasker asked. "Mason's new ads attack Kerry's reform proposals."

"That just shows Kerry's willingness to make a decision," Frank said. "Even if Dick says Kerry's going to cut benefits, Mason's approach is too 'old politics' to work anymore."

"People aren't that stupid," Jack Sleeper concurred. "Our polling shows they know Social Security's in trouble. And more gen X-ers believe in extraterrestrials than that they'll ever see a nickel from Uncle Sam. Dick comes off like the smarmy principal all the kids know is lying."

On the screen, another ad appeared.

"Americans know," Dick Mason said, *"that I'll fight to protect their air and water . . ."*

The picture shifted to a view of the Vice President walking on an oil-befouled beach in hip boots. *"For the last four years,"* the voice-over said, *"Dick Mason has accepted more contributions from corporate polluters than any previous presidential candidate."*

On the beach, Dick Mason shook his head in dismay.

"Sorry, Dick," the voice said again. *"It's too late . . ."*

"None of us want to run too many ads," Clayton observed.

"Rather than blur our message, I say we stick to using Kerry. Dick looks pretty stupid in the hip boots, but not as dumb as Dukakis in the tank."

Frank glanced at Jack Sleeper, then, surreptitiously, at Nat Schlesinger. "There's one more spot, Clayton, that Frank and I wanted to talk about."

He sounded unusually tentative. "What's that?" Clayton asked.

"It goes back to our focus groups," Frank said. "Okay, Kerry's got no wife, no kids, and, for political purposes, no mom. But what he does have going, at the risk of being irreverent, is the Holy Ghost."

Clayton looked from Frank to Jack. "James Kilcannon," he said in a flat voice.

"Look," Jack Sleeper urged. "Think about what made Bobby Kennedy work. Part of it was the association with his brother and, in an odd way, the hope of reincarnation.

"Maybe, people thought, we can bring Jack back to life—make it up to the Kennedys, and to ourselves. In a way, repeat history.

"Some people found Bobby strident and authoritarian. Like Mick was saying, some people think *Kerry*'s a little scary—too combative and confrontational. But emotion and Jack Kennedy took Bobby a long way. Even if he was never President, James Kilcannon can help carry his kid brother across the river . . ."

"The river Styx?" Clayton asked. "What are you suggesting?"

Jack Sleeper stood, hands resting on the back of his chair. "We've focus-grouped James Kilcannon—how voters remember him. His favorables are something like eighty-three percent." He looked around the table. "Frank's preparing an ad using clips from Jamie's last campaign. It'll be ready tomorrow."

"What will we call it," Nat Schlesinger inquired. " 'Necrophilia'?"

They turned to him, silent, waiting. It was Nat Schlesinger who, as James Kilcannon's press secretary, had been there when he died; Nat who had announced his death to the press corps, with tears in his eyes. "I loved James Kilcannon," Nat said in the same quiet voice. "Oh, he was a pretty cool character, but I always figured he had his reasons, and he would have made this country proud.

"But that's not why I have such a problem with this. Jamie was also the smartest politician I've ever known—smarter than Kerry, which, in some ways, is to Kerry's credit. And what James Kilcannon would say if you managed to resurrect him is that this is a question of touch, and that you don't need to beat folks over the head to remind them Kerry is his brother. Voters won't like it."

"Not just *voters*," Clayton added bluntly. "Kerry. Where have you two been?"

"It works," Frank Wells shot back. "You can look at Jack's polling data. Dick Mason would do this in a nanosecond."

"You tell Kerry that, Frank. That'll turn him around."

Frank's diplomat's face was harder now. "He's gotten himself in trouble on abortion. He should think about getting himself out before Mason kills him with it.

"I have a favorite metaphor, Clayton. If all your friends came to you with a red box and told you that you had to hold it for four years and never drop it, because if you dropped it the whole goddamned world would blow up, you and every other normal person we know would hand the box back in a heartbeat.

"But every four years there are ten guys who come forward and say, 'Give me the fucking box.' And the guy who wins is the one who'll kill all the other guys just for the chance to hold it.

"To me, that guy's still Dick Mason. It's time for Kerry to stop treating his brother like a forbidden subject." Frank leaned forward. "I'll show him the ad. Jack will show him the polling data. We'll take the heat for it. But you let *Kerry* decide how much he wants the box."

Clayton stared at him. "All right," he said. "We'll do that. Tomorrow. It will absolutely make Kerry Kilcannon's day."

Frank's gaze broke, and he looked suddenly weary. "Whether or not we run that ad, there's the question of whether we go for it—sink our money into California, or not. Which is part of the same question."

"Maybe not," Mick Lasker countered. "I know Ellen Penn is calling every other day, saying go for broke. But that's about *her* reputation; she doesn't want Kerry to embarrass her by losing in her state, and she doesn't want to be blamed if he does.

"California isn't winner-take-all. Kerry could lose a close election here and still pick up almost half our delegates."

"If Kerry loses," Jack Sleeper snapped, "it's over. Haven't we been claiming that the party *has* to ditch Dick Mason because only Kerry can win."

Clayton did not comment. Instead he got up, removed the tape from the television, and turned on CNN.

On the screen, Dick Mason was standing in front of the abortion clinic, speaking in a strong, clear voice. "*In the name of those who died here, I say to the purveyors of terror and violence: No more. Not one more life, not one more woman deprived of her legal rights . . .*"

Clayton turned from the television. "Spend the money," he said.

FIVE

Sean Burke stood alone on the corner.

Van Ness Avenue was slick with rain; a moment before, a Muni bus filled with commuters had splashed through a puddle of water and soaked the bottom of Sean's jeans. Chilled, he gazed at the abandoned auto showroom across the street, papered with signs that read "Kilcannon for President."

Sean felt disoriented. It was nine in the morning; by this time yesterday he had killed the abortionist and his accomplices, three time zones away. All that seemed real was the woman he had spared.

Sean could see her frightened green eyes, could imagine her describing to the police artist a killer who had babbled nonsense while the receptionist bled on the carpet. Soon they would show the sketch to members of Operation Life.

Who would be the one to give him up? he wondered. Which one would see a reproach to his own cowardice and, out of shame, look up from his portrait and put a name to Sean's face?

Perhaps Paul Terris. He would remember their disagreements and, in tones of false reluctance, say, "It's a little like Sean Burke." And then the police would go to Father Brian and find that Sean had vanished.

The plane ticket would bring them here. His last hope was that he had vanished in the maze of a new city, under a new name, long enough to do what must be done.

Seven days, and he could not make himself cross the street.

Hands in his pockets, Sean felt the cool drizzle on his face and hair, smelled the exhaust fumes of a hundred cars. San Francisco was ugly, he decided: low-slung buildings, cheap restaurants, no trees, an anonymous dirty six-lane avenue that could have been anywhere.

A patrol car stopped at the curb beside him.

Sean stepped back, looking for a place to run. There was nothing but a grid of streets he did not know.

Heart racing, he looked back at the police car. It had only stopped for a traffic light; the cop in the passenger seat gazed ahead, sipping coffee from a styrofoam cup. This was a warning, Sean realized. The lining of his stomach felt bloody and raw. His pocket seemed empty without a gun.

When the light changed, Sean crossed the street and forced himself to enter Kilcannon headquarters.

The building felt as vast as a church, was as shabby as an old hotel. Voices issued from behind cheap partitions and echoed from tile floors to fifty-foot ceilings, filigreed with fading gold.

A receptionist of indeterminate race and age sat at a cafeteria table. Her skin looked dry, her face severe; her black eyes were opaque as obsidian. Remembering the eyes of another receptionist in her last moments of life, Sean looked away.

"I'm here for Senator Kilcannon," he said.

"All right. Please have a seat and fill out a volunteer form."

It took some moments. With the awkwardness of a child

learning cursive, Sean wrote the name "John Kelly." The only address he gave was "Golden Gate Motel."

The next section asked for his activity preference. The list of tasks meant nothing to him; all Sean cared about was that Kilcannon would come to San Francisco, that headquarters must surely know his schedule. He put a check mark near any job that might keep him in this building.

The last question was "Best times to volunteer."

Carefully, he wrote "Every day until next Tuesday" and gave the form to the receptionist.

Silent, she read it. "Looks like you've got some time for us," she said, and picked up the telephone.

As the plane took off from San Diego, Kerry murmured to Kevin Loughery, "Miles to go before we sleep."

He was tired yet fully awake, like someone on a coffee jag. He had already done *Good Morning San Diego* and given his first speech. Ahead for the day were stops in Sacramento, then Oakland, then Los Angeles, and finally a cocktail party in Beverly Hills, where film stars and studio heads would lecture him on public policy. "All most of them want is proximity to power," Clayton told him. "Maybe a sleepover in the White House. Just worry about the ones who want to sleep with *you*."

Tomorrow morning, Kerry realized, Lara would be in the rear of the plane.

Somehow he would make himself meander through the press section, chatting with the others, until he reached where Lara was sitting and, as twenty reporters listened, say how nice it was to see her. The moment would feel like death—pretending that he had never looked into her face and wished their lives were different . . .

He stared out the window.

Kerry did not know how much time had passed before he noticed that the ground beneath was green and fertile, rich fields of crops bisected by irrigation ditches. It was no longer two years ago, when Lara and he could still make choices: the only question he faced now was "Are you good enough?" That was the question he asked himself in the privacy of flight, watching the lights of a city at night; or crossing the gray, jagged Rockies; or, as now, passing over farmlands that fed so many so well.

Are you good enough?

Twelve years ago, tomorrow, Jamie had died before he could find that out.

Next to Kerry, Kevin Loughery was quiet.

For another moment, Kerry watched the earth below them, coming closer. "Have you been back to Vailsburg lately?" he asked.

Kevin shook his head. "Not since Christmas," he answered. "I took my mother to Mass at Sacred Heart, and things were so different it brought tears to her eyes. When she lived there, she said, the church was overflowing; even the balconies were full. Now it seems like a ghost town to her—rows of empty pews, and only a few of the old faces, the ones who couldn't leave."

Kerry thought of Liam Dunn, now buried near the church; Kerry had taken Kevin on the journey of politics much as Liam had, towing Kerry to the bars on Sunday. "It was a fine place," Kerry answered. "If only we could have adapted instead of moving away. I wonder about that, now and then."

He fell quiet again. Then the wheels touched down, bounced once, and settled onto the runway. The motorcade was waiting.

The man who emerged from behind the partitions had curly hair, a high forehead, and a pleasant, easy smile. In T-shirt and blue jeans, he was loose-limbed, lean; he could not have been much older than Sean. He glanced at the form and then gave Sean a firm, dry handshake.

"Rick Ginsberg," he said. "It's great you're giving us so much time."

Sean stared at the tiles. "I'm kind of on vacation."

"You're not from here, I guess."

Sean shook his head. "New York City. Since I was twelve."

Ginsberg smiled again. "Yeah? I went to NYU. Which borough you live in?"

This morning, Sean had studied the guidebook again; the name of the traditional Irish section was as close to truth as he could come. "Manhattan," he said with hesitance. "Yorkville."

The word had no more meaning to him than a name on a Monopoly board.

Ginsberg cocked his head. "Really changed, hasn't it. Yuppified."

Sean thought of his own childhood. "They're all like that." His voice was soft, a monotone. "People move away. But maybe I'll go back . . ."

The sentence trailed off. As if concerned that Sean felt tentative, Ginsberg said, "Not for seven days, I hope. Kerry Kilcannon *needs* us."

Sean shoved his hands into his pockets. "I've always liked him."

Ginsberg nodded vigorously. "The first time I saw the senator," he told Sean, "he was trying to sell a roomful of college kids on compulsory national service. 'This country's given us so much,' he said. 'We owe it more than paying interest on our charge cards.'

"Afterward, I talked with him. He has this quiet way of listening, like he's taking in everything you say, and his eyes never leave you. It sounds intense, but there's something almost gentle about him, and he has a terrific sense of humor." Ginsberg shrugged, as if helpless to explain. "It makes you wish that everyone could meet him."

Slowly, Sean nodded. "I want to. Sometime."

Ginsberg paused, letting the hope linger, and then touched Sean on the shoulder. "Come on," he said. "Let's find you something to do."

It was not until Kerry Kilcannon finished his speech—a call for expanded day care—that Nate was able to phone his editor.

He stood outside the filing center, a makeshift tent by the landing strip at Mather Field, speaking into his cellular as softly as he could.

"Lara Costello's coming here," he said. "The regular NBC guy broke his ankle."

For a moment, Jane Booth was silent. "I just can't believe her arrogance, Nate. Or her lack of integrity."

Nate looked around him; about thirty feet away, Lee McAlpine had emerged from the tent, squinting in the sun.

"Maybe Lara was stuck," he murmured to Jane. "Who would want to do this . . . ?"

"No one *should* do this. Period." Jane's tone was cool, insistent. "You're not doubting it's a story *now*, are you?"

The question did not require an answer. "Have you gotten to her counselor?" Nate asked.

"Sheila Kahn is out in Maryland now, trying to talk to her." Jane paused again. "When is Costello showing up?"

"This afternoon."

"Because *you're* going to sit down with her. A drink after hours—two old colleagues meeting on the road."

Nate hesitated, imagining Lara's face as he slid the memorandum across the table. Still quiet, he asked, "You want me to confront her? This soon?"

"I won't know how soon until I hear about this counselor. Call me at home, as close to nine eastern time as you can make it." Jane's voice slowed a little. "You know, I really can't believe she let them send her. Not if the story's true."

Lee McAlpine was watching him, Nate realized. "If the story's true," he answered, "how could Lara tell anyone?"

SIX

Sean stood with Rick Ginsberg in a vast open area where perhaps twenty volunteers sat at long tables with telephones in front of them. The volunteers placed call after call, reading from a script; these were the disembodied voices Sean had heard in the reception area.

"We've been open since January," Ginsberg explained. "But with only seven days to go, our job is to identify the Kilcannon voters and get them to the polls. This is where we need you."

Sean was silent. That the volunteers were as young as he made him feel even more apprehensive, and many were Asian or Latino or black, the ones his father had despised. It was like the first-day-of-school feeling when he was eleven— wondering what the others knew about him, or thought they knew. The loneliness had never left him.

"You have a lot of people here," Sean said. It was part obser- vation, part argument; perhaps Rick would find him something else to do.

Ginsberg nodded. "We have more people come in at night, the ones with jobs. But our outreach coordinator has done great at finding college kids and minorities, which is something the senator wants."

Sean stayed quiet, looking restlessly around him. But Gins- berg did not seem to notice. "Anyhow," he went on, "it's pretty simple. Each volunteer is given a list of voters, coded by precinct, neighborhood, party registration, and, if possible, eth- nicity. By election day every precinct captain should have a list of identified Kilcannon voters to get to the polls—either by mail or in person.

"This election is too damned close. But if every volunteer in every headquarters does his or her job, I think Kerry Kil- cannon's our next President." He turned to Sean, resting one hand on his shoulder. "Once you're up and running, the goal is twenty calls an hour. All you need is to follow the script we give you."

Sean fought his desire to recoil, felt desperate to leave. He would never get close to Kilcannon *this* way, trapped making calls like some salesman.

Behind the volunteers, a slim Asian man stood watching them. "Who's that?" Sean asked.

"Jeff Lee, the phone bank supervisor. He'll show you what to do."

Still Sean hesitated. Rick studied him a moment, then said, "I'll start you out, John. It won't take but a minute."

Walking across the room, Sean felt like a prisoner. It was like joining Operation Life, he tried to tell himself; after that, people started to accept him. At least for a time . . .

Rick found him a seat at the end of a long table, next to a

slender strawberry blonde with a ponytail and a sweatshirt with "USF" in red block letters. Hanging up the telephone, she made an entry in her log; in profile, her face was delicate, like china, her eyes cornflower blue.

"Okay," Rick said, pointing to Sean's place. "By every telephone is a computer list of names to call; a form to total up the number of contacts for that day and who's for Kilcannon or Mason; and a script. Just place the call, follow the instructions, and record what happened—contact, no contact, who each contact's voting for." Ginsberg angled his head toward the supervisor. "Any problems, Jeff will help you."

He patted Sean on the back and left.

Motionless, Sean read the script in front of him, line by line.

"Hello. My name is [volunteer name] and I'm calling from the Kilcannon for President campaign.

"Is [voter's name] home?"

If no, "May I leave a message?"

If yes, "Great! I'm calling to see whether you intend to support Kerry Kilcannon for President . . ."

Yesterday, Sean thought, he had executed three people in the name of life. Now he was about to shill for an immoral man who sanctioned killers like Dr. Bowe.

Sean felt the eyes of the Asian man, watching. Next to him, the blond woman placed another call. "Hello," she said brightly. "I'm Kate Feeney . . ."

Sean picked up the telephone, stabbing out the first number on his list.

The phone screeched, the sound of a misdialed call. Sean put down the phone and dialed again.

Screech.

Sean slammed down the telephone. His face was red, his anger like a pulse.

Kate Feeney seemed to hesitate, then turned to him. In a pleasant voice, she said, "I guess Rick forgot to tell you about the phone system. You dial nine first."

Caught in his frustration, Sean did not know what to say. Smiling, Kate reached over, hit 9 on the phone pad, and listened for a dial tone.

"Here," she said. "It works."

Sean took the phone from her hand. Her skin, grazing his, was cool. "Thanks," he managed to say. "That was stupid."

"The phone system's stupid," she answered. "What are we supposed to do—call each other?"

Reluctantly, Sean turned from her and dialed the number again: Robert Walker, 2406 Miles Avenue, Oakland.

"Hello?" a black voice answered.

Sean swallowed. "This is John Kelly. I'm calling to see if you're supporting Kerry Kilcannon for President."

"Oh, yes," the voice answered promptly. "He reminds me of his brother."

All at once, Sean felt relieved. "Would you like to vote by mail?" he asked. "We can send you a ballot."

"Sure, Mr. Kelly. That would be just fine."

It was strange, Sean thought; suddenly he was connected to this man. He took Walker through the questions and then, thanking him, hung up.

Kate Feeney looked up from her computer log. "A Kilcannon voter on your first hit," she said. "Not bad."

Sean paused for a moment. Picking up the telephone, he felt more confident.

"Hello," he began. "My name is John Kelly, and I'm with Kilcannon for President."

After the plane took off, Kerry called two supporters, and then Kit Pace returned from the press section and sat across from him.

"Want to see a tape of Mason's speech?" she asked.

Kerry smiled wearily. "I don't know, Kit. Got *Forrest Gump*?"

"More or less," she answered, and put the tape of Mason into the TV monitor.

Together, they waited—Kerry, Kit, Kevin, and two agents from the Secret Service—and then Dick Mason's face appeared.

He looked somber, dignified, and his voice was quiet and measured. Kerry knew at once that Dick would find the right aura, the right tone.

"We have come to Boston," Mason began, *"to decry the*

tragedy which happened here—the death of three innocent people, a man and two women.

"The only greater tragedy would be to strip their deaths of meaning.

"In the deepest sense, it does not matter whether as individuals we favor or oppose the right to choose. What matters most is that we all agree that violence has no place in this debate, and that murder must end."

The camera panned wider. Standing behind the Vice President was a slender woman in black—the widow of Dr. Bowe. Her face was pale, stoic. Kerry felt for her loss, and that her grief was on public display.

"Who but Dick would ask her?" Kerry murmured.

Kit shrugged. "Maybe she wanted to. Anyhow, it's effective..."

"But these murders," Mason said with sudden sternness, *"did not happen in a vacuum. In a society whose laws protect the right to choose, that choice must be made in the privacy of our homes and in the depth of our hearts—with care, compassion, and, we hope, a due appreciation of all that is involved.*

"But the time for public equivocation has passed. It is imperative that those in public life protect this private right—without hesitance, without apology, without exception—or we ourselves become responsible."

"I guess that's me," Kerry said. "Hesitant, apologetic. I might as well have murdered them..."

"No more." Pausing, the Vice President gazed into the camera. *"In the name of those who died here, I say to the purveyors of terror and violence—*no more. *Not one more life, not one more woman deprived of her legal rights—"*

Kerry stood, snapping off the monitor. Turning, he said, "I think I get the drift."

Kit gazed up at him. "That's the lead on the six o'clock news, Kerry. All you can do is stay out of Mason's way."

Kerry sat, feeling his anger become determination. "All I can do," he said, "is go to Los Angeles and speak about battered women. Maybe some of it will filter through the lens."

* * *

When they landed in Los Angeles, Nate Cutler saw a black stretch limousine waiting near the press buses.

Nate paused, letting his colleagues pass him. Debarking wearily from the rear of the plane, they straggled toward the press buses as if they were bound for a detention camp. As always, Kilcannon left from the front. The senator was a distant figure, shaking hands with local politicians, shepherding a congressman to a black Lincoln.

As Nate watched, the rear door of the stretch limousine opened.

Stepping onto the tarmac, the slender, dark-haired woman watched the candidate. She stayed quite still, Nate saw, until Kilcannon disappeared inside the Lincoln. Glancing at the press buses, Nate realized that the first two had filled.

Satisfied, he walked across the airstrip and boarded the last bus.

Sara Sax and Lee McAlpine were sitting in front. Stopping, Nate said, "So what do you think?"

Lee shrugged. "So far, Kilcannon's a little off—good but not great. Maybe he thinks Mason's preempted him and this is a wasted day."

Nate grimaced. "Not many days to waste," he said, and walked to the back of the bus.

The tape in the PA system was playing "The Sound of Silence." It seemed appropriate, Nate thought: he was stuck on a patch of asphalt on a hazy Los Angeles day, waiting to pursue a story that no one else imagined.

He felt tense, detached from the others. No one seemed to notice his withdrawal; they had been together so long that it was like a group marriage, with all the tacit understandings that make marriage possible. Silence was not a privilege but a right.

Checking his watch, Nate glanced at the door of the bus, but did not see her.

He leaned back in the seat and closed his eyes, listening to the desultory chatter around him: Mason's speech; Kilcannon's day; a reporter's two-year-old son who had flushed about forty of her tampons down the toilet and caused a plumbing crisis that was driving her husband crazy. "David didn't know they could *expand* like that," Ann Rush was saying. "The plumber sent a probe with a miniature camera up the pipes, and now we've got a video David calls 'The Tampon Dam.' That and a water bubble in the wall of our dining room."

Nate heard Lee McAlpine's distinctive laugh. "It's like Kilcannon's been warning us, Ann—the infrastructure in this country is going flat to hell."

Nate felt himself smile, and then, quite suddenly, the bus became quieter. He opened his eyes.

Lara Costello stood at the front of the bus with her producer, looking for a seat.

Lee McAlpine got up. *"Lara,"* she said, and went to hug her.

Lara smiled, and the two women embraced, Lara several inches taller. "How *is* this?" she asked Lee.

"Terrible. One long list of human rights abuses—lost underwear, crummy sandwiches, sweatshop hours. It's gotten so bad we're looking at pictures of each other's kids. You need to let the world know."

Lara smiled again. " 'For three hundred dollars a day,' " she paraphrased, " 'you can feed this girl. Please send money to Operation Chargecard.' "

Lee laughed; perhaps only Nate noticed that Lara's eyes did not smile. They were cool, he thought, detached.

"Oh, well," Lee said. "And here I thought I'd look so good on the side of a milk carton."

"Maybe Ben and Jerry's," Lara answered, and gave Lee's arm a quick squeeze. "I'd better find a seat. If we can ever make sense of this schedule, let's have dinner, okay?"

Lara proceeded down the aisle. Now and then she stopped to say hello, but many of the faces, Nate realized, were ones she did not know: the press corps was young and turned over quickly. Nate thought that it must be strange to vanish, spend two years abroad doing God knows what amidst great suffering and privation, and then return suddenly famous, with a salary ten times that of everyone else here. The print media were not immune to resentment—of fame, of money, of greater access to the candidate, of the cachet conferred by network television— and some were inclined to see their TV colleagues as all surface and no substance. This would have been difficult for Lara even if she were not, as the notes in Nate's pocket suggested, concealing a secret that could ruin both her and Kerry Kilcannon.

Then Lara saw him.

"Nate," she called. Her pleasure seemed quite genuine. When he stood, she hugged him fiercely, then leaned back to study his face.

"You look good," she said, and then cocked her head. "Except for the haircut."

Gazing back at her, Nate felt that same combination of deep liking and sheer male desire which, two years before, had made him feel uneasy in her company. But nowhere as guilty as he felt now.

"You never called," he said lightly. "You never wrote. You barely said goodbye."

She smiled a little, shaking her head. "It was a funny time for me. I took the NBC job and suddenly there I was, in Bosnia. Everything else—Washington, the Hill, the *Times*—felt like trying to remember the worst drunk you threw in college. Nothing seems quite real—" She stopped herself, then kissed him gently on the cheek. "Anyhow, I'm sorry."

She *was* sorry, Nate sensed. "No matter," he said. "You look good too."

But *not* the same, he thought. Lara appeared leaner, like a sliver of steel; her eyes struck him as older, more watchful. She seemed confident, quite self-possessed, and maybe a little haunted.

"Tell me about *your* life," she said.

Nate shrugged. "Nothing to tell. No wife, no kids. My life is Kerry Kilcannon."

Something flickered in Lara's eyes, and then she smiled again. "Everyone's life, it seems. At least until next Tuesday."

Nate paused, trying to conceal his discomfort. "That doesn't give us much time to catch up. Can I buy you a drink later on?"

Her face seemed to relax, and she touched him on the wrist. "I'd really like that, Nate." He could hardly look at her.

SEVEN

Clayton Slade stood next to Peter Lake, the special agent in charge, waiting for Kerry's last speech of the day.

They were on the campus of a junior college in Los Angeles, selected because of its outreach program for battered women. It was five o'clock; the sky was a cloud-streaked blue, the palm trees were deep green in the fading sun. The plaza where Kerry was to speak was set amidst a spacious lawn, which slanted upward on both sides; the knoll where Clayton and Peter were standing offered the best view.

To Clayton, everything appeared in order—the Service people siphoning the crowd through magnetometers; the volunteers gathered in front of the platform, holding two-sided "Kilcannon for President" signs; the press bleachers set up on the other side of the plaza. There was only one three-story building overlooking the plaza: Clayton knew from experience that the Service had already secured the rooms facing the speakers' platform and placed sharpshooters on the rooftop. The PA system worked: upbeat rock music pumped through the speakers, and a young Latina county commissioner had just assured the crowd that "the next President of the United States will be here in ten minutes." The schedule was holding; with luck, Kerry's speech would make both the early and the late evening newscasts.

"Seems like good advance work," Peter observed.

"At least so far," Clayton answered. "What's funny is I couldn't pick the advance man for this event out of a lineup—they're always on to the next one. The only signs this guy is real are the charges on his credit card."

Peter smiled. "Stiffing the campaign, is he?"

"Uh-huh. According to our chief of advance, his girlfriend dumped him for spending fifty-seven straight days on the road. He finally made it back to their apartment in D.C., and she put his suitcase in the hallway and told him that New Hampshire was due north. Now his only address is a sky page number and a bunch of room service bills for Roederer Cristal. I can't even find the sonofabitch."

Though Peter smiled again, Clayton noted that he never stopped watching his agents. But their interchange was cordial, even warm. Kerry Kilcannon was what the Service called a "high-risk protectee," and Clayton felt fortunate that Peter Lake was running the detail.

At fifty-three, Peter had the stocky frame and broken nose of the linebacker he had been in college. But he was many other things—a lawyer by training, a reader of the classics, and a deeply religious man. He had first been drawn to the Service when, at thirteen, his father had taken him to see John F. Kennedy speak. His father had adored Kennedy, but what fascinated Peter was the Secret Service detail. "I guess I missed the point," he'd remarked dryly to Clayton, but Clayton had come to know better. The desire to protect was the deepest part of Peter's nature.

Sometimes this had led to conflict—it was in *Kerry*'s nature to be a Secret Service nightmare. What Kerry feared most was to look fearful: this drove him to plunge into crowds; to change his schedule on impulse; to refuse to wear a Kevlar vest despite several requests from Peter Lake.

At length, Peter had told Clayton, "The senator's a fatalist. My job is *not* to be one. I'm going to need your help." This conversation had two results: Kerry Kilcannon's Secret Service detail became as large as the President's own, and Clayton made it his personal business to keep Peter informed.

Now, waiting for Kerry to appear, Clayton saw Peter scan the roofline of the three-story building. Outdoor events were the most dangerous, Clayton knew. The Service could control an auditorium, but there were too many ways to shoot a candidate in the open—from a building, a car, any vantage point that afforded a line of fire to a marksman with a high-powered weapon. *That* was what Peter Lake remembered about Jack Kennedy.

Peter had fifty agents assigned to Kerry Kilcannon, running in three eight-hour shifts, with teams leapfrogging California to cover each event. Planning Kerry's protection was as stressful as the protection itself, and in this way, it was like advance work—one error by an advance man could ruin an event; one error by the Service, and Kerry might be dead. "The presidency is the biggest nut magnet in the world," Peter had told Clayton. "And some of these would-be assassins don't care about themselves. All they want is to get close enough."

Now, waiting for Kerry, Clayton saw Dan Biasi and Joe Morton standing in front of the speakers' platform, watching the crowd. That both wore sunglasses was a backhanded tribute to John Hinckley. After Hinckley shot Reagan, the Service had identified him in prior films of a speech given by Jimmy Carter, mingling with the crowd. When questioned, Hinckley had admitted planning to shoot Carter. What had stopped him was a Secret Service agent wearing sunglasses. Unable to see his eyes, Hinckley believed that the agent was watching him.

"Maybe he *was*," Peter Lake had told Clayton. "What we look for is any face that's not part of the crowd experience— serious while everyone around him is cheering, watching us instead of the candidate. Review those films, and Hinckley's face is just *different* from anyone else. You don't even have to know who he is."

Behind the speakers' platform, Clayton saw the lead car of the motorcade coming to a stop. He looked at the press platform and, for the first time, spotted Lara Costello, with her cameraman. Then Kerry Kilcannon stepped from the black Lincoln, flanked by Secret Service agents, and headed for the platform.

The crowd began to cheer.

"Kerry, Kerry, Kerry . . ."

Standing beside Clayton, Peter Lake was intent, unsmiling. All at once, Clayton thought how drained Peter and his agents must feel at night—they were as taut as the assassin they were watching for. "You always wonder," Peter had told him over a drink, "which time it will be."

Clayton placed a hand on Peter's shoulder. "Six more days," he said.

Edgy, Lara Costello waited for Kerry to appear.

Next to her, Lee McAlpine was showing Nate a love letter from an Ethiopian security guard who had seen her once on C-SPAN. "Dear Genius Woman," the letter began. What followed was a tortured poem describing the despair of living in Ethiopia—the absence of food, of opportunity, of the hope of a better life—and an offer to become Lee's "lover and guard dog." Lee found this quite amusing; Lara had been to Ethiopia and knew that what the poem described was true.

Lee turned to her. "C-SPAN," she said. "Amazing. You must get letters like this all the time."

That she had seen more than Lee, Lara reminded herself, did not make her Mother Teresa. "From Ethiopia?" she answered. "Some. But most of them just want food. And they don't write nearly as well."

Lee gave her a brief quizzical look, then put the letter in the pocket of her jeans.

Scanning the crowd, Lara distracted herself by noting details she might use: that an angry-looking pro-life woman was holding a sign which read "Abort Kerry Kilcannon"; that the crowd was young and multiracial; that, knowing they had an attractive candidate, the Kilcannon signs used Kerry's picture. Then she spotted a young black man with a hand-lettered "KFK" sign. At once, she remembered Kerry on the beach during that last weekend, smiling when she asked him why he refused to use his initials.

"Change one letter," he had told her, "and I'm someone in a white hood. Or maybe a bucket of fried chicken."

"Or a Kennedy," she answered.

Kerry had stopped smiling. "I'm a policeman's son from Newark. All I've got in common with the Kennedys is a murdered brother." He stuck his hands in the pockets of his windbreaker and stared out at Nantucket Sound, adding softly, "I hate the way people romanticize death. One look at the back of Jamie's head . . ."

They never spoke of it again. Perhaps, Lara thought, if she had known how little time was left . . .

"Kerry, Kerry, Kerry . . . ," the crowd began chanting.

Suddenly he was on the platform, perhaps a hundred feet away, a slim figure in shirtsleeves, his tie unknotted.

Lara felt the briefest pulse, the tightness of a caught breath. She could not see his face well. At this distance, he was all energy and movement, sending a current through the crowd. The visuals were good, Lara thought: waiting on the platform were a black congresswoman from South Central and several advocates for battered women.

Kerry paused, talking with each of them, and then walked to the podium. Perhaps, Lara thought, she only imagined that Kerry waited until he saw her, or that this moment—Kerry suddenly quite still—lasted more than a few seconds. But in that brief time she experienced two years' worth of regret, loss, the guilt that never quite left her. Then she shut it down, like a curtain drawing closed, and Kerry began to speak.

A few minutes into his speech, Kerry noticed them—a handful of women scattered among the cheering volunteers. Their faces were tense, and they did not join in the applause. Kerry had a preternatural sense of crowds; had it not been for the impact of seeing Lara, he would have spotted them at once.

Now, as he spoke, they edged closer to one another.

"It is not just battered women who suffer." Kerry paused, scanning the faces before him. "The children who witness the brutality of a father to a mother are scarred by that experience forever; by the helplessness they feel, by the anger it breeds, by the prospect—borne out by bitter experience—that many of those who witness abuse as children will practice abuse as adults."

The crowd was quiet now. Kerry saw an Asian woman with tears on her face and wondered what emotion he had touched, what experience of pain had come to the surface. But that group of women still watched him intently, seeming detached from the excitement surrounding them.

"Should children be punished," Kerry asked, "because their father is abusive and their mother has no skills? Should *women* be abandoned because, after a good-faith effort, the one way to protect themselves is to leave?

"I think this country is better than that . . ."

Suddenly forming a line, the women held their banner aloft for the TV cameras.

"Abortion Is a Right," the banner read, "Not a Favor."

The women began a chant—their voices ragged but audible enough for the press to hear.

"We will not apologize," they called out. *"We will not apologize."*

Watching from the bleachers, Nate Cutler felt the pieces fall into place: the memo in his pocket; Mason's speech in Boston; the demonstrators now.

Next to him, Lara Costello seemed taut. "Who *are* they?" she asked.

"Anthony's Legions, I expect—militant pro-choicers. Kilcannon's advance team fucked up somehow, and now *this* is what gets on the news."

When he turned to her, Lara was quite pale.

Lara felt Nate watching her.

"I'm not asking you to apologize," Kerry told the women. "Neither is anyone here."

Quickly, a trim woman with glasses and long gray hair called out to Kerry, "We want to be heard."

Kerry hesitated, then nodded. "Come on up."

"Risky," Nate murmured.

Lara shook her head. "He can't blow them off—not after Boston." All around them, the television Minicams followed the woman's progress to the speakers' platform.

Kerry gestured toward the podium. Nodding curtly, the woman stepped to the microphone. Amplified by the PA system, her voice was high, nervous.

"On behalf of pro-choice women," she began, "we want answers to our questions.

"You've said a fetus is a life. Does it have legal rights? Do you believe that a woman who has an abortion is, effectively, a murderer?"

Tense, Lara watched Kerry's face. But at this distance, all that she could see was how intently he seemed to listen.

The woman turned to him. "You also say, Senator Kilcannon, that *you're* pro-choice. Does that mean you believe a woman has an absolute right to choose?

"Do you support the right to a partial-birth abortion?

"Do you support the use of the abortion pill RU-486, to protect women from potential violence like at the Boston clinic?

"Do your personal and religious beliefs mean that a Kilcannon presidency would be a risk to pro-choice women?"

Abruptly, she faced Kerry. "In the last two years, the right to choose has been eroded in Congress and in the courts. Your party is *our* only protection. The Vice President's position is clear. We feel threatened by your recent statements on choice, and we need to know just who you really are."

The questions were straightforward, each a perfect sound bite. For a moment, Lara shut her eyes.

"My turn?" Kerry asked politely, and walked to the podium. The crowd was silent, waiting.

"First," he said crisply, "I support the right to choose.

"I support the use of RU-486.

"I support the partial-birth abortion to protect the life or physical health of the mother.

"My personal and religious beliefs are just that—I don't propose to force them on anyone, let alone make women and their doctors outlaws. Only a woman can make this difficult judgment, based on her *own* life and her *own* beliefs."

Kerry turned to the woman. "Those positions are as clear as I can make them. They're the same as Dick Mason's, or any of the thousands of politicians in this country who call themselves 'pro-choice.'

"And," he added, "they are absolutely devoid of moral content or *any* thought too complicated to fit onto a bumper sticker."

"Jesus," Nate said. "He was almost out of this." But those listening seemed rapt; Lara felt herself stand straighter.

Kerry faced the crowd. "In an environment where pro-life fanatics use harassment and even violence, to concede how complex abortion is may seem like a step backward. I sympathize with those fears. But having an abortion is the most wrenching decision some women will ever have to make, and no 'position' *I* take will ever change that.

"Why are so many people so uncomfortable with partial-birth abortion? Because it makes it so painfully clear that an abortion is not just another operation and that the words we use to avoid that truth—like 'procedure' and 'choice'—beg the difficult questions each woman must face alone."

His voice grew soft. "Any parent who has ever seen a sonogram, or listened to the heartbeat of an unborn baby, or thanked God for the doctor who saved their premature child, knows that."

"Oh, Kerry," Lara said under her breath. The crowd was utterly silent.

"I didn't come here to talk about abortion. I wish it weren't an issue. It's not the proper business of a senator—or a President—to force pregnant women to have children." Once more, Kerry turned to the woman. "Your rights are safe with me. You needn't apologize for anything. But *I* refuse to apologize for believing what I believe."

For a long moment, there was silence. And then the applause started, slowly building—a solemn sound, different than cheers. To Lara, it was the sound of respect.

Beside her, Nate was quiet.

EIGHT

Checking his watch, Nate saw that it was nearly six o'clock.

As the crowd drifted away, the print reporters hurried to the press filing area, a canvas tent on the knoll overlooking the plaza. But Nate had no deadline; his responsibilities were to write a weekly article and to accumulate materials for *Newsworld*'s special "Campaign 2000" issue, covering the early primaries to the November general election.

Today's incident would be part of that, he was certain. But the deeper story could become the campaign's central drama, rich in character, irony, and, to Nate, something akin to tragedy. Though part of Nate recoiled, he could imagine that, for the rest of his life, he would be known as the reporter who had brought down Kerry Kilcannon.

On the field near the press tent, he spotted Lara.

She was setting up for a shoot. At a distance, she seemed to be practicing her lines as she paced, waiting for her cue. He could not resist watching.

Crossing the field, he stood to one side.

Lara stared at the ground, oblivious to anything but the cameraman, the instructions coming through her earpiece, her own thoughts. "When I say 'private trauma,'" she said through her microphone, "that's your cue to roll the tape."

She cocked her head, as if listening. "All right," she answered, and faced the camera.

A moment passed. "Speaking in Los Angeles," Lara began, "Kerry Kilcannon capped a day devoted to issues targeting female voters—education, day care, support for battered women. But his appearance outside a women's shelter was interrupted by pro-choice militants, demanding that he clarify his recent statement that a fetus is a 'life.' His response was to suggest that abortion is a public right but—at least for some women—a private trauma . . ."

Abruptly, Lara stopped. Nate realized that the technicians in the NBC sound truck were running the tape. Listening, Lara was intent, motionless. Then she raised her eyes to the camera.

"This was *not* the speech," Lara continued, "that Kerry Kilcannon had planned. In the California primary, the women's vote is critical, and the campaign had hoped to avoid further problems on the abortion issue.

"Senator Kilcannon *did* strongly affirm his pro-choice stance. But by implying that those views begged deeper moral questions, he may have said more than he needed to. The question is whether voters will remember his public position or his personal qualms—and how they will feel about either.

"Lara Costello, NBC News, with the Kilcannon campaign in Los Angeles."

Lara was still for a moment. When she turned to him, Nate realized that she had been aware of him all along. Her gaze was level, cool.

"Well?" she asked.

At once, Nate felt uncomfortable. "Kilcannon went too far."

Something changed in her eyes; her answer was at once soft and sardonic. "I guess that's his fatal flaw, isn't it."

Nate nodded. "I'll see you at the hotel," he said, and went to call his editor.

In the stairwell of the building's emergency exit, Nate spoke into his cellular phone, hoping no one would overhear.

"Did you get to the counselor?" he asked.

"We did." Jane Booth sounded wired. "Her name is Nancy Philips. She confirmed that Costello was a patient, that Costello met with her in confidence, that Costello talked about the affair with Kerry Kilcannon.

"According to Philips, Costello was devastated."

"Yeah," Nate said softly. "That's pretty clear from the notes."

"The problem is that Philips won't talk on the record. What I get from Sheila Kahn is that Philips feels almost as guilty about what she's doing now as about what she *used* to do."

"Why shouldn't she?" Nate asked. "I mean, violating Lara's right to privacy is one thing. But ruining her life should give this lady at least a little pause. Even in *these* tawdry times."

Jane was briefly silent. "You still don't like this, do you?"

Nate gazed at the dank stairwell. " 'Don't like' is too simple. To borrow from an old southern congressman I knew, I'm like a bird looking at a snake—both fascinated and repelled. At moments, I can see myself on Larry King."

"Forget all that," Jane answered. "And stop worrying about Lara Costello. Nobody made her sleep with him."

"I never said my feelings were important, Jane. Just that I have them." Nate stood, restless. "Will this counselor say who she gave the memo to?"

"No. But Philips admits having joined the local chapter of the Christian Commitment. Which *may* mean something."

"So now you're thinking it got to the GOP and *they* slipped it to Katherine Jones? Because I'm not so sure it's them anymore." As he spoke, Nate began pacing. "Jones gives me this memo, Mason goes to Boston, and now these demonstrators disrupt Kilcannon's speech. I can imagine Mason's people looking at the returns in Oregon last night and deciding it was time to go for broke—"

"So you think Mason *shot* those people too?"

Briefly, Nate laughed. "I didn't say he wasn't lucky."

"Not *that* lucky." Jane's tone became clipped, businesslike. "We need another source, Nate. We don't have a story yet."

Nate hesitated. "And you want me to do what, exactly?"

"Confront Lara Costello. Ask her all the questions about Kilcannon."

Pausing, Nate imagined Lara's face. "Before I show her the memo?"

"I'd say so, to see what she says without knowing you have it. She may tell the truth or, far more likely, get caught in an obvious lie."

"*Or* she may tell Kilcannon."

"She may." Jane spoke more quietly now, as Nate did. "But as you pointed out, we run the same risk by talking to Costello's neighbors, which we'll start to do tomorrow. And if Kilcannon begins avoiding the press, *that's* interesting too."

"To *us*. But it doesn't make him Lara's lover—"

"We don't have much time," Jane interrupted bluntly. "They could give this story to someone else. Especially if it's Mason."

Nate stopped pacing. "From Mason's point of view, the woman who confronted Kilcannon couldn't have been better. When she said 'we need to know just who you really are,' it was eerily coincidental."

Jane seemed to consider this. "Coincidence or not," she finally answered, "*our* job is to answer her."

As the motorcade sped down a six-lane freeway on the way to Beverly Hills, Clayton sat with Kerry and thought of a maze leading nowhere. Kerry stared out the window; at his request, the staff had spared him another ride with yet another politician. He had not spoken for several minutes.

"Mason killed me today," Kerry said at last. "God help anyone in this party who says abortion involves more than the right to have one."

Clayton frowned. "Your response was honest, at least. But it won't come across in thirty seconds of airtime."

In profile, Kerry was pale, his face etched with weariness. "Oh, I knew that. It just wasn't my day for pandering. But if I were a pro-choice activist, I might not like me, either."

Kerry was angry, Clayton knew. But what struck him was Kerry's ability to detach, to see himself as others saw him.

Once more, Kerry fell silent.

Pensive, Clayton watched his face. "You saw her, I guess."

Kerry did not turn. "Yes," he answered. "I saw her."

Sean Burke looked at his watch.

It was eight fifty-five. The long cafeteria tables were jammed with well-dressed professionals who had come from work, and the cavernous room echoed with voices reciting the same script at various speeds and rhythms, like a ragged Gregorian chant in a vast cathedral. At nine o'clock, the volunteers would stop phoning; Sean had time for one more call.

In twelve hours, he had dialed one hundred ninety-seven telephone numbers. There had been no time to find a gun.

Next to him, Kate Feeney talked on the phone, her face intent while her slender frame, slumped with fatigue, was supported by both elbows on the table. As the day had worn on, Sean had felt a tenuous connection grow: for an hour they would not speak to each other, and then, seeing that he was off the phone, Kate would offer a word of encouragement or, as he gained confidence, a wry smile that acknowledged their mutual imprisonment. At midafternoon, she had shared her turkey sandwich.

"Great," Kate was saying in a cheery voice. "I'm calling to see if you're supporting Senator Kerry Kilcannon for President . . ."

Her words shook Sean from his reverie; when he stopped to think, as he had when watching Kate, hesitance overtook him.

The only way to conquer his fears was to dial one number after another, like a robot.

Sean hit nine and made his last call, hoping to get an answering machine.

"Hello?" the woman responded.

Sean could feel the dampness on his forehead. "My name is John Kelly . . . ," he began, then stammered at the lie. "From the Kilcannon campaign. Is this Louise Degnan?"

"It is." Her voice was middle-aged, polite but reserved. "I haven't decided, if that's why you're calling. I doubt I'll decide much before Tuesday."

It was his mission, Sean thought, to make sure the Tuesday election never came. Suddenly he saw himself stepping toward Kerry Kilcannon, gun raised to fire. In a hollow voice, he asked, "Do you plan to vote in the primary?"

"Yes." The woman's voice warmed slightly. "I don't mean to discourage you, Mr. Kelly. I don't favor Vice President Mason, either. I'm just listening to what they both have to say. Do you know if there'll be a debate?"

Mason had called for one, Sean remembered. "I'm sure that Senator Kilcannon wants to debate," he ventured, and then remembered the stacks of campaign literature he had perused during a ten-minute break. "You know about the senator's stands on women's issues, right? Like protecting battered women and children . . ."

The woman paused. "I'm not sure I do, actually."

"Well, he's always been like that." The pit of Sean's stomach felt empty now. "I mean, his first job was prosecuting men who beat up women. He even saved a kid's life . . ." Abruptly, Sean felt Kate Feeney's gaze—they were not supposed to argue with voters or deviate from the script. His voice fell off. "Maybe we can send you some pamphlets."

"That would be fine, Mr. Kelly."

Sean closed his eyes. "Thank you," he said, and then remembered the script. "Thank you on behalf of Senator Kilcannon."

When he hung up, his fingers felt clumsy, the telephone heavy. It was nothing like the remembered feel of the weapon in his hand, light and slender and lethal. He would not look at Kate.

"That was good," he heard her say. "What you told her about Kerry."

When he turned to her, Kate's eyes seemed guileless; wisps of blond hair fell across her pale brow. Sean felt his face redden. "We're not supposed to say anything."

"You were nice, though, and you were sincere. People feel that."

Kate was smiling a little. But Sean could not tell whether it was pity or deception. He remembered the first time he had realized that, with girls, there was something he did not quite comprehend. It was like listening to distant music on his old car radio when he drove in the remoteness of the Berkshires—notes too faint to hear, words fading until the station vanished altogether.

He would never forget her name—Ann Regan—and the way she looked: strawberry-blond hair, light freckles; her full mouth, when she smiled, framed dimples at both corners. She sat near him in religion class; lying in his bunk bed at the boys' home in Charlestown, he would listen to the boys around him stir as they slept, and safe in the darkness, he dared to imagine that she liked him.

One morning, leaving the boys' home on a crisp spring morning, he decided to wait for her after school.

Each class that day was an agony of suspended time, of looking at his watch. In religion class, two hours before school ended, he studied her for signs. She did not seem to notice him until Sister Helen asked if he was praying or merely day-dreaming. Ann Regan had laughed with the rest, and Sean, humiliated, had bowed his head in shame . . .

Looking into Kate Feeney's face, Sean felt a hand on his shoulder.

He flinched, startled. Kate's eyes widened at his reaction. Quickly, Sean turned to see who had found him.

Rick Ginsberg smiled down at him. "Jeff Lee says you did a great job, John. Thanks for staying."

Staring at the coordinator's pleasant face, Sean felt surprise, then relief, and then a wrenching wave of gratitude. Rick squeezed his shoulder. "Keep coming back, and maybe you *will* meet him. Sometimes we can arrange that for volunteers."

Rick hurried on. Sean stayed next to Kate, muted by the fresh, sudden image of facing Kerry Kilcannon. All around them, women in suits or men with loosened ties had begun to chat among themselves, freed from the telephones in front of them. A T-shirted student with tousled black hair put a stack of pizza boxes on one corner of a table.

"Can you stay?" Sean heard Kate ask. "This is where you get to know people."

Once more, the fear of being known struck Sean like a blow to the chest. He shook his head, not daring to meet Kate's eyes. "No," he mumbled. "I can't."

NINE

Ten minutes before she was to meet Nate Cutler at the bar, Lara heard a knock on the door of her hotel room.

She was in the bathroom, fresh from a shower. Unhurriedly, she put on her blue robe and then, at the second knock, opened the door.

It was Nate. For an odd moment, Lara thought that his thin face, his wire-rimmed glasses, made him look ascetic. He stood there, silent and unsmiling.

"Can I come in?" he asked.

Studying his face, Lara felt surprise war with apprehension. She nodded, backing away. Nate closed the door behind him with exaggerated care.

"Is something wrong?" she asked.

Nate watched her. "It's about Kerry Kilcannon."

His voice erased whatever ambiguity the words might have had. Sickened, Lara suddenly pictured the two of them as solitary antagonists, trapped in a room overlooking a darkened city.

As she struggled for clarity, the mastery of thought over emotion, Lara tilted her head in silent inquiry. She would not help him by speaking.

The mirthless smile at one corner of Nate's mouth seemed to acknowledge this. "We know you had an affair with him, Lara. It ended two years ago, when he was still married. Just before he decided to run for President."

Instinctively, Lara turned away. She was overwhelmed by the swiftness of this, two years of silence shattered, her own emotions breaking loose. Walking to the window, she gazed out at Los Angeles, its irregular grid of lights flickering in the night. Though there were tears in her eyes, her voice was soft, clear.

"If you know all that, why come to me?"

The question was foolish, a way of buying time. Nate's tone was level, relentless. "You know why. We're asking you for comment."

She turned on him, and then anger overtook her—at the devastating consequence of his question, at his betrayal of their friendship. "You're asking me for *help*. It's the reporter's oldest trick: say whatever *might* have happened as if it's true, then hope your victim confirms it."

Nate watched her eyes. "This is hard for me," he said at last. "It's also my job. You've done this to people a hundred times. You'd do it to me if you had to."

She had put him on the defensive, Lara saw. It gave her more time to consider who could know about Kerry—snoopy neighbors were not enough. "You won't do anything to me, Nate. Because you don't have anything, and you *can't* have anything."

"Is that a denial?"

Lara's thoughts moved quickly now. "I won't dignify this, on *or* off the record. You float some innuendo that could ruin two lives, planted by God knows who days before the election, and you expect an *answer*? If you want anything from me, tell me what you think you've got and where it comes from."

Nate crossed his arms, silent. Lara felt a momentary confidence: Nate needed two credible sources and could not have them. Then he said, "You'd better sit down, Lara."

The words held a compassion that unnerved her more than

what had come before. Slowly, she crossed the room and sat on the edge of the bed.

Nate sat next to her. Then he took some papers from his pocket—two pages, stapled together—and placed them in her hands.

Lara read the first words.

Shock came, then nausea. A film of tears kept her from reading more. "Leave," she said. "Please."

Nate folded his hands, as if to stop himself from reaching for her. "You know I can't. Not yet."

Lara turned from him and waited until she could read again.

The counselor's notes were scattered, digressive. But for Lara, each line was devastating shorthand for all that she had repressed. She saw herself as she was then, helplessly sobbing in the counselor's office, with no strength left for herself. All that she had wanted was for Kerry to be with her . . .

She forced herself to finish reading. Nate's patience felt like that of a cat watching its prey.

Softly, Lara asked, "Why do you assume this is authentic?"

"Come off it, Lara—"

She spun on him. "*You* come off it. Any sick or malicious person can make a lie look more authentic by writing it down. I could *say* that you fuck elephants. And if I *write* it, it's still bullshit."

Nate rested one finger on the memo. "This is *you* talking, Lara. I can hear your voice." His own voice was quiet. "I remember how you acted, how quickly you left the *Times*. This is why, isn't it?"

Lara remembered it all—the fierce desire to get away, to bury herself in something so new, so completely divorced from the past, that it would block out all thought of Kerry Kilcannon. She could not face Kerry again. Far worse was imagining the day when she would have to go to him for a quote, or an interview.

"*You* can fuck elephants, Lara," Nate said evenly. "But you don't get to cover the circus. Then or now."

It was as if Nate had heard her thoughts. By reporting on Kerry Kilcannon, she erased any doubt that their involvement was a story. For Kerry, Lara Costello was more than a painful memory—she was an albatross.

Lara stood, the papers clutched in her hand. "If this is true," she told him, "someone has violated my privacy in a terrible way, for rotten motives. Shouldn't that bother you just a little?"

Nate seemed to have found his bearings now. "Personally, yes. Professionally, it can't. This story's too important." He stood to face her. "It *is* true, isn't it?"

Lara made herself detach, think like a reporter. Someone might have seen her leaving Kerry's apartment, but this proved nothing in itself and could even be a mistake: two years ago, strangers did not recognize her face. *Newsworld* was aggressive but not unethical—though press standards had eroded, they still needed more than they had.

"Well?" Nate asked.

Lara remembered Kerry's agonized voice on the telephone. Even if she had no career to protect, she could at least protect his privacy, the freedom to pursue his ambitions. In her heart, she owed him more than that.

"It's not true, Nate." Her mouth felt dry. "Not about Kilcannon."

"You did see this counselor."

"Off the record, yes. I'd had an affair. But not with Kerry Kilcannon." She paused, searching for the words that might protect them both. "He was a source, a good one. I liked him—as much as a reporter can like a politician. We were friends, in a way. But that's all it ever was."

"You weren't lovers?"

For a moment, Lara thought of Kerry's eyes after the last time they made love. The hurricane had passed. The beach outside was littered with rocks and debris, like the ruins of some other world; the house itself was hushed. Kerry lay on the pillow, touching her face.

"I love you," Kerry said. "More than anything in my life . . ."

Lara drew a breath. "We weren't lovers," she told Nate in an even tone. "That part's a terrible lie."

She was lying, Nate sensed.

He had watched her. She understood everything—the position she was in, what he was trying to do, what he needed from her. But it could not change the wound he saw in her eyes, the delay in answering, sometimes brief, as she struggled with how she felt.

"He never came to your apartment?" he demanded. "Or you to his?"

Lara stood straighter. "No more questions, Nate. It's time for you to leave." Abruptly, she walked to the door. Just before she opened it, she turned to him again. "But thanks for asking me out for drinks. It's been wonderful to see you."

Inwardly, Nate winced. He made himself walk to the door and then, quite gently, took the memo from her hands. "You're sure about this, Lara."

"Wouldn't you be?"

Her voice was clear, determined. Nate had always liked her poise under pressure; even now, as he watched her for clues, part of Nate was half in love. He might never understand Kerry Kilcannon, Nate thought, but he could imagine Kilcannon's feelings very well.

"If you want to talk . . . ," he began, and then saw her expression.

Leaving, Nate heard the door close behind him with a muffled click.

Inside, Lara leaned her face against the door.

The only sound was her own breathing. When the sickness came, she barely made it to the bathroom. Her body trembled as she vomited.

Just like *then*, she thought.

Slowly, she got up and lay across the bed, face buried in her pillow.

What had happened with Kerry could get out now. Even if *Newsworld* never printed it, their reporters would interrogate her neighbors and Kerry's, ask her friends if she had confided in them, spreading rumors as they went. Soon the affair might be gossip at cocktail parties, then a story in the tabloids. The only question was whether to warn Kerry.

The vomit tasted bitter in her mouth.

She was still a journalist, Lara told herself. But she hardly felt like one; she had betrayed her profession first by being Kerry's lover and now—tonight—by doing something worse. To pass word to him would draw her still deeper into the story, make her the corrupted reporter whose only concern was Kerry Kilcannon's interests. Nate would watch Kerry's people for signs; Lara was not sure what good it would do to burden Kerry, when she had already given him what he needed most. A lie.

The telephone rang.

Lara hesitated. When she lifted the phone off the nightstand and answered, she sounded as ill and wary as she felt.

"This is Clayton Slade." His voice was deep, polite. "If you have time, I need to see you."

Lara closed her eyes. "Why not," she said at last. "I wasn't sleeping, anyway."

TEN

Clayton Slade went to a chair and sat, silent for a moment, gazing at Lara with frank curiosity. It felt to Lara as if, through Kerry, they knew each other, yet each represented a corner of his life the other did not know—one his former lover, one his closest friend and manager.

The man Lara saw was heavyset, with a salt-and-pepper mustache, wide perceptive eyes, and a look of keen intelligence. The fact that he was in California told her how devoted he was to Kerry; since the accident, Kerry once had told her, Clayton Slade hated to leave his family. Ambition alone would not have made him take this job.

She sat down on the bed. "You know," she said. "Everything."

Slowly, Clayton nodded. "Yes."

"You've come here to protect him, I suppose."

Clayton's eyes narrowed. "I came to say that I appreciated your call. And to ask you to be careful—for *both* your sakes."

Lara gave him a sardonic smile. "Maybe I can help here, Clayton. You want me to stay away from him. You expect me to adhere to the highest standard of journalistic ethics. And if I don't, you'll personally make sure that I wind up in Des Moines, covering the sewage commission."

Clayton's own smile flashed and vanished, a reflex. "My speech was more polite. You've got the substance, though."

Through her exhaustion, Lara felt a spurt of anger. "What do you think I am? Even if I didn't give a damn about him, I have to live with myself. This is the last place on earth I want to be."

Clayton was silent for a moment. "Is it?" he asked.

Lara felt the anger drain from her. "It's torture," she said at last. "You can't know."

Clayton's gaze softened. "Oh, I think I have some idea."

Lara's throat felt tight. She fought a battle with herself and lost. Quietly, she asked, "How is he?"

Clayton's smile was ironic. "Kerry, you mean? Oh, he's fine—the best candidate the party has seen in years: attractive, passionate, and he actually gives a damn about people other than himself. If he doesn't fuck it up somehow, he'll be the forty-third President of the United States." Abruptly, his voice fell, and his face became serious. "He hardly mentions you. He doesn't have to."

Lara touched her eyes. "*I* don't have to either, Clayton. If that's what you want to know."

Lara felt Clayton watching her, trying to divine her meaning. "There's something I need to ask you," he said.

"What?"

His gaze was level. "Who else knows about this? Besides the person who *had* to know?"

Lara stood, arms folded. Her stomach felt empty, raw; the choice was between the last betrayal of her principles and yet another lie, this time to Kerry Kilcannon. His best friend watched her, waiting.

Lara turned to him. "*Newsworld* knows," she said simply.

* * *

For twenty minutes, Clayton listened. When she was finished, Lara's face was ashen.

Out of kindness, he tried to conceal how appalled he was—for Kerry, for her, even for himself. His first words were practical and direct. "You believe it's this counselor?"

"Or someone with access to her files." Lara looked down, her expression pensive, haunted. "Ever since Nate left, I've been trying to remember her. I was such a wreck she could have been anyone, as long as what I told her never left that room. I can hardly see her face now." She looked at him, voice suddenly hard. "Don't even *dream* of going to her, or I'll break this story myself. I've gone too far already."

Clayton's tone was crisp. "If we did that, Mason's people would find out. Your ethics don't enter into it."

Slowly, Lara sat on the bed again. In the dim light of the hotel room, she looked wan; without makeup, her most striking feature was intense dark eyes. "Why do you think it's Mason?"

"Timing. The Republicans would sit on this."

Lara faced him. "Whoever it is, we're never talking about this again. You're on your own."

Studying her, Clayton tried to sort out his feelings. In the last few hours, her world had collapsed, her past had returned to haunt her, and she had compromised—twice—everything that was important to her as a journalist. Yet Lara tried to keep a tight rein on her emotions, preserve some sense of self. What she evoked was far from pity—it was admiration.

Clayton drew a breath. "Do you want me to tell him anything?"

Her eyes met his, and then she looked away. "No. Nothing."

Clayton hesitated. "Well," he said finally. "I've got a job to do."

Lara stood with him, hands in the pockets of her robe. "Good luck."

Clayton was quiet for a moment; there was nothing left to say. "You too," he answered, and left.

When Clayton opened the door of his room, there was a white envelope on the floor. It took him a moment to realize what was inside—Jack Sleeper's numbers, the nightly tracking poll. This seemed so pointless that he almost laughed.

Sitting, he made himself scan the data. The first discipline he must impose was on himself: reviewing the numbers was his job, and Jack Sleeper was waiting for his call. He could not let Jack sense that anything was wrong.

Stretching out on the bed with the papers laid in front of him, he called the pollster.

"It's about what I'd expect," Clayton told him. "Mason three points up—statistically, a tie. The debate could make the difference."

"What about pro-choice women?" Sleeper asked. "We're down six points in the San Francisco Bay Area, down two among pro-choice women statewide, and that was before Kerry stepped in it today. I think Mason's getting traction."

"Could be a blip. One night's numbers don't tell us enough—"

"I think we should be proactive," Sleeper interjected. "Ask Ellen Penn to help put together an event with all the prominent women who support him. Maybe in San Francisco."

"Let's watch the numbers the next couple of nights, see if this is really a problem. Believe me, Kerry wants to change the subject."

"He *should*." Even over the phone, Jack's worry was audible. "Tomorrow's the anniversary of his brother's assassination. Hopefully, we'll get a shot in the arm from that. Metaphorically speaking."

"I wouldn't try that one out on Kerry."

"There's no wind so ill, Clayton, that doesn't blow a *little* bit of good. The senator knows it too. No matter what he says, or doesn't say."

"Oh, he *knows*," Clayton said, and got off.

He sat up on the bed, back against the wall. Pro-choice women would have to wait.

Eyes shut, he considered whom he needed. Kit Pace, certainly. Nat Schlesinger, for his experience and contacts. Both of them he trusted.

Finally, reluctantly, he added Frank Wells to the list—Wells was too savvy to ignore, and he knew the media too well.

He would call the three of them tonight. The person he would not call was Kerry; he needed rest, and there were countless reasons why, if told, Kerry would not sleep at all. The morning was soon enough.

Picking up the telephone, he awoke Kit Pace. "Sorry," he said brusquely. "There's a problem. We're meeting in my room tomorrow morning, at seven. Don't mention it to anyone."

When Sean turned on the news, the picture seemed blurred and faded. It was the bedside lamps, he realized; too bright, they cast reflections of the bare motel room across the anchorman's face. Moving closer to the screen, he kept the lights on.

It had happened when Sean was seven, this darkness he could not escape. He still remembered knocking over the wine as he reached across the dinner table; the red drops spattering across his father's T-shirt; the lightning flash of anger on his face. His father had wrenched Sean from his chair, dragging him across the living room carpet. In the dim hallway, his father opened the closet door.

"Inside," he ordered. His voice was thick as blood.

Gazing up into his father's eyes, Sean made himself stop crying. He knew his mother would not help him.

Slowly, the boy walked into the darkness. The door shut behind him; with a soft metallic click, the lock turned.

It was pitch black. Sean stood there, eyes shut, crying so uncontrollably that his body shook with the effort to make no sound. Finally, the spasms stopped.

When Sean opened his eyes, he was blind. The air was hot and close.

Panic came, and then a deeper anguish. Fearful, Sean groped in the darkness around him. The first thing he touched was thick and rough; he recognized the feel of his mother's wool coat.

Fumbling, the boy pulled the coat from the hanger, spread it on the hardwood floor beneath him. He lay down, knees curled against his chest; suddenly he could imagine her on the other side of the closet door, eyes bleak with drink and bitter helplessness. Often they did not seem to see him . . .

Last winter, when his mother was pregnant, the baby had been a small bulge in her stomach. Leaning against her on the park bench, Sean could feel it through the wool coat. Sometimes he hoped the baby would never come.

In the closet, Sean swallowed, remembering . . .

Drinking wine, his pregnant mother had asked his father if they could find a bigger apartment. Drink made Sean's mother careless; from their arguments, overheard at night, Sean sensed that her request was foolish, that his father resented having another mouth to feed. For several hours thereafter, he drank and brooded in the living room as Sean watched with silent dread; when his mother asked again, too drunk to gauge her husband's mood, his father rose from his chair in a whiskey-soaked rage and punched her in the stomach. His mother doubled over in shock and pain, too nauseated even to cry. After she had gone to the hospital, Sean saw drops of blood on the carpet; when she returned, there was no baby . . .

Even through his mother's coat, the closet floor felt hard. Sean shifted, body aching, unable to sleep, afraid that he might suffocate. His bladder hurt. Finally, in agony, he wet himself, careful not to wet his mother's coat. When at last she opened the door, his father was gone, and it was morning; soiled and shamed, the boy stumbled from the closet, blinking in the light.

Now, sitting against the bed, Sean gazed blankly at the television.

"*After a dramatic cross-country trip to Boston,*" the anchorman said, "*Vice President Richard Mason spoke in front of the Boston Women's Clinic, responding to yesterday's tragic murders.*"

Mason appeared on the screen. "*In the name of those who died here,*" he proclaimed, "*I say to the purveyors of terror and violence . . . not one more woman deprived of her legal rights.*"

Suddenly Sean felt a rush of pride, mingled with contempt for Mason. To Sean, the Vice President's anger did not seem authentic—not like Sean's own. The wonder was that this man spoke at the site of Sean's act. Mason was words; yesterday Sean had become much more.

Mason's voice rose. "*We will devote every resource of our government to find this cowardly murderer and make him face the nature of his crime.*"

Reflexively, Sean looked around him. The door was latched,

the chain in place; the curtains were drawn. In one day, or two, they might start looking for Sean Burke. There was not much time.

A woman appeared on the television. Though her surname was Irish, Sean had always thought her exotic, almost Latin. *"Speaking in Los Angeles,"* she began, *"Kerry Kilcannon capped a day devoted to issues targeting female voters . . . But his appearance outside a women's shelter was interrupted by pro-choice militants, demanding that he clarify his recent statement that a fetus is a 'life.' His response was to suggest that abortion is a public right but—at least for some women—a private trauma."*

On film, Kerry Kilcannon appeared slight, embattled. But Sean could feel his directness through the screen.

"The words we use to avoid that truth—like 'procedure' and 'choice'—beg the difficult questions each woman must face alone." Kilcannon's voice softened. *"Any parent who has ever seen a sonogram, or listened to the heartbeat of an unborn baby, or thanked God for the doctor who saved their premature child, knows that."*

Sean stiffened with rage. You *know that,* he thought. *You're Roman Catholic, and you've abandoned your roots and everything you know is right to become what Paul Terris called you—"abortion with a human face . . ."*

Sean stood and began pacing. He had a sudden, visceral memory—his father's eyes, the last time Sean had seen him.

"Lara Costello," the woman finished, *"with the Kilcannon campaign in Los Angeles."*

Kerry Kilcannon splashed water on his face.

Exhausted, he had fallen asleep thinking of Lara and then awakened from his dream of Jamie. The dream ended just as Jamie had—in a funeral home in Newark as his younger brother, the next United States senator from New Jersey, gazed into his waxen face.

The face Kerry saw in the bathroom mirror looked haggard; he saw little resemblance—as if there ever had been—to the youthful savior some had imagined.

Kerry Kilcannon, the hero who had saved a small boy's life.

That was what the newscasts had said. In the mirror, Kerry studied the scar on his shoulder as if, like the heroism, it belonged to someone else.

At tonight's reception in Beverly Hills—in the glass-and-light showplace of a wealthy art dealer—Kerry had spoken of minorities and the poor. Gazing at the affluent crowd in front of him—celebrities; lawyers; well-fed dealmakers who watched each other like mirrors of themselves—Kerry found that his sense of irony made him more pointed and impassioned. The last irony was that they liked him for it.

Afterward, a young actress-of-the-moment, doe-eyed and flirtatious and intelligent enough that this was flattering, had hinted that she might sleep with him. What Kerry replied was not "no," only "not now"; he knew that she wanted to sleep with a President, not a man.

For Kerry, his own face vanished.

In its place was Lara. And then, a long time later, other faces—Meg; Liam Dunn; a small, dark-haired boy who had worshiped him; and, as always, Jamie.

"I see my life go drifting like a river," Yeats had written, "from change to change . . ." But to Kerry, his life felt like a series of wrenching accidents, sudden and incalculable, of which Lara was the last. "Life plans are foolish," he had told her once. "It's all so contingent . . ."

At twenty-six, he had not known how true that was.

Newark

1984–1988

ONE

Though he could not have known this, Kerry had foreordained the Musso case, a woman's murder, and his own near death at the moment he told Vincent J. Flavio to go to hell.

When Liam Dunn had gotten him the job, defying the Essex County prosecutor had been the furthest thing from Kerry's mind. He was simply grateful—to Liam for helping him through college and law school at Seton Hall; for the discovery that, in addition to a surprising gift for poetry, he had a decent head for law; for the softness in his mother's eyes at his private swearing in, administered, at Liam's request, by the venerable Judge Thomas Riordan in his spacious oak-paneled chambers.

Two years before, Mary Kilcannon had found her husband, Michael, slumped in his living room chair, dead from a massive heart attack. Though the neighborhood was changing, Mary remained in the house where she had raised her sons. Kerry watched over her; Jamie was now a distant figure, seldom seen in Vailsburg yet a subject of great pride—the handsome senator whose cool intellect and gift of eloquence, more Ivy League than Irish, might take him to the presidency at a younger age than Kennedy.

But Kerry had little interest in Jamie or his world. His ambitions were much simpler: to prosecute criminals and warrant his mother's pride. Except for one college trip to Florida, he had seldom been more than a hundred miles from Newark. He had no thought of leaving.

Just as Newark had become a place of contrasts—modern glass towers next to abandoned buildings and shops, the glorious city hall that housed a nearly bankrupt government—so was the Essex County Courthouse. The first time Kerry climbed its steps as a lawyer, he stopped at the foot of the massive pillared structure, gazing up at the words "Law," "Justice," and "Peace" chiseled above the doors, then at the quasi-Greek statuary atop the portico. But the interior, though vast and awe-inspiring in design, had fallen into dinginess and disrepair. Like other assistant prosecutors, Kerry shared a ten-by-ten cubicle along a dim hallway with offices on both sides; crammed within were a filing cabinet, two metal desks with laminate wood tops and rickety wooden chairs that, in the phrase of Kerry's red-haired officemate, Tommy Corcoran, were cursed by the ghosts of prosecutors past.

Their office faced the inside corridor and sweltered during the summer. For privacy, Kerry and Tommy covered its only window with movie posters, so that the witnesses they interviewed did not grow more paranoid than they already were. But even the lawyers were a little paranoid. Though Newark was a violent city, neither the courtroom nor the prosecutor's office had security or even a metal detector; like a number of the other prosecutors, Tommy kept a gun in his desk.

Kerry himself had no feeling about guns. But he could not imagine getting shot for prosecuting the endless run of misdemeanors that were a rookie's lot—traffic offenses, petty vandalism, minor breaches of the peace. And the incumbent county prosecutor, Vincent J. Flavio, was not looking to inflame passions.

"Flavio's a time-server," Liam had told him. "The one thing to never forget is how long he's wanted to be prosecutor and how hell-bent he is to keep it. Threaten *that*, and he's as mean as a snake. Worse, the man knows enough secrets to persuade the last two governors—a Democrat *and* a Republican—to reappoint him. The only way we'll be rid of him now is to indict him. Unless we make him a judge."

This last was said with a touch of humor, Liam's wry acknowledgment of the world's imperfections. Then his face turned serious. "Vincent's no admirer of your brother—sometimes I think God created Jamie just to make politicians like Flavio feel resentful. 'When did he pay his dues?' they wonder. So make sure you pay yours, Kerry.

"*We* know you're there to learn your trade. But to Flavio, just the name Kilcannon makes you someone to watch out for, maybe with enough influence to take his job. Treat him with respect, and let him know about whatever seems important. And should some reporter take an interest in anything you do, remember that every mistake is your own, every triumph a reflection of Vincent J. Flavio's leadership and wisdom."

Kerry did not think this unreasonable. Better than Vincent Flavio could know, Kerry understood how Jamie could make someone feel inadequate. In many ways, Kerry thought, he had more in common with Flavio than with his brother: education at Seton Hall, the "contact" school which bred Newark's lawyers, politicians, and judges; deep roots in the community; a sense of his own limits. Like Flavio, all that Kerry wanted was respect.

On his first day, Flavio's chief assistant, Carl Nunzio—a bald man with a face as creased and hard as a walnut—escorted Kerry to the prosecutor's office and shut the door behind them. Vincent Flavio sat at his desk. He was a big man, built like Kerry's father, but there the resemblance ended. His shoes shone, his curly graying hair had a whiff of the barbershop, and his gold cuff links and monogrammed tie tainted his attempted air of gravitas—steepled fingers, raised head—with a touch of vanity.

As Flavio rose to greet him, Kerry sensed that the vanity, far from being droll, marked the most dangerous thing about him. Vincent Flavio's handshake was firm, his smile so broad that it crinkled the corners of his eyes. But the eyes themselves bored into Kerry's with an invasive intensity. It was as if, Kerry thought, Flavio had trained his mouth and eyes each to serve different functions. Kerry felt small, uncomfortable.

Flavio sat down again, framed by his own face smiling from the wall behind him, pictures taken with a governor, two senators, and, to Kerry's surprise, Luciano Pavarotti. "So," the prosecutor said, "you're here to become a trial lawyer."

Kerry nodded. Reticent, he searched for phrases of gratitude and reassurance. "Maybe someday I'll open my own practice. But this is the only place to learn. I'm lucky to be here."

Flavio's smile appeared again, a display of white teeth. "No luck involved, Kerry. Liam Dunn thinks well of you." Kerry caught the silent message beneath the words; Kerry was here not through his own deserts but on Vincent Flavio's sufferance, as a favor to Liam. Kerry imagined the long list of supporters whose kids or cousins or nephews had lost this slot to Kerry, and, as Flavio no doubt wanted, he felt defensive.

"I'll do the best I can," Kerry said, and disliked himself for it.

As if warmed by Kerry's discomfiture, Flavio's voice grew hearty. "I'm sure you will, Kerry. I'm sure you will." But what Kerry heard was *however good that is.*

Awkwardly, Kerry stood. "Thanks for giving me a chance, Mr. Flavio."

Flavio did not stand. " 'Vincent,' Kerry. As long as you're here, the door is always open. Keep me informed, all right? Or Carl."

Leaving, Kerry realized that the prosecutor had never mentioned Jamie. The message was clear enough: Kerry had entered the world of Vincent J. Flavio, where James Kilcannon held no sway.

That was fine, Kerry thought with fresh determination. All he cared about was trying cases.

For the next year, he labored doggedly. There would always be smarter lawyers in the office, he decided, with quicker minds and better instincts. But no one would outwork him. Petty crime by petty crime, Kerry learned to make cops trust him, to deal with the polyglot array of witnesses afflicted by the accidents of urban life, to weather judges so rude and bored and cynical that their courtrooms were a lawyer's purgatory. Tommy Corcoran marveled at Kerry's hours, and even Vincent Flavio took notice; by the time the year was over, Kerry had tried more misdemeanors than anyone else. He might not be a brilliant lawyer, Kerry thought, but he was becoming a decent mechanic.

Then Carl Nunzio came to his office and handed Kerry an empty envelope. "It's for the flower fund," he said.

Kerry gazed up at Nunzio, fighting back dismay. He was not Liam's pupil for nothing; when he returned the envelope, it would not be empty. With feigned innocence, he asked, "What's the flower fund?"

Nunzio's eyes, narrowing slightly, signaled his annoyance.

"To help Vincent with office expenses," he said at last. "I'm asking his lawyers to water the flowers, so to speak."

Kerry was trapped, he realized. Liam lacked the means to get rid of Flavio by himself; in the tacit division of spoils that held the party together, the prosecutor's office was Italian, and those with the power to get rid of Flavio feared him instead. Kerry wondered whether his money would go toward Flavio's clothes or to his condominium in Florida, and what part spilled over to Nunzio.

"How much?" Kerry asked bluntly.

Nunzio tilted his head, as though appraising Kerry for something he had missed. "Ten percent of gross pay."

Silent, Kerry added two hundred fifty dollars a month to the four hundred he already sent to his mother, and realized that he might have to find a cheaper apartment. Nunzio's tone was deceptively gentle.

"It's voluntary, of course. But we're hoping for one hundred percent participation."

Cornered, Kerry filled with anger at his powerlessness. Liam's friendship and his brother's name would only save him from being fired; his choice was to go along or face professional death—certain transfer to some office backwater, shuffling paper. Kerry's training as a trial lawyer would end.

Kerry nodded slowly.

To his surprise, Nunzio took Tommy Corcoran's chair and sat across from Kerry. "There's something else."

Kerry's instinct for silence was deep. He simply waited.

"You've got a file," Nunzio went on. "The Frankie Scaline case. It's up for prelim next week."

Kerry had numerous cases; he did not know this one. But the name Scaline was familiar. "I haven't read the file yet," Kerry said.

Nunzio spread his hands. "Domestic quarrel—wife gets upset, tells a cop the husband whacked her. Who knows?"

Kerry felt his eyes grow cold. "Who cares?" he asked softly.

Nunzio stared back at him. "The case is weak. They always are. I don't want to waste your time."

Kerry paused. Voice still quiet, he said, "Give it to someone else, then."

Nunzio sat back, hands folded beneath his chin. "I think you should dismiss it."

At once, Kerry understood. If something later happened to the wife, a reassignment might look peculiar; Flavio wanted Kerry's fingerprints on this one, not his own. "Maybe I should interview the wife," Kerry answered.

For a moment, Nunzio was silent. "I understand she's sorry now." His voice had an undertone, the hint of patience lost. "No point in bothering this lady. It's *her* marriage, not yours or mine."

Kerry felt his chest tighten. The woman had persisted, and someone had placed a phone call. That was how it was done.

"Let me read the file," he said.

Nunzio stood. "You do that, Kerry. By tomorrow."

When Nunzio was gone, Kerry sat very still, staring at nothing. A half hour passed before he picked up the telephone.

"Who's Frankie Scaline?" he asked Liam.

"Peter Scaline's boy," Liam answered. As was typical, he asked no questions.

"That's what I thought," Kerry said.

"You should know," Liam continued evenly, "that Peter is a great supporter of Vincent Flavio. Vincent's also Frankie's godfather, if memory serves."

And you're mine, Kerry thought. "Thanks, Liam."

There was silence, Liam weighing his obligations. "Things all right over there?"

Liam had done enough for him, Kerry thought. To intervene with Flavio would squander a piece of the political capital Liam needed for more important matters. "Things are fine," Kerry said, and got off.

He found the Scaline file in a stack atop the filing cabinet.

According to the police report, Frankie Scaline was twenty-four. His wife of less than a year, Elaine Scaline, had locked herself in the bedroom and called 911. Arriving, the police saw a bruise on her face, a slightly swollen lip. She claimed that Frankie had slapped her for refusing oral sex; her husband, embarrassed and belligerent, claimed that she had tripped. To men like Vincent Flavio, a comedy, a favor to be done.

Putting down the file, Kerry touched his eyes.

It was Elaine Scaline's second complaint. Through the wooden prose of the report, Kerry had an image of her plight; intuitively, he believed that Frankie was a wife beater and that his wife knew he would grow worse. That was why she had not backed down.

It was the last case Kerry wanted.

He faced the reasons. For others, it would be enough that domestic violence cases were the dregs of the office—losers, pitting one witness against another, often abandoned by the complainant herself. Most of them would gladly do as Nunzio asked. But Kerry knew that his own reasons went far deeper: the habit of silence, passed from his mother to Kerry, the need to forget.

That part of his life was over. He had no wish to go back.

The morning of the preliminary hearing for Frankie Scaline, Kerry went to court.

Everything went as planned. Speaking for the State of New Jersey, Assistant County Prosecutor Kerry Kilcannon asked that the case be dismissed. Frankie was absent, and so was his wife. The hardest part was done—Kerry's phone call to Elaine Scaline, explaining that her case was problematic. Frankie Scaline's lawyer did not have to say a word.

As they left the courtroom, he shook Kerry's hand and thanked him.

Solitary, Kerry stopped on the courthouse steps. He did not know what he would do, or even where he was going.

At the end of their conversation, Elaine Scaline had started to cry.

Torn between anger and self-hatred, Kerry went to his office. The envelope was still on his desk.

Tearing a scrap of paper from his notepad, Kerry scrawled three words and slid the paper in the envelope. Then he walked the maze of corridors to Vincent Flavio's corner office and opened the door.

Flavio was on the telephone. Looking up at Kerry, he neither waved him to a chair nor cut short the conversation. Kerry waited.

Hanging up the phone, Flavio studied him, a silent reproach for his rudeness. "What is it?" he demanded.

Kerry walked across Flavio's Oriental rug and placed the envelope in his hand. As Flavio removed the scrap of paper, Kerry watched his face turn red.

"*State v. Scaline,*" Kerry had written.

Kerry's voice shook. "That's my contribution, Vincent. It seems like enough."

Before Flavio could answer, Kerry turned and left.

He did not have long to wait. Within hours, they dispatched his friend Tommy Corcoran to share another office. Tommy's replacement was a heavyset black lawyer, Clayton Slade, with his own inclination toward quiet.

Two days later, Carl Nunzio called Kerry to his office. "I'm giving you a new assignment," he said, and waited for Kerry's question.

There was none.

"We've been taking some heat on domestic violence," Nunzio went on. "Vincent thinks we need a specialist." For once, amusement played on his wizened face. "Of course I thought of *you*, Kerry. After all, you've got experience."

TWO

Two weeks later, the Musso case came in.

Bridget Musso was the victim. When the cops arrived, her husband was gone; she was sprawled on the living room floor, unconscious. Her face was bruised and several teeth were broken. But the detail Kerry found most chilling was that her eight-year-old son sat next to her, so uncommunicative that at first they thought he was retarded. His only words to the police were "I think my mommy's dead."

They rushed Bridget to the hospital and her son to a Catholic home for boys. This made sense to Kerry; in the Vailsburg apartment house where the Mussos lived, the father had a reputation for drunkenness and fits of temper. When the police tracked down Anthony Musso in a bar, he claimed that his alcoholic wife had tripped in the bathroom, smashing her face against the sink. He did not ask about his son.

The second problem, it seemed, was Bridget herself.

The admitting report from the hospital showed traces of drugs in her system, and a blood alcohol content well above the legal limit. The drugs were prescribed for epilepsy but, combined with too much alcohol, they produced an incapacitating haze.

That was how the neighbors frequently saw her—dazed, remote, with a vacant stare that made them feel invisible. It seemed John Musso had no parents worth the name.

The other thing it meant, Kerry knew, was that a good defense lawyer might impeach Bridget Musso. That drunks can stumble and injure themselves was emblazoned in Kerry's memory.

Before anything else, he must interview Bridget.

When they discharged her from the hospital, she was afraid to go home. She and her child were living in a shelter run by the city; over the telephone, Kerry confirmed that she was drinking again. He reserved a witness room and sent the police to escort her in.

She was red-haired, Irish-looking, and the file said she was thirty-five. But ill health and addiction seemed to have sapped the life from her. There was a softness to her chin, a slackness to her face and body: her pale skin was blotchy, and Kerry noticed burst blood vessels beneath the surface of her cheeks. Though it was eleven-thirty in the morning, Kerry could smell whiskey on her breath.

"Can you tell me what happened?" he asked.

She touched her face, as if this would help her remember. Beneath her delicate fingers, the swollen bruise was fading to green-yellow. When at last she spoke, Kerry saw her ruined teeth, the stitches on the inside of her lip. "Anthony did this," she said dully, and then she shrugged. "He's no different than anyone. Sometimes men get angry."

The words left pinpricks on Kerry's neck. "Your father beat your mother?" he asked gently. "Or you?"

For a time, she just looked past him. "Both."

Sweet Jesus, Kerry thought in despair. But he stifled the impulse to ask about this; already, she seemed enervated. "That night," he asked, "what did your husband do to you?"

For almost an hour, question by question, Kerry negotiated the minefield of her memory—bursts of vivid clarity, surrounded by black holes. The memory of a drunk.

By the time it was over, Kerry was exhausted, the night, as he pieced it together from Bridget and the file, indelible.

She was alone in the shabby living room. John was probably in his room—about this Bridget Musso had no curiosity. The light from the living room lamp receded into darkness. The acrid smell of burned pasta sauce reminded her, vaguely, that she had not turned off the kitchen stove.

Anthony had not come home for dinner.

Waiting, Bridget poured more whiskey into the plastic glass. The music on the soft-rock station seemed to come from far away, a note at a time. She barely heard the sound of a key opening the apartment door, the door softly closing.

Her husband was a large form in the darkness.

Bridget jerked upright. He stood over her, very still, his face still in shadows. "Why do you do this to me, Bridget?"

His voice was mournful, a whisper. That was how Bridget knew to fear him.

Numb, she shook her head.

"Why?" he asked again.

His eyes were dark pools, his beard a neglected stubble. Like her father's . . .

Frozen, Bridget felt the urine run down her leg.

Her husband gazed at the stain she had made, spreading

across the cushioned chair. "Like an animal." His voice was hoarse now. "A dog."

Bridget began to cry. When he jerked her from the chair, she screamed in pain . . .

The world went dark.

She was in the bathroom now, dress pulled up around her waist, spraddled across the toilet. Her husband slapped her so hard that her head hit the wall.

"Now you can piss," he ordered. "Go ahead—*do* it."

Closing her eyes, she tried, her body trembling with the effort.

His voice rose. "Do it *now*."

Dazed, she felt the tears on her face.

He slapped her again. Falling sideways, she clawed at the sink with one hand.

She caught herself, pulled upright to stand, underpants around her ankles. In the cracked mirror above the sink, her husband's face broke into pieces.

With one powerful hand at the base of Bridget's skull, he smashed her face into the sink.

Bridget cried out in shock and pain. Reeling, she lurched toward the bathroom door, spitting fragments of her teeth.

Her son stood in the doorway, his eyes filled with terror. Bridget stumbled past him, into darkness.

She remembered nothing more. It was her eight-year-old son who had called 911.

Drained, Kerry studied her across the table. The cubicle they sat in was pale green in the fluorescent light. The air felt hot and close.

Kerry kept his voice soft. "I need you to testify."

Mute, she shook her head, staring at the rings of coffee stains on the battered wooden table. At last, she murmured, "If I do, he'll kill me."

Kerry's mouth felt dry. "Bridget," he said quietly, "he'll kill you if you don't."

Her greenish eyes, Kerry thought, were close to dead. Only her tears said that she had heard him.

* * *

When he returned to his office, Kerry loosened his tie and sat back in his chair, eyes half shut with weariness. He took no notice of Clayton Slade.

In Mary Kilcannon, Kerry thought, he had been luckier than he knew.

"So," he heard Clayton ask, "how was she?"

Surprised, Kerry turned to him, wondering how much Clayton had divined from Kerry's calls to the shelter, the hospital, the police. "A mess." Suddenly Kerry realized that it would be a relief to talk like a professional, a lawyer. "Major gaps in memory. Past the legal limit when it happened. Scared to testify."

"What about the injuries?"

"*She* says he slammed her face into the sink. *He* says she fell, so drunk she pissed all over herself. Which she did."

Frowning, Clayton folded his hands across his stomach. "You're going to need the kid," he said.

That night, Kerry went to his apartment, put on some tapes of Bruce Springsteen and Southside Johnny, and began taking inventory of his life.

He was twenty-seven and single, the less gifted younger brother of a senator, with a boss who was his enemy and a docket of domestic violence cases. The sole escape was James Kilcannon; during Kerry's first trip to Washington, Jamie had offered to secure him an entry-level position in the Senate bureaucracy. But Washington had no allure for Kerry, and becoming Jamie's dependent would condemn him to a life in his brother's shadow, having nothing of his own.

"You're going to need the kid," Clayton Slade had told him.

Unbidden, the image of his father came to Kerry's mind.

In his last years, Michael Kilcannon had been a quiet brooding figure, drinking alone, ashamed of what he had become, unable to apologize to his wife or sons. For Kerry, his father was dead before he died; content that his mother was safe, Kerry hardly spoke to him. Then he was gone, and Kerry, to his shock, wept from loneliness and unresolved anger—he had desperately wanted a father, he realized, but all he had was the terror of his father's violent moods, the determination never to be like him.

John Musso was eight years old.

Against the habit of a lifetime, Kerry forced himself to remember.

At eight, Kerry had known there was no help for them: Jamie had turned his back, and his mother feared calling the police. If she had done so, Kerry wondered, would he have had the courage to speak for her? But Mary Kilcannon had not been a pathetic drunk, as hopeless and indifferent as his father was brutal.

For Kerry to put Anthony Musso in prison, he must persuade this boy to believe in *him*.

From the first moment, sitting with Kerry in the witness room, John Musso could not look at him.

He was pale, Kerry saw, with lank, dark hair and the habit of clenching his jaw, as if to withstand whatever might happen next. His fear showed in a convulsive swallowing.

"My name is Kerry," he said gently.

John would not look up. The only sign of his having heard was that his head became quite still; only his throat moved. No wonder, Kerry reflected, that at first the cops had thought this boy autistic.

"I work with the police," Kerry went on. "My job's to help you and your mom."

John was silent. Kerry took a rubber ball from his pocket and placed it on the wooden table, resting it beneath his fingertips.

The boy's eyes moved, surreptitiously, to the ball. "Do you like balls?" Kerry asked.

No answer.

"I'm giving it to you," Kerry said. "Hold out your hand, all right?"

For a moment, the boy remained still, blue eyes fixed on the table. His hand slid toward Kerry, as if it had a life of its own. When Kerry placed the ball in his open palm, John flinched, and then his fingers clutched the red sphere so hard that his knuckles turned white.

"Roll the ball to me," Kerry said, "and I'll roll it back. It's a game."

John swallowed again; at once, Kerry saw that he did not want to let go. "It's okay," Kerry told him. "You can keep it."

More from fear than a sense of play, Kerry thought, the boy let the ball slip from his fingers and roll across the table. Kerry took the ball and placed it in John's hand.

"Again?" Kerry asked.

As if in answer, John rolled the ball to Kerry. Rolling it back, Kerry wondered who played with this boy. John regarded others with suspicion, his second grade teacher had told Kerry, and his grades and attendance were abysmal. In school, his only animation was flashes of anger.

Silent, they rolled the ball back and forth. For John Musso, the dismal witness room was a refuge, Kerry realized—a few moments with a stranger who, whatever he wanted, did not seem to pose a threat. Kerry let the silence grow around them; the few times he had thrown a ball with his father, he remembered, there had been no need to speak.

What to say? Kerry wondered. When the answer struck him, its difficulty gave Kerry a window to the boy's soul, and his own.

"Can I tell you something?" Kerry said at last.

The ball froze in John Musso's hand. "When I was eight," Kerry began, "my dad did things to my mom."

The boy was still.

"He hit her. Like your dad does. I couldn't make him stop."

The boy swallowed again. His mouth, Kerry noticed, was not as tight. Kerry's own mouth was dry.

"I'd lie in bed," Kerry went on, "and wish that someone could help us."

John was silent. His hand clutched the rubber ball again.

For the first time, Kerry took the ball from his grasp, then rolled it back to John. "I hated what Da did to my mom. I know you hate it too." Kerry kept his voice soft. "If I can make him stop, maybe your mom will get better. But I'll need your help for that."

Kerry stopped there, letting the hope settle in John's mind.

The boy's swallowing seemed convulsive now. Then his fingers loosened, and the ball slid from his hand.

Taut, Kerry watched it roll into his own. "You remember that night, John, when the police took your mom to the hospital? How did your dad hurt her?"

There was a long silence, and then John Musso looked up into Kerry's eyes, lips trembling, shutting his eyes just before he whispered, "He smashed her face into the sink."

This time, Kerry drove to the shelter to visit Bridget Musso.

It was a warm spring morning, and Kerry had the top down on his ten-year-old Volkswagen. The weekend promised to be a fine one, reminding Kerry that he had no girlfriend, no dates, no plans. That was another way he was unlike his brother, Kerry thought ruefully. But one look at Bridget Musso, and he forgot all that.

She was lolling on a battered couch, slack-faced again, and the tip of her nose was red. Quite deliberately, Kerry glanced around the barren meeting room, as depressing as a flophouse hotel, then asked, "Is this what you want for your son? Or you?"

She stared through him, wordless. Kerry sat beside her on the couch. "He doesn't want you beaten anymore, Bridget. He doesn't want you drunk anymore." He paused, softening his tone. "Do you *hear* me?"

Almost imperceptibly, she nodded.

"Then *listen*." Kerry's eyes bored into hers. "Even though he's frightened, your eight-year-old son is willing to go to court for you. Will you go for *him*, Bridget?"

Her lips parted, but she made no sound. Sensing her uncertainty, Kerry put aside the fact that John Musso had not yet promised to testify, that he was using each of them to strengthen the other. "What is that boy worth to you?" Kerry asked. "Anything? Because unless you change things, all he'll ever know is all *you've* ever known. And all he'll ever *be* is like his father."

The woman blinked, turning away.

Kerry wanted to grab her by the shoulders, make her look into his face again. He forced himself to be still. "*Look* at me, Bridget."

Slowly, she turned.

Kerry's face was inches from hers. "If you help John," he said, "I'll put Anthony in jail. After that, he'll be afraid to hurt either of you again."

For a long time, she stared into his eyes. Then, as if Kerry had willed it, she nodded.

THREE

That evening, self-doubting and far more lonely than he cared to be, Kerry decided to drop by McGovern's for a beer.

To Kerry, McGovern's was the last great Irish bar. Vailsburg had changed so quickly that its own bars were dying off, turned to shops or meeting places or, in one startling twist, a black apostolic church. But McGovern's remained as it was in the 1930s, with Irish memorabilia on the walls and fire and police hats suspended from above its oval wooden bar. Its rules were as timeless. Smoking was fine, but a man would be thrown out for cursing in front of a lady. There was no television to impede conversation, argument, or the chance to meet a prospective mate under acceptable circumstances: this was not a pickup bar, everyone knew, but a social club, and the common saying was that "more marriages are made at McGovern's than in church." The jukebox featured Irish tunes, and its longtime proprietor, an immigrant given to dancing the occasional jig, might stand a round or two. Because McGovern's was near the law schools at Rutgers and Seton Hall, it was a favorite haunt of court-room types; the bar's ad in the law school newspapers read "McGovern's—the only bar you'll never want to pass." More than one legal hopeful, Kerry thought wryly, had passed out at McGovern's after failing the bar exam.

It was a Friday, and McGovern's was filled with smoke, laughter, the sound of debate or gossip or flirtation. To his surprise, Kerry saw no one from the office. He thought about leaving, then contemplated another night spent with Southside Johnny and took the one empty seat at the bar.

Instantly, the proprietor, Bill Carney, a trim man of sixty with bright eyes and a gray mustache, appeared with a cool bottle of Kerry's favorite, Killian's Red. " 'Kerry Kilcannon,' " he said, smiling, " 'the fighting prosecutor, valiant for truth.' "

Kerry grinned. They had been playing this game since the night Kerry was sworn in, and his every appearance required a new billing. " 'Bill Carney,' " Kerry answered, " 'tax chiseler, refugee from the law, and scourge of the English Crown.' "

Bill laughed. "Would that it were true—the tax chiseler part, especially." He poured Kerry's beer. "So how *are* things on the frontiers of urban justice?"

Kerry sipped his beer and chose to tell some semblance of the truth. "Tough cases, long days. Today, especially."

Bill gave him a quick shrewd look, born of ten thousand nights spent divining moods in an instant, and his eyes moved from Kerry to the woman on the next stool. "Do you two know each other?"

Kerry had hardly noticed her. She turned, giving him a quick, mock-critical appraisal. She was pretty, he saw at once—short auburn hair, a snub nose with freckles, large green eyes, and a generous mouth that formed dimples as she smiled at Bill. "Should I?" she asked.

Bill gave an elaborate shrug. "Jury's still out on that one. Some days I hardly know him myself." He turned to another customer, leaving Kerry and the woman to fend for themselves.

Somewhat embarrassed, Kerry said, "Bill's at work again."

Once more, the dimples flashed, this time in a smile that seemed slightly sardonic. "My parents met here," she said wryly. "Bill thinks that's a heartwarming link in a great tradition. I've no heart to tell him how miserable they are."

The remark was so unexpected that it made Kerry laugh. With a few candid words, the woman had taken what might be a sentimental story and inverted it, easing Kerry's sense that Bill

Carney had assigned them to each other. "I'm Kerry Kilcannon," he said, and held out his hand.

Her own hand was cool and dry. "Meg Collins. And I *do* know you. From school at Sacred Heart." She smiled again. "You were much older. Maybe ten."

Kerry gave her a puzzled look and then made a connection of his own. "I saw you at a law school party, I think. Aren't you Pat Curran's wife?"

"You *did*. And I *was*. We barely outlasted the party."

"I'm sorry," he said, and meant it.

"Oh, it's all right, really." She spoke with brisk good humor, as if to ward off sympathy. "Without children, it's more like a train wreck than a lingering illness. Suddenly your husband's gone, and you never have to talk to him again."

What had happened? Kerry wondered. But the empathy that made him curious kept him from asking; all he could offer was honesty. "Some days, being alone is better than others, I guess. There's no one to talk to, but you can do what you want."

Meg nodded. "That's what I'm trying to learn," she said. "Like going to the movies without a girlfriend, or coming here. It's amazing—they don't teach women that, do they?"

Beneath her question, Kerry heard an undertone of resolve, then wondered if he was in the way. "You shouldn't feel stuck with me," he said, then tried to ease this by adding, "You know, like on that game show where the date some woman's picked comes out from behind the screen, and she looks at him like 'There's no way *this* guy is ever getting near me.'"

Smiling, Meg touched his arm. "If I'd wanted you to leave, you'd know by now. My eyes get really blank, like by the end of one of Father Joe's homilies." She took another sip of beer. "That show *is* awful, though. The point must be to give you someone else to feel sorry for."

Beneath his own smile of relief, Kerry had an unwelcome thought: *As long as I'm working domestic violence, I'll never need them.* What he did need, Kerry realized, was to talk about John Musso. But this was not a subject for a first meeting, and it felt too close to his own life. "So what are you doing now?" he asked.

"I'm a legal secretary." Again, Meg made her tone indifferent. "I'd do that till Pat got through law school, the plan was, then be free to finish college. Instead I'm getting my teacher's certificate at night."

The indifference was practiced, Kerry sensed; sheltered by her guise of fatalism, Meg was still back in the marriage, sadly pondering its end. "I guess Pat didn't quite make a husband," he ventured.

She looked at him, suddenly pensive, then gazed down at the bar. Around them the smoke and talk and laughter afforded a cocoon of privacy. "He was young," she said. "He kept wanting change, excitement, new things. Marriage isn't like that, I discovered."

For a moment, Kerry's heart went out to her; she had offered him a piece of honesty in return, a brief glimpse of her own heart. But he had no experience to offer, knew too little about Meg's to say. They sat together in silence.

"Anyhow," she said at last, "I really should go home. Finals start on Monday."

Wondering if this was true, Kerry felt hesitation overtake him. But Meg *was* pretty, and he was curious about her. Standing, he asked, "Can I take you home, at least?"

Meg paused, considering him, and then she smiled again. "You always *seemed* nice, Kerry. At least to girls."

She lived on the bottom floor of a duplex in Down Neck, the old Portuguese section, now favored by some young people for its low rents and good restaurants. On the way, they chatted about Vailsburg and common memories. "You looked so serious," Meg told him. "Sometimes I wondered what was wrong." But Kerry had learned the uses of humor. "Not serious," he answered. "Prayerful. It was my only hope of decent grades."

Arriving at Meg's duplex, Kerry walked her to the porch. They stood facing each other in the cool night air.

"This was nice," she said. "Seeing you again."

The evening was over, Kerry knew. But she had not dismissed him, quite.

Looking into her face, he gently cradled her chin. Her eyes were wide, questioning. As he bent his head to hers, they closed.

Her mouth was soft and warm. He felt the smallest shudder of her body, and then, slowly, she ended the kiss.

Her gaze was serious, direct. "That was nice too," she said. Then she backed away slowly and opened the door behind her, still looking at Kerry.

Driving home, he felt an unfamiliar lightness.

For the next two weeks, they went to movies or dinner, met at McGovern's after work. Meg laughed easily now, spoke readily of her parents. With a certain dryness that did not quite conceal her resentment, Meg portrayed her father as an authoritarian misogynist, puzzled that any woman went to college. The unspoken subtext, Kerry sensed, was that her father and her husband had made her wary; she might consider marrying again, but not at the risk of losing herself. Though she sometimes seemed drained by the stress of job and school, the next day Meg would bounce back, cheerful in his company.

They slowly learned about each other—likes, prejudices, the outlines of their lives. But she seldom spoke of her marriage, and though she often asked, Kerry found it hard to speak of his work. Part of his reluctance was the Musso case: as he headed for trial, Kerry felt so responsible for both son and mother that the fear of losing kept him awake at night. He wanted Meg to be separate from his concern for the Mussos, his anger at Vincent Flavio, his bleak vision of a stalled career; at the end of a day, the mere sight of her raised Kerry's spirits.

One warm summer night in June, they went to Iberia, her favorite restaurant. Amidst the colorful trappings of Portugal, the sound of fado music, they drank sangria and shared radicchio, skewers of delicious meat. Meg was vibrant, laughing, full of life.

"My friends are right," she said.

"About what?"

Meg looked at him across the table, eyes smiling. "You're better-looking than your brother. He's much too perfect."

Surprised, Kerry felt slighted that Jamie mattered—that even with Meg, he could not escape comparison. With sudden intensity, he wished that she simply had *known* this, then realized that, if she did not, perhaps the fault was his. "So I'm the un-Jamie," he said at last. "But what does that make *me*?"

Meg seemed to study his expression, and then she touched his hand. "Human, Kerry. It makes you human."

They went back to her apartment.

When Kerry kissed her, he was torn between anticipation and another feeling, less joyful: the desire to prove himself to Meg. Her remark about Jamie still unsettled him; for a moment, he had an image of two strangers, driven by whatever needs, hidden from the other, that their separate lives had created. Then Meg kissed him more deeply, and he put this out of his mind.

When he unzipped her dress, she pressed against him, and Kerry knew that she had decided to trust him this much further.

Her skin was lightly freckled, her breasts full. Dropping her panties to the floor, she gazed at him with uncertainty. "Be patient," she said. "It's been a long time for me."

Kerry could feel the beating of his own heart. "For both of us," he answered, and reached out for her hand.

Together, they walked to her bed.

In his desire, Kerry felt unsure where best to touch her, how to know when she was ready. Meg tried to murmur her pleasure or approval, a kind of guide. At last, still tentative, Kerry entered her.

Even as their bodies moved together, he felt too conscious of her for quick excitement, too aware of all the ways in which they still did not know each other. Suddenly Meg felt rigid beneath him, emitting one small cry. A moment later, Kerry was still.

In his arms, Meg fell silent. It was as if, Kerry thought, she had gone away. "Are you okay?" he asked.

"You were sweet, Kerry." Softly, Meg kissed him. "The first time's always hard, they say."

Quiet, Kerry lay beside her. What more, he wondered, did he want her to say or do?

"Pat," he said at last. "What happened with him?"

She looked away. "Why does it matter?"

Gently, he touched her bare arm. "Look at us, Meg. Three weeks ago we'd barely met, and now we're here."

Meg turned on her stomach, gazing at the wall behind him. "He left me," she said in a monotone. "For a woman in his office, a lawyer. She was more interesting, he said. I'd stopped being fun."

The last words were muffled. Kerry traced her spine with his fingertips, barely grazing the skin, until she curled her back against him. He could feel her crying.

Later, Meg slept. Kerry did not. They were two children of bad marriages, he thought, with little way of knowing how things should be. It was no wonder if they stumbled.

Kerry held her close.

FOUR

Waiting for Bridget Musso and her son on the steps of the Essex County Courthouse, Kerry recalled Clayton Slade's advice.

He could not call Clayton a friend—they spoke only about work, and sparingly at that. But Clayton was older than Kerry by three years, all spent trying cases, and seemed to sense Kerry's anxiety.

The day before the trial, Clayton had watched Kerry outline his examination. "Mom's clean and sober now?" he asked.

Kerry looked up in surprise, and then nodded. "Three months."

"What about the boy?"

Kerry hesitated. "I don't know what he'll do," he confessed. "I *won't* know, until the moment I put him on."

Clayton frowned. "Tell the jury that up front. If the kid folds, at least they'll be expecting it."

Imagining John facing his father across the courtroom, Kerry drew a breath. "If he *doesn't* fold, I have to win. Or God knows what will happen to them both."

Now Kerry watched John Musso climb the steps, holding his mother's hand.

It was remarkable, Kerry thought: he had believed this woman beyond redemption, yet here she was. Though still pallid, Bridget's skin was less blotchy, her eyes clear. This was not entirely a mercy, Kerry reflected, for she had nothing to numb her fear.

"I knew you could do this," he told her. When she raised her head, Kerry saw that he had been right: reminding Bridget of what she already had achieved was better than promises she knew he could not make.

He knelt beside her son.

For hours, Kerry had worked with him. But the boy's eyes, veiled by dark lashes, were fixed on the stone steps. Gently, Kerry said, "I'm glad you're helping your mom."

John did not look up. Yet Kerry saw his shoulders square; an attachment, tentative but touching in its hope, had grown between son and mother. When they began climbing the last steps, John Musso took both his mother's hand and Kerry's.

Grasping the small fingers, Kerry felt a stirring of unease, wondering what he might symbolize to an eight-year-old boy. Within hours, John Musso would be forced to choose between his father and his mother. Between his father and Kerry Kilcannon, who had put him there.

A social worker met them at the top of the steps. With a calm he did not feel, Kerry told the boy again that she would take him and his mother to a room with toys, until their turn had come.

For the first time, John's fearful eyes met his. In a thin voice, he asked Kerry, "You'll be there, right? In court?"

Nodding, Kerry clasped his shoulder. "When you answer the questions, just look at me. Nothing else."

Watching son and mother leave with a stranger, Kerry was still. Then he went to the courtroom alone.

It was empty. Through the airy ceilings, inlaid with gold, grids of clear glass filtered light onto the marble bench of the judge, the jury box. Five rows of hand-carved benches were flanked by oil paintings of judges and a fresco of Lady Justice and her suitors. Not unlike his feelings in the sanctuary at Sacred Heart, where he still took his mother on Sundays, Kerry's first moments in this courtroom filled him with a sense of awe and mystery. How much more awesome, he reflected, would it seem to a child.

Sitting at the defense table, Kerry waited for his first glimpse of Anthony Musso, a man he had never met but already knew to hate, and who, in the three months of jail awaiting trial, had no doubt learned to hate Kerry.

Slowly, the courtroom filled, stirring to life—the bailiff; the clerk; the prospective jurors; the public defender, Gary Levin, a sharp-eyed veteran who affected bow ties and gray flowing hair; Judge Frederick Weinstein, balding, cadaverous, and given to sarcasm. Then, at last, Anthony Musso.

He was shorter than Kerry had imagined, barely taller than Kerry himself, though barrel-chested and much stockier. But there was little of the swagger of the bully; sitting next to his lawyer, Musso was unnaturally still. The olive surface of his face was flat, as if hammered on an anvil, and his hair was as black as his eyes. When at last he turned those eyes on Kerry, they were unblinking, implacable, beyond reach. It was like looking into the eyes of a horse.

Staring back, Kerry imagined himself as John Musso, gazing up at his father. The fear he felt was not only of sudden violence but of what lay behind this, infinitely worse—a terrible remoteness of feeling, an indifference to the lives he warped. Suddenly Kerry was a young boy in the doorway, watching Anthony Musso smash his mother's face into the white porcelain sink. The sound of teeth breaking, the spittle of blood, had not changed the father's eyes at all.

I'll get you, Kerry promised him across the courtroom, and then the trial began.

The morning went quickly. The jury was impaneled; largely forced on the lawyers by Judge Weinstein, it was a fair cross-section of Newark, though heavier on males than Kerry would have liked. His opening witness, the first cop on the scene, described Bridget's injuries and Anthony Musso's story; on cross-examination, Levin established that John Musso had said only that he thought his mother was dead. The emergency room doctor could not add much; though the injuries to Bridget's mouth and teeth were severe, he could not be certain how this happened, and Bridget's epilepsy and blood alcohol content suggested the possibility of motor impairment, perhaps even fainting, which could have caused her to fall by herself. At two in the afternoon, Kerry had no case.

Gazing at the jury, he called Bridget Musso.

A courtroom deputy escorted her in. As she walked between the benches, empty of spectators, Kerry saw Bridget will herself not to look at Anthony Musso. Instinctively, Kerry went to her, touching her elbow, and then she took the stand.

Her green eyes were fixed, her face a frozen mask. "Make the jury see her fear," Clayton had counseled; an emotionless victim could lose the jurors as surely as one who was shrill and vengeful. But even sober, Bridget was sparing of both words and feelings; against all her instincts, and in the presence of the man she feared, Kerry must re-create that night.

For the first few questions, she did not look up, and her voice was toneless, a whisper. "Before Anthony came home," Kerry asked, "where were you?"

Bridget's eyes narrowed; though Kerry had scoured the corners of her memory, every detail was a strain. "The living room," she said at last. "It was dark."

"And you'd been drinking."

Still downcast, Bridget's eyes grew vague. "Yes."

Kerry walked closer, hoping he could somehow reach her. "Where was John?"

Bridget hesitated. When she spoke, her tone was shamed. "I don't know."

Look at me, Kerry silently implored her, moving nearer still. "How did you know," he asked, "when Anthony came home?"

To Kerry's right, from the defense table, Anthony Musso stared fixedly at his wife. Almost whispering, Bridget answered, "At first he was a shadow. Then his face came into the light."

"He was standing over you, wasn't he? Just like I am now."

Bridget nodded. It was as if the two of them were alone now, the jury merely eavesdroppers. Quietly, Kerry asked, "What did you do?"

Swallowing, Bridget answered, "I peed myself."

Kerry exhaled. "Your husband saw?"

Her head bowed. "He called me an animal."

"Did he say it like this?" Suddenly Kerry's voice cracked like a whip: " 'You're like an animal—a dog.' "

Bridget flinched, turning sideways. *"Objection."* Behind Kerry, Levin's voice was sharp. "Leading."

Kerry kept watching Bridget. Only part of him was aware of the jury; the sharp gaze of Judge Weinstein; Anthony Musso's unremitting stare. "Sustained," Weinstein said.

Kerry ignored this. "After your husband called you an animal," he asked Bridget, "what happened?"

She hunched, closing her eyes, briefly shuddering. "He dragged me to the toilet by my hair. Then he pulled my pants down and told me to start pissing." In profile, Bridget sat straighter, her jaw tightening in a pantomime of fright and determination. "I tried . . ."

Kerry moved to his right, closer to her line of vision. After a long moment, Bridget's eyes met his. Still quiet, he said, "Did that make him angry?"

"He slapped me." Bridget winced, as if from a blow. "My head hit the wall."

To his side, Kerry saw a juror—a black woman—touch her throat. "Then he hit you again, didn't he?"

"Yes." Bridget's words were choked, husky. "I caught the sink, trying to pull myself up. His face was in the mirror . . ." Once more, her eyes closed.

Please, Kerry thought, *stay with me.* "What did Anthony do, Bridget?"

For the first time, she glanced at her husband. Her mouth opened, making no sound, and then the tears came to her eyes.

"What did he do?" Kerry repeated.

She turned back to him, drawing a breath. "He pushed my face into the sink—"

" 'Pushed'?"

"My teeth broke." Her voice caught, quavering. "There were pieces in my mouth . . ."

Kerry waited a moment. "What happened then?" he asked.

Bridget folded her hands, lips trembling. "I was in the hospital . . ."

No, Kerry thought. He forced himself to pause again, waiting for her eyes to meet his. "*Before* the hospital, Bridget, do you remember anything else?"

Bridget blinked, seemingly lost to him. Kerry felt his stomach tighten.

"Bridget?"

Sudden tears ran down her face. "My son," she said softly. "John was standing in the bathroom door."

By the time Gary Levin rose to cross-examine, Bridget appeared drained, bloodless. Levin stood next to Anthony Musso; the tactic, Kerry saw at once, was to make her look at her husband.

"That night," Levin began crisply, "what alcohol were you drinking?"

Bridget looked away. "Whiskey."

"How much?"

Fidgeting, Bridget touched the hem of her skirt. "I don't remember."

"Over two drinks? Or three?"

Bridget gave a listless shrug. "I don't remember," she repeated.

"You don't *remember*?" Levin's voice and posture—hands on hips, gazing at Bridget—conveyed how unimpressed he was. "You were drunk, weren't you? In truth, you were drunk throughout your marriage."

Bridget hesitated. But for three months, she had gone to AA meetings, learning to confront her shame. Dully, she said, "I'm an alcoholic."

"And when you drink, you lose your memory."

"Objection," Kerry snapped. "Which time? Every time? *All* the time? Surely Mr. Levin can't mean *that*."

From the bench, Judge Weinstein stared at Kerry. "Are you trying to convey, Mr. Kilcannon, that the question is overbroad?"

Kerry flushed. "Yes."

"Because I sustain objections, not speeches." He turned to Levin. "Sustained."

Smoothly, Levin said to Bridget, "You don't remember that night, do you? The night you blame your husband for."

In confusion, Bridget looked from Weinstein to Kerry. "I remember it," she said with belated stubbornness.

"Do you remember when you talked to the police?"

"Yes."

"But you didn't tell them about urinating, did you?"

"I was *scared*—"

"Or about your husband shouting at you."

Bridget touched her forehead. "I don't remember . . . ," she began, then heard herself. "I was afraid."

"In fact," Levin cut in, "all you told the police was that your husband hit you."

Bridget shook her head. "I was scared," she insisted.

"You were drunk, weren't you?"

Bridget shook her head. "Not then."

Levin glanced at Kerry. "But you didn't 'remember' any of those details until you met with Mr. Kilcannon, correct?"

Bridget stared into some middle distance, unable to look at Kerry, Levin, the jury. "Mr. Kilcannon helped me. For John."

"John," Levin repeated. "When all this supposedly was happening—the drinking, your husband coming home, you urinating down your leg—you don't remember *where* John was, do you?"

Bridget's eyes shut. "No."

"And then, with your teeth broken and your mouth bleeding, about to pass out—*then* you remember seeing John?"

"Yes."

"But you didn't tell the police *that*, either."

Bridget seemed to hug herself. Watching, Kerry wished he could stop this, but to ask for a recess might, for the jury, be worse. Levin's voice rose. "Is there some reason you won't look at me, Mrs. Musso?"

All at once, Kerry's temper flared. "Maybe," he said to Weinstein, "it's because Mr. Levin's standing next to her husband. Or maybe because Mr. Levin is *acting* like him."

Weinstein leaned forward, red suffusing the papery skin of his face. "Counselor . . ."

"He can ask her without bullying." Kerry stood, his voice as angry as Weinstein's stare. "One bully is enough."

The judge paused, lips working, as if he had tasted something bitter. "If you want to be cited for contempt, *Mister* Kilcannon, please do that again." Slowly, he turned to Levin. "The witness can look anywhere she wants, Counselor. Get on with it."

Levin walked slowly toward the witness. Kerry watched the jurors follow him, their faces intent. In his most pleasant voice, Levin asked, "You also suffer from epileptic seizures, don't you?"

Bridget nodded. "Yes."

"When you have seizures, you pass out, correct?"

"Yes."

"Sometimes you fall and hurt yourself."

"Yes."

Levin skipped a beat. "And lose your memory?" he asked.

Frozen, Kerry watched Bridget marshal herself, knowing that the truth would hurt, resigned to telling it. "Yes," she answered. "Sometimes."

Even before the defense lawyer's eyes flickered to Kerry, Kerry knew that Levin had done enough. As of now, there was reasonable doubt.

"No further questions," Levin said, leaving Kerry's case to rest on the shoulders of an eight-year-old boy.

FIVE

That night, Kerry lay awake.

At his request, Judge Weinstein had recessed without calling John Musso. Kerry's stated reason—an eight-year-old should not suffer two days of testimony—was true. But it was the other reason that stole Kerry's sleep and shadowed his conscience: the balance between the child's interests and Kerry's own.

Even now, he could dismiss the case; perhaps Anthony Musso, intimidated by the courtroom, would leave his wife and son alone. Then the sole humiliation would be Kerry's, and John would be spared the choice between helping to jail his father and endangering his mother. Remembering Anthony Musso's eyes, Kerry imagined in his tiredness that he held John's life in his hands.

Why had he done this? Kerry wondered. Where did the Mussos end and Kerry begin—his own ego and ambition, his own bitter memories, his own childhood wish for a savior? When he looked into John Musso's face, did he see himself reflected? Or was he better than that—a man who had never wanted this case but knew, from hard experience, that there would be no end to violence unless he ended it?

To be eight, he had said to Bridget Musso, was hard enough without fearing your father, fearing for your mother.

Reaching out, Kerry turned on the bedside lamp. Dim, it cast shadows in the room; he thought first of his own childhood, his father's footsteps on the stairs, and then of Anthony Musso, standing over Bridget as his face came into the light.

What he had now was instinct—that Anthony Musso, unlike Kerry's own father, was insane.

Rising, Kerry prepared for court. He had come too far.

As he took the witness stand, John Musso's throat twitched.

His father stared at him from the defense table. John would not look at him; his glances at the lawyers, the jury, the seeming vastness of the courtroom, were surreptitious, as if the shafts of sunlight hurt his eyes.

To counteract this, Kerry had placed Bridget on the bench behind him. The primal symbolism—a child choosing between mother and father—seemed to highlight the boy's frailty. He looked pallid, close to nausea, and his face was a yellowish hue. His feet did not touch the floor.

Careful to keep his father from the boy's line of sight, Kerry stood close to him.

The first problem, Kerry knew, was whether he could qualify John Musso as competent to testify; the second was to ensure that his testimony—if John had the courage to give it—did not produce a mistrial or an appeal. "Kid witnesses are tricky," Clayton had told Kerry. "They don't understand they're only supposed to testify about what the charges are, not everything they ever saw." Before trial, Weinstein had precluded any evidence that Anthony Musso beat his wife beyond the night in question. It frustrated Kerry that presenting the truth—that Anthony had beat Bridget for years—could set Anthony free, making his son's testimony an even greater risk.

Kerry faced the boy, hands in his pockets. "Can you tell Judge Weinstein your name?" he asked.

John swallowed. His voice was slight, reluctant. "John Musso."

"You know me, right?"

The boy paused, and then his eyes lit on Kerry as if he were his refuge. "You're Kerry," he answered.

The simplicity with which he said this had undertones—that Kerry Kilcannon was important to him, perhaps a central figure in his life, surely the reason John was testifying. Feeling the weight of this, Kerry stood next to the boy, speaking softly.

"Do you know why you're here?" Kerry asked.

When John swallowed again, it racked his body. "I'm here—" John stopped, then started again. "I'm here to say what happened to my mom."

"Did anyone tell you what to say, John?"

John hesitated, gazing at Kerry as if for clues, then answered, "You did."

Kerry tensed; for the judge or jury to misinterpret John's answer could be fatal. "What exactly did I tell you?"

"To tell the truth." For an instant, Kerry experienced relief, and then John added, "If I did that, you said you'd put my dad in jail."

Kerry felt his nerves jangle. From the bench, Weinstein gave him a sharp look and then asked John, "Do you know what the truth means, John? Is the truth what Mr. Kilcannon told you to say?"

Taut, Kerry watched the boy turn his fearful gaze to Weinstein. He could not seem to speak.

More sharply, Weinstein asked, "Did Mr. Kilcannon tell you what to say?"

John's throat twitched again. In a slight voice, almost inaudible, he said, "Kerry told me to say what happened."

Moving between Weinstein and the boy, Kerry faced the judge, holding up one hand to intercede. Reluctant, Weinstein nodded. Turning to John, Kerry asked, "You know what happens to people who lie, don't you, John? You told me about that."

Emphatically, John nodded. "Telling lies is a sin against God. Jesus punishes liars."

Turning to Weinstein, Kerry raised his eyebrows. Satisfied, the judge nodded. "Go ahead, Mr. Kilcannon."

The jury, Kerry saw, was watching intently, for the next few questions could decide the case. Facing John, Kerry asked quietly, "Do you remember the night your mom was hurt?"

For the first time, John sneaked a look at his father. Glancing at the defendant, Kerry imagined the fright Anthony could induce in this boy by the simple, but inhuman, act of never seeming to blink. Kerry could only wait, wondering if the child would collapse. Behind Kerry, Bridget watched her son with parted lips, and then the boy looked up at her.

"I thought my mommy was dead," he answered, and Kerry heard the fear, the helplessness, that the boy must have felt. The same fear Kerry had felt for his own mother.

"So you called 911," Kerry said.

"Yes."

"Do you know *how* your mommy got hurt?"

John's shoulders curled in, and he looked away; Kerry recognized the posture of a boy who had learned that his position was hopeless, that speech was dangerous, that trust was hurtful.

"John," Kerry asked, "did you understand my question?"

John turned to him; in his flickering eyes, Kerry saw him weigh all his experience of life against his experience, much briefer, of Kerry Kilcannon. "I was in my room," he said.

Kerry drew a breath. "And what happened?"

John closed his eyes. "He was shouting—"

"Who?"

Eyes still shut, John's face worked. "My dad."

The jury was rapt now; whatever John might tell them, there could be no doubt of his fear. Gary Levin watched him intently, eyes narrowed.

"Did you stay in your room?" Kerry asked.

The boy nodded. "I pulled the covers over my head."

Kerry froze; the answer was a surprise, and if it held, his case was over. He struggled for a question. "Then how did you know your mommy was hurt?"

The boy stared at his folded hands and then looked sideways at his mother, as if to see if she was still there. "I heard Mommy screaming."

Kerry walked to the witness stand; laying one hand on its arm, he stood next to John, a friend, so that the jury could see their faces. Softly, he asked, "Were you afraid for her?"

The boy's eyes opened slowly. "Yes."

"What did you do?"

John folded his arms, seeming to shiver. "I got out of bed."

"Where did you go?"

"The living room. But no one was there."

"Then what happened?"

The boy swallowed again, then started coughing so violently that his body was racked and spittle came to his lips. Kerry went to him, bracing both of John's shoulders until the coughing subsided. Gently, he wiped the boy's mouth with a tissue. "Are you all right, John?"

Opening, John's eyes were pools of fear and, beneath this, pleading. Kerry felt wretched.

"Would you like a recess?" Weinstein asked.

Kerry looked into the boy's face. John Musso wanted to leave, Kerry suddenly knew, but once he did, he might never return. "No," Kerry said coolly. "I have only a few more questions."

John blinked; he was not fine, this said, and Kerry was forcing him to stay here. "When you went to the living room," Kerry asked, "did you *hear* anything?"

Kerry gazed into the boy's eyes, demanding an answer. John swallowed again, then murmured, "They were in the bathroom."

"What did you do?"

The boy licked his lips, still looking at Kerry. "I went there."

"Did you see your mommy?"

Slowly, John nodded, gaze suddenly downcast in mortification. "She was on the potty, crying."

"Was your dad there?"

The boy's eyes closed again. "Yes."

"And what did he do?"

John looked at his mother. Across the courtroom, tears welled in her eyes. The boy gazed at her, then glanced briefly at his father. He spoke to the floor. "My dad hit her."

Kerry exhaled again. "What happened to your mom?"

John looked up at his mother again. "She fell off the potty."

"Did she get up?"

"Yes."

"And then what happened?"

In the long pause that followed, the boy closed his eyes again; the jury leaned forward; his mother, tear-streaked, bowed her head in the attitude of prayer. Kerry felt the sweat on his forehead, a hollowness in his stomach. When at last John spoke, it was in a dull monotone, to Kerry.

"My dad grabbed Mommy's hair and smashed her face into the sink."

* * *

Slowly, deliberately, Gary Levin walked toward John. His line
of approach forced the boy, if he looked at the lawyer, to see Anthony Musso behind him.

"You don't have to look at him," Kerry had said. "Look at
me, or your mom. All you have to do is tell the truth."

Hands folded, John gazed at Kerry, the man to whom he had
just given his trust and, more than that, his loyalty. "Your
mommy drinks whiskey," Levin asked, "doesn't she?"

John shook his head. In a tone of faint pride, he said,
"Mommy doesn't drink anymore."

"But she used to."

"Yes."

Pausing, Levin adopted a tone of kindly inquiry. "Sometimes
your mommy hurt herself."

The boy paused. Tense, Kerry felt time stop; this was a
process he could not control, and fearful that John could not absorb too much coaching or subtlety, he had not warned him of
what he should not say. How could he ask this boy to tell the
truth, he had said to Clayton, as long as it was *only* the truth that
Kerry needed? Whatever else the boy had seen and heard,
Kerry must hope, would remain locked inside him.

John folded his hands. "Mommy has epilepsy," he said with
a certain dignity. "The fits make her fall down."

"And that's how your mommy hurts herself, isn't it?
Falling."

Behind Levin, Anthony Musso stared at his son with what
seemed, to Kerry, a chilling admixture of hatred, command, and
indifference to the boy's ordeal. Seeing his father, John looked
away, his voice anxious. "Sometimes."

"And when you called 911, you just told them your mommy
might be dead."

John swallowed. "I don't remember."

"But isn't that all you said when the police came?"

John shook his head, confused, unable to answer.

Levin moved forward now, voice and manner kindly. "John,"
he said in a tone of understanding, "you like Mr. Kilcannon,
don't you?"

Looking at Kerry, the boy nodded. "Yes."

"And you want him to be proud of you."

The boy looked from Kerry to Bridget. "Mom, too."

Levin smiled. "They'd want you to tell the truth, right? That's all that Mr. Kilcannon wants."

The boy nodded. The seduction was beginning to work, Kerry saw; caught in a rhythm of answers, Levin's seeming approval, John had his eyes on the lawyer now.

"So," Levin said, "isn't it the truth that you met with Mr. Kilcannon and found out it would please him if you said your dad hurt your mom?"

For a long time, John hesitated, and then he said, "I wanted to help him."

Levin nodded. "So you did, John. By telling him your dad pushed your mom into the sink. But you don't really *know* what happened, do you?"

John folded his arms again. "I do *too* know."

His voice was stubborn, angry. Edgy, Kerry felt himself begin to rise.

Almost pityingly, Levin said, "Your mommy drinks, doesn't she? And then she hurts herself."

John straightened in his chair, looking at the lawyer with a sudden rage that startled Kerry. "Daddy hurts her. He hurts her all the time—"

"Your Honor," Levin called out, but now John Musso had turned to the jury, voice piping and insistent. "He punches her in the face and in her stomach—"

In the jury box, Kerry saw the black woman shudder.

"Your Honor," Levin said at once, "I move for a mistrial."

They sat in Weinstein's airy chambers—the judge, Kerry, Levin, and a court reporter.

"The testimony's prejudicial," Levin insisted. "The charge is whether my client is responsible for a single incident—the only one *ever* reported to the police. Suddenly he's this brute who routinely uses his wife as a punching bag. There's no way he gets a fair trial."

Weinstein turned to Kerry. "I agree with Mr. Levin—there's

a problem here. Why go on and risk getting reversed on appeal?"

Kerry paused, gathering his thoughts. "Let Mr. Levin appeal, Your Honor, if he thinks that flies. But a mistrial? *I* didn't ask John the question, although John's answer shouldn't surprise anyone—especially Anthony Musso's lawyer." Pausing, Kerry turned to Levin. "Mr. Levin pushed and pushed an eight-year-old boy—"

"You *put* him there," Levin shot back, red-faced. "It's up to you to tell him what the rules are."

That this might be true only made Kerry angrier, more impassioned. "Your Honor," he said to Weinstein, "Mr. Levin effectively called this boy a liar, a pawn in my vendetta against his dad. The boy fought back with the only weapon he had—the truth. The defense got what it deserved." He lowered his voice. "What it *doesn't* deserve is a mistrial. This boy has seen enough and suffered enough. To put him through all this again would be an act of cruelty."

Slowly, Weinstein nodded, and then spoke with what, to Kerry, was surprising compassion. "I agree with Mr. Kilcannon. The testimony wasn't his doing, and it's painful to watch this boy. If he has to come back here again, it'll be because the court of appeals says so, not me." He turned to Levin. "Mr. Levin, I'm instructing the jury to disregard all testimony about any other alleged acts of domestic violence. Motion denied."

Levin frowned. "For the record, Your Honor, if Mr. Musso is found guilty, I'm taking this to the court of appeals."

Weinstein shrugged. "That's what it's there for," he said, and the conference was over.

On the way out, Kerry put his hand on Levin's shoulder. "Why don't you put Musso on the stand, Gary. Have him explain why he stepped over his wife's body on the way to the local bar, leaving his eight-year-old son there, afraid she's dead. That'll fix everything."

Levin flushed, clearly angry. He stalked back to the courtroom without answering.

In the clearest possible terms, Judge Weinstein instructed the jury to disregard John Musso's answer. But Kerry knew that they could not; the damage was there, in the transcript of the trial, a ticking time bomb. To spare the Mussos further agony, he would have to win twice—here and on appeal.

Resuming his cross-examination, Levin was cautious. "Isn't it the truth, John, that you never told anyone that your dad beat your mom until after you met with Mr. Kilcannon?"

Swallowing, John looked at Kerry. With a small nod, Kerry gave his permission.

"Yes," John said.

"And you've met with Mr. Kilcannon a lot."

"Yes."

"And gone over your story, again and again, to make sure you get it right."

"Yes."

Levin put his hands on his hips. "Mr. Kilcannon made a promise, you said? That if you helped him, your dad would go to jail?"

A glance at Kerry, a nervous bob of the head. "He promised me."

"And that's what your mom says she wants too. Your dad in jail."

Suddenly John Musso looked exhausted; the question went to the choice he had made and, because of this, shamed him. "Yes," he answered in the voice of a guilty child or, perhaps, a liar.

Levin, Kerry saw, had gained back a little ground. As if sensing this, the lawyer said, "No more questions."

Kerry stood, irresolute. With luck, he could repair the last few minutes. Looking back at him, John Musso's eyes pleaded for relief.

Gently, Kerry said, "Thank you, John. It's over," and the case for the prosecution was done.

SIX

From the first words of his closing statement, Kerry felt off balance, defensive.

Gary Levin had not called Anthony Musso to the stand; it deprived Kerry of his aggressive edge, the chance to show Musso for what Kerry knew him to be. At once, Kerry sensed that Levin would make *him* the issue, resting his hopes on the assertion that Kerry had fabricated the case and, if Kerry won, using John Musso's blurted accusation as grounds for appeal. For that, Kerry blamed himself; suddenly the trial seemed far too much about him—*his* passion, *his* mistakes.

Now, facing the jury, Kerry tried to be the calm professional, marshaling the evidence: that John Musso's story buttressed Bridget's, that Anthony Musso—as confirmed by the police—had not called 911. "All I ask," Kerry concluded, "is that you find Anthony Musso to be what *he* knew he was when he fled that apartment—guilty of a brutal crime against a defenseless woman, witnessed by a helpless child."

Sitting down, Kerry was depressed. The jurors appeared neither antagonistic nor persuaded, as if reserving both their judgment and their emotions. The quiet of the courtroom seemed distant from the night that Kerry imagined, filled with rage and violence.

Gary Levin got up—calm, confident, unapologetic.

"All of us," he said, "deplore the acts described by Mr. Kilcannon. But that's the problem, isn't it? Because while this is very much Mr. Kilcannon's *case*, he himself is not a witness." Briefly, Levin turned to Kerry. "His witnesses are a damaged woman and an eight-year-old boy."

179

Once more, Levin faced the jury. "Bridget Musso," he continued, "merits our pity. On the night of her injury she was, as she admits having been throughout her marriage, drunk. She was also what she will be for the rest of her life—epileptic, with frequent blackouts and a propensity for falling.

"*Alcoholic* and *epileptic*." Levin shook his head. "The combination is devastating. Especially to memory, as Bridget Musso so clearly demonstrated.

"Forget her performance as a witness, though that should be proof enough. Remember this: within hours of her injury, when the trauma as described by Mr. Kilcannon should have been fresh in her mind and branded in her memory, Mrs. Musso remembered nothing.

"Ask yourself this: why did she tell the police nothing and yet, a month later, tell *Mr. Kilcannon* more than reason suggests she could remember?"

Levin paused, hands in his pockets. The jurors seemed troubled and deeply attentive; the woman who had seemed sympathetic to Bridget sneaked a glance at Kerry and then looked away.

"Which brings us back," Levin said, "to Mr. Kilcannon and his other witness, a young and impressionable boy.

"When the police arrived, John Musso told them that he thought his mother was dead." The lawyer's eyes swept the jury. "He was able to articulate a child's worst fear—the death of a parent. Yet *at no time* did he tell the police how this fearful tragedy occurred.

"No." Levin's voice became sad. "No, he told *Mr. Kilcannon*.

"Even more than his mother, John Musso deserves our compassion, and far beyond the life he has led or the damage that may have been done to his sense of who he is. From the moment Mr. Kilcannon brought him to the courtroom, the boy faced a terrible choice." Levin stopped, pointing to Anthony Musso. "The choice between a father he has not seen for over three months, and the mother he has lived with every day. The choice between a man now locked in jail and the man he has spent hours trying to please—Mr. Kilcannon."

Looking around him, Kerry saw Bridget Musso, humiliated

and clearly frightened; her husband, watching her with a soulless, heavy-lidded calm; the jury, seeing neither of them, listening to Levin with new intensity. Then Kerry thought of John Musso waiting in a small room with a stranger and a box of toys, and felt a deep rage at Levin's perversion of a truth he knew in his bones—that the cry for help might take months, or years, or never come at all.

"I make no excuses," Levin went on, "for Anthony Musso. I do not claim that he has been a model husband or father, or that this family can or should be a family anymore. But he does deserve what the law accords us all—reasonable doubt. You cannot find that the 'truth' presented by Mr. Kilcannon through a troubled child and a woman with no memory is, beyond a reasonable doubt, true."

In the jury's pensive quiet, Levin sat.

Kerry stood, walking toward the jurors. Suddenly he was less aware of the faces in front of him than of his own memory of a small boy and, as painful and more fresh, his image of this one. The words came to him without thought.

"You're eight years old," he said softly.

"You're alone in your room.

"The apartment is dark, and your mother is drinking. Your father is out somewhere—probably in a bar, you know. You've got no one at all.

"Then you hear the front door open, and know it's your dad.

" 'Dad's home,' " Kerry said, more quietly yet. "You know other boys in school who would run to the door to give their dad a hug. But you—you're different. You already know better.

"You hear his voice, and pull the covers over your head. And then you hear your mother scream."

Kerry paused, scanning the faces before him—an Italian sanitation worker, an Irish mother of six, a Jewish accountant, the black woman he had been so conscious of.

"You know who your mother is," Kerry went on. "You know all her problems. But, God help you, you need someone in your life to love, and to love you back.

"When your mother cries out, you feel it on your skin, in your stomach. You're afraid to move." Kerry lowered his voice. "But you're alone, and you're afraid of having no mother.

"So you crawl out of bed and, against your will, start toward the sound of your mother's cries."

Slowly, with the faltering steps of a small boy, Kerry walked toward the jury.

"The living room is dark. The only light is in the bathroom.

"You go there, hoping that no one will see you. Afraid of what you'll see.

"What you see is your father pushing your mother down on the toilet, screaming at her while tears run down her face."

Suddenly Kerry stood tall. " '*Now you can piss,*' " he shouted at the jury. " '*Go ahead. Do it.*' "

In front of him, the accountant flinched.

"You shrink back in fear," Kerry told him with new quiet. "But you can't stop watching. Because they're your father and mother, all that life has given you.

"He slaps her. Her head hits the wall. He slaps her again. She falls sideways, catching herself on the sink. She bends over the sink, underpants around her ankles." Kerry's voice became hoarse and slow, stretching out each word. "And then your father takes your mother by the hair and smashes her face into the sink."

The courtroom was hushed. "Your mother staggers past you," Kerry went on relentlessly. "Her mouth is bloody; she's spitting pieces of teeth; your father is behind her.

"So you shrink back into the darkness. Hide, so he can't see you. Hide, with tears in your eyes, unable to move or make a sound. Hide, until your father leaves.

"Then the only person you've got in the world is lying on the living room floor, and you're the only one to help her.

"So you go to the telephone, like they told you in school, and call 911."

The Irish woman was crying. Kerry spoke to her now.

"When the police come," he said, "you tell them you're afraid she's dead. But there's something locked inside you that you're more afraid to say. And someone you're more afraid of than anything in the world."

Kerry stood straighter. "*You* know what happened," he said, and turned to point at Anthony Musso. "*You* know what this man is."

In the silence, he stared at Anthony Musso until Musso's unblinking eyes filled with rage, and then Kerry turned to Bridget Musso. "For three months," he said, "Bridget Musso has gone without a drink. She's done her part. You do yours." Now Kerry almost whispered. "Protect this woman. Protect her son."

Across the courtroom, Bridget sat straighter, with a dignity Kerry found touching. At once, he realized that he was the first man in Bridget's memory ever to speak for her. But when he faced the jury, his last thoughts were of the boy, alone, waiting.

"Please," he implored them, "tell John Musso that what his father did was wrong. Tell him he was right to save his mother." Pausing, he looked at each juror in turn, and then he finished gently. "Tell John Musso that, like other boys, he deserves a life."

Without another word, Kerry sat down.

When the jury instructions were finished and court was adjourned, Kerry said goodbye to Bridget and prepared to face a long night of waiting. Then, to his surprise, he saw Clayton Slade at the back of the courtroom.

"How long were you here?" Kerry asked.

"Some of the mom, most of the kid. All of the closing arguments."

As usual, his face was inscrutable; Kerry could detect no reaction to what Clayton had witnessed, and had little hope of praise. But he was sure by now that Clayton would be honest and that, for better or worse, his advice would be worthwhile. "Have time for a beer?" Kerry asked.

Clayton nodded. "All right."

Kerry drove them to McGovern's, edgy at Clayton's silence. The bar was beginning to fill; Kerry saw a few looks of surprise at the presence of a black man, which he sensed Clayton absorbing without acknowledgment. They sat at a table in the corner and ordered two beers.

"Well?" Kerry asked.

The question needed no explanation. Clayton sipped his beer and then sat back, looking steadily at Kerry. "You made some mistakes," he answered. "You worked well with the boy. But Levin's appeal's got a decent chance, and you should have brought out on direct *why* Bridget didn't tell the cops—fear, just like her kid. That was where he began to learn it."

Both points were so true that it deepened Kerry's self-doubt. "So," he said finally, "who wins?"

Behind his glasses, Clayton's eyes became bright, the first hint of amusement. "Oh," he answered, "that one's simple. You do."

"Why?"

"Your closing argument." Clayton's face was serious now. "At first I thought you were over the top, especially when you acted out Musso shouting at his wife. Then I realized the problem was *me*—I'd never try to do what you did, and I'd never seen anything like it. In seconds, you went from an adequate lawyer to connecting with that jury so completely that Levin didn't matter anymore." He paused, studying Kerry with open curiosity. "You didn't rehearse that, did you?"

Feeling less flattered than disconcerted, Kerry shook his head. "I'll never do it again, either. It just happened."

Clayton took another swallow of beer, thoughtful. He looked around, as if to ensure their privacy, and then looked back at Kerry. "So," he asked, "what's domestic violence to you, anyhow?"

The question was so direct that it took Kerry by surprise; he had never talked about this to anyone. Across the table, Clayton's look was unabashed. Staring at the bottle of beer in front of him, Kerry found himself saying, "My mother."

There was a tremor in his voice, Kerry realized. For a moment, Clayton was quiet. "So that's the answer," he said simply.

Kerry looked up at him. "What do you mean?"

"Find the thing that you can feel. Because if *you* care, you can make a jury care. That's the gift you have."

Kerry felt a great relief—that Clayton would not abuse his confidence with intrusive questions or instant psychoanalysis; that perhaps Kerry might become a better lawyer than he had imagined. And then he realized something else: that beneath Clayton's quiet intelligence was a deep, ineffable kindness.

"Let me buy you dinner," Kerry said.

* * *

The next afternoon, the jury found Anthony Musso guilty.

For Kerry, the moments following were a blur: the clerk reading the verdict; the polling of the jury; Weinstein setting a date for sentencing. Bridget and John were not there; what Kerry would remember was that Anthony Musso no longer watched anyone but him.

Then two deputies took Musso away, and Kerry went to the witness room.

In the corner, John played intently with a Lego set; he did not look up, as if fearing what Kerry might say. Bridget's red-rimmed eyes were anxious, her body rigid. Kerry sat across from her.

"Guilty," he told her.

Her hand went to her throat; for a moment, it seemed that she could not breathe. Then, tentative, she reached across the table and placed her fingers on Kerry's wrist. "You saved my life," she said.

"*You* saved your life," Kerry answered. "You, and John."

John became still and gave Kerry a sideways glance, as if hesitant to believe. Kerry went to him, kneeling.

Slowly, the boy faced him. "It's over," Kerry promised. "He can't hurt you now."

John's blue eyes simply stared at him, as if he had not heard. Then he put his arms around Kerry's neck and, hugging him fiercely, began to cry without making a sound.

When Kerry returned to his apartment, there were balloons Scotch-taped to the door.

He stood there in surprise, looking for a note, and then opened the door.

The living room was quiet. Slinging his suit coat over his shoulder, Kerry walked to the bedroom.

Meg lay naked across his bed, holding out a glass of champagne. Kerry was startled; this was so unlike Meg that it made him uneasy.

"Congratulations," she said, and laughed so hard at his expression that she spilled champagne on his sheets.

Bewildered, Kerry took the glass and placed it on his

nightstand, next to the bottle she had chilled for them, then he sat beside her. "How did you know?" he asked.

"I called your officemate. Clayton." She took his hand. "I know how worried you've been—the other night you hardly slept. I'm really happy for you, Kerry."

Kerry looked into her face, and then a sense of well-being overwhelmed his doubts: the Musso case, so all-consuming, was over; Bridget and John were safe, perhaps even saved. His loneliness fell away; Meg had understood, after all, without his needing to explain. And she was here with him.

"So," she said, "want to go to the movies?"

Smiling, Kerry shook his head.

Meg unknotted his tie; Kerry did the rest. When he was inside her, she wrapped her arms and legs around him, as though she would never let him go.

Their lovemaking was far sweeter than ever before— intense, passionate, without reservations. Afterward, moist and spent, they lay in each other's arms, Meg's head on his chest. "I can feel your heartbeat," she told him.

Perhaps, Kerry thought, the difference was in *him*. Perhaps it was Meg, patiently waiting all the while, who had caused this. What he knew for certain was that this was what he had always wanted, first for his parents, now for them.

"Marry me," he said.

SEVEN

In the next year, Kerry brought twenty domestic violence cases and won seventeen.

This was a dead end, many of his colleagues warned; the smart move would be to mend relations with Flavio and exit this legal ghetto, any way he could. But Kerry did not listen. He visited battered-women's shelters; worked with the police; lobbied for more progressive legislation. Forcing himself to become a public speaker—a role that did not come easily—he made the rounds of civic groups to call for compassion for victims, harsher punishment for abusers. He was relentless in pursuing his cause, and for the first time, some labeled him ruthless, too willing to put men in jail to advance his own agenda. Though Kerry found this hurtful and perplexing, he rejected the easiest way to soften the impression others had of him—to talk about his mother. Except to Clayton Slade, he never spoke of his own childhood.

As his involvement deepened, Kerry thought much more about politics, not as a path for his own career—for he did not want the loss of privacy—but because government affected the things that mattered most to him. It was one thing to prosecute abusers case by case, but that did not ensure that their sentences were longer, that there was funding to help their wives, decent day care for their children. He became an early advocate of barring convicted abusers from buying guns; in turn, this spawned an incident that some found admirable, others intemperate and even chilling.

Kerry had visited the local office of Ralph Shue, a pompous suburban congressman who was positioning himself to run for the Senate but was also a tacit ally of the gun lobby. Kerry's proposal was, to him, simple and appealing—surely even advocates of gun ownership would agree that wife beaters should not be armed. Finding Shue evasive, then resistant, Kerry inquired whether donations from the NRA had affected his position. When Shue became angry, Kerry snapped, "Life is cheaper than running for the Senate, isn't it? Just remember this—the next time one of these animals shoots his wife and kids, you helped him pull the trigger."

With that, Kerry stalked from Shue's office, leaving behind an enemy and an anecdote.

The follow-up to this, a conversation with Clayton Slade, was something no one ever heard about. But its effects on Kerry were profound. Over a beer, Clayton said, "Shue's an asshole. But if you can't disarm every guy who beats his wife, what about trying to educate them?" His tone grew firm. "They can't *all* want to be the way they are, Kerry. And even if they do, you come off sounding a little less vengeful."

Kerry sat back, silent and withdrawn. For him, his father had been the paradigm of violence without reason. Yet by now Kerry knew that many of those he prosecuted had learned rage from their own abusive fathers; he sensed, too, in a way that made him uncomfortable, that his own anger—channeled into prosecutions—mirrored Michael Kilcannon's. He made no answer to Clayton. But counseling for men who wanted it became part of every speech, scrutiny of his own motives a greater part of Kerry himself.

Vincent Flavio began to watch him. At one of their frequent dinners, Liam Dunn remarked, "Vincent can't believe you're doing all this for the exercise. He thinks you may be positioning yourself, and it makes him nervous." Finishing, Liam looked at Kerry shrewdly, leaving him to wonder if the question was also Liam's own.

"Why," Kerry replied, "does Vincent Flavio think everyone wants to be *him*?"

His godfather's look of appraisal lingered, and then Liam chose to cover this with a smile. "Vincent's a wee bit paranoid, Kerry, and your last name *is* Kilcannon. If *he* were you, he'd make some use of it."

It was the last thing Kerry wanted.

His own contacts with Jamie were infrequent. His brother visited the office only once, making a courtesy call on Vincent Flavio, as cursory as decorum allowed. "An hour with Vincent," he observed to Kerry, "is an hour closer to being dead, and seems much the same experience." He paused, glancing around Kerry's shabby office. "Still, there's probably something I can say to him. How much more domestic pathos can you stand?"

Kerry simply stared at him. "As much as I have to."

Jamie gave him a fleeting smile, though his eyes were serious and a little quizzical. "Ah, Kerry," he said at last, "are you never leaving home?"

Kerry stayed in domestic violence: even if nothing else had

held him there, the Musso case would have. After all, he had paid Vincent Flavio to keep it.

By Flavio's fiat, appeals were handled by lawyers in another section; feeling his responsibility to John and Bridget, Kerry wanted—even needed—to handle the Musso appeal himself. But when he went to the head of the appellate section, the reply was "If you want to keep the Musso case, go see Carl Nunzio."

Reluctantly, Kerry did so.

The amusement in Nunzio's eyes, heightened by a hint of malice, reminded Kerry of the day he had refused to pay Flavio's tribute, and Nunzio had exiled him to domestic violence. At length, Nunzio said, "You're asking for a favor, Kerry? Then it's time you joined the team."

Kerry stifled his own rage. There was Meg to consider, he told himself: in a few months, they would marry. But it was not Meg he envisioned as he weighed his answer; it was the look on John Musso's face, just before he wrapped his arms around Kerry's neck.

Slowly, Kerry nodded.

Nunzio smiled. "If it will make things a little easier," he said, "maybe Essex County can give you a raise. In the public interest, of course."

Leaving, Kerry felt dirtier than before.

As months passed, and the time for arguing the Musso appeal drew closer, Kerry kept in touch with Bridget and John.

In many ways, their lives were difficult; without income from Anthony's construction jobs, they were poor, and Bridget's health problems and lack of skills made her depend on public assistance. But she stayed sober, and John's school attendance was far better. One Sunday, Kerry took them to Manhattan to visit the zoo in Central Park; Bridget seemed almost serene, and though quiet and still guarded, John plainly had come to depend on her. She was taking courses in bookkeeping, Bridget told Kerry; she had a facility with numbers, and John's grades in mathematics suggested that he possessed it too. Their lives were far different than with Anthony, and Kerry believed they would be better yet. It was one achievement of which he felt proud.

Another was his friendship with Clayton Slade.

In time, Kerry acquired a sense of his friend's life. Clayton was the son of a silent and unloving city bureaucrat and a well-meaning but somewhat feckless mother; observant from youth, Clayton viewed both parents with detachment. His deep capacity for affection was channeled toward his wife, Carlie, sharp-tongued and irreverent, and their rambunctious five-year-old twin daughters. "The coven" was what Clayton called them, in a dry way that confirmed, rather than concealed, how much they meant to him.

The Slade family lived at the edge of Vailsburg, a few blocks from Mary Kilcannon. One of Kerry's pleasures was going to their home for dinner: he and Clayton felt no need to force conversation; Carlie came to treat Kerry much as she treated Clayton, with a certain wry affection; Kerry discovered from the twins—Kelsey and Marissa—how much he wanted children. He loved them for their sense of play. One night, rounding up the troops for dinner, Carlie had found Kerry in her clothes closet, hiding on his hands and knees behind her dresses, the object of the twins' elaborate game of hide-and-seek. "Well," she said with raised eyebrows, "at least you're not *wearing* one. But if either of those girls asked you, you probably would."

Kerry admired both husband and wife. A junior college teacher, Carlie was smart in her own right, and she shared Clayton's unvarnished way of thinking and speaking. Clayton was a superior trial lawyer—systematic, thorough, and far-sighted, particularly good at complex cases. Kerry never saw him make an obvious error in judgment; it seemed that Clayton could understand any situation, no matter how complicated or novel. His sense of office politics was as sure as his reading of personality and motive; guided more by intuition and impulse, Kerry came to know the times he needed Clayton's advice. When a large Newark law firm hired Clayton at twice his salary, Kerry was not surprised.

Though they enjoyed each other's company and shared a common sense of irony, Kerry was far less certain of what Clayton admired in him. But it was not the kind of thing they talked much about. "At first," Clayton once conceded, "I thought you were just another Irish primitive—you know, the kind of scrappy, narrow kid who likes a fight and can't imagine anything outside his neighborhood and the Church. Then I saw how dumb that was." But Kerry never asked *why* Clayton thought so much better of him, and Clayton never said.

They seldom discussed race. But the subject was all around them: the Irish were fleeing Vailsburg, and there was no question that the neighborhood was deteriorating, the sense of community fading too. Boarded-up homes of families Kerry had known for years became crack houses; there were tensions between blacks and whites; Mary Kilcannon, who kept their old house spotless, now complained of roaches in the kitchen.

"She wants to move," Kerry told Clayton. "Doesn't feel safe, she tells me."

They were sitting in Vailsburg Park after a touch football game among some local lawyers; vainly diving to deflect the winning touchdown pass, Kerry had skinned his arm and now was using his Seton Hall sweatshirt to wipe dirt from the wound.

"*Is* she unsafe?" Clayton asked.

Touching his raw skin, Kerry winced. "Nothing's ever happened to her. But she can't understand what's happened to Vailsburg."

Clayton fell quiet. Then he drew a breath, saying with weary patience, "And if the Irish could get off the boat and turn their kids into lawyers and senators, why not 'the blacks.'"

"Something like that." Kerry paused and then added with reluctant candor, "I used to wonder too."

Clayton gazed across the park. "When your parents showed up from Ireland," he finally said, "they came to a community a lot like home—same culture, same church, same family structure, with friends or relatives waiting to give them jobs. Though I guess you could say African Americans had jobs waiting for them, too."

The tone of quiet irony lingered. "I understand that," Kerry said defensively. "Even if the first wave of Irish were pretty near the bottom of the barrel. But what about now?"

"Oh, no excuses. There's work to do, and in these days there's not going to be a lot of help. And the glowing example of the family Kilcannon is not a lot of help, either." He turned to

Kerry. "Prejudice against folks who look different is hard-wired in the human brain. In ten years, maybe white kids will be imitating James Kilcannon like they used to imitate JFK. But I'm damned sure they won't be imitating Jesse Jackson, or even Denzel Washington. You know it too."

Kerry looked at him steadily, then at the neighborhood surrounding them. "Still, it's a shame."

"But not the only one," Clayton said bluntly. "And for sure not the worst one. After all, your old friends are in the suburbs now, where no one can reach them."

It was Kerry's turn to be quiet. "I've never wanted to talk about this," he said at last.

Clayton shrugged. "I don't care if we talk about it—that's part of the deal. I just want you to think about it."

"I guess that's part of the deal too," Kerry answered, and stood. "Think Carlie's got something I can rub on this arm? Your kids are always banging into walls."

When Kerry and Meg were married, three days before Kerry's twenty-ninth birthday, Clayton was best man.

After the wedding, Kerry put the top down on his VW Rabbit and, filled with elation, the anticipation of a new life, drove a smiling Meg to Manhattan for a four-day honeymoon.

The trip was a change of plans. For once, Kerry had taken his more worldly brother's advice. "Florida's where people go to die," Jamie had told him. "Book a room at the Pierre, see some plays, eat at a couple of nice restaurants with the money you'll save on airfare. God knows that's what *I'd* do with a certain woman if it wouldn't cost me a hundred thousand votes."

Still unmarried, James Kilcannon was embarked on a cross-country tour, which would culminate, the media predicted, in an announcement that next year he would seek the presidency. Jamie's rueful reference to the pitfalls of his romantic life— a rumored involvement with the beautiful rock singer Stacey Tarrant—made Kerry glad that his own life was private, his choices were his own. Gazing at the Manhattan skyline, Kerry took Meg's hand and said, "There's no one I'd trade places with."

The room at the Pierre was small but tastefully appointed,

with a view of Central Park. Drawing the drapes, Kerry turned
to his wife, filled with wonder.

Gently, she kissed him. "Can we go out for a while?" she
asked. "I'm still pretty wound up from the wedding."

Kerry fought back disappointment; though they had slept together for a year, this would be special to them—their first lovemaking as husband and wife. But Meg, Kerry reflected, might
have other memories, more painful. "We'll go anywhere you
want," he told her. "There's a whole night still ahead of us."

They walked for over two hours—Kerry recalling the high
points of their wedding, Meg admiring various unaffordable
extravagances in Fifth Avenue store windows—and then found
the restaurant Jamie had suggested, La Côte Basque. Amidst
the colorful murals and muted elegance, Meg took his hand; savoring the ambience, the attentive service, she asked if they
could linger for dessert, then for a glass of port to toast their
wedding. By the time the check came, it was close to midnight,
and the crowd had dwindled to the Kilcannons and a foursome
finishing a long business dinner.

Wincing at the impact on his credit card, Kerry paid the bill,
eager to be alone with Meg. But when they reached the Pierre,
Meg glanced at the bar and asked if they might stop in for a
brandy. *This* must be special to her, Kerry told himself, a
memory unique to them, a fresh start for Meg herself—their
first evening out as a married couple, the luxury and excitement of Manhattan. It was one o'clock before they reached
their room.

In the dim light of a bedside lamp, Meg began unpacking.

Kerry watched her find drawers or hangers for every gar-
ment. As Kerry undressed for bed, Meg disappeared into the
bathroom.

For a half hour, Kerry waited, anxious and alone.

She emerged without speaking. When Kerry reached out for
her, she slid into his arms, turning her back to him.

Tentative, Kerry kissed her neck and then was overcome by
his own feelings. This was the start of their life together, the
path to family and children, to a deeper understanding. Slowly,
he slid the straps of Meg's nightgown down her arms.

Her bare shoulders curled in. "I'm so tired," she said.

Kerry's arms tightened around her. "This is our wedding night, Meg. We can always sleep in."

She did not answer. Gently, Kerry removed her nightgown. With what could have been a sigh or a shudder, Meg lay on her back.

For the next few moments, Kerry was possessed by his own emotions. He barely noticed that Meg opened her legs as if giving in to him, that her movements seemed less passionate than before. Caught up in the softness of his new wife's skin, her breasts, her hair, he murmured, "I love you, Meg Kilcannon."

Beneath him, Meg began to cry.

Kerry stiffened; the sudden knowledge of their separateness—her distress, his obtuseness—was like a slap in the face. "My God, Meg—what is it?"

She slid from beneath him, sitting on the side of the bed, her head bowed. "I'm so sorry," she said in a muffled voice. "I should have known."

Heart pounding, Kerry knelt beside her. "Sorry for what?"

She closed her eyes. "This room feels like a prison, Kerry. Please, let's go home. Things will be better there."

The next morning, confused and disbelieving, Kerry drove his wife to their new flat in Down Neck. Arriving, Meg picked up the phone and called a girlfriend from work, someone Kerry barely knew. Kerry stood in front of her until she hung up.

"We have to talk, Meg."

Meg took a deep breath. "It's not you, Kerry. Maybe it's Pat. Maybe I'm afraid of being hurt again."

Kerry felt a lump in his throat. "*I'm* your husband now," he said. "Not Pat. Please, give us time."

A week later, his spirits leaden, Kerry argued the Musso appeal before a three-judge panel. They listened to Kerry's plea—that Judge Weinstein's admonition was sufficient, that an eight-year-old boy should not be subjected to a second trial for a single blurted accusation—with an impassivity that gave no clue as to how they might rule. When Kerry arrived home, depressed and anxious to talk, there was a note on the dinner table. An old girlfriend was in town, Meg had written. She hoped the argument had gone well and couldn't wait to hear about it.

* * *

In Kerry's months of waiting for the Musso decision, his life with Meg became better but never quite what he had pictured.

He was watchful, attentive; their marriage sometimes seemed a matter of his sensing Meg's shifting moods. But when he tried to confront their problems more openly, Meg would withdraw, hurt. Kerry felt her offer a tacit understanding: as long as they made love on weekend mornings, perhaps Kerry would be assured that their marriage was untroubled. On the good days, when Meg laughed with him, he felt happy and filled with hope. And sometimes she left notes in his briefcase, wishing him luck on a case or simply saying "I love you." Sitting at his desk, Kerry would read the notes and smile.

At times Kerry wished that he could talk to Clayton about it. But the two couples were friends, and whether with the Slades or at parties, Meg was different—smiling, vivacious, eager to meet new people—from the woman Kerry sometimes saw. He felt a bewildering mix of pride, relief that others did not discern his own confusion, a buried resentment that Meg could switch personae so persuasively. Only Kerry suffered her withdrawals, or the long, silent weekends that came without warning, when she would stay in bed well into the afternoon. Only Kerry knew what she had told him about children.

They were in the kitchen, making dinner. Kerry had returned from a visit with John and Bridget Musso; proudly, John had showed him a model aircraft carrier he was building and asked Kerry to help him finish it. "Being with a kid is so amazing," he remarked to Meg. "For John, the only thing that mattered in the world was finishing that ship together. After a while, it was all that mattered to me."

Meg gave him a thoughtful look. "It's nice you can have fun with him, even with all his problems. Did you ever think about joining Big Brothers?"

On the surface, her comment was benign; that they would have children had always been a given. But by now Kerry was alert to Meg's defenses, her need for indirectness. "Oh," he said with feigned nonchalance, "I've thought more about our own kids. When would you like to fit one in?"

Meg's gaze lowered to the stovetop. "I don't know," she answered. "Not now."

Kerry felt himself tense. But the subject was too important to drop. "Not now? Or not ever?"

Cornered, Meg looked at him. "You're very traditional," she said. "I'm not sure *what* I am anymore."

The next morning, the court of appeals granted Anthony Musso a new trial and ordered his release from prison.

EIGHT

The morning of the second Musso trial was drizzly, bleak.

Kerry brought John and Bridget to court. For their protection, Kerry had persuaded Judge Weinstein to enjoin Anthony Musso from visiting their apartment or Bridget's new place of work, the office of a small moving company. The week before, leaving work, Bridget had noticed Anthony waiting across the street, though he did not approach her. Bridget had not seen her husband since; John had not seen him at all. But the incident hardened Kerry's resolve.

As they climbed the marble steps to the second floor of the courthouse, the dim light seeping through the ornate dome reflected the gloom outside. John Musso was quiet and pale. Kerry still remembered the moment he had explained that Anthony was free—the primal look of fear in this boy's eyes, as eloquent as Bridget's tears. At the door of the courtroom, Kerry took John's hand. "One more time," he promised, "and this will be over."

Watching John gaze up at him, his mother brushed back the boy's hair. "We know that," she told Kerry. "You've always taken care of us."

Kerry looked at them, mother and son, the woman sober now, the boy more trusting of her, less trapped within himself. *You're so close,* Kerry thought. *If I can keep you safe this time . . .*

He never finished the thought.

Anthony Musso walked toward them down the hallway, right hand in the pocket of his heavy woolen jacket. Only Kerry saw him; only Kerry had time to register his slow, tight-muscled walk, his heavy-lidded stare at the back of Bridget's head, and to sense that Anthony had not come for a retrial.

No one else was near. From the corner of his eye, Kerry saw a sheriff's deputy, drinking coffee and chatting with someone in the doorway of an office. Musso stopped. With calm deliberation, he drew a black handgun from his pocket.

Kerry could not move or speak.

The next seconds were slow motion, a series of impressions: Musso raising the gun. The utter quiet as he aimed at Bridget. Her lips parting as she saw the look on Kerry's face. As the hollow pop sounded, John's fingers twitched in Kerry's hand.

Bridget's head snapped forward.

Her eyes widened. Through the third eye in her forehead, blood and brains spattered Kerry's face.

As Bridget stumbled toward Kerry, Anthony Musso aimed at him.

A woman screamed. In a sudden reflex, Kerry dived for the door, John's hand still clasped in his.

Searing pain shot through his shoulder. His head struck the heavy door with a thud, knocking it open; dazed, Kerry heard a second thud, Bridget's body hitting the floor as he did.

Kerry rolled on his back, John in his arms now, blinding spots before his eyes. Bridget lay beside them. More gunshots echoed; as if struck from behind, Anthony slumped in the doorway. The last thing Kerry remembered was John Musso lying beside him, shrieking uncontrollably at the sight of Bridget's face.

Kerry was a hero.

The sheriff's deputy had seen him save John Musso's life. That was what the media reported. That was what Vincent

Flavio told him when, trailed by reporters, he visited Kerry's bedside.

Kerry lay there with his right arm in a sling, his collarbone shattered by Musso's bullet. His thoughts, shamed and solitary, were so remote from Vincent Flavio's false solicitude that Flavio left quickly. Only Liam's tart remark—"Vincent prefers his heroes dead; he's less afraid they'll take his place"—kept Kerry from confessing the truth as he remembered it. Myth, like cowardice, had its uses.

A woman was dead, a boy orphaned.

"They're looking for the nearest relative," Clayton told him. "There's a great-aunt somewhere—Bridget's mother's sister."

His friend sat beside him in the cool, quiet room. Kerry stared at the ceiling. "God help him," he said at last. "God help me."

Clayton shook his head. "There's nothing more you could have done."

Kerry turned to him, wincing from the pain that shot through his shoulder. "I could have saved her," he said. "I saw the gun, and I froze."

Clayton studied his face. "It took two seconds, Kerry. No one could expect that."

"I did, though. From the moment I saw him." Kerry faced the ceiling again; he could not look at his friend. "You know what I think it was? 'Better her than me.' The only accident was saving John."

Clayton rose from his chair, standing over him. "You don't know that, Kerry. You'll never know. It was too fast."

Kerry did not answer.

After a time, Clayton laid a hand on his arm. "You'll never know," he repeated. "Maybe the deputy made you into someone you're not. But you don't have to do that to yourself."

Kerry looked up at him. "Just live with it, in other words."

Clayton nodded. "You've got a *life* to live. Enough bad has come out of this already."

For a long time, Kerry was silent. "I want to see John," he said.

*   *   *

For two days more, Kerry healed, floating in and out of sleep. His brother called from California; reassured that Kerry would recover, Jamie quipped, "I hear you forgot to duck."

"No," Kerry answered. "I remembered. Just not in time."

Thinking this a joke, Jamie laughed. "Next time, Kerry, you'll do better."

When Kerry put down the phone, all that he could think of was Bridget's face, exploding into his.

Ceaselessly, he replayed those last few seconds in his memory, as he had ever since awakening to realize that Bridget's death was not a dream but a living nightmare, for which he was responsible. Even now, he would awaken as in his former life, before Anthony Musso had pulled the gun from his pocket; for a blessed moment, Kerry was blameless, and then he would remember Bridget's face and hear a young boy's cry . . .

When he woke again, the room was dark, and Meg watched him, wordless.

There were fresh tears on her face, Kerry saw. "What's this?" he asked.

She took his hand, answering in a muffled voice, "I could have lost you."

Kerry managed to smile. "And then where would you be?"

"Don't joke about it, Kerry. Please."

Her face was shadowed with desperation. He felt compassion for her, and then wonder. "It's over, Meg, and I'm still alive. What else can I do?"

Meg could not seem to stop crying. "That man nearly killed you," she said with sudden vehemence. "Promise me, please, that you'll get out of domestic violence."

Thinking of Bridget Musso, Kerry flinched inside. "I can't."

"Please." She squeezed his hand tightly. "At least promise you'll never take a chance like that again."

Kerry closed his eyes. Then he sat up, wincing at the pain in his shoulder, and his tone became as patient as a parent's to a child. "It was an accident, Meg. I'm a lawyer, not a policeman, and from now on there'll be metal detectors at every door of that courthouse."

Meg shook her head, unpersuaded, and her expression took

on the cast of stubbornness. "Promise," she repeated. "That's not too much for a wife to ask her husband."

Weary, Kerry lay back on the pillow, still holding her hand. "All right," he answered, and closed his eyes again.

Mary Kilcannon came once a day, staying briefly. It was as if she sensed that Kerry was troubled by more than she knew, and that she did not wish to burden him. Her hair was steel gray now, just a few black strands remaining, and her face quite worn; thinking of all that she had suffered, Kerry felt a deep gratitude for what she had tried to give him as a child, the restraint she was showing now. Jamie might become President, he knew, but Kerry was the son Mary loved most deeply, the one in whose face she saw her care reflected. And yet she refused to worry in his presence.

What parents do for their children, Kerry thought in wonder. *What* mothers *do . . .*

One more time, he had said to John, *and this will be over.*

In the doorway, Clayton touched the boy's shoulder, then nodded toward Kerry. "You can see now, John. Kerry's fine."

For once, the boy could not keep his eyes off Kerry; what Kerry read there went so far beyond relief that it was painful. Tentative, the boy came to him.

Glancing up at Clayton, Kerry nodded. "I'll be down the hall," Clayton told them both, and vanished.

John placed his hand on the sheets, a few inches from Kerry's arm. His eyes were sunken, his face was stunned; since John had stopped crying, the social worker had told Kerry, he had been almost mute. He had not asked about his father, or his mother. They gave him pills to sleep.

What to say, Kerry thought, *that could make any difference?* He clasped John's hand in his own. "Your mom loved you very much, you know. She always will."

The boy swallowed, then looked away. Kerry sensed how little use to him a dead mother—whose love John had known for barely a year—would be in the years to come. But all that Kerry could do was to grasp his hand still tighter. Just as he had done at the moment Bridget died.

Perhaps, Kerry thought, the same memory made the boy's lips tremble, as if to speak.

"What is it?" Kerry asked.

John laid his face on the bed, not daring to look at Kerry. "I want to stay with you," he whispered.

Kerry's throat tightened. A whisper, so that Kerry might not hear him. So that John could hardly hear himself.

I want to stay with you . . .

Did he mean tonight, Kerry wondered, or forever? And why not—wasn't this what Kerry owed John Musso? Who could believe that an aging woman in another city would know enough, or even live long enough, to mend the damage done to him?

Gently, Kerry touched the dark crown of John's head. There was so much to consider, he knew—his work, his marriage, his own fitness. He recalled his last impulsive decision, so entwined with this one; how little he had known about love when he asked Meg Collins to marry him, how dimly he understood it now. Just enough to know that the reasons she could not love him must have begun, not with Pat, but in her childhood, planting the seeds of her own subconscious wish—and this Kerry felt more sure of—never to have children. Not their own, and certainly not this child.

He must not temporize, Kerry knew. If he could not save Bridget Musso, or take John's life into his hands, nothing was left but truth.

Softly, Kerry began to explain about the boy's new home, the great-aunt who was waiting for him. John said nothing more. When Clayton came for him, he did not look back.

NINE

In the weeks after his release from the hospital, Kerry threw himself into his rehabilitation and his work. Had he been a split-second slower, he often thought, the bullet would have struck him in the head. Every hour since was a gift: his unspoken guilt only fueled his new intensity. Calling the office to find Kerry working past ten o'clock on a Monday night, Clayton said to him, "It's not your fault that you're still alive." But Kerry would not listen. At home, there was only Meg; here, there were cases to win, causes to help him remember or, perhaps, to forget.

When he called John's great-aunt, the boy would not speak to him.

John was so withdrawn, the woman told Kerry, that she never quite knew what to do. She seemed decent, humorless, and wholly unimaginative. Every week, John refused to come to the telephone; every week, her report was the same. Her aged voice combined helplessness with a certain fatalism: John Musso was her cross to bear, Kerry detected, and it was not for her to question the burdens God imposed. Kerry thought about flying to see them and then realized with bitter certainty that reappearing in John's life now was the last cruelty left undone.

At times Kerry thought of Jamie. Striving for the Democratic nomination, Jamie had fought his opponent—a former Vice President—to a virtual draw. Then, to Kerry's astonishment, Jamie made public his involvement with Stacey Tarrant; that a potential President was involved with a rock singer—however intelligent and socially aware—was deeply controversial. With a fervor that surprised him, Kerry hoped this candor marked a change in Jamie, a willingness to love at any cost, and not a mere recalculation of political advantage. But all that Jamie told him in their one brief conversation was "If you were reckless enough to take a bullet, the least I can do is date in public."

It was the last time they ever spoke.

On a warm April night, Kerry worked late. Once more, he had called John Musso's aunt; John was much the same, she told him. Hanging up, Kerry vainly wished that the damage of childhood were not so hard to heal. To his surprise, these reflections brought him back to Jamie.

He was in California now, campaigning, so the media said, to the point of exhaustion. Unless Jamie won the primary, the nomination would slip from his grasp; on a film clip two nights before, Jamie had looked so depleted that Kerry was shocked. Perhaps, at eleven, he would switch on the news . . .

The telephone rang.

Meg's voice was stunned, hollow. "Your mother called," she told him. "It's your brother. He's been shot."

Kerry felt numb. It was a moment before he could ask, "How bad is it?"

"They're not sure yet. It just came on the television."

"Go to Mom's," he said. "I'll be right there."

Like an automaton, Kerry walked down the bleak corridors to Vincent Flavio's office, footsteps echoing on the worn tile floors.

The television was in a corner, atop an antique hutch. Kerry pushed the button; in the darkness, the picture flickered to life.

Jamie stood on a concert stage, fingers touching Stacey's. The crowd was frenzied; the arena echoed with his name.

"Kil-cannon . . ."

With a dazzling smile, Stacey turned to him. They stood at the intersection of two spotlights, as if suspended in darkness. The crowd blessed them with its cry.

"Kil-cannon . . ."

Smiling, Jamie stood taller. All sign of fatigue was gone. Stacey stood aside, giving him the crowd.

Jamie raised his hand.

From one corner of the stage, a slender man stepped forward. Watching, Kerry flinched.

As if in a trance, the man raised his gun. Only Kerry seemed to see him.

Amidst the chant, Kerry saw Stacey Tarrant's mouth open in a silent scream . . .

The gunman took one last step, and fired.

Still facing the crowd, Jamie froze. The hair on his crown seemed to rise.

He crumpled, falling on his side, then his back. Stumbling forward, Stacey dived across his body. Then the Secret Service agents surrounded them, the TV camera searching for Jamie between their arms and legs.

When they found him, Jamie's lips were moving. Blood glistened beneath his head.

As the television cast a glow on Vincent Flavio's Persian rug and vanity photographs, Kerry stood motionless, watching his brother die.

They brought him home to Newark.

At Mary's request, Niall Callahan, the funeral director, prepared Jamie to be buried. Mary was stoic, tearless, sustained by prayer and Kerry's presence. When Niall was finished, she insisted on seeing her oldest son.

"Let me go see Niall," Kerry said. "Then I'll bring you."

Mary nodded. He did not need to explain.

With a few soft words, Niall led Kerry to the room where Jamie lay and left him there.

Alone, Kerry gazed into his brother's face.

In death, Jamie was waxen, and the crown of his head was missing. By now Kerry understood too well the wreckage an autopsy left; he knew that the lean body beneath the senatorial pinstripe was hollow and riddled with stitches. The man who had been his brother was gone.

My God, Jamie. What was it all for?

For a long time, Kerry stayed with him, tears in his eyes, fists balled in the pockets of his suit coat.

I hear you forgot to duck.

I remembered. Just not in time. ·

So much death, Kerry thought. *And now you. How much I wish that I had known you or, God help me, loved you. How*

*much I wanted never to be like you when, all the while, part of
me hurt that I was your younger, lesser, brother. How much, I
wonder, did any of that ever matter to you?*

"But you mattered to me," Kerry told him. "Always."

It was hard, Kerry found, to turn his back and leave.

When he returned with his mother, Mary leaned against
Kerry's shoulder, staring at her older son. "It's not what he
would want them to remember," Mary said simply. Beneath the
hushed words, Kerry heard another sadness—that long ago,
James Kilcannon had ceased to belong to his family.

Leaving, Kerry found Niall Callahan. "Close it," he said.

Jamie's aide, Nat Schlesinger, oversaw the funeral arrangements. Soldiering on through his own grief, Nat treated both
Kilcannons with a deep kindness. When Nat asked Kerry if he
wished to give the eulogy and Kerry answered, "He deserves
someone who knew him," Nat seemed to understand how
Kerry meant this.

It was Nat, as well, who made arrangements for Stacey Tarrant. But the morning of the funeral, Kerry asked to see her.

She was alone in a hotel room, with a bodyguard outside.
Passing through the door, Kerry wondered at the life she had
chosen, that Jamie had chosen—so public and yet, in some terrible way, so isolated. When she stood to shake his hand, quite
formally, Kerry was struck by her composure, her look of keen
perceptiveness.

"I'm sorry," Kerry told her.

Her grave blue eyes registered brief surprise—perhaps that
he was consoling *her*—and then comprehension. "Jamie spoke
of you often," she told him.

Kerry did not ask in what way, or care to press the point. It
struck him that all he shared with this beautiful woman, his peer
in age but from a different world, was a man both knew only a
part of—she, Jamie's present; Kerry, his past.

Their talk was polite. It was only when Kerry asked what she
might do next that her composure slipped.

Staring at the floor, she slowly shook her head. "I can't
imagine," she said softly, "that I'll ever perform in public. I feel
so responsible . . ." Her eyes shut. "All that I can think about are

those last few moments, Jamie trying to talk to me, knowing it was finished."

What, Kerry wondered, did Jamie need to tell her? Perhaps it would explain him, make clear what Kerry had never understood.

Hesitant, he asked her.

The look she gave him was guarded. Beneath this, Kerry detected a fresh hint of pain. "Just as they reported," she said. " 'Is everyone all right?' "

Kerry thought of the film clip, his brother's lips moving. "That was all?"

Stacey studied him. "No, not all." Pausing, she inhaled. " 'Such a joke,' he said to me. 'But what does it mean?' "

They buried Jamie in Princeton. The President was in Europe, but Vice President Bush came, many congressmen, most senators. They filed gravely past Kerry and his mother, like emissaries from Jamie's life; Kerry thought that Mary Kilcannon took some consolation from that, and in her prayers for Jamie now, for the afterlife of his soul. Throughout, Liam Dunn was a silent presence, attentive when they needed him but, Kerry sensed, nursing thoughts of his own.

A week later, Liam called.

Could Kerry come to see him? he wondered apologetically. There was a private matter to discuss, which it seemed could not wait.

Entering the spartan office Liam maintained as Essex County chairman, Kerry thought how different it was from Vincent Flavio's: for Liam, the trappings of power had never mattered; only its uses. With unwonted gravity, seemingly born of Jamie's death, Liam motioned Kerry to sit.

"How's your mother?" Liam asked. "I've been wanting to call on her."

"Resigned." Kerry tried to find words for what he saw. "It's like she has some immutable core, something that can't be reduced to ashes. God, perhaps."

Liam nodded. "And you?"

"I have work."

Liam gave him a long, almost cool appraisal; it was so different from the way his godfather had ever looked at him that it made Kerry uneasy. "I have something to ask you," Liam said at length. "And it's not an easy thing to ask. Probably not a fair thing. But then politics, like rust, never sleeps."

"What is it?"

"There's still an election this November, Kerry. Someone will fill Jamie's seat now." Liam's voice became quieter. "You'll recall Congressman Shue. The gun lobby's best friend."

Kerry watched his godfather's face. "You've heard the story, then."

"What I heard, Kerry, was that you virtually called Ralph Shue an accomplice to murder. Is it true?"

"Yes. It's true, and he is."

Liam folded his hands. "He's also taking Jamie's place. After a decent interval, our governor's appointing him to the United States Senate. Pending the election."

"They'd put that whore in Jamie's seat? He'll never win."

"He *will* win. He's got a cartload of suburban voters and all the money he needs." Pausing, Liam's voice was gentle. "There's no one who can beat him."

The sentence ended abruptly. What Liam had not said, suddenly did not need to say, hit Kerry in the pit of his stomach.

Liam looked at him calmly. "I've talked to the state chairman, and most of the committee. We know what we're asking, son. But it's you we're wanting."

Kerry sat back, shaken. "I've never wanted this, even when he was alive. I surely don't want it now, like *this*."

Liam watched his face. "Then all I ask, Kerry, is that you tell me that tomorrow."

A swirl of emotions brought Kerry to his feet—shame, anger at Liam, a feeling of betrayal. "All I've got to offer is a dead brother and the name Kilcannon. They'd be voting for a corpse, not for me. Why should they?" Kerry's voice grew quieter. "They don't know *me* at all. But there's one thing *I've* always known, ever since I was old enough to know anything. That I'm not Jamie."

Liam gave him a bleak smile. " 'My arms are too short to box with God.' Is that what you're feeling?"

Kerry flushed. "It's simpler than that. I've got no qualifications."

"You've made yourself a fine prosecutor, Kerry, a friend to women. You're a hero. And yes, you're Jamie's brother. All things to be proud of. Together, they can make you a senator." Liam paused. "If you decide to be one."

Kerry felt the irony come crashing down on him—so many assets, none earned. He slowly shook his head.

Liam's voice was still gentle. "You've gone through a great deal, yourself been wounded by a madman. You've your mother to consider, and a wife. You've every right to say no. But before you do, ask yourself one question, for your own sake. Ask how you'll feel if you turn your back on this." Pushing up from the chair, Liam stood to face him. "You understand politics well enough, Kerry. I raised you to. But you've never understood just how much you can do."

Kerry looked into his godfather's face. "The other day," he said at last, "I learned what Jamie said before he died. The last part."

"And what was that?"

Kerry told him.

For a moment, Liam was quiet. "Pray on it," he said.

TEN

When he told his mother of Liam's request, she fell into deep silence, eyes veiled. Perhaps, Kerry thought, she was praying.

They were sitting in her living room. It was late afternoon and the room was shadowed; so little of this had changed, Kerry thought, since Jamie had lived here. Now only the two of them were left.

"What answer have you given him?" she said at last.

"I haven't."

She raised her eyes to him. "And you were expecting me to tell you no?"

He touched her arm. "I know how you feel, Mom."

Tears came to her eyes. "Since you were born, I've prayed for your safety, like any mother. But I've always thought there was a reason for things, one that I can't quarrel with." Her hand covered his. "Search your heart, Kerry. Whatever you find there, then that's what you should do. Because I know God loves you even more than I."

Kerry entered the sanctuary at Sacred Heart.

At this hour, five in the afternoon, it was close to empty. He knelt before the altar, crossing himself, waiting for the vastness of the sanctuary, its hush, to calm the terrible force of his emotions.

Jamie hardly dead a week, and now they wanted him. Kerry shut his eyes.

Such a joke, he thought to himself. *But what does it mean?*

They wanted *Jamie,* not him. What obligation did he have, because his brother had died, to live his brother's life for him? And badly at that: Kerry could never be James, and the cost would be what Kerry dreaded most—endless comparisons to his brother; the merciless scrutiny of a thousand eyes along a path not of Kerry's choosing; the jeers of those who thought him callous and an opportunist; the disappointment of others who projected onto Kerry all their hopes for Jamie; the fantasies that no man could fulfill.

You're next, Kerry—if you can get your grades up a little.

How Kerry had despised him for it. How deeply, now, did he wish him still alive. How could they ask him to take Jamie's place, when he might never sort out his feelings about Jamie himself?

They'd put that whore in Jamie's seat? he had asked. *He'll never win.*

He will win . . .

What was he most afraid of, Kerry wondered—Jamie's shadow, or his own incapacity? Perhaps his brother had simply been a mirror in which Kerry saw his own truth more clearly than anyone else could see.

You're a hero.

Once more, in Kerry's memory, Anthony Musso raised the gun.

Perhaps that was his deepest fear, Kerry acknowledged. Another madman with a gun, driven by some warped circuitry that Kerry would never know.

You've every right to say no.

One more time, he had promised John Musso, *and this will be over.*

It's not your fault, Clayton had said to him, *that you're still alive.*

Kerry closed his eyes again, and prayed.

When, at last, he opened his eyes, Kerry saw Father Joe Donegan standing in the doorway behind the altar.

Rising, Kerry acknowledged him. The priest hesitated and then came forward.

"The quiet," Kerry said. "It helps me think."

Father Donegan studied him. It was thirteen years, Kerry thought, since Father Joe had vainly tried to dissuade Michael Kilcannon from brutalizing Kerry's mother. Now he was gaunt, graying, growing older in the service of the Church as he watched his parish dwindle.

"Would you care to talk?" the priest asked gently.

No, Kerry thought, *not about this. Of all the people in the world, there's only one to whom I'd say all this.* "I've been wanting to thank you," Kerry answered. "For looking after my mother."

"Mothers don't expect to bury sons, Kerry. Sometimes faith in God is the only answer. That's why she comes."

"She's *always* come." Pausing, Kerry looked around them. "But it's changed, hasn't it?"

"That it has."

Kerry shoved his hands in his pockets. "What would help, I wonder."

"The parish, or the community . . . ? We need so many things—compassion, reconciliation. And then there are the

more practical forms of help, like renewing abandoned buildings or simply tearing them down. They're breeding grounds
for all the things that corrupt our children." The priest sighed.
"Truth to tell, the kids are what worry me most. Not this parish,
love it as I do."

Kerry nodded and, touching the priest's shoulder, left.

Driving home, Kerry thought of Liam.

*You understand politics well enough. I raised you to. But
you've never understood just how much you can do.*

He found Meg in the living room, studying for her last exam;
by fall, Kerry reminded himself, Meg would be an English
teacher. Her job was already set.

As calmly as he could, Kerry explained what had happened.

Meg's eyes widened. "My God, you're really thinking about
it, aren't you? After all that's happened."

"It deserves at least that much, Meg. Whatever I decide, I'll
be a long time living with it."

"You *hope*." Meg stood, arms folded. "You've just buried
your brother, Kerry. How can you do this?"

"Please, I haven't said I will. But there's a reason Liam
asked. If I don't run, he thinks, Ralph Shue takes Jamie's seat.
That's the last thing I'd want."

She stared at him in incomprehension, her voice choked with
emotion. "*Ralph Shue?* He'd be one senator among a hundred."
She caught herself, then came to him, laying her head against
his chest. "I'm sorry, Kerry. I nearly lost you . . ."

Torn, Kerry stroked her hair. "I'm sorry too."

"Please." Her voice was muffled by tears. "You promised me."

"I know," he murmured. "But Jamie was alive then."

Kerry felt her stiffen, looking up into his face. "And now you
want to *be* him. Because he's dead?"

Kerry drew a breath. "No, Meg. I don't want to be Jamie."

She pushed back from him, her face tear-streaked. "I'm
sorry. But if you do this, I won't help you. I've got a life here,
and a job I've worked hard for. Even if I weren't afraid for you,
I hate what politics does to women." Meg shook her head, as if
stunned by all that had happened, and then she spoke more

quietly. "I won't stand in your way, Kerry. If you go to Washington, I'll come there when you need me. But I won't go with you."

Kerry looked at her. "Well," he said softly, "at least our kids won't miss me."

Tears sprang to her eyes again. Turning, Meg left the room.

That night, they lay next to each other, silent. Kerry never slept.

In the morning, Kerry called Clayton Slade. "There's something I need to ask you," he began.

Four days later, schooled by Liam Dunn, an apprehensive Kerry met with Liam and three members of the party's state committee—its chairman, Joseph Auletta; Walter Shipman, the head of an important union; and Carl Cash, a black former civil rights activist and a friend of Newark's mayor. Looking around the table, Kerry reflected on the shrewd instincts that had enabled Liam, and Jamie, to survive among competing forces. But all of them wanted to keep the seat, and Kerry was the instrument at hand.

"There's no point in my running," he told them, "if the sixty other Democrats who're better qualified start saying so in public. Which is surely what Shue's hoping for, if he's caught wind of this."

His directness seemed to take Auletta by surprise. "Under these circumstances, Kerry, there won't be any primary. If Senator Kilcannon hadn't won the presidential nomination, he'd still have been our nominee for Senate." Auletta paused. "No guarantee. But if you commit to us now, I think we can head off any problems."

Kerry glanced at the others. "Do you agree?"

They nodded, watching Kerry.

"What else?" Auletta said.

"Money. Will there be enough?"

Auletta nodded. "There's your brother's network, Kerry. I know where the organization is, *and* the money. In that way, Senator Kilcannon left you in good shape."

Senator Kilcannon, Kerry thought to himself. How long might it be, if ever, before these men thought of him as anything but Jamie's surrogate. "I appreciate that," he answered. "But if I do this, I'll be running as me—whatever *that* turns out to be—not as some poor imitation of my brother. Everyone will know why you've come to me. Why make it worse?"

Auletta nodded his agreement. This was meaningless, Kerry knew; what they expected was a malleable amateur, appealing enough—with proper coaching—to win by running under his brother's name.

"There's one more thing," Kerry said. "I'd expect to name my own campaign manager. And I'd want it understood that everything, and everyone, goes through him."

Auletta raised his eyebrows. "Do you have someone in mind?"

"Clayton Slade. We worked together in the prosecutor's office."

Watching Kerry, Auletta idly touched his nimbus of gray-black hair. In a dubious tone, he said, "I don't know him. Has he ever run anything?"

"No. But he's a very quick study. All he'll need is help from you."

Auletta gave him a long look of appraisal. *Take your time,* Kerry thought. *We both know who asked me here, and that I can walk away.*

"All right," Auletta said at length. "We can put some good people around him. But you need to decide, Kerry—soon."

"By tomorrow." Kerry looked around him, speaking to the group. "One question, just for my own curiosity. The two senators pretty much control who the President appoints for U.S. attorney, right? Including in the district covering Newark."

Not even a senator, Kerry could see Auletta thinking, *and you're already dispensing patronage.* "You'd have a lot of influence," Auletta replied. "Assuming that a Democrat's in the White House."

"That's what I thought," Kerry said.

They shook hands all around. It was only after the others left that Liam asked, "You're going after Vincent Flavio, aren't you? Your U.S. attorney would indict him."

Kerry gave his godfather the smallest smile. "You forgot Nunzio," he answered.

* * *

It was not easy.

"A Senate seat is not a bequest," the *Newark Star-Ledger* editorialized, "however tragic the loss." Its political columnist was more direct: "The Democratic Party has determined to replace a potential President with an Irish machine politician whose name, curiously enough, also happens to be Kilcannon."

Kerry and Clayton worked hard to overcome this. But Kerry's inexperience showed—there were issues he did not yet grasp, constituencies he did not understand—and Ralph Shue hammered relentlessly on Kerry's lack of qualifications, his own years of experience. Frustrated, Kerry burst out at a rally, "Where did Mr. Shue learn to roll over and do tricks whenever the gun lobby whistles? Or drool like Pavlov's dog when polluters ring the dinner bell? It must be all that *experience* . . ."

Almost instantly, Kerry regretted this; to his list of adjectives for Kerry, Shue now added "intemperate" and "immature." For some voters, followers of Jamie, nothing Kerry could do or say was excessive; for others—and much of the press—Kerry seemed too volatile. When Auletta suggested that Kerry contact John Musso and his aunt, hoping for a TV ad to soften his image, Kerry refused. For several weeks thereafter, hamstrung by caution, he suffered Shue's attacks, delivered from the lofty vantage point of the man's knowledge and years of service.

The climax occurred at their last debate. Now leading by a point, Shue, emboldened, decided to attack with new force—Kerry would either lose his temper, as before, or suffer the attacks in silence. Finally, Shue turned to Kerry and said, "If your name was Kerry Francis, sir, your candidacy would be a joke."

For a moment Kerry was silent, gazing into Shue's square, smug face. "If my name were Kerry Francis," he answered softly, "my brother would still be alive."

Shue blinked. With an otherworldly detachment, Kerry realized that the last man he had seen this wounded was his own father, on the night when Kerry had beaten him. Only Clayton, perhaps, would understand how much the answer cost Kerry himself.

At thirty, the same age as his brother, Kerry narrowly won election to the United States Senate.

The Campaign

Day Two

ONE

Telling Kerry about Lara—the counselor's notes, Cutler's question, her lie in return—Clayton watched his friend closely.

Kerry's stillness was so complete that he seemed not to breathe. His thoughts could have been anything—a terrible regret; the fear of discovery; the potential destruction of his hopes for the presidency—except for the look in his eyes. So that it did not surprise Clayton that Kerry's first words were "How is she?"

They sat across from each other in Kerry's suite. It was a little past six; Kerry had just come from the gym, and his hair was mussed, his forehead damp. Surrounding them was the hush of a giant hotel in the moments before the clatter of room service carts began, the muffled sounds of doors opening and closing. They had led this life for so long, uprooted from home yet surrounded by people, that Clayton sometimes forgot the utter solitude at its core.

"Devastated," he answered simply. "Because of then, and because of now. Though she's trying not to show that."

Kerry seemed to wince. His pain for Lara was so naked that Clayton looked away.

"She didn't lie just for you, Kerry. She did what was best for both of you."

Kerry folded his hands. "That's what she thought two years ago. Does she still think it was, I wonder?"

Clayton was silent. "Whatever else," he said at last, "you could never have become President. She left you free to choose. Just like now." He paused again, then added quietly, "She doesn't want to see you. For your sake as much as hers."

This time, it was Kerry who looked away.

For a moment, Clayton let him be. They sat together in silence.

"So," Clayton said at last, "there's only one decision left for you to make."

Kerry did not answer. The only sign that he had heard was the gaze he directed at Clayton, level but impenetrable.

"*Newsworld,*" Clayton continued, "will try to break this before Tuesday. That means Cutler's coming to you next. Kit can try to buy you a little time. But it won't be long until you're face-to-face with Cutler, and have to make a choice."

"*Have* to?" Kerry stood, suddenly angry. "What happened between Lara and me has nothing to do with whether I'm fit to be President. Answering validates his right to ask."

To Clayton, the response revealed how shaken Kerry was: unlike many politicians who, faced with trouble, create their own reality, Kerry had always been willing to acknowledge whatever difficulties he faced. "A 'nondenial denial'?" Clayton asked. "Everyone knows that means 'I did it.' That won't stop *Newsworld* from trying to get your cell phone records, questioning your neighbors, finding any maître d' who ever saw you two together. What are you going to say when Cutler asks why you called her at three in the morning, or left her apartment at six—'None of your business'?" Clayton stood to face him. "There'll be enough to make you look bad. Without a flat denial, he prints it all."

Kerry folded his arms. "So I let Nate Cutler make a liar out of me."

"Or lose the primary."

Once more, Kerry was still. Only his questioning look betrayed surprise.

"Lose," Clayton told him, "and the story goes away. But if you win the nomination and *then* the story comes out, you'll be the ruined candidate who dragged his party to disaster." Clayton's voice softened. "Forty-two years old, Kerry, and a ghost. How many more regrets do you want to live with?"

Kerry stared at him. After a time, he asked, "Just how do we ensure I lose, when we're not even sure how I can win?"

"I pull the TV ads we committed to, explaining we need the

money for between now and the convention. Without more air-time, Frank Wells and Jack Sleeper think Mason wins. I agree." Clayton gave a first bleak smile. "They've got their reputations to protect. Once I cancel the ads, they leak it to the press, and I become the idiot who cost you the nomination. Next time you'll know to hire someone better."

Kerry tilted his head, studying him. Clayton could feel his friend thinking of what this would cost Clayton himself: two years of his life; his own pride in reputation; his hopes to be attorney general. For his own sake, Clayton realized, he wanted Kerry to lie. "You're young," he finished. "You've made a great run, when almost nobody gave you a chance. In four years, or eight years, you could run again. If you want that."

"And if I lie?"

"No guarantees. But *Newsworld* still has standards: does it print the story when all it has is innuendo? At least you can hope this gets pushed down a level, to papers that don't count as much. Maybe even the tabloids, so we can call it sleaze."

"Even though it's true."

"Give them the 'truth,' Kerry, and Lara loses her reputation, and her career. So do you." Clayton's voice became slow and emphatic. "If you don't want to lie, lose the primary. But first ask yourself this: are you willing to sacrifice everything you've campaigned for, let down everyone who's worked for you, so that whoever is trying to destroy you—Dick Mason or some Republican—can be President? Then ask yourself which sin you want to live with."

Kerry walked to the window, opening the drapes. A sun-streaked smog sat over Los Angeles; to Clayton, the office towers surrounding their hotel, random in their shapes and colors, looked like the careless work of a willful child. Kerry's tone was bitter. "I can't be with her, but I can ruin her. All because I think I'd be a better President than Dick Mason." He shook his head, and his voice became softer, a mixture of irony and sadness. "What would my brother have done, do you suppose?"

Twelve years ago today, Clayton reflected, James Kilcannon had been murdered. He waited a moment longer. "In five minutes, Kerry, I'm meeting with Kit, Nat, and Frank. What should I tell them?"

Kerry did not turn. "Tell them to stall," he said at last.

At six o'clock, Sean Burke stood in front of the glass door beneath the "Kilcannon for President" sign.

The dawn was sunny; the clouds that had covered San Francisco were gone. At Sean's back was the hum of urban traffic running normally, the squeal of brakes, the arrhythmic snarl of motors. After a moment, Rick Ginsberg, the volunteer coordinator, appeared like a specter through the glass. Then Sean opened the door and stepped inside.

Though his eyes were bruised with sleeplessness, Rick managed a smile. "Thanks for showing up early, John."

Rick's quiet words echoed; with few others there, the cavernous showroom had a shadowy hush, even more churchlike than before.

"Come on back," Rick said. "I've got the morning *Times* and the *Chronicle* spread out on the table."

Sean followed him. Their footsteps echoed from the Spanish tiles to the ceiling, fifty feet above. Over his shoulder, Rick asked, "Did you see Kerry's speech last night? When he was talking to the demonstrators?"

Even Kerry Kilcannon's name, Sean found, made him edgy. "Yeah," he murmured. "I saw it."

"I hope they understand—Kerry's pro-choice; he's just got his own feelings." Rick's voice was doubtful. "With this creep who murdered those people in Boston, you wonder who's listening. Mason's sure using that every way he can."

Sean felt his skin crawl. How much longer would it be, he wondered, until they traced him to San Francisco, put photos of the "creep" on television for fools like Rick to see. And still he had no weapon.

The coordinator stopped by a Formica-top table covered with newspapers next to two pairs of scissors. "Start with the *Chronicle*," Rick told him. "We clip out anything about the campaign, or issues, and fax it all to state headquarters in L.A."

Sean placed his hands on the table, leaning forward as he

scanned the papers. On the front page of the second section, he saw the headline "Kilcannon to Tour Bay Area Tomorrow."

Sean stared at the words. "After I'm done," he mumbled, "I may have to go out for a while. Maybe an hour."

Mechanically, Sean picked up the scissors.

"Jesus," Nat Schlesinger murmured.

It was seven o'clock. Clayton sat in his hotel suite with Nat, Kit Pace, Frank Wells, and two pots of coffee; Nat's voice was the first sound since Clayton had finished speaking. Now Clayton watched them sort out the pieces: the counselor's memo; Nate Cutler's visit to Lara Costello; Lara's denial. The gloom was palpable.

It was Frank Wells who spoke next. "Well," he said, "this takes care of the gay rumors, doesn't it?"

No one smiled. Kit's round face looked puffy, as if she had been aroused from sleep; Clayton watched her struggle to jump-start her thoughts. Carefully, she asked Clayton, "If Nate goes to him, what will Kerry say?"

Kit, Clayton knew, would not ask if the story was true. Nor would the others; like criminal defense lawyers, they did not wish to know and would never talk of this to Kerry. That was Clayton's job.

"Right now," Clayton said, "he doesn't see why he should answer at all."

Kit's coffee cup froze halfway to her mouth. As she stared at Clayton over the rim, he saw her recover. "That won't fly," she said bluntly. "How you deal with a scandal can make it better or worse. One way or another, Kerry has to respond." She sipped her coffee, then added more quietly, "Deciding things has never been his problem."

Clayton felt the others watching. Each, he was confident, assumed that Clayton knew the truth, and was waiting for cues. "He's had less than an hour to live with this," Clayton answered.

Kit put down her coffee cup, eyes veiled. *So it's true,* he saw her think.

"What about this woman?" Frank Wells asked. "The

counselor who wrote the memo? Can we send someone to talk to her?"

Clayton gave a curt shake of the head. "That makes her look more credible. If *Newsworld* prints this, our visit could become part of the story. And there's no controlling what this counselor might say about it."

"At least run her through the Internet," Kit put in. "If we're lucky, she's a political activist or files nut lawsuits. Something we can discredit. Any way you look at it, what she's done is shitty."

"*You* know the first rule," Frank Wells said to Clayton. "If you've got a problem, get it out and live with it. Then hope you can find something about Mason that's even worse."

"What would *that* be?" Kit demanded. "Whoever slipped this to Cutler knows how it would look—that Kerry is so ruthless and amoral he'll do *anything* to save himself." She turned to Clayton. "*That's* the problem, isn't it?"

"*I* think so," Clayton admitted, then turned to the others. "Does anyone here disagree that if *Newsworld* can source this, it's a story? Or that it would ruin Kerry's chances to be President?"

Narrow-eyed, Frank Wells stared into some middle distance past Clayton's head. "Voters are more tolerant now," he said finally. "I can imagine a candidate saying that this is an agonizing moral dilemma, one he feels he shares with thousands of others."

"You mean make this *Kerry's* tragedy?" Kit's voice, though quiet, was incredulous. "*And* hang Lara Costello out to dry? Women would hate him for it."

Frank spoke to Clayton. "At least we could focus-group it—quick and dirty and somewhere far away, like Massachusetts. Make the hypothetical candidate some married guy who wants to run for Congress, script a few versions of a *mea culpa*, see what people think. Why close down our options?"

With this, Clayton knew, the conversation had taken a decisive turn; more blatantly than Kit's, Frank's suggestion assumed that the story was true. "That would take a week," Kit rejoined. "If Kerry's still deciding a week from now, it's the worst mistake he could make. And this *is* Kerry Kilcannon we're talking about, not some narcissist on a talk show. The confessional style just isn't him."

Stress, Clayton saw, was becoming antipathy: Frank was talking past Kit to him; Kit was telling Frank that he had no grasp of the candidate. It was time to end this. "The story's deadly," Clayton said. "Period. Once it's printed, there's only one thing he could say that isn't hopeless: 'It's not true.' And if he's waited until *then*, it's probably too late. So let's talk about the next few days."

There was silence again. They gazed out the window, watching the towers of the city, surreal amidst the haze. "Then we should sum up what's going for us," Kit said at last. "First, whatever problem is here, its not characterological. Unlike our current leader, no one's going to claim that he's been doing a volume business in women."

Clayton shook his head. "That's not him, either."

"Okay. Second, Kerry's divorced now. Adultery's not an on-going issue . . ."

"What about the ex-wife?" Frank Wells asked. "What would *she* say if *Newsworld* went to her?"

It was a good question, Clayton knew. Quietly, he said to Frank, "I don't think Meg knows anything about this. But if someone needs to talk to her, I will."

The ambiguous comment hung in the air, and then Kit resumed her analysis. "Third," she told them, "—and *this* is the biggest thing—*we* already know that Lara's denied it. That's a huge advantage: other than Kerry, *she's* the only one who knows for sure. Cutler may not believe her, but even these days *Newsworld* has to be ambivalent. They won't be comfortable with one unnamed source and a memo that could be a political dirty trick. So Nate has to come to us.

"He can't do *that* in public." Her voice grew sardonic. "Can you imagine him shouting at Kerry along the rope line: 'Have you fucked any NBC reporters in the last three years?' Nate would lose his exclusive.

"The problem is when *Newsworld* goes to Lara's friends, just like to Kerry's ex. 'We *know* you're close to Lara Costello,' they'll say. 'We *know* that she was having an affair with Senator

Kilcannon. What did she tell you about that?' The questions go on from there."

True enough, Clayton thought. "As to Lara," he told her, "they won't find anyone."

Kit sat back, steepling her fingers. "She told you that?"

"Yes."

For a moment, Kit dropped her crisp manner. "God, I feel sorry for her."

"So does Kerry. He doesn't want us to do anything which tells Cutler that Lara came to me."

"How do we avoid that?" Kit asked. "Until Nate tips his hand, or Kerry decides what to do, we can't have Kerry any-place where Nate can corner him. And one of the things the press likes about Kerry is that he's accessible: walking through the airplane, saying hello—"

"It's not that bad," Frank Wells interjected. "Our guy's tired, that's all. We've already said that we're saving his time for the California media. For a couple of days, at least, it won't look like we're singling out *Newsworld*." His tone, though strained, became ironic. "With luck, they'll think we're waiting until Kerry's comments on abortion die down."

"That's how it'll have to be," Clayton said to Kit. "We need to buy him some time."

"Until next Tuesday, you mean? That only works if Kerry in-tends to deny it, or he loses. Otherwise it's worse."

Once more, Clayton found himself appreciating how sharp Kit was. "He knows that," Clayton answered quietly.

Suddenly Kerry was a palpable presence. Clayton could feel the others imagining his conversation with Kerry; adjusting their view of the candidate; wondering how their unspoken knowledge would affect his relations with each of them. And last—because this was politics, and they were professionals—he felt their sympathy for Kerry the man.

"Isn't it amazing," Nat mused. "We just accept that they can do this to him—ask it, and print it. There's no sense of outrage anymore."

"Oh," Kit responded, "I don't have any illusions about these people. They're not our friends, or even an audience—they're usually not open to persuasion, and they're too obsessed with scandal. But they've got their job to do, and I do my job best by respecting that. Sometimes they fuck up, but they're generally pretty close to the mark. If this is true, they've got their arguments: the ethics of Lara covering Kerry, the fact he may look like a hypocrite, the ruthlessness thing. I even think Nate Cutler's a decent guy. Why bother being pissed off?"

"Because *Kerry Kilcannon*'s a decent guy," Clayton answered, "and this election should be about what he offers the country." He turned to Nat. "You know the publisher of *Newsworld*, don't you? And you're friends with the editor in chief?"

"Uh-huh. In fact, I was in his wedding." Nat gave a faint smile. "His *first* wedding, before he dumped Janie and the kids for a reporter from the *Baltimore Sun*."

Kit Pace emitted a brief, somewhat harsh laugh. "Touché," she said to Nat.

"So," Clayton asked him, "what would you say to your highly moral friend once Cutler knocks on Kerry's door?"

"That they've got one off-the-record source. That a topflight newsmagazine needs a higher standard of proof—something like 'beyond a reasonable doubt'—before it effectively decides the most critical primary election in recent memory. That in these times of media feeding frenzy they're all the more obligated to get it right. That there's still time between the convention and the general election to do more checking."

Nat paused, looking at the others, then spoke with new force. "That if they print this story now, as thin as it is, they're deciding that they want Dick Mason over Kerry Kilcannon. That they'd turn the campaign into the kind of mudslinging nightmare that requires us to retaliate against Mason or the other guys any way we can. And that the public is so sick of that *and* them only half of us vote now, and this 'scandal' would be one more step toward flushing presidential politics down the toilet."

All of them had moved past shock, Clayton thought; the conversation was both feeling and practical. "Then maybe you fly to New York," he said to Nat, "as soon as Cutler comes to us, and tell them so."

Nat leaned forward, graying and rumpled, a man who had seen it all and still hoped for the best. "But Kerry has to deny this, and the denial has to stick. Otherwise it'll boomerang on us with a vengeance." He drew a breath. "It's the old gotcha game. Nobody's going to admit to fucking their dead grandmother, but once they ask the question and you *lie*, the press has an absolute obligation to expose you as a liar. I can hear the *New York Times* right now."

"The *Times* editorial page," Kit said with quiet contempt. "The epicenter of conventional wisdom." She turned to Clayton. "If Cutler gets sat on, he could leak enough dirt to a lesser paper to have *them* print it. Then Nate can print *his* more complete story without *Newsworld* being responsible for breaking it. I've seen reporters do that."

Clayton saw Nat Schlesinger's rueful shake of the head; he was sixty, Nat's expression said, and had entered journalism in another age—in Nat's opinion, a better one.

"A question," Clayton said to him. "Who fed this to Cutler in the first place?"

Nat frowned. "The GOP. It's *their* issue, after all."

Frank Wells shook his head. "Mason. It fits with the past two days." He turned to Clayton. "Which gets me back to my cynical question: Are our oppo-research people looking for the magic bullet we can use on Dick?"

"That's what they're for. But all we've found are rumors. Although they're bad ones."

Clayton heard the others stir. Frank raised his eyebrows. "About what?"

Clayton shook his head. "If they're more than that," he said firmly, "I'll let you know. But if they're not, this is something that could backfire."

There was silence, acceptance. "All right," Clayton said. "Let's sum this up. For now, Kerry avoids Cutler by avoiding the press. If Cutler wants to see him in private, Kit demands to know what it's about. And once Cutler pops the question, Nat goes to *Newsworld*. But only if Kerry's prepared to make a firm denial."

The others nodded. "When you talk to Kerry," Nat said softly, "emphasize the last part."

No response, Clayton knew, was necessary. With equal quiet, he said, "Then I've got one more thing to say.

"What we've talked about today is Kerry's political future. It's also personal, and involves my closest friend.

"Your first obligation is to look upbeat, as if nothing has happened. The second is to say nothing about this to anyone. To me, that's not just loyalty—it's morality.

"*My* moral distinction is not between one decision Kerry might make or another. It's between campaign consultants who are loyal to their candidate and those who leak. The culture of Washington rewards disloyalty: a political consultant is never wiser than when he's screwing his boss. Show me the consultants with the best reputations among the press, and I know who the treacherous pricks are." Now Clayton looked directly at Frank Wells. "Of course, the *real* art form is to leak and spin simultaneously—to dump on your candidate for not doing all the things you recommended and then suggest how badly that reflects on his judgment, and how well on yours.

"I don't *ever* want to see that happen to Kerry Kilcannon. Especially about this." Clayton's tone grew softer yet. "But if it does, whoever leaks this meeting had better bury him. Because if Kerry becomes President, no one will have to worry about how long *my* memory will be."

Frank Wells gazed at him steadily. Clayton let the silence build, and then he looked at all of them. "All right," he said. "The general meeting's next, and we've got work to do. Among other things, Jack Sleeper's polls say we've got a little problem on abortion."

TWO

"We're still weak on abortion," Jack Sleeper said. "Last night's numbers show you slipping with pro-choice women."

Kerry looked around the hotel conference room: among the five others—besides Clayton—Kit Pace, Frank Wells, and Nat Schlesinger were trying to seem normal. Perhaps only Kerry could see the artificiality of their smiles, the too-bright looks of interest with which they tried to cover their unease. His relations to the three of them were now forever changed by something they could never mention. To Kerry, the two others—Jack, his pollster, and Mick Lasker, the California manager—seemed like innocents.

"What do you have in mind?" Clayton asked Jack.

The pollster glanced at Frank Wells. Leaning forward, Frank spoke directly to Kerry. "Your antiviolence message got lost yesterday. What we need to get across is that you've saved the lives of women *and* their children—literally."

Kerry's eyes met Frank's. Softly, he said, "Not all of them."

Frank seemed to hesitate. "You saved the kid, Kerry. What's Dick Mason ever done?" Rising, he went to the VCR and pushed the button. "Here's the spot I want to run instead of the one we saw yesterday. Jack and I think it's stronger."

On the screen, a younger Kerry appeared: a news photo, Kerry thought, taken when he declared for the Senate. After Jamie, before Lara. He looked at himself, young and obviously daunted, and thought of all the things this man had yet to learn.

The narrator, a woman, began quietly.

"On February 12, 1988, a young lawyer went to court.

"Already he had dedicated four years of his life to protecting women from violence. Now he had come to protect another woman, and her son.

"But someone else came to court that day—a man with a gun. The woman's abusive husband."

There was a soft percussive pop, like the sound of a bullet firing, and then the picture changed.

Kerry stared at the screen.

The photographer had arrived in the first seconds after the courtroom guard killed Anthony Musso. His photograph caught the deputy standing over Musso. Next to them was Bridget's body, her arms outflung. Mercifully, her face was turned from the lens.

The picture moved to Kerry.

He was lying in the doorway, his eyes shut, blood seeping from his shoulder, the other arm crooked around a boy whose own eyes were widened in horror.

"Kerry Kilcannon," the woman's voice finished. *"Because caring is more than talk."*

Kerry could not take his eyes off the screen. Next to him, he felt Clayton's quiet.

You'll never know, Clayton had told him then. *It was too fast.*

The picture went dark.

"Caring is more than talk," Kerry said at last. "I don't even know what happened to the boy. Do you?"

Pausing, Frank studied his face. "Kerry, one photograph of you pulling a dead seagull out of a polluted waterfront is worth ten half-hour speeches on saving the wetlands. Nobody *heard* you yesterday. But they'll get this."

Kerry was silent. "One other thing," Clayton put in. "I'm re-thinking all this money for television. If we're broke between now and the convention, Kerry's completely off the air. It's the problem Dole had last time."

Frank came back to the table, sitting with an exaggerated slump. "Clayton," he said wearily, "we've already been here. Lose California, and Kerry's off the air for good. I can just hear Ellen Penn."

"We'll talk about it." Though quiet, Clayton's voice had an edge. "Later. Tell me what else you've got."

Frank looked from Clayton to Kerry. *Is he dropping out?* Kerry saw him wonder. "That last spot," he said to Kerry, "also helps you with the kid thing. But you need to do more."

"The kid thing?" Kerry asked.

"That you don't have any."

"Oh," Kerry said. "That. Is it too late to adopt?"

Only the unaware—Jack Sleeper and Mick Lasker—smiled. "It's all those pictures of Dick and Jeannie," Frank responded at last, "with the three golden-haired kids—the perfect albino family. If your number one value is being a good parent and a good spouse, you like the candidate who seems to be one. That's Mason.

"But it's got a downside. We've done some mall intercepts, and the single women—"

"Mall intercepts?"

"Yeah. It's like a focus group, only quicker. We go to a mall, pull some folks who look like what we want into a rented room, and ask some questions with the videotape on. In the post-O.J. age, no one seems to mind."

Kerry smiled in bemusement. "You know what this country *really* needs, Frank? A sense of shame. Instead everyone wants an agent."

Frank gave a sour smile of his own. "Then this was real value—they did it for free. Anyhow, to single women, the idea of someone single as President is almost like a civil rights issue. They're sick of hearing about 'family values,' like *they* don't matter.

"So what I want, Kerry, is to put you back in the studio and tape another spot about kids." Frank hesitated, glancing at Jack Sleeper. "We'll use *your* line: 'At the least, a civilized society should spend as much on the first five years of a child's life as on our last two weeks when we're old.' Only you need to personalize it more."

"How, exactly?"

"You look into the camera and say you've always wanted kids and hope someday to have your own. But that as President, you mean to help every child in the American family."

Kerry felt himself freeze. From the corner of his eye, he saw Frank Wells look down.

"I won't do that," he said. "What I may have wanted, and whether I'll ever have it, is no one's business but mine."

Frank glanced at Jack. "Can we at least use the first one?" he asked Kerry.

There was a long pause, and then Kerry said softly, "I got shot, it's true. No one can take that away from me."

Jack pursed his lips. "All right," he responded carefully. "There's one more issue that resonates with women—guns. They want something done about them."

Without a word being said, Kerry felt the subject of his brother's death enter the room. "So do I," he answered.

"The question is what." Sleeper's tone remained tentative. "Like it or not, a lot of people distinguish between handguns and assault weapons. Some have handguns in their homes, for self-protection. But they think only nuts own AK-forty-sevens."

Next to him, Kerry saw Mick Lasker begin to speak, think better of it. "Did you have something, Mick?" he asked.

Mick hesitated, then nodded. "I think Jack's right. Handgun control is volatile here, at least with a vocal minority. With the new open-primary law, some might cross party lines just to vote against you. Assault weapons are the safest line of demarcation."

"Not for my brother," Kerry answered gently. "And not for the woman in the picture you just saw. They were killed with handguns. Looking at them afterward, it was hard to appreciate the distinction."

In the silence that followed, Frank Wells spoke quietly. "*They're* how we make it, Kerry. Not by focusing on the weapon itself." He stood again, walking to the television. "I want to show you another spot. Before you react, please think about what you've seen."

There was a certain grim determination, Kerry thought, in the media consultant's manner. Kerry nodded.

Frank started the VCR.

On the screen, James Kilcannon appeared.

"*Kilcannon . . . ,*" the crowd was chanting. Releasing Stacey Tarrant's hand, Jamie stepped forward. As he had that night, as he did in Kerry's nightmare, a gunman appeared at the corner of the screen. Unknowing, James Kilcannon smiled, savoring the last seconds of his life.

The picture froze.

The close-up was of Jamie's smile. Then his face dissolved, becoming Kerry's.

"*It changed our history,*" the narrator intoned, "*and it changed his life.*

"*Kerry Kilcannon—he'll protect us if it's the last thing he does.*"

The spot ended.

Nat Schlesinger, Kerry saw, was slowly shaking his head. Kerry's mouth felt dry. "Not the last, I hope. I'm having children, remember?"

Frank spoke with equal softness. "I understand your feelings on this. But we asked our focus groups two questions about your brother: 'What do you remember him for?' and 'How do you feel about him?'

"The answers were: 'I cared about him' and 'He died too young.' When we showed this spot, several cried, most of them women.

"Dick Mason has Jeannie and the kids. For the voters, Kerry, James Kilcannon was *your* family, and you lost him to a maniac with a gun." He paused, looking around the room, then back at Kerry. "It's too powerful a message to ignore. Show this spot, and a lot of people won't care *how* you feel about abortion, or much of anything else Dick Mason may say. And they'll be with you on handguns without your ever saying a word about them."

There was a silence, people turning to Kerry; their gazes seemed so uneasy that, to him, it was as if sunlight had hurt their eyes. "I think I can speak for Nat here," Clayton interposed, "if not for Kerry. It's too exploitive. The newspapers will hammer us."

"No one will care about *them*, either," Frank retorted. "Because it's a simple statement of fact, and it's completely overwhelming. And for *Mason* to complain would be like spitting on James Kilcannon's grave."

Once more, the other faces at the table turned to Kerry. "You remind me of something," Kerry said evenly. "Twelve years ago, before I declared for the Senate, Liam Dunn advised me to visit my brother's grave site. I knew he meant to alert the press, that there'd be pictures.

"Last year, just before I declared for President, your predecessor suggested the same thing." Pausing, Kerry finished, "They didn't know that I *never* visit Jamie's grave. What I do, I do in my own way, for my own reasons. No one else's."

Kerry stood to leave.

"Is that your answer?" Frank asked stubbornly. "Go with what we have?"

Kerry turned to him. Frank had his own integrity, Kerry knew; this could not be easy for him. It was that, and Kerry's memory of using his brother to wound Ralph Shue, which kept his temper in check. "After this is over," Kerry answered, "I mean to go to Jamie's grave. For my own sake, when no one else is there. But I could never run that film."

With that, Kerry thanked them all, and was gone.

After the meeting, Clayton asked Frank Wells to stay behind.

"Don't push him," Clayton said. "Not on this. Stacey Tarrant's introducing Kerry in Sacramento this afternoon, and it was hard enough to get him to do *that*. Besides, he's right.

"Everywhere he goes today, the media will do the brother thing. He won't have to say a word." Clayton leaned forward. "Kerry has his principles, but he's not a fool. His instincts are worth a month of polls."

"That's why I'm so amazed," Frank rejoined, "about this whole mess he's made on abortion. As of this morning, it seems like a death wish."

Clayton shrugged. "The definition of a *faux pas*, Liam Dunn once told me, is telling the truth at the wrong time."

"The *worst* time." Frank's gaze was level. "What you said about pulling the ads—you're covering for him, aren't you? In case he decides it's best to lose."

Clayton studied him. If Kerry Kilcannon was not a fool, he reflected, neither was Frank Wells.

After a time, Frank's mouth formed a crooked smile. "You think I'm going to roll over on him, don't you? Once the whole thing goes south."

It was the moment of truth, Clayton knew. "You're in this to make a living, Frank. You don't want to suffer for some candidate's mistakes. So you leak."

Frank's eyes grew hard. "Let me disenchant you," he said with asperity. "I could make a better living selling Tide. I'm in politics because I'm a romantic. You're *not* one. But Kerry is. To be a good candidate, a good leader, you have to be. Because then you not only want to make a difference, you imagine that you can."

Standing, Frank went to the coffee urn, poured himself a cup, then turned back to Clayton. "For me, Dick Mason would have been the smart choice—he rarely makes a mistake, and he'd kill his mother to win. And if I told Mason to run a spot on his own agony *after* he killed Mom, and had the poll numbers to back me up, he'd do it.

"But I'm a *romantic*, Clayton. Kerry's passionate and honest—to him, polls exist to figure out how to get people to go with you, not to figure out who you are." Frank's voice lowered. "I only hope that we don't lose him. Because he's the kind of candidate someone like me waits twenty years for."

Quiet, Clayton watched him.

"All right," Frank conceded. "He frustrates me, too. But you know who wears out the people in my business? Candidates like Mason. Because they're empty, and they want you to fill them up."

Frank sat across from Clayton again, looking at him intently. "You're Kerry's best friend, granted. But not his only one. Dump on Kerry Kilcannon, and I'm dumping on myself." Frank paused, his voice muffled with sudden, surprising emotion. "Can you understand that?"

For the first time that morning, Clayton felt himself relax. "Yeah," he answered. "I can understand that."

THREE

Waiting for takeoff, Lara sat in the press section, weary after a sleepless night, edgy from two cups of coffee in a stomach too nauseated for food.

Around her, the plane buzzed with the crazy energy of fifty uprooted people, the nomadic press. A couple of rows back, Lee McAlpine was asking Sara Sax if she'd scored a Secret Service agent the night before and, if so, to describe the experience "for those of us who've forgotten whether tab A still goes into slot B." Moments before, Nate Cutler had taken a seat across the aisle without noticing where Lara was; she had turned to him, expressionless except for the coolness in her eyes. *How could you?* Lara had thought. For that moment, feeling his betrayal, she was not a reporter. Nate had possessed the grace to look away.

The danger, Lara realized, was that others would sense their chill. It was beyond her to feign friendship. Somehow she must blot out Nate's existence, the humiliation of what he knew; must be a professional, hour by hour, until she could get off this plane and return to whatever life was left after *Newsworld* finished scavenging.

Sitting back, Lara closed her eyes.

She was alone in her apartment, two years before. The room was dark; Kerry pleaded with her on the answering machine. "Lara," he said, "can't you see what this will do to us . . ."

Think about something else.

You were a good reporter after that—more driven but, you hoped, more compassionate. It wasn't like *this*: a horde of bright and gifted people, spending huge amounts of money grubbing nuance out of routine stories. You could make a difference.

Kenya. Potentially Africa's richest country, wallowing in tribalism, its arbitrary borders drawn by white exploiters in the age of colonialism, now run by black exploiters who let the roads break down and communications languish, depriving their people of the means to rise against them. A friend of Lara's, a Kenyan lawyer and a devotee of Thomas More, had asked to go on-camera to protest the treatment of political prisoners—the use of cattle prods, genital and dental torture. Lara had agreed, and her friend had gone to prison. No one protested; the administration in Washington was indifferent. Finally, when Kenya's president had visited Washington in search of aid, Lara had persuaded NBC to run a major story on Kenya's human rights abuses, focused on her friend's imprisonment. Both the Kenyan president and the administration were embarrassed; the Kenyans had released her friend, and the use of torture—at least temporarily—lessened.

She would not have had to explain this to Kerry. No one had to ask him to imagine pain; it was one of the many reasons why he, not Mason, should be President. And now Lara might bring Kerry down.

The press would be so moral, Lara thought, when it came to Kerry himself. But the campaign swirling all around her was a dance of ethical light and shadow: the hired guns who migrated from one candidate to another; the staffers and reporters who traded secrets after sex; the sources whose half-truths, leaked for their own benefit, gave reporters a story which justified their existence for that day. Was her lie any worse, Lara wondered, when she would have told the truth—whatever the damage to herself—if it could save him?

She wished she could tell him this. Give him that much, at least. But Kerry was on his own. Two years ago, that had been what she thought was right; now, it was how this had to be.

Lara stared out the window.

Waiting for Kerry's motorcade, the press pool clustered on the tarmac, a clump of reporters, Minicams, boom mikes. Four years before, briefly covering Dick Mason for the *Times*, Lara had learned what reporters called it: the death watch.

The stated purpose of the pool, of course, was to provide coverage for everyone else—file film; stray quotes from the candidate; snippets of news. But, since the murder of John F. Kennedy, the second purpose was to cover an assassination. It was to the pool that history owed the photographs of Bobby Kennedy dying, the maiming of George Wallace, the wounding of Ronald Reagan. Of James Kilcannon, lips open to speak, moments from death.

Everyone knew what day this was.

The pool would be more alert, their nerves on edge. Four years ago, covering Mason, Lara had imagined each step in case the candidate went down: calling in extra reporters on her cell phone; sending others to whatever trauma center received the wounded man; getting close to see how bad the wounds were, who the assassin was, what happened around the body; dictating the story to her paper. It was always a question in Lara's mind: once the gunshots sounded, would she recoil, or would she observe and report, as was her job? Even before she loved Kerry, she prayed that nothing would happen and, if it did, that she would not be in the pool.

This was up to fate. Day by day, the pool rotated alphabetically by news organization: the networks, magazines, newspapers, and radio each had their representatives. Sometime before Tuesday, Lara and her cameraman would be among the pool.

The motorcade arrived.

Lara watched the pool scramble toward Kerry's black Lincoln. He got out, a distant figure with wavy ginger hair, appearing slight next to his protectors from the Secret Service. In a crowd, Lara knew, the press pool was part of the Service's calculations—they recognized the pool reporters and could concentrate on strangers. There were even rumors that the Service considered the pool as potential human shields. "It should be *their* ass," she had heard one reporter grouse, "not mine."

Now they milled around Kerry, a single wriggling organism. Yesterday afternoon he had stopped to chat with reporters, shake hands with the local police. Now Kerry rushed past, flanked by the Service and his aide, Kevin Loughery, with Kit Pace hovering to hear any stray remark so that she could break in, deflect it, spin it. In less than a minute, Kerry was inside the plane.

So this was what they would do now. It would not take long for the press to notice that they were no longer seeing anyone but Kit, for Nate to guess that Lara had gone to Kerry or someone close to him. If she were Kit, she might put out some diversionary rumors about threats, fears of violence centered on the anniversary of his brother's death. That might help for a day or so.

The plane began cruising down the tarmac. Moments later, they were in the air; only then did Lara realize that she had spoken to no one except, in her imaginings, Kerry.

Boarding the bus on Van Ness Avenue, Sean sat alone.

His stomach churned. Surreptitiously, he took an antacid pill from inside the pocket of his jacket, slid it into his mouth, and began chewing it to chalk.

It was ten forty-five. In less than two hours, he had placed thirty-eight phone calls, made twenty-three contacts, identified eleven voters for Kerry Kilcannon. Kate Feeney had worked alongside him. Even as he dialed, Sean was aware of her face, pale and delicate in profile; her fresh skin; the sheen of her hair, pulled back in the same blond ponytail. But girls had never liked him, never understood the way he wanted to protect them, to make them better. When Kate smiled at him between calls, he hovered between confusion and distrust.

Eyes veiled, Sean glanced around the bus.

The faces seemed alien; the polyglot mix of whites, Asians, Latins, and blacks intensified his sense of being adrift in a strange city, his fear of being known. It was like entering the boys' home where the social worker had taken him. Alone at fourteen, he would lie awake in the bunkroom, afraid that they would learn about his father and his mother, about Sean himself. For Sean already knew that the people you wanted love from abused you, or abandoned you, or died.

Even Father Brian, whose faith he had come to share, would betray him if he knew what was in Sean's heart. For a moment, as he remembered, tears came to Sean's eyes.

The boys' home had been clean and orderly, the safest place Sean had known. Father Brian had understood that his fights were to protect himself, or someone younger. It was the priest who taught him that God loved the weak, the young, the innocent. The unborn child.

It was like a flash of lightning in the brain. When Sean was sixteen, the meaning of his life was suddenly so clear that he was shaken, then uplifted. God had blessed him with the gift of anger, not for random fighting, but to be His soldier.

Now, through the window of the bus, Sean read the street sign: "McAllister."

The block was dingy—sex shops, decaying stores, flophouse hotels. Sean saw a bearded man with a shopping cart, then a woman who sat on the steps of a hotel, vacant-eyed from drugs, mouthing words to no one. You can see the soul of a society, Father Brian once said, by the people it leaves in the street. But Sean felt only revulsion; there were such places in Boston, streets where men could buy a woman's body, anything at all. This woman's face was like his mother's . . .

When Father Brian had suggested in his gentle way, shortly

before graduation, that God might not mean for him to be a priest, Sean had applied to join the Boston police. Then the police psychologist had shown him pictures, asked about his parents, even about his dreams. A few weeks later, they denied his application. Out of pity, Father Brian had given him a job.

Sean Burke, the soldier of God, was to help maintain the boys' home and the church whose name it bore, Saint Anne's.

Alone in the sanctuary, Sean had prayed for answers.

It was a chill Boston morning, Sean recalled—much like the morning, two days ago, when he had executed the abortionist. But God had given him no sign. Torn between hope and bitterness, Sean had stepped from the church, feeling the mile-square Irish enclave of Charlestown envelop him. The neighborhood seemed changeless: the shabby triple-deckers with a family on each floor; the small and darkened bars, many without signs; the stubborn code of silence that prevented one townie from betraying another to the cops. A man could be born in Charlestown, go to the parish school, find work at the naval yard, marry a girl from Saint Anne's, eat and drink, procreate and die, all within a few blocks of his birthplace. Sean stood on the steps of his church, imagining his own death—the caretaker, disappearing like a raindrop in the ocean.

At the bottom of the steps, a man waited for him.

He was about thirty, with tightly curled brown hair, a gaunt face, and black eyes so intense that Sean thought of an archangel. The man came toward him, holding out a piece of paper.

Sean froze.

The man placed the paper in Sean's hand. "Please," he said. "Read this."

Though his voice was soft, it held an urgency, as if much depended on Sean's answer. Sean took the leaflet. Seeing its first words, he felt a current pass from the stranger to him.

If life is sacred, the leaflet asked, *how can we tolerate murder?*

Slowly, Sean looked up into the stranger's eyes. "I'm Paul Terris," the man said. "From Operation Life . . ."

The bus sighed to a stop.

Startled from thought, Sean saw first the street signs, Second and Harrison, and then the storefront he was looking for. The Gun Emporium.

Eyes downcast, hoping to preserve his anonymity, Sean got off the bus.

On the flight to Fresno, Nate Cutler checked his watch. Perhaps he only imagined Lara watching him from across the aisle.

For the last three hours, he had been trying to accost Kit Pace. But on the plane and on the ground, Kit seemed surrounded by, or busily in search of, representatives of the California media. Now she stood at the front of the press section, two rows from him—just enough distance that to call out to her would make Nate conspicuous. "This is always a bad day for Kerry," he heard her murmur to the earnest young woman from the *Sacramento Bee*. "Every year. I'm not sure you'll be seeing him back here. But he'll make time for you up front on the flight to Sacramento . . ."

The Sacramento *fucking* Bee, Nate thought.

At seven this morning, his editor had authorized him to ask Kilcannon the question.

As Nate rose to speak to her, Kit vanished through the curtain.

Alone in his hotel suite, Clayton Slade stood abruptly. "Can you confirm that?" he said into the telephone.

"We don't know," the head of opposition research answered. "We're trying to get the files. But they're over twenty years old, and it looks like Mason's had them sealed."

Clayton paused; waiting on his second line was an urgent call from Tony Lord, the lawyer negotiating the debate rules with Mason's people. "Other than breaking the law," Clayton directed, "do everything you can."

The cavernous store was empty but for a stocky man with wiry hair, polishing a rifle on the counter.

The sound of his own footsteps on the wooden floor made Sean stop. Self-conscious, he gazed at the racks of shotguns on the wall, the glass cases filled with handguns, shining a metallic black or silver beneath the fluorescent lights.

The dealer put down his shotgun. "Can I help you?" he asked.

Sean walked toward him, watching his face. The dealer's eyes, a liquid brown, combined with his smile to give him the pleasant aspect of a man who gave his spare change to the homeless.

"I was thinking about a handgun," Sean murmured. "To protect myself."

The man nodded briskly—no explanations were needed here. "What kind?"

"Nine millimeter, maybe."

Stooping, the man unlocked a gun case, then placed a slender black gun on the counter.

Sean flinched; the gun was so like the one he had used in Boston that he could feel its lightness in his pocket, see the mist of his breath in the chill morning air. For a moment, Sean was certain that the dealer must know who he was.

Mute, he took the weapon in his hand.

"You like this one?" the dealer asked. "Just sign the forms, and in fifteen days it's yours."

Startled, Sean blinked.

The dealer appraised him closely, eyes narrowing. "You know about the waiting period, right?"

Slowly, Sean shook his head.

"Fifteen days." The man's tone was flat, disgusted. "State law—been that way since after that guy shot Kilcannon. *This* one's brother."

Sean stared at him, speechless.

"Yeah," the man said. "I know. Maybe someone can do us another favor."

Sean felt his skin tingle. "Fifteen days," he murmured.

"Uh-huh. Some animal rapes your wife on the fourteenth day, you get two free tickets to the ACLU dinner dance. *If* she lives."

Eyes shut, Sean let his fingers graze the trigger. "What if you need it?"

"Ask the politicians." The man paused, and then his voice grew quiet. "You buy one on the street, brother, or maybe in a pawnshop if they're willing to chance it. Whatever piece of crap you can find, from whatever piece of crap is selling it. But *we* can't break the law."

Sean put down the gun. "In fifteen days," he murmured, "I'll be gone."

The man's mouth worked, showing his frustration. "Maybe you're coming back."

Sean jammed both hands in the pockets of his coat and walked away.

Outside, he stopped, startled by the brightness of the noonday sun. The dealer would remember him, a strange man wanting the same gun that had killed the abortionist. For two blocks, Sean half walked, half ran, until he saw the bus coming and swerved across the street to catch it.

The doors hissed open. Eyes averted, Sean dropped six quarters in the till and took a seat behind the driver.

Tomorrow Kerry Kilcannon would be in San Francisco. Sean was unarmed, unaware of Kilcannon's schedule, running out of time. A soldier of God without a weapon.

Trying a pawnshop, Sean knew, might increase the risk still more.

Through the window, the neighborhood turned rancid again. "Talk to a naked woman," a sign said. "Seventy-five cents a minute."

You buy one on the street, brother . . . Whatever piece of crap you can find, from whatever piece of crap is selling it.

Sean pulled the cord. A bell chimed; at the next corner, the bus came to a stop, jerking abruptly, and Sean stumbled onto the street.

FOUR

"Prepare to step through the looking glass." Tony Lord's voice was crisp and a little sardonic. "Was it only a couple of months ago, Clayton, when you proposed that the senator and Mason debate under the Lincoln-Douglas rules? A free-for-all, where the candidates can question each other directly?"

"In New Hampshire. Dick's people ran from *that* one like Dracula from garlic." Pacing, Clayton felt constricted by the telephone cord. "Kerry's quicker on his feet, and Mason's more programmed. The last thing Dick wants is spontaneity."

"Not anymore. The new Dick Mason wants four prechosen topics for ten minutes apiece, and the last twenty minutes left open to anything. Mason and Kerry can ask each other questions on every topic, and the questioner gets to follow up. Just like Honest Abe."

In his own silence, Clayton could almost hear Tony's thoughts. Softly, he said, "That makes no sense at all."

"Then let's figure out what they think is different."

"Not the candidates," Clayton answered. "Kerry's instincts are better, and he knows more. If Kerry challenged Mason on comparative state welfare reforms, the only question is which dies first—Dick's memory or his audience." Clayton's voice grew testy. "It's the difference between real and unreal, and Mason's handlers know it."

"Any reason they'd be feeling desperate?"

"Not *that* desperate. Our polls show Mason winning by a point or two. I'm sure his show the same."

"Well, *something's* changed. Before I go back in that

meeting and tell them how much we love this, I'd be curious to know what it is."

Though pleasant enough, Lord's tone was pointed. Until four years ago, Stacey Tarrant's husband had been a first-rate criminal lawyer, and though he had abruptly walked away from his practice in favor of public interest work, his perceptions remained keen. That was why Clayton had asked for his help.

"You tell me, Tony. You're the one in the room with them."

Tony paused, gathering his thoughts. "They seem more aggressive," he said. "In the last two days, Mason's seen Kerry stumble on abortion, and he's been quick to capitalize. Maybe he thinks Kerry's been lucky, that he can take him after all—"

Interrupting, Clayton laughed briefly. "A lot of people have thought that. Dick's the only one still standing."

"And maybe," Tony continued in the same calm voice, "Mason thinks he's got something on Kerry Kilcannon, and has chosen this moment to share."

Clayton sat down. "What could *that* be, I wonder."

On the other end, Tony was silent. "I can propose a town meeting," he said evenly, "where citizens ask the questions. A civic-minded discussion of what the people want to know, in front of a crowd looking for civil answers. It makes personal attacks much harder."

Tony Lord, Clayton realized, did not believe him. "No," he answered. "If we refuse what we asked for in New Hampshire, Mason feeds it to the press. More important, it's not in Kerry's nature to hide. He'll take his chances, always."

"So I make the deal."

"Yes."

Slowly, Clayton hung up the telephone.

Sean stood alone on the sidewalk, shifting his weight from foot to foot, a clean-shaven stranger amidst the sex shops, a slum hotel, a dingy Vietnamese restaurant, the liquor store with neon signs for cheap wine and whiskey. The street smelled of garbage and urine.

The last fifteen minutes had seemed like a preview of hell, a parade of human detritus that filled Sean with loathing—the homeless straggler with rags for shoes and trembling hands; the woman on the stoop jabbering vacantly to no one; the small, furtive man who scurried through a red door to "talk to a naked woman"; the scraggly-haired prostitute with sores on her face, pale and wasted, who sickened Sean by offering him oral sex. Now and then he saw younger men who seemed to belong here: the skinny black kid who jaywalked with exaggerated languor, owning the narrow street; the mahogany-faced Latino who darted past with an edgy urban energy, perhaps from drugs. Hands shoved in the pockets of his sweatshirt, another young black leaned against the hotel across the street; ignoring the jabbering woman, he inspected Sean with contemptuous leisure. Sean ached for the gun he could not buy.

In a seeming act of will, the black man stood erect and, counterfeiting aimlessness, ambled in Sean's direction.

He stopped on the sidewalk three feet away, gazing around him. He was smaller than Sean, slighter, with ears that stuck out beneath his pea cap. But when he turned to Sean at last, his dark eyes were hard as bullets.

"Lookin' for somethin'?"

His tone was impatient, as if Sean was occupying someone else's space. Through his nervousness, Sean felt himself bristle. He cocked his head, looking down at the black man.

"Like what?" he asked.

The man gave a fractured shrug. "Maybe a rock?"

Sean moved closer. "Not drugs."

The man's eyes narrowed; when he spoke, his lips seemed barely to move. "I don't do that shit. Maybe I can find someone."

It took Sean a moment to understand, and then he flushed with shame and anger. "I want a gun."

The man looked around him, quick, darting glances. "A piece."

Sean nodded.

The man's eyes bored into Sean's. "You a cop?"

"No."

"Well, I don't know about no piece, man." Pausing, the black man assumed a certain sarcasm. "Selling you a piece is against the *law*."

Sean stared at him, unsmiling. "A hundred dollars."

The man gazed at the sidewalk, lips forming a silent, reflective whistle. "Someone find you a piece," he asked, "what kind you want?"

"Handgun. Nine millimeter."

One side of the man's mouth twisted. "You think I own an arsenal? Fucking West Point or something?" He looked up at Sean again. "Want a piece, you take what you can find."

"Tomorrow morning." Sean's voice was tight now. "I want it before nine."

The man shrugged. "That's not my office hours."

Sean clutched the front of his sweatshirt. "Nine o'clock."

Deliberately, the man removed Sean's fingers and stared into his face again. "You want a piece that bad, make it four."

Sean felt a helpless anger. "Four," he said finally. "Right here."

"That's what I'm saying."

Without another word, the man turned and sauntered across the street as if Sean did not exist.

When Clayton's telephone rang again, it was the special agent in charge, Peter Lake.

"Where are you?" Clayton asked.

"Fresno. About to go to Elk Grove, then Sacramento. That's what I'm calling about. Three local stations there just got the same death threat."

Clayton sighed. "No reason today should be any different. What did *this* threat say?"

"What the receptionists wrote down was: 'Don't you know what day it is? We're going to kill him on the six o'clock news.' That probably means Sacramento."

"What do you want me to do?"

"Talk to the senator." Peter's voice was dispassionate, professional. "Probably it's some fraternity kid. But this is the day his brother got shot, and the place where he's chosen to talk about gun control. The gun nuts have been all over the Internet, asking people to show up there for the rally, egging each other on: 'Term limits isn't good enough'—that kind of thing. It could be pretty tense."

Clayton stared out the window. Since the death of their young son, his deepest fear was for Carlie or the twins, as powerful as superstition. The long nights at the hospital were engraved in his memory—Carlie's sunken eyes, Kerry's quiet presence, more eloquent than words of grief he knew they could not stand to hear. Once Kerry had entered the primaries, Clayton's second fear had been a stranger with a gun, another tragedy without reason. There was never a day that Clayton did not think of it; never an outdoor rally that Clayton did not suffer through until Kerry was back in the limousine.

"We can't cancel the event," Clayton said at last. "And Kerry wouldn't. You can hear him now, can't you—'If I don't speak, they've already won.'"

"I'd never ask him *not* to speak. Just to factor in safety in deciding *when* to speak, and where." Peter paused a moment. "I know we've had this discussion before. But I'd have put this rally indoors, not in a park."

"Kerry wanted it there. You know why."

"Then maybe it's time he wore a vest. Starting tonight." Peter's voice was soft. "He's no good to anyone dead, Clayton. Including himself."

The comment was as oblique, Clayton realized, as it was acute. "I'll fly on up," he answered.

FIVE

The flight to Sacramento, Nate Cutler reflected, had begun to remind him of *Lord of the Flies*, a descent into the Hobbesian state of nature.

Everyone seemed restless. Other than the pool reporters, no

one had seen Kilcannon up close; he had not visited the press section at all. Even Kit Pace was more brisk than normal, guiding local reporters to the front. Needing amusement, the guy from *Newsweek* had taken a plastic food tray and butt-surfed down the aisle on takeoff, drawing whistles, scattered cheers, and one wadded napkin tossed at his head. Watching him whiz by, Lee McAlpine observed, "That's the tough thing about this gig—it really spoils you for coach class on United."

Next to her, Sara Sax was scrawling on a grapefruit with Magic Marker, vowing to "penetrate the iron curtain." Proudly, she showed off her handiwork. The grapefruit now asked: "Senator K—do you favor partial-birth abortion to protect the psychological health of the mother?"

With a flourish, she signed it "Love, Sara," stood, and rolled the grapefruit beneath the curtain separating the press from Kerry Kilcannon.

Edgy, Nate stood in the aisle, looking about him. Around the table where the food was laid out, four reporters were playing a desultory game of hearts, and in the special section at the rear of the plane, the camera guys were bitching that the new woman reporter from Fox, by ripping down their *Hustler* pinups, had "pissed on the First Amendment." Heading for a sandwich, Nate felt something hit his foot.

Looking down, he saw the grapefruit.

Nate picked it up. Beneath Sara's question were the words "I don't know, Sara—how crazy are you?" In his distinct scrawl, the candidate had signed it "Kerry."

Solemnly, Nate presented it to Sara. "I can't be sure," he told her, "but there seems to be life in the front cabin."

Reading Kilcannon's answer, Sara grinned. "It's a sign," she proclaimed, and began passing the grapefruit among her colleagues. Only Lara Costello, Nate noticed, read it without smiling.

As Nate watched her, Rich Powell from Reuters, who had known Lara in the Congo, knelt beside her in the aisle, kissing her hand with the grave obeisance that befit a new princess of the media. "Millions," he said in tones of awe. "*TV Guide* said you're getting millions. Can this be true?"

Lara smiled. "Every word. Tomorrow I'm incorporating,

and endorsing my own line of panty hose. You get two free samples."

Rich placed his hand over his heart. "Used, I hope."

Lara tilted her head. "How *are* you, Rich?"

"All right. If I had to draw a candidate, I'm glad it's Kilcannon." He paused for a moment. "You know him, right?"

Watching her, Nate felt her awareness of him, standing two rows away. *"Knew,"* she answered. "I haven't seen or spoken to him since he decided to run."

"Big decision, if you're him." Rich sat in the aisle, crosslegged. "See Stacey Tarrant's introducing him in Sacramento? That's kind of amazing, I think. Or maybe just manipulative."

Lara shrugged. "The subject's right, for both of them. And the day. She'll certainly help draw a crowd."

"That she will. But I want you to know something, Lara: I'd rather sleep with you than Stacey Tarrant, any day."

Lara gave Rich a wan smile, patting him on the arm. "I don't think I'll be on the ship of fools quite long enough. But thanks for asking."

Rich shook his head, mournful. "Still monastic."

"Uh-huh. How can I do my job if all I think about is you?"

Rich laughed at this. Turning, Nate sat down again, reflective.

Lara's tacit message was clear enough: she had not seen or spoken to Kilcannon; by leaving the campaign, she was taking her ethical problem with her. That would be part of Clayton Slade's argument to Nate's editors when—once Nate asked the question—the Kilcannon people tried to kill the story. As Nate was certain they would.

Time was running: in five days, the voters would go to the polls. The real story of the California primary, hidden from all his colleagues but Lara, was the dark corner in which Nate and Kerry Kilcannon now competed for control. Resuming his silent watch for Kit, Nate felt an intensity that bordered on obsession.

This was not personal, Nate felt sure—no matter what Lara might suspect. Though he had almost never voted for a Republican, Nate had achieved a certain detachment from his own beliefs, and there was little any politician could do to either offend or please him. Nate's job was to interpret, to separate rhetoric from reality, to cut through the mind-numbing repetition, the robotic determination to avoid error, the protective armor of spin, through which most candidates try to obscure hard truths and manipulate the news. If Kerry Kilcannon was often better than that, it made no difference now. Nate had a legitimate question to ask; for reasons he understood but could not honor, he believed that Kilcannon was trying to avoid him.

The curtain opened.

Instead of Kit Pace, it was Sara's new love object, Dan Biasi, the Secret Service agent. From Dan's look of deep preoccupation, Nate guessed that he was searching for an empty bathroom. As Dan hurried past, Nate rose from his seat and casually followed. But for Lara, no one else looked up.

When Nate got to the rear, the bathroom door was locked.

Nate leaned against the baggage closet, as if waiting his turn. The door opened and Dan Biasi emerged, his dark hair freshly combed.

"Better?" Nate asked.

Dan laughed good-naturedly. "Too much coffee. The senator says I've got the smallest bladder in the Service."

For Dan, Nate realized, the airplane was a zone of relaxation, relief from the terrible alertness the Service must show on the ground. Beneath the young agent's eyes were the etchings of fatigue.

"Now that your head is clear," Nate said amiably, "can you tell Kit Pace I need to see her, ASAP? There's a fact I need to check."

Dan's smiled faded. Scrupulously apolitical, the agents avoided anything that fell outside their mission. "Yeah," he said at length. "I can do that. Unless she's tied up with someone."

"Thanks. Appreciate it." With that, Nate stepped inside the bathroom, waited for a moment, and then returned to his seat.

He resumed watching the curtain.

A few minutes before landing, Kit appeared. She knelt by his seat with a professional smile that conveyed neither warmth nor its absence. "I hear you're fact-deficient, Nate."

"Uh-huh. Can you give me a couple of minutes in Elk Grove, after the speech?"

Across the aisle, Nate saw, Lara seemed to study her nails. Kit's smile narrowed fractionally. "I'll try. But no promises. If I leave Kerry by himself too often, God knows what he'd say."

Nate did not smile. "It won't take long," he answered.

The rally at Elk Grove was in a stretch of the American heartland, a patch of dirt near some stables that could have been a fairground. The platform was surrounded by tractors and bales of hay, and in the distance, Lara saw silos and wavy fields of grain she supposed were wheat. Her lack of agrarian knowledge reminded her of a piece of family lore she had once shared with Kerry: the day that the nine-year-old Lara, a child of the city, had driven with her parents past a field of grapes. "Look," she had told them, "wine plants." For minutes, her father could not stop laughing. Hearing the story, Kerry had eyed her with feigned puzzlement. "Why?" he had asked her. "What else do they call them?"

Remembering, Lara smiled briefly to herself, thinking of Kerry in this setting.

She stood on the press bleachers, surrounded by her colleagues with their tape recorders, laptops, Minicams. The PA system blared Bruce Springsteen singing "Born in the U.S.A."; it was a point of pride that Springsteen, another New Jersey boy, supported Kerry. The candidate himself was climbing the speakers' platform. Filling the fifty square yards between the platform and the press was the kind of eclectic crowd that Kerry seemed to draw: farmers, small-business owners, Asians, high school kids, some Mexican farmworkers. It was four o'clock, and a waning sun fell gently on the platform—a metaphor, Lara thought suddenly, for the last days of a campaign, perhaps of a career.

A few moments before, Lara had checked her voice mail in Washington. There had been one message—from her first roommate, a friend from Stanford now working on the Hill. A reporter from *Newsworld* had called, Maria explained, asking about Lara and Kerry Kilcannon. But Maria had told them nothing, had nothing to tell. What *was* this? her message asked.

Nothing, Lara must tell her. Nothing at all. Suddenly she felt a piercing loneliness: she and Kerry, trapped within their secret, could not even speak.

Two steps behind her, Nate stood with his tape recorder.

He would stay close, Lara knew. For the next five days, her world would be claustrophobic.

To rising cheers, Kerry walked to the podium holding a scrap of paper, no doubt with the names of the local worthies he should acknowledge—the mayor, the county commissioners. But when he set down the paper, it blew away in the wind.

Kerry froze, eyes following the paper as it drifted into the crowd, a pantomime of the nonplussed politician. "Oh, no," he said, "there goes my farm program."

It was a risky joke, Lara knew—self-parody with a core of truth. But there was a chorus of good-natured laughter, from farmers most of all. Flawlessly, Kerry acknowledged everyone on the platform.

There was a soft buzz in the pocket of her sport jacket. Watching Kerry, she took out her cell phone and answered, "Yes?"

"Lara?" The mere sound of her bureau chief's voice startled her; for a sickening moment, Lara thought she had been exposed. "There's been a death threat," Hal continued, "against Kilcannon. Someone phoned our affiliate in Sacramento."

Lara felt numb. "What did they say?"

"That they'd kill him on the six o'clock news. We think that means at the rally in Sacramento."

Lara took a deep breath. "I'll ask the Service about it. Kit too."

"Good. By the way, I liked your report last night."

Still speaking softly, Lara thanked him, then slid the telephone back into her pocket.

Quickly, she surveyed the area for vantage points—trees, the roofline of the stables. She saw the billed caps of three Secret Service sharpshooters on the roof of the barn, then the top of one's head, his eyes trained on the platform. How, she wondered, must it feel to be Kerry?

She turned to watch him. The crowd was silent now, solemn.

"The death penalty," he said, "is one of the most painful questions facing a civilized society.

"Once, several years before I was a senator, I toured a prison. I saw the faces of men waiting to be executed, and I thought of the sadness, the loss, the waste of those lives. And if it were humanly possible, I would have an America where no life is so blighted, so warped, that its defining act is the taking of another life."

Kerry, Lara realized, was not speaking from notes. His voice, though quiet, carried easily.

"For a time, *that* was all I could think of. But I since have had occasion to think of all the faces I would *never* see: those of the men, women, and children these men had killed. For when we give up the notion of private revenge, we do so with the expectation that our laws will pay proper tribute to the value of an innocent life: that, if warranted, the death of the murderer may follow the murder of the innocent."

How they had argued, Lara recalled—for hours, alone in Kerry's apartment because they could not be seen together. "Like college," Kerry had said with gentle humor. "Beer, pizza, and the death penalty."

She knew why Kerry felt the way he did. Even without the pressure of politics, perhaps he could not have felt otherwise. But still she had challenged him. "Murder is murder," she had argued. "There's no such thing as a public service killing, or where does it end?"

"Murder is murder?" Kerry had rejoined. "Perhaps the Senate's made me a connoisseur of irony. My pro-life colleagues love them till they're born but don't mind a righteous execution afterward. Whereas death row is where many of my pro-choice friends at last develop scruples, even if they're saving Charles Manson . . ."

As Lara watched, the crowd was still, attentive.

"But before we take a life," Kerry went on, "we must be certain that the race or status of the murderer can no more count than that of the victim.

"The least the death penalty *demands* of us, if we choose it, is fair jury selection, a just trial and a just review, and a scrupulous regard for the rights of the accused. Because if we follow the siren song of law and order—a shortcut here, a right abandoned there—we will surely be complicit in the murder of the innocent. And that is too great a price for *any* of us to pay . . ."

It was a moment before Lara felt Nate next to her.

"Did you two ever talk about this?" Nate asked. "I remember how *you* felt."

Lara turned to him. *You bastard,* she thought. "No," she answered coolly. "Why would we?"

She turned away, looking for her cameraman.

The question had hurt, Nate thought. He could see in her eyes that it struck too close to home.

She was lying, had to be. But his near certainty, however important, gave him little pleasure.

He went to find Kit.

She did not have the excuse of sticking with Kerry Kilcannon, he quickly saw; the Service had hurried him to his limousine. Kit stood near the speakers' platform amidst the pool, its members slowly dispersing to their bus. Though Nate was only a few feet back, Kit seemed not to see him.

Hands shoved in his pockets, he waited her out.

When only two reporters remained, Kit acknowledged him with her eyes. After the others had left, she walked slowly to Nate, squinting against dust kicked up by the wind.

"What was that movie?" Kit asked. "*The Grapes of Wrath?* Or was it a book?"

Nate smiled; like most of the reporters, he admired Kit for her tart humor, and for her professionalism. She might duck, but she seldom lied.

"So," Kit said, "what can I tell you?"

Nate looked around them. "I need to see the senator," he answered.

Kit frowned. "Not until after Tuesday, Nate. It's not that we don't love you, but most of your readers aren't California voters, and we love *them* best of all."

Nate shook his head. "What I have won't wait that long."

Kit raised her eyebrows. "Donations from extraterrestrials? Right now, 'won't wait' doesn't get it."

"The question I have is sensitive." Nate kept his tone low, patient. "It's something he should answer directly."

Kit folded her arms, gazing at the dust around her feet. Carefully, she asked, "Are we talking about some sort of illegal activity?"

She knows, Nate thought; she's trying to be a filter for Kilcannon. "It doesn't involve a crime. It's about the senator's personal life." His voice became harder. "So when do I get to see him?"

Kit looked up again, her eyes less friendly. "As soon as you tell me what it is. And why it's credible enough to take Kerry's time before Tuesday."

"Quit being the Stepford Press Secretary, Kit." Nate made his voice soft again. "You don't want me asking him along the rope line. If this is something Kilcannon can deny, he'll want to do that in private. I'm trying to give him that chance."

"Or?"

"Or we go with the story next Tuesday. Based on what we have."

Kit studied him. If Nate was right, and Lara had gone to Kilcannon, he could imagine Kit's calculations: *Did* Newsworld *have enough to print?*

"I'll think about it," Kit said finally. "*You* can think about telling me more."

"Seventy-two hours," Nate repeated.

Kit smiled slightly—whether in belief or disbelief, Nate could not tell. Then she walked away.

Nate went to the press tent to type up his notes. When he next saw her, Kit was standing alone near the barn, talking into her cell phone.

SIX

"God," Stacey Tarrant murmured in bemusement. "Jamie would be amazed at all this, don't you think?"

Kerry smiled. "Maybe at me. 'What are you doing?' I can imagine him saying. 'Do you have to learn *everything* by experience?'"

They were in the back of Kerry's limousine, cruising toward the skyline of Sacramento; at Kerry's insistence, the motorcade had met her plane at a private airstrip, so that the two of them would have time to talk. Since Jamie's death, they had seen each other rarely, but a certain affinity had developed, a shared understanding. Stacey was a perceptive woman who did not mind quiet; to a degree that surprised him, Kerry could be direct with her, at ease. It reminded him of Lara.

"Oh," Stacey answered, returning his smile, "he always thought you had *ability*. He just wondered what it would take for you to figure it out."

"I'm glad he didn't know." Kerry turned to the window, watching the towers of the city, light and shadow in the failing sun. "'Such a joke,'" he added softly. "'But what does it mean?'"

For a moment, Stacey was quiet. "Do you ever get frightened?" she asked.

Kerry nodded. "Who's out there? you ask yourself. Someone. But you don't know who, or where."

Stacey tilted her head. "Then why did you decide to run?"

"Other than what I always say—to make America a better place?"

"Yes."

Kerry appraised her; Stacey's candid blue eyes were probing, but not unkind. She had suffered a great deal once, he thought, for the sake of his brother's ambitions. A sense of his own ambitions was all that he could offer her.

"It's complicated," he said at last. "Some of it has to do with my personal life—things I've had, things I've lost, things I may never have. If I'd had a woman I loved, or children, would I have done this, knowing what happened to Jamie? I'm not sure." He paused, trying to explain as much as he was free to explain. "A couple of years ago, I came to a decision point. There was no one to ask but me. Because I was his brother, some people had always wanted me to run, some part of me had always felt I should. But for *what*, I had to decide—wasn't it enough that, as a senator, I could help bring about things I believe in? Why should I be President?

"Then I looked at the others. The Republicans have all the answers, but too often we simply disagree. Mason *has* no answers. What does he believe? I wonder. What does he even *feel*? I've seen him mist up at the funerals of people he despised, show righteous indignation because some pollster told him to, waffle on gun control so he could beat me in New Hampshire. I can't tell which are more promiscuous—Dick's emotions or his beliefs." Slowly, Kerry shook his head. "I question if there's anything that really reaches him, any principle for which he'd risk losing. Any moment in which Dick Mason truly has an authentic self, and knows who that is.

"People are cynical, Stacey. We've helped make them that way. We try to flatter *them*, we smear our opponents, and we lie about ourselves. Dick Mason as President would be one more nail in the coffin." Kerry caught himself and smiled faintly. "I can think of others who might be better than both of us. But they can't win. So here I am, doing the best I can."

Unsmiling, Stacey gazed down, her expression pensive. "But you wonder if you're good enough."

"Yes. All the time."

Turning, she gave him a long, thoughtful look. "That's something Jamie could never admit."

"Why should he have?"

"Your brother?" Her voice was quiet again. "So cool and

self-possessed? Because he was afraid of all sorts of things, including being known. That was what his wit was for—his own protection. I think Jamie was afraid he was this terrible fraud, a self-invented Kennedy, the son of people he could never talk about. But you were probably too young to see that."

The image of a tormented Jamie startled Kerry; it was as if she had taken his memories and, like a kaleidoscope, changed their form. "Maybe there were clues," he said at length. "But I could never read them." He paused a moment, then asked, "Why did you love him, then?"

Stacey's smile seemed wistful. "Because he *wasn't* a fraud. But I'd have given a lot to hear him say what you just did. Though I might have waited all my life." Her smile faded, and she appraised him. "Self-knowledge is a gift, Kerry, if you've got the courage for it. It's another reason you should be President. Or even, God help you, a parent."

In the slipstream of the motorcade, the hushed efficient progress toward their public moment together, Kerry considered her anew. She seemed more settled, at peace; her career was still successful, her marriage seemed a happy one, and she and Tony Lord had recently adopted a daughter, born in China, who must now be close to three. "How *has* that been?" he asked. "Mothering."

"Indescribable." Stacey smiled again. "I've learned a whole new definition of love—reading aloud when you're tired, from the same damn book about the cat and the dog, without skipping a single word. Even though your daughter might never know."

"Integrity," Kerry said. "Trust. A willingness to sacrifice. Would you consider becoming Vice President?"

Still smiling, Stacey shook her head. "No, thanks. I'm happy where I am."

For a moment, too private and too sad to speak of, Kerry thought again of Lara. And then he felt the motorcade slow and saw that they had slid into the city, toward the park.

The park was in Old Town Sacramento, near the statehouse, on a tree-lined street of wood-frame homes that, though not imposing, bespoke comfort and serenity. Clayton was quite certain that the shooting there one year ago, which had resulted in the death of a child, had shaken the neighborhood quite badly.

The park itself was three blocks square, with a generous lawn, picnic tables, and swings and a slide where the murdered boy had fallen. The Secret Service had roped off the borders and was funneling the people with tickets issued by the campaign—many of whom were advocates for gun control— through magnetometers. Since early morning, Kerry's detail had swept the park for bombs, closed the windows of adjoining houses, secured those homes with a line of fire to the speakers' platform. Once more, the Service's perimeter system was in place: the outer perimeter, with sharpshooters on the rooftops, and agents scanning windows and vantage points; the middle perimeter, in which they screened the crowd and everyone else in handgun range; the inner perimeter, its agents near the rope line and around Kerry himself—the place where it was most likely, as Peter Lake put it, to be "game day."

Clayton stood with Peter on the platform, watching the press pool with their microphones and cameras; the swath of lawn jammed with supporters carrying "Kilcannon for President" signs; the bleachers for remaining press; and, to one side, a section for the uninvited, the curious, the hostile. To Clayton, there were far too many men with grim faces and hard eyes, too many signs like the one that read "Terminate Kerry Kilcannon." The air crackled with tension.

"Stacey Tarrant," Peter murmured to Clayton. "The anniversary of his brother's death. A speech on gun control. For nuts, it's like an alignment of the planets." He nodded toward the crowd. "That's the local militia and gun clubs out there, the groups that follow Sarah Brady around, trying to intimidate her. The Internet was full of stuff like 'Every gun owner should give Kilcannon the reception he deserves.' You're working for a 'left-wing totalitarian,' Clayton, in case you didn't know it."

Clayton turned to him. "Did Kerry tell you why he wouldn't wear the vest?"

Peter surveyed the crowd, gray eyes watchful in his solid face. "All he said was 'It wouldn't stop a head shot, would it?' It was the nearest he's come to mentioning his brother." Turning to the adjacent houses, he murmured, "He's right, in a way. A guy with training and a weapon, like one of these crazies out there, could get him from a hundred yards. But not on my watch."

Spotting the eager visage of a young college girl with a Kilcannon sign, Clayton felt the chasm between the crowd's excitement and his own fears. "How does it go wrong?" he asked.

Peter drew a breath. "Other than a sharpshooter? Could be anything. A malfunction in a magnetometer. A member of a privileged group, like press or staff, who one of your people vouches for but isn't what he's supposed to be. We're damned careful about press credentials and background checks for anyone who's hanging around a campaign. But if you folks don't give us enough notice ..." He shrugged. "It could happen. Especially with someone who doesn't care if he lives or dies."

Against his will, Clayton turned to look behind the platform.

The ambulance was there. At their first meeting, Peter had laid out the plan should Kerry be shot. The nearest agents would cover his body, the others maintain their posts: there might be a second shooter, and Malcolm X had died because his security, diverted by a disruption, did not protect him. They would try to secure the assassin—alive, if possible—then get Kerry to the ambulance. At every event, the Service knew how to reach a hospital within ten minutes; within that time, with a wound not mortal, there would be a better chance of saving him. But, as Kerry had intimated, there had been no saving James Kilcannon.

"Stacey Tarrant," Peter asked. "How did you get her here?"

Clayton turned. "She thinks Kerry should be President. But what I said to her was 'Dick Mason has his wife and kids—Kerry has you.' After that, she said she would."

Peter fell quiet.

Clayton gazed out at the demonstrators, their numbers swelling as they waited for Kerry.

Especially with someone who doesn't care if he lives or dies...

Peter had meant an assassin, not Kerry himself. But there were several things Clayton could not tell him: That Kerry had endorsed an antigun initiative now on the ballet, embittering gun owners, against Clayton's advice. That Clayton had implored him not to do *this* event, in *this* place. And Clayton's most haunting suspicion—that beneath Kerry's insistence was a death wish, the need to face danger, the unspoken belief that he would be worthy of his brother, or the courage of Bridget Musso, only if he died.

Whatever the reason, Clayton had known since New Hampshire that Kerry would not back down.

The state chapter of the Gun Alliance of America had invited all candidates to a public forum in Manchester, to explain their stand on gun control. All six Republicans had accepted, and Dick Mason had declined; in a state where the tradition of gun ownership was so strong, Mason's pro-gun-control positions, however tepid, were a liability. "Imagine the arrogance," Kerry said to Clayton. "We're running for *President*, and these one-issue fanatics want us to come crawling. What do they expect me to say—'Guns don't kill people, *slingshots* do'?"

Clayton nodded. "I'll tell them you're busy."

Kerry turned to him. "No," he snapped. "I'm going."

It was a cold January night; as they walked from the van toward the cavernous meeting hall, their feet crunched on the icy snow and their breath was silver mist. The president of the state chapter, Walt Rogers, a white-haired man plainly suspicious of Kerry's presence, escorted him with stiff civility to a stage with a line of folding chairs where the other six candidates already sat, as Kerry murmured to Clayton, "like prisoners waiting to be executed."

Clayton stood near the press and the cameras. One by one, the moderator introduced the Republicans; as reasonably as they could, the first five advocated measures to keep felons from buying guns and then affirmed their belief in gun ownership for everyone else, two including a repeal on the assault weapons ban. The sixth brought the crowd to its feet by proclaiming that "if King George had enforced gun control, our capital would still be in London. But the slogan of patriots has always been 'Ride to the sound of the guns!'"

When at last Rogers introduced Kerry, the tepid applause was matched by boos and catcalls.

Calmly, Kerry gazed at the crowd. "Those boos must have been for King George," he began, "because I haven't said anything yet." He smiled. "Don't worry, you'll get your chance. Just give me mine."

As the room grew quiet, Kerry turned to the other candidates. "For the last hour, I've watched six intelligent men try to pretend that violence with guns isn't a problem. It's as embarrassing to watch as it must be to do." Here, Kerry grinned at the last speaker. "Except for Pat, of course. Saying things like 'lock and load' makes up for all the time he didn't spend in the army during Vietnam. And there's always the militia vote to consider."

The crowd remained silent, perhaps at Kerry's effrontery. He faced them again. "By the way," he asked with mock innocence, "where's Dick Mason? Hiding out with King George? Or riding to the sound of the guns?" There was mild laughter, acknowledgment of a point scored. "Well," Kerry said more quietly, "I guess I'll have to do this without him.

"I'm running for President of the United States, not president of the Gun Alliance. My only obligation to anyone is to tell the truth as I see it." His voice softened. "All of you know my personal history. I can't imagine that anyone doubts how I feel about gun control, or that I have a right to feel that way, however much you may disagree. But since you've asked me here, I'll spell it out.

"Too much senseless violence in this country stems from guns. Three weeks ago, as you'll remember, a man walked into a day care center in Manhattan and murdered six children, including his own son, with an assault weapon. A gun whose only purpose is to kill people as quickly as possible. *People,* not deer or rabbits. In this case, children." Once more, Kerry scanned the other candidates. "As my six friends here know, he wasn't a convicted felon. Nothing any of them proposed would have prevented this tragedy.

"For me, the right to live is more important than the right to own whatever weapon someone may want. And there is no punishment after the fact which will restore those murdered children to their parents." Pausing, Kerry stood straighter. "When you oppose any law to limit this insane trafficking in weapons of death, you assume responsibility for tragedies like this one. If I'm elected President, I'll make it a priority to prevent them, any way I can.

"In the next few months, I'll spell out how. So keep listening."

Kerry turned to Walt Rogers, nodding politely. "Thank you for inviting me," he said, and walked offstage.

There was momentary silence, and then the antagonism of the crowd—boos, jeers, catcalls—closed around him. Reaching Clayton in the press of reporters and Secret Service agents, Kerry said under his breath, "I'll bet those six other guys wish they were me—*I* get to leave."

Clayton glanced around them. Some faces were stony, others distorted by hate and anger. A gaunt, mustached man in a camouflage cap shouted, "You're a dead man, Kilcannon." Kerry did not seem to hear him; only his pallor suggested that he felt the hatred, that his candor had come at the price of his own fear.

Quickly, the Secret Service hustled Kerry out the door and into the waiting van.

Clayton and Kerry sat in the rear with Kevin Loughery, silent. Kerry had lost himself votes, Clayton reflected, perhaps the primary. Then Kerry broke into his thoughts.

"Dick Mason," Kerry murmured, "just missed his chance."

It was later, in Florida, when Kerry started to win, that Clayton began to agree. But Clayton was never sure how much of what Kerry did at any given moment was impulse, how much a dead-on political intuition, and how much the work of Kerry's ghosts . . .

Now, Clayton watched Stacey Tarrant appear on the stage.

Slender and erect, she waited out the applause, then let the silence hold for seconds, which seemed longer. The only sound was the distant jeer of a demonstrator: "One down, lady, and one to go."

Stacey stared out at him, and quiet fell again, more terrible for the interruption. "Many of you," she told Kerry's supporters, "are survivors of tragedies involving guns, who've had to go on with your lives. No one needs to explain that to Kerry Kilcannon."

It was a graceful beginning, Clayton thought; left unsaid was the reason that no one had to explain this to Stacey, either. "I wanted to be with Kerry today," she continued. "And Kerry wanted to be with you." Turning to Kerry, she finished simply, "The President we deserve, Kerry Kilcannon."

SEVEN

Standing in the press bleachers, Lara was closer to the demonstrators than to Kerry. *Why,* she had always wanted to ask him, *would you ever run for President?* She would think of this as she sat across from him at dinner, when they watched the sunset on Martha's Vineyard, when she awoke in the morning and saw his sleeping face, the rise and fall of his breathing. But she was not his wife. Lara had a life of her own, a reporter's life; she had no standing to define *his*.

Kerry stepped forward. "You're next," the same rough voice called out amidst the cheers. "You're next."

Amidst her fear and anger, Lara fought to retain her reporter's instinct. Whatever else he was, Kerry was a practical politician. Knowing the emotions he would stir, Kerry had chosen to be here, perhaps because there would be demonstrators.

"Today," Kerry began softly, "is the anniversary of a death." The crowd was hushed.

"His name was Carlos Miller," Kerry went on, "and he was nine years old. He was murdered in this park, in a drive-by shooting, committed by a racist with an AK-forty-seven.

"He died, as people die every day in this country, cherished by his family, little noticed by the rest of us, quickly forgotten by the media." Kerry paused, and then his voice rose. "Because the carnage is so great that only a mass slaughter, or the death of a celebrity, even makes us pause.

"Over forty thousand Americans were killed with firearms last year. One hundred and ten people *every day*." Kerry lowered his voice again. "And on this day a year ago, Carlos Miller was one of them.

" 'Guns don't kill people,' the gun advocates tell us, '*people do*.' So let's ask how many people around the world last year killed other people with, say, handguns.

"Thirty-six people in Sweden.

"Thirty-three in Great Britain.

"One hundred twenty-eight in Canada.

"Thirteen in Australia.

"Sixteen in Japan." For an instant, Kerry paused. "And, in the United States, thirty *thousand* four hundred and ninety-five.

"In *our* country, people armed with handguns committed over one point one million violent crimes.

"In *our* country, guns are the leading cause of death for black males under thirty-five.

"In *our* country, fifty-three percent of the victims in spousal murders died from gunshot wounds.

"In *our* country, the annual firearm-injury epidemic—due largely to handguns—is ten times larger than the polio epidemic in any year in the first half of the twentieth century."

The staccato delivery of fact upon fact, Lara thought, was devastating. The demonstrators were silent.

"What causes this terrible slaughter?" Kerry asked. "Are Americans less humane than the Japanese, or the Australians, or the Swedes? Do Americans consider mass murder a small price to pay for the unfettered right to buy and sell guns?" Now Kerry's voice became almost gentle. "Or that the life of Carlos Miller is a small price to pay?

"We do *not*. These tragedies occur because, despite the wishes of the vast majority, our efforts to control the flow of weapons are among the most feeble in the world. So there is something else which must be said, out of respect to Carlos Miller and the countless others who have died for no good reason." At last, Kerry turned to the demonstrators, voice rising in anger. "The notion that James Madison wrote the Bill of

Rights so that racists and sociopaths and madmen could slaughter innocent men, women, and children with assault weapons *or* handguns is one of the most contemptible notions that an irresponsible minority has ever crammed down the throats of its potential victims."

There was a startling riptide of emotion: Kerry's supporters screaming their support; the demonstrators trying to drown them out, faces filled with rage. Lara saw a squat man balanced on a folding chair and shouting through a megaphone, *"Where's your brother?"* His hatred was so visceral that Lara felt it on her skin.

"No," Lee McAlpine whispered. When Lara turned, she saw that Lee's usual insouciance had vanished; her face was pinched with apprehension.

"I don't care about the politics," Lee said under her breath. "He'll never live to be President, and I don't want to be there when it happens."

Instinctively, Lara scanned the rooftops, then turned to watch Kerry again—a distant figure, looking almost frail, who had made himself a vortex of passion.

Why, she asked him. *Why?*

"In the last half of this last century," Kerry said into the cacophony, "men with guns stole our future by killing the best of our leaders, again and again—in one single tragic year, Martin Luther King and Robert Kennedy. And day after day, death upon death, they steal our dreams by killing the people we love. *"Enough."*

Abruptly, Kerry's voice changed again; to Lara, it sounded lilting, eloquent, faintly Irish. "Today I ask you to share a dream too powerful to kill, too important to let die: the day when we have eradicated the misery caused by assault weapons and illegal handguns as surely as we eradicated smallpox."

Kerry paused, letting the crowd absorb this. "In New Hampshire," he told them, "I promised you a program. Here it is.

"*First,* everyone who owns a gun should be required to carry a license, conditional on completing a course in firearms use and passing a safety test . . ."

Once more, the demonstrators unleashed a wave of jeers and catcalls. "That's what we do with automobiles," Kerry snapped. "Why is a drunk with a gun safer than a drunk in a car?"

Waving their signs, Kerry's supporters cheered him on. *"Second,"* he continued in a steady voice, "we should ban any weapon whose sole purpose is to kill other people—assault weapons, cheap handguns, cop-killer bullets." Turning to the demonstrators, he said, "No 'sportsman' uses weapons that can kill twenty deer—or twenty people—in less than thirty seconds. No 'marksman' needs a bullet designed to tear another man's insides to shreds."

"The bullets are for *you*," the squat man called through the megaphone.

His voice carried across the park. "No," Kerry answered simply, "the *laws* are for *you*."

He faced the crowd again. "It should be a felony," he went on, "to sell *any* gun to anyone not licensed to have one.

"But that brings us to the heart of the problem—that Robert Kennedy, and Carlos Miller, were killed with guns bought and sold illegally. To end the slaughter, we have to put gun traffickers out of business. So here's what I would do."

Again, Kerry gazed out at the demonstrators. "I'd limit gun purchases to one a month, so that illegal traffickers can't resell in bulk.

"I'd require manufacturers to install a code in every gun, like a home alarm, so that only the licensed owner could use it. And finally, I'd go after the people who hoard weapons for illegal resale, for organized crime, and for so-called militia groups . . ."

With a primal roar of anger, the demonstrators began shouting from behind their barriers, waving their fists and their signs. One sign near Lara read "Stamp Out Kilcannon, Not Guns."

"He's making himself a target," Lee murmured to Lara. "Doesn't he know how nuts these people are?"

Taut, Lara folded her arms. "That's clearly his point. They'll be on the news tonight, for everyone to see."

The Secret Service agents, Lara noticed, scanned the roiling knot of demonstrators. Through the public address system, Kerry's voice carried above their taunts. "Every person who owns more than ten weapons should be required to have an arsenal license. No license, no gun collection—a felony, plain and simple. And if you sell a single gun outside the law, your license goes."

"*You* go," a demonstrator shouted, and then the cry became a ragged chorus. "*You* go, *you* go, *you* go . . ."

"Who will object to this?" Kerry asked. "Very few of us. Fully ninety percent of Americans support the ban on assault weapons, and eighty percent support the regulation of handguns.

"No, we have an epidemic of death because our government has been bullied and bribed by a powerful lobby which values guns more than human life."

Quickly, Lara scanned the roofline. *"We'll get you, Kilcannon,"* the man with the megaphone called out.

Stopping, Kerry stared at him. "Do you think it ends with me?" he demanded. "If that were so, the world would still be ruled by all the other cowards who tried to murder truth—the Nazis, the Communists, the dictators—and wound up on the trash heap of history."

Kerry paused, his voice, though measured, filling with passion. "There is a long and committed line of people who will never rest until the violence ends. Every murder in this country creates *more* of us. So that the loss of any *one* of us will only hasten the day when the fight is won where it should be won—at the ballet box, in the Congress, and in the presidency itself."

Once more, Kerry took in his audience. "For Carlos Miller," he said, "and for all those who have died, we have work to do."

The applause rose, drowning out the jeers, the catcalls, the shouted threats. Suddenly Kerry was in the crowd, shaking hands, stopping to talk to the families of victims, looking into each face as if no one else were there.

Get back in the car, Lara silently implored him.

Next to her, Lee McAlpine expelled a breath. "Well . . ."

Lara could feel the moisture on her forehead, the beating of her own heart. "I'd better set up," she said, and went to find her cameraman.

* * *

Ten minutes later, Lara stood on a swath of grass facing the camera. Her producer, Steve Shaffer, stood chatting with Nate Cutler.

Lara felt quite certain now that the subtext of Nate's story would be how Kerry's lover had reported his campaign. *Newsworld* would scrutinize each broadcast, parsing every word she said. The press, self-referential as it was, would find her downfall as compelling as Kerry's: Lara Costello, once NBC's rising star, now its deepest embarrassment. In the cool air of early evening, the dampness of her skin felt chill.

Ignoring Nate, she reviewed her scribbled notes. Through her earpiece, a technician asked, "Ready?"

Lara nodded. "The roll cue," she said into her microphone, "is 'demonstrators as foils.'"

Standing straighter, Lara gazed into the lens and began.

"In a speech punctuated by the angry shouts of pro-gun demonstrators, Kerry Kilcannon made an impassioned plea for a society free of handguns and assault weapons. His proposal is possibly the most far-reaching ever made by a member of Congress—comprehensive licensing for gun owners or collectors, a ban on all assault weapons, Saturday night specials, and cop-killer bullets, and the denial of guns to anyone with a record of violence, not just those convicted of felony offenses."

Now came the time for her analysis. "In the short term," she continued, "these proposals have little chance of becoming law. But Kilcannon's speech neatly balanced his earlier support for the death penalty with an issue that appeals to liberals, even as it showcased his gift for using demonstrators as foils . . ."

In the sound truck, the tape began to roll. Lara could hear the angry calls of the gun enthusiasts, and then Kerry.

"*In the last half of this last century, men with guns stole our future by killing the best of our leaders . . .*"

"Today," Lara said to the lens, "was the twelfth anniversary of James Kilcannon's death. Kerry Kilcannon never spoke of this. But then he didn't have to. From his introduction by Stacey Tarrant to his last plunge into the crowd, his message was clear: 'I'm the candidate with a moral mission, standing in my brother's place.'"

"Lara Costello, NBC News, with the Kilcannon campaign in Sacramento."

Finishing, she was still for a moment.

Kerry would despise her closing, she knew—it hit him where he was most sensitive. But she could not cut him slack another reporter would not; his speech had shaken her too much already.

"Nice," Steve Shaffer said.

Removing her microphone, Lara turned to him. Nate was still there.

"Perfect," Nate opined. "You nailed both the politics and the calculated symbolism."

Lara gazed at him evenly. "It's what I live for," she said, and turned to chat with her cameraman.

EIGHT

Guided by Agents Joe Morton and Dan Biasi, Kerry headed toward his limousine. With every step, he reminded himself to walk slowly, to mimic unconcern. But when he slid inside, to find Clayton rather than another politician, Kerry slumped down in the seat, letting the relief wash over him.

Clayton was silent. After a time, they were gliding down the highway toward the airstrip, causing traffic jams on the entry ramps blocked by motorcycle cops. Gazing out the windows, Kerry imagined the frustrated commuters, late for dinner with their families.

"I hope you put those 'Mason for President' stickers on our bumpers," he said to Clayton.

Clayton emitted a short laugh, but his tone was without

humor. "I should have. Maybe that way they won't shoot. Seeing how you won't wear a vest."

Don't you *understand?* Kerry thought. But when he turned to Clayton, ready to be angry, he remembered that his friend understood a great deal. "I can't let them change me," he said simply.

"Who's 'them'?" Clayton shot back. "Peter Lake and all the others who try to keep you from getting killed? Every time you wade into a crowd, you make their job that much harder."

"That wasn't just a *crowd*, dammit. Some have lost people they loved to guns, and I'm not supposed to *be* with them? Then why am I running?"

Clayton stared at him, his round face somber. "To get elected, I used to think."

"Can the pop psychology," Kerry snapped, and then reined in his temper again. "Today was hard enough."

"I *know* it was hard, Kerry. So what does risking your life do for anyone?"

Kerry sat back. "You can't run for President," he said at length, "and hide from people. But look what's happened to me.

"In New Hampshire, when nobody thought I'd win, we didn't have this entourage. I could talk with people, see their faces. Now I'm surrounded by the Secret Service, the press, all the handlers.

"It's life in the bubble: limousine, airplane, hotel room . . . The last 'real' people I spent time with were a bunch of rich film producers in Beverly Hills, and I was asking them for *money*, not votes." He turned to Clayton. "When you start learning about people from tracking polls and 'mall intercepts,' *you're* not real, either. You're a TV pitchman for someone else's product."

"Well," Clayton answered, "you met some 'real' people today. Like that psychopath with the megaphone."

Turning, Kerry gazed out the window. Twilight was thinning to gray smoky dusk; in the distance, the lights of Sacramento were barely visible. "What makes someone like that?" he murmured. "So many reasons, I suppose. Like the guy who murdered Jamie."

It was strange, Kerry reflected; after twelve years, he still could not speak the name Harry Carson. Perhaps it was the dream . . .

"All the more reason," Clayton was saying, "to stop playing chicken. If you could melt down all the guns tomorrow, and turn them into steel girders in a chain of public libraries, that would be one thing. But you can't. You're going to have to live awhile."

Kerry faced him again. "I may not have that much time," he answered. "It would be that much worse if I pulled punches, waiting for it to happen."

In the enveloping shadows, Clayton stared at him in genuine alarm, and then comprehension dawned. "Cutler?"

Kerry nodded. "I look at what he's doing—to Lara and to me—and it's hard to distinguish Cutler from our friend with the megaphone. Politically, the intent's pretty similar." Kerry's voice, though soft, had an edge. "*Newsworld* must think this is very important to our nation's future."

Clayton folded his hands across his stomach. "Cutler cornered Kit today. He wants a private moment with you, to discuss a 'personal matter.' You've got three days, he says, or they'll go with what they have."

Kerry felt his anger return, harder and more certain. "Will they now? Without specifying the question? Tell Kit to wait him out—he'll be back, I'm sure of it. And we'll have bought some time."

Clayton studied him. "Unless you've decided what to do, time doesn't help."

Kerry gazed at the floor. "Would *Mason* have done that today?" he finally asked. "Will he do that if he's President? No, he'll show up at the funeral of some poor victim, to hug the survivors. And after that, he'll go on to whatever trivia the polls tell him is safest. Maybe preschool training in pedestrian skills." After a moment, he looked up at Clayton. "Run those ads, pal. I don't want to lose this race."

Clayton's gaze was unflinching. "Then you'll have to lie."

Kerry fell silent. "Imagine being Lara," he said at last. "Waiting for me to decide. For both of us."

Clayton's eyes were veiled, perhaps from a sense of irony he need not express aloud. "There's something else. About Mason."

Kerry turned to him. "What is it?"

"We have a tip from a cop in Darien, where Mason started out in politics." Clayton's voice was quieter yet. "It's wife beating, Kerry."

Kerry could feel his own astonishment. "Jeannie?"

"She called the police, our man says, then filed a complaint. But Mason had the files sealed."

Kerry exhaled. After a time, he asked, "Do we know whether he did it again? Or where the files are now?"

"About the files, they're in storage." Clayton's tone was even. "If Mason's guilty of domestic violence, even once, he's a dead man. Or at least severely wounded."

"Jeannie Mason," Kerry murmured. "This must have been years ago."

"Over twenty. We're checking everywhere they've lived since then, to see if there's something fresher. Unless you tell me to stop." Clayton paused a moment. "If Mason's the one who fed the Lara story to *Newsworld*, this incident alone should be enough to keep him from giving it to anyone else. Assuming it's still under their control, the Mason people will make a deal. They'll have no choice."

"*If* it was Mason," Kerry retorted. "But we don't know that."

"What about their debate proposal? It fits with everything else—those hecklers yesterday, Mason flying to Boston, Lara. Mason's coming after you, Tony Lord thinks, and Tony doesn't know what we do." Clayton's voice became emphatic. "If Dick beat Jeannie, and it happened more than once, does it matter *who* leaked Lara's story? It won't matter to the press."

Kerry stared at him. "It matters to *me*."

"But should it? The result's the same—he looks worse than you do." Clayton's tone was soft again. "I know that you don't like this. Neither do I. But I'm trying to be practical. You don't deserve to lose because of Lara. The country deserves better too."

Kerry turned from his friend. The adrenaline rush from his speech—the crazy combination of elation and fear—had vanished. He watched the headlights of the motorcade cutting through the darkness, lighting palm trees and military barracks, the edge of Mather Field. On the tarmac was the distant shadow of his plane, the *Shamrock*, waiting to fly them to San Francisco. But what he thought of was Jeannie Mason and her family, and then his own family long ago.

"The President was right," he said. "You think you know what it takes to run. But you don't."

Beside him, Clayton stared ahead. "And so?"

"So I'm a Catholic, not a Quaker. Find out what else is there."

"So," Kate Feeney asked Sean, "how did you do?"

The question startled him. He had been absorbed in his search for a gun—the dealer who could not help him, the street hustler he did not trust. But Sean found himself still sitting in Kilcannon headquarters, at nine in the evening, after hours of calls to strangers.

"I did all right," he managed to say. "But there's lots of undecideds."

Kate frowned, thoughtful. "Some of mine are waiting for the debate. That's good for Kerry, don't you think?"

Sean nodded. It was hard to speak.

"Well," she said, "Kerry's coming here tomorrow. That should help."

Sean stared at the table. "I wonder if we'll get to meet him."

"God, I'd *love* to." Kate no longer sounded tired. "I think he's the best thing that could happen to this country. He's so caring and honest, and he doesn't play political games."

So caring, Sean thought bitterly. *So honest.* What did she really know about this ally of abortionists, breaker of promises, traitor to his own religion? Standing, he shoved both hands in the pockets of his blue jeans.

Kate looked up at him. Her guileless expression held pity for his awkwardness, Sean suspected—or, worse, concealed disquiet. "Aren't you sticking around for pizza?" she asked.

For an instant, Sean wished to stay. Just to be alone with her, to have her understand his silence. Then his own distrust, the fear of rejection, hit him like a slap in the face.

"No," he said. "Tomorrow I'm coming in early."

He turned and walked away.

Rick Ginsberg stood amidst a knot of people—listening, nodding, providing guidance. Sean waited, a few feet distant, not wanting to be part of them.

At last, Rick noticed him. He wiped his glasses, looking weary, as the mahogany-skinned receptionist told him they were nearly out of leaflets. "I'll call them," he said tiredly. "First thing."

Satisfied, she headed toward the pizza. Rick put on his glasses, regarding Sean with a wry, complicit smile. *It never ends,* the smile said. *You know how it is.*

"What's up, John?"

"Nothing, really. It's just that Senator Kilcannon's coming tomorrow, and I wondered . . ." He shrugged, eyes on the tile.

"You want to meet him." Rick's tone was patient. "That might be tough, tomorrow. We've already got people going to the events, and you've been great on the phones."

Sean looked up at him. "It would mean a lot."

Rick studied him. Quietly, he answered, "Then I'll see what I can do."

It was nine-thirty in San Francisco before the weary band of re-porters reached the Saint Francis Hotel, another hour before Nate was able to retrieve his luggage and locate his room. That made it one-thirty a.m. in Washington; when he called his editor at home, it took her five rings to answer, and her voice sounded thick and dazed.

Without apology, Nate said, "Your message read 'urgent.'"

"Yeah," Jane answered. "There's something more." Abrupt-ly, she seemed to have awakened. "Sheila Kahn talked to one of Costello's ex-neighbors—a retired army colonel who detests Kilcannon's politics and told Sheila he 'knew the little bastard on sight.'

"Anyhow, this man claims he was walking his greyhound one fine spring morning, and who should come out the front door of the building but Kerry Kilcannon, wearing a tuxedo. Kilcannon saw him, the colonel says, and looked the other way. Then he walked to an old compact car with New Jersey plates saying 'USS' and drove off."

Was it *that* night, Nate wondered. "Did this guy ever see him with Lara?"

"No. Never with her. And only that once."

Nate lay back in his bed. That the memory was so clear did not surprise him; in a white evening dress, Lara had looked so slim and elegant that she had, figuratively speaking, stopped his heart. It was the moment when Nate had stopped deluding himself and begun wondering what to do. "This would have been three years ago," he asked, "right?"

"How did you know *that*?"

"Lara and I were both at the *Times*. She'd invited Kilcannon to the Congressional Correspondents Dinner—a real coup for a rookie. But I didn't figure they were fucking."

"Well, they were, it seems. Staying over at her place wasn't smart."

For another moment, Nate was quiet. He could also remember when Lara had first mentioned Kerry Kilcannon, months before that dinner. How soon after that, Nate wondered, had Kilcannon begun to see Lara as he did?

"It's not enough," Nate said at last.

"Of course not." Jane's tone was filled with impatience. "But surely for a question, or to catch Kilcannon in a lie. When are you meeting with him?"

Nate could feel his own frustration. "Kit Pace is stonewalling me. When I tried to tell her this was for his ears only, Kit did the old 'tell me why I should bother him at a time like this . . .'"

"Because you're *you*," Jane snapped. "And from *Newsworld*, not the fucking *Wichita Bugle*. Don't they know what we can do?"

"Of course. I even gave her a deadline—seventy-two hours." Pausing, Nate made himself sound less defensive. "Maybe Lara's told Kilcannon. Kit figures we can't run this without telling them what it is, and she's playing for time."

There was silence on the other end. "She's right," Jane answered tersely. "And we don't have time. Tell Kit that we want Kilcannon tomorrow, and what we want to ask him. In case Kit's forgotten what she already knows." Jane's voice filled with real anger. "It's totally unethical: Costello's not a reporter, she's Kilcannon's fifth column. She deserves whatever happens as much as he does."

NINE

At ten forty-five—one forty-five in Newark—Clayton told Carlie how much he loved her, and slowly put down the telephone.

They had a deal: no matter how late, Clayton could call. She missed him, of course, but there was something else neither needed to say—that Clayton did not sleep well without hearing that, as far as Carlie knew, the twins were fine. No matter that they were in college now; since Ethan's death, for Clayton not to ask felt like an act of carelessness. It was deeper than superstition, much more than a habit.

Tonight, as so often, after Clayton asked about the twins, Carlie asked how Kerry was.

This association, too, was something they both understood. When they were at the hospital, waiting for their son to die, Kerry had stayed up with them. His wife was the one person with whom Clayton had shared the deepest secret of Kerry's life and how it had begun. So that two nights before, when Clayton told her Lara was back, Carlie had emitted a long sigh. Not for the politics of it but for Kerry himself.

Go back to Washington, they had told him after Ethan's funeral. *We'll be all right . . .*

If Kerry had stayed with them, Clayton wondered now, would it ever have happened? But this was hindsight: they—and perhaps Kerry—had known nothing.

Restless, Clayton turned on the television, the nightly tracking polls strewn next to him on the bed.

In five minutes of channel surfing, he saw two "Mason for President" ads stressing the Vice President's "consistent support for every woman's right to choose." But the local CBS station featured Mason himself.

The Vice President had flown back from Boston to San Francisco the night before, Clayton knew, and the news clip showed him at a breakfast for entrepreneurial women. As Clayton watched, Mason looked up from his text and said firmly, *"By the way, I want to emphasize what I've said many times before—economic opportunity for women goes hand in hand with reproductive freedom . . ."*

The telephone rang.

"Looked at the numbers?" Jack Sleeper asked without preface.

"Oh, yeah," Clayton answered. "Still down three percent statewide. But Kerry was strong all day, and he says to run the ad where he gets shot. I've already told Frank."

"Thank God," Jack said fervently. "Kerry could win the whole fucking thing. Not just this, but the presidency."

Except for *Newsworld,* Clayton thought. Jack's relief was so evident that he was glad the pollster did not know.

On the screen, the well-dressed businesswomen rose to applaud Mason. *"The highlight for many,"* the reporter's voice broke in, *"was Mason's linkage of economic progress with reproductive choice . . ."*

"You've seen Dick's ads," Clayton said to Sleeper. "The stuff on choice."

"He sees what we see, Clayton. Among pro-choice women, the gap's widening—we're down another three in the Bay Area." The pollster's voice was firm. "I was right last night. Do a pro-choice event in San Francisco, where the problem's worst."

Tired, Clayton stared at the poll numbers. "I'll talk to Senator Penn," he said at last. "San Francisco's her base, and we damn sure need her help."

Sean Burke stared at the television, transfixed.

He was in shirtsleeves, standing on a platform before a crowd of farmers, suddenly speaking from Sean's heart. *"I am*

quite certain," Kerry said, *"that someone who chooses to take
the life of another human should forfeit his right to live . . ."*

He understands, Sean thought. *He knows that I am coming
for him, that God's law imposes death on the murderers of children. That his own death is retribution.*

Absolved, Sean shivered.

The picture changed. Now Kerry stood in a park, his every
word an accusation . . .

*"The notion that James Madison wrote the Bill of Rights
so that racists and sociopaths and madmen could slaughter innocent men, women, and children with assault weapons or
handguns is one of the most contemptible notions that an irresponsible minority has ever crammed down the throats of its
potential victims . . ."*

Sean felt a sudden wave of nausea.

He hurried to the bathroom. When he bent over the sink,
spasms racking his body, his spittle was flecked with blood.
Kerry's voice accused him still.

Sean dried his face. The lesson life had taught him, he remembered, was to trust no one. Least of all the street kid who
had promised him a gun.

Wiping his mouth, Sean swallowed an antacid pill.

The knife was in his suitcase. He had bought it when he
bought the gun, unsure of why he needed it, simply because he
liked to feel its balance in his hand.

Sean walked past the television. As he opened the tiny closet,
he imagined himself locked inside, heard the angry voice of his
father.

"Do you think it ends with me?" Kerry asked.

Fingers trembling, Sean slid the knife inside his jacket.

As Kerry watched, Lara's face filled the screen.

"In the short term," she was saying, *"these proposals have
little chance of becoming law. But Kilcannon's speech neatly
balanced his earlier support for the death penalty with an issue
that appeals to liberals, even as it showcased his gift for using
demonstrators as foils . . ."*

The impact of seeing her was so intense that, for an instant,
Kerry felt he could reply. *Why so cynical?* he wanted to ask.

Have you forgotten so much about me that what I say comes down to neatness and balance? . . .

How could you run, he imagined Lara asking in return, *knowing what might happen?*

The question had always been there, unspoken. He could see it in her eyes the morning after their last fateful lovemaking, when the hurricane had passed and the world outside was silent. Could feel it in her fingertips as she gently touched his face.

On the screen, Kerry's own face appeared.

"In the last half of this last century, men with guns stole our future by killing the best of our leaders . . ."

Because of *this,* he answered her now. And because of you.

That final weekend, she did not answer the telephone. Kerry had lost track of the times he had called her from his hotel room: at some point, pain and desperation had become the slow death of hope, then a terrible certainty, and he knew what she had done. Finally, the message on his home telephone, her voice weary, toneless. That it was over. That her feelings no longer mattered. That—for both their sakes—she could never see him again.

As if he were someone else, Kerry had gone downstairs, to give the speech he had promised. As he spoke, another death occurred inside him.

She was here *now,* in this hotel. Alone.

Please, Kerry. Don't try to contact me. It's finished.

The two years since came back to him: his decision to run, his debt to Clayton and to all those who believed in him. And, when none of this was quite enough, his respect for her wishes—the near certainty that, with all that had happened and was happening now, she would flinch at the sound of his voice.

Her voice filled the room.

"Today was the twelfth anniversary of James Kilcannon's death. Kerry Kilcannon never spoke of this. But then he didn't have to. From his introduction by Stacey Tarrant to his last plunge into the crowd, his message was clear: 'I'm the candidate with a moral mission, standing in my brother's place.'"

Kerry turned off the television, and then the lights.

* * *

Alone in her room, Lara could not stop crying. It was as if all her strength had been for those who watched her watching Kerry, and when they were gone, she had none.

He'll never live to be President, Lee McAlpine had said.

And if he lives, Lara thought now, he still may never be President. Because of what lay between them.

I love you, she had imagined telling him. *I want to be with you.* Imagined this a thousand times, after it was too late. Imagined being selfish, no matter what the cost.

Imagined it now. Like a child who did not like the story she had heard, and wished to change the ending.

Except that it was *their* story—Kerry's and hers—and she had written the ending herself.

Washington, D.C.

May 1996–April 1997

ONE

The first time Lara Costello met Kerry Kilcannon left her intrigued and more than a little curious.

Though she was new on Capitol Hill, prominent politicians had long since ceased to impress her; she had experienced enough in California to develop an ear for fraud and hollowness, a sense of how political posturing affected ordinary people. It was her focus on the inner landscape of her subjects that separated Lara from some of her peers. And this was partly what had brought her to where she was on that late-spring afternoon, waiting by the "Senators Only" elevator while the Senate debated a proposed constitutional amendment barring desecration of the flag. No subtleties here, Lara thought; the fascination was watching opponents pretzel themselves to avoid looking unpatriotic. All she wanted was a quote or two, and her story was complete.

The door to the Senate swung open, and Ted Kennedy emerged, then Kerry Kilcannon. "What we really need here," Kilcannon murmured to Kennedy, "is a mandatory death sentence. None of this 'three flags and you're out' stuff."

Kennedy turned to his colleague and, seeing Kilcannon's mischievous grin, began to chuckle. It was a nice moment, Lara thought—two Irishmen, standing in the shadowy elegance of the Senate, sharing a laugh about the vicissitudes of their job. Which one to approach? Lara wondered, and then Kennedy headed toward the Senate meeting room, Kilcannon toward the elevator.

"Senator?" Lara said. "Lara Costello, *New York Times*."

Kilcannon stopped. He was not tall—five feet ten, at most.

But what struck her was an incongruous youthfulness—a thatch of tousled hair, the slender build of a teenager not yet grown into his body—and then the startling contradiction of his eyes: their green-flecked blue irises were larger than most, giving Lara the unsettling sense of a man who had seen more than someone twice his age. It was an illusion, Lara thought, abetted by her knowledge of his history.

"I guess you're new," he said, and held out his hand.

His handshake was cool and dry. "Two weeks," Lara answered.

Kilcannon smiled. "Another two, and you'll have had enough." He took a few steps and pushed the button to the "Senators Only" elevator. "What can I do for you? If anything."

"I wanted to ask you about the flag amendment."

Kilcannon gave a mock wince. "Isn't it sufficient that I have to *vote* on this thing? Now I have to tell you what I *think*?"

Lara could not tell whether this was teasing, the somewhat quirky humor of someone willing to laugh at his own dilemma, or an outright refusal. "I've never noticed voting was the same as thinking," she ventured. "It's nice when someone does both, and even nicer when he shares."

Kerry cocked his head, appraising her. "Oh, well," he said. "Why don't you ride with me to the Russell Building."

She followed him into the elevator. Together, they descended to the bowels of Congress, the gray basement corridors where the Senate subway waited. Walking quickly, Kilcannon waved Lara into an open minicar. There was an energy about him, Lara thought, less the grace of an athlete than a certain restless vigor. But when he sat across from her, Kilcannon lapsed into stillness, preoccupied.

The car began moving. "The flag amendment," Lara said.

Kilcannon looked up. "Oh," he said, "*that*. Do you know how many actual cases of flag desecration we've had since 1776?"

"No. I don't."

"Roughly forty. About one every five years. Hardly an epidemic." Kilcannon shrugged, as if to himself. "They trot this out as a distraction. It's so much easier than feeding kids, or giving them proper medical care. Cheaper, too. And when you've been caught out shilling for the tobacco companies, as several of the sponsors have, it's good to become a patriot."

Surprised by his candor, Lara took out her notepad and began scribbling. "Does that mean you're against?" she asked dryly.

Kilcannon did not smile. "A million or so people," he answered, "have died for this flag, not because they liked its colors but because it stood for something. Like the right to express yourself, even in ways that are ill-advised or outright stupid." Pausing, he added with a trace of humor, "As I'll exemplify tomorrow, when I speak in opposition."

So his reluctance had been feigned, Lara thought, an extension of the joke. "Do you think you'll win?" she asked.

"Sure. The proponents need a two-thirds vote, and most of my colleagues think it's a bad idea. The only problem is selecting the lucky ones who get to say so." His smile flashed. "As you can imagine, the competition's pretty intense."

The car shuddered to a stop. Again, Kilcannon moved to the elevator with a purposeful stride, Lara following. "Then why take a leadership role?" Lara asked.

"Oh," he said, "I've always wanted to be the ACLU's poster boy. Willing to die for principle." He tilted his head again, this time in inquiry. "Off the record?"

Lara hesitated. "All right."

"Because I can provide some of my colleagues cover, at little cost to me." When the elevator arrived, he held the door open for Lara and they stepped inside, leaning against the wall. "The people of New Jersey aren't going to chuck me over *this*. That's not necessarily true for, say, the junior senator from Idaho. And if the Republicans say I've gone Communist—well, they never liked me anyway." Pausing, he gave her a considering look. "But then I'm telling you what you already know. Again."

Of course she knew, Lara thought; she was already calculating the advantage to Kilcannon of having grateful colleagues, especially if—as was widely whispered—he meant to run for President someday. But it was not politic to say so. "It sounds familiar," she answered. "Of course, Sacramento's the capital of political courage."

The elevator door rumbled open, and they stepped onto the

marble floors of the Russell Building. "You're from California?" he asked.

"Uh-huh." Lara kept walking toward the front door; she had her quotes now and needed to file. "Born, bred, and educated."

"And 'Costello' is Irish, the last time I noticed."

"So am I, on my father's side. My mother's Mexican."

They stopped in the doorway. "Then you *can't* be a Republican," Kilcannon said in a tone of mock challenge.

Lara smiled slightly. "I'm totally objective—no beliefs, feelings, or opinions. Like all reporters." She held out her hand. "Thanks for your time, Senator. It really was a help."

"*De nada,*" he answered. Turning, he gazed out at the street, the sunlight, the trees and swatches of green. It gave Lara a chance to study him more closely. There was a scar near his left eye, and his face was bony yet fine-featured. He was not conventionally handsome, she decided; the aura of a potential President made his looks seem more arresting than they were. That, and the eyes—the sense of deep intuition, of secrets withheld. A slight breeze ruffled his hair, red-tinted in the light.

"Not too bad a day," Kilcannon observed. "And here I've been trapped in the Senate, listening to *that.* An hour closer to being dead, and for what?"

Lara did not quite know how to respond, or if she was expected to. He faced her again. "You may not need this. But if you want to spend a half day with me sometime, watching how this place works, give my AA a call." He smiled. "For orientation, not publication. That way I get to say what I want."

Once more, Lara was surprised. "I'd like that."

Kilcannon nodded briskly. "Then I'll be seeing you," he said, and was gone.

"Take him up on it," Nate Cutler said to Lara. "If you can get some kind of relationship going, it can only help."

Lara pulled up a chair next to Nate's desk, jammed in a corner of a rabbit warren filled with other desks. She barely knew him; at first meeting, she had thought he had the intense, almost ascetic look of a Jesuit or a bomb thrower. But Nate was experienced and, Lara was learning, endowed with balance and good sense. "Like the golden days," she replied, "that all the old white guys reminisce about. Where some famous senator pours them drinks in his office and tells them a lot of stuff on background. Male bonding in the seat of power."

Nate shrugged. "Access isn't so bad: you can learn things that way, as long as you remember who you are. And who *he* is."

Lara tilted her head. "I'm sure it's an illusion, but there's this sense of contempt for consequences. Like he couldn't be bothered trying to mislead me."

Nate smiled. "Well put," he answered. "What I've never been able to figure is whether it's principle, or ego."

"How did he get to be such a force here? The name?"

"That's how he *got* here. When he first arrived, Kilcannon seemed almost tongue-tied, and everyone took him for the underequipped kid brother, out of his depth. Later I decided he'd just been watching—the man doesn't seem to miss much, and I realized he'd figured out how the Senate operates. He's got a pretty good political sense, wherever it comes from. Plus, he's always worked like a dog, and people respect that."

Pausing, Nate reflected. "There's another thing that helps him—passion. When he finally did start speaking out, it was for people he seemed to view as powerless: kids, or minorities, or workers left behind by new technology. He was surprisingly eloquent, and when something engages him there's a relentless quality. But I don't know where it comes from." Nate gave her a curious look. "What did *you* make of him? Personally, I mean."

"God knows." For a moment, Lara tried to gather her impressions. "Sometimes I wasn't sure whether I was talking to a politician or a character in a novel. You can't tell what he's thinking, and you start to wonder. It's distracting."

Nate smiled. "He'll slip away on you, just go off somewhere. There's this directness, plus a sense of whimsy—the dark and light of the Irish. You think you almost know him, and then you realize you don't at all." Nate removed his wire-rim glasses, inspecting them for smudges. "My current thinking is that he's really not a complex man at all. Just four or five simple ones."

"How do you mean?"

"Two examples. Last year I went to hear Kilcannon speak at Georgetown. He's going along great, about job training, and suddenly he's off his text and onto the plight of Native Americans—lack of education, fetal alcohol syndrome, years of white neglect and broken promises, then describing a sick baby he'd seen. And the memory is so strong that he seems absolutely devastated—he's *there*, not here." Nate slid his glasses on again. "Indians. Where are the votes in that?

"Then there's Kerry the ruthless. We usually don't get to meet *him*. But every now and then there'll be a sighting." Interrupting himself, Nate checked his watch; he was so wired, Lara had begun to notice, that he seemed to time his own conversations. "Do you remember that story last week—where Newark's ex-prosecutor got sent to jail?"

Lara smiled. "Jail for a Newark politician? That *is* news."

"You know who got *this* particular politician? Kilcannon."

"Why? And how?"

"Before his brother got shot, Kilcannon worked for him—Vincent Flavio. Somehow Flavio pissed him off." Eyes brightening, Nate warmed to his story. "Kilcannon waits four years, until there's a Democrat in the White House, and then gets a friend of his appointed U.S. attorney—a black guy who ran Kilcannon's Senate campaign. Supposedly their deal was that if Kilcannon gets his pal Slade the job, he goes after Flavio like hell wouldn't have it.

"He did, for three years. The first jury hung. So they try it again, and Flavio and his bagman get ten years. When I asked Kilcannon about them, all he said was 'Even *Newark* can do better.'"

Lara smiled at this. "So was Flavio a crook?" she asked.

"Probably. But some Democrats find that story a little dark—the revenge of Kerry Kilcannon. And Kilcannon won't talk about the rumors. Let alone give reasons."

Pensive, Lara found herself fiddling with an earring. Take someone as elusive as Kerry Kilcannon seemed to be, she reflected, and people begin inventing their own truth.

"Well," she said to Nate, "maybe someday I'll ask him."

TWO

At nine in the morning roughly two weeks later, Lara introduced herself to Kerry Kilcannon's receptionist and settled into a plush leather couch. "The senator will be out shortly," the young woman told her.

Waiting, Lara studied her surroundings. The reception area was elegant—high ceilings, a gilt-edged mirror, two crystal chandeliers. But there were none of the vanity photographs typical of public men, no pictures of a wife or parents or children, nor any of James Kilcannon. From the evidence, Kerry Kilcannon could have been an orphan.

Turning to the entrance, Lara saw a pale young man hesitate in the doorway.

His dark gaze was darting and indirect, as though he could not look at other people without making them, and himself, uneasy. His face was damp, and the gray sport coat, too short for him, appeared borrowed. In a tremulous voice, he told the receptionist, "I came to see Senator Kilcannon."

The woman seemed to stiffen. Cautiously, she asked, "Do you have an appointment?"

The man shook his head. He could not be over twenty, Lara thought; his hair was lank, badly cut, and his shirt and pants were ill-fitting and drab. Watching, Lara noticed that his hands shook.

The receptionist frowned. "The senator has a full schedule today. If you'll just leave your name—"

"*No.*" The man spoke through clenched teeth now, his voice pleading, a near whisper. "I need to *see* him. *Please.*"

The receptionist's olive skin looked suddenly clammy. As

she reached for her phone, Lara felt the woman's instinctive fear, the shadow cast by James Kilcannon's murder.

Next to her, Lara heard a door open.

Turning, she saw Kerry Kilcannon, his shirtsleeves rolled up, come to retrieve her.

He took in his assistant's apprehension, then its object. The man froze, staring at Kilcannon with such a seeming hunger for recognition that Lara guessed he must live within his imagination, fixating on a public figure. Kilcannon stepped forward, standing between the man and his receptionist.

"How can we help you?" he asked.

The young man blinked, swallowing. Speechless, he reached into the inside pocket of his sport coat.

Lara tensed, watching his hand. The receptionist half stood. Only Kilcannon remained still.

Slowly, the man withdrew a pamphlet.

Lara could see its cover—a hideous portrayal of a partial-birth abortion, the crushed skull of a fetus. As the man pressed it on Kilcannon, tears came to his eyes.

"How can you abandon children?" he asked simply.

Looking from the pamphlet into the young man's stricken gaze, Kilcannon's own eyes narrowed. The silence grew, the pale young man and the senator studying each other.

Two uniformed officers arrived, shattering the frieze. As if awakened from a dream, Kilcannon seemed to start. "It's all right," he told them. "This man just wanted to give me something."

An officer took the young man's arm. To Lara, he looked pitiful now. His mouth opened, but he could form no words.

As they led the man away, Kilcannon stared after him.

Abruptly, he remembered Lara. "Sorry to keep you waiting," he said with a show of humor. "But the fun never stops."

Thanking his receptionist, he led Lara through a suite of offices, occupied by assistants, to his own.

"He *did* seem a little off," Lara said as they walked. "Don't you ever worry about security?"

He gave her a quick ironic glance. "*You* came through the metal detector, I hope."

"Yes."

"So would he have. Unless someone slips up." He put the pamphlet on his desk, motioning Lara to a chair. "We get used to drop-ins here, and some have a certain charm. My current favorite is the eighty-five-year-old World War Two veteran who wanted a hundred percent disability. For impotence." Kilcannon's tone became wry. "His particular war wound had occurred in Italy, in 1944, when he was hit in the groin by a soccer ball. But when I asked when he'd become impotent, guess what he told me. Two years ago."

"A gradual case, I suppose."

"Very. And it was a very delicate task suggesting it was because he was eighty-three, and not because he'd been nailed with a soccer ball forty-two years and six kids ago. But what's a senator for, if not to make tough calls?"

Lara returned his smile. Part of his persona, she was learning, was an appreciation of the human comedy and a perspective on his own place in its cast of characters. But his humor also defused subjects that might become more personal. Glancing around his office, Lara saw only three photographs: a white-haired woman who resembled James Kilcannon; a blunt-faced man with shrewd eyes and red-tinged gray hair; then a black family of five—a stocky father and a slender mother, merry-looking twin girls in their early teens, a sweet-faced boy who could not be over four. "Your parents?" Lara asked.

"My mother." Kilcannon's voice was soft. "The man's my godfather, Liam Dunn. Much of what I learned about politics, or anything else, came from him."

Still no pictures of dad, Lara thought, or brother. Or, for that matter, Meg Kilcannon. "And the family?"

"Friends of mine. Clayton's the U.S. attorney in Newark."

Lara turned to him, hesitant, and then decided to take a chance. "The one who indicted Vincent Flavio."

Though his eyes turned cool, Kilcannon's face held no surprise. "Not just indicted," he answered. "Jailed."

That was not a matter, Kilcannon's tone made clear, which was open for discussion. Almost idly, he picked up the pamphlet on abortion, studying it in silence and, from his expression, deepening reflection. It was as Nate Cutler said, Lara

thought; Kilcannon was there, and then something made him
slip away.

He stood, suddenly restless. "Come on," he said. "I'll explain our schedule on the way."

For the next nine hours, Kerry Kilcannon was constantly in
motion—subcommittee meetings; huddling with aides to make
quick decisions on various bills and amendments; granting a
CBS interview in his office to discuss the administration's exit
strategy in Bosnia; a visit from the foreign minister of Vietnam,
in which Kilcannon showed great tact, listening far more than
he spoke; a press conference on the lawn in support of school
lunch programs; a private visit to the Senate office of the Vice
President—with whom Kilcannon was known to have differences of temperament and policy—to discuss, Lara guessed,
Kilcannon's role at the upcoming convention; lunch in the
Senate dining room with a group of parochial school boys from
New Jersey, which Kilcannon seemed to enjoy, even though the
main topic was why the New Jersey Nets were so lousy.

Kilcannon was far quieter in private, Lara noticed, than in
public. But his sense of humor remained keen, his attention to
each person unflagging; his staffers called him Kerry—unusual
in the Senate—and their own energy and dedication seemed as
high as his. As hours passed, Lara found herself impressed: Kilcannon showed an excellent memory, an ability to switch subjects without effort, to ask the right questions and make
decisions on the spot. "It's a defense mechanism," Kilcannon
told her. "Otherwise I'd have to think."

To her surprise, he made her day not just interesting but en-
joyable. At each new stop, he introduced her graciously. Often
he would seem preoccupied and then, as they hurried around
the Hill with a series of legislative aides, would surprise her by
anticipating those points about which she was most curious.
Lara was smart, his manner suggested—little comment was required of him. "After all," he said with a smile, "you've been
covering Willie Brown." And then he was off again, at six in the
evening, leaving her with his office manager as he rushed to the
Senate floor.

Two hours later, Lara found herself chatting with his owlish

AA as they watched Kilcannon on C-SPAN, criticizing human rights abuses in China. "Why is it," Kilcannon demanded, "that the less business we do in a particular country, the more vehement our denunciation of its human rights offenses? Or have we started measuring freedom of speech in earnings per share?"

The pointed question, Lara thought, was bound to make the current administration—Dick Mason included—unhappy. Intrigued, she began wondering what Kilcannon was up to, when he entered his office alone, suit jacket slung over his shoulder.

He stopped, gazing down at her in astonishment. "*You're* still here?" he asked. "I'd have thought you'd tire of this."

Lara smiled. "You were right, Senator. The fun never stops."

Smiling quizzically, he glanced at his watch, then seemed to come to a decision. "For me," he answered, "it stops when I'm hungry. The least I can do is buy you dinner."

Kilcannon's car was an aging Ford Taurus, ennobled by the USS 1 plates issued to New Jersey's senior senator. When he turned the ignition, a grinding sound, not unlike a pencil sharpener, made him wince in mock dismay. "I *still* meet people," he observed, "who think we're in it for the money. When you consider the hours, and throw in the loss of privacy, we don't drive a very hard bargain."

Kilcannon began steering them toward Pennsylvania Avenue. It was twilight; the dome of the Capitol glowed behind them, a tourist's dream. "Then why," Lara asked, "do you fight to stay?"

" 'We' generically? In part because we're more interested in doing good than voters imagine. That's one of the most depressing things about politics in the nineties—this contempt so many voters seem to have for us as irrelevant, petty figures, concerned with nothing but self-preservation. Abetted by the press, of course. Worse, we have a 'shoot to kill' political culture premised on permanent scandal, where people in both parties don't just try to win but to destroy each other with charges and countercharges. And I've stopped counting the number of special prosecutors there are." His voice became thoughtful, a kind of self-admonition. "But what's still just as pernicious is the overwhelming sense of your own power and importance, reinforced in a thousand ways. Unless you're careful, it becomes an addiction."

"But how does anyone avoid that?"

"My friend Bill Cohen writes—it helps give perspective, he tells me. But I'm a little less gifted." For a moment, Kilcannon was quiet. "For others, I suppose, it's family."

Did he mean children? Lara wondered. After all, Kilcannon had a wife. "And what do *you* do for perspective?" she asked.

He shrugged. "Other things. Stuff that has nothing to do with this place."

"Such as?"

"Good works. Saintly acts." In the darkness of the car, she could not read his expression. "But if I talked about them to you, then they *would* have to do with this place, wouldn't they? Another senator on the make, tending his image as a sensitive human being."

This was fair enough, Lara thought. But Kilcannon might simply be taking her seduction to the next level, drawing her in with carefully packaged candor. Her doubts, Lara realized, reflected the divide between politician and journalist—in this case, between Senator Kerry Kilcannon and Lara Costello of the *New York Times*—which made any interaction seem double-edged, a prelude to manipulation or betrayal. It struck her that this was also true of relationships between politicians; in Washington, there was no safe place for Kerry Kilcannon.

"It must seem pretty solitary," she ventured. "Always being so guarded."

In the silver glow of oncoming headlights, Lara saw his sardonic smile. "Are you a journalist," he asked, "or a psychiatrist?"

To Lara, Kilcannon's tone implied that she had overstepped her bounds; despite his smile, she felt slightly patronized. "It was an obvious question, Senator. We were talking like real people, I thought."

In his silence, Lara watched them slip past the Washington Monument and the Ellipse, the White House appearing from between the surrounding trees, so familiar, yet so distant behind its wrought-iron fence, the barricades blocking Pennsylvania Avenue. "It's odd," he murmured. "Lately I catch myself sounding like my brother. You could go a lifetime, and never know what he really thought. Or felt."

What Lara felt was genuine surprise; Kilcannon's public reticence on the subject of his brother was well known. There was something wistful in the veiled apology, a trace of puzzled self-reflection. She decided to let him be.

"Solitary?" he said at last. "Sure. You know your peers, but seldom very well. Because almost every relationship is based on mutual calculation—what will this do for me, and what will it cost?

"It makes you less human. So does the fact that so many people are focused on *you*—your staff, your supporters, the reporters who cover you. It becomes too easy to see them only in terms of your own needs.

"But often that's how they see *you* too. The press is merely the most obvious. There isn't a local politician living who doesn't have *some* story about how well they know you, the time that you relied on them—some claim of ownership, true or not, which enables them to use your name.

"Most of them mean well enough. But your life and reputation become the coin of exchange." Briefly, Kilcannon nodded in the direction of the White House. "The higher you go, the worse it gets. No one sane ignores the price."

Lara turned to him. "So you're not running for President?" she asked with quiet skepticism. "Not even, say, in the year 2000?"

He smiled a little. "I don't expect you to believe this. But I *am* sane, I like to think. And barring disaster, the President's going to win reelection this fall, which leaves Dick Mason in very good shape for 2000. If that ever changes, it'll be because of things I can't anticipate. Or control."

"So tweaking them about China . . ."

"Was because I think it's right. I try to do that, every now and then." Turning a corner, Kilcannon pulled up in front of the restaurant, adding softly, "That's another thing Jamie left me. Not a legacy—a lesson."

Once more, Lara was surprised. "What was the lesson, then?"

Kilcannon stared out the windshield, as if speaking to

himself. "For as long as I can remember, Jamie always had a goal, always believed that he controlled his fate. I don't think he ever imagined that what happened *would* happen." Pausing, he slowly shook his head. "I learned from my brother what it wasn't given Jamie to learn: not to plan or play it safe. Because the only thing you control is who you are."

Sitting with him in the quiet of the car, Lara felt a fleeting intimacy; through some quirk of circumstance—the lateness of the hour, perhaps regret that he might have seemed condescending—she sensed that Kerry Kilcannon had shown her a glimpse of himself. Then the parking valet approached, and Kilcannon turned to her as if nothing had happened. "Come on," he said. "I can taste the fried calamari."

THREE

Kinkead's had a light, airy atmosphere, attentive service, and well-prepared entrées with an emphasis on fish. Recognizing Kilcannon, the young woman at the front found them a corner table on the second level, darker and more private.

"Power," Lara told him, "is never needing reservations."

Kilcannon smiled. With his public day ended, he seemed at ease; the absence of people competing for his time must be a luxury. "Now that we've got the table," he answered, "I'm tired of being me. I know all about myself, and if I ever forget something, I can read the *Times*. But all I know about you is that you're curious about what makes people the way they are. As much as we can know that."

You know, Lara found herself thinking, *or at least you try to know.* "What else should I tell you," she parried, "that I'd ever want you to know?"

He laughed at this, softening his retort. "Why you're bothering our nation's leaders—questioning our motives, discovering awful truths. Wasn't there a *law school* where you went?"

"That *is* patronizing, Senator. And there was, actually—Stanford Law School. I even thought about it. But it was time for me to work."

The directness of her answer erased his smile. "Why?" he asked. "For someone as bright as you are, I'd have guessed there'd be scholarship money."

Lara nodded. "That wasn't the problem—I'd been on scholarship since second grade. I needed to *make* money, not take more."

Kilcannon began to ask something when the waiter came, a stout, bearded man with an Australian accent. They chose their entrées, and after consulting with Lara and discovering that the waiter knew more about wine than either of them, Kilcannon ordered an Australian chardonnay. It was not until their second glass that he asked, "So you were tired of being broke?"

No, Lara thought. *At the time I'd have given a lot to go to Stanford Law.* She was not sure she wanted to tell him this—it seemed like a confession of weakness. Perhaps it was his patience, his stillness across the table, his comfort with silence. Perhaps, even, her second glass of wine. "No," she answered. "I was tired of my *mother* being broke."

Kilcannon tilted his head. "What does she do?"

"Clean other people's houses, watch other people's kids. And raise four more of her own." Even now, Lara realized, she could not speak of her mother's sacrifice without emotion, imagine the faces of her younger brothers and sisters without a rush of affection. "I love them all," she added quietly. "When things are hard, there's less room for sibling rivalry. You need everyone to help, and you want everyone to do well."

"And your dad?"

Was a tall man with eyes like mine, Lara thought, *younger in my memory than you are now.* "Who knows?" she answered. "When I was ten, he took off with someone else. He might even have been sober enough to know what he was doing." She gave a dismissive shrug. "I've tried hard to make him irrelevant."

She felt Kilcannon study her. "You never can, I think,"

Kilcannon said. "Better to ask what that did to you than pretend it was nothing."

His eyes held no judgment, only interest. Suddenly Lara realized that this was a remarkable conversation; when politicians wanted to ingratiate themselves, she had learned, they would offer what they thought you wanted most—a piece of themselves, usually predigested for easy consumption. No politician had ever asked Lara for a piece of *herself*.

"It's hardly profound," he added. "But sometimes I think that people are the most dangerous—to others and to themselves—when they deny that their past has anything to do with their present."

The thought was more important than he admitted, Lara felt sure—perhaps because of his brother, or himself. "What was it Wordsworth wrote?" Lara asked. " 'The child is father of the man'?"

"Something like that." Briefly, Kilcannon smiled. "My father was a difficult man. Still is, in fact."

The delphic remark made Lara smile in return. "Actually, you've hit a prejudice of mine. The last thing I want is to be my mother, or for my father to be the model for my husband. If I ever have one of those, I'm demanding self-knowledge on arrival."

Kilcannon laughed. "How old are you? Twenty-seven, twenty-eight? You may have to wait awhile."

"Are you speaking from experience?"

"Of course." Though he still smiled, Kilcannon's tone was softer. "When I was twenty-eight I was married, and even more clueless than I am now. As Meg could tell you."

It was his first reference to his wife, Lara realized; though amiable enough, it revealed little. "Does *she* want you to be President?" she asked.

"Meg?" he answered. "With her, it's an obsession. Some girls grow up wanting to be Miss America, or maybe an astronaut. Meg's fantasy is to be First Lady. No sacrifice is too great—including me."

Lara smiled politely. The tongue-in-cheek response was so preposterous that she saw it as a matter of hiding in plain sight: because everyone knew that the Kilcannons had a commuter marriage, Kilcannon was well prepared to duck any questions this might raise. But understanding the recesses of his life was part of her job. "So she doesn't," Lara persisted.

Kilcannon shrugged. "Would you? Like Meg, you've got your own life. It's part of what makes politics so hard."

This was going nowhere, Lara realized; his defenses were far too good to be pierced by yet another curious reporter. And perhaps the truth was no more complex than that of a hundred other congressional marriages, built on compromises between men and women who balanced their separate lives with a life together. Only the absence of children made the Kilcannons' marriage less usual, and there was no simple way to probe that.

"Anyhow," Lara said, "that's one reason I became a journalist and not a lawyer. So I could help out."

"And you're still sending money home."

She nodded. "For a while. My youngest sister, Tiffany, starts college next year."

"Tiffany Costello," Kilcannon repeated with a smile. "Is there *really* a Saint Tiffany?"

"Her middle name is Joan—as in 'of Arc,' so we're covered." Lara sipped her wine. "My mom has a weakness for the movies. When I was born, she'd just seen *Doctor Zhivago*. So she named me Lara, after the woman with whom he has this heartbreaking affair." Putting down the wineglass, Lara smiled. "With what my dad did later on, she probably wished she'd named me Hester Prynne."

"Gloomier book," Kilcannon answered. "Worse movie."

Dinner arrived. As he offered her a portion of his calamari, accepting a little of her tuna in exchange, the waiter brought an extra glass of wine for both of them. "So," Kilcannon said, "I still don't know how you became a journalist."

Sitting back, Lara took in the light and shadow of the restaurant, felt the glow of the wine. "Just everything else about me."

"Yeah. I thought I'd finish up."

Lara rolled her eyes. " 'How I Became a Journalist,' by Lara Costello. 'I became a journalist because . . .' "

"Yes?"

"Because when I was small I liked to read—everything, even the newspaper. Naturally, that meant I was the 'smart one.'

So our parish priest in San Francisco helped me get a scholarship to one of the best schools in the city, Convent of the Sacred Heart, right through twelfth grade. With only girls in class, I developed a very rich fantasy life, with me at the center. The school encouraged me to sublimate through writing." She smiled. "In between writing bad short stories and imagining I was Gabriel García Márquez, I became the star of the school newspaper. In the end, reality beat out fantasy."

"Are you sure?" Kilcannon said lightly. "Or have you just found a way to combine them?"

Lara shook her head. "Writing fiction usually doesn't pay. When you've got no money, you know things like that. Even in high school."

"So you don't wish you could go back, do something else?"

"No. I like journalism a lot. If I 'went back' anywhere, it might be to where I started."

Kilcannon put down his fork. "Why? You've got a great job here."

"But that's Beltway thinking, isn't it?" She had talked too much already, Lara thought, and to a nominal adversary, one she barely knew. But that was part of it, she told herself: properly managed, a friendship with Kerry Kilcannon would be a good thing for any reporter to have. "I think politics is important," she went on. "And the *Times* is the best. Those are reasons to be here. But another reason is that, with my background, it felt counterintuitive to turn down a promotion."

"What would you rather do?"

"Maybe something more about people and what they need, not just politicians." Lara finished the last glass of wine. "When I first worked for the *Chronicle*, I did a series on migrant workers—I speak fluent Spanish, so it helped. I wrote about the conditions in the fields, and now the UFW is coming back again.

"It got attention for *me*, too, and a state journalism award. The only problem is, four years later, it's still the work I'm proudest of."

Saying this, Lara realized it was so. She felt Kilcannon watch her across the table. "If that's true," he said after a time, "you won't want it to be true four years from now. It seems you've done enough for other people."

To her surprise, the simple statement touched her. Was he also talking about himself? she wondered. Then came a more unsettling thought: that she had enjoyed Kerry Kilcannon's company more than she had her recent run of male friends. In combination, they had been too young, too anxious about their careers, too horny for what Lara could manage to feel for them. It was odd that she seemed more comfortable with a well-known senator, except that he felt more comfortable with himself. And, married, was not a problem *that* way.

"It's nice," she told him, "to be absolved of the sin of selfishness."

This made him smile again. When the waiter came with the check, Lara felt surprised.

"Let me," she said.

Kilcannon shook his head. "It's all covered by campaign funds," he assured her. "From foreign donors."

"A story," Lara answered. "At last."

Leaving the restaurant, they stopped on the curb outside. The air was balmy, with a hint of rain to come.

"Can I give you a ride?" Kilcannon asked.

The thought of asking for anything more set off an internal alarm in Lara, renewing the fear that she had lost her distance. "No," she answered. "I can take a cab. You've had a long day already." She held out her hand. "Thank you, Senator. I really enjoyed my orientation. Dinner too."

Kilcannon gave a mock wince. "Kerry," he said. "And whatever you decide, Lara, good luck."

FOUR

The next time Lara spent any real time with him was in August 1996, at the Democratic convention in San Diego.

Lara had never covered a convention before, and her reaction ranged between amazement and amusement. Around the modern convention center there was security everywhere—cops on motorcycles, streets blocked off, cars being checked for explosives. Outside, anti-abortion demonstrators kept a constant vigil, denouncing the delegates as "murderers." Inside the hall was another world altogether, insulated and surreal: balloons and banks of klieg lights hanging from the rafters; skyboxes for the networks—NBC, ABC, CBS, Fox, CNN, C-SPAN; hospitality suites for major donors and lobbyists, awash in liquor and canapés, come to watch the hollow spectacle like Romans at a triumph. And it was hollow, Lara wrote; the mass of delegates hugged each other and traded addresses like any conventioneers, half listening to empty rhetoric about the "party of prosperity for all." The only purpose was to recoronate the President and Dick Mason with as little fuss as possible; the only problem was Kerry Kilcannon.

She saw him on the convention floor, surrounded by delegates who wanted to shake his hand, to get an autograph, or simply to touch him. The electricity surrounding him reflected Dick Mason's well-known belief: that Kerry was positioning himself to fight Mason for the presidential nomination in four years' time. The Vice President's minions had already punished the New Jersey delegation for Kerry's anticipated sins in the petty, telling ways through which an incumbent could play hardball: bad hotel rooms, well away from the convention hall;

limited invitations to parties and outside events; cramped meeting rooms.

But Kerry's immediate sin was his refusal to submit any speech he might give to Mason's handlers for approval. The result was that—unless Kerry relented—he was scheduled to speak for no more than ten minutes late Tuesday night, well after the network coverage had stopped. It was, as Nate Cutler quipped to Lara, "a special place in media purgatory."

Now, as Kerry approached, she darted between two delegates and confronted him, tape recorder in hand.

Kerry gave her a sardonic grin, then gazed up at the skyboxes. "Like a trough for special interests, isn't it? Imagine the migrant workers they could feed."

As was often true with him, Lara thought, beneath the irony lurked a more serious point. "I hear you're staying at a Motel Six, Senator. In Tijuana."

He laughed with what seemed genuine amusement. "Only until they find us something worse."

You don't mind this, Lara thought suddenly. *You think Mason looks scared, and you enjoy being an underdog.* "Do you attribute that to the Vice President?"

Kerry looked up at the four-sided screen hanging over the convention floor, magnifying the images the President's convention managers wished to showcase. The image of the moment was Dick Mason, seated in a VIP section with Jeannie and their three children, waving to people on the floor below, his face alight with pleasure. Kerry's own expression was quizzical. "Why should I?" he answered. "I can't imagine that the Vice President of the United States has time to worry about room reservations, can you?"

The question had a subversive innocence, Lara thought; it could be taken either at face value, as a gracious dismissal, or as a tacit comment on the emptiness of the office and the pettiness of the man. "Really," she said, "don't you think that your problems over speaking time have to do with the year 2000?"

Kilcannon still gazed up at Dick Mason's enormous electronic head. "Is Big Brother watching me, you mean?" He looked at Lara, then spoke in a different voice, more serious. "If this were only about hotel rooms, or personal ambitions, I'd have stayed home."

"What *is* it about?"

"Issues. The President and Vice President have an election to win, and I'm here to support that effort. It's just that sometimes there are differing priorities. I didn't go into politics just to hold an office, or secure a place on prime-time television. People expect better."

"Have you said that to the Vice President?"

"Oh, I think he understands." Kilcannon smiled, adding, "It's nice to see you again." And then he was off, shaking more hands, talking into a microphone shoved at his face. It was only much later, when they truly knew each other, that Kerry told her about his meeting with Dick Mason, an hour before she saw him.

At Mason's request, the meeting was private, without aides.

They sat in Mason's suite, two blocks from the convention hall, late-afternoon sun falling on the bright floral displays sent by numerous well-wishers. Kerry looked around him at the flowers. "Did you die, Dick? No one told me. And you look so natural."

Mason gave a good-humored laugh; his blue eyes, crinkling with amusement, signaled his appreciation at Kerry's sense of humor, his fondness for Kerry himself. "It comes from clean living, Kerry. And short commutes."

"Yes," Kerry said lightly. "Sorry to be late. It's rush hour in Tucson." He sat across from Mason. "So here we are, like a pair of scorpions, and for what?"

The Vice President sat back, hands folded, gazing at Kerry with disarming candor. "The President and I want a unified party. After that, I may want to be President myself. I'd rather have you as an ally than an adversary."

"But first," Kerry responded, "you thought you'd get my attention."

Mason smiled again, though now his eyes did not. "There are thousands of delegates to satisfy, dozens of governors and congressmen and senators clamoring for a prime-time slot. And you're the only one who insists on saying whatever he pleases, rather than playing your part in a coordinated message."

Kerry met his gaze. "Dick," he answered, "I don't need to speak at all. And you don't need *me* to read whatever part of the message you had in mind—'reinventing welfare,' was it? Especially when I don't believe in it."

Mason leaned forward; he had a thousand postures and expressions, Kerry thought, to signal how much a particular conversation engaged him. "We *do* need you. You've become a strong voice in the Senate. You represent a legacy . . ."

"Ah, that."

"Yes, *that*. Your support carries a great symbolic power." Mason's voice became soft, sincere. "When I first ran for Congress, your brother campaigned for me. I had a deep admiration for him, as I do for you. And I'm sure that Jamie would have muted whatever differences there are."

Despite himself, Kerry felt stung; there would always be a part of him that felt inferior to Jamie, that doubted his own instincts. It made him squirm that Dick was shrewd enough to see this, even as he resented Mason's inherent condescension—the belief that this knowledge would change what Kerry did.

"But I'm not Jamie." Pausing, Kerry tried, for once, to reach Mason on a deeper level. "When I took his place, I knew I couldn't be Jamie. All I could do was take this terrible accident and give it some kind of meaning, in the way that seemed best to me.

"If I'd wanted this life, yes—maybe what you're saying would make sense to me. But when you try to use Jamie to make me shrivel, all it proves is that you don't know me at all."

There was the first flicker of doubt in Mason's eyes, the fear that an unblinking knowledge of his own motives could not help him grasp Kerry's. "Look," Mason said in a reasonable tone, "we all know campaign finance is a terrible problem. But the other party's worse; until we fix it, every dime we raise is in self-defense. And what about our union friends, and all the money *they* raise to run ads on our behalf? For you to challenge our fund-raising in a convention speech, when we need *more* money for November, is like cutting our balls off with a butter knife."

"How do you know," Kerry retorted, "that they're not already missing?" When Mason flushed, angry for the first time, Kerry held up his hand. "You're about to step in it, Dick. Your people are so hungry to raise cash that they've stopped caring how they get it or where it comes from. You're going to wake up some morning and find Saddam Hussein sleeping between you and Jeannie.

"Voters already think we're on the take—that the way we raise money is a slightly more elegant version of the kind of bribery I saw in Newark. When are we going to find the guts to change that?" Kerry lowered his voice. "If we don't change things soon, Dick, what does it matter *who* becomes President? Except maybe to you."

Mason stared at him. "That's easy to say," he responded, "from the shelter of a safe Senate seat. It's harder when you want to run the government, and the alternative is turning it over to Bible thumpers and reactionaries." He paused a moment. "Who do you want to be, my friend? Jerry Brown, wearing denim shirts and sniping from the sidelines, a popgun in the wilderness? Or someone who helps make the hard decisions, with the wisdom to know how hard they really are?"

Mason gathered his thoughts, his tone reasonable again, avuncular. "I *will* win the nomination in 2000, Kerry—no sitting Vice President has lost one, ever. The question is whether you force me to marginalize you to protect my interests, or start asking yourself a *better* question."

"And what's that?"

The Vice President smiled slightly. " 'When Dick Mason becomes President, who takes *his* place?' "

Silent, Kerry studied him, a pleasant-faced man imploring Kerry to be as practical as he. Detaching himself, Kerry had a second, sadder image—two men of decent intentions, trapped in mutual incomprehension, who might be led by circumstance to tear each other apart. *I don't want this,* Kerry thought, but it did not serve his interests, or the things he believed in, to take the pressure off now.

"I'm sorry," Kerry said. "And I appreciate your candor. But I'll take my place with *Nick at Nite*. Or whenever you've got me scheduled."

Frowning, Mason shook his head. "I'm sorry too, Kerry. For both our sakes. But four years is a long time."

"It is that."

They stood, shaking hands, and then Kerry heard the door open.

Turning, he saw Jeannie Mason in a smart blue suit that matched her eyes, her blond hair newly cut. She smiled at Kerry with unaffected warmth.

"Hello, Kerry." She walked over, kissing him on the cheek, and then leaned back to look into his face. "I haven't seen you since the last time you refused to take me away from all this. How *are* you?"

Kerry returned her smile. "Fine. Morphing into Jerry Brown, Dick tells me."

Jeannie grinned; even in her mid-forties, she reminded Kerry of a homecoming queen with a wicked sense of humor. "Jerry Brown?" she asked. "I don't think I've ever heard of him."

Kerry found himself laughing. "That was Dick's point, actually."

"It's the convention," Jeannie said cheerfully. "It brings out the best in everyone." Her smile narrowed. "Is Meg here?"

"No. At home."

Dick stood beside them, seemingly amused. But Jeannie's eyes became serious and, Kerry thought, kind. "In my next life," Jeannie said to him, "I want Meg's deal."

Kerry smiled again. "I'll tell her that." But when he left, heading for the convention hall, what he felt was not worry about his future, or even about what he would say tomorrow. It was envy of Dick Mason, and a piercing loneliness.

FIVE

The next morning, Kerry spoke to three different delegations before nine o'clock, promising to campaign for statewide candidates in the fall. Lara followed him—at each stop, he made a mocking reference to himself as "the convention's answer to Conan O'Brien," a veiled jab at Mason which drew chuckles from his audience.

If Kerry wasn't preparing to run for President, Lara thought, he was doing more than enough to make Mason nervous: Kerry was highly visible, the most popular figure on the convention floor, and his schedule was jammed with meetings with delegates and party leaders from around the country. There was about him the crackle of prospective candidacy—the frenetic pace, well covered by the media; two aides to keep him on time and remind him of names; the burst of applause from bystanders in the lobby when he emerged from the Hyatt; even the air of cheerful defiance he carried from place to place. Despite her posture of detachment, Lara felt disappointed and a little cynical. His air of coyness was a ruse, she was coming to believe; Kerry was doing what any ambitious politician did at a party's convention—simply better.

All of which, to Lara, made the absence of Meg Kilcannon more striking. Politics was a viciously public business, and never more so than at a convention, where appearances are paramount, rumors fair game, one politician's weakness another's target of opportunity. Everywhere Kilcannon went, Lara saw some operative for Mason watching from the crowd; everywhere the Vice President went—and his schedule was equally busy—his attractive wife was with him. With the growing sense of barely concealed conflict, it was inevitable that the comparison harmed Kerry. "Where's his wife?" Lara heard a woman delegate from Texas ask. "We need a candidate with a *family*, not just an *arrangement*."

At nine-thirty, Lara saw Kerry emerge from another meeting at the Hyatt, his fourth of the day, and murmur something to one of his aides.

The young man, seemingly startled, began to remonstrate about the senator's commitments. Kerry stilled him with a long, cool look and then said pleasantly, "So call me the defiant one, all right? But I'm going."

Kerry hurried off, pursued by Lara.

"Going where?" she asked.

He turned to her. "Watsonville," he said over his shoulder. "Want to come along?"

Lara was startled. Watsonville was about five hundred miles north, in the farm country near Salinas; she knew of it only because of her series on migrant workers. "Why are you going *there*?" she asked.

"To impress you, of course." He pushed open the glass door and stood on the sidewalk amidst the palm trees and bright morning sun, hands shoved in his pockets, looking for a limousine. "There's a United Farm Workers rally. The president of the UFW phoned yesterday, and I've decided that's where I want to be."

"What about your schedule?"

Restless, he scanned the line of black Town Cars. "What are a few offended delegates? It's a perfect chance to firm up my credentials as a centrist." He turned to her, eyes serious now. "Think what you want, Lara—the press always does. But there's not a single major politician from our party who's agreed to come. Besides, I was suffocating in there."

So *that* was what he was thinking about last night, gazing up at the luxury boxes. *Like a trough for special interests,* he had murmured. *Imagine the migrant workers they could feed.* But whether this sudden trip was an act of impulse, conscience, or politics—or some uneasy combination—Lara could not guess.

A Town Car pulled up in front of them, and a driver popped out. "So," Kerry asked her, "are you coming?"

He was serious, Lara realized. "I'll have to call my editor."

The driver opened a rear door for them. "You can do it from the car," Kerry answered.

An hour later, they were flying north in a small private jet, alone in a rear cabin that shuddered with the fearful grinding of the engine. Unknotting his tie, Kerry grinned. " 'Free at last.' "

He seemed lighthearted, Lara thought, caught up in a great carelessness that made him look even younger than he was—the school rebel, cutting religion class to go to a Yankees game. "So you're dropping out," she asked, "like Dustin Hoffman in *The Graduate*?"

He laughed. "The Costello women have this thing about movies, don't they?" He settled back in his seat, sipping from a bottle of cranberry juice. "You know where I was scheduled to go for lunch? A party for delegates given by a tobacco company, on John Wayne's old yacht. Am I missing something here, or didn't the Duke die of lung cancer? It certainly wasn't hostile fire."

Lara smiled. "Freed up his yacht, though."

"Yup. The problem with the tobacco folks is they have no sense of irony. And now they're selling to kids and the third world to make up for the fact that their clientele is, quite literally, dying off. 'Death—our most inconvenient by-product.' " Smile fading, he added softly, "That way they can afford a few more politicians. Campaigns are expensive, so we don't come cheap."

His mordant comment, the sudden change of mood, seemed the hallmark of some unspoken thought. But Lara no longer found this disconcerting. Together, they gazed out the oval windows at the low mountains of coastal California, golden brown in summer. "So," she asked after a time, "why *are* you doing this?"

He continued to inspect the terrain, a silent landscape beneath the snarl of the engine. "There's been so little idealism," he said at last. "The nineties are light-years away from the days of Cesar Chavez, when farmworkers were a romantic cause. People want grapes, people eat them.

"The farmworkers are struggling. Agribusiness still exploits them, and the canning industry whipsaws factory workers by threatening to move across the border. Just as you wrote in your articles."

"You read them?"

"Nexus is a wonderful thing, isn't it." Kerry turned to her. "They were good—accurate too. Four years later, conditions are hardly better. But so few of us seem to care."

Lara felt surprise mingle with skepticism. She was used to politicians—males, particularly—saying fulsome things about her astuteness. But if Kerry was trying to flatter her, he was going to extraordinary lengths.

"You know what some people will write," she told him. "That you're preparing for a run at Mason in the California primary. Trying to build some sort of minority coalition."

Kerry sighed audibly. "And others will say I'm reckless. The problem with being in politics is that you're not entitled to be believed, even if you have beliefs." He turned to her again. "Is that what *you're* writing, Lara?"

She looked at him levelly. "I'm keeping an open mind."

He studied her for a moment. His eyes, Lara realized, were his most arresting feature; they seemed to take her in, though Lara was not sure what she read there. "Oh, well," he said. "It really doesn't matter."

"Then why did you ask me to come?"

Kerry hesitated and then smiled. "If I hadn't," he asked, "would the *Times* have covered this?"

Or you, Lara thought. But she was no longer confident that his motives were so transparent, or even simple—his invitation had seemed as impulsive as the trip. "Maybe not," she answered.

He gave a curt nod and began staring out the window again.

"About the President thing," he said after a while. "First more Latinos have to vote. They haven't been, enough."

The plane began slipping downward, its motor slowly quieting. Until they landed, neither spoke.

The rally took place in a barren patch of field near Watsonville—dusty and arid, reminding Lara of a Steinbeck novel—with fields of strawberries in the distance, the pickers in white shirts barely visible in the shimmer of hot sunlight. The crowd was light, only a few thousand workers and young people braving the searing heat which beat down on Lara, making her regret that she was wearing a dress and panty hose instead of jeans. But in her compassion for the farmworkers, and her interest in Kerry Kilcannon, she felt gratified to have escaped the air-conditioned cavern of the convention—the well-fed delegates, the innocuous soft-pop music on the PA system, the endless jockeying for advantage.

Perhaps, she thought, this was how Kerry felt. Standing in shirtsleeves with the union leaders, he looked curiously at home, with none of the awkwardness of a politician visiting foreign territory. Though his presence had drawn more local media, he was careful to cede center stage to the union leader, Raul Guerrero. When it became Kerry's time to speak, his words were simple.

"I'm here," he began, "because it is right to be here.

"Farmworkers need better wages. They need more water in the fields, proper sanitation. They need medical care, and retirement, and the simple right to bargain. The things which give work dignity.

"Their children need schooling. They need proper health facilities, and the hope of a better life. The things which make their parents' work worth doing."

Pausing, Kerry scanned the crowd. "For too long, we've allowed the exploitation of immigrants—legal or otherwise—by businesses in search of profits and politicians in search of votes. But if our history proves anything, it's that those who speak to the best in us defeat those who speak to the worst in us.

"Those who've come here today already know that. If we *each* do what we're able to do—organize, boycott, send money, call our leaders to account—there'll be more of us tomorrow, and next month we'll be that much closer . . ."

When his speech was over, Kerry slipped into the crowd, not merely shaking hands now but listening and talking, alternating English with awkward Spanish. To Lara, he seemed liberated, free from the politician's tyranny of schedule and repetition. But there was also this, Lara thought again: if he was ever to run against Mason, he would need to turn out minority voters, the people Mason did not seem to reach. And nowhere was this more true than in California.

It was not until five-thirty that Kerry found her again. "Come on," he said, smiling. "I've got another speech to give. In San Diego."

SIX

Four hours later, at nine-thirty, Kerry Kilcannon walked to the podium.

It was half past midnight in the East; the network television coverage had ceased hours before. Watching from the press section with Nate Cutler and Lee McAlpine, Lara could see that the delegates were tired. But no one knew what Kilcannon would say, and his surprise visit to the UFW rally seemed to have stirred emotions deadened by a litany of platitudes so numbing that, as Lee had remarked, "you can hear television sets clicking off all over America." By setting himself apart, Lara sensed, Kerry symbolized what many delegates were craving—daring, conviction, spontaneity. What was harder for her to grasp was how much of this was calculated.

"Ker-ry . . ."

It began as a ragged chant from the New Jersey delegation, slowly spreading.

"Ker-ry . . ."

More rose to their feet now. With a diffident smile, Kerry held up his hand, signaling the crowd to stop.

"Ker-ry, Ker-ry, Ker-ry . . ."

"Please," he called out. "People are trying to sleep . . ."

There was a wave of laughter. From where Lara sat, Kerry was a distant figure, but his smile flashed brighter on the screen above her. "Seriously," he added, "I'd like to thank you for staying up with me . . ."

More laughter. Next to Lara, Lee McAlpine smiled. "Maybe he should thank Dick Mason," she murmured.

Kerry held up his hand again. "I've got ten minutes," he said wryly, "and then they turn off the lights. So I'll try to be succinct.

"I'm here to support the President and Vice President. They deserve all the commitment we can offer. And I will do everything in my power to help ensure their reelection."

Waiting, Kerry let the applause build, the sense of reassurance, and then said crisply, "But I also want to talk about the future."

"Well," Lara said, "so much for fervent praise."

Kerry's face was intent now. "There is a terrible disconnect in this country. People don't trust their leaders. They believe we manipulate their emotions and lie about their problems.

"Too often, they're right."

The crowd was still now—surprised, Lara thought, and engaged.

"The *other* party's great lie," Kerry said sardonically, "is that if you cut welfare, foreign aid, and the National Endowment for the Arts, you'll have a balanced budget and a better life. And if that doesn't work, you just tighten the screws on immigrants.

"*Our* time-honored deception has been that if you tax the rich and cut the defense budget, you can save Medicare and Social Security without any cost to anyone else.

"More and more people realize that those things aren't so. But they don't believe we have a program for change. They're no longer sure what we stand for."

Nate whistled softly. The delegates from Connecticut—Mason's people—seemed suddenly restive. But Lara could feel the feedback growing, Kerry touching his audience.

"If this party deserves to lead," Kerry went on, "we must embrace certain truths which separate a compassionate society from one that is selfish and complacent:

"That racial discrimination still exists, and that we need the courage to challenge it, and to end it.

"That gay men and women are not on a crusade to change the

behavior of others, and that protecting them from violence and discrimination is moral, not immoral."

The delegates were rapt, gazing up at Kerry. Around Lara, the reporters had fallen silent.

Kerry's voice became staccato. "That guns are too available, and kill far too many people.

"That too many children are denied proper medical care and a proper education.

"That too many of their parents are trapped in dead-end jobs.

"That too many lives are warped by violence, inside and outside our families.

"That too much of our prosperity is built on low wages and shattered dreams.

"That, in the end, *we* are a family, charged by decency and self-interest to care about every American."

Though he spoke to thousands, Kerry's tone became direct, intimate. To Lara, his cadence gave no sense of a speaker waiting for applause. "No issue," he continued, "is more bitterly divisive than abortion. Yet it seems to me that this is a prime example of the narrowing of our minds and the hardening of our hearts.

"To our opponents, who have made their position a litmus test of decency, and yet would cut programs for our poorest children and our most endangered adults, I quote Joseph Cardinal Bernardin: 'Those who would defend the right to life of the weakest among us must be equally visible in defending the quality of life of the powerless among us, the old and the young, the hungry and the homeless, the undocumented immigrant and the unemployed worker.'

"And for those of us who defend all women's right to choose, I say this: we must also give women the choice of having children who, because we care, will have a lifetime of choices.

"Maybe," Kerry went on, "if we not only say these things, but act on them, we will regain the trust we've lost. But we will never be free to act on them unless we face one more fact—that the way we raise campaign money is hopelessly corrupt."

Pausing, Kerry gazed up at the skyboxes and luxury suites, and then his voice cracked like a whip. "How can we inspire trust," he demanded, "when the best we can say for ourselves is that the other party's worse? No wonder people are so fed up."

The audience was silent—startled, Lara thought, by his bluntness, the implicit demand that the President and Mason take the lead. Kerry stood straighter, scanning the convention floor. "Half of our citizens have already stopped voting." Now Kerry's voice became cutting, angry. "What else do they need to tell us? How much more clearly can they spell out their despair?

"It's about *freedom*, the special interests say. But how many of *you* are 'free' to spend ten thousand dollars to influence a political party?

"This is the freedom to corrupt, and it is slowly destroying our democracy."

"Well," Lee murmured. "He's off the reservation now."

"Ending it," Kerry went on, "is a moral imperative. And the beginning of the end is a constitutional amendment which says, 'Nothing in the Constitution shall prohibit Congress from passing laws to regulate the funding of campaigns for federal office.'

"Pass this amendment, and the lobbyists and politicians will have no place to hide, no excuse to offer. And if they oppose it, we have the right to know what reforms they offer in its place."

The proposal was another surprise, at least to Lara, and a gamble; to many, amending the Constitution would seem too radical and too difficult. But on the screen, she saw a black woman in the Illinois delegation mouthing the word "yes."

Kerry's tone became passionate, imploring. "In our party's past," he said, "there is much to be proud of. But we can only be proud of our future if we give Americans back their government.

"I ask all of you to join me in that effort . . ."

There was a moment's silence, and then the applause began, echoing to the rafters, delegates clapping, stomping their feet, standing on chairs to acclaim a party leader who—for at least this moment, long after most Americans were sleeping—had transformed their convention. After several minutes, it showed no sign of ending.

"Impressive," Lee McAlpine said. "And it was actually about something."

Nate looked at his watch, timing the applause. "He'd better enjoy it now," he remarked. "Mason will cut his throat, if he can. And if Kilcannon wants to run, where's the money coming from?"

Lee turned to him. "Of course he's running, and he'll find the money somewhere. He's got the name, after all."

It was more than the name, Lara thought. As she remembered him, James Kilcannon had been handsome, elegant, cautious. Kerry was the passionate one, the dangerous one, the Kilcannon who might change the party and challenge the system, perhaps destroying himself in the process. If he decided to run for President, she had begun to think, he would be driven as much by his emotions as by cool cerebration. Watching him, a slight figure in a maelstrom of his own creation, Lara felt a new and puzzling emotion of her own—fear for Kerry Kilcannon.

"*Maybe* he's running," she told her colleagues. "But I'm not sure he'll know more than a minute before we do."

For the next two days, Kerry was back in rhythm again, doing a steady stream of appearances and interviews, while Lara waited her turn. Reading the press reports, she saw that he had developed a mantra: "I have no plans to run in the year 2000. My speech was about policies, not personalities, and I expect to help the President and Vice President have a successful second term." Which was what he told Lara Thursday night, with a palpable air of weariness and boredom.

They were in a pressroom off the convention hall. The President and Mason had just given their acceptance speeches, carefully crafted to minimize risk, and the conventioneers were straggling from the hall in an atmosphere of anticlimax, like air leaking from a balloon. "Really?" Lara answered. "You damned near stole the convention."

He gave a reticent shrug, as if tired of talking about himself. "Then that's a sad commentary, isn't it."

"But suppose you *do* decide to run," she persisted. "Later on. If you have to raise millions of dollars, won't that create a credibility problem? And won't all the special-interest money go to Mason now, for sure?"

Kerry gave her a sideways look. "What makes you think I care?"

"Because you have to. You didn't win New Jersey twice because you're a virgin. What about all the donations from the trial lawyers and the teachers unions?"

Kerry's eyes flashed. "I guess that defines me, doesn't it?" He paused, then told her in a flat voice, "The press is such a safe place. You sit on the sidelines, where everything we do is cynical and self-serving, and the only risk is believing anything we say." He stood abruptly, hands shoved in his pockets, looking down at her. "You were right a few years ago, Lara. Write about 'real people,' not us. That way *you* can be real, too."

Stung, Lara felt an anger of her own. "If you don't want to answer questions tonight, just say so."

Kerry stared at her intently, and then his shoulders slumped. "I'm sorry," he said. "That wasn't fair."

Lara's anger subsided; in its place she felt exposed, disconcerted by the hurt his words had caused, puzzled that they bothered her at all.

"Just walk with me awhile," he asked her. "Okay?"

Without waiting for an answer, Kerry left the room; Lara hesitated, then followed.

Silent, they passed the hospitality suites on the mezzanine, walking among the last wave of lobbyists and delegates and politicians. Briefly, an aging, bespectacled congressman from Pennsylvania took Kerry aside. Lara watched Kerry listen intently, studying the congressman's face, then touching him on the shoulder.

"What was that?" Lara asked when he returned.

Kerry shrugged. "He wants my help this fall. He's in trouble in his district, and he's scared. You can always see it in their eyes." His voice held both compassion and puzzlement, Lara thought; there were worse things than losing office, it suggested, and Kerry had seen some of them.

Leaving the hall, they stepped into the balmy subtropic air. Beneath the full moon, a clump of anti-abortion demonstrators stood sentinel, holding signs with pictures of aborted babies, blurred mercifully by the semidarkness.

"I can't imagine it," Kerry murmured.

"Abortion?"

"It would be so hard, I think. Knowing that *my* child . . ."

His voice trailed off. Lara turned to him. "It wouldn't be just you, though."

He did not answer. They walked among the great hotels, grids of light in a cloud-streaked sky. After some time, they found a bench on the wooden pier, in the shadows of chartered yachts. Kerry gazed across the harbor, a pool of ink, listening as the sounds of the last parties mingled with the lapping water.

"If you really care to know," he said at length, "I'll tell you what I think I'm doing. Off the record."

Lara nodded.

"Mason's a tactical politician," Kerry went on. "He reacts to pressure, not to core beliefs. If I reach people he's not reaching, maybe he'll begin taking campaign reform and the inner cities more seriously, just to head me off. I'll have moved the party without ever having to run."

"Do you think you can?"

"Perhaps." Kerry's gaze remained fixed on some middle distance. "The problem with confrontation is picking the right issues. Or else I'm just a nasty little Irishman who likes a fight. I don't want that."

There was a hint of self-doubt in his voice, Lara thought— perhaps the worry that he liked a fight too much. "But you think campaign reform's a 'right issue.' "

"Yes. These people plan to win by not running on anything. That creates an agenda vacuum, and what flows into political vacuums tends to be scandal—in this case, the way they're raising money." Kerry smiled. "By this time next year, with a little help from friends like me, Dick's going to be a dedicated reformer. Especially if you folks do your job."

It was a much cooler analysis than Lara had expected. "But a constitutional amendment . . ."

"Is like pushing a boulder uphill, and tomorrow all the law professors will be screaming bloody murder. But if nothing else happens, *it* could. So let's see what the President and Dick come up with, and whether—if they do—the Supreme Court finds it constitutional." His tone became ironic. "Those justices may pretend to be virgins too, but they read the papers like anyone else. The threat of an amendment might prod them a little."

Lara watched his profile, reflective and quite still. "What if Mason doesn't respond?" she asked.

"He has to have *some* sort of record. Otherwise what's his rationale for running—'It's *my* turn'?" Kerry faced her. "The world's full of former statesmen who used to be unbeatable. Dick's people are getting lazy in office—smug, slow to act, protective of their own turf. I'm not sure how they'd do against a grassroots campaign run by community activists, plugged into their own states, who believe in what they're doing."

Lara met his eyes. "And in what *you'd* be saying. It would have to be you, wouldn't it? There isn't anyone else."

Turning, Kerry gazed at the dock, eyes hooded. In his quiet, Lara heard the ocean swirl beneath them, splashing the wooden legs of the pier. "By then there may be others, Lara. In four years, who knows what happens to any of us." His tone was pensive. "Becoming President was Jamie's dream. It doesn't have to be mine."

Once more, Lara thought, she heard the echo of self-doubt and wondered, in spite of his denials, whether the line between his brother's life and Kerry's own was quite so clear to him. Feeling his reflectiveness, she nerved herself to pose the other question that remained.

"What about your wife, Kerry? Does she figure in here?"

Kerry gave her a level look. She sensed him preparing his stock answer: that like many couples of their generation, they had their own careers and their own lives. And then he turned away. "Oh," he said softly, "if I'm inaugurated, I expect she'll come."

SEVEN

Two months later, Liam Dunn died, the victim, as Kerry's father had been, of a sudden, massive heart attack.

He had risen early, Kerry's mother told him, for his usual walk around Vailsburg, surveying the parks and the conditions of the streets, the empty houses or those that were declining, along, perhaps, with the families who lived there. As on every day, the walk had ended at Sacred Heart, where Liam asked God for the wisdom to be a decent man in a complex world. And then Liam had driven downtown, to party headquarters, and died at his desk.

"What better way?" his mother asked simply.

"No better," Kerry answered. But when he put down the telephone, he asked that his calls be held, and he sat alone in his office in the Senate, his brother's before him, the place Liam Dunn had secured.

You understand politics well enough, Kerry. I raised you to. But you've never understood just how much you can do.

Slowly, Kerry Kilcannon shook his head, feeling the hole in his heart . . .

Something seemed to move in Liam's eyes. "Your mother . . ."

Kerry could not look at him. He felt Liam's large hand on his shoulder. "If you want to fight, Kerry, then you need to learn how . . ."

For a moment, vivid as yesterday, Kerry was a boy again, afraid of his father, fearing for his mother, as lonely as Senator Kerry Kilcannon felt now.

Ah, Liam. When was the last time I picked up the phone to call you? Three weeks ago?

Tears filled Kerry's eyes.

You had sons of your own, so I could never say how much I loved you. Did you know that? Do you know it now?

Resting his forehead on clasped hands, Kerry closed his eyes. The world around him vanished.

When his intercom rang, he started. Angry, he grabbed the telephone.

"I'm sorry to interrupt you," his receptionist said. "But Ms. Costello's here. She'll only take a moment, she says."

Kerry was still.

"Kerry?"

"Yes. Send her in."

He composed himself, staring at the door. When Lara entered, she took a few steps forward and then stopped, fingers resting on the back of a chair. Her eyes were grave, he saw; she made no move to sit.

"What is it?" he asked.

She drew a breath. "I saw the news come over the wire. About your friend Liam Dunn." Her tone was neither impersonal nor presumptuous. "I was coming to the Hill, and I just wanted to tell you I was sorry."

He was not prepared, Kerry realized. Not even for the simple words, or the look on Lara's face—compassionate, all sense of probing gone.

"Thank you," he managed to say. "It's hard, I'm finding."

Lara nodded. "I've never lost anyone. Not that way."

She must mean her father, Kerry realized. Perhaps, too, she was thinking of Jamie.

She tilted her head, studying him, plainly hesitant. "Well," she said, "I guess I should go."

Belatedly, Kerry stood. "I appreciate it. Really."

She gave him a first faint smile. "I understand."

The door closed softly behind her.

He had needed her to leave, Kerry thought. But the office was too quiet now, and he felt lonelier than before.

Palms on the desk, he stared down at the green desk blotter. There was much to do, he told himself. Call Liam's widow, then his oldest son. Find out the funeral arrangements and what help they needed. And then, of course, tell Meg he was coming home.

Kerry did those things. Then he sat at his desk and, after many cross-outs and erasures, drafted a brief statement—the words a senator should say on the death of a party leader.

When they held the service for Liam Dunn, Lara went with the local *Times* reporter. Liam Dunn had been an important man in New Jersey politics, and Kerry Kilcannon's mentor; surely, the *Times* believed, there was a story in his passing and, perhaps, the passing of an era.

Sacred Heart was overflowing as it had not been for years. There were floral displays from friends and local merchants, even one from a tavern in County Roscommon. The mayor and the governor sat in the first pew, as did several congressmen. Next to Liam's family was Senator Kerry Kilcannon, with a gaunt, handsome woman Lara recognized as his mother and a pert, pretty one with auburn hair—his wife, Lara assumed. Meg did not seem to speak, Lara noticed, nor did she turn to console her husband.

The priest's tribute was warm, as were the eulogies given by Kerry and by Liam's oldest son, a bluff, graying Irishman whose part it was to speak of Liam the husband and father. When Kerry rose, it was to recall the public man.

"In Vailsburg," Kerry said with a smile, "we all counted on Liam Dunn to do the best for us. And in *my* case, he outdid himself."

There was a ripple of laughter, an appreciation of Irish self-deprecation and, more than that, the common memory of what Liam had meant to them all. Kerry's face turned serious. "But he left me—and us—far more than a legacy of kindness: the belief, in spite of all we hear and read, that politics could be 'an honorable adventure.'

" 'Telling the truth when it's hard,' he once said to me, 'is what political capital is for.' "

There was more laughter, softer now. "Liam knew," Kerry went on, "that in politics courage and practicality need not be enemies, and that without the other, either one is insufficient.

Just as Liam—the practical man, and the courageous one—knew and said that blacks and whites *must* not be enemies."

The church was quiet, mourners of both races nodding. "We are lucky," Kerry told them, "when a leader's courage and practicality is informed by simple decency. That was Liam Dunn." His voice became a gentle replica of an Irish lilt. " 'Do the right thing, Kerry, and things tend to come out right in the end. But the first is the only part you control. And sometimes going to bed square with yourself is a day-to-day kind of thing . . .' "

Lara saw tears forming in the eyes around her; to her surprise, she felt the loss of a man she had never known. There was brilliance in what Kerry was doing, she thought. By summoning Liam back to life, Kerry gave those who remembered him a second chance to honor what some had not acknowledged—that Liam had reached across the racial divide.

As Kerry's gaze swept the church, their eyes met.

He looked incalculably sad. In that moment, Lara thought she understood him better: that who he tried to be, and what he tried to live up to, involved far more than a murdered brother. And, believing that, she felt for Kerry; there was so much left inside him that he could not say to others.

" 'Day to day,' " Kerry finished quietly, "Liam was the best of us."

The mourners came to the two-story wooden home Liam had never left. Reporters were welcome, Liam's son Denis assured her; his father respected the press, knew they had a job to do. "Some of you," Denis said wryly, "he even liked." And so Lara found herself there, late into the night, nursing an Irish whisky, talking to neighbors and old local politicians, listening to an Irish band, and hearing how Newark and Vailsburg had been when the two Senators Kilcannon were boys. "That Jamie," an old woman told her, "could run like the wind and charm the birds out of trees. And what a smile he had, like a film star."

The house was jammed with people—old and young, children and grandchildren—and the tables were covered with food and drink and photographs of Liam. The mood was as complex as death itself—brave, nostalgic, sad—and laughter mingled in the air with the softer voices of recollection. Lara had no chance to talk to Kerry. He was trapped in his role of public man—shaking hands, listening to complaints or advice, suffering those for whom his presence made their own grief more important, something to be shared with a senator. But for the fact that, to Lara, he appeared drawn, Kerry looked contained—speaking softly, touching and being touched, smiling when that was called for. The others left him no time for his wife.

Meg, Lara found, was an enigma.

She seemed quite different from the subdued woman Lara had noted at the funeral. Here, she was animated, seeking friends out, her warmth and energy offset only by a somewhat short attention span, a smile that seemed to flash and vanish. In this, she was the opposite of Kerry, who appeared to slow down, to look into faces. But it was not until Lara returned to the buffet that she found herself next to Meg.

"Pardon me," Lara said. "You must be Meg Kilcannon, the senator's wife. I'm Lara Costello."

It took Meg a second to react, as though she had been startled from some private world. "I'm from Washington," Lara explained. "I cover Congress for the *Times*."

The warmth in Meg's eyes receded. "That must be interesting," Meg said. "What brings you here?"

"Liam Dunn. He and the senator seemed so close."

Meg nodded. "Kerry really cared about him."

It was a reasonable enough remark, Lara thought. But the distance in Meg's tone puzzled her; she could have been talking about a rumor she had heard, rather than something she knew and felt. Then Meg was off to seek new company, smiling again.

It was time to go, Lara thought.

Glancing around the living room, she looked for Kerry, hoping to put in a word. But he was talking to a black couple Lara recognized from the photograph in his office. Kerry appeared tired now; head bent, he said something muted, and the woman kissed him on the cheek. Then the man touched his shoulder, as if in valediction, and Kerry walked out the front door, alone.

Puzzled, Lara went to take leave of Denis Dunn, then stepped into the night.

On the lawn, Lara saw a slim figure in shirtsleeves, gazing up at the moon.

She hesitated, and then walked toward him. A few feet away, she stopped.

Kerry did not turn. "Liam had a long run," he murmured. "But still . . ."

When she stepped closer, Lara saw the tears on his face.

"Without him, Lara, I don't know what would have happened to me. When I was nine—" His voice broke, and then was soft again. "When it comes to death, I'm no philosopher. It's a weakness, sure."

Lara's fingertips grazed the sleeve of his shirt. "It's not a weakness," she said, and left.

EIGHT

After Liam's death, Lara felt a subtle change in her relationship to Kerry Kilcannon.

They never spoke of Liam, or the night of his funeral. But Kerry seemed to accept her as more than a journalist. To Lara, they had entered that ambiguous zone of friendship in which a politician and a reporter use each other for their own purposes, and yet self-interest is tempered—and complicated—by genuine liking. Without saying so, they made up their own rules: personal conversations were always off the record; deceptions were forbidden; each would call the other with useful information. Lara was free to drop by his office; sometimes, when Kerry was restless, they might walk around the Capitol.

"You've become the Kilcannon expert," Nate told her. "With a lot of luck, you'll be White House correspondent."

Even Kerry, who understood her colleagues well, teased her about this. "If I decide I'm never running," he told her, "you can always cultivate Dick Mason."

"Just let me know," she had answered. But Lara found Kerry intriguing for his own sake, a complex mix of toughness and sensitivity, fatalism and calculation. "He's like a work in progress," she told Nate over drinks at the Monocle. "Or a house where they keep adding rooms."

Nate took off his glasses, inspecting them for smudges; by now, Lara recognized this as a nervous tic, perhaps the residue of shyness. "Does he ever talk about his wife?"

"No. Not really."

Nate glanced up at her, smiling slightly. "Eight years in Washington is a long time to spend alone. Do you think maybe he's got someone, after all?"

"Based on what?" Lara answered with some asperity. "Besides, for Kerry Kilcannon, sin actually exists. In *this* crowd, it's part of his appeal."

It was true, Lara thought, but for reasons beyond Catholic guilt. Kerry deeply wanted to be good, as a politician and as a man, and doubted that he was. To violate his own moral sense would be to wound himself; however blind his wife might be to this, Meg Kilcannon was a beneficiary, and so was Lara. Though she liked him for it, it made her a little sad.

"Do you ever want kids?" Kerry had asked her the day before.

They were sitting on the lawn in front of Capitol Hill, enjoying the first break of spring; Lara had brought sandwiches and, between bites, had been asking why flood relief for North Dakota was held up in the Senate. The conversation had meandered to Lara's biggest news—for the first time, she had become an aunt. "It's hard to believe," Lara told him, "that I'm related to this midget." Kerry laughed; his question had followed, asked with the detached curiosity of one friend to another.

"Me?" Lara gazed out at the cherry blossoms, trying to form an honest answer. "I think so. But it scares me, too."

Kerry tilted his head. "Why's that?"

"Because if I let it mean too much to me, maybe I'll get married when I shouldn't. I'm only twenty-eight. I need independence, my own reason for getting up in the morning." Lara's voice grew pensive. "I guess I think about my mom. *We* were the only reason she got up."

"Does it have to be one or the other?"

His tone was serious, genuinely questioning; Lara guessed that the subject had meaning to him. "Part of it, I guess, depends on who I'm with. I still haven't figured *that* out."

Kerry was quiet. Never, Lara realized, did he ask about her social life, nor did she ever speak of it. "Well," he said at last, "thank God you have choices. At your age, my mother believed hers were already made. Mostly, she was right."

Lara had an instinct for hurt; she could still remember coming home, a ten-year-old, and discovering her father was gone—that he had not loved his wife, or her, enough even to warn them. The same instinct told her not to ask about Michael Kilcannon and yet, perversely, spurred a question she could not resist.

"What about you, Kerry? Did you ever want kids?"

Kerry picked a blade of grass. "Yes," he said. "It just never happened. And with politics . . ."

It seemed to trouble him, Lara thought. *If you want children,* she almost asked, *why not have them?*

As if he had heard her thoughts, Kerry looked up. "At least I get to be godfather," he said, "to Clayton and Carlie's kids. And there's a boy I see here, whenever I can. A five-year-old."

" 'See'?"

"I take him places. On Sunday afternoons whenever I'm here."

Lara felt the freshness of discovery. "Is it some sort of secret?" she asked. "I've never read anything about it."

Kerry shrugged, as if discomfited. "Why should you have?"

All at once, Lara was deeply curious—it was as though she had discovered another missing piece of him. On impulse, she asked, "Do you ever let anyone come with you?"

His eyelids lowered, and then he looked at her directly. "If someone wrote about this, it wouldn't be about Kevin anymore. And I'd guess he wants me to himself." His voice softened. "The sad thing is that it takes so little. One interested adult can make such a difference, and many kids don't even have that."

Lara turned to him. "How did you meet Kevin?"

"At a day care center I was touring. Every time I turned around, he was there." As if reliving this, Kerry shook his head. "Sometimes you can look at kids, and see the problems in their eyes. Kevin didn't have to say a thing."

There was a flatness in Kerry's voice, the tone he sometimes used, Lara had learned, when he was trying to gain distance from his own feelings. "What do you do when you can't be here?"

"I call him. Once you start this, it can't be a hobby."

What would it have been like, Lara thought to herself, to have had a father who cared, even enough to pick up the telephone and call. "It's good you feel that responsible," she said.

"The harm you can do . . ." His eyes narrowed, as if at some distant memory. "Ten years ago, when I was a prosecutor, a young boy got attached to me. I invited him to." His tone became quiet again. "I learned not to create too many expectations, and to know the ones I could keep."

The recollection was hurtful, Lara sensed. "It sounds like you're pretty good with kids, Kerry. In fact, I was thinking you were prime father material."

In profile, Kerry was still; Lara felt him deciding whether to respond. "At some point," he said at last, "Meg realized she didn't want a family. Perhaps politics makes it look worse to her—being Jeannie Mason's not for everyone." He turned to her. "I mean, can *you* imagine being Jeannie?"

How honest should she be? Lara wondered. "No," she answered. "But then I can't imagine marrying a politician."

"That's just it. Meg didn't." His voice had the trace of irony that Lara had come to know as his response to sadness, the inscrutable works of fate. "To understate the matter, my career was an accident. One Meg wanted no part of."

Lara gazed at him, a youthful man of thirty-nine, and tried to imagine Kerry nine years before, faced with his brother's death. "So the price you pay . . ."

"Is having a wife who doesn't want to give up her own life— friends, career, predictability—to be an afterthought in someone else's. Who can blame her?" As if listening to himself, he said more softly, "The truth, Lara, is that I'll always feel guilty about coming here when our marriage needed my attention most, and I'll always resent Meg for the feeling. I've never known who to blame, or whether it would have been different."

And how will it be next year? Lara wondered. Or the year after that: early in its second term, the administration was beset by allegations of illegal fund-raising, raising anew the potential that Kerry could challenge Mason. "What if you *do* run?" she asked.

Kerry's expression became almost bleak. "It would make the human cost that much worse—for Meg and for me. A friend once told me, 'To want any one thing too much is barbaric.' Run for President, I think, and you learn how true that is." Kerry looked directly into Lara's eyes. "You're part of the cost—you and your friends in the press. If I ran, you'd pick over Meg and our marriage until there was nowhere left to hide."

Lara met his gaze. "No one's comfortable with that," she said evenly. "Not you, not us. But Nixon and then Gary Hart changed the rules. We can't know *what* decisions a President might be asked to make, but we can ask what kind of man is making them, and why."

Kerry shook his head, smiling faintly. "Easy for you to say. You'll never be on the other end of the telescope."

"Because I'd never choose to be. But anyone who runs for President does." Her voice softened. "Would that really keep you from running, do you think?"

Turning, Kerry gazed at the lawn, its shadows lengthening in the afternoon sun. "Oh, it should . . ." For a long time, he was silent. "After I was shot, and then Jamie died, I wondered why it had happened that way. Why not me? I asked myself. Every day since then has seemed like a gift. Now the question I ask myself is 'What are you doing to deserve it? And what *should* you do?' "

Oh, Kerry, Lara found herself thinking, *there should be more to your life than that.* Briefly, she touched his arm. "You've already paid your debts, Kerry. You deserve a life of your own."

When at first he did not answer, or look at her, Lara thought she had gone too far. "I have part of a life," he said pensively. "I came here as Jamie's brother, and somehow turned into me. It's just that a piece is missing, sometimes."

Lara felt a strange sensation, the smallest catch in her throat. Then Kerry glanced at his watch, breaking the moment. "Time to go," he told her.

NINE

A few days later, Lara stopped by Kerry's office. "I came by to ask you out," she told him.

Kerry cocked his head; with his shirtsleeves rolled up, his tie loosened, he looked less like a senator than like the young and harried lawyer he once had been. "Dinner and a movie," he asked, "or *Meet the Press*?"

Lara smiled. "The Congressional Correspondents Dinner. It's six weeks from now, so this is sort of like asking Brad Pitt to the Winter Prom in 1999. But I know how popular you are, and this will give you plenty of time to rent a tuxedo."

"I *have* a tuxedo," he said with feigned hurt, and then adopted a teasing tone. "But don't you have a boyfriend or something?"

"You mean bring some guy I'm *dating*?" Lara answered in mock horror. "People would think I didn't *know* anyone. Whereas *you're* at the top of the food chain."

Kerry laughed. "It's a sick society, here inside the Beltway, and you've already learned the rules. Leave, Lara, while there's still time."

Lara felt a moment's doubt. "If Meg is coming . . ."

He shook his head. "Oh, no, don't worry about that. The fun has worn off for her." Smiling again, he added, "Really, I'd be happy to go."

Leaving, Lara stood on the steps of the Russell Building, savoring a warm spring day.

It would be fun to spend an evening with him, she thought, sharing part of a world he knew well. Much, much better than a date . . .

Five days before the dinner, Kerry called her at home.

From the first few words, Lara knew that something was terribly wrong. "I'm sorry," he said, "but there's a problem. I'm in Newark, and I don't know whether I'll be back for the dinner. If you want to ask someone else . . ."

Lara felt a stab of disappointment. Instinctively, she asked, "Is it Meg?"

"Oh, no. Meg's fine." His tone grew weary. "It's Clayton and Carlie's five-year-old, Ethan. He was climbing a tree in the backyard and just fell somehow. The fall broke his neck."

On the other end of the line, Lara felt the tragedy in the pit of her stomach. "Oh, no," she said, and then asked softly, "Is he still alive?"

She heard Kerry draw a breath. "Yes. As of now, that's all they're hoping for." There was a long silence, and then Kerry said, "He's paralyzed, Lara."

Inwardly, Lara winced. Is there anything I can do? she was about to ask, and then she realized that she did not know the Slades and, in this private part of Kerry's life, had no place. "Oh, Kerry," she said. "I feel for them all."

"You just can't know—" His voice caught, then went on. "They're here at the hospital, waiting, while their son lies in an oxygen tent, not moving or making a sound. All I can do is be with them, for as long as they want me."

What to say, Lara wondered, when nothing is adequate? "Don't worry about the dinner," she said at last, and then added quietly, "If you have a chance, call me. I mean, if you want to . . ."

"Yeah." His voice was barely audible. "I'd better go."

When she hung up, Lara closed her eyes. It was strange how clear her image was of Kerry at this moment—pulling himself together, then walking down the bleak corridor of a hospital at night, to be with his stricken friends.

The next time he called her, Ethan Slade was dead.

It was the morning of the Congressional Correspondents Dinner. Telling her, his voice was uninflected.

At her desk, Lara spoke in an undertone, so that Nate and the others would not hear. "How are your friends?" she asked.

"As you'd expect." He paused. "They'd have taken him any way but dead, Lara. I don't know how anyone gets past this."

He sounded utterly dispirited; nothing in his own experience of death, Lara sensed, had quite prepared him for this. "I'm so sorry," she said softly. "For you, too."

He was quiet for a moment. "After the funeral, watching them, I knew it was time to leave. Some things, they wouldn't want even *me* to see."

Once more, Lara sensed how much this family meant to him, his feeling of lonely helplessness. "Where *are* you?" she asked.

"Here, in Washington. There were things I had to do, and it's better than doing nothing." Then, as if in an afterthought, he told her, "If you haven't traded me in, I'll come with you tonight."

Lara hesitated, surprised that he would go, and at her selfish desire to see him. "Are you sure?" she asked. "With what's happened, it seems like a lot."

There was a moment's silence. "No," he said. "It would be better for me, I think."

Lara felt relief, the warmth of being able, perhaps, to help someone she cared for. "Then we'll make it an early night," she promised.

The dinner was in the banquet room of the Grand Hyatt—several hundred men in black tie and women in evening dresses, looking about to see who else was there and with whom. The *Times* had reserved several tables for its correspondents and their guests, including the secretary of defense, the ambassador to the United Nations, the governor of New York, an eminent British actor with an interest in politics, and, sitting beside Lara, Senator Kerry Kilcannon.

To her now-practiced eye, Kerry looked drawn, a little tired. But he was good company, holding his own in conversation, laughing in seeming amusement at a comedian's after-dinner speech. "Whenever I see Netanyahu and Arafat," the comedian gibed, "it gives me insight into others of our recent history's warmest friendships—Michael Eisner and Michael Ovitz, Dick Mason and Kerry Kilcannon . . ."

Laughter broke out. At a nearby table, Mason stood, giving Kerry an exaggerated bow, while Kerry, entering the joke, folded his dinner program into a paper airplane and lobbed it in Mason's direction, miming dismay as it fell short of the target. "I modeled it after the B-2 bomber," he said audibly, alluding to one of the administration's recent weapons orders, and there was another wave of chuckles. Grinning, Jeannie Mason retrieved the paper plane and presented it to her husband, as the comedian said, "Senator Kilcannon wants you to play at *his* house, Mr. Vice President. And you'll never guess the address."

Gazing up at the dais, Kerry smiled faintly, but his eyes were distant. It was not a night, Lara felt certain, when he had much interest in his own ambitions, or in the rituals of Washington. And, knowing this, she felt something akin to guilt. Leaning over, she whispered to him, "If you like, feel free to skip the after-dinner party."

As he turned to her, Lara had a sense of intimacy, a private moment amidst a very public event. "Do you need a lift?" he asked.

Lara nodded. "That would be nice."

When the dinner broke up, they left the room, stepping into the cool night. She had been proud to be with him, she realized, and this deepened her sense of selfishness. "I never got to ask about the Slades," she told him.

Kerry handed his parking stub to the valet. Turning to her, he slowly shook his head. "It was hard."

To Lara, the understatement bore the weight of his emotions, a hint of his solitude. For much of the ride, they were quiet.

Lara lived in a converted brick town house just off Connecticut Avenue. To her surprise, Kerry found a place in front.

Turning to her, he said, "Thanks, Lara. For asking me, and for leaving."

She hesitated. "Can I give you a cup of coffee?"

Kerry looked down, reflective. Then he glanced up at her again. "Do you have any cognac?" he asked.

Lara's apartment was on the second floor—living room, a small kitchen, a bedroom that caught morning light. She did not have much furniture, given the money she still sent her family, but everything was neat and of good quality. Entering with Kerry, Lara realized to her surprise that she wanted him to like it.

He glanced around, openly curious, as though looking at another facet of her life. "Well?" she asked.

Turning, he answered, "I was thinking how much nicer this is than my first apartment in Newark. Or my apartment here." He smiled. "Thirty-nine, and still living like a college kid."

"Forever young," Lara told him, and went to the kitchen.

She poured the cognac into her only wineglasses. When she returned, he was sitting on the couch. It stopped her for a moment; unlike with the other men she knew, the sight of Kerry Kilcannon in her living room unsettled her. Lara handed him the glass, taking the chair across from him and placing her cognac on the table between them, waiting until he took a sip. "Tell me about the Slades," she said quietly. "After you called."

Kerry gazed at the wineglass in his hands. "Ethan died an hour later." He shook his head. "To see Clayton and Carlie sit beside him . . .

"The next morning, we rode with Ethan to the funeral home. They were like automatons, both of them—very soft-spoken, very precise in telling the funeral director what they wanted. No one cried until we got to the car, and then Carlie broke down entirely." Kerry's eyes closed. "She couldn't stand to leave Ethan alone, she said. Clayton got in the back seat, to hold her, and I drove them home.

"When we got there, Clayton stood in front of the house— this beautiful Tudor in South Orange, the place they'd worked so hard to have. I could see him thinking if they'd only chosen some other house . . ." Kerry took a deep swallow of cognac.

"So I put my arm around his shoulder, and he leaned his head against me. No one said a word."

His voice, soft and very sad, made the Slades' grief palpable to Lara. "Did the funeral help at all?" she asked. "It does, sometimes."

"Not here. Though I'm not sure what would have helped." Kerry looked up at her. "The minister tried. But the twins looked hollowed out—Ethan was their little brother, their pet. Carlie couldn't stop crying, and Clayton never cried at all.

"He was like that until we got back, lost in this deadly kind of quiet. And then he took out a chain saw, went to the backyard, and methodically turned that tree into kindling.

"Carlie watched until she couldn't stand it anymore." Pausing, Kerry winced at the memory. "This time, *I* held her."

Except at the death of Liam Dunn, Lara had never seen Kerry's emotions so exposed. But that had been a chance encounter; this was not. Now, she realized, he had come to her. "Will they survive this, Kerry?"

"I think so. They have two daughters, a twenty-year marriage, a strong relationship. They love each other and they've overcome a lot . . ." His voice turned flat. "That funeral, Lara. Maybe there's nothing that can explain to me the death of a five-year-old boy. But for me it was hollow and inadequate, as so many rituals are. I kept thinking of how I felt when our party chairman put on this memorial dinner to honor Jamie—so empty, so meaningless, so full of platitudes. The sheer heartlessness of it would have made him laugh."

She watched him, a slender man with ginger hair, no longer just a senator, but somehow part of her life. "Your brother," she asked softly, "what was it like to lose him?"

He looked at her steadily; for a moment, she expected some deflective remark. "Ennobling," he answered. "Of course. They asked me to take Jamie's place, and I sacrificed myself out of love for him and a sense of duty. Isn't that how the story goes whenever my media people tell it?"

"Except," Lara ventured, "that you didn't really like him."

He swirled the brandy in his glass, watching it. "It's all so complicated," he said at last. "Then, and now.

"Suddenly Jamie was dead and there I was, caught in my

own ambivalence. Perhaps even my envy. Although I told myself that I'd little more want to be as cold as Jamie than as mindless and brutal as our father." The simple statement startled her; tonight Kerry's reticence had vanished. "All those things I've said to you about politics, Lara—the loss of self, the tunnel vision of ambition, the sacrifice of people you love—to me, Jamie was all these things and, even worse, he knew it."

Lara was overcome by curiosity, the absence of barriers. "Why did you take his place, then? Let alone position yourself to be President?"

Kerry gave a mirthless smile. "Survivor guilt, isn't that the theory? Jamie would have been President, and if you inherit the crown, you have to make something of it. Sometimes I think even Clayton believes that." His voice was quiet again. "But it's more complicated than that. Because when I took this job, I discovered a pride in doing it which is my very own.

"Did I want what he had, after all? Was Jamie better than I thought, or am I more like him than I know?" Kerry shook his head. "And what *was* he like, when he never let me know him?

"I don't know the answers. And there's one more answer I never want to know." Once more, Kerry looked at her. "If I could bring Jamie back again, and give up what I have because he died, would I?"

The nakedness of his admission, the sheer pain of what he carried with him, left Lara at a loss for words. In her silence, Kerry seemed ashamed. "*Look* at me," he said with a trace of self-contempt. "Here it's Clayton's son who's dead, and I'm maundering on about Jamie. About myself, really." His voice softened. "Except that I seem to have lost the habit of hiding from you. Or even wanting to."

Suddenly Lara felt conscious of everything—the distance between them, the dim light, the slight chill of the room on her bare shoulders. "Who *do* you talk to?" she asked.

He looked away. At length, he answered, "These aren't easy things to talk about. To anyone."

Lara gazed at him again, torn between caution and the desire to reach out to him. Quietly, she said, "There's me, Kerry. Now there's me."

Their eyes met, and then Kerry turned away. He stood

abruptly, trying to smile. "Then I'd better go, Lara. Before I tax your patience."

In her confusion, Lara was still. "You don't have to," she said at last. "Not yet. Unless . . ."

Kerry looked down at her. His lips parted, as if he was startled in mid-thought.

Slowly, Lara stood.

Her eyes were wide, self-doubting. Kerry could feel the pulse in his own throat.

"I'm not sure," he managed to say, "that you know how I feel."

Kerry saw her surprise, her fear, as clearly as he felt his own. "I think I do," she answered.

They were inches apart, not touching. Kerry gazed into her face, stunned and pale and so lovely that now, this close, it almost hurt to look at her.

"Are you sure?" he asked. Then his fingers grazed the nape of her neck, and her eyes shut in answer.

Her mouth was soft, warm.

Kerry pressed against her, wanting the heat of his body against the cool of her skin, feeling his lips in the hollow of her neck now, saying her name. For a moment, her breath caught.

After a time, it was not enough.

Why didn't you know? he asked himself. But nothing mattered now—not Meg, not his career. Only her.

When he slid down the straps of her gown, fingertips grazing her skin, Lara trembled. "Wait," she whispered. "They'll see us."

Pulling away, Lara went to the bedroom. Then she turned to him, dress around her waist.

She was beautiful. "I never thought . . . ," Kerry murmured.

Lara managed to smile, though her voice tremored. "If you don't come to me, Kerry, we never will."

Fumbling, he switched off the light.

In the shadows of the bedroom, Kerry knelt, kissing her nipples, her stomach. His nerves twitched with wanting her.

When they slid into bed, the sheets felt crisp and cool. And then she was against him, murmuring, "Kerry," and he no longer felt alone.

Gently, Kerry touched her hair with his fingertips, looking into her face.

Do you know how I feel?

Yes, Lara realized. *God, yes.*

His mouth slid slowly down her stomach, and then Lara was lost.

The rest was instinct, his and hers, a craving that felt months deep. When he was inside her, she shuddered.

"Kerry," she said again. Then the room went dark, and Lara could not say anything.

Afterward, she lay against him until she fell asleep.

When she awoke, it was close to two.

Kerry stirred beside her, restless. She felt shaken, adrift.

Everything had changed.

Her thoughts were a collage: Meg, and the guilt he must now feel, that Lara herself felt. All that divided them—his ambitions, her profession. The breach of her standards, the terrible risk if they continued. Even regret at all the insights into Kerry Kilcannon that she, as a reporter, could never use.

It was strange, Lara reflected, to believe that he could sense her thoughts. Just as she believed, without his saying so, that he had never before been unfaithful to his wife. As he must know that she had never been part of infidelity, and never wished to be.

If you want me tomorrow, or the next day, what will I say to you?

She lay next to him, unable to sleep, afraid to speak. In the darkness, she felt his fingers curl around hers.

The Campaign

Day Three

ONE

Just before dawn, Lara awoke.

In the dimness of her room, the confusion of past and present, Kerry was still with her. She could feel the turmoil of his emotions, the touch of his fingers, the soft timbre of his voice.

I want to see you again, he had said.

They seemed so innocent to her now. Fearful, but unknowing, blind to what awaited in the ambush of time.

Tell me about Meg, she heard herself say.

Not "no." Not "we can't." Not the things she could have said to spare them this.

Tell me about your wife. Give me a way to be with you. The plea of a million women, less smart and knowing than Lara had been. But not as knowing as she was now.

Rising, she went to the window, opening the blinds.

Not Washington at all. The sprawl of Oakland Harbor, green water, the distant towers of San Francisco appearing in the dawn, silver fingers in the wisps of morning fog. A city she had always loved.

In an hour, she would call her mother. Anna Costello's voice would rise at the sound of Lara's, and then the questions would come in her mother's rapid cadence—about the promise of her new life in Washington, the excitement of the campaign, old reporter friends re-met. About whether her friend Senator Kilcannon was still the same. Because she loved her mother, Lara would contrive answers, then ask about her brothers and sisters, her three-year-old niece, Clara. About them, there were no secrets.

She had held her own secret so close, for both their sakes. And had been betrayed.

Tell me about the campaign, her mother would ask.

I'm afraid for him, she would want to say. *Afraid that I'll destroy him, afraid of what I saw him do yesterday. Afraid of fanatics with guns.*

Where's your brother? the squat man had called to him. A voice swollen with hatred and unreason.

All it would take was one.

She could have stopped this, too. *Yes,* she could have said to Kerry, *if you're willing to face this, I will.* But she had not, and now she was alone, and Kerry was here.

Turning from the window, she went to her suitcase for a fresh set of clothes.

Folding his clothes with one hand, Nate tossed them in the suitcase as he spoke into the phone. "What about his wife?" he asked.

"Ex-wife," Jane Booth corrected. "And probably a good thing, given her reaction. Where are you, incidentally?"

"In my hotel room." Nate glanced at the room service tray—coffee, the remaining crusts of wheat bread, half-eaten cantaloupe. "I ordered in, so I didn't have to use the cell phone. Anyhow . . ."

"Anyhow, Sheila knocked on the door and asked Kilcannon's ex if she knew about Lara Costello. When Meg looked blank, Sheila spelled it out for her—right down to the date of the counselor's notes. Apparently Meg got very quiet, and then said, 'That explains it, doesn't it.'"

Nate could not help but feel squeamish; the use of Lara's counselor's notes to confront an unwary wife might be good investigative journalism, but he could imagine Meg Kilcannon's face, her feeling of betrayal. "Meaning?" he asked.

"The divorce. Kilcannon asked her one week later. It was a surprise, Meg said. I guess all he told her was that it was time."

"But was it? With Lara on her way to Africa?"

"That's what Sheila asked. 'You don't know Kerry,' she says Meg answered. 'He has an endless capacity for guilt.'" Jane's voice became dry. "It sounds as if she's bitter."

"Well," Nate said quietly, "I'm sure she is now. Probably enough to go on the record."

"We think so." Jane's tone was willfully oblivious. "But she doesn't know anything except for what we told her—either Kilcannon's good at cheating, or the flames of passion were so dead that Meg never noticed. The pressure's still on you, Nate."

Not just me, Nate thought. "I'll get to Kit," he answered. "This morning, if possible."

Kerry faced them around the coffee table in Clayton's suite—Jack Sleeper, Frank Wells, Kit Pace, Clayton. It was seven a.m.; the subject of Lara Costello hovered over the meeting, unspoken.

"For two nights running," Clayton said abruptly, "the numbers show us soft with pro-choice women. It's worst in San Francisco. Jack wants us to do an event, and Ellen Penn wants it too."

"When?" Frank asked. "And what?"

"The what," Clayton answered, "is a rally featuring Kerry and all the prominent women who support him. I'm not committed yet—I want to see another night's worth of polling. But there's a hole in our schedule the Sunday morning after the debate. We can start Kerry in a black church, then go directly to the rally."

"On Sunday morning in San Francisco?" Frank shot Kerry a dubious look, as if to ensure that he was listening. "No one's working, nobody's downtown, and we've only got two days to organize a crowd. Advance and Senator Penn will have to do one hell of a job with turnout, or we've got a major embarrassment and the press will be all over it—'Kilcannon Rally Fizzles.'" He faced Kerry again, speaking more softly. "It'll become a metaphor, Kerry, for all your problems on choice. You don't need that."

Kerry was quiet for a moment, and then turned to Clayton. "What's Mason doing?" he asked.

Clayton frowned. "Yesterday he spoke to women's groups, hammering you on choice and Medicare reform—that you're too big a risk to take. Today is back to basics: an endorsement from the state teachers' unions, a speech to Silicon Valley execs, saving old-growth redwoods—"

"But without losing a single job," Kit put in sardonically. "Don't forget that."

"What's he supposed to say?" Jack Sleeper inquired. " 'I think that I shall never see a job as lovely as a tree'?"

Frank's smile was thin. "Kit's right, though—it's pablum as usual. Where Dick's playing rough are his new TV spots: Kerry's not a grown-up; Kerry's not pro-choice enough; Kerry's too extreme. The whole pitch is that Dick's calm, he's tested, he's ready. Like Ward Cleaver."

And faithful to his wife, Kerry could feel him thinking. He thought of Jeannie Mason, trying to imagine her as a battered woman.

"So," Clayton said, "any thoughts about this San Francisco rally?"

"Aside from great advance," Frank replied, "you're going to need the volunteers to turn out the crowd. If they can't do it . . ."

Clayton nodded. "We can call the guy in San Francisco— Ginsberg. Mick Lasker says he's pretty good."

"Lay the groundwork," Frank responded. "But don't decide until you've checked this out. There may be other uses for that time."

"That raises another problem—the Secret Service." Clayton glanced at Kerry. "The more last-minute an event, the less Peter Lake is going to like it. He sets a premium on planning."

Kerry picked up his coffee. "Wait a day," he said to Clayton. "Until Tuesday, every minute counts, and we don't need a bad event. The Service will have to roll with it."

In Clayton's silence, Kerry heard an echo of their argument the day before. Then his friend shrugged. "At least we can let Peter know we're considering this. Maybe get some advice on a site."

Kerry took another hit of coffee. "I'll be over in San Francisco this morning. Any chance I can run by headquarters?"

Clayton frowned. "A spontaneous drop-in? We'd better ask Peter *and* advance. You're flying to L.A. at one, and the speech in South Central is key. Meeting the converted isn't worth a blown schedule."

Kerry nodded. "I understand. These people work hard, though, and I don't often get a chance to say I'm grateful. And if we're asking them to build an event overnight . . ."

"This speech in South Central," Jack Sleeper put in, "what's the theme?"

Sipping more coffee, Kerry watched Clayton over the rim. "Education," his friend answered. "Inclusion. Economic security."

"All good and worthy goals, Clayton." Jack's gaze and voice were level. "As long as it's done right."

"Meaning?"

"That Kerry's getting squeezed here. Gun control drives men away, so Kerry has to get that many more votes out of minorities and women. But now we have a choice problem. And if Kerry seems *too* pro-minority, you lose more whites than you can afford." Jack turned to Kerry. "Black voting tends to be matriarchal, so Head Start and nutrition are good issues. You don't need to be stepping on land mines like affirmative action."

Kerry smiled. "But how will people know which one's *me* and which one's Dick? Unless I keep on being as reckless as he says I am."

"Which people, Kerry? South Central's still volatile. To a lot of voters, it still reminds them of Rodney King and that white trucker who got beaten up, even how they felt when O.J. was acquitted. Isn't it enough you're going there?"

Kerry sat back, looking at the others. For a moment, he had an image of five bright people trapped in a vacuum, mapping out reality as if it were a game of chess. "If our leaders can't campaign in South Central," he said, "where are we as a country? I'm not in this for just the pleasure of beating Dick Mason. When was the last time a candidate for President talked honestly about race instead of mouthing platitudes?"

"Honesty is one thing," Frank Wells interjected. "But suicide helps no one—not you and not the people you want to help, black or white. Just how well would affirmative action fly in your old neighborhood? And most opponents would tell you they're upholding the most basic American value—fairness."

"Oh, I know," Kerry said softly. "And you know. And Dick Mason knows. Everyone in the world knows."

"So hold your base," Jack Sleeper responded. "But don't let any more white votes slip away. Especially women."

"Oh," Kerry rejoined, "I'll try not to throw them overboard. We've worked so hard to *be* white, after all."

To the side, Kerry saw Clayton's smile. "I'll call San Francisco," he said at length.

Kerry nodded. "Good. And when you do, tell them I may be dropping in."

Putting down the telephone, Sean Burke felt a hand on his shoulder.

Sean flinched. All his fears assaulted him—failure, prison, claustrophobia. Being locked up with animals and sodomites, loathed by a world indifferent to the death of children. He turned, expecting the police.

Rick Ginsberg smiled down at him. "Don't get your hopes up," he said, "but Senator Kilcannon may be coming *here*. To headquarters."

Still flushed with apprehension, Sean stiffened, unable to speak. "Really," Ginsberg told him. "Today."

Next to him, Sean felt Kate Feeney turning. "What time?" she asked.

Four o'clock, Sean thought. That was what the street punk had told him. "If it happens," Rick told them both, "around noon."

"God." Kate sounded crestfallen. "I'm signed up to be at our outdoor table. In Union Square."

Rick gave her a rueful smile. "Sorry, Kate. One of us has to be there. If you can find somebody else . . ."

Instinctively, Sean patted the inside pocket of his army jacket, feeling for the knife. "Of *all* the days," Kate groaned, "Kerry would have to pick this one."

TWO

From the press section, Lara watched Nate Cutler stalk Kit Pace.

It was nine o'clock, Kerry's first event of the morning. They were in an auditorium at Boalt Hall, the law school at U.C. Berkeley. Kerry was speaking to minority students; Nate was among the pool today, in a cluster of reporters at the side of the stage trying to edge toward Kit. Seemingly unaware of him, Kit busied herself whispering to local reporters, no doubt dispensing the favors—a piece of information, a slot to interview Kerry—she had reserved for them. But what this meant, Lara noted, was that Kit was never alone, and that there were always several bodies between her and Nate. Lara was torn between apprehension and admiration—Kit's performance was a small piece of art, as intricate as dance.

As for Kerry, he was challenging his audience. "As a country," he told them, "we ask very little of our brightest young people. Except, of course, that you repay your student loans."

There was a ripple of laughter. "Isn't that enough?" a young black man called out.

Kerry grinned. "Too much, for some of you. When John F. Kennedy asked what you could do for your country, he wasn't thinking about compound interest."

The laughter grew. "But that's the point," Kerry went on. "When you graduate from this school—a publicly supported school, by the way—most of you with loans will be able to repay them. For many of you, the cost of your education will be a down payment on a place among America's elite—the

351

wealthiest, the best educated, the most respected. Whether you are white or a person of color."

Sitting behind them, Lara watched the students stir in their folding chairs. Next to her, Lee McAlpine whispered, "There's something absolutely perverse about Kilcannon at times. Shouldn't he be talking about racial justice?"

"I don't think he will," Lara murmured. "They're too comfortable." Quickly, she glanced at Nate; he had paused to take notes. As if sensing this, Kit Pace stopped moving away from him.

"In World War Two," Kerry went on, "we believed that common sacrifice for the common good was the duty of all our citizens. But somewhere in the last half of this century, the ideal of common citizenship vanished from our public life."

Kerry paused, eyes sweeping the crowd. "One of the ugliest truths of Vietnam was that the Americans who died there were disproportionately poor, disproportionately black, disproportionately less educated. And one of its ugliest legacies is the elitist notion that the only men and women who now need serve our country are those for whom the military is a jobs program. Those people, to be blunt, who are far less fortunate than you."

Lara saw the young black man who had been Kerry's questioner stiffen in his chair. "A country," Kerry continued, "is more than a place to live. And justice is more than ensuring that you keep more of what you earn.

"Justice, to be sure, means equity among the races and between men and women. But it also means this: that all young persons who are able should give some small part of their lives—their passions, their energies, their ideals—in a common cause. Or we will exacerbate this growing division—the America of the inner city, the worst schools, the least hope; the America of the shopping mall, the gated community, the best education money can buy. The kind of education you're getting . . ."

Turning, Lee McAlpine leaned her head near Lara's. "This is either incredibly nervy," she murmured, "or a very clever way of not pandering to minorities."

It's far simpler, Lara wanted to say. *When Kerry does something unorthodox, you want to reduce him to a more evolved*

Dick Mason, instead of a man with an eye for social irony and contradiction, and a preference for the truth. The thought startled her: for that moment, she had thought of the press as "you."

In the pool, Nate Cutler had resumed his pursuit of Kit Pace. Now all that was between them was an *L.A. Times* reporter, one arm on Kit's shoulder, whispering urgently.

At the podium, Kerry glanced at his notes and then gazed out again. "What I propose today is a national service requirement. Two years, at any time before you turn thirty, to be spent in any way—the Peace Corps, charitable foundations, the military, or a wide range of public interest work—that you feel embodies *your* best contribution to our country and to a better society."

"Pandering?" Lara remarked to Lee. "Unless I misunderstood him, he's just reinstituted the draft."

"I don't expect all of you to welcome this," Kerry was saying. "But I implore you to consider it, not just for your country but for yourselves. Because I've never known anyone who helped a child to read, or an old person to feel loved, who thought less of himself for doing that. Just as I've never known anyone whose sense of self was strengthened by ignoring those in need." As Kerry's eyes swept the crowd, he continued in a softer voice. "As Robert Kennedy told another generation of Berkeley students, 'In your hands, not with Presidents or leaders, is the future of your world and the fulfillment of the best qualities of your own spirit . . .'"

Kerry's questioner stood, applauding, then others. And in that moment, Lara saw Nate Cutler catch Kit Pace.

Lara watched them. Forehead next to Kit's, he briefly whispered; except for a nod, almost imperceptible, Kit was still.

Lara was suddenly aware of Lee McAlpine, following her gaze. Turning to Lee, she asked, "What did *you* think?"

Lee gave her a quizzical look, then smiled faintly. "I think he got away with it, don't you?"

Lara nodded.

Afterward, they left the auditorium, stepping into the sunlight. Leaning against the press bus, Nate talked to Kit alone, his face and gestures a pantomime of quiet urgency. Walking beside Lara, Lee murmured, "What's that about, I wonder?"

Lara felt the same sick feeling—alienation, fear, shame. "I wonder too," she answered.

Nate watched Kit's eyes narrow in restrained anger. "Where did you get this, Nate?"

Though tense himself, Nate managed to smile. "Come on, Kit. All I want is time with him."

"And all I can do is ask if he wants to dignify this crap, which you seem to have gotten off a bathroom wall. He's running for President, after all. That tends to take up his time."

Nate stared at her, face hard, voice low. "Do you people really think you can sit on this? If they had a relationship, we'll find it . . ."

"*What* relationship? Warm looks? A dinner or two?"

"You don't make love at dinner, Kit. Or *we'd* be even closer than we are."

Kit's eyes became distant, opaque. Her tone held muted disgust. "And that's what you want to ask him."

"Among other things." Nate's voice was a staccato whisper. "She's on the fucking *bus* with us, *covering* him. If he refuses to answer, we've got every right to print *that*, too. And everything else we know."

"Such as?"

Nate felt his temples throb. "You've got forty-eight hours, Kit. Me and the senator, alone."

Kit stared at him, then nodded. "I'll get back to you," she said, and walked away.

As a young state rep was about to slip into the car with him, Kerry saw Kit Pace place her hand on the man's arm.

"I'm sorry," she told him, "but I need to talk to Kerry."

Briefly, Kerry apologized. Even before Kit sat beside him, uncharacteristically subdued, he knew what this was about.

Kit glanced at Joe Morton and Dan Biasi, sitting in the front seat, seemingly oblivious. "Cutler's in the pool today," she said. "This won't wait."

It was a moment that Kerry had hoped would never come. He tried to imagine what Kit thought of him, how she might interpret what she knew. But there was no way to ask, or to explain.

Once more, Kit's eyes flickered toward the two agents. "Nate's spelled out his area of inquiry," she told him. "Unless you give him an interview in forty-eight hours, he says your refusal is a story in itself."

Kerry turned away, staring out the window as the Berkeley campus slipped behind them. "Will Cutler accept you as an intermediary?"

"No." Kit's tone was candid, unflinching. "You can see the problem here."

Turning, Kerry managed a slight smile. "I used to be a prosecutor, Kit. If you can't prove the underlying charge, trap your target in a lie."

Kit nodded. "Whether she went to your place. Whether you went to hers. Anything they think they can prove that looks damning."

Kerry looked down. "It really is Hobson's choice, isn't it? If I say no, maybe I'm a liar. If I say yes, she came to my place, it's 'Why? What hours? When did she leave?' It never ends."

He heard Kit exhale. "I don't want to know anything about this, Kerry, and I don't care. We bought a day, and now *Newsworld*'s spelled this out, just as I demanded. So I need an answer for Cutler."

"*Cutler,*" he said disgustedly. "Can we stretch this out any more, I wonder?"

Kit frowned. "I don't know," she answered. "But that forty-eight hours isn't an arbitrary deadline. It's the last day *Newsworld* can get a story into print for next Tuesday's edition. After leaking the story on Monday, so everyone will read it."

Even as he nodded, Kerry struggled with his disbelief that loving Lara had come to this. That two years of grueling effort, spent on the brink of exhaustion, could now mean nothing. That his hopes of becoming President could rest on what he told Nate Cutler.

"I keep thinking of something I read once, Kit: 'Character is who you are in the dark.' " His tone was musing. "It's why I try hard not to lie. In this business, you have to have some idea of who you are, or you're lost. That's always been Dick Mason's problem."

Kit's voice was firm. "That's why it's better you be President than Mason, Kerry. No matter what you say to Cutler."

For a long time, Kerry gazed out the window as they crossed the Bay Bridge, watching the skyline of San Francisco move closer. "Tell Cutler I'll see him on Sunday," he said.

THREE

By the time the motorcade reached the Mission District, Dolores Park was bright with sun, its line of palm trees a vivid green against a flawless blue sky.

Lara and Lee McAlpine trundled off the press bus with the others, heading for the bleachers at the far side of the crowd. The speakers' platform was flanked by blocks of houses whose windows faced the park. It was a Secret Service headache, Lara knew—too many lines of fire. But the crowd was large and festive, primarily Latin, men and women in jeans and cotton shirts or dresses chatting in English or Spanish. Here and there were groups of kids let out of school, waving colorful banners. Spotting a cluster of nuns, Lara smiled to herself, knowing that Kerry would like seeing them.

"Did you see the Field Poll this morning?" Lee asked. "Forty-two to forty-one in favor of Mason, with seventeen percent undecided. They say it could be the closest primary ever."

"Depends on turnout," Lara answered. "Kilcannon's got to get minorities to the polls. Latinos in particular."

Lee scanned the crowd, swelling to cover the sweep of grass. "At least three thousand, I'd guess. Not bad."

Lara nodded. "You know what's sad, though? What's happened to this neighborhood. This park's a microcosm—drug dealing, gang murders at night, people afraid to come here. It's been like this since I was in high school, slowly getting worse."

On the speakers' platform, Kerry appeared in shirtsleeves.

Lara experienced the now-familiar ache; the sense of loss; the jarring fear for his safety. The strange complicity between two people who could no longer speak, yet knew the truth of a relationship that could, in a moment, end his chances. Then a Latina county supervisor began Kerry's introduction, her amplified voice cutting through the hum of the crowd, and Lara saw three middle-aged women raise a banner. "Senator," it asked, "if an unborn child is a 'life,' why commit murder?"

For an instant, Lara was still. Turning again to Kerry, she tried to screen out everything but her job.

Twenty feet away, Nate watched Kilcannon's face, trying to gauge whether he seemed dispirited.

"This," Kilcannon began, "is a community under siege.

"There is a certain class of politician, in this state and in this country, who try to win elections by finding a minority group to run against. For some, that target has been Latino immigrants—whether legal or illegal." Stopping, Kilcannon surveyed the crowd. "Because politicians looking for a scapegoat don't want to make distinctions, or admit the facts."

This speech would be aimed at galvanizing Latinos, Nate knew, but what was more notable was that Kilcannon was not afraid to polarize. This was the great secret of American politics, Nate believed. True leaders make choices; the moral difference is which ones. It was something Kilcannon seemed to understand, and Mason did not.

"But the facts," Kilcannon went on, "are appalling.

"We've cut off the elderly and frail from government services for the sin of immigrating legally.

"We deny the children of illegal immigrants—those exploited in the dirtiest jobs—any chance to rise above where they started.

"We force adults not to be immunized.

"We force mothers not to seek prenatal care."

The crowd was silent; Kilcannon's face had a passion so visceral that Nate could feel it. "But for every person," he said clearly, "to whom we deny basic health care, we double the threat of public contagion and the cost of emergency treatment. For every child we deny an education because we think it the son or daughter of illegals, we add to the population of gang members, criminals, the illiterate and the hopeless. For every adult we scare away, we will pay the price in dollars and in human misery—not just among immigrants but in the population at large."

Nate watched the crowd again. Kilcannon had them, Nate thought; most seemed to listen intently, almost hungrily, eyes fixed on the candidate.

"Ask any cop," he told them, "any doctor, any teacher. Ask anyone who deals with the consequences of these blindly punitive policies." Pausing, Kilcannon added softly, "Ask yourselves.

"Ask yourselves, and then ask yourself *this* question: Isn't it time to take matters into your own hands?

"I want you to support me, that's true. But no leader can help a community unless it takes enough pride in its own people and its own streets to fight for itself, vote by vote and block by block.

"Tell your state and city government what you need and are willing to do to improve your own lives. And, if that doesn't work, tell *me* . . ."

Nate started at the hand on his shoulder.

Turning, he saw Kit Pace, her face an amiable mask for those around them. "He'll see you on Sunday," she murmured. "When I know his schedule, I'll give you a time."

At the corner of his vision, Kerry saw Kit with Cutler. Hastily, he faced the crowd again as a yellow banner rose above it, demanding to know how he could murder the unborn.

He stopped speaking, just for a moment, and then blocked it out of his mind.

"Please," he implored, "don't let apathy and despair be as real for your children as it may seem to you."

Pausing, Kerry found his coda, a link between his own life and theirs. "You, like my immigrant parents, and all the children of immigrants I knew when I was young, have helped to make this a stronger, better country. Now help each other, help your families, help yourselves."

As Lara listened, Lee McAlpine said, "When he's like this, Kilcannon seems like a real person."

Lara gave her a small smile. "Compared to what?"

"Compared to Mason. Who seems like a real politician. All the time."

It was true, Lara thought. But what she could not tell Lee was that *this* was closest to who Kerry was; that it was the politician in Kerry who seemed to her more invented.

She began looking for her cameraman, to file her report.

It was as if, for this moment, the applause was not for Jamie, but for him.

Grinning, Kerry turned to Supervisor Susan Estevez, a community activist whose hair had gone from black to gray in the years between his brother's death and now. Together, they stepped off the platform and into the crowd, the police and Secret Service agents scrambling after them.

There were outstretched hands in front of him, children thrust out to hold. Kerry touched everyone he could reach, looking into faces, saying "Thank you," over and over, hugging a small girl he had noticed. Next to him, Susan Estevez said, "They love you." Nodding, Kerry murmured, "I feel that."

Slowly, they worked through the crowd to the edge of the park, Susan greeting her constituents in rapid-fire Spanish. "I'm hungry," Kerry told her. "Aren't you?"

Susan smiled. "There's a *taquería* on Guerrero Street. No fancy restaurants, remember?"

Laughing, Kerry answered, "Let's go."

Moving down Seventeenth Street, Kerry felt the press of bodies around him—the Secret Service, the pool of reporters, the crowd that followed. He touched more hands; he had time, Kerry decided, and he was sick of life in the bubble, of worrying about *Newsworld* and a past he could not change.

At the corner of Guerrero and Seventeenth, he followed Susan inside the *taquería*.

It was small and dark and smelled of pork and cooked

vegetables and seasonings. Kerry sat at the counter with Susan. The proprietor, a mustached man with gray-brown hair and a smile that crinkled his eyes, held out his hand.

"Senator," he said, "I'm Frank Linares. For you, the lunch is free. As it was for your brother."

Behind the counter, Kerry saw a picture of Jamie and Linares. In his surprise, Kerry was quiet. His brother smiled back at him. "How long ago?" Kerry asked.

Linares's eyes turned serious. "Twelve years."

Just before he died, Linares did not add. But Kerry could see it; in death, Kerry had noticed the crow's-feet at the corners of Jamie's eyes, the new streaks of silver at his temples. As he saw them now, in Jamie's picture.

Belatedly, Kerry noticed the press pool crowding in the doorway, Nate Cutler among them.

When Kerry turned again, Linares had placed an empty beer glass on the bar.

"Too early for me," Kerry said with a smile. "Drink a beer, and I'll fall asleep."

Linares gave him a shy look. "Your brother drank from that glass. I've kept it."

Kerry gazed into the man's brown eyes, and saw what this meant to him. "What did Jamie have?" he asked.

"Dos Equis."

Kerry nodded. "Share one with me."

Next to him, Susan Estevez smiled. Frank Linares poured Kerry a few inches of beer, then some for himself, and touched his glass to Kerry's. "To you, sir. May you become President."

As your brother never did, Linares left unsaid. Within the toast was a prayer, a benediction.

"Thank you," Kerry said softly, and sipped his beer. After a moment, he turned to Susan Estevez. "This has been a good day," he told her. "Before we leave, I'd like to visit headquarters."

Sean Burke hung up the telephone and, for a moment, was in Boston.

It was the last call from Paul Terris, the local leader of Operation Life; the time was close to ten at night, and Sean was in his room.

"Sean," Terris said simply, "please don't come to meetings anymore."

Sean's fingers clasped the telephone. Answering, he found that his chest was tight. *"Why?"*

"You know why. We may agree about goals, but we're far apart on means."

Sean stood. The sparely furnished room—a bed, a desk, some drawers, the crucifix on the wall—felt shabby and too small. "Because we're cowards," Sean said angrily. "We're like witnesses to the Holocaust. We stand outside these chambers of death while they keep on killing babies."

"So what is 'militant action'? Acts of violence?" Terris's voice was so quiet and patient that Sean felt he was being treated like a child. "If we believe abortion is murder, how can we advocate murder?"

He had never told Paul exactly what he meant, Sean realized. But now it was clear to him. "Because these murderers choose to violate God's law," he answered. "America executes murderers all the time. Except for the abortionists."

"Sean," Terris said coldly, "if any of us says that aloud, decent people will turn their backs. And if one of us acts on it, Operation Life may cease to exist."

Sean felt the dark fear of rejection, of isolation, of scorn. And then, in his pain, he saw the truth of his solitude—alone Sean Burke was free to act. He would show this club for pacifists the courage they lacked.

"What difference would *that* make," Sean asked with bitter scorn, "to all the children you watch die?"

Hands trembling, he put down the telephone, severing his connection to the man who, for four years now, had given his life its meaning and its mission.

Deep in the night, an image came to him.

It was the man who had murdered Rabin, that traitor to *his* cause. Stepping from the crowd, the executioner had aimed his gun at the traitor's back, and by this lone act had changed the history of a region and the spirit of a people . . .

"John," Rick Ginsberg said now. "He's coming."

"Who?" Sean asked, then flushed at Ginsberg's smile.

"The senator. He'll be here in fifteen minutes."

Sean swallowed. No gun, he thought. Only a knife, with Secret Service agents between them.

"Dammit," Kate Feeney said behind him. "I have to go."

How long would it take, Sean wondered, to pull the knife from inside his jacket and plunge it into Kilcannon's heart? He clenched his jaw, imagining his hand falling short, the bullet entering his brain. "Are you all right?" Ginsberg asked him.

He was *afraid*, far more so than when he executed the abortionist. Afraid of the look on Kerry Kilcannon's face. Afraid for himself, dying at Kilcannon's feet.

Panicky, he turned to Kate. "You stay here," he said in a trembling voice. "I'll go."

Her eyes widened, surprise and hope struggling on her face with the wish not to be selfish. "Are you sure?"

Sean nodded curtly.

She hesitated another moment, as if trying to read his face. "Do you know which bus to take? You just go on Geary to Powell."

Fifteen minutes, perhaps less. Sean stood to leave. "I'll find it."

Heading for the door, he heard Rick call out behind him. "Wait, John. Let me tell you what to do."

The trace of impatience in Ginsberg's voice made Sean more anxious. He stood there, unable to leave, glancing over his shoulder at the showroom windows facing the street. "There'll be pamphlets on the table," Rick told him, "a sign-up sheet for volunteers, and a list for people who want us to get them to the polls. Make sure you ask everyone if they want to help us, or how we can help them."

Sean felt the fear of being trapped here, and then the dread of meeting people in person, torn from the anonymity of the telephone. All he could do was nod.

Rick placed a hand on his shoulder, freezing him. "It's nice you're doing this for Kate. I know how much meeting the senator means to you. If there's some way I can make it up, I will."

Sean found he could not answer. Ginsberg's brow furrowed,

as if sensing his words were inadequate. "There are three more days, John . . ."

As Rick patted him on the shoulder, Sean turned toward the door. His footsteps echoed in the cavernous room.

Through the glass, he saw people clustered on the sidewalk—the receptionist, other volunteers, men in sunglasses who looked like Secret Service agents. Then, as if in a silent film, a black limousine glided to a stop in front of them.

Three feet from the doorway, Sean froze.

A second car pulled up, filled with men who looked like Secret Service agents. They spilled from the car, surrounding Kilcannon's limousine. As an agent opened its door, Sean's heart raced.

Slowly, Kerry Kilcannon got out.

Utterly still, Sean watched him through the glass.

Kilcannon waved briefly to the crowd, his grin curiously shy, as if their applause surprised him. They moved toward him as one.

As though caught in their vortex, Sean went out the door, eyes locked on Kilcannon's face.

Next to Kerry, the agents in sunglasses watched the crowd. Sean stood behind the cluster surrounding Kilcannon, watching Kerry greet the mahogany-skinned receptionist. He could get to him, Sean suddenly thought, thrust the knife toward Kilcannon's throat before the agents shot him.

If only he could see their eyes.

Reaching out toward Kate Feeney, Kilcannon saw him. He seemed to hesitate . . .

Sean flinched, turning away, and scurried down the sidewalk.

Who was he? Kerry thought. Pale, shrinking from contact, with a face unlike the others—hungry, possessed, unsmiling. What was this odd flicker of fear, of recognition.

It was false *pre*cognition, Kerry thought, the instinct for danger that made him study faces, looking for the eyes of a man who, like the one who murdered Jamie, wished to take his life. But Kerry had looked into ten thousand faces and had no time to wonder, or remember.

Jamie. Perhaps what had driven Kerry here to headquarters was the wish to thank those too young to remember, who worked not for a myth but because they believed in Kerry himself. He could feel what he meant to them, was learning what they meant to him.

Turning, he looked at the blond-haired girl in front of him. She was delicate, Irish by the look of her, poised between shyness and naked wonder at his presence. He reached out to her, smiling. "I'm Kerry Kilcannon," he said. "I wanted to thank you."

She took his hand, her touch soft, and then began grinning like she might never stop. "I'm Kate Feeney," she told him.

Kerry squeezed her hand. "Thanks, Kate. I'll remember you."

Sean ran away.

Chest pounding, he fought the sour sickness rising from his stomach to his throat, as he dodged pedestrians startled by his panic.

Stopping abruptly, he began to gasp.

He bent, wheezing, clasping his knees as his body shook with coughing. Eyes moist with anguish and humiliation, he stared at the spittle at his feet, stained with blood.

Coward, he told himself. The frightened child he once had been had returned to claim him.

As the press bus shuddered to a stop three blocks short of Kerry's headquarters, Lara saw him—a lone man, perhaps drunk or mentally disturbed, retching saliva as others passed him without looking. A sad piece of urban detritus, like so many Lara had seen here, people with stories that broke the heart. She could not seem to look away.

The man's body trembled, and then he straightened, staring wildly at the bus as if he had just noticed it.

Eyes narrowing, Lara leaned her face against the window.

She had seen him before, she was certain. But not recently, and she could not remember where. It could only have been here, she thought, in San Francisco.

Wheeling abruptly, the man ran away, vanishing from Lara's

vision and, moments later, her thoughts. The motorcade began moving again, toward the airport.

FOUR

It was past three in the afternoon when Kerry arrived in South Central Los Angeles.

The air was hot, dense with smog Kerry could feel on his collar. He stood on the steps of the Third Baptist Church, a plain stucco building dating to the thirties, transformed by the Reverend Carl Wills into a social center that provided food for the urban poor, day care, after-school programs in sports and remedial reading. Though Wills's congregation was mainly black, it reached out to Asians, Latinos, progressive whites, the urban poor. In a city marked by racial conflict, this set Wills apart.

For months, Kerry had worked to get Wills's endorsement; the minister, a calm but strong-minded man who would not be used by anyone, had deflected Kerry's appeals. When Wills's call had come, days before, it was a surprise. "Well," the minister told Kerry dryly, "guess you got a chance to win. I take that as a sign from God." His voice softened. "Don't let Him down, Senator. Or us."

Now Wills stood beside him—a gray-bearded man with a benign countenance and shrewd brown eyes—speaking to a group of his supporters, the pool, and, well behind them, the remaining press.

"When no other congressman or senator would come to this state and say ending affirmative action was wrong, Kerry Kilcannon *did*.

"When no other candidate dares to stand up for the farmworkers, Kerry Kilcannon *does*.

"When no other of our politicians strives to save our cities, Kerry Kilcannon *will*.

"And when almost every President tries to hide from the problems of race, Kerry Kilcannon *won't*." Wills raised his hand. "This country needs a leader, not a pollster; a healer, not a wheeler-dealer; a conscience-raiser, not a fund-raiser."

Slowly, Wills lowered his hand, placing it on Kerry's shoulder.

"This is the man," he said. "This is the one."

The two men turned to each other. It was a moment the boy Kerry Kilcannon, a parochial Irish kid in a city divided by race, could never have imagined.

"Don't let Him down," the minister repeated quietly.

Kerry smiled. "Perhaps Him," he answered. "But never you."

Wills nodded, looking at him intently, and then Kerry stepped up to the microphone. The crowd was mostly African Americans, some in suits or dresses, some not, but also Asians, whites, Latinos. In their faces, Kerry found his theme.

"When I meet a man like Carl Wills," he began, "when I see the work of this church, I wonder how anyone can seek office by asking us to vote against each other."

From a distance came the faint whine of a police siren. Kerry raised his voice. "Too often," he said, "we're told that politics is a matter of black versus white, suburbs versus city.

"It's the era of the frightened white man, we're told, of the endangered middle class. That's true. Many white Americans have a right to feel threatened—they're working hard for less money, and their kids go to lousy schools. And it is not their fault." Pausing, Kerry said succinctly, "Nor is it the fault of Asians, Latinos, or African Americans. Many of whom face the same problems.

"I hope the day comes when bigotry ends. But that day is not in sight. And every day that a politician claims that the only discrimination left favors minorities, and that the problems of white Americans will vanish when we end affirmative action, the *real* solution to our common problems slips further from view."

At the edge of his consciousness, Kerry heard the wail of

more sirens meet above the grid of treeless streets he had passed through in his limousine: rows of small stucco houses with barred windows; oil-stained asphalt lots; burned-out buildings; seedy strip malls; men loitering with boom boxes. But here and there were neighborhoods with well-kept lawns and no graffiti, where neighbors organized community-based day care and health centers. It was this that gave him hope.

"I'm here to answer your questions," he finished. "But I want to promise you this much—that I will always speak out for this community. And for hope, not fear."

The crowd applauded, a sound fainter than Kerry was used to, dissipating in the void: bare concrete, debris, abandoned storefronts, and, Kerry thought to himself, years of rhetoric that had left no trace. Looking into their faces—hopeful, wary, reserved—Kerry said, "Now tell me what's on your minds."

In the pool, Nate Cutler glanced at his watch.

It was three-thirty; he wanted to call Jane Booth, check on whether they had found anything new about Kilcannon and Lara Costello. But working the pool meant dogging the candidate, the absence of time or privacy.

The wail of sirens grew louder, more insistent. The Secret Service agents guarding Kerry seemed to tense.

What was it? Nate wondered. The air in South Central still crackled with volatility—too much crime, hopelessness, distrust or outright hatred between blacks and Asians and Latinos. Kilcannon could say what he wanted, even mean it, but the motorcade would move on.

Near them, a young black man in denim, with gold-rimmed glasses and the intense air of activism, demanded of Kilcannon, "What does affirmative action do for *us*?"

"For this community?" Kilcannon asked. "For many of you, damned little." Kilcannon unknotted his tie. "You obviously know that, or you wouldn't have asked the question. So let me ask *you* a question: How would *you* give people in *this* community choices and chances? And how can people in this community take better advantage of the opportunities they have?"

The man shook his head. "What about you, Senator? Have

you thought about it? Or do you think ripping off Martin Luther King's enough?"

Kilcannon's eyes seemed to flash. "Better Martin Luther King," he retorted, "than Louis Farrakhan. But your first question's worth answering."

Watch it, Nate thought. His interest suddenly intensified; there was about Kilcannon, most reporters believed, a whiff of buried anger which could hurt him. Whereas if Dick Mason had a temper, almost no one claimed to have seen it.

"Government can't transform South Central," Kerry said more evenly. "Or truckloads of cash. If they could, the war on poverty would be over, and this would be a garden spot."

There was a small ripple of cynical laughter. "One thing South Central needs," Kerry went on, "is more and better jobs. Private jobs, not make-work, based on training which encourages employers to come here, and stay here for the next generation.

"A lot's been written about what's wrong with black families, and a lot of it's unfair. Families—black or white—often break up because there's no hope, no jobs, no future. But churches like this one show how local institutions can help change things for the better. Especially if Washington cares to listen, and to learn." Stopping, Kerry looked around him, his demeanor transformed into sudden mocking innocence. "Where's Dick Mason, by the way? Does he ever call? Does he ever write? Did we only imagine him, like the Wizard of Oz?"

The crowd laughed more openly; they had begun to enjoy Kilcannon's edginess, Nate thought, his willingness to engage. "Well," he said to his interrogator, "for the moment you're stuck with me. And I believe we're both responsible for the future of South Central. So let me tell you what I think we can do together . . ."

The sirens were louder now, Nate realized. And then, abruptly, they were silent.

It was the silence that told Lara there was trouble. She could see that Wills sensed it too; standing still, he seemed to cock his head, listening for something he could not hear.

As Kerry finished, she saw a squad car pull up. A cop got

out—by the look of his gold braid, a senior officer—and hurried toward Carl Wills.

The officer was heavyset, with brick-red skin, a seamed, alert face, pale-blue eyes. Cop's eyes, Kerry thought.

Wills seemed to know him. As the crowd watched, anxiously speaking among themselves, the cop placed a hand on the reverend's shoulder and began talking in a low voice.

"Damn," Wills said under his breath. *"Damn."*

"What is it?" Kerry asked. He felt the Secret Service surround them.

The cop turned, grim-faced. "We have a shooting incident, Senator, involving a Korean grocer and a black kid. In the last year, the grocer's been held up twice, he says, by black men with Saturday night specials. So he bought himself a shotgun."

He spoke now to both Wills and Kerry. "Today two black kids came into his store after school, one thirteen, the other ten. The thirteen-year-old pulls out a plastic toy gun—as a joke, he says now—and asks Young for a box of Snicker bars. Next thing the kid knows, he's looking at the barrel of a gun.

"He drops the toy and begins running. On the way out the door, he hears a shotgun blast. Since then, nobody's seen the ten-year-old. He may be dead, wounded, or a hostage. We just don't know." The cop faced Wills again. "The grocer's locked up the store and pulled down the metal screens behind the doors and windows. Now there's a crowd, and the boy's mother's there, screaming at us to get him out. We may want your help."

Wills nodded. "We need calm here. All of us."

Kerry remembered Newark—the fortitude of Liam Dunn, the shells of buildings, the residue of hatred. "I'd like to go with you, Carl."

"Senator—" Dan Biasi began to protest, and then the cop cut in. "I'm sorry, Senator. The Secret Service doesn't want it, and we don't, either. We've got all we can handle, and we can't guarantee your safety."

So that's it, Kerry thought. *I just run away.* "There are no guarantees," he told the cop and Dan. "And I don't expect any." He turned to Wills again. "Maybe I can make a difference by coming. I can't tell people I care about what happens here, then drive off in a limousine."

Wills glanced at the policeman, and then the cop's face turned hard. "There are people in the crowd with guns, Senator, and some of them have been drinking. There aren't enough forms in the world to get rid of the liability. And I wouldn't put you in that crowd if you signed them all."

Nodding, Wills turned to Kerry. "Something happens to you, and this neighborhood, maybe race relations, get set back a long ways."

Kerry did not answer. Perhaps, he told himself, he had expected this before he asked to help.

As Wills rushed off, the Service closed around Kerry, hurrying him to his car.

When Sean Burke reached the Tenderloin, it was twenty minutes until four, and the street punk was nowhere in sight.

Sean felt wasted, shamed, pathetic in his self-hatred. He had run from his moment; now Kilcannon was in another city, safe in his cocoon of security, and Sean had become the walking dead.

For two hours, he had sat at a table in elegant Union Square, the sun beating down on him, the sweat on his face like a fever. A delirium overcame him; he was barely conscious of the people who stopped, of what he said. The Asian woman who took his place seemed more a dream than a person.

A death, a kind of death.

A lifetime ago, some other man had walked into an abortion clinic with a gun. Now all that was surreal fragments—a woman with a red hole in her forehead, the abortionist falling into a file cabinet, the supine body of a nurse. What felt real was flinching as he looked into Kilcannon's eyes.

Sean was already dead—putting a bullet through his brain would be no different than withdrawing life support from wasting flesh. Across the street, the prostitute with sores on her face and eyes like burn holes loitered on the sidewalk, a figure from hell; that she seemed to look right through him was no surprise.

A dead man.

Sean felt hard fingers on his shoulder.

Turning, he saw the black street punk. His eyes were like marbles—glassy, opaque. "I got your piece," he whispered.

The words jolted Sean. The black man touched the pocket of his pea coat. "In here," he said, "but I ain't gonna sell it to you on the street."

Yesterday, in another life, there was no way Sean could have trusted this man.

"Come on," the punk said.

Following him, trancelike, Sean stayed close.

Between the liquor store and a tenement hotel they found an alley lined with garbage cans, its pavement smelling of urine and rotten scraps of food. The man slowed, walking next to Sean, then a little behind, prodding Sean deeper into the alley. The dank sunlessness seemed to change the chemistry in Sean's brain, sending a current to his nerve ends.

The man was at his back now. "Turn around," he said.

Even before he complied, Sean could feel the gun against his stomach.

The soulless eyes stared at him. "Your wallet, man."

Dead, Sean thought. Though his fingers trembled, his mind felt calm, almost peaceful.

"It's not in your back pocket," the punk hissed. "I seen that. So you just tell me where it is."

Slowly, Sean reached for the inside pocket of his army jacket. As he found the handle of the knife, he watched the man's eyes. Their faces were so close that the smell of whiskey filled Sean's nostrils.

Take your time, Sean told himself. *You're already dead.*

Beneath his jacket, he pulled the knife up to his collar, still hidden.

"Careful, man. Don't make me waste you."

With a flick of his wrist, Sean turned the point of the knife to the street punk's throat.

"We're both dead," Sean whispered.

The punk blinked; through the blade of the knife, Sean could feel his throat twitch. Split-second calculation darted through the black man's eyes: if he pulled the trigger, Sean's knife might cut his throat. If he didn't . . .

Sean's fingers tightened on the knife.

"Man...," the punk mumbled.

Sean jammed the knife into his throat.

Pain shot through his wrist, metal hitting teeth. Sean's eyes shut against the bullet that would rip his stomach apart; he felt the punk's whiskey breath in his face, expelling a terrible squeal of agony.

The gun clattered on the sidewalk.

Slowly, Sean opened his eyes.

Impaled on the knife, the punk stared at him, eyes stricken, a foam of blood and saliva on his parted lips. The knife was stuck in his palate; all his power of movement seemed to have gone to his knees, buckling and twitching as blood seeped from his throat.

Placing a hand beneath the man's chin, Sean wrenched the blade out in one convulsive motion.

The man crumpled, falling on his side.

Repelled, Sean stepped back, staring. The punk's eyes were still open. His mouth made small gurgling sounds, and his breathing was shallow; Sean thought of a fish his father had thrown on a wooden dock, to die there.

Dropping the knife, he glanced toward the mouth of the alley.

No one there. A car drove by, so quickly that it was gone before Sean flinched.

He was alive.

Sweating, he picked up the punk—twitching, still alive—and awkwardly dumped him facefirst in a half-empty garbage can. The can teetered as skull struck metal.

Sean turned away.

Lying in a patch of oil was the knife and, near that, the gun.

Sean wiped the knife on the sole of his boot and put it in his pocket. As he reached for the gun, he saw the blood spatters on the sleeve of his coat.

The gun was oily, cheap-looking. But when Sean curled his fingers around the trigger, he saw the moment again, but somehow transformed: Kerry Kilcannon, eyes widening in fear as Sean aimed his weapon.

A faint cry came from the garbage can.

Sean looked up. The man's legs made spastic kicking movements, like those of a drowning child. But Sean felt no pity; the man had meant to rob him, perhaps kill him, and his death had brought Sean back to life.

In his other life, as John Kelly, people waited for him.

He was frightened, confused. All he knew for certain was that to run again was living death.

Slipping the gun in his pocket, Sean left the alley behind.

FIVE

In his hotel room, Nate Cutler watched a film clip taken from a helicopter—a police car, the Korean grocer inside, moving without resistance through a restive crowd. "Have you seen this?" he said into the telephone. "It's on CNN. I was in the pool today and heard Kilcannon ask to go."

"That's been reported," Jane Booth answered. "Sheer grandstanding, and so irresponsible. What happens if he gets hurt?"

Nate watched the screen. "What's happened so far," he pointed out, "is that no one else got hurt. Because Wills was prepared to go there."

"And Kilcannon," Jane said grudgingly, "gets credit for *wanting* to go. Maybe now he gets elected, so he can try to perform these wonders every month or so, taming the unruly. That's what we have Presidents for, after all." Her voice became caustic. "And Vice Presidents, in case things don't work out."

Nate gave a mirthless laugh. "Then maybe we're saving Kilcannon from himself," he said. "Does Sheila have anything more for me? It's less than two days before I interview him."

"One thing," Jane reported crisply. "But it's good—from a woman who lived on Lara's floor. She only saw Kilcannon once, she told Sheila. But he was banging on Costello's door, obviously upset, the woman says. This went on for several minutes, Kilcannon not caring who saw or heard him." Once more, Jane's tone became acid. "No wonder she moved—her boyfriend had no judgment. As he proved again today."

In her supercilious mood, Nate found, Jane was getting on his nerves. "When was this?" he asked.

"About the time Costello spilled it all to the counselor, Sheila thinks. Just before, the neighbor remembers, Costello took the job with NBC and left the country."

What was Kilcannon doing there? Nate wondered; this curious business of judging lives left him poised between queasiness and fascination. "Interesting," he said. "I don't suppose we're any closer to knowing who slipped the counselor's notes to our friends from Anthony's Legions."

"Not really, although there's the relationship between this woman Philips and the Christian Commitment. What remains ripe for speculation, as the pundits say, is what inspired one of America's most fervent anti-abortion groups to give it to their pro-choice enemies."

"Or who was in the middle." Nate gazed out the window at the skyline of downtown Los Angeles. It had always struck him as surreal, arbitrary, like a giant Lego set dropped suddenly from the moon. "To me," he went on, "that's as important as proving what happened with Lara and Kilcannon."

"Do you think so?" Jane asked dubiously. "Doesn't it depend on *who* the 'who' was? If anyone."

On the screen, the film shifted abruptly—paramedics bearing a litter covered by a white blanket to a waiting ambulance. "If the 'who' was Mason or the opposition," he answered, "it matters quite a lot. Because if either is using us to destroy Kilcannon's political future, people should know that, too. Then they can decide for themselves who's worse."

"Oh," Jane said tartly. "That one's simple—*us*. We're always the ones people blame. For what politicians do, and for our obligation to print that."

It was too simple, Nate thought. "They blame us *all*, Jane. It's another reason they don't vote."

"Perhaps." Jane's voice was filled with irony. "But they *do* read these things, don't they. And they never, ever blame themselves."

When Sean reentered headquarters, he stopped, looking around him.

Talking on the phone, the receptionist noted him with her eyes, then began writing a telephone number on a pad of paper. Numb, Sean walked past her; at the phone bank, Kate Feeney was making notes on the computer run, and a couple of early arrivals from work were sitting down in shirts and ties. To Sean, the air of normality was haunting.

Putting down her pen, Kate Feeney saw him and stood.

Sean froze. As she hurried toward him, he thought of his blood-spattered sleeve, the twitching body in the garbage can.

Kate began grinning. *"You,"* she said, "are *so* great." With skittering half-steps, she came to him, giving him an awkward hug.

Confused, Sean felt the sparrow lightness of her body against his chest, the fear that she would feel the gun still hidden in his jacket. Then Kate leaned back, grasping his sleeves with both hands. "I *met* him," she said. "Kerry."

That was it, Sean thought—Kilcannon. In a strained voice, he asked, "What was he like?"

"So nice. Really friendly. And those eyes . . ." She shook her head, as if trying to find words. "It's like he can look into your soul."

Sean could only nod.

Looking down, Kate seemed to focus on his sleeve. "What happened?" she asked.

Sean swallowed, repeating the response he had practiced on the bus. "Coffee," he answered. "When I was handing out leaflets."

Kate frowned. "I'm so sorry you missed him. Really. But as long as I live, I'll never forget."

How long, Sean wondered, would it take someone to find the body?

"John." It was Rick Ginsberg's voice, hearty with the good cheer of the motivator. "I've got some news, maybe."

Sean faced him, apprehensive.

Rick was smiling; to Sean, the pervasive good humor felt unnatural, untrustworthy. "I've gotten two calls today," Rick said. "From Clayton Slade, of all people—Kerry's national campaign manager. Kerry may schedule another event in San Francisco, after the debate. If he does, he'll need our help."

Sean was speechless. "After the *debate*?" Kate asked. "That's tomorrow night."

"It would be the next day," Rick amended. "Sunday morning. *If* they do it."

Kate bit her lip. "When will they decide?"

Still silent, Sean turned to Ginsberg.

"Tomorrow morning, at the latest." Rick smiled at Sean. "If it happens, it'll be crazy around here. But at least you get another chance."

In that moment, Sean was acutely aware of everything: the gun in his pocket, Ginsberg's demented cheer, Kate's eyes on his face, the memory of her body against his, the dead man in the alley, the dryness of his own mouth. He felt too much to speak.

Kerry lay back in the bathtub, achy and exhausted, reflecting on the tragedy in South Central and his own reaction to it. He had not wished to go, he knew; the mention of guns had silenced him.

Across from him, Clayton closed the lid over the toilet and sat. "Sorry," Clayton said. "But there's no rest for the weary."

Kerry raised his head. "What's this about Dick Mason?"

Clayton clasped his hands in front of him. "We've got the arrest records," he said. "From Darien. All I can tell you is that *we* didn't break the law to get them."

Pushing with his hands, Kerry sat straighter. "What do they say?"

"They're from 1978, two years before Dick went to Congress. Jeannie Mason filed a complaint—Dick was drunk, according to Jeannie. He'd hit her before, she told the police, and this was one blow too many."

What might have happened, Kerry found himself wondering, if his mother had called the police when he was young—or felt she could have? How might their family, might Kerry himself, be different? "What did they do?" Kerry asked. "The cops."

"Went to the DA. Who, as it happens, was a friend of Dick's. There was a quiet resolution—charges dismissed, Dick agrees to counseling. It never got to court." Clayton's voice became clipped. "Explains a few things, doesn't it. Like the fact that Dick drinks apple juice because it 'makes our family life more wholesome.'"

"Is there anything more recent?" Kerry asked.

"Not yet."

Kerry wiped his face with a washcloth. "I still remember, back at the prosecutor's office, you telling me to place more emphasis on helping abusive men. Maybe Dick got helped. If he hadn't, do you honestly think Jeannie would have stuck it out?"

"I don't know her." Clayton stood, arms folded. "What I'm pretty sure I *do* know is that Mason's behind this Lara thing. That's why it's coming out now, and that's why he wants these crazy debate rules. To confront you before Tuesday."

"So plant this, you say. And hope somebody prints it."

Clayton frowned. "If I'm right, why is Mason entitled to anything better than he's done to you?"

Once again, Kerry thought of holding Lara, the debris of what once lay between them, the potential ruin of two lives now. Roused from torpor, the anger inside him felt like a living thing. "Prove to me he did this, Clayton, and I'll think very hard about screwing him. Jeannie or no Jeannie."

Clayton's eyes met his, and then his friend gazed downward. "Speaking of wives," he said, "I talked with Meg today."

Startled, Kerry asked, "*Meg?* Why?"

"Why do you think? *Newsworld* came to visit her. Seems like they just had to share."

Kerry felt his anger merge with regret, then sadness. "Bastards," he murmured. "I never wanted her to know."

"Neither did she. 'Tell Kerry,' she said to me, 'that I don't want to hear about this anymore. From anyone.'"

Kerry rubbed the bridge of his nose. "What does *that* mean?"

"That she's not going to help them." Clayton's voice was soft now. "She says 'good luck,' by the way."

For a brief, depressing moment, Kerry had an image of Meg and himself before the first time they made love, ignorant of the gulf between them, the blasted hopes to come. "If you talk to Meg again," he said at last, "tell her thanks."

"Which brings me back to Cutler, Kerry. We're sending Nat Schlesinger to see his bosses in New York. To ask if they really know what they're doing."

"Oh, they know." Kerry looked up again. "Do we have a statement about the killing in South Central?"

"Uh-huh. Kit wrote it the way you wanted: that this is a tragedy caused by guns and urban crime; that your prayers are with the victims' families; that you're glad no one else got hurt; that great credit goes to Reverend Wills and the people of South Central. And that you have nothing else to say."

"What else *can* I say? Anything more, and offering to go there turns into a campaign stunt. Some will call it that, anyhow—after all, this is about a murdered ten-year-old, not me." Pausing, Kerry shook his head. "I guess my message of racial progress got a little lost."

"What you tried to do was stupid," Clayton said in his flattest voice. "I guess you know that. So you're right that the only choice now is heroic modesty." He gave a first, thin smile. "With any luck, and some graceful silence, you'll be up a point by morning."

" 'Heroic,' " Kerry said wearily. "I learned about *that* from you as well, after the Musso shooting. The less a 'hero' says, the better. Especially when he *knows* better."

Clayton sat again. "If you're waiting for a day without scrutiny, Kerry, you'll be waiting for a long time. Unless you give up on running for President."

Kerry felt the truth of this settle over him. Quietly, he answered, "I can't give up. Not now."

"Then consider what I said about Mason. The standard here

isn't legal—'guilty beyond a reasonable doubt.' It's political, which means 'best guess.' " Clayton's voice was quiet again. "We can't find anything on this counselor, Kerry—at least nothing that makes her look bad. Making *Dick* look bad is the best alternative."

Kerry felt his mind recede into the world of practical politics—constituencies, polls, the new ambivalence of pro-choice women toward Kerry himself. The cost of speaking what, to him, was a painful, complex truth.

"What about this rally in San Francisco?" he inquired at last. "Ellen Penn thinks she can help us draw a crowd, and I don't want to infuriate her more than I already have. But the mayor's for Dick, so we get no help there."

Clayton's eyes grew thoughtful. "In about three hours," he answered, "we'll have Jack's tracking numbers. Then we can decide."

SIX

When Lara arrived at Citrus with Lee McAlpine and Sara Sax, Nate Cutler was waiting at their table.

Lara had a jarring sense of betrayal; dinner had been for three, not four. "I decided to join you," Nate told Lee, "when I found out Lara was coming." He smiled up at Lara. "I see these guys every day. But after Tuesday, you vanish from our lives."

You prick, she thought. *Now everything I say tonight will end up in your story.* She managed to return his smile. "But you'll be in my thoughts, Nate. Never doubt it."

Her eyes met his, sending a brief signal of anger and dislike, and then the three women sat down. Four reporters, Lara thought sourly, resting from the pressures of the day in an up-scale L.A. restaurant. But there would be no rest for her now.

"So," Nate asked as they ordered drinks, "what do you make of Kilcannon chasing fire trucks? Or trying to."

Lara determined to remain silent; if Nate planned to make Kerry the subject, she wanted no part of it. "With Kilcannon," Lee answered, "the question is always *why* he does what he does. When you report that Kilcannon asked to attend a riot, you're barely scratching the surface."

Nate sipped his daiquiri. "My editor says the answer's simple—votes."

"But what do *you* think?"

Nate smoothed the tablecloth in front of him. "Kilcannon doesn't want to be irrelevant. He sees Mason practicing the politics of gestures, and to him politics demands the willingness to take risks."

"Do you honestly think there *was* a risk?" Lee retorted. "The cops didn't let him anywhere near."

"But if they *had* . . ." Nate shrugged. "Dick Mason would have waited until South Central burned to the ground, and then shown up with federal money for the Derek Baker Memorial Youth Center. Or whatever this dead kid's name was." He turned to Lara. "Any opinions, Ms. Costello? You knew him when."

Lara's smile was cool. "I'm with your editor," she said in her flattest voice. "Never give these people credit for anything. Why risk disappointment?"

As Nate looked at her, Lara felt Lee's quick glance. "For me," Lee said to Nate, "dissecting these characters is the fun part. The more I'm around them, the more I'm detached from what they say. It's *who* they are that matters. I mean, look at the President. You can't tell me his personal problems aren't about something deeper."

Nate nodded. "That's why my editor's wrong, with all re-spect to Lara. At least about Kilcannon." Glancing around the table, he let his gaze settle on Lara. "Take this abortion thing, for example. Politically, what Kilcannon said about a fetus being a 'life' was dumb, especially within his party. So there has to be some other reason."

This sudden clammy feeling, Lara realized, reminded her of the night when Nate had first confronted her. "Maybe he believes it," she said simply. "Despite what you and I might think. Or think expedient."

Nate cocked his head, a man who had won a point. "Then you *do* give him credit for principles. Even though you told me once that the key to Kerry Kilcannon was life experience."

Lara felt her face harden. "It was a theory, Nate. Formed at the time I was a charter member of Lee's school: reportage as psychoanalysis."

"And now you don't believe that?"

Lara shrugged. "In Africa it seemed a little less pertinent, that's all. Witnessing starvation tends to reorder one's priorities." She sipped her gin gimlet. "So, Nate, we know why Lee does her job. Why do you do *yours*?"

It was a diversion, Nate must know. But he gave Lara a considering glance, as though he owed her a serious answer. "This may sound like a Fourth of July speech. But I went to J school believing that if you tell the American voter what's going on, he'll make the right decision. Or at least a better one."

"Well," Lara said, smiling, "you've come a long way."

Nate stared at her. "The American voter," Sara Sax put in, "is impossibly stupid and incredibly apathetic. But I still love the game. When they launched the anti–affirmative action initiative out here and its supporters ran ads quoting Martin Luther King, I found myself laughing out loud. It's completely reprehensible, of course, but it's *so* much fun."

"That's *another* thing Kilcannon opposed," Nate responded. "Repealing affirmative action. He has this taste for underdogs, and losing causes."

"But *why*?" Lee asked. "He won't talk about himself, except to joke, and you're left with all these questions. What was he like as a kid? Did he love Mom and Dad? What did his brother really mean to him?"

"Or," Nate said, "for that matter, what happened to his marriage?"

Lara watched him across the table. Softly, she asked, "Does it matter to you so much, Nate?"

He gave her a long, level glance. "Depends on the answer. But, as a reporter, I think I'm entitled to know. Then I can make a judgment as to whether the public needs to know."

Like God, Lara thought in anger, and then realized that four years ago, she would have said much the same things. "So what's your test of need? Is it an ad hoc judgment, based on competition? Or, as our critics would suggest, circulation."

Lara felt Lee study her; the conversation had taken on a sense of covert hostility, with Nate and Lara as antagonists. "There's no bright line," Nate said evenly, "but I'll give you the most obvious test—hypocrisy. Where a politician's private life is at odds with his public statements."

How can you know that, Lara wanted to ask, *when I'm the only one who knows?* She felt Nate drawing her in, and struggled for a means of deflecting him. "Then let me pose a hypothetical," she said. "For everyone.

"We have a governor of Florida—strong on family values, married twenty years, a nice-seeming wife and two nice kids. The voters love him for it.

"There's only one problem: you've just found out that he's passionately in love with his chief legislative aide. A guy.

"He's not a gay baiter; as much as the politics of Florida permits, his public attitude toward gays is pretty benign. But seventy percent of Florida's voters would consider that being homosexual is pertinent to his qualifications for governor. In other words," Lara finished dryly, "the folks Nate is looking out for, but who Sara thinks are dumb, are dying to know about the inner life that Lee believes is so critical. Do we run the story?"

Lee scowled at the tablecloth. "If he's not a hypocrite—"

"Why ruin his life?" Lara finished. "Exactly. But consider this: all of us are sympathetic to gays, and many voters aren't."

"So we're elitist?"

"Of course. And inconsistent too."

"But are *my* standards the public's?" Nate broke in. "And if so, *which* public? The people who read the *National Enquirer*?"

Smiling slightly, Lara turned to him. "That's a really good question, Nate. I'm not sure I know the answer."

For the first time, Nate seemed to flush. "The man's not a hypocrite, you say, or a liar."

"Oh, but you can make him one." Lara strained to keep her voice and demeanor calm. "One day, you corner him in an interview, allegedly about Cuban immigration. Instead you've got notes from a psychiatrist, where he pours out his heart about how much he loves his aide but can never tell the truth.

" 'Now's your chance,' you say to him.

"But you know better, of course. The truth will ruin his marriage and career. So he lies, like you expect him to." Her voice was soft. "Then you nail him with the confession of a former boyfriend and run it as a cover story. Because the governor of Florida *lied* to you."

Nate gazed at her steadily. "I don't think I'd do that, Lara."

Lara smiled again. "No? Just checking." She looked around the table. "Which one of us rolls over on the governor?"

There was silence. "No one," Sara said.

"An act of mercy," Lee chimed in, and then their somewhat epicene waiter arrived.

As the others ordered, Lara looked around them. The glittering room, the flashy crowd, seemed unreal. Lara had no appetite; she ordered a salad and an appetizer—for form—and felt Nate still watching her.

"Chardonnay," he said to Lara. "Is that still your favorite?"

"That's fine," she answered, and handed the waiter her menu.

"A bottle of the Peter Michael," he said, smiling. "And keep another cold."

The waiter left. "Expensive," Sara Sax remarked.

"We work hard," Nate said, "and suffer greatly. Speaking of which, Sara, did you *ever* seduce that Secret Service agent?"

Sara summoned a melancholy smile. "If I had, would I be *here*?"

"Sure," Lee answered, "because you'd be hungry. That's what happens to me—onion rings at midnight."

"Really?" Nate asked. "For me, it's chocolate mints." Once more, he turned to Lara. "Speaking of sex, I've been working on another hypothetical. Interested?"

Watching his eyes, newly intense, Lara said nothing.

"Sure," Lee answered.

"Okay." Nate glanced around the table. "Same governor of Florida, same wife, same two kids. Only now he's heterosexual and a raging pro-lifer.

"His youngest kid is ten, and his wife has a good job—doing TV interviews, let's say. Plus, she's sick of kids.

"One day, to her horror, she discovers that her diaphragm let her down." Pausing, Nate faced Lara. "Another baby would be simply too depressing. So she decides on an abortion. And on the morning her husband tells a group of ministers that abortion is unacceptable even in the case of rape or incest, she has one." His voice softened. "What do you think, Lara? Do we print *this* one?"

Lara's skin felt cold. "Ask Lee and Sara. Why should I have all the fun?"

Turning to Lee, Nate raised his eyebrows.

"What does the governor say afterward?" Lee asked, then stopped herself. "I guess that doesn't matter. If he's still pro-life, he's a hypocrite. If he softens his position, the public has a right to know that it comes from personal experience. One a lot of women have had."

"What about her privacy?"

Lee frowned. "That would be a factor, normally. But she's married to a public official who's vocal on the subject. That trumps privacy."

As Lara sipped from her water glass, Nate turned to Sara Sax. "What about you?"

"I'm pro-choice, period. So I have a bias here." Sara folded her hands in front of her, brow furrowed. "Yeah, I'd run it. What's so fucked up is the gap between what these moral crusaders want to impose on other people, and what they want for themselves. There's a total absence of humanity."

"Two to zip." Nate looked across the table at Lara. "Back to you, I think."

Lara's eyes met his. "Aren't we forgetting something?"

"What's that?"

"Whose choice it was."

Nate gave her a thin smile. "The woman's choice, I think all us secular humanists agree."

"Then tell me how *he* felt," Lara said, "and I'll give you an answer."

Nate's smile lingered. But his eyes were serious now, reflective. In his silence, the waiter returned with the wine.

Nate sipped it. "Perfect," he said. "Worth every penny *Newsworld* spends."

The others laughed. When, Lara wondered in despair, did she stop feeling part of this? The first time Kerry touched her, or just a moment ago—Nate stalking her amidst the banter. Yet they were good people, she knew. Competitive, certainly; with strong egos, certainly; but professionals who worked hard and cared about what they did. Only *she* was no longer one of them.

"Speaking of lies," Lee asked, "and expense accounts, which newsworthy figure am I having dinner with tonight?"

"Kerry Kilcannon," Sara Sax suggested brightly. "Of course."

Nate's gaze flickered to Lara. "Not credible. Kilcannon's been avoiding us."

Following his eyes, Lee's own glance at Nate was sharp. "Why not Kit Pace? *She* still seems to have time for you."

With an innocent smile, Nate raised his glass. "To Kit."

Lara left her glass where it was.

SEVEN

Alone in his hotel room, Sean Burke checked the gun for bullets.

It was full. A belated fear washed over him, like the aftershock of a bad dream: the street punk could have killed him; the corpse in the alley could have been Sean's. He closed his eyes, cradling the gun in his hand, the sound of the television as muted as prayer.

He was running out of time. Once they traced him to San Francisco, only the name "John Kelly" stood between Sean and the police. His last chance was thirty-six hours away and rested in the hands of Kerry Kilcannon.

Kilcannon, Sean thought with fresh anger—a man who defended blacks instead of unborn children. It was incomprehensible to Sean: one group so rife with drugs, idleness, immorality; the other so innocent, so unsullied.

From the television, a voice broke through.

"On February 12, 1988, a young lawyer went to court."

Sean's eyes flew open.

On the screen, Kilcannon's face appeared. *"Already,"* the voice-over continued, *"he had dedicated four years of his life to protecting women from violence.*

"Now he had come to protect another woman, and her son . . ."

Sean walked to the television, fixated on the screen.

"But someone else came to court that day—a man with a gun. The woman's abusive husband."

There was a pop, the sound of a bullet firing. The gun twitched in Sean's hand.

The picture changed.

A guard stood over a dead man. Near him, sprawled in the doorway of a courtroom, was the body of a woman.

Slowly, the picture panned away.

Kilcannon lay beside her, bleeding from his shoulder. His other arm sheltered a traumatized dark-haired boy.

"Kerry Kilcannon," the woman's voice finished, *"because caring is more than talk."*

Tears blurring his vision, Sean placed the gun to the glass screen, to Kerry Kilcannon's head.

In the bathroom, Kerry splashed water on his face. Briefly, he considered his pallor, the puffiness beneath his eyes. For the debate tomorrow, he told himself with resignation, the makeup people might finally have their way with him.

A voice disrupted his thoughts.

"In Boston," the local NBC anchorwoman said, *"police released the first sketch of the man who murdered three people on Tuesday at the Boston Women's Clinic . . ."*

Curious, Kerry walked to the living room, gazing at the young man in the ski hat.

He felt a certain unease, perhaps at the crime itself, perhaps at the face on the screen. It was remorseless, and its fierce, killer's eyes had a somewhat Asian cast: Kerry wondered whether this was an accurate depiction of the man himself or represented the fears of the woman who had seen him.

"He is described as a slender man in his early twenties," the voice-over continued, *"roughly six feet tall, with dark hair and pale skin. Police caution that this composite is based on the description provided by the lone survivor . . ."*

Studying the picture, Kerry felt a kind of frisson. Then he heard someone knocking on the door.

He turned off the television and answered.

Holding a sheaf of fax paper, Clayton entered. He glanced at the briefing books for the debate, strewn across the coffee table.

"I hope you've memorized it all," he remarked.

Kerry grimaced. "This stuff on balance of payments gives me a headache. If I'm elected, can we find someone else to worry about that?"

"All sorts of people. The pain in the ass will be sorting them out." Sitting on a chair next to the couch, Clayton smiled fractionally. "As of the moment, your chances of *that* are a little brighter. Jack's tracking numbers put you ahead of Dick for the first time. A one percent margin's not much comfort, but maybe there's a trend."

Kerry sat across from him, torn between caution and excitement. "Where are we gaining?"

"You're galvanizing your base, as they say—at least among minorities. It's a combination of the ads we've run and your last couple of days' campaigning. South Central may end up working for you: a significant plurality think you'd be better at resolving racial problems."

Kerry nodded. "How many undecided?"

"Almost twelve percent." Clayton's face was serious now. "Three days before an election, that's pretty high. Jack thinks the debate's frozen a lot of them—that they'll decide after watching you tomorrow night."

Kerry winced. "If you're trying to help me relax, try something else."

Clayton leaned forward, expression grave. "Dick's got to be seeing these numbers, too, and imagining his entire adult life going down the toilet. He's going to be desperate, Kerry. Be prepared for anything."

Kerry thought of Lara, tear-streaked, absorbing the shock on her lover's face. "I've tried to imagine it," Kerry said softly. "I've spent hours wondering how Dick will do this. Perhaps a hypothetical . . ." Pausing, he looked up. "Where are we with pro-choice women?"

"Still soft. Especially among those to whom choice means the most."

Narrow-eyed, Kerry placed a finger to his lips. "Schedule that rally," he said at last. "Sunday morning, after I meet with Cutler. I'll call Ellen Penn myself to tell her how much I care."

Clayton nodded. "And I'll call San Francisco."

After Clayton left, Kerry sat in the living room.

He was a practical politician, with a practical problem. And all that he could manage was the pointless wish to turn back time.

Putting down the telephone, Lara closed her eyes.

She had called her voice mail at NBC. There was the usual run of messages—a meeting about her new show, a request to speak to a Hispanic women's group, another marriage proposal from the same unstable fan—except for one.

It was from a former neighbor, oblique and carefully phrased, as if the woman was afraid of being overheard or, perhaps, of her own conscience. But the essence was clear enough.

A reporter from *Newsworld* had visited, and the woman, disconcerted, had described something that perhaps Lara had never known: a man who resembled a prominent senator, standing in the hallway—upset, anxious, unwilling to leave. He had called Lara's name through the door.

No, Lara thought, she had never known. She was already gone; there was no one on the other side of the door to hear him.

If only she could have seen their end in their beginning.

Tell me about Meg.

Washington, D.C.

April 1997–September 1998

ONE

Awakening, Kerry looked into her face with a sense of wonder. They lay together, silent, the lines of their bodies touching; her gaze was so serious that he was afraid the next moments would end them, that he would never see her like this again, or talk to her as he had the night before, holding nothing back.

"I never knew what loneliness was," he said at last, "until just now."

Her eyes were grave, questioning. "Do I mean so much to you?"

He hesitated, then realized that his sense of solitude, so familiar that he had come to accept it as his fate, had now, with Lara, become unbearable. "The night of Liam's funeral," he told her, "I wanted you to stay there with me. Not Meg, not Clayton—you. You wouldn't have had to say anything, or do anything. And still I tried to believe that you were just a reporter I liked. Maybe I was afraid to face what I'm facing now." He caught himself, fearful of scaring her off. "I know you don't want a politician, any more than Meg did. But I hope to God there's some part of me you do want."

She covered his hand with her own. "There's so much wrong with this," she finally answered. "Most of it I don't need to tell you, including that the President's personal life has only raised the stakes for us. But there's one thing you should know—it's not in me to be with you like this and be with anyone else. And someday I would need to, because someday I'll want a life." She paused and then said, "That could hurt us both, Kerry. Much more than stopping now."

Kerry struggled with his own emotions—a sudden swift

possessiveness; a fear of loss so searing that now, at their beginning, he could only imagine it; the fierce desire to be happy. "You're an honest person," he said simply. "I'll trust you to tell me when that is."

She looked away, long dark lashes cloaking her eyes. "It could be," she answered, "the day you decide to run for President. Because this would be impossible."

The mention of politics, the complex calculus that bound him to the Vice President, made Kerry feel bleak. "Lara," he said gently, "we've just made love. We can talk about my career any other day—I'll even want to. But right now, all I want is to see you again."

Lara drew a breath. "I don't know, Kerry. I don't know what's best to do."

The thought of losing her jarred him. He held her close, her face against his chest. For minutes, neither of them spoke, or wanted to speak.

"It's getting late," she murmured. "And harder to let go. At least for me."

He did not answer. She slid back from him, leaving a space between them. Taut, Kerry saw the hesitance in her eyes, all the personal and professional barriers that kept her silent, the warnings of ethics and self-preservation, her own deep fear of hurt. But when she spoke, it was not to mention any of that.

Gently, Lara asked, "Tell me about Meg."

For the next hour, she listened, trying to comprehend what had brought him to her.

The subject of Meg was difficult, Lara saw. Much was still unclear to him: Meg had let him live his life without protest. But, Lara sensed, he had not quite come to terms with his own hurt and anger, or, perhaps, a deeper truth: that an absent husband, burdened by guilt and obligation, would not demand more than Meg knew she was able to give.

"You've been lonely," she told him. "It's Meg who made me possible."

As he looked into her face, his vulnerability was palpable. But it was part of what made him see and feel for others, a quality which touched her so much that, however difficult, it required more from her than wanting him. "It's hard for me to say this," she said, "but if you don't want to be with Meg, you should find someone who wants to share the life you've chosen to lead, to share *both* your lives with all the other people who may want or need a piece of it. She exists, I know, if you were free to look."

He gazed at her, silent for a time, and then his hand held hers. "I've found her," he said. "It's just that I'm not sure she wants me."

But think of where that leads us, Lara thought sadly. *We can offer each other only pieces of what we may come to want, each a stepping-stone to the final piece, where the weight of all we've tried to ignore comes crashing down on us.* It was just that having found him, she could not bring herself to throw away those moments.

"Oh," Lara answered, "she wants you. And it would be so much better if she didn't."

Month by month, a year passed.

They came to need each other's company, each other's thoughts. Sometimes days went by without her seeing him, sometimes—when Kerry traveled—a week or more. But every day they would talk on the phone with the frustration of thwarted lovers, the directness of good friends. "I can't imagine not wanting you," she told him once. "But the idea of never *talking* to you . . ."

Lara had never felt this close to anyone.

Whenever she needed him to listen, he did, whether it was about her career or her family or the harsh demands of their affair. "When you're away," she told him after a few months, "I think about you with Meg. Even though you say you never sleep with her."

Kerry's look was gentle, querying. "Would you *be* Meg, Lara, if you could be?"

She took his hand. "I've wondered," she acknowledged. "In spite of everything—my career, the fact that we'd be a scandal. But who you are, the person I want so much, is inseparable from everything I don't want." Her voice became quiet. "You've been a senator since you were thirty. I can't imagine you as anything else, can you? Unless, perhaps, as President."

He looked down. "If that's true, Lara, then I've become what I'm afraid of being. Someone with no other life."

"Maybe you've just become what you are. I don't want you to lose that, Kerry." She kissed him. "I think you know how I feel, or I couldn't be here. But if I'm ever married, I'd want a career, a husband who's got time to be an equal partner, and children who see both of us. That's not a senator, or a President. Either you'd lose those things by being with me, or I'd lose you to *them*." She turned away. "And knowing that is so painful that sometimes I hate what we both do . . ."

By unspoken consent, their days were spent in the present, and, in the present, there was little they didn't share. But often they just made each other smile. One night, at the height of their lovemaking, the sound of a clattering garbage truck beneath Kerry's window turned passion into a race between fulfillment and complete distraction, until the shudder of their climax dissolved into mirth, two lovers holding each other, laughing helplessly.

"Timing," Kerry said at last, "is everything. Two seconds more, and we'd have missed out."

Lara kissed him. "And it was *so* romantic," she said dryly. "Like we had a panel of judges with stopwatches."

Rolling on his back, Kerry grinned. "I can't imagine making love in the quiet of nature. Where's the challenge?"

Lara turned to him. "Maybe," she said to her own surprise, "we should try."

Leaning on his elbow, Kerry stroked her hair. "An escape?" he asked. "No lovemaking in the urban cocoon, to the mellow sound of boom boxes and the hum of traffic on East Capitol?"

He was smiling. But in their life, lived hour by hour, the idea of a few days alone seemed precious to her. "If you can," she said simply.

His smile vanished, and he looked into her face. "I'll try."

For over a year, Lara had escaped discovery.

If anything, her reporting on Kerry Kilcannon was more penetrating, analytical, alert to the prospect that his growing conflict with Mason over Kerry's causes—campaign reform, health insurance for children—might lead him to seek the presidency. Sometimes Kerry would joke about this, in passing. But he knew better than to complain; the edge to her coverage was more than protective coloration. In Lara's mind, it preserved her integrity, at least enough to make them possible.

"I think you're right," Nate Cutler told her at lunch one day. "He's going for it. The positions he's taking are like a blueprint for running against Mason."

Lara finished her bite of seared tuna. "Maybe he believes in them. I'm sure he does, actually."

Nate nodded. "Then he's that much more likely to do it, and save us all from boredom. Races in both parties—a reporter's dream."

Lara looked down, appetite lost.

Watching her, Nate hesitated; misinterpreting his silence, she was certain that he somehow knew about her affair with Kerry. "Listen," he said, "I was wondering if you'd like to have dinner this Friday."

He was fidgety, she realized, uncomfortable as she was, but for different reasons. "The two of us?" she asked lightly. "You mean, like people who go out together?"

He tried a smile. "Something like that. Unless you think there's an incest taboo."

Lara smiled in return. "Haven't you read the data on office romances? Tragic, and the woman always pays. Just like the President's chief economic adviser, out of her marriage *and* her job." When he grimaced, she touched his arm, voice softening. "It's not just that, Nate. And it's certainly not you. There's someone else."

He looked up from the table. "You never said anything. Is this relationship some sort of mystery?"

Lara summoned another smile. "Completely," she answered. "Even to me. Someday I may need a friend like you."

When she went to Kerry's apartment that evening—fearful, as always, that someone might be following—the conversation was still on her mind.

Kerry was late. She went to his kitchen nook, slid the wine

she had brought into the refrigerator, next to the marmalade she reserved for predawn breakfasts, before she had to leave.

His apartment was barren—a couch and a television, a few magazines and pictures—and felt empty without him. As empty as Lara might feel after he was gone.

He's going for it.

Nate thought so too. And for the right reasons—the more Kerry's beliefs widened his fissure with Mason, the more impelled he would feel to run. And then it would all close around him: the need for Meg, the Secret Service, the heightened scrutiny of Nate and all their peers. There would be no place left for her.

The door opened. Kerry walked in, tie askew, a look of disgust graven on his face.

Quickly, he kissed her. "Sorry," he said. "I was at the old EOB, discussing our nation's future with America's greatest almost-living Vice President. A man truly worthy of the office."

Lara handed him the glass of chardonnay she had poured to share with him. "No help coming?" she asked.

He sat next to her on the couch. "It was ridiculous, Lara. The man's so pleasant that the depth of his cynicism takes your fucking breath away." His voice held quiet anger. "He's everything that's wrong with politics in the nineties—cowardice masked as cleverness, leadership by poll, symbolic gestures, careful attention to special interests. What's so depressing is how little Dick Mason matters to anyone but *them*. And himself, of course."

It was happening, Lara thought. Mason was mishandling Kerry—perhaps because he still could not imagine that Kerry's motives were any different from his own.

"Tell me about it," she asked.

The old Executive Office Building was all wood and marble and filigree, beautifully restored. Mason's decor reflected a certain need for borrowed gravitas: a desk that once belonged to Henry Clay, royal-blue curtains trimmed with gold, a delicate vase from a recent trip to China, a pen set used by John F. Kennedy. Dick Mason, Kerry thought sardonically, had already entered history.

With gracious authority, Mason waved Kerry to a chair. But Kerry was in no mood for anything but business.

"We need to pass campaign reform," he said bluntly. "You know why, morally and politically. The system's so corrupt that it's breaking down entirely, and the Republicans are killing us with pictures of you and Arab arms dealers."

Mason gave him an indulgent smile, though his eyes were keen. "I didn't know *who* they were, Kerry, and I regret it. But these things fade."

"Maybe by 2000," Kerry said. "And maybe not. But 1998 is already here. We've got off-year elections in six months." Pausing, he softened his voice. "I'm not here to lecture you . . ."

Mason raised his eyebrows. "Not even to threaten me?" he asked in a jocular tone.

Kerry stared at him. "I *do* threaten you," he answered. "Even when I'm not trying. And it's getting in the way."

Mason touched his chin with tented fingers and then smiled again. "If I'm still the problem, Kerry, tell me how I can fix this."

Kerry leaned forward. "Support my bill in the Senate. I don't mean lip service. I mean getting out front, asking my colleagues for help—putting yourself, the party, and the administration on the line for this." Kerry's voice grew urgent, imploring. "You can do so much, Dick. Help me, and all the shady contributions won't make a damn. You'll be a born-again reformer, whose own innocent experience with the way things are have proved to him that it's unacceptable." He paused, and then finished bluntly. "The President's in trouble, Dick—this thing about him breaking up Beth Slater's marriage isn't going away. You need more to set you apart from him than Jeannie and the kids. And campaign reform is 'moral' with a capital M."

Mason's smile was that of a tutor for a slightly dull pupil—kind, patient, and somewhat condescending—tainted by suspicion. "Have you thought about the politics, Kerry? Not enough Republicans will support you; they raise even more money than we do. For some of them, corporate bribery helps offset the parlous effects of letting ordinary people vote—"

"So reform is in our interest," Kerry interjected.

"So," Mason continued, impervious, "we need every senator

on our side of the aisle, and we'd still lose in the House. Then I'm the guy who got fucked twice—not bright enough to turn down the money, not strong enough to fix things."

"Dick," Kerry said in a low voice, "this isn't just about you."

Mason stopped smiling. "True. It's the Kilcannon-Hawkins Bill we're talking about."

"And either way," Kerry snapped, "you lose. That's all that matters, isn't it." He felt a hopeless anger wash over him. "You figure I'm running in 2000 and that you've got enough money to squash me like a bug. So campaign reform's my little gimmick to choke off all the cash and steal your place in history."

Mason's face became opaque, a mask. "The thought never occurred to me, Kerry. But clearly it's occurred to you."

Kerry stared at him. "Do you ever feel like a pygmy, Dick? With every minute we spend together, I feel myself getting shorter."

Mason returned his stare, then shrugged. "See me as you like, Kerry. I don't think people out there care enough to justify the risk. And I've never thought leadership meant lost causes and self-inflicted wounds." For an instant, his eyes grew hard, and then he smiled again. "That's really more your department, I think."

Kerry simply looked at him, the slightest smile of his own appearing in his eyes. "If that's what you believe, Dick, I don't mind." He stood. "Please give my love to Jeannie, by the way."

Mason stood, shaking his hand. "Always," he answered lightly. "And to Meg. When next you see her."

Finishing his account, Kerry poured another glass of wine.

They sat together, evening shadows filling the apartment. There was little Lara needed to say. Both of them understood the implications: campaign reform was dead this session, and in the perverse synergy between Mason and Kerry, the Vice President had drawn him that much closer to running.

"Remember what you said," he asked her, "about an escape?"

At first, Lara was surprised, and then she realized that he, like she, must feel time closing in on them. "I remember," she answered softly.

TWO

Lara sat on the beach, leaning back against Kerry's chest, and watched the sun, descending, burnish the ebbing waters.

They had been on Martha's Vineyard for a day. "Here," she said to Kerry, "I feel we're a couple."

For four days they could live without worry: the house, off Dogfish Bar, was at the end of a dirt road near Gay Head, so quiet that few people knew how to find it. Unconstrained as they were by apartment walls, the need to hide, their time took on a careless quality: that morning they had stood in water swelling to their waists, feeling the light breeze on their faces, the warming sun. Kerry looked young, contented, filled with life.

"I've discovered something," she had told him. "You're a nature sensualist. Cities have been bad for you."

Hands shoved in the pockets of his windbreaker, Kerry laughed, savoring the scent of seawater, the bracing cool of the Atlantic. "I'm a Lara sensualist," he answered. "I'm only tolerating this."

Lightly, she had splashed his face with water. "If you want me," she announced, "I want lobster. On the beach."

He wiped the water from his eyes. "You mean there's takeout?"

They spent the rest of the day as they pleased: A climb in the foothills above Menemsha, ending in a panoramic view of the sound, speckled with white sails, the Elizabeth Islands green patches in the spreading blue. Then a walk in the town itself, a fishing village where, in sunglasses, Kerry seemed to go unrecognized. Finally, the purchase of two lobsters. "A down payment," Kerry said, as he put them in the refrigerator.

Holding hands, they walked to the bedroom.

From the windows, no one could see them. They lay naked in the sunlight, unhurried, touching as they looked into each other's faces. She traced the scar on his shoulder with her fingertips, then the thin line of hair running between his breast-bone to his waist. But it was his eyes that had always drawn her; a deep blue-green, they gazed at her, a window to his emotions.

I'm in love with you, she thought with sadness. *I'll never love anyone this much again.*

The sudden certainty, held at bay for months, was like a catch in her throat. His eyes were intent now, questioning. "What is it?" he asked.

"De nada," Lara murmured. The words he had used the afternoon Lara had met him, two years before.

Two years, and now you're so much a part of me I don't want to let you go.

He kissed her throat. "Oh," he murmured. "It's hardly nothing."

Later, she lay in his arms. Would a life for them be possible, she found herself wondering, if Kerry never went beyond the Senate?

"Penny for your thoughts," Kerry said.

Gazing at the ceiling, Lara shook her head. "I seem to have lost control of them."

"Why? And over what?"

"Give me time," she answered. "To sort things out."

Kerry did not press her. He had the grace of silence, Lara thought, another gift she valued. But it was more than that, now. Kerry simply knew her.

"I'm hungry," Lara said after a while. "I think *that's* what it was."

Together, they planned dinner, then went to gather driftwood on the beach.

It was a mile of white sand and half-buried rocks, stretching toward the final red-clay promontory on which the Gay Head lighthouse stood, a distant spike against the blue of early evening. They found a spot free of rocks and scooped an indentation with their hands, then started a fire with the help of matchsticks and dried sea grass. Within moments, they were sipping chardonnay from paper cups as they waited for the lobster pot to boil.

Tender, the lobsters tasted of lemon Kerry had squeezed, the drawn butter Lara had melted in a pan. They sat back in the sand, drinking wine, pleased with their achievements. "Not bad," Kerry said, "for a couple of urbanites."

At dusk, they watched the sun backlight a thin line of clouds, the sky fade to cobalt. Things seemed so much clearer, Lara thought, when she slowed down, altering the pace and rhythm of her life. And then a truth about her relationship to Kerry struck her so hard that, to her surprise, she spoke it aloud. "Something's changed for me," she told him.

"What is it?"

She shook her head. "It's hard to explain, Kerry. But all my life I've been afraid of being like my mother was with my father—lost to herself. Even after he took off with someone else, she loved him so much that she kept his picture in a drawer, just to look at.

"I never told her that I knew. But I promised myself I'd never be like her. That I'd have my own life, some irreducible self that belonged to no one but me.

"I've lived that way, until now. No one would ever make me forget who I was." Pausing, Lara realized that it was better like this—talking to the water instead of facing him—and made herself go on. "When we started, no matter how strongly I felt about you, I knew we had our limits. I wasn't going to be a political wife, or someone like my mother. The rest of my life, my career, went on as it had. And I tried to believe that, when we ended, the core I'd kept would help me face that."

"And now?"

"I know I've been lying to myself." The sting of tears caught her by surprise. "It's too good being with you like this. *You're* too good, and I'm having a hard time with that."

His arms tightened around her. Silent, they watched the sun vanish. A night wind, stirring to life, cooled their skin.

"Lara," he said at last, "I never thought you wanted more than what we have. But if you ever do . . ."

"I'll tell you. For now, I just need to be quiet with this."

For a long time, she was.

The night closed around them. Burrowing against him, Lara gazed at the star-streaked sky, brighter for the absence of a city, listened to the deep spill of the ocean, the crackle of red, dying embers. "I'd like you to tell me something," she said finally. "*Are* you running for President?"

Behind her, she felt Kerry shift his weight, his chin resting lightly on the crown of her head. "It's too soon, Lara."

"You'll *know* soon—after the off-year elections. Either the President and Dick repair the damage, or the party stays in the minority." Tilting her head, she gazed up at the stars. "I think it will. And so do you. That's part of why we came here now, isn't it?"

His silence, Lara thought sadly, was a tacit acknowledgment that what she'd said was true. "I look at Mason," he said at last, "and I think of all I'd do if I were in his place. But even if the President and Dick are the last passengers on the *Titanic*, the cost of running is so high." His voice dropped into a lower register—pensive, thoughtful. "And then there's this endless cycle of myth-making and myth-destroying. It's the one thing Jamie escaped."

"Because he's forever a myth?" she asked.

"Yes. God, how people still love him for dying young."

Quiet, Lara listened to a surf she could no longer see, felt again her fear of losing him; the fear of standing in his way; the sense that fate and circumstances were slowly, sinuously, drawing Kerry toward the race. "Are you afraid of that?" she asked. "Dying like Jamie, because some sick person wants to join his name to yours?"

For a moment he said nothing, and then he leaned his face next to hers. "Never more than now," he answered.

After a time, the wind cooled.

In the warmth of the beach house, they made love again. They fell asleep to the sound of the ocean, the breeze coming through the window screens, the smell of salt.

The next morning, on the radio, Kerry heard the first warning of the hurricane.

Listening, Kerry looked out the window. In blue jeans and a Stanford sweatshirt, Lara sat on the deck, drinking coffee and watching the ocean sparkle with morning sunlight. For a moment, he did not wish to tell her.

When he walked outside, she took a deep breath of ocean air, shivering with pleasure. "I love this," she announced.

He put both hands on her shoulders. "We may have to leave," he told her. "There's a hurricane on its way. It was supposed to hit the Carolinas. But now it's veered."

She looked up at him awhile. Finally, she asked, "How long do we have?"

Gently, Kerry rubbed her shoulders. "Three days, they think."

"That feels good," Lara murmured. She leaned back, looking up at him. "Do you have to decide now? If this hurricane veered once, maybe it can veer again."

Kerry smiled. "Tomorrow morning," he said, "I'll turn on the radio again."

"Good. Do you think you could keep on rubbing? Maybe a little higher."

But she seemed pensive after that. It was only when he brought her a second cup of coffee that she said, "There's something I've been meaning to tell you."

Her tone was serious, soft-spoken. He sat beside her on the deck, cross-legged, his own cup of coffee a centrifuge of warmth in his hands. "What is it?"

"I've had a feeler from NBC. Believe it or not, they may want me to do television."

"Oh, I believe it. How do *you* feel?"

"Ambivalent. I did a little of that in college, so it's not completely bizarre." She sipped her coffee. "On one side, there's not the depth of print reporting. On the other is what they may be prepared to offer."

She did not look at him, and her tone of reticence, unusual for Lara, unsettled him. "A lot more money?" he asked.

Lara nodded, still gazing at the water. "There's that," she

answered, and then turned to him. "They'd send me overseas, Kerry. If that's what I prefer."

It startled him. "Do you?" he asked.

She paused, a troubled look in her eyes, as if she felt the shadow in his soul. "I would," she said quietly, "except for you. I've been telling myself how stupid that is."

Kerry looked down. *Be fair,* he admonished himself. *Be her friend.* "I know," he said at last, "that you've always wondered if this job's right for you. I've known since the first time we really talked."

He felt her hand, gently touching his arm. "And that was two years ago, Kerry. How much more political intrigue can I cover?" Her tone was soft. "The real irony is, if you ran for President, the *Times* would probably ask me to cover *you.* And I couldn't."

Looking up at her, he tried to smile. "Then I've lost my reason to run."

Lara gazed into her coffee cup. "I didn't look for this. But we knew that sometime . . ." She shook her head. "I don't expect you to do anything about this. I don't even want you to. But our careers are getting all tangled up with *us.*"

Kerry took a deep breath. "I can't tell you what to do, Lara. All I know is how good you'd be. If it's what you want."

Slowly, she intertwined her fingers with Kerry's.

For the rest of the day, they did not talk about it. But to Kerry, their lovemaking had a desperate quality.

The next morning, the hurricane was one day closer, and every plane, every ferry to the mainland, was booked.

Lara phoned her office. Then, knowing that Kerry had to call Meg, she walked the beach alone.

Illicit lovers, she thought sadly, develop a strange tact; she would never make Kerry lie in front of her. Upon her return, he said, "It's done. I'm staying here a little longer, trapped in my solitary retreat."

She took his hand. "Then you should make the most of it."

Afterward, they spent their time preparing for what would come. Lara drove to the Chilmark General Store for flash-

light batteries, canned goods, candles, and bottled wate.
moved the furniture to the center of the room. Returnin₃, Lara
saw this and, for a time, felt irrationally cheerful. "It's an adventure," she said. "Like camping out."

Kerry grinned at her. "Oh, yeah. And I'm an Eagle Scout.
Did you bring your cell phone, by the way?"

Outside, the winds had risen, and then the rain began.

For another day, the storm closed in on them.

There was no one on the beach now, no boats on the water.
The sky, close and dark, seemed to merge with the ocean.

At dusk, the lights went out.

Kerry had a memory from childhood—a dead tree fallen
across a power line. "It could be like this for days," he said
to Lara.

Kneeling, she lit a candle on the coffee table. "I don't mind,"
she answered. In the background, the radio, powered by batteries, continued its mournful narrative—a lone announcer,
playing disks and counting down the hours.

The rain came in sheets now, gusts of wind rattling the windows. They were squares of black; nature could no longer
be seen, Kerry reflected, only heard. He turned to Lara.
"There's too much glass out here. When it hits, we should be in
the bedroom."

In the candlelight, her face was sculpted, her eyes black.
"Well," she said, "we wanted to be alone."

Kerry smiled. "Got our wish, didn't we."

He went to her, holding her close.

From the radio came the first bars of "A Summer Place."
"Someone," Lara murmured, "has a sense of humor. Or maybe
it's prom night."

Kerry kissed her. "Care to dance?"

"In a minute." Stepping back, she unbuttoned his shirt. "We
are alone, after all."

His shirt fell on the floor, and then Lara's blouse. "There,"
she murmured, putting her arms around his neck. "Like this."

The wind became a low, insistent moan. In light and shadow,
the senior senator from New Jersey and the congressional

correspondent for the *New York Times* danced to the thin sounds of their radio, bodies lightly touching, confident for once that they could not be seen.

To Lara, the storm, when it hit, felt as awesome as Creation.

There was an eerie stillness. Then it seemed the house would come apart—a shrieking wind, glass shattering, the rafters creaking, straining, as sideways rain struck the wood like gunshots. She shivered in Kerry's arms.

"Ignore it," he murmured, "and maybe it'll go away."

She could not see his face. Only feel his mouth, slowly, gently, as it traced her chin, her throat. As he did, she shivered again, suspended between fear and the first faint glow of wanting him.

His mouth moved further. As the wind screamed, Lara shut her eyes. And then, for a time, she felt a part of everything around them.

Kerry held her until the storm passed.

At dawn, the world had changed. One of the windows had shattered, and slivers of glass glistened in the rain-soaked living room. Outside, electric air crackled like sheets hanging in the wind, and the beach was ruined—rocks and debris driven into the sea grass, the sand devoured by roiling waves. Lara leaned against him. "I love you," she said simply. "No matter what."

THREE

The morning after Lara's first meeting with the president of NBC News, she knew.

She had been tired for several days—unusual for someone with her energy. But going to bed early had not helped; this morning, her nipples were sore, sensitive. She felt nauseated.

Suspended between dread and disbelief, she walked to a pharmacy on Connecticut Avenue and bought a home test kit. Then she called in sick and waited for the kit to confirm what, with uncanny certainty, she already knew.

It must have happened the night of the hurricane.

Seized by emotions she could not yet grasp, she returned to the bathroom and saw that the stick of paper had turned pink at the tip.

Though she could scarcely imagine it as real, she was pregnant with Kerry's child.

Listless, she tried to catalog the reasons she must put an end to this. She sat on the bed, elbows propped on knees, so stunned that minutes passed with Lara motionless, so overwhelmed that her emotions seemed to have the gravity of prayer.

There was only one solution. But her thoughts kept slipping to where they should not go—imagining Kerry, laughing and careless as he had been on Martha's Vineyard, carrying their baby on his shoulders. Kerry, cast in the role of one of her friends' yuppie husbands, a picture from an album. The fantasies of a woman who knew the truth—for both of them—even as her heart recoiled.

This was not an abstraction. She had come to love Kerry far more than she thought he knew, and to give him up was hard enough. To abort their child was more than she should have to bear.

Yet she must, and without involving Kerry. What could he offer her but guilt; what could she give him but anguish?

The telephone rang.

"Hi," he said. "Playing hooky?"

"Can I see you?" she heard herself ask, and realized that she was weaker than she knew.

As long as she lived, Lara thought, she would never forget his face at that moment.

Speechless, he gazed at her with such confusion, guilt, and

love that no words could have captured it. *I know,* she thought. *I know.*

She leaned her face against his shoulder.

After a time, he murmured, "We need to think about this."

As he held her, Lara closed her eyes. It was painful to feel the consequences hit him, already knowing where they led. Leaning back, she took his face in her hands, wanting to spare them both. "There's nothing to decide," she told him. "I've had a few more hours to live with this, and I know that."

Gently, he removed her hands and went to the window, gazing out at a crisp fall afternoon that Lara knew he should be spending in the Senate. Instead he was here, in a sad corner of his secret life, with the lover no one knew he had. For the world, Lara thought, this will never have happened.

Turning, he said softly, "There *is* something to decide. I want you to marry me."

Lara sat quiet, stunned. Tears of shock came to her eyes; she felt herself caught between irrational hope and the harshness of their reality. "I can't," she managed to say. "You're already married, remember?"

Kerry bowed his head. "I'm well aware of that. But Meg and I should have divorced long ago."

"I think so too." The quiet edge in Lara's voice surprised her. "But you didn't. I don't want you because of a birth control mistake."

He came to her, grasping her wrists. "But *I* want *you.*"

She looked away from him. "Please, don't make this worse. This isn't what you want. If it were, you'd have asked for it."

Cradling her chin, Kerry turned her face to his. "*You* were the one who didn't want a politician. If you'd said to me just once, 'I want to marry you,' do you think an affair would have been enough for me?" He caught himself, softening his voice. "I'm in love with you, and I want our child . . ."

"At any price?" Intently, Lara looked into his eyes. "Instead of running for President, you'd be a running joke on Letterman: Kerry Kilcannon, the man who knew what the *Times* really meant when it promised home delivery. Does the name Gary Hart mean anything to you?" Pausing, Lara battled a fresh wave of nausea. "You'd probably lose your Senate seat in 2000, and you're the only one who doesn't know how much that defines you. How can the ruin of your career be the premise for our marriage?" Lara drew a breath. "I don't want that for you," she finished simply. "And I don't want that for me."

"Do you think that little of me, Lara? If I'm only what I do, and not who I am, how can you have loved me at all?"

She turned from him. "Because you're all those things. I can't separate them, and you shouldn't try . . ."

"There's something else." His voice had the first hint of accusation. "Not *my* career. *Yours.*"

After a moment, she nodded. "I'd be done too, Kerry—the journalist who fucked the senator she wrote about. Maybe I deserve that, but . . ." In an act of will, she forced herself to meet his eyes. "Part of us is who we are in our own lives. And what you claim to want would end that."

"There's another life involved here." Kerry pulled her close, her forehead resting against his. "It's not what we'd have chosen, I know that. But it's here, staring me in the face.

"I want you much more than I've ever wanted to be President. And if the Senate is the price I pay for our child, I'm willing to pay it."

For the first time, Lara felt angry. "Do you think this is easy for me?" she demanded. "You can say anything you like, and *I* still have to decide what's best. And then live with it."

Kerry considered her. Quietly, he asked, "What else do you want from me?"

"I want you to *support* me, dammit." Tears sprang to her eyes again. "If you want me to thank you for offering to help ruin both our lives, I will. But I know what's right, and *you* know what's right. Please, don't make me do the right thing by myself."

This time, Kerry turned away. "Am I supposed to lie about my feelings," he asked, "because *you're* the one who's pregnant? Doesn't this involve *me*, too?"

The justice of his question undercut her anger, even as she saw, with aching sadness, the chasm opening between them.

She was the one whose body was already different, whose spirit might never be the same.

"Please, Kerry. Just be my friend."

He took her hands. "Give us two weeks, all right? We'll be a long time living with this. Whatever you decide."

Lara felt wrung out, without peace or consolation. All that was left was to let him hold her, to wish, with bitter longing, that she had never told him.

At four o'clock, Kerry had to leave.

He had four speeches to give in the next few days, Lara remembered—in Philadelphia, Chicago, Denver, San Francisco. It reminded her of the possibility enveloping them both that, until today, Kerry had willingly preserved: a race for the presidency, which would put an end to them. The world outside their secret spun on as before.

As Kerry left, he kissed her. "I'll call you," he said. "Every night."

For two years, she had counted on it, even as she worried that each call added to the paper trail of their affair. Now she felt a chill, an instinctive sad finality.

"I love you," she said. "Remember that."

"And I love you," Kerry answered, and was gone.

Give us two weeks, he had asked. But every day she felt the life grow inside her, and nothing changed but her attachment, the vividness of their imagined child.

For three nights, he called, not pressing. Every night, she asked herself how she would answer if he said, "No matter what you decide, I'm leaving Meg." Every night, she wondered why he had not.

Lara called a clinic, did nothing. She sleepwalked through her days, her decision growing harder, more scarifying. Until she acted, her life was about nothing but Kerry's phone calls, the other life inside her.

We'll be a long time living with this, he had said.

Waiting, she found, was even worse.

The day he arrived in San Francisco, she stopped answering the telephone.

* * *

Sleepless, he called every hour.

He would hear five rings, and then the answering machine. "Please," he implored the spinning tape. "Wait until I get back." Kerry did not say the rest: that whatever she chose, he wished to marry her. That, he would say in person.

By the morning, he had called twelve times. His hopes for their child had turned to ashes.

He went to the banquet hall, heart leaden, and began his speech.

In the waiting room, Lara stared at the forms, her mind echoing with the sound of Kerry's voice. *Please, Lara, don't do this.*

Name, address.

She had driven to Maryland alone. The clinic had promised Lara privacy; like the room, it was small, discreet, anonymous. No one else was waiting.

As if by rote, Lara printed her name.

Please, I love you. I don't want you to face this alone.

Did she want counseling? the form asked.

I want Kerry, her mind answered, even as her hand scrawled "No."

A nurse appeared—stout, benign, motherly. "Have you filled everything out?" she asked.

Mute, Lara handed her the form.

Looking from the papers to Lara, the nurse touched her gently on the shoulder. "Then we're ready."

Standing, Lara thanked her.

They went to a small room without windows. Silent, Lara gazed at the operating table.

In a calm voice, the nurse explained what would happen. When Lara did not respond, she felt the woman study her.

"Afterward," she told Lara, "some women are relieved. Others need more support."

No, Lara answered, she was fine. All she wanted was for this to be over.

Then you need to undress, the nurse said. The doctor was with another patient; he would come once he was finished.

Alone, Lara took off her clothes, folding them neatly on a chair.

I'm in love with you, and I want our child.

Gently, she traced the curve of her stomach. Soon, she thought, the doctor would be here.

There was a hospital gown on a hanger. With awkward fingers, Lara draped it over her body, and then lay down on the table.

I want you to marry me.

The door opened and the doctor came in—a young man with a mustache, as mild in manner as the nurse. "Good morning," he said.

Lara tried to smile. Behind him, the nurse pushed a four-foot steel canister across the tile floor.

Ignore it, she remembered Kerry murmuring, *and maybe it'll go away.* Her stomach was a knot of sickness.

As the doctor instructed, she placed her feet in the metal stirrups.

Lying exposed, Lara listened to the drone of his voice. They were giving her an injection, he explained, to deaden the pain. Head averted, Lara saw the clear plastic tube coming from the canister. It ended in the nurse's hand.

There's another life involved here . . .

With a speculum, the doctor opened her. The nurse passed him the tube.

Tell me about Meg.

Through the anesthesia, Lara felt the tube push inside her, and closed her eyes.

Someone flipped a switch.

The machine began whirring like a vacuum. Lara started; there was a sudden jolt, the shock of suction inside her.

Her eyes snapped open. Beside her, the clear tube filled with red.

No.

The doctor placed a hand on her stomach, slowly increasing the pressure. As Lara watched, a clump of tissue shot through the tube.

"I'm sorry," Lara whispered. "I'm sorry." She did not know to whom.

The nurse wiped her forehead with a cool, damp cloth. "It's

all right," she murmured. Trembling, Lara felt the nurse's fingers curl around hers.

"We're almost done," the doctor promised.

The tube was clear now. The whir became a scream in Lara's head. "Can you turn it off?" she begged them. "Please."

The whining stopped. In a soothing tone, the doctor said, "There's just a little more."

With an instrument, he cleaned out the rest.

Teeth gritted, Lara held herself stiff. The instrument slid from inside her. As she turned to vomit, the nurse held out a plastic dish.

Blind, she felt the nurse's soft touch on her shoulder. There was deep silence, nothing but the sound of Lara's breathing, the nurse cooing words of comfort, as if to a baby. Lara still imagined hearing the machine.

The doctor, Lara realized, had vanished.

After a time, she lay back. The nurse stayed with her, patient, unhurried.

Groggy, Lara sat up, then somehow she got to her feet.

For the first few moments, she felt hollow, light-headed. The nurse supported her until she could dress.

"Our counselor's here now," she said in a tentative voice.

The cramping had begun. Dazed, Lara said, "I think I just need to be with someone. Anyone."

The nurse helped her down a narrow hallway.

Inside the last office, a short, middle-aged woman with dyed brown hair sat behind a desk. As Lara sat, the counselor gazed at her with deep compassion. "I'm Nancy Philips," she said.

The door shut behind her, and Lara and the woman were alone. Tears ran down Lara's face.

"This can be hard," the woman said. "I know."

Lara told her everything.

When she returned to her apartment, a few hours later, there were three more messages from Kerry.

Dully, she listened to them.

The operation that had emptied out her body had drained her

of all ability to defend herself. She had violated ethics, broken trust, for the sake of a hopeless love affair. And now she had done *this*.

From somewhere, she summoned the strength to call NBC News, and then the *Times*.

Her last call was to Kerry.

Alone in his hotel suite, Kerry listened to her voice on his answering machine, sickened.

She was leaving—first to see her mother, then to go abroad. He should not feel guilty; they had loved each other, and no one had intended this. But now it was done.

"No," he said aloud. *"No."*

"I have to start over," Lara's voice went on. "Please, if you still love me, the one gift you can give to me is not to make it harder . . ."

Her voice broke. There was muffled crying, then the click of a connection breaking.

Kerry hurried to the airport.

The drive to her apartment was shards of consciousness: half-remembered streets; the broken words of his lover; the desperate litany in his own brain.

I'm leaving her. Marry me. Nothing else matters. We can always have more children. All I care about is that they're ours.

Parking by a fire hydrant, he ran to the apartment. He reached her door, out of breath.

Softly, he knocked.

No answer. He rested his forehead against the door, heard nothing stir inside the room.

In a low, insistent voice, he began to call her name.

Two weeks later, Lara left the country.

She next heard of him on the BBC, alone in a cramped apartment in Sarajevo. Senator Kerry Kilcannon and his wife, the clipped voice said, were divorcing.

Throat constricted, Lara listened.

Kilcannon had no comment, the report went on. But the

divorce was not expected to prevent him from running for President, as was widely anticipated since his party's defeat in the off-year elections.

At least there was that, Lara told herself. If he had not lost everything, then neither had she.

The Campaign

Day Four

ONE

"This is Lara Costello, NBC News, with the Kilcannon campaign in Los Angeles . . ."

Kerry Kilcannon bolted upright in his bed, breaking through the gauze that separated sleep from consciousness.

Lara's face vanished from the screen.

Hours before, Kerry realized, he had fallen asleep with the television on, two briefing books for the debate beside him on the bed. Now the sheets were a disordered mess, tangled by the last panicky moments when he fought to escape the new climax of his nightmare.

For the first time, it did not end with his brother's death. As in life, Jamie's killer came from backstage. Yet now the assassin was not Harry Carson but someone else, his face obscured by shadows. And Kerry stood in his brother's place.

As the assassin fired, Kerry awakened.

Dawn was breaking. Kerry struggled to dismiss the dream, retrieve the pieces of his life, the bricks and mortar of reason.

Lara was an image on the television, out of reach. He was in Los Angeles, on the morning of a debate that could determine his candidacy and in which—if Clayton's instincts were right—Dick Mason meant to trap him. It was six o'clock; he had twelve more hours to prepare.

And after that? A confrontation with Nate Cutler that might destroy his hopes if Mason did not. And then a rally in San Francisco, to tame the demons Kerry had unleashed by saying that a fetus was a life.

Take each in turn, Kerry told himself; until after the debate was over, Cutler did not exist. Focus was the candidate's best friend, panic his worst enemy. He supposed this must also be true for Presidents.

Someone knocked on his door.

Slowly, Kerry got out of bed and went to answer.

Already dressed in a suit and tie, Clayton stood between the two agents who guarded Kerry's suite. "Don't you ever sleep?" Kerry asked.

"Don't you?" Clayton rejoined. Closing the door behind him, he gave Kerry—mussed hair, damp forehead, boxer shorts—a glance that combined humor with concern. "You look like you've taken up boxing again."

"Bad night," Kerry answered. "What's up?"

Clayton took a chair, wearing a look of mild apology. "This San Francisco rally tomorrow. Ellen Penn and the advance people want it outside, in a plaza near the financial district. The Service says do it indoors: thirty hours is too short notice to make an outdoor site secure. Peter Lake insists it's serious enough that only you can make the call. He's as close to pissed off as he allows himself to get."

Kerry made himself be still. With a fair show of calm, he asked, "What are the arguments?"

"Ellen and the chief of advance think the outdoor site will help them draw a crowd on a Sunday—there's an open-air market nearby and restaurants where yuppies will be having brunch. Plus, the visuals are better: the candidate bathed in sunshine, meeting the folks with a backdrop of the city. Maybe even the Bay Bridge if the camera angle's right." Clayton's tone became dry. "It's a made-for-TV event, they keep reminding me, and we need good production values to impress the viewing audience."

Kerry raised his eyebrows. "What if I *don't* draw a crowd? Give me a hundred people in an outdoor plaza, and it'll look like the world's worst company picnic, held for the handful of pro-choice women who still support me."

Clayton adjusted his glasses. "Ellen claims she can turn people out, and this guy Ginsberg—the local volunteer coordinator—thinks they've got enough volunteers to help form a crowd *and* to leaflet anything that's open near the plaza.

Use an indoor site, and you lose passersby and people in the area."

"And Peter?"

Clayton shrugged. "An indoor site's more secure. Obviously."

Kerry gave a mirthless smile. "Jamie," he said softly, "would be interested to know that."

Clayton's gaze was even, his voice firm. "The Service has been monitoring the Internet, Kerry. The gun-nut vitriol is getting worse. There are literally a thousand windows surrounding the plaza, and elevated lines of fire from every conceivable angle. And we need a lot more volunteers outdoors, which Peter sees as another complicating factor." Clayton paused. "Ellen Penn may want this site. But if *she* gets shot, it's an accident."

Kerry's eyes met his. "So you say play it safe."

"Yes. For once."

Kerry went to the window, staring out at the orange-red specter of a smudged Los Angeles dawn. "Electric cars," he murmured. "It's the only hope for this place."

Behind him, Clayton was silent.

Arms folded, Kerry experienced a moment's superstition, the residue of his dream. It was as if the nightmare had been meant to tell him something. But whether the danger lay in defiance or in letting fear control his conduct, he could not decide. And each moment of daylight took him that much further from knowing.

What was left was a politician determined to defeat Dick Mason, and a man who wished desperately to be unafraid. Turning to Clayton, Kerry said, "Do it in the plaza."

Clipping the last article from the *San Francisco Chronicle*, Sean Burke saw Rick Ginsberg, hurried footsteps echoing in the cavernous room as he went from volunteer to volunteer. For once, Sean thought, the man's air of benign calm had left him. "He's coming," he blurted to Sean. "Kerry. How much of the next day and a half can you give me?"

Sean felt Ginsberg's excitement hit him like a current. "All of it," he managed to say. "I don't sleep much."

Shock, Sean realized, had made his tone almost dull. But this seemed to have a calming effect on Ginsberg. The volunteer coordinator rested a hand on his shoulder. "There are so many ways to fuck this up," he explained in a softer voice. "In the next twenty-nine hours we'll need bleachers, leaflets and people to pass them out, car pools, a crowd, all of us to make as many phone calls as we need to make sure we *have* one. Plus, we have to work with the Secret Service."

A second jolt hit Sean—fear—and then a vision he could hardly believe: his mission opening up for him, if only he could hide the gun. "I can build bleachers," he said impulsively. "At home, I was a handyman."

Rick shook his head. "San Francisco's a union town, and there are companies that do events. But everything else I need you for." He gave a crooked, half-crazed grin, and Sean realized how little sleep he must have had. "You've got a second chance, John. This time you'll meet him, for sure."

TWO

Three hours into the debate preparation, Clayton thought Kerry looked distracted, tired, enervated by the handlers and their constant coaching.

They were in a room usually rented by the hotel for business meetings and wedding receptions, now turned into a facsimile of a TV studio. In a blue suit, Kerry sat opposite his senatorial colleague and friend Bob Kerrey, who had flown in from Washington to provide advice and do his Dick Mason impression in a "debate" moderated by Tony Lord. In Clayton's view, Dick Mason was having the best of it.

From their expressions of concern, the handlers thought so too. They sat in folding chairs in front of the pseudo-soundstage—

Frank Wells, Jack Sleeper, Kit Pace, Mick Lasker, and Senator Ellen Penn—offering advice and scripting prepackaged lines, hoping one would become as immortal as the "You're no Jack Kennedy" gibe with which Lloyd Bentsen had wounded Dan Quayle twelve years prior. "When you're talking about the economy," Frank Wells interjected, "don't forget the 7-Eleven quotient."

Kerry waved his hand. "I know, I know—the price of a loaf of bread and a quart of milk. Maybe Rough Rider condoms . . ."

In the swivel chair next to him, Bob Kerrey smiled. "Skip the condoms," Jack Sleeper answered tartly. "When it comes to teenage sex, most parents believe that abstinence is the only answer."

"Then they should take up prayer," Kerry murmured, so inaudibly that only Clayton, sitting beside him, could hear.

"Mason's totally isolated," Frank Wells continued, pursuing his point. "For the last eight years he's been surrounded by Secret Service. He hasn't driven a car, gone to a video store, or shopped for groceries. A few 'real-life' details can make him seem out of touch."

With a small smile, Kerry looked around him. *Real life,* Clayton could hear him thinking. *What's that?* Catching Tony Lord's eye, Clayton nodded.

They were near the end of the "debate." Under the rules originally proposed by Kerry and suddenly adopted by Mason, there were four ten-minute segments on a single subject—the economy, foreign policy, crime and social justice, protecting the American family—with the last twenty minutes on any subject. The candidates were free to question each other, and the moderator to interrupt; pretending to do so, Tony Lord read from a slip of paper.

"Senator Kilcannon," he began—parodying the plump-pudding tones of a network anchorman, heard nowhere else in life—"the current administration signed into law the Defense of Marriage Act, barring so-called gay marriages in one state from being recognized in any other. And yet, while signing, the President intimated that the legislation was a politically motivated attempt to exploit bias against gays and lesbians. Vice

President Mason seems to agree. Where do *you* stand on this and other issues involving gay rights?"

Kerry gave Lord a look of mock adoration. "Could you ask me that again, Peter? I just *love* the way you talk."

Clayton smiled; after a moment's struggle to maintain his composure, Tony Lord laughed aloud. "The candidate," Bob Kerrey observed from the side, "is punchy."

"Still too quick for *you*, Dick," Kerry said, spinning abruptly on his friend. "This is another example of your hypocrisy and lack of leadership. If the bill is homophobic, and you don't like homophobia, don't sign the bill and then say 'those bullies in Congress made me do it.' " His voice slowed, becoming serious. "We'll tolerate a lot from a leader who actually leads, even if we don't agree with him or her on some issue or another. And if you can't stand up to this, how can you stand up to some defense contractor who's given money to the Democratic Party and wants something in return . . ."

"But where do you stand?" Bob Kerrey shot back. "That's the question. What's your answer?"

Kerry paused for a moment. "*Someone* should have the courage of your convictions, Dick. I'd veto the bill and tell the American people why. Because it's both homophobic *and* unnecessary—"

Frank Wells leaned forward—taut, unable to restrain himself. "*I* know that, Kerry. We *all* do, in this room. But Joe Six-pack thinks 'the gays' are out to turn his son the quarterback into a cross-dresser. Even if you win this primary, the GOP kills you with this in the general election. There's a difference between moral leadership and driving off a cliff—"

"So now *I'm* Dick Mason," Kerry said, and hooked a thumb toward Senator Kerrey. "I thought *Bob* was Dick."

The senator from Nebraska, knowing his colleague well, did not smile. Kerry's gaze at Frank was cool, and to Clayton, his tone had the strained patience Kerry used when reining in his temper.

"Let's take a break," Clayton said.

By the tacit conspiracy of everyone in the room, Kerry knew, he was being given a few minutes' reprieve, to keep from becoming too frayed. But it did not surprise him when Kit, her expression tentative, approached him. Kneeling by the chair, she murmured, "Frank's right, you know. With all respect. And appreciation."

Tilting his head, Kerry looked at her with genuine affection. Kit did not have to mention the ironic subtext of her advice— the moment two days before the crucial Florida primary, when Kit had approached him in the campaign plane and requested a seventy-two-hour leave of absence.

Her timing could not have been worse. Kerry had lost the early primaries and was trailing here. Everyone agreed that another loss would end his hopes: to Kerry, the mere question had felt like a betrayal.

"Why?" was all he could say. "Getting your résumé out?"

She glanced around the plane, then summoned the nerve to look at him again, quite steadily. "It's personal."

Kerry said nothing. His silence, he knew, spoke for him.

Her own gaze flickered. Quietly, she said, "I have a partner. There's been a bad diagnosis, and now there's going to be surgery."

It took Kerry a moment to understand; that Kit had a personal life was something that, in his preoccupation, he had never considered. "Partner," he finally answered. "As in 'domestic.'"

"Yes." Kit's voice was hushed, almost choked. "She's having a mastectomy, Kerry. It's a surprise—to me, and to Bev. We just found out this morning."

Beneath her professional air, Kit was, Kerry saw, quite bereft, made even more vulnerable by her admission of something that—even now—might make her a political pariah to candidates who feared a backlash. "I'm sorry," he said. "Of course, go. Come back when you can."

"Thank you," she said simply, eyes briefly closing in relief. When they opened again, she asked with hesitance, "You didn't know, did you?"

"No." Kerry smiled faintly. "About things like this, I'm usually the last to know. I hope it's because I don't give a damn."

Kit smiled as well. But her eyes held both sadness and appreciation. "I *always* knew," she answered. "And I always knew it was a problem."

"Not to me," Kerry answered.

On the day of the operation, Kerry had managed to find out where Bev was, and send her flowers. It was the day of the Florida primary . . .

Now, in California, he and Kit were in the last days of the last primary, trying to win it all.

"Well," Kerry told her dryly, "the Pilgrims came here nearly four hundred years ago so we'd never have to talk about sex again. It's a great tradition, sure."

"And still alive." Kit's face was serious. "When it comes to job discrimination, people are getting better. But there's still a lot of fear about adoption, or gays in the military, or Social Security benefits. And gay 'marriage' terrifies them even more. I *know* that—whatever I might wish for."

For a moment, Kerry looked around them—first at the "soundstage," then at the gaggle of handlers. "You know what Dick Mason is," he said at last. "He's the symbol of a whole generation of politicians who are so handled, so removed from what got them started, that they no longer have an idea of their own. Every issue seems equally important, and equally fatal to their chances to survive." His voice softened. "Some of the people here forget—if they ever knew—that I've been around politics since I was ten. Every senator and congressperson who voted against the Defense of Marriage Act was reelected. Plus, five percent of the Democratic voters in this state are self-identified as gay, and their lobbies are loyal and hardworking. There are times when telling the truth is merely brave, Kit—not suicidal. And bravery is something people respect."

Kit's silent gaze was complex: relief that Kerry, the practical politician, had thought the matter through; worry that her candidate, so vulnerable because of Lara, was too inclined to risk-taking. She touched his sleeve.

"Still," she said, "tread lightly."

Nodding, Kerry braced himself for another three hours of debate and second-guessing—the anxiety of others, added to his own.

"We had a visitor yesterday," Jane Booth said long distance. "Nat Schlesinger."

"Surprise." In his hotel room, Nate Cutler sat tethered to his telephone, wishing that he could pace. "Let me guess: The process of invading the private lives of public figures has gone too far. There's too much gossip, no accountability, and we run in packs. We're changing the face of politics, and unless we act responsibly, we'll change the face of this campaign by recycling scurrilous gossip planted by the Republicans, or Mason. Is that about it?"

"Yes," Jane answered crisply. "You almost sound like you believe it. And it seems to have made an impression on our distinguished publisher."

"Oh."

"He wants us to be sure we 'have the goods.'" Her voice held bitter irony. "Why do they let him go to bad movies about reporters? It's enough he owns a magazine."

Nate felt renewed tension—from the threat to their story and from his own ambivalence. If he understood what Lara had told him at dinner, between the lines, Kerry Kilcannon had not wanted an abortion. "So how do the great man's scruples affect *us*?" Nate asked.

"They don't—if the story's good. In the end, our leader wants to be one of us. Just as long as he doesn't get *paid* like us." Her tone became businesslike. "We're trying to get ahold of Kilcannon's phone records, track down every dinner they ever had, every sighting at funny hours. Everything we find, I'll fax you by tomorrow morning at six. So you have it when you meet with him."

"And then?"

"If *she* lies, Nate, that's one thing. But if he lies about stuff like this, it goes to the integrity of a candidate for President."

Once more, Nate thought uncomfortably of dinner, his veiled confrontation with Lara. "What if he refuses to answer?"

"At some point, that becomes a story too. If the details start to pile up, calling us sleazebags isn't going to keep this out of print." Booth paused a moment. "We're not through with *her*, either. What do you think she'll do if we say, 'Either you answer our questions, in detail, or we're going to NBC with what we have'?"

Despite himself, Nate felt a chill. "Laugh in our face, for

one thing. Because we'd be giving up our exclusive, and she knows it."

"Tell me," Jane said evenly, "do *you* think Costello warned him?"

Nate considered the evidence. "Kit was pretty subtle," he answered. "And so was Kilcannon's disappearing act. But yes, probably."

"Then maybe he's *seeing* her, Nate. Have you considered that?"

"No way," Nate promptly responded. "Far too big a risk, unless it was passed off as an interview. And then she'd need to have something to show for it."

"What about late at night?"

"No." Nate spoke more slowly now. "If nothing else, because of me."

There was a long silence. "Start watching her," Jane ordered. "Especially at night. You can always sleep on the plane."

THREE

An hour before the debate, Clayton and Kerry waited alone in a hotel suite, Clayton in his suit, Kerry lying on the couch in blue jeans and a Bruce Springsteen T-shirt. Clayton could feel his friend's anxiety.

"Go get him, champ," he said dryly. "I'm behind you, all the way."

Kerry examined the ceiling. "Any other helpful remarks?"

"Yeah. If he starts to win, bite his ear." Watching Kerry, Clayton spoke more softly. "Seriously?"

"Of course seriously." Raising his head, Kerry turned. "This is pretty much it for us, pal."

Clayton folded his hands across his stomach. "Just a few things. Like stay calm, within yourself, no matter what Dick says or does. Remember that abortion isn't just about Lara. Any more than gay rights is about Kit, or race in America about me."

Kerry's eyes became hooded. "Or wife beating just about my mother?"

Clayton studied his face. "We can kill him with it, Kerry. We've got the court documents. And you know, and I know, that Dick's behind the leak to Cutler."

"I *don't* know that, Clayton." Kerry looked up at his friend. "And Dick had twenty years to smack Jeannie around again, but there's nothing to suggest he ever did. How I wish my father could have changed like that." When Clayton did not answer, he finished, "Has running for President changed *me* so much that I use this?"

"It's a question of *how* you use it, Kerry. I'm not saying feed it to the tabloids—yet."

Kerry rubbed his temples—the sign, Clayton knew, of the headaches he sometimes got when his energy reached bottom. "Before we leave," Clayton admonished, "eat a candy bar."

Kerry gave no sign of hearing. "My mother called," he finally said. "Three days ago, after the abortion clinic shooting came up, and I got myself in trouble by using the dread word 'life.' Do you know what she asked me? Whether I wanted her to tell the press how I saved *her* life by beating up the old man."

Beneath his quiet words, there was an undertone of wonderment, of pain. "And you said no," Clayton responded.

"Of course, and as gently as I could. But what have we come to that even *she* knows to ask the question?" Kerry lay back again. "Oh, she also feels guilty about how I grew up, and wants to make it up to me. But it's too late for that, and not the right place."

Clayton's tone, though muted, was hard. "And Jeannie's not your mother. She's the wife of a man who's trampling on someone else you loved—and, I think, still do. You owe no debts there, except to Lara. And yourself." Pausing, Clayton asked, "What happens when, in the middle of this debate, you suddenly realize that it *was* Dick all along? What do you do then?"

Kerry was silent a moment. Then he turned to Clayton again. "Go ahead," he answered. "I'm listening."

In the press bus to the studio, Lara checked her watch.

Forty minutes to go. Two rows down and across the aisle, Nate Cutler sat with Lee McAlpine. In profile, he looked tense, ascetic, preoccupied, like a cloistered monk desperate for salvation. She devoutly hoped that what he was inflicting on her, and on Kerry, was exacting its price from Nate himself.

Next to her, Rich Powell asked, "Taking bets?"

She turned to him. "Not on this, Rich. All I think is it won't be dull. Mason didn't want these rules for nothing—he's going after Kilcannon with all he's got."

Rich frowned. "But what would it be?" he asked.

Surrounded by the Secret Service, Kerry and Clayton arrived at the studio.

It was like all TV studios, Clayton thought, cheap, sterile, and brightly lit, smaller than it appeared on-screen. The audience—Asian, Latino, white, African American, men and women, young and old—was a carefully selected cross-section of Los Angeles. The moderator, a longtime anchorman in the city, was talking with Dick and Jeannie Mason and, of course, their blond-haired children. They were three young adults, really—two boys with a girl in between—all seemingly quite stable, normal, and at ease with both their mother and their father. In itself, Clayton knew, this might give Kerry pause about using what he knew. As Kerry shook hands with the Mason kids, Clayton could sourly imagine the photographs in tomorrow's *L.A. Times*—the lone candidate versus America's next First Family.

To Clayton, these moments were another hollow ritual of politics: the candidates making idle chat, pretending that this was their idea of fun, that they were not so gripped by tension that each body part felt screwed on too tight, that they had not come here, figuratively, to cut each other's throats. *Oh, well,* Clayton thought, and headed for Mason's campaign manager, Bill Finnerty, ready to fulfill his role in the charade.

A shambling white-haired Irishman from the Boston school

of bare-knuckle politics, Finnerty stood behind Jeannie Mason. As Clayton approached, Jeannie gave Kerry a brief hug and kiss. With a sheepish grin and a roll of her eyes, she murmured, "God, it's all so phony, isn't it? Reminds me of sorority rush."

No wonder, Clayton thought, that Kerry liked her. With a genuine smile, Kerry answered, "It's not too late for the two of us. We can just drop out and leave Dick to his own devices."

Jeannie smiled back. "Tempting, Kerry. But I've sort of gotten used to him. As bad as this can be." Her expression turned serious. "Good luck, though. As far as I'm concerned, the country could do worse than either one of you. Deep down, Dick thinks so, too."

Was this just a graceful remark, Clayton wondered as he passed them, or a subtle suggestion that Kerry might yet be her husband's choice for Vice President? It could be either; whatever else Jeannie Mason was, she was a clever woman, a full partner in her husband's career. But Clayton already knew Kerry's answer—the presidency or nothing.

"Hello, Bill," Clayton said, shaking Finnerty's hand. "How's tricks?"

Above his thin smile, Finnerty gave Clayton a quick, speculative glance. "Just dandy. Your man ready?"

Clayton shook his head. "He's too damned passive. I wouldn't be surprised if he winds up endorsing Dick."

Finnerty stopped smiling. As one professional speaking to another, he said, "It's been a tough race, I know. Things happen, and you just have to go with it." He lowered his voice. "Tell Kerry we're sorry about what we're going to have to do to him tonight. I don't know if he'll ever accept this, but it really isn't personal."

Against his will, Clayton felt himself freeze, heard his own silence as he stared into Finnerty's ice-blue eyes. Was this affirmation, Clayton hurriedly thought, or the hoary stunt of spooking the opposing candidate in the last minutes before a debate? Or, worst of all, both.

Calmly, Clayton put his hand on Finnerty's shoulder. "Don't worry about Kerry, Bill. He'll be fine. But maybe you should apologize to Dick."

Finnerty gave Clayton a look of silent appraisal, and then

stuck out his hand again. Even before he shook it, Clayton had decided not to tell Kerry: for better or worse, Kerry's mind should be as clear as possible.

Crossing the soundstage, Clayton heard Mason say, "Well, Kerry, this is it." Then, on cue, the stage cleared, and the debate began.

FOUR

For the first thirty minutes, Lara thought, Mason dominated the debate.

Anxious for Kerry, she was aware of Nate Cutler sitting directly behind her in the press section, watching her reactions. She controlled her nerves by taking copious notes. "American family," she scribbled now, and glanced quickly at the stage.

Sitting beside Mason, Kerry listened as the Vice President continued to underscore that he was a parent and that Kerry was not. Kerry seemed watchful, cool, almost preternaturally still.

"Talk is cheap," Mason said dismissively. "But for Jeannie and for me, our children have been the focus of our lives. That's why we've taken the lead in fighting for family leave, better day care, better schools—"

"*Public* schools?" Kerry finally interrupted. "Because as a parent—as opposed to a politician—you've never seen the inside of one.

"Like most parents, you don't want your own kids going to schools that are overcrowded, underfunded, and unsafe. The question is what happens to *other* people's kids." Leaning toward Mason, Kerry ticked off points on his fingers. "I support school vouchers to help parents send their kids wherever they can. You oppose them.

"I support charter public schools, free of the rules that protect bad teachers and students who deal in drugs and violence. You oppose them."

Behind her, Lara heard Nate's low, soft whistle.

"I support higher standards for teachers," Kerry went on. "You oppose them.

"Why? Not because parents don't want them. Not because our kids don't need them. But because the teachers' union— one of your biggest financial contributors—opposes them, too. Even though many of our best teachers would tell you that the union's wrong, and that *they* deserve better, too."

For Kerry, aggressiveness was second nature; to Lara's relief, and for the first time, Mason looked momentarily off balance. The risk was that Kerry might appear more prosecutor than President. As if sensing this, the Vice President drew himself up with an air of dignity.

"I have to wonder, Kerry, what choices for your children you'd have made—*if* you'd ever had to make them. I won't apologize for ours." He turned to the camera with an air of deep sincerity. "I mean to stop the drift toward two Americas—one for the elite and one for everybody else. That's why I've proposed an Educational Bill of Rights, in which every high school graduate in America receives one thousand dollars a year to attend the two- or four-year college of his or her choice." His voice slowed. "Who among this generation's children might find a cure for cancer, or bring peace a little closer, if we help remove the barriers to universal college education? How many millions more would have a better life?"

As if they were still just fellow professionals, Nate murmured over Lara's shoulder, "When it comes to hypocrisy, no one can touch Mason."

Tensing, Lara ignored him. "All that, Dick?" Kerry responded with a quizzical smile. "For a thousand dollars a year? Why not *two* thousand, and buy world peace right now?"

There was a ripple of nervous laughter. *Don't push him too far,* Lara silently warned.

"A thousand dollars," Kerry said in a more serious tone, "is window dressing where rising tuition has completely overwhelmed the income of the average working family—which, in real dollars, has *fallen* twenty cents an hour during this administration.

"That's why I've called for interest-free loans—up to ten thousand dollars a year for any student at a four-year college who pledges to devote two years to public service, military service, or a wide variety of charitable causes." Now it was Kerry who faced the camera. "Not only would more young people finish college, but they would help bring peace—if not to our world, at least to our recreational facilities, our day care centers, and our neighborhoods—"

Despite herself, Lara smiled. "Proposals like this," Mason broke in, "will explode the deficit and choke off programs like Head Start which we've *now* been able to increase—"

Kerry wheeled on Mason. "We can *find* the money, Dick. The problem, so very often, is where *you* find the money.

"Last year I introduced a bill to provide universal health coverage for children under eighteen, to be fully funded by a dollar-a-pack tobacco tax. You didn't raise a finger to support it. And now the tobacco lobby—through something called Citizens for Responsible Reform—has funneled money to your campaign—"

"It's irresponsible," Mason shot back, "to pay for health care by taxing an addiction that is dangerous to health *and* life." Once more, Mason faced the camera. "If we achieve *our* goals for discouraging tobacco use through education, there will be no one left in America who smokes."

Only in the third world, Lara answered for Kerry, *where the tobacco industry is free to pursue new customers in the millions. Which is why the tobacco lobby supports you as much as they dare.*

"You say your contributors don't matter," Kerry responded. "And that you're too worried about the budget to fight for better health care.

"Let's look at that. In the last budget deal, a mysterious provision suddenly appeared, delaying cheaper generic drugs from going on the market. Letting them go wouldn't hurt the budget. It involves no taxes on anyone. The only people opposed to it are the pharmaceutical companies." Kerry jabbed a finger at Mason. "*And* you. Could it be all the campaign money you've received from these same companies? Let's go through the list . . ."

Kerry was doing real damage now, Lara saw. She felt a hand on her shoulder.

Flinching, she turned to Nate. As he leaned forward, his voice was soft, almost apologetic. "I need to talk to you, Lara. Alone."

Despite her surprise and apprehension, Lara managed to keep her tone equally quiet and, she hoped, controlled.

"Fuck you," she said, and turned to watch Kerry again, filled with fear of what Nate might make public before Tuesday, of what Mason might say tonight.

Sitting to the left of the stage, Kerry's side, Clayton checked his watch. Twenty minutes to go, and they were out of this free-for-all unscathed.

Kerry had become quicker, crisper, and every comparison he made was tied to a central theme—that he was the innovator and that Mason was too compromised to lead. But the more Kerry damaged him, the more desperate Mason might become; Clayton could not stop second-guessing his decision to keep Finnerty's warning to himself.

"What these examples point to," Kerry concluded, "is the need for comprehensive reform of our corrupt system of campaign finance. A fight in which you, Dick, have been conspicuously AWOL . . ."

"Gentlemen," the moderator interjected, "as is my privilege, let me redirect this somewhat intense discussion of family issues to another subject that excites no emotion whatsoever: the rights of gays and lesbians."

The dry remark drew a smile from Kerry and, somewhat belatedly, from Mason. "In recent years," the moderator went on, "federal legislation to outlaw job discrimination against homosexuals has been narrowly defeated, while Congress passed the Defense of Marriage Act, barring same-sex marriages. Now Californians are hotly debating Proposition 244, which—if passed—would ban so-called special rights for gays and lesbians." He turned to Mason. "Starting with the Vice President, where do each of you stand on the issue of gay rights?"

Mason leaned forward, achieving an expression of sober thoughtfulness. "Our administration," he began, "opposes discrimination against citizens who pay taxes, hold jobs, and contribute to our society. That means *any* citizen, regardless of sexual orientation. And we will rededicate our energies to win the fight against AIDS."

Pausing, Mason leaned toward the camera. "But Americans aren't ready to change the definition of marriage, which is thousands of years old and derives, not from government, but from the Old Testament and beyond." He turned to Kerry. "You've accused me of being AWOL, Kerry. But when the Defense of Marriage Act came up for a vote, *you* were conveniently absent. So let me ask you this: how *would* you have voted?"

Duck it, Clayton silently implored. *There's only fifteen minutes left.*

Kerry smiled. "Of course, I was in China at the time, inquiring into human rights abuses. On which *you've* been virtually silent."

"Not true . . ."

With a slight shrug, Kerry continued, seemingly quite relaxed despite the touchiness of the question. "I've read the same polling data you have, Dick. So I know that you're right to suggest that if you ask most people if they're against 'gay marriage,' they'll say yes.

"The difference between us is that's where it ends for you—with the polls."

Don't do this, Clayton begged. He saw a look of undisguised astonishment flash across Mason's face, as if he had not dared to hope that Kerry would hand him such a gift. The audience was intent, still, as if straining to hear.

"What if we ask the question differently?" Kerry said to Mason. "What if we asked people whether, because someone is born gay or lesbian, we're going to treat that person *worse* than everyone else? That's never been the kind of thing that Americans agree with.

"I don't know if you need to call it 'marriage.' But there is a cluster of rights that go with legalized partnership—health benefits, the right to visit a loved one in the hospital, the right to make medical decisions, the right to pass on your estate, the right to Social Security.

"These are not 'special rights.' I mean, who among us really wants to deny gay people the right to visit a dying partner in the hospital? Very few of us, I think." Kerry's tone softened. "It's as if you've forgotten, Dick, that Americans are a compassionate people. And once you've forgotten that, you can't help bring about the same healing that's already happened in so many American families who have accepted a daughter or a son for what they were born to be."

The faces around him, Clayton saw, wore various expressions—open, even moved, skeptical, unpersuaded. But everyone listened intently; Mason looked frustrated, as if he saw a defining moment slip away.

"I don't accuse you of bad will," Kerry said to him. "I don't even think you believe in this bill. But you *did* advocate signing it.

"I'd have vetoed it. And that's the difference between us."

The ripple of applause caught Clayton by surprise. Clearly stung, Mason spoke through it. "The difference," he retorted, "is that I respect what the American people in their settled wisdom believe marriage should be. And I don't need any instruction from *you* when it comes to opposing discrimination. I was leading that fight when your brother held the seat that you hold now and you were still in law school . . ."

Mason was genuinely angry, Clayton saw, and so—at this condescending reminder of his debt to Jamie—was Kerry. His eyes narrowed, and he fixed Mason with a chill stare. "So would you have signed this bill," Kerry snapped, "if *you* were President? Would you have spoken out for it as a senator? Would you have introduced it? Or is it just another 'problem' you wish would go away?" Kerry leaned forward. "Suppose I introduce a bill to repeal the Defense of Marriage Act. What will you do *then*?"

Abruptly, Kerry had changed the terms of the argument—it was about whether Dick Mason was a leader or an equivocator. And unless he waffled again, many of his gay and lesbian supporters might switch to Kerry Kilcannon. Nervously checking his watch, Clayton saw that only ten minutes remained.

Mason leaned forward, voice tight with strain. "Let's talk about something that's not quite so speculative, Kerry. Let's talk about a woman's right to choose. Everyone's watching, and now's the time for truth."

Kerry stared at Mason.

Three feet separated them. For the first time, Kerry could see the unbounded fear of losing etched on Mason's face, hear a tremor in his voice which jangled Kerry's nerves.

"A woman's right to choose," Mason said accusingly, "is newly threatened by the Supreme Court itself. If you were President, would you appoint justices who share *your* belief that a fetus is a 'life'?"

Kerry willed himself to stay calm. "I'd appoint justices who share my belief in the right to privacy—"

"That means nothing," Mason said harshly. "What if they agree with you about 'life'? Would you appoint them? Or would you decide that a justice who shared your beliefs is too dangerous to a woman's most basic right?"

It was clever, Kerry realized: if such a justice was "dangerous," so was Kerry himself. "I'm not interested in personal beliefs," Kerry retorted, "but in legal philosophy."

"So you'd select nominees who disagree with your deep personal beliefs, and reject those who agree with you?"

"You're not listening, Dick—"

"I've been listening," Mason interrupted. "You say you're pro-choice, but your real message is that women should be ashamed of choosing. How can they trust *you* to protect them?"

"Because I've committed myself," Kerry retorted. "And I'm not in the habit of lying—"

Suddenly he heard himself, and stopped.

"Not in the habit of lying," Mason repeated, his voice now quiet. "What if the choice involved you?"

Stunned, Kerry froze.

Mason seemed to hesitate, as if looking into an abyss. With a tense, terrible certainty, Kerry thought, *It was* you. The space between them seemed to have closed; the moment felt visceral, as if the studio, the audience, the press, no longer existed.

For a last instant, Mason looked as appalled as Kerry felt, and then he pressed on in a tighter voice. "Suppose *your* girlfriend wanted an abortion. What would you say to her?"

In a blinding instant, Mason's intentions became clear to Kerry—to shake him so badly that he completely lost his composure. *And even if you don't,* Mason had just warned him, *your only choice is to withdraw.* The sole question was whether Mason would end by asking, *What if the baby would damage your career, Kerry? What would you do then?*

Sickened, Kerry drew a breath. The two men's eyes met, and Kerry felt Mason stretch out the moment. "Is *she* entitled to choose, Kerry? Or would you insist on your own beliefs?"

He must stop this now, Kerry knew. Abruptly aware of the audience, Kerry felt the feral atmosphere, a collective intake of breath. "Is this the level to which we've sunk?" he asked softly. "Should I ask if you still beat your wife?"

Startled, Mason blinked.

Kerry watched his face, just as he had watched Anthony Musso in a Newark courtroom. He saw doubt become fear, then certainty, sapping Mason's energy like a blow to the stomach.

"No answer?" Kerry inquired. "Then let me answer *you.* I support a woman's right to choose, period. But anyone with an ounce of compassion must acknowledge how hard that choice can be.

"That's what I'd feel—compassion. And, I hope, love."

Watching, Lara swallowed. She looked as sickened as Nate Cutler felt.

"Mason," he murmured, as much to himself as to Lara.

She could not answer, or even think.

"I'd be grateful that she *had* a choice," Kerry continued, "and that it was safe. And deeply sorry for the anguish she—and perhaps I—might suffer." Reining in his emotions, Kerry saw the sweat on Mason's face. "If making something that can be so painful sound cut-and-dried is a qualification for the presidency, then I'm not qualified to serve. But I don't think it's a qualification, and I doubt many women do, either."

Mason hesitated, the moment hanging in the balance. Then he drew himself up, turning from Kerry to the camera. "I don't believe in code words," he began. "I won't hide behind vague statements about judicial philosophy to obscure my own beliefs. The first question I'll ask any judicial nominee is whether he or she supports the right to choose . . ."

Kerry inhaled, more deeply now. Smoothly, Mason was back on message, scoring his usual points on choice. What lay between them would be settled elsewhere.

For Lara, the last few minutes were a blur.

The debate became mechanical, prescripted lines delivered to the camera, confrontation kept to a minimum. Mason's closing statement focused on "experience, maturity, a tested capacity to lead." Only at the end of Kerry's closing statement did Lara regain her concentration.

"I want to win this election," he said. "I want to become your President."

"But I'd rather you vote against me than not vote at all. Because that's the first step to ensuring that your government belongs to you—not to special interests, and not to less than half of us . . ."

In the applause that ended the debate, Kerry waited for the sound system to switch off.

He stood first, extending his hand to Mason. With a wan smile, Mason took it, and then Kerry moved within inches of the Vice President, resting one hand on Mason's shoulder as he looked up into his face.

"Pray, Dick," Kerry said under his breath. "Pray you can put the genie back in the bottle. Because if you can't, I'm going to take this very dirty stick and jam it up your ass."

Tense, Nate Cutler followed Lara to the "spin room," where the campaign spokespeople were stationed, ready to explain to the media why their man had decimated his opponent.

His mind was moving rapidly again. Tracing the letter to Mason would complete the story, exposing not only when personal issues become public ones, but how Mason had treated Kilcannon's private life. *Then* let the voters decide.

Ahead of him, Lara still looked shaken. Never, Nate was quite certain, could she have imagined that her affair with Kerry Kilcannon would be used in a veiled public threat by Mason himself. And there was a second threat Nate could not miss: *Print this, or we'll go to someone who will.*

"So," Lee McAlpine said, catching up with him. "What was all *that* about?"

Nate considered how best to conceal what he knew. "Hard to say," he said finally. "It was out of character for Mason to be so overbearing—it was like the 'what if someone raped Kitty' question Bernie Shaw asked Dukakis in the '88 debates. And Kilcannon handled himself well."

Turning, Lee looked at him with sudden directness. "What's the story you're working on, Nate?"

Nate flashed a reflexive smile, still glancing at Lara. "Kilcannon's affair," he answered. "With Jeannie Mason."

Lee gave him a narrow-eyed glance, unamused and undeflected. Together, they entered the spin room, where Lee made a beeline for Bob Kerrey and Ellen Penn. Turning quickly to ensure that Lee was occupied, Nate resumed following Lara, to see how she did her job.

For the cameras, Jeannie gave Kerry a perfunctory handshake, her blue eyes grave and deeply troubled. "What are you *doing*, Kerry?" she murmured. "Is it what I think?"

Suddenly Kerry felt tired, drained. Glancing around them, he saw that they had a moment's privacy. "This doesn't just involve me," he answered. "There's someone else he could hurt, quite badly. Do you know what *Dick's* doing?"

She gave a brief shake of the head. "No," she said in a flat voice. "But he's frightened. He never thought you'd come this far."

Kerry exhaled. "And you never thought I'd stoop this low?"

For a moment, her eyes shut. Then she opened them, looking into his. "He never did it again, Kerry. You should know that."

Heart heavy, Kerry nodded. He watched her return to Mason's side, smiling for the cameras.

FIVE

Watching Kilcannon on the screen, Sean felt isolated, as if the enthusiasm of Kate Feeney and the others came from a party he was watching through a window.

When Kate took his hand, he flinched.

"Don't you think Kerry was good?" she asked. "He's so human, and Mason's like this stiff."

Sean said nothing. Rick Ginsberg emerged from the celebrants, suddenly quite businesslike.

"You two," he said to Sean and Kate. "Stick around—we've got a countdown meeting with the advance team and the Secret Service to plan tomorrow's rally. We can celebrate on Tuesday."

Sean could only nod.

"Based on a preliminary sampling of two hundred Californians," the anchorman said, "forty-five percent of viewers feel that Senator Kilcannon won the debate, thirty-nine percent feel the Vice President did better, and sixteen percent called it a draw. Critically, women choose Kilcannon by forty-six to thirty-six . . ."

"You pulled it out," Frank Wells told Kerry. "The bastard's really hurting now."

They were huddled around the television screen in Kerry's suite—Frank, Kit Pace, and Kerry. But Frank's tone was more worried than elated; he knew too well what Mason had threatened, but not how Kerry had stopped him.

"Well," Kerry said, "we'll see how it affects Jack's tracking polls. If at all."

"Oh, it will." Kit's look mingled affection with a sadness that Kerry understood: at the height of his achievement, Kerry might be driven from the race. "You were gutsy and compassionate, Kerry. It's not in Mason to match that."

The last phrase had a bitter undertone; the one unalloyed emotion in the room was hatred of the Vice President. "Perhaps the most dramatic moment," the anchorman was saying, "was when the Vice President confronted Senator Kilcannon on the issue of choice . . ."

The picture switched to Mason. In a thick voice, the Vice President demanded, *"Suppose your girlfriend wanted an abortion . . ."*

Softly, Frank asked, "Where's Clayton?"

"Don't know," Kerry answered. On the screen, he told Mason, *"If making something that can be so painful sound cut-and-dried is a qualification for the presidency, then I'm not qualified to serve. But I don't think it's a qualification, and I doubt many women do, either . . ."*

"You were so good," Kit murmured. To Kerry, the words seemed retrospective, as if his campaign were already over.

Kerry smiled faintly. "It sounds like a eulogy, Kit."

She turned to him, shaking her head, her mouth set in a determined line. "Not to me."

The door opened, and Clayton walked in.

Everyone looked up. "The networks are saying you won," Clayton informed Kerry. "Dick looked too shrill, and unhappy doing it. Someone should have told him what any trial lawyer knows—don't try to be someone you're not."

"A prick?" Kit asked. "He's much better at it than he looks."

"So are we," Clayton answered, and glanced from Kit to Frank. "Mind if I take a few minutes with Kerry?"

Frank looked at him a moment, questioning and perhaps a little annoyed. Then he and Kit congratulated Kerry again, and left.

Unknotting his tie, Kerry felt tired. Faces flashed across his mind—a startled Mason; Jeannie with her eyes shut; and, most of all, his imaginings of Lara watching the debate. Then his thoughts returned to the present, the practical.

"Finnerty?" he asked.

"Uh-huh." Clayton sat across from him. "I spelled it out for them. They're very sorry, of course."

Kerry leaned forward, fingers tightly interlaced. "How sorry?"

"They're laying off you and Lara. They'll return the counselor's notes, with no leaks to anyone else."

"A little late," Kerry said with fresh, cold anger. "The story's pretty close to the surface, and *Newsworld* spreads it just by digging. And Mason can't control that counselor, either."

Clayton frowned. "At least they're motivated. I told Finnerty that if this hits print, we're giving Dick's police files to the tabloids." He paused, eyes meeting Kerry's. "He believed me."

Kerry examined the rug. "I don't think I could," he said slowly. "Not for Dick's sake, but for Jeannie's. Though I was careful not to tell her that." He looked up again. "How did the counselor's notes get to them, and how did they leak this?"

"They got them through the Christian Commitment. Finnerty didn't want their fingerprints on it, so he gave it to Katherine Jones—the executive director of Anthony's Legions." Clayton's voice was soft. "Jones is a lesbian, by the way. I hope her man's performance tonight left her at least a little embarrassed."

Kerry felt his stomach clench. "Jones isn't the problem," he answered. "If I'm the nominee, where else are pro-choice groups like Anthony's Legions going to go?" He stared at Clayton again. "You already know what the problem is. You explained it to me two days ago."

"The Republicans." Clayton puffed his cheeks. "Likely the Christian Commitment went to someone in the party with this, and *they* decided they'd rather run against Mason than you . . ."

"Which means that they can use this to cripple me in the general election. I'd be a ghost at the age of forty-two, I think was how you put it. And I'd have shafted my own party." Kerry's voice softened. "So it's over. We pull our ads off television and, if I still manage to win, I find an excuse to withdraw."

Clayton's face took on a stubborn cast. "There's nothing we

can do right now," he finally answered. "Let's think about it overnight."

Despite his gloom, Kerry felt empathy for Clayton, and fondness—it was his pragmatic, earthbound friend who, for once, did not want to face reality.

"Somehow we'll go on," Kerry told him. "I've got the Senate, and you've got Carlie, two great daughters, a fat bank account, and a rather promising career."

Clayton shook his head, shoulders slumping with the weight of his own weariness and disappointment. "Well," Kerry said with an ironic smile, "at least you and I have come a ways since we worked for Vincent Flavio."

"Vincent Flavio," Clayton said, and then looked up at Kerry. "Did I tell you Frank Wells still wants to try and find John Musso?"

Kerry smiled without humor. "That won't be so easy. A few months after John moved away, his aunt decided that if she changed his name, he could leave the past behind. As if any of us can do that." Kerry's voice grew quiet. "Don't bother telling Frank. If there's one thing I can do for John Musso, wherever he is, it's to make sure he's left in peace . . ."

The telephone rang.

Slowly, Clayton rose to answer it. To judge from the clipped dialogue—a series of pointed questions, clearly directed at Jack Sleeper—Clayton had managed to sound much like himself.

Hanging up, Clayton turned to Kerry. "Jack has you up three points," he said with dispassion. "And now you're holding among women."

In frustration, Kerry stood, hands jammed in his pockets. "Shit," he said. "Mason doesn't deserve this nomination. *I* do."

"It sucks." Kerry felt Clayton watching him, trying to read his thoughts. "Your life just caught up with you, Kerry. The whole thing—your marriage, and Lara."

Kerry turned to him. "I have to see her," he said at last. "If she's willing."

It was not a question. With a level gaze, Clayton answered, "You know what I think."

Kerry folded his arms. "Well, things have changed, haven't

they." His voice lowered. "Imagine how she feels tonight. What would you do, if you were me?"

Clayton shook his head, still watching him. "I only know what *you'd* do, Kerry."

There was silence. "Tell Peter Lake I need him," Kerry said.

Two hours later, after meeting with Bob Kerrey and Ellen Penn, Kerry sat across from Peter Lake. It was a little past eleven o'clock.

"Sorry to cut into your sleep," Kerry said. "You and I don't get much, do we?"

Shrugging, Peter smiled. "Sleep's for sissies, Senator. And I needed to talk to you anyhow. About this event in San Francisco."

Oh, that, Kerry thought. After tonight, the rally seemed so pointless that it had slipped his mind. But despite his smile, Peter's voice had an undertone of urgency.

"Sure," Kerry said.

"Your advance team," Peter continued in a flat voice, "wants the speakers' platform facing a slough of office buildings. That way there's a picturesque backdrop for the cameras, they think—a clock tower in front of the Ferry Building. The problem is that you'd be facing over a thousand windows, and some terraces besides." Peter paused, and any trace of humor vanished. "Security-wise, Senator, it's a nightmare."

Kerry restrained his impatience—at the moment, all that seemed important was calling Lara. "Where do *you* want the platform?" he asked.

"Against the nearest building. It eliminates most lines of sight."

"What do my advance people say?"

"Too cramped-looking, too much glare from the glass. Bad for television."

Though he was trying to be objective, there was an edge in the agent's voice. Kerry felt a wave of sympathy; Peter worked hard, and the Service had already lost Kerry's brother. They did not want to lose *him* as well.

Quietly, Kerry said, "I haven't made things easy for you, have I?"

Peter hesitated, as though wondering how far to go. "Not too easy," he answered with another fleeting smile. "But I guess that's not your job."

Kerry studied him. "Tell my advance folks," he said at length, "that I can live with a little glare."

Above the bruises of fatigue, Kerry could see the relief in Peter's eyes. "Good," the agent said slowly. "Good."

Kerry paused a moment. "I've got a favor to ask you, too."

"Sure."

"There's a reporter I'd like to meet with—tonight if she's available. But the rest of the pack can't know." Kerry hesitated, trying to sound matter-of-fact. "I need a way to see her in private. Without signing off security, I hope."

For an instant, Peter stared at him, to assess whether he was joking. "Signing off protection," he said finally, "is *not* a good idea."

Kerry tilted his head. "Don't you guys work out all the ways some psychotic with a gun could get to this floor? *One* of them ought to work for an unarmed woman."

A trace of Peter's smile returned. "We could probably bring her here, Senator. If that's what you're asking."

Once Peter left, Kerry began pacing—arms folded, lost in thought.

What would he say to her? he wondered. How would her voice sound? How would she feel when she heard *his* voice?

He could find no speech to give, no words that gave him confidence. All he had was how he felt.

Throat constricted, he reached for the telephone.

SIX

Close to hyperventilating, Sean could not stop watching the Secret Service agent.

His name was Ted Gallagher. White-haired, affable, and alert, he sat next to the advance person, Donna Nicoletti, at the head of three tables usually reserved for phone banks. The others occupied folding chairs along both sides—three San Francisco cops; two scruffy guys in T-shirts who were sound system specialists; a representative of the event company that would set up the bleachers; several volunteers. Pinned to a sketchboard was a hastily drawn diagram of Justin Herman Plaza, with a schedule for the rally.

"11:45 a.m.," it read. "Candidate arrives from Los Angeles."

Nicoletti pointed to the diagram. "Here," she said to Gallagher, "is where we want the volunteers with signs. Right behind the press pool, so they show up on TV."

From there, Sean thought anxiously, *he might get close enough.*

Gallagher eyed the diagram. "I want a list of these volunteers," he said to Ginsberg, "for a security check. Names, addresses, and Social Security numbers."

Sean's hands felt clammy. "I can give you a partial list," Ginsberg answered. "Maybe the rest tomorrow morning."

Gallagher shook his head. "It's Saturday night. Computer checks take longer on a weekend, and this event is thirteen hours away."

Ginsberg put a finger to his lips. With some reluctance, he answered, "I can have someone call people at home."

"I'm afraid you'll have to. In case we can't complete the security check, I'll want a couple of your people near the platform to help ID the folks who belong to you. Anyone your people don't know, we'll keep out."

How, Sean wondered desperately, could he avoid giving his Social Security number? Eyes fixed on the table, he heard Ginsberg ask, "Who else should be on the list?"

"Anyone who'll be near the candidate—onstage, backstage, or with a sign. That includes the events folks and the people running the sound system." Gallagher looked around the table. "For those who haven't worked with us before, all of you will be given pins with numbers and color codes, identifying who's permitted within the various perimeters of security. That defines where you're allowed to go and how close to the senator you'll get.

"This event is very last-minute. We're rushing magnetometers up here; we may not have them all in place as soon as we'd like, and some may have calibration problems. Plus, we have to sweep the area before *anyone* gets inside." Pausing, he glanced at the events supervisor, a stocky man in a San Francisco 49ers windbreaker. "If you want this to come off on time, we'll need the bleachers and sound system in place by seven a.m."

"They will be," Donna Nicoletti said, with an admonitory glance toward the sound people. "We've already started work."

Sean half listened now. He had no criminal record: obsessively, he wondered how close the Boston police had come to him; whether the name Sean Burke was now on a computer or otherwise known to the Service; whether, in the next moment, Gallagher would spot him. To be so close . . .

"All right," Nicoletti was saying. "Let's go through this, step by step.

"By seven o'clock, the platform is in place and the sound system is set up. We need the sound system connected directly to the press bleachers, so they don't pick up ambient noise." Standing, she touched the diagram, saying with veiled displeasure, "At the request of the Secret Service, the platform will be here, in front of the office building marked 'Embarcadero Four.'"

"Good," Gallagher said blandly.

"By nine a.m.," she continued, "the barriers for the various perimeters will be in place, as well as the magnetometers, right?"

"Hopefully. Between nine and ten-thirty, we sweep the area for guns and explosives. During that time, the plaza will be empty. At ten forty-five, we start letting people in." He looked at Ginsberg again, pointing at an area near the plaza marked "Parking." "I'd have your buses and car pools already here, so we can sweep them. Then we can admit these folks right away, to help minimize backup at the magnetometers."

Next to Sean, Kate Feeney looked somewhat awed. "They're really thorough," she whispered.

When Sean reached for the Diet Coke in front of him, his hand shook. Awkwardly, he clutched the aluminum cylinder so hard that he indented its side, causing a metallic click which made him wince.

No one seemed to notice.

Standing next to the diagram, Gallagher traced a line from a point marked "end of Sacramento Street" to the speakers' platform. "This chute," he said, "is about a hundred feet long. It'll be lined with agents and police. The only people allowed to use it are the volunteers with signs, the press pool, and Senator Kilcannon and his party, including Senator Penn." His finger jabbed a checkpoint near the platform. "Two agents and your two volunteers will be right here.

"At eleven o'clock, we start checking off the folks with signs. When we're finished, your two people can join the rest. At eleven-thirty, the press pool arrives. *They'll* have been swept before they got on the bus."

Finishing, he turned to Nicoletti. She looked around the table for emphasis. "At eleven forty-five," she said, "Senator Kilcannon arrives from the airport. Accompanied by Senator Penn, he proceeds from Sacramento Street into the chute, shaking hands as he goes. He'll be surrounded by prominent women supporters, which makes for good visuals." Pausing for breath, she continued: "The pool proceeds to the front of the platform. At eleven fifty-five, Senator Kilcannon should be at the checkpoint.

"And at twelve o'clock, if all goes well, Senator Penn introduces Senator Kilcannon. To thunderous applause."

Where, Sean wondered, should he be? The security seemed daunting; it was hard to imagine, especially from a mere diagram, how it would be possible to conceal a gun. Let alone assassinate Kilcannon.

"Any questions?" Nicoletti asked.

Sean barely listened. The back-and-forth was like the drone of a television. "We'll need to do a walk-through," the agent was saying to Ginsberg and Nicoletti.

Sean looked up. "When?" Ginsberg asked.

Gallagher checked his watch. "Soon."

The meeting broke into clusters, people standing, talking among themselves. Sean stayed where he was, irresolute.

As if sensing his isolation, Kate Feeney asked, "What do you want to do tomorrow?"

Sean gave a twitch of the shoulders. "I just want to meet the senator."

"You *should*." Enthused, she squeezed his arm. "Maybe the two of us can check through the volunteers. That way we'll be close to him."

She was trying to look after him, Sean thought. He turned to her, confused yet touched, unable to speak. Dully, he noticed again the pale skin, the delicate features, the light down at the nape of her neck.

"Let's talk to Rick," she urged him.

Without awaiting an answer, she clutched his sleeve, standing. Together, they walked toward Ginsberg, who was quietly talking to Gallagher. "This is a real fire drill," Ginsberg was saying.

The agent nodded. "We like more notice—this makes things harder. But we know how campaigns can be."

Noticing Kate, Ginsberg turned. "What can I do for you, Kate?"

"We'd like to check the people with signs through. If we do, maybe John would meet Kerry."

Ginsberg hesitated. "*You* know everyone, right?"

"Right."

"Then sure." He faced Sean. "You might not meet the senator until afterward. Is that okay?"

Sean nodded, forcing himself to speak. "Are you going to the plaza? Maybe we could go with you."

Sean sounded the way he felt—nervous, overwhelmed by a sense of responsibility. Ginsberg frowned, eyes narrow with thought. Turning to Gallagher, he asked, "Can these guys walk through with us? There's a lot to think about on the volunteer side, and maybe it would help if a few of us went."

Gallagher looked at Sean, then Kate. "I'm Kate Feeney," she said, extending her hand.

He took it, expression softening. "Ted Gallagher," he said, and turned to Sean. "And you're . . . ?"

Sean licked his lips. "John Kelly."

To Sean, Gallagher's eyes seemed to linger. Turning away, the agent asked Ginsberg, pleasantly enough, "You can vouch for these people, right?"

Ginsberg smiled toward Kate and Sean. "Sure," he said. "They're superstars."

"Okay," Gallagher answered. "Let's go."

He headed toward the others, who were already gathering at the center of the room—Nicoletti, the events and sound people, two police officers. Sean went to the corner where he had left his jacket folded in an empty desk drawer, in order to conceal the gun.

SEVEN

There was a soft tap on the door, then another.

Inside, Kerry stopped pacing. Pausing for an instant to prepare himself, he went to answer.

Lara stood in the doorway, with Peter Lake at her side.

Her eyes were dark pools, solemn and unblinking. Kerry made himself look at Peter.

"Thanks," he said. "I'll call you."

He turned to Lara again. It struck him that neither was able to pretend, for Peter's sake, that this was an ordinary meeting. Then Kerry moved aside to admit her.

She hesitated a final moment, and then stepped inside. The door closed behind her.

She stood in the artificial light, dressed in jeans and a sweater, as he was. It had been almost two years, he thought again, since the last day he had seen her, fresh from the shock of discovering her pregnancy. Lara looked older—to Kerry, more beautiful than ever, but tempered by experience. She seemed quite determined to wait for him to speak.

For Kerry, a slight smile was easier.

At this, she came closer, two steps, and rested the crown of her head against his chest. "I'm sorry," she murmured. "For everything."

He clasped her shoulders, his touch light, tentative. "I came back to D.C.," he said softly, "to ask you to marry me, no matter what you decided. But you were gone."

Her head bowed. When she looked up again, there were tears in her eyes. "Oh, Kerry, it's too late for this. Why hurt each other more?"

Her tone was weary, helpless. She backed away from him, shoving her hands in her pockets, as if retracting her own feelings. Quietly, she said, "There was just so much."

Kerry's stomach was a knot; he felt constricted, as though two years of emotions had nowhere to go. "Please." Her voice had a desperate quality. "Let's talk about something else. We used to be able to talk."

He gestured toward the couch. She sat at one end, facing him; he sat at the other. It was instinctive, he realized—this was how they would sit in his apartment at the end of a day, each with a wineglass, sharing whatever had happened since they were last together. Only, now she looked tentative, like a bird about to take flight.

"I'm seeing Cutler tomorrow," he told her. "No choice."

Somehow this subject seemed easier for her. "What are you going to do?"

"About Cutler? Lie, of course."

"I mean about the campaign."

"Withdraw, probably. We've found a way to back off Mason. But I think the Republicans know, too."

He watched her take that in. Beneath her stillness, Kerry sensed a shiver. But when she looked at him again, her gaze was cool and direct. "Have you ever considered," she said, "that the truth might be an option? You never wanted me to do it, after all."

Briefly, the thought made Kerry angry. "Throw you to the wolves, career and all, and explain what a stand-up guy I was? No way." Pausing, he softened this with a smile. "Besides, Clayton says it wouldn't work."

He saw the answering trace of humor at the corners of her eyes. "How *is* Clayton these days?"

"Tired. Like me."

She looked away, pensive again. "Do you know what's so terrible?" she told him. "I don't even remember what this woman looked like. It was just that what I went through was harder than I expected."

Kerry watched her. "Maybe that's because," he answered, "you didn't do it just for you. There was the small matter of my career."

Lara tilted her head, as if to readjust the focus of her thoughts. "What has it been like, Kerry? Running for President."

She needed to know, Kerry thought: his candidacy was the culmination of her decision. But she was also finding her emotional bearings, he guessed, and the subject of his endangered quest, however fraught, was less damaging than all they had lost together. For a moment, he looked about the suite—its neutral colors, its look of a furniture showroom, way station for a thousand strangers who left no trace—and sadly realized that he and Lara had always been in hiding.

"The word that comes to me," he said at last, "is 'more.'"

"More pressure—what you say and do affects so many people, and the scrutiny's so relentless.

"More intoxicating, because you become gripped by a vision of yourself at the center of the world. Everything and everyone else is all about you—the choices are yours, you get all the credit and all the blame—and it occurs on such an epic scale." It was a relief to say what he felt again, Kerry realized, in a way he had never done with anyone else. "The President once warned me about the sheer enormity of running: how demanding it was and, sometimes, how degrading. He was right—there's no way to imagine it. But there's something that's even worse.

"I've come to believe that who I am, and what *I* believe in, is what the country needs." Pausing, he finished quietly: "It's embarrassing to say it aloud. Even to you."

Her gaze was soft. "Embarrassing? Or painful, now?"

She was right, Kerry knew: the thought of giving up ravaged him. "No one could have tried harder, Lara. Ever since I was a kid, there's never been any other way for me." He looked into her face. "But I've also done things far worse than lying to Nate Cutler, things I never thought I'd do. Things I'd never *had* to do, because Jamie had done them for me.

"In the last few days, for the first time, I've begun to comprehend him: he was the one who had to make it on his own. And I wish I could talk to him now."

She sat up, intent, more the woman he remembered. "What would you say?"

"That I finally understand what he said before he died: 'But what does it mean?' And that it's helped me. Because the only reason to go through all this is to make it *mean* something." His voice was quiet again. "Every day, I've tried to do that."

Somehow, the last phrase seemed to echo with his loneliness. Lara looked away.

"Overseas," he asked her. "Was it what you hoped?"

Lara put her feet up on the couch, sitting crosswise. "By the time I went," she said in an even voice, "I was hoping for so many things. One was to be so absorbed in work that I forgot you.

"The work was good. But what I saw—especially in Bosnia and Africa—was terrible.

"Those places weren't a game, like the Hill sometimes

seemed to me. It was a matter of antediluvian prejudice, psychosis, ego, brute ignorance." Her voice hardened. "Bosnia didn't need to happen. It was ripped apart by people who did it on purpose: in their own way, Karadžić and Milošević were as evil as Hitler—they had just had a few million less victims to work with. Rwanda was pretty much the same. And the world at large donated its usual proportions of bumbling, cowardice, and indifference.

"I would say it was unbelievable, Kerry, but I came to believe it. The day I knew that for sure was when I interviewed a Tutsi woman in Rwanda while she identified the bodies of ten members of her family, mostly children, chopped to pieces with machetes by her Hutu neighbors." Lara's tone grew quieter. "I did the interview, and we filmed the bodies. Because I wanted the world to know."

The quality of the experience, Kerry saw, was difficult for her to convey. It seemed that Lara did not believe anyone could understand; she stared at the couch in front of her, and her voice became a monotone. "They didn't know, really, because they didn't want to. Sometimes I could still get something done— maybe prod the government to help get food to people. But I never knew what became of the ones I saw." She gave the smallest shrug. "I had airplane tickets, credit cards, a passport—the freedom to come and go. It was like being a voyeur, only I was watching things most people turn away from."

As if to reach her, Kerry touched her wrist. "Did you have *anyone*?" he asked.

She looked at him with renewed directness. "The choices were other journalists or someone from whatever country you were in. And there were problems with both.

"There was a night in Sarajevo, after the war started again. I went to dinner at the apartment of a guy from AP—a bunch of other journalists, mostly, and a college professor I'd brought.

"Paul was my age—a Serb, very perceptive, handsome in his mustached, dark-eyed way—and quite political. We'd become friends, as much as you could with anyone in such a crazy place, and he sat next to me at dinner. There was the sound of shelling nearby; all of us ignored it—we were drinking cheap wine and telling stories, getting drunker and drunker as the sound of explosions moved closer. Beneath the table, Paul held my hand.

"A shell hit the building.

"The walls rattled and the lights went out. Suddenly Paul pulled me under the table, holding me, and then a second shell hit, and we were kissing each other quite desperately. It was too dark to see—I think I could have made love to him right there." Briefly, Lara's fingers grazed her throat; Kerry had the sad sense of remembered surprise, of widowed desire. Softly, she finished. "Then I thought of the hurricane, and you."

Silent, Kerry covered her hand.

She looked up at him. "It wasn't only that," she said simply. "Paul was part of the story. I never wanted to be part of the story again."

The words had a painful resonance—by covering the campaign, Lara was part of the story, so badly compromised that she might never see herself as a reporter after this. Or be one.

"What happened to him?" Kerry asked.

"He was murdered. By Karadžić's people."

Kerry removed his hand—a gesture of consolation seemed pointless and, from him, ill-timed. He wondered if it was possible, now, to know her.

"I've imagined seeing you again," he said finally. "A thousand ways. But in my heart, it was always as if the last two years had never happened. That somehow we'd still be us . . ."

Her gaze was penetrating, just as he remembered. This much was familiar—her inability to look away for long. And then Kerry realized what he was sure of.

He took both her hands. "Do you remember what I said once, about running for President? That the love of any one thing is barbaric?"

She smiled faintly. "We were driving to Kinkead's. In that beat-up car of yours."

"My saving grace, Lara, is that I love two things. The other one is you."

It was past midnight when Nate knocked on Lara's door.

He did not feel right about this. But his directive was not

simply to watch Lara—it was to question her further, the better to prepare himself for tomorrow morning's confrontation with Kilcannon. What Mason had done might make her more susceptible; certainly, it had made her that much more a target.

No answer.

Pausing, Nate leaned the side of his head against the door. He heard nothing stir. Puzzled, he took the elevator from the sixth floor to the lobby and called her from the house phone—once, then twice, for ten rings each.

He put down the phone, reflective. She had to be out; a reporter might not answer the door, but a late-night phone call could be too important to miss. He meandered through the lobby, a miracle of brass and mirrors, to the bar.

There was the usual collection—bored businesspeople, a handful of his colleagues, a few politicians who supported Mason or Kilcannon. But no Lara. Nor had Nate expected to find her; he could not imagine that, tonight, she would want to be with anyone there.

Could they be that *foolish?* he wondered.

Kilcannon was ten floors above her; there would be agents in front of his suite, on the stairwell, by the elevator. Nate collected himself, then walked to the elevator and punched the button for sixteen.

The elevator whistled upward, glided to a stop, and opened with a metallic chime.

There were three agents waiting. To Nate's surprise, one was Peter Lake; as special agent in charge, Peter did not pull protective duty, and he tried to sleep when things were quiet.

Peter regarded him impassively. "What can I do for you, Nate?"

Nate felt edgy. "What are *you* doing up? Is there a problem?"

"No problem. But this floor's off-limits. As you know."

Nate shrugged, eyes not moving from Peter's face. "I was going to meet Lara Costello," he said. "Is she already with Kilcannon?"

Nate saw a split-second's hesitance, and then Peter shook his head. "You also know we don't answer questions. But when the Pope shows up, I'll ask Kit to phone you."

Pressing the elevator button, Peter placed a comradely hand

on Nate's shoulder. The door slid open. Unresisting, Nate said good night and entered.

Once the door shut, he pushed the button for Lara's floor.

Trailing behind the others, Sean walked through the darkened chute where, tomorrow, Kerry Kilcannon would enter the plaza.

The barriers were already up, creating a narrow gauntlet that passed between a hotel and an office tower. Looming above, the lights from hotel rooms and office windows formed an irregular grid. But at ground level the shops were dim, their windows near-opaque; the street was bare except for a homeless straggler pushing a shopping cart, metal wheels scraping the sidewalk. Darkness imposed its own quiet; ahead, Ted Gallagher murmured to Donna Nicoletti and Rick Ginsberg.

Sean tried to imagine himself as Kerry Kilcannon in the last, unknowing moments of his life. But there were no crowds, no cheers, and the night felt close and chill; Sean thought again of his father, a closet door closing between them, and shivered.

Ahead, a slim figure paused: Kate Feeney.

She fell in beside him, not speaking. Instinctively, Sean found the outline of the handgun, hidden in his jacket. He had been so conscious of it that, a passenger in Kate's car, he had felt she must sense its presence; for a confusing moment, it was as if they conspired together.

Sean heard the hollow sound of a hammer striking wood. Then, emerging from between the buildings, the chute ended at an open plaza.

At night, the plaza was a bowl of shadows. From the rear, a large, twisted form emerged—a contorted concrete sculpture, Sean realized, twenty-five feet high. Behind it was a broad deserted street, the looming face of a clock tower; in the distance, the Bay Bridge was a bracelet of lights, suspended from its cables.

Searching out the hammering sound, Sean turned to his left.

Against the office building, a wooden platform had begun to rise. It was skeletal in the darkness—like the remnants of some earlier civilization, Sean thought, the workmen like archaeologists.

The advance group formed a cluster, facing the bare plaza.

"Where's the checkpoint?" Sean heard Rick Ginsberg ask.

Turning, Gallagher stood at the end of the chute. "You'll be right here," he said to Sean and Kate, "with our agent. As soon as we finish the sweep."

Because of the sweep, Sean realized in despair, he could not hide the gun. He felt new fear course through him.

Crossing the plaza, the group stopped in front of the platform. Disheartened, Sean followed.

"*Here's* where the volunteers with signs will be," Nicoletti said. "Right behind the press pool."

Gallagher gazed up, surveying windows. Sean kept his eyes on the platform.

Pausing, a silent figure faced them, a workman. In the darkness, he was not unlike Kilcannon.

Instinctively, Sean moved closer.

The distance between them was thirty feet, he guessed. His sole chance would be from here, and only if he could somehow breach security.

Sean felt Kate Feeney touch his sleeve, affirming their shared duty.

EIGHT

Stunned, Lara gazed at her hands in Kerry's, then into his face again.

"I love you," he said. "Still."

She felt her eyes close. How many times had she wished she could have the last days of their affair to live again, to choose some other path. But now she felt diminished, trapped by the harsh reality of the decisions she had made. Tears welled in her eyes.

"Tell me, Lara."

She looked at him—older now, wearier, but still so emotion-ally immediate, so much the same man she had loved, that at first this recognition overwhelmed her. She stood, her hands in Kerry's, shaking her head.

"No," she managed.

He rose, hands on her waist now, face inches from hers. "Why?"

She turned from him. "Aside from all the guilt and regret—yours *and* mine?"

"I don't blame you for that. Please, *listen* to me."

"You listen to *me*." She turned on him, caught between anger and despair. "We can't sneak around anymore. And once we're out of the closet, the vultures will pick our bones. When did our affair start—tonight?" Slowing, her voice became a prayer for reason. "It would be all Nate Cutler needs, Kerry. You might as well admit the truth—"

"And if I did?"

"Then whenever you looked at me you'd see a lost baby and a lost chance. How many months would we last?"

Kerry thrust his hands in his pockets. His tone, though quiet, was etched with frustration. "That's what you said two years ago. Look how well it's worked."

She gazed at him steadily. "Then let's have the rest of the conversation, Kerry. Two years ago, I said you wanted to be President. I was right, wasn't I?"

He looked down, then met her eyes again. "I suppose you were."

"Well, there's no supposing now." Her voice softened. "You *do* love two things, Kerry. I watched your face tonight: even after what Mason did, you haven't given up, have you? You're still wondering how to bury this."

He shrugged, silent. At length, he said, "It's hopeless."

"If we go public, it will be. For good." To ease the hurt, she went to him, clasping his arms. "We'd be on the cover of every magazine in America, and you'd be the punch line on Let-terman and Leno I said you'd be two years ago. Because I made a decision for both of us, then told a stranger instead of you."

He shook his head. "I'd rather risk it than be with anyone else. Whenever I looked at her, I'd wish she were you."

Briefly, Lara tried smiling. "You really *are* a romantic, aren't you?"

"No," he said flatly. "Just too practical to live the way I have." He cocked his head. "Are you being practical, Lara? Where does *your* career figure into this?"

She had felt so bleak, so compromised that—tonight—she had given it no thought. Moving away from him, she sat on the couch, alone. "I'd give a lot," she said, "not to feel like such a whore. That's part of what going overseas was about—penance. But, after tonight, I don't know what it would take to feel like myself again."

He fell quiet. She watched him, standing in the middle of a strange room, so much the captive of his own thoughts and feelings that minutes seemed to pass. "Maybe," he said finally, "we could wait. You could go back to your job, get a grip. I deal with what I have to deal with. Then, after some time has passed . . ."

"We begin dating?"

"Something like that. No one needs to know that I've called you every night." His voice grew soft again. "I've missed that too."

"So have I, Kerry." Lara struggled to find the truth. "But no matter how long we waited, Nate would wait us out—Nate, or your potential enemies. And imagine how ripe our story would be if you somehow managed to become President."

"I suppose I'd have to marry you," he answered. "Then the whole damned country would be stuck."

Suddenly his unwillingness to *see* made Lara angry at him. "And what a gift I'd be to fanatic right-to-lifers: the First Lady of the United States, symbol of heartless abortion. I wouldn't do that to you, me, *or* other women—never mind that, for myself, I've come to hate what I did." She stood again. "These people play for *keeps*, Kerry—on both sides. They'd use me to destroy you."

"Lara . . ."

"Of course," she said relentlessly, "there's all the joy we'd have in the meantime, waiting for them to do it. While your anxious handlers tried to make me into a Barbie doll . . ."

"How can you imagine," Kerry snapped, "that I'd ever let them do that? Or that *you* would?" He crossed the room, kneeling by the couch. "You could be the best thing for this country, and for all the things you care about—like starving children. You could make such a difference—"

"That's what you say to *yourself*," she interrupted, "isn't it?" She saw the hurt on his face and made her tone more gentle. "Listen to yourself, Kerry—suddenly we're in the White House. You haven't let it go yet. Maybe you can't."

This left Kerry silent. "You know I'm right," she told him. "There'd be no safe place for us, ever."

"So I'll withdraw," he answered. "How many times do I have to ask? Please, give us a chance."

Heartsick, Lara slowly shook her head. "It's not up to me anymore, Kerry. And they *won't* give us a chance. No matter what we do." She touched his face. "Why do you always make *me* see the truth? Why can't *you*, for once . . . ?"

The quiet words seemed to pierce him. "I did see the truth," he answered. "Two years ago. But you weren't ready to listen."

She looked away. "Sometimes I wish I had," she said at last. "Sometimes I wish I'd believed you were content to stay a senator. Maybe then you'd never have learned what really *is* true." She caught herself, voice pleading again. "Please, let's stop this. Before we do more damage."

Kerry touched her face. "Tell me one thing, then."

"What is it?"

He looked into her eyes. "Do you still love me?" he asked.

Despite herself, Lara felt the tears well again. "Oh, Kerry," she murmured, "that's such a sad question."

He took her hands again. "Why?"

For a moment, she considered telling the truth. And then she found a second, easier truth. Softly, she said, "Because the answer doesn't matter."

For a last painful moment, she let her hands rest in his. Then she gently disengaged and, rising, stood by the door again.

"It's time to call Peter," she said simply.

* * *

Nate sat in the alcove of the sixth floor, reading a *New Yorker*. It was more comfortable than sitting in her doorway and, at one in the morning, less odd and less revealing. Besides, he could see Lara's door from here.

He had been waiting for forty minutes. It was a good thing their colleagues were so tired, he reflected; no one had seen him.

Restless, he reread a particularly scathing film review. "Ms. Draybeck," the reviewer said of a supposedly hot actress, "uses both of her expressions frequently." It almost made him smile.

What was Lara doing? Nate wondered. He tried to imagine the psychic devastation Dick Mason must have wrought and then, for his own sake, tried not to. He gave up; in the next pitiless moments, Nate also saw himself, stalking a woman who once had been his friend.

Suddenly there was a soft metallic sound—heavier, somehow, than the opening of the door to a hotel room. Putting down the magazine, Nate rose and quickly turned the corner marked "Exit."

Ten feet away, Lara Costello slipped through the heavy metal door from the stairwell.

Turning, she saw him.

His nerve ends jangled. "Hello, Lara."

Though she was still, her expression was strangely emotionless, unsurprised. She seemed to nod, as though confirming something to herself.

"Where've you been?" he asked.

"Running up and down the fire escape," she answered coolly. "Twenty times, and I'm not even sweating. You should try exercise instead of skulking in hallways."

"Kilcannon," he ventured, and then Lara began walking toward him. She stopped, two feet away.

"You saw him," Nate said.

With steely deliberation, Lara drew one hand back and slapped him hard across the face.

Startled, Nate heard his teeth click, felt pain run through his jaw. He managed to keep looking at her.

She was breathing hard now—a sudden release of tension—and her eyes were molten.

"Don't say his name to me," she told him. "Not you."

He did not answer. She stared at him, her hatred plain. Then she walked past him, to her room.

NINE

Silent, Kate Feeney drove Sean to his motel.

He, too, was quiet. Surreptitiously, he watched her as they turned from Broadway onto Van Ness, her face lit by the few cars that—even at this late hour—sped down the other side of the six-lane avenue. A few more hours, and it would be dawn.

Just before leaving, Rick Ginsberg had asked for their Social Security numbers.

They had been alone in the plaza, the last three to leave. Promptly, Kate had given hers; squinting in the darkness, Rick scribbled the numbers on the back of a business card.

"John?" Ginsberg asked.

Tense, Sean hesitated; the number would expose him as Sean Burke. "I can't remember," he finally mumbled. "My card's at home—New York."

Rick frowned. "Can you get it from someone? I'll need it first thing tomorrow, or the Service won't let you do this."

Sean nodded. He had felt chastised, suspect; perhaps he only imagined Kate studying his face.

"Can you find your number?" she asked now.

Remembering the artist's sketch, Sean folded his arms, afraid to look at her. "My mother knows," he lied.

Bending forward, he hugged his own chest. The bloody acid

sourness snaked from his stomach to his throat. "My mother knows," he repeated. "She knows everything . . ."

"John?"

Kate's voice had filled with concern. Did she care for him, Sean wondered, or fear him? He stared at the floor, tears misting his eyes. "I feel sick," he murmured.

Turning onto Lombard Street, Kate gave him another quick glance. "We'll be fine tomorrow," she said in a soothing tone. "Everything will go fine."

Was she *with* him? he thought with fearful wonder. In his riptide of panic and hope, the street looked surreal, its glowing electric signs—a gas station, a bar, a hotel—the guideposts to a seedy world filled with enemies and strangers. He did not know whether to hide from Kate or to beg her to come to his motel, to await the morning with her arms around him. As his mother had done after she stopped drinking . . .

Sean coughed spittle into his hands.

"Are you all *right*?" Kate asked now. "Should we stop?"

Hands covering his face, Sean shook his head. Kate continued down Lombard faster, headed for Sean's motel. He had pills there, Sean thought desperately. All he needed was to get to them.

Helpless, he felt the sickness rise within him. He sensed, but could not see, Kate turning into the motel parking lot.

As the car came to a stop, fear and nausea overcame him. Shuddering with shame, Sean retched miserably into his hands.

He felt Kate reach for him.

Gently, she dabbed at his face with a tissue, then tugged at his jacket. "You need to get this off," she told him.

Docile, Sean let her ease one arm from its sleeve, the left side of his jacket falling free.

The sudden silence in the car felt like a cry suppressed. He could feel her stillness.

Turning, Sean stared at her.

Her lips were parted, and she gazed down at the seat, stunned. His eyes followed hers.

His gun lay between them, a dull metallic shape.

Kate's eyes moved from the gun to his face, appalled. "What is that?" she managed.

Swallowing flecks of vomit, he reached for the gun.

I had to stop him, he had said to the red-haired woman. *Your sympathy should be with your baby, the life I came to save . . .*

"*John . . .*" Kate's voice was hoarse now. "What are you *doing*?"

Hand trembling, Sean raised the gun. For a split-second, he saw the street punk, the last threat he had faced.

Gingerly, he placed the gun to Kate's throat.

There was no one but them—the parking lot was dark, the motel a dim shadow with a flickering, fluorescent sign. In the cocoon of Kate's car, her shocked eyes shone with tears; her throat twitched where the metal touched it.

She said his name again.

Do you love me? he wanted to ask.

"Please," Kate whispered. "I won't tell anyone."

Please, I only came here for an IUD.

The woman had given the police his portrait. If Kate turned on him, they would find him quickly, and then what meaning would his mission have? Sean's hand shook more violently; he could feel her breath on his face.

"*Please . . .*"

Her eyes were beautiful, blue. He could no longer look at them.

"Please . . ." To Sean, it sounded like a prayer.

Closing his eyes, he pulled the trigger.

There was a popping sound, swallowed by the darkness, by whatever the bullet had struck.

Shaking, Sean looked into her eyes again.

They were shocked, stricken. The smallest sound came from her blood-flecked lips. Above her on the ceiling was a glutinous sheen.

Sean turned away, sickened.

He heard Kate slump against the seat; there was a last pitiful sound, then nothing. The car smelled of more than vomit.

Across the parking lot, a car cruised down Lombard.

Eyes half shut, Sean touched the nape of Kate's neck, pushing her head below the dashboard. Her skin was moist, warm.

Quickly, he withdrew his fingers.

You had no choice, you had no choice. The repeated words swirled in his brain—a mantra, a plea for absolution. The hum of traffic came to him as if from a great distance.

Her keys were in the ignition.

Opening the door, he slid out the passenger side. He stood, frozen by car lights, and then circled the car with jerky steps and flung open the door against which Kate rested.

Her head fell toward him, faceup, staring at him. Her neck hung over the seat, hair spilling from the car.

Sean swallowed. Kneeling, he shoved her by the shoulders, pushing her into a half-sitting position and then into a fetal ball, curled where Sean had sat.

Sean slid behind the wheel, slamming shut the door, and switched on the ignition.

Blindly, he turned onto Lombard, Kate lying beside him.

He did not know where he was heading. Blocks passed, intervals of dissociation. And then he saw a looming swath of darkness.

A grove of trees, Sean realized, was blocking the moon and stars.

By instinct, he drove toward it. Then he saw the markers directing where he should exit: "Presidio National Park."

Slowly, he entered the park.

It was an abandoned military base, he saw—neat signs pointed out a former hospital, an officers club, a base headquarters, a cemetery, all now shadows. To his right was the inky blackness of San Francisco Bay, distant lights flickering beyond; through the towering eucalyptus trees he saw a sliver of a distant glowing span—the Golden Gate Bridge.

For uncounted moments, Sean drove toward it, deeper into the park. He felt the darkness close around him.

Cautiously, he steered down a hill, then up again, afraid to stop. The bridge was closer now, more visible. Soon, he sensed, the park would end.

To his right he saw another sign: "Fort Point." Beside it was a smaller road, dipping steeply.

Hesitant, Sean turned.

Winding down the side of a hill, the road traced the edge of the bay. At its foot, Sean saw a large prisonlike rectangle by the water's edge, its backdrop the massive concrete pillars of the bridge. In the beam of his headlights, the dark shape beside the building became a parking lot.

There were no other cars.

Sean parked in the shadow of the bridge. He still could not look at Kate.

As he opened the door, a chill wind swept through the pilings. Sean shivered, lonely in this strange place; the only sounds were the cars on the span high above him, the harsh current slamming against rocks.

A memory came to him, from a film. Alcatraz was in the middle of this bay: no one could escape from it—the current, too swift, would sweep the strongest swimmer through the bridge and out to the Pacific.

Kate.

Circling the car, he opened the passenger door. She lay there, face averted, as if she had fallen asleep.

Pausing, Sean inhaled. Then he lifted her from the car, awkwardly cradled in his arms. He felt sick again, weak. Sweat chilled on his face.

He could not help this, Sean told himself. She would have betrayed him—no, betrayed the cause in which he was God's soldier. Sometimes even bystanders must choose, and sometimes they must die.

He stopped, panting, at the edge of the rocks.

The water swirled beneath them, twenty feet below. For a moment, he did not want to let her go.

At last he loosened his grip. As if by her own volition, Kate slid from his arms and plummeted into the bay.

Tears blurred Sean's vision again. Then he saw her far below, a vague form, at first swirling, and then slowly, half submerged, drifting inexorably toward the pillars of the bridge.

Sean turned away.

His mission was still before him, paid for with her blood.

He locked the car and walked away into the dark. Half lost, he retraced his route by instinct. Several hours later, hungry, sick, exhausted, he at last heard the traffic sound and then found the mouth of Lombard Street again—a lone man, the blood and vomit on his army jacket concealed by the dim neon light.

In the first red streak of dawn, Sean reached the motel.

The Campaign

Day Five

ONE

Facing Nate Cutler, Kerry was gripped by the ironic thought that, six hours earlier, Lara had sat where the reporter sat now.

It was seven a.m. The time suited both their purposes—neither wanted the press to know. Nor could Kerry do this any later: five hours and four hundred miles away, in San Francisco, he had another speech to give. But that could not matter now, any more than Kerry, sleepless, could dwell on the hopelessness he had felt in the hours after Lara left his suite. Survival is our most basic instinct, he thought with a certain bleakness, no matter how dismal our life may seem.

He let the silence stretch, Nate's question linger unanswered.

With some satisfaction, he watched Cutler's own discomfort: the nervous rubbing of the fingers of one hand, a defensive look in the intelligent dark eyes behind the wire-rim glasses. At Kerry's insistence, the two men were alone.

"Let me understand this," Kerry said at last.

"You've gotten some notes from a psychologist who—by her own admission—has violated her legal obligation of confidentiality to advance her own political agenda. You've stolen my cell phone records. You've been telling people—though you can't know this—that Lara Costello and I were lovers. And you're doing all this, among other reasons, because you're worried about *her* professional ethics."

Nate seemed to tense. "Are you going to answer the question, Senator?"

"Are you?" Kerry asked, and then his voice became sardonic. "Oh, I've forgotten. You're draped in the First Amendment, like a communion dress. So nothing you do matters. But I'm accountable to you for every aspect of my life, no matter how private—"

"She was *here*," Nate interjected. "Last night."

Kerry gave him a long, chill look. "Was she, now?" he answered. "And you're here this morning. Just think of the implications."

Briefly, Nate flushed. "Were you having an affair?" he persisted. "I need a quote."

With exaggerated patience, Kerry looked at his watch, then into Nate's face again. "No," he said at length. "I hope that's not too upsetting."

Nate leaned forward, taut. "Then how do you explain this memo, describing in detail Lara Costello's anguish over aborting *your* child?"

Imagining Lara's solitude then, her horror at this betrayal now, Kerry fought his own anger. "I don't," he answered with a fair show of calm. "I didn't write it. And I can't begin to explain anyone who would give this memo to *you*."

Nate clasped his hands in front of him. "We have records of long-distance calls from you to her, at all hours of the night. We have neighbors who saw you leaving her place in the morning. Others who saw her leaving *your* place."

Kerry fixed him with the same unblinking stare. "We were friends," he said. "And I liked her very much. You did too, I thought."

Nate sat straighter. "I'm not a candidate," he answered. "And I didn't stay at her place, or she at mine."

Kerry gave him a cold smile. "Well," he said, "that's a relief. All of it. As for me, if what you *do* have—phone calls and visits—is news, print away. This race has been focused on the issues for far too long."

Nate shook his head—refusing, Kerry saw, to rise to the bait. "Do you deny, Senator, starting an affair with Lara after the correspondents' dinner?"

"An affair? Yes, I deny it. For the second time, and for the record."

"You were *seen*. Leaving Lara's building the next morning, still wearing a tuxedo."

Kerry stood. "What's the question? Where I rented the tuxedo?" His tone became cutting. "In case you haven't noticed, I'm busy. The question was whether Lara and I were lovers. I've answered it. I'm not going to account for every UFO her neighbors might have seen." His voice flattened. "If that's the price of public office, I refuse to pay it. Maybe Mason will.

"We're through here, Nate. I have only one more thing to say to you." He paused again, his words low and emphatic. "I don't expect much for myself. I don't expect my political opponents to be any better than they are. But I expected better from *you* than what you're doing to Lara."

Despite himself, Nate found that the words—delivered with plain anger and contempt—stung him. He stared up at Kilcannon.

"You talk about issues," he snapped. "Abortion is a central issue in this because you've helped make it one.

"I didn't ask for this story, Senator. But if it's true, you're either a hypocrite who chose to sacrifice a 'life' to your ambitions, or unable to separate your own distaste for *Lara*'s choice from abortion as a broader question."

Kilcannon considered him in silence, his wiry frame quite still now. "Or neither," he said at last. "And you can never know. So it comes down to a matter of conscience, Nate—first mine and now yours.

"You can rationalize this as news, just the way you have. But you also know all the pressures to rationalize it that *aren't* about news—that magazines like yours are losing out to newspapers and television, that tabloids have lowered the standards until it's hard to find them, that scandal sells more advertising space than articles on the budget." Kilcannon paused, as if for emphasis. "That this 'story,' if you print it, stands to benefit your career as surely as it will destroy Lara's. And, perhaps, mine.

"You know what kind of person she is. And you know—at the least—that I'm not unstable, uncaring, corrupt, a substance abuser, or any of the other things that clearly *would* affect what kind of President I'd be.

"If I were Richard Nixon, and using the power of government to subvert the law—*then*, you'd have an obligation to print the truth, and nothing you did to uncover it would be too much.

"But *this*?" Kilcannon paused again, shrugging. "This isn't just about who I am, Nate. It's about what 'news' should be, and who and what *you* are."

Nate regarded him in silence.

Gazing down at the reporter, Kerry felt his anger drain, recalled again how exhausted he was. The self-righteousness left him, replaced by the knowledge of his own failings, his lies, the image of Lara, still so present in the room.

In a quiet voice, Nate asked, "Are you telling me it *is* true, Senator? But that we shouldn't print it in good conscience?"

For a moment, Kerry wanted to answer honestly, as one human speaking to another. But this was about far more than him, and he knew too well that his plea for reason would instead become part of Nate's cover story. *They're not your friends,* Kit Pace was fond of saying. *They're not even an audience.*

"What I'm saying," Kerry answered simply, "is that it never happened. Your conscience is your own concern."

Nate watched his face. And then, ambiguously, he nodded.

"You'll excuse me, then," Kerry said. "I've got a plane to catch."

The reporter stood to leave. Nate had the grace not to thank him.

Afterward, Kerry sat alone, quite still, took some minutes more to refocus on the speech in San Francisco. Then Kevin Loughery knocked on the door, and Kerry's public day began.

Disoriented, Sean waited for the bus on Lombard Street.

His stomach felt as though it had hemorrhaged; his jacket, still damp from his frenzied efforts to remove Kate's blood with a wet cloth, seemed to draw the morning chill into his bones. The cold reminded him of those last moments in Boston, breath misting in the air, as he wondered if he could take a life.

Five days now, five deaths. He could still feel Kate's warm skin beneath his fingertips.

There had been no choice. He was the protector, the shepherd: with all his heart, he wished that Kate could understand. Perhaps today he would give meaning to her death.

The cold and fear made him shiver. He was alone, and enemies surrounded him. The Secret Service. The security check. The magnetometers. The protective shroud in which Kerry Kilcannon escaped God's judgment.

The street in front of him appeared as swatches of reality—half-noticed cars, an old man walking into a coffee shop with a newspaper in his hand. Sean kept his head down. How much longer would it take them to realize that Kate was missing, to find her car?

Three hours to go . . .

At any moment, the police could trace him from Boston to here. Perhaps they already had; one computer check—nine damning numbers—and the Secret Service would discover him.

A bus rumbled to a stop in front of him and, with a hydraulic whisper, opened its doors.

Lara sat with her cameraman on the pool bus as the motorcade cruised toward the airport. She made no effort to chat with him.

Kerry was somewhere ahead of her. Today would be hellish: spent in his presence, a few feet away, both pretending that there was nothing between them, that last night had never happened. *I'm not even in my life anymore,* she thought. All that seemed real was *him,* and how impossible *they* were.

Leaning her head back against the seat, Lara steeled herself.

Work was her salvation, she decided. Not its meaning—its details: all the focus the pool required; listening for quotes; scribbling notes; distributing morsels to the press corps; preparing to react to some terrible mischance. A series of rote steps, which she must treat as if it were a drill that had no human meaning. And then another day would have passed.

Idly, Lara touched the chain around her neck—the press pass, the service tag—and then the ID pin on her blazer.

Two more days, and she would escape. But to what? More regrets, more sham, more days and weeks of anxiety, which would end, if at all, only if Kerry lost or withdrew. To the certainty of being hunted, watched, her past fingered casually by any reporter assigned to investigate their secret. Somehow she would have to withstand it; she could not snap as she had last night, with Nate.

At least *he* was not in the pool, she told herself with bitter humor . . .

I could hit *Nate,* she suddenly thought. *Why couldn't I have held Kerry and let him hold me? When we'll never be alone like that again.*

Lara closed her eyes to ensure that she would not cry. When she was a semblance of herself again and looked around her, they were entering the airport.

At the sterile outbuilding for chartered planes, the Secret Service swept the press again.

The *Shamrock* sat alone on the runway, dull silver in the sunlight. Nate watched the pool join the usual contingent of cops and agents; among them, Kerry Kilcannon moved like a magnet that drew a swarm of followers toward the steps of the airplane.

Hastily, Nate went to the pay phone and called Jane Booth again.

She was in. "I got your message," she said in a clipped voice. "Do you believe him?"

Nate glanced over his shoulder. A few feet away, Lee McAlpine was chatting idly with Sara Sax, pretending not to watch him. "No," he said softly. "He won't—can't—respond to all this stuff that looks funny, except to say we're contemptible for digging it up. But he's right that we can't *know.*"

"So," Jane answered, "we're going to have to decide whether we can go with what 'looks funny'—a counselor's contemporaneous notes, sightings at odd hours, scores of late-night phone calls, Kilcannon calling to her through the door . . ."

Nate glanced at Lee, openly watching him now. "You know what *I* think?" Nate asked, more quietly yet. "Kilcannon didn't want her to do it, and was willing to risk his career. So he's not a hypocrite . . ."

"Maybe not. But maybe that's why it keeps spilling over into his campaign." Jane paused briefly. "The pressure's building. We may decide to go with what we have, on Tuesday. Sheila's got the first draft written."

Lee and the last stragglers began filing toward the plane. "Talk to me first," Nate said hastily, and hung up.

TWO

Sean found Rick Ginsberg standing outside the barriers on the edge of Justin Herman Plaza.

There was a platform now, a sound system, and, across the plaza, press bleachers. In the distance, buses full of volunteers had begun to arrive and were waiting in a holding area. But the plaza itself was eerily empty; inside the barriers, a few Secret Service agents with sleek dogs or metal detectors walked slowly through the area, eyes downcast, like archaeologists on a dig. Feverish, Sean felt the weight of the gun inside his jacket.

Ginsberg checked his watch. "Where's Kate?" he asked.

Sean shook his head.

Ginsberg stared at him, openly worried. "She gave you a ride last night, didn't she?"

This time, Sean nodded. He did not trust himself to speak.

Ginsberg seemed to scrutinize him further, eyes briefly moving to his speckled jacket. "Did you get your Social Security number? I'm going to need it."

Reaching into his back pocket, Sean withdrew a slip of paper and handed it to Ginsberg; in pencil, Sean had scribbled the number 486-24-2119.

Ginsberg glanced at it and, without comment, began to look for Ted Gallagher.

The agent was near the press bleachers, talking on a cell phone. At the edge of the barrier, Rick waited for him to get off the phone, then called out.

Sean watched helplessly.

Gallagher walked to the barrier and took the paper from Rick's hand. Ginsberg inclined his head toward Sean; Gallagher glanced over, nodding, and squinted at the numbers.

It was the Social Security number for Sean Burke.

Sean felt his fingers twitch as if he were fondling a string of beads. Fervently, he prayed that the check would be delayed, that Gallagher would not hear back for another hour and a half. Or that the name Sean Burke, whatever the Boston police might now suspect, would not yet appear on the computer system for the Service.

Holding the paper in front of him, Gallagher dialed his cell phone again.

Tense, Sean saw the agent seem to repeat the numbers.

Before Sean was aware of it, Ginsberg was at his side again. "Damn Kate," he said impatiently.

It was the first time Sean had seen the volunteer coordinator fretful, and it increased his own agitation: he could not tell if this was the pressure of a last-minute event, or something else.

"What's wrong?" Sean blurted.

Rick grimaced. "All their magnetometers aren't here yet, and *you* can't help them check our people through, not by yourself—you don't know enough of them. So *I* need to vouch for them all."

Sean hung his head, assaulted by the confusion of his roles: shame at not being valuable to Ginsberg; fear of the computer; shock at his frightening good fortune.

All their magnetometers aren't here . . .

Then, across the plaza, Sean saw Gallagher walking toward them.

They know.

Sean felt his knees buckle. He stood there, unable to move, ignoring Ginsberg. Following his gaze, the volunteer coordinator turned to Gallagher. The agent's last few steps, closing the distance, seemed unbearably slow.

He looked first at Sean, then Ginsberg. "We're through with the sweep," he said. "Time to start letting your people in."

Sean swallowed.

Were they still checking? he wondered. How many minutes would it be until he felt Ted Gallagher's hand on his arm? For a fearful instant, he wished for that. And then Gallagher gave him a staff pin and a tag to wear around his neck.

Turning, Rick Ginsberg put a hand on Sean's shoulder, as if to apologize for his curtness. "Come on," he said. "We'll get these folks checked through. You can hand out the signs."

Sean followed him for nerve-racking minutes, circling the plaza, the complex scheme of barriers erected to thwart car bombers and filter the crowd through checkpoints. And then, for the second time in twelve hours, Sean was walking through the chute, as he had in the dark, with Kate.

In another hour or so, Kerry Kilcannon would pass through this same passageway—toward him, if somehow Sean had not been caught.

Two more agents in sunglasses waited at the rear end of the chute. In front of one were three boxes of signs with "Kilcannon" printed on both sides.

Ginsberg took a checklist from an agent. "We'll have all the magnetometers here soon," the man told Ginsberg. "But for now, you have to vouch that these people match their name and number."

Sean pulled out a sign. A trickle of volunteers—mostly young, some older, a cross-section of sizes and races, similar only in their eagerness—started through the chute.

Behind him, Sean could feel a crowd building, the people who had filled the buses now moving through the checkpoints. Nervous, he patted the gun inside his jacket.

Suddenly Sean saw two heavy-set men in suits hurrying between the volunteers. The first, large-framed and graying, wore the pin that identified him as a Secret Service agent. But it was the black man with him who made Sean freeze.

They've come for me, he thought.

Rick stepped out to meet them. "Mr. Slade?" he said. "I'm Rick Ginsberg, the volunteer coordinator."

The two men shook hands. Behind them, the volunteers had bunched, waiting. Sean stared at the ground.

"John," Ginsberg was saying, "this is Clayton Slade. The senator's national campaign manager."

Clayton, glancing at Sean with shrewd black eyes, stuck out his hand. Limply, Sean took it. Then the agent with Slade shouldered between them, speaking to his colleagues. "We should have a magnetometer here," he told them. "In about ten minutes."

Clayton Slade regarded Sean for another moment. Then, glancing at the volunteers behind them, Slade said to the agent, "I think we're holding up progress here."

Together, the two men walked through the checkpoint. Mechanically, Sean handed a sign to a smiling black woman, who thanked him.

Waiting for Kerry, Clayton stood with Peter Lake on the speakers' platform.

At their backs was a thirty-story office building with at least five hundred windows; the row of buildings to Clayton's right had perhaps a thousand more. But Peter had been correct: placing the platform at the foot of this building had eliminated countless lines of fire.

Clayton was restless. He had preceded Kerry here this morning and still had no account of the meeting with Cutler. Based on the debate, the momentum was with Kerry now, and Ellen Penn was urging Clayton to buy all the airtime the campaign could afford. Clayton could find no graceful exit strategy: to lose the race, he thought wearily, was proving harder than he once had thought.

Next to him, Peter watched the crowd form; once more, Clayton noted with appreciation, the Service had secured the site, swept the area, closed the windows, identified the sight lines, made a car or truck bomb effectively impossible. "Sorry for the late notice," he said to Peter. "But this was what we needed to do."

Peter kept eyeing the crowd, the placement of his agents. "The senator helped us," he answered.

There was a certain wryness in Peter's voice. Clayton turned to him, asking, "For once, you mean?"

Peter smiled. But his only response was to say, "Nice crowd."

It was. The volunteer coordinator had done well, and, it seemed, a number of the curious from local restaurants and the farmers market, slowly filtering through security, were helping to swell the audience. The plaza was filling; a banner floated over them, proclaiming "Kilcannon—The Woman's Choice," and volunteers with signs continued to trickle through the chute and take their places in front of the platform. At the rear of the plaza, a few kids in jeans and T-shirts had climbed the twisted concrete sculpture to get a better view.

"Look at that sculpture," Clayton remarked to Peter. "It's Nazi Stonehenge."

Peter gave a second, brief smile. Following his gaze, Clayton saw two sharpshooters positioned behind the clock tower of the Ferry Building, perhaps two hundred fifty feet away. "We just got notification from the FBI," Peter said at length. "A possible suspect in those Boston shootings apparently flew out to San Francisco. Right after it happened."

Clayton turned to him again. "Do they think he's still around?"

Peter shrugged. "They don't know. They've started to look, but it's pretty low-profile—they don't want to warn him. Still, they wanted to alert us, and Mason's detail too. For a right-to-lifer gone insane, an event like this could be a lightning rod."

Clayton gazed out at the barriers, the checkpoints, the sharpshooters, and thought again how dedicated Peter Lake was to his mission. "Two more days," he said, "and they're holding an election. *Then* what will you do?"

Peter rested a comradely hand on his shoulder. "I'm going snorkeling, Clayton, in the British Virgin Islands. With the woman who—as far as I know—is still my wife."

For a moment, Clayton allowed himself to envision some unbroken time with Carlie, who was tending their now-empty nest. This made him think sadly, as he so often did, of Ethan. Then he had another thought: that Peter had not mentioned Lara Costello, either directly or by implication. And never would.

When Clayton looked at his watch again, it was close to eleven-thirty.

Sean glanced over his shoulder.

Perhaps twenty feet away, at the corner of the platform, Clayton Slade talked quietly with the gray-haired agent. They did not seem to notice him.

Sean passed out another sign. Next to him, Rick Ginsberg checked off names on the list, thanking each volunteer.

A magnetometer was on its way, and Sean was trapped here.

"Rick?" someone called.

Turning, Sean saw the sound specialist from the countdown meeting, now wearing a Grateful Dead T-shirt and an expression of intense worry.

"Hold our people here," Rick said to Sean, and went to the checkpoint.

From behind the two agents, the soundman said to Rick, "There's a problem with the sound checks. The mult-box isn't working."

"What the fuck is a mult-box?"

"Never mind *what* it is," the soundman said with equal impatience. "We need it to get good sound for the press and the TV people. I can have one here in fifteen minutes. The question is how my guy's going to get *through* all this mess."

Quickly, Ginsberg glanced at one of the agents. Narrow-eyed, the tall man told the sound specialist, "Have your man come to the head of the chute. We're going to have to sweep him." Then he turned to Ginsberg, asking, "Can you meet him up there? We don't want someone new inside."

Ginsberg faced Sean, nodding toward the head of the chute. "Wait for this mult-box guy, okay? Folks can grab their own signs."

Swallowing, Sean nodded. "All right."

He began sliding against the traffic, the stream of volunteers. Then the stream ceased altogether.

At the head of the chute, more volunteers waited for two Secret Service agents to install a magnetometer.

* * *

For long moments, Nate waited patiently with the rest of the cattle—the press corps, slowly filing through the checkpoint for the press platform. Next to him, Lee McAlpine clutched his sleeve. "Share," she murmured. "After all, we're friends."

Nate merely smiled.

Soon someone else would sniff this out. That was the fear Jane Booth was feeling, and Mason's veiled warning to hurry seemed to make the competitive pressures on her unbearable. He could imagine the fevered conference calls—Jane in Washington; the publisher and the managing editor in New York; perhaps others. Nate wondered how much difference it would make that Mason had plainly leaked the memo; while it mattered to Nate himself, and seemed crucial to the story, there had been no real chance to hash it out with Jane.

Lee still waited next to him. Then Nate passed through the checkpoint and climbed up into the bleachers, away from her.

It was hard to see this as just another event—Kilcannon's effort to mend his fences with pro-choice women—when the theme itself was so resonant with irony, its painful subtext so near the surface. But Nate would try. He stopped to scribble on his notepad that it was a fresh spring day, a seeming metaphor for the new hopefulness of Kilcannon's supporters. Climbing the bleachers, he stood on the uppermost board, pad in hand, satisfied that he had a clear view of the crowd, the signs, the speakers' platform.

"A beautiful day," Kerry remarked to Ellen Penn.

They sat in the rear of Kerry's limousine as it glided to a stop on Sacramento Street. The junior senator from California, dark-haired, diminutive, and feisty, answered, "This is San Francisco, Kerry, not some toxic waste dump near Passaic. There'll be a good crowd too. All you have to do is tell them where you really stand." Her grin was somewhere between cheerful and challenging. "Or do I have to remind you?"

This is San Francisco, Kerry thought reflexively, *where Jamie died.* But last night the dream of his own death had not plagued him. He supposed that was the upside of sleeplessness.

"I know where I stand," he assured Ellen with a smile. "Three steps behind you, like Prince Philip."

Ellen gave a satisfied laugh. Then their driver turned to say, "About two minutes, Senator."

Nauseated, Sean stopped short of the magnetometer.

The device was like the one he had passed through at Logan Airport, the nuisance that had made him leave a far better gun behind. Through the metal frame he could see the line of black Lincolns parked at streetside, waiting, then reporters and cameramen climbing from a large bus with a cardboard sign in its window marked "Pool."

Waiting in one of the Lincolns, Sean knew, was Kerry Kilcannon. Just as Sean knew that to pass through the magnetometer would be fatal.

The last of the volunteers came through the frame. Behind them, Sean saw an anxious-appearing Asian man holding a metallic box in his hands while an agent swept his body with a metal baton. Another ritual followed, partially obscured from view: the box was swept, inspected, sniffed by a dog, put through an X-ray machine. Sweating, Sean tried to believe in the power of his staff pin.

He took two steps forward—as far as he dared—stopping at the threshold of the magnetometer.

A mustached agent, weathered as a cowboy, steered the Asian man to the frame. Only the device itself separated Sean from the soundman, the box in his hand.

"You John Kelly?" the agent asked Sean.

Sean nodded. The Asian man stepped through the frame, setting off a buzzing sound, and handed Sean the box.

"Hurry," he said.

Jerkily, Sean turned and slithered back through the chute, passing the line of volunteers.

At the end of the chute, Rick Ginsberg waited, the soundman just behind him.

"Grab a sign," Rick snapped at Sean.

Sean took a sign, hurrying past Ginsberg and the two agents, handing the mult-box to the soundman. And then, quite suddenly, Sean was amidst the volunteers.

To his right, he saw Clayton Slade again, still talking with the gray-haired agent.

Averting his eyes, Sean edged through the volunteers, blending among them. The speakers' microphone was above and to his right, fifteen feet away; the end of the chute to his left, near the stairs to the platform where Clayton stood. Four Secret Service agents were stationed at the base of the platform, facing Sean and the other volunteers.

Sean glanced around him. The others had already started cheering—an Asian woman with glasses, a Latin man, a blond lawyer Sean recognized from headquarters. Wordless, Sean raised his sign, to conceal his face from Clayton Slade.

Lara and her cameraman stood with their backs to the magnetometer, waiting with the others for Kerry to emerge from the black Lincoln.

It was like a frieze, she thought—the stillness of the cars, the Secret Service agents beside them. Only the pool, wrestling for position, seemed to move. Then an agent took the cell phone from his ear and stepped toward the rear door of a limousine.

Briskly, he flung it open.

A small woman emerged, Ellen Penn. And then, behind her, Kerry. More notable women came from the other cars, to join them: Susan Estevez; a local congresswoman; Dolores Huerta, vice president of the UFW, wiry and energetic, with her silver-streaked raven hair; the mayor of San Jose. Kerry greeted each of them, smiling, and then the party headed toward the passageway, the pool first backing into the chute, cameras aimed at Kerry's face. In the semi-chaos, Lara did not think Kerry saw her.

It was not a frieze anymore, she thought—more like the running of the bulls. Kerry was ten feet away.

"Senator," someone called out. "Do you think you're ahead now?"

Surrounded by agents and his women supporters, Kerry smiled. "Wasn't I before?" he joked.

Suddenly Lara found herself inside the plaza. She became part of a file of pool reporters moving between the platform and Kerry's supporters. Spotting Dan Biasi and Joe Morton at the base of the platform, she drew a breath. The chaos had ended; the presence of the agents, as always, reassured her.

* * *

With Senator Penn, Kerry emerged into the light.

Seeing him, the volunteers erupted in cheers, the sound passing like a contagion to the outer limits of the crowd. As he stopped at the foot of the stairs, Kerry watched Ellen Penn climb them, preparing to introduce the others, then Kerry himself. He noticed Clayton a few feet away—solid, loyal, watching over him as he had since the last days of the Musso case. Their eyes met and, despite everything, Kerry smiled.

THREE

When Sean saw Kerry Kilcannon, everything changed for him.

The cheering crowd, the Secret Service agents, Ellen Penn— all were far away, like split-second images in the slipstream of a car. The plaza was noiseless; the hush of prayer seemed to enter his soul.

As if knowing his fate, its justice, Kerry seemed to smile.

Sean lowered the sign.

All of his dreams, his planning, the luck with which God had graced his last days and hours, had brought him to this moment. He had no thought of living past the next few freeze-frames, already imprinted in his mind like a silent film: raising the gun, the shock on Kerry's face when he recognized Sean at last, then his look of resignation as Sean emptied the gun into his head and body.

How many times, in how many ways, had Sean imagined their final meeting. He felt a new lightness, a flood of transcendent rapture, and wondered if this was how death would be, the soul slipping from the body, toward eternal peace.

That action was imperative Sean must not doubt. Frozen by cowardice, his own people—the Church, Operation Life—had become complicit in mass murder. Now Sean would share the light occupied by Kerry Kilcannon; united in death, they would save the lives of children, shame the compromisers who had been immobilized by fear disguised as moral qualms.

Slowly, Sean let the sign slip from his hands.

Catching Kerry's eye, Clayton edged toward him.

He wanted to tell him something, Kerry thought. He felt Dan Biasi step aside, making room for Clayton. From the platform, one by one, Ellen Penn introduced the women who had come with them to vouch for his pro-choice credentials.

Just before Clayton reached him, Kerry saw Lara.

She was behind Clayton, in Kerry's line of sight, framed by the crush of volunteers with signs. He looked into her face and allowed himself the smallest smile, a private, rueful signal of his pain and loss. And then Clayton blocked her from view.

His friend's face, Kerry thought, mirrored his own fatigue. They had been through so much together, and now, most likely, it was almost finished. That the reason was Lara Costello made the juxtaposition of these two faces, both dear to him, seem all the more sad. But this was no time to say so.

"The great leader of the United Farm Workers," Ellen Penn was proclaiming, "Dolores Huerta . . ."

The crowd erupted in cheers, volunteers waving their signs up and down. Kerry put a hand on Clayton's shoulder. "They've done well here," he murmured.

"Yes," his friend answered. "They have."

Kerry still watched the crowd. Behind Lara, a dark-haired volunteer had dropped his sign.

"Peter just told me something," Clayton was saying.

Kerry half listened. The man's expression was different from the others, he thought, as unsmiling as the women demonstrators in Los Angeles.

"This nut," Clayton continued, "the one who did the Boston murders. They think he may be here in San Francisco . . ."

There was something more, Kerry suddenly knew—a fever in his eyes, then a terrible familiarity.

The man stepped forward.

Sean felt their eyes meet.

Kerry's face froze. There was a new focus in his gaze, a stillness in his body; in that moment, Sean felt Kerry acknowledge him at last.

It was their time.

Sean's throat tightened. Light-headed, almost suffocating, he reached inside his jacket.

Kerry watched the movement of his hand.

"So," Clayton finished, "no plunging into crowds, okay? Just as a precaution . . ."

The man held a gun now, aimed at them both.

Kerry felt himself turn to lead. "What is it?" Clayton murmured.

The quiet words jolted Kerry. With a sudden effort of will, he pushed Clayton away from him.

"John," Kerry called out. *"No . . ."*

A pop shattered the air, and then Kerry felt the bullet strike him.

There was a searing pain, a blinding whiteness. Kerry's legs went out from under him.

He dropped into a sitting position. Shock ripped through his body, numbing the sticky warmth on his chest. All he could see was that one face, its expression now sickened and appalled.

"John," he whispered.

"Gun . . ."

As the screaming crowd recoiled, John Musso saw the stain on Kerry's white shirt, the emptiness in his eyes. Kerry's lips moved, and then he fell back, two agents covering his body.

Another two pushed toward John.

Putting the gun to his throat, John thought of Kate Feeney. But the last image in his brain before the bullet tore through it was of Kerry Kilcannon in a witness room, reaching across the table toward an eight-year-old boy.

*   *   *

Lara felt the shriek die in her throat.

All she could see were Kerry's legs, twitching reflexively. The crowd emitted a collective moan of horror; the agents collapsed around Kerry, shouting to each other; the pool reporters were still, stunned by an instinct more basic than their job. Then a photographer began snapping pictures, a reporter started chattering into her tape recorder.

Dropping her notepad, Lara rushed forward.

Thrashing blindly, she reached the edge of the crush surrounding Kerry, saw the two agents covering him, more agents sealing off the crowd. Then she found herself in Peter Lake's strong grip.

"No," he said in a low voice. "You can't."

His face was sickly gray. In near hysteria, Lara began to fight him, her voice choked. "Let me go . . ."

At the end of the chute, two paramedics ran forward with a stretcher, convoyed by more agents. Still holding Lara, Peter turned to them. "Damn you," she spat out, "I have to *be* with him . . ."

"Let her go," someone called to Peter.

It was Clayton, tears streaking his face. "Take her with him," he said thickly. "For chrissakes, get him out of here . . ."

Kerry lay on the stretcher now—unconscious, eyes shut, chest moving rapidly, arrhythmically. Quickly glancing from Clayton to Lara, Peter began to snap out orders.

The stretcher rose from the ground, and the agents and paramedics started rushing Kerry back through the chute. Lara felt Joe Morton's hand on her arm; she began running with him, heart pounding, leaving behind the chaos, the dead assassin, her work.

From the bleachers, Nate could see both the madness and the discipline: the animal fright of the crowd; the controlled frenzy of the agents swarming around the candidate and clearing a path for his stretcher with quickness and brute force. Cries of fear and grief and panic rose from the squirming mass of bodies.

"No," Nate murmured, thinking automatically of James Kil-cannon. "Not another one . . ."

Lara Costello scurried behind the stretcher, an agent at her side.

"What's she *doing*?" he heard Lee McAlpine blurt.

Nate turned to her. Pale, Lee began scribbling notes, still watching Lara.

"God," he heard Sara Sax say baldly. "I wonder if he's dead."

It was a reminder of what Nate needed to do. Taking out his cell phone, he called Jane Booth at home and told her to get someone to the hospital, more people to the site. Then he phoned the office and began dictating his story. His voice, Nate thought with professional detachment, sounded quite steady, his opening paragraph quite coherent.

FOUR

The paramedics laid the stretcher in a waiting ambulance, Joe Morton and Lara scrambling in after them.

It felt like madness—the sudden acceleration; the nightmare shriek of sirens; the sense of careening wildly, a fun-house ride gone out of control. The white-coated strangers bent over Kerry's body, blocking him from view. Then, beneath the sirens, Lara heard the terrible sucking sound.

Sliding sideways, Lara found a place near Kerry's head.

His eyes were open, lifeless. Blood spread from the right side of his chest; a ragged hole in his shirt and skin showed the white jagged edge of shattered bone. The sucking sound came from the hole, as if the wound itself were gasping for life.

One paramedic, a smooth-faced black man, glanced quickly

at the brunette woman who was his partner. "His lung's col-lapsing," he said.

The ambulance struck a pothole; Kerry's body bounced like a rag doll's, with no volition of its own. *Please, God,* Lara prayed in silence. *Please.* The repeated prayer, the awareness that the Service had rehearsed this, were her only threads of sanity.

From behind him, she bent her face to Kerry's.

His eyes seemed wider now, as if fighting their own sight-lessness. The sucking sound grew ragged, perfunctory.

Do you still love me? he had asked her.

Oh, Kerry, she had answered, *that's such a sad question . . .*

"I still love you," she told him now.

The paramedics did not seem to hear. Intent, they monitored Kerry's pulse, his pressure, their eyes like slits, barely seeming to breathe themselves.

The wound took a final gasp, shallow now, and was silent. Kerry's chest no longer moved.

The woman inhaled sharply. "No pulse," she said.

Through a film of tears, Lara watched Kerry begin to die. Then she felt the ambulance slow, heard the sound of the sirens expiring with him; it was as if, she thought, death had overtaken them.

Abruptly, the ambulance stopped.

The rear doors flew open. Leaping out, the black paramedic grabbed the stretcher at Kerry's feet. Then, quickly, Kerry's face slid from beneath Lara's, head lolling, and the stretcher was outside, run by paramedics and Secret Service agents toward a metal double door. Instinctively, Lara grabbed Joe Morton's arm.

"Please," she said.

Lara saw the compassion in his eyes and remembered what he must have heard her say. Suddenly, Joe took her elbow; they slid out of the ambulance, running after the others. Lara was barely aware of the clipped phrases with which Joe guided her past a gauntlet of agents and through the door. It was only when they stopped that Lara saw Kerry again.

He was on a table, shirt ripped open, surrounded by doctors

and nurses. A gaunt young doctor said tersely, "Tension pneumothorax."

Someone shoved a metal clamp on his hand. With controlled savagery, he jammed the clamp through Kerry's wound.

Lara heard the sudden sucking sound, so loud and desperate that her hands flew to her mouth. From between the nurses, she saw Kerry's chest shudder, trembling.

Deftly, the doctor removed the clamp and inserted a thin plastic tube through the bullet hole. Kerry's body convulsed again.

"I have a pulse," someone said.

Lara slumped against Joe Morton, watching the rise and fall of each new breath. It was some moments later when she learned what she had seen and that Kerry's life still hung in the balance; minutes more until she knew what she must do.

Clayton and Kit could only wait.

The hospital had given them a cubicle near the emergency room, equipped with a television. Until a doctor came for them, there was nothing for Kit to tell the press; the reporters waited outside the hospital, with one of Kit's aides to tend to them. In the agony of helplessness, Clayton and Kit watched the screen: now NBC played a tape of the shooting—Kerry freezing, then abruptly pushing Clayton aside, mouth opening just before the bullet struck him. As Kerry fell backward, eyes wide with shock, Clayton looked away.

"Reporters at the scene," a newsman's voice said, "tell us that Senator Kilcannon appeared to see his assailant and to push his campaign manager out of harm's way. By one account, he called out a name . . ."

"Did Kerry *know* him?" Kit asked with quiet incredulity.

With equal softness, like a story recited to a child that served also to distract a parent from his own heartache, Clayton offered his grim surmise.

"Jesus . . . ," was all that Kit could say.

They sat there, silent in the sterile room, the harsh light, the first moments they had shared that were beyond ambition, calculation, the intense concentration Kerry's quest had required.

"He tried to save me," Clayton said at last. "He's seen me through so much . . ."

When his tears began, he did not try to stop them. Perhaps Ethan, and now Kerry, had taught him at least this much. And then Dick Mason appeared on the screen.

He looked diminished, the flesh somehow loose on his face, as though the persona of good cheer had vanished and left nothing in its place. The setting was a television station; his voice husky, Mason kept glancing at a piece of paper.

"I know that California and the nation," he began, *"share my horror at the tragic wounding of a gallant leader—my friend Senator Kerry Kilcannon. In these crucial hours, Jeannie's and my prayers, and those of our children, join with the prayers of countless others around the globe—"*

Abruptly, Kit stood, voice trembling with fury. "Fuck *you*," she said to the electronic face. "*You* wanted this . . ."

"This terrible crime," Mason continued, *"has no place in a process based on ideas and on issues, openly expressed and fairly contested . . ."*

"Issues," Clayton said quietly, "like a lover's abortion . . ."

As he thought it would, his comment, rather than inflaming Kit further, seemed to deflate her. He watched her body slump with the knowledge of her own helplessness, the pointlessness of unreasoned anger.

"She had to be with him, Kit."

Neither the "she," nor the remark itself, needed explanation. Kit kept watching the screen.

"Accordingly," the Vice President concluded, *"I am suspending all campaign activities until further notice . . ."*

"As if you had a choice." The quiet contempt in Kit's tone matched Clayton's now. Turning, she said, "We're going to need Frank Wells here. If Kerry's all right . . ."

Kit did not finish the thought. Nor did Clayton, as wounded as he felt, resent it. Kit Pace was not a religious woman; her practicality was a form of prayer for Kerry's life.

"Get him on the phone," Clayton answered, and closed his eyes.

* * *

Lara stepped inside the phone booth. Dialing the number, she observed through the glass two nurses gliding by, like silent ghosts in white.

Her bureau chief sounded startled, then angry. "Where the hell *are* you?" Hal Leavitt demanded.

Lara steeled herself. "At the hospital."

Without explanation or apology, she told Leavitt what she had seen and that Kerry Kilcannon was still alive.

Leavitt's own voice became a newsman's, clipped and focused. "What about brain function?"

Lara's eyes clouded. "I don't know. I'm not sure *they* do."

Leavitt was briefly silent. "They've sealed off the hospital," he told her. "You're the only one inside. I want you to go live, by telephone."

It was what Lara had anticipated. "I'm ready now," she said.

In shared astonishment, Clayton and Kit watched Lara's photograph on the screen, listened to her reporter's voice, as cool and factual as it had sounded from Africa or Bosnia, tell them what they did not know.

"As of ten minutes ago," Lara said, *"Senator Kilcannon was still alive . . ."*

Kit gave a small gasp; silent, Clayton bit his lip.

"When he reached the emergency room," Lara continued, *"the senator was close to death. He had stopped breathing, his blood pressure was zero, and he had no pulse.*

"He was suffering from a trauma called tension pneumothorax. My lay understanding is that the bullet wound closed up, and the air from the senator's damaged lung could not escape.

"The result is a buildup of gases escaping from the lung into the chest cavity. When the pressure becomes too high, it collapses the veins to the heart, blocking the flow of blood and causing a massive cardiorespiratory collapse . . ."

"Jesus," Kit murmured with distaste and fascination. "How can she do this?"

Clayton shook his head. "Think about it, Kit. She's trying to save our ass."

Intently, he listened, and then the door opened and a gaunt-faced doctor entered the room.

Finishing, Lara told the studio producer, "Give me Hal."

Promptly Leavitt was on the line. "Nice—"

"Hal," she cut in, "get someone else out here."

"Why?"

"Because if he dies," Lara said simply, "I won't be able to re-port it."

It was another hour before the Service admitted the press, under heavy security, to a hot and crowded room. The sole reason, given without explanation, was that Kit Pace would make a statement; filled with a sense of foreboding, Nate edged inside the room, flanked by Lee McAlpine and Sara Sax.

The podium was empty.

Speaking in hushed voices, the reporters sat in folding chairs or—like Nate—stood at the back of the room. He looked about for Lara, but could not find her. Then Kit appeared, advancing to the podium.

Nate felt the tension, his colleagues straining with him to read her face. All that he could observe was that her eyes appeared puffy.

Clearing her throat, Kit seemed to draw a breath. "As NBC reported earlier," she began, "Senator Kerry Kilcannon is alive.

"The senator has undergone an emergency procedure to restore his respiratory functions. While his vital signs are stable, he has not regained consciousness and remains in critical condition . . ."

"As to life?" someone asked.

Kit drew another breath. "Within the next half hour," she answered, "we'll have medical personnel available to answer your questions more precisely. But the senator is young and fit, and I'm advised that the prognosis for survival is good."

"What about mental functioning?" Sara Sax asked. "The trauma as you described it involves oxygen deprivation to the brain."

Kit nodded. "What I can tell you is that thanks to the efforts of paramedics, the Secret Service, and this hospital's trauma unit, there was a relatively short period between the loss and restoration of respiratory function. Obviously, that minimizes the prospect of brain damage."

"If he recovers," the *Sacramento Bee* asked, "will Senator Kilcannon continue his run for the presidency?"

Kit gave the woman a look of silent astonishment. "There's been no opportunity to consider that," she said in a flat voice, "and only the senator can say. Obviously, our first concern is for his life . . ."

"Kit," Nate called out, "all of us saw Lara Costello of NBC attempting to reach the senator. We've now heard her report. Could you tell us why Ms. Costello accompanied the senator in the ambulance and was present for the efforts to save his life?"

Watching Kit, Nate could feel the others studying her intently. "Certainly," Kit answered with professional calm. "Ms. Costello responded as a reporter, and we responded in kind.

"While all of us may deplore it, this will become part of our history. As you know, the violent deaths of public figures— John and Robert Kennedy, Martin Luther King, and the senator's own brother, James Kilcannon—have been accompanied by conflicting accounts, factual confusion, and a proliferation of conspiracy theories.

"The senator's closest friend and campaign manager, Clayton Slade, made the immediate decision that—should Kerry Kilcannon die—this confusion is the last legacy he would wish to leave us. Ms. Costello was simply the instrument at hand."

It was the most artful "fuck you" Nate had ever received, a subterfuge so elegant that—amidst the sadness and tension of the hour—he almost laughed aloud. Instead, with equal professionalism, he asked, "Where's Ms. Costello now?"

Kit shrugged wearily. "In the hospital *somewhere*, I'm sure. At the moment, I can't be more precise."

Kerry felt his eyes open.

He could not see. There was a frightening darkness—either blindness or a place so alien that he could not imagine it. He struggled to escape.

He felt paralyzed.

"Kerry . . ."

There was something gentle, fingertips touching his forehead, as they had when he was a child. Perhaps his mother . . .

He struggled to draw a breath, and then he saw her.

"It's all right," Lara told him.

His eyes filled with tears, just before he slipped away.

The Campaign

Day Six

ONE

When Kerry next became conscious, he drifted in the twilight between sleep and waking, dream and thought. The images that came to him were from his deepest past—Vailsburg, his mother and father, Jamie, Liam Dunn. A small dark-haired boy, an angry man with a handgun. For a time, this confused him; he was in Newark again, and Anthony Musso had shot him. And then, quite suddenly, he was wholly awake.

There was a tube in his chest, and his throat was raw, swollen on the inside. He felt feeble, not himself; gingerly, he tried to puzzle out the relationship between his brain and his body. He raised one hand slightly, then another, then managed to move his head. Shivering, he inhaled.

His feet.

With a terrible effort, he moved his right foot. A searing pain ripped through his chest and ribs.

"Everything working all right?" someone asked. "No reason why it shouldn't."

Kerry turned his head slightly. Standing near him was a red-haired man in surgical scrubs. "I'm Dr. Frank O'Malley," he said.

Kerry tried to pull his thoughts together. "Well," he heard himself murmur, "at least you're Irish."

The doctor laughed. "And you still have a sense of humor. But I wouldn't try playing the tuba just yet, or talking too much, either. You came by that sore throat the hard way: until about an hour ago, you've been breathing through a tube in your trachea, attached to a ventilator."

Kerry swallowed once, painfully. "What happened to me?"

O'Malley folded his arms. "To cut to the chase," he said with a studied bluffness, "you arrived here dead, and now you're alive." His tone softened. "You're a tough man, Senator, and a lucky one. The bullet missed your spine, the major arteries, and—other than a lung—any vital organs. And they revived you very quickly, as the chat we're having suggests."

Kerry closed his eyes. A fathomless gratitude washed over him, which he lacked the strength to express; he felt too overcome by the knowledge that, hours before, he had stopped living.

"Barring the unexpected," O'Malley continued, "you'll be fine. In a couple of days, you'll be standing; in a couple of months, you'll be running. Including for President, if that's what you want, though I've never understood why anyone would." The doctor's voice slowed again. "Even before yesterday."

Kerry did not answer. He lay back on the bed and allowed his soul to catch up with his body. He was alive and his life, and his future, belonged to him again, perhaps more profoundly than before. But he had come too far to sort this out alone.

To Kerry, Clayton seemed slow, almost sluggish, like a man moving underwater. The sheen in his eyes revealed his emotions.

Kerry was so glad to see him that there were no words. Clayton took Kerry's hand in both of his. "You meant to push me out of the way, didn't you?"

Kerry managed to smile. "The plan was to duck behind Ellen Penn," he whispered. "I was using you for leverage."

When Clayton did not smile, Kerry exhaled. "It was a reflex, Clayton. There was no time to *mean* to do anything."

"Then maybe," his friend answered, "that was what happened before. Your 'reflex' was to protect John Musso."

All at once, Kerry felt a terrible weight. In a guttural voice, he asked, "It was *him*, wasn't it?"

Clayton took a chair from a corner and sat next to the bed, as if settling in for a hard conversation. "He was the Boston shooter," he said at last. "They also think he killed a girl who worked for your campaign, the night before. Kate Feeney."

Kerry's stomach tightened. "Kate Feeney," he said. "She was a strawberry blonde, wasn't she?"

"You met her?"

"I think so, yes." Kerry felt a fresh wave of horror, of pity. "God, Clayton, why did he do *that*?"

"They're not sure. Maybe she found out who he was."

Kerry lay back, the weight becoming despair, the memory of a boy coming to a wounded man in a hospital, much like this. "What did I do?" he asked. "God help me, what did *I* do?"

Clayton seemed to sort through his thoughts. "You tried to save him. But he'd already seen so much, sustained so much damage . . ."

"Dammit," Kerry rasped. "You know what I mean."

Clayton's tone grew firm. "You were a prosecutor, pal—not an adoption agency. You'd just been shot, and your wife didn't even want her *own* kids. And John had a great-aunt in Boston. Who seems to have died, unfortunately, a couple of years after he moved."

Kerry turned his head on the pillow. With renewed quiet, he murmured, "But he came after *me*, didn't he. Because I was what he'd needed, and I'd turned him away."

Clayton looked at him steadily. With veiled irony, he answered, "He believed in the sanctity of life."

For Kerry, the words had a resonance beyond John Musso. Once more, they opened up the pain he had lived with for the last two years, the complex world he had occupied the last five days.

Clayton seemed to track his thoughts. "Do you remember what Liam told you after Jamie died? That politics, like rust, never sleeps?"

Jamie, Kerry thought, and then realized that there was now another difference between them: Kerry had survived.

"It still doesn't." Clayton's pause signaled his reluctance to go on. "There are hundreds of people standing beneath that window over there, and millions more who are praying for you—that you'll still run, or simply that you'll live.

"You're a hero again, and a near martyr to anti-abortion fanaticism. All you need to win this primary is to show that you're all right, and say that you still want it." Pausing, Clayton let the implicit question linger, and then he finished quietly: "But you're also a free man."

"How do you mean?"

"You nearly died, Kerry. Recuperation will take some time. No one blames you if you withdraw.

"If you do that, *Newsworld* probably goes away—once you're not a candidate, they don't have much of a story, and the distaste for it goes sky-high. And in four years, or eight years . . ." Clayton shrugged. "Maybe it's a different world.

"Right now, *you're* the only story. But if you decide to run, you and Lara are the story again." His voice lowered. "When you were shot, she tried to get to you. She was with you in the ambulance, the emergency room—"

"How?"

"Because I told them to take her." Clayton's smile flickered. "If I'd known you were going to live . . ."

He let the sentence die there. Once more, Kerry felt the depth of his friend's kindness, his capacity for love.

"Anyhow, Kerry, we're stuck with it. We've concocted some eyewash about a reporter and a campaign answering history's tragic call. Lara phoned in to NBC, so maybe we can gull the others. Maybe I can even back off the Republicans: they might not want to be caught out doing this, not with you so sympathetic, and their probable nominee is a very decent man. But *Cutler*?"

Kerry gazed into Clayton's face. Softly, he asked, "What does *she* say?"

Clayton looked down. "She'll stick to the story, if that's what you want. But to have a prayer of making it work, you can never see her again."

Kerry lay back, his eyes shut.

"I don't expect you to decide now," Clayton said at last. "That wouldn't be human. But you needed to know, before you saw her."

Kerry felt exhaustion overtake him. "I have to rest," he said at last. "Then I want her here."

He heard his friend rise to leave. Kerry opened his eyes. "Find out where Kate Feeney's parents are. When I'm better . . ."

Nodding slowly, Clayton left.

TWO

Lara stopped a few feet from the bed.

There was a nakedness to her expression such as Kerry had never seen before. Though she was still, he could sense that very fiber of her being wanted to touch him.

He held out his hand.

So quickly that it startled and overwhelmed him, she came to the bed and kissed him, gently and for a long time. He closed his eyes, feeling the warmth of her breathe new life into him.

When their mouths parted, he opened his eyes.

Fingers curled, she laid her hand on his cheek, looking into his face. Her own eyes were ravaged with sleeplessness.

"Clayton says you came here with me."

In silent acknowledgment, her eyes shut. Kerry could feel his own pulse.

He swallowed, trying to speak again. "Well," he murmured, "I guess we're out of the closet."

She took his hand in hers and, with the smallest shake of her head, pressed it against the side of her face.

"Lara . . ."

She seemed to shiver. A moist film appeared on her eyelashes; Kerry saw her jaw tense, as if she was determined, despite everything, to say what she had come to say. "If I just go away," she began in a near whisper, "Clayton and I think what's happened may help you out of this . . ." She paused, then finished in a low voice. "Without me, you might still be President."

Despite himself, Kerry felt a desperate impatience, as though there were very few moments left to them. "For once, Lara, tell me how you feel."

She looked past him, seeming to slip far away. Then he saw her shoulders square, and she looked at him with new directness.

"I'm in love with you," she said. "So much that it hurts. No matter what, I'll love you for the rest of my life."

He felt his throat constrict. Gently, she brushed the hair back from his forehead.

"You need to know this," she said at last. "From the beginning, I was drawn to you—more, I realize, than to anyone in my life. And I came to trust you, to feel you were the person I could say anything to, and still be understood. So I started making excuses to see you." She closed her eyes. "That was so frightening for me, Kerry. Not just as a reporter, but because of who I am. I wanted to lie to myself. But I couldn't.

"I felt that before I ever made love with you. After that, the feeling was like a hunger, so deep that it scared me even more. I knew we had to end, *should* end. But I kept making deals with myself, stealing hours, days, weeks." She inhaled, voice becoming thin. "And when it was over, I felt completely hollowed out. It was the hardest thing I've ever had to do. Until now . . ."

He touched her face. "And now?" he asked.

She seemed to gather herself. "Before I answer, *I* need to know something. After all of this, do you still want to be President?"

He hesitated, but only for a moment. "Not if it means never seeing you again. Nothing's worth that."

"But suppose you could have us both." Her voice was firm now, insistent. "No scandal, no abortion—the presidency and me, free and clear. Isn't *that* what you really want?"

He gazed at the white nullity of the ceiling. For a time, the tragedy of John Musso mingled with the trauma of his own near death, making all ambition seem pointless. But then Kerry found a hard kernel of truth, which Lara must already know, that whatever else these things might change, the man within had come to believe that he should be President, and no longer could—for better or worse—believe any less. And, realizing this, he owed Lara nothing less than honesty.

He turned back to her, saying quietly, "I'd have you both."

Once more, she looked away. "Then giving you up is the next hard thing I have to do. Again."

He did not ask why, nor could he quarrel with the justice, or the dignity, of her belief. Instead, he said simply, "That's not a choice you have."

She became quite still, lips parted.

"If it takes giving up the race to be with you, Lara, then I'll give it up." He paused, feeling the rawness in his throat. "Or I'll run, and we can take our chances. I think we're strong enough, but that involves some other things I haven't the right to choose for you. So you decide."

Her eyes misted again. "For both of us?"

"As long as, this time, we're together."

She took both his hands in hers, looking intently into his face. At last, she said with quiet certainty, "Then I guess we're running."

Kerry felt his flesh tingle. "You're sure . . ."

"Yes." Her voice was clear now. "The last time, I decided alone, for both of us. I did what I thought was best. So if we're caught out, I can hold my head up, as long as you can.

"But you did with your life what I thought you should. And now I'm choosing to be part of it." For the first time, Lara smiled. "The worst that can happen to me is that you'll be elected and reelected. At the end, I'll only be thirty-nine. There must be something that used-up First Ladies can do."

Kerry felt a flood of emotions: wonder; belief in her strength of character; a deeper love than he could now express. Then Lara's smile vanished and she shook her head, as though astounded at her own unsteadiness. "I nearly lost you, Kerry. I can't lie to myself anymore."

Watching her, tears came to Kerry's eyes. Then, as he knew he would for as long as he lived, he thought of John Musso, of the incalculable fate that had ended the boy's life, yet now had brought Kerry to this. "How alone he must have felt," Kerry murmured.

From her expression, he knew that Lara understood the complexity of his emotions, how one thought flowed from another. "Tell me," she asked after a time. "If John Musso had lived, would you have wanted *his* life taken?"

"No," he answered. "God, no. Not for me." Touching her cheek, he finished quietly, "But Kate Feeney's parents might feel otherwise."

She looked into his face again, and then kissed his forehead. "I'll go find Clayton," she said.

THREE

In a few terse sentences, Clayton explained to Kit Pace and Frank Wells what Kerry had decided.

The sequence of their expressions mirrored the emotional cross-currents in which Clayton himself had swirled—sheer relief that Kerry had lived; delight at having a campaign to run again; an almost superstitious fear for the candidate's future safety; and then, hearing about Lara, intense distress. "That last one," Frank said in somber tones, "is going to take some work."

"Not all gift horses are free," Clayton answered crisply. "At least Kerry isn't gay anymore."

Frank's contemplative silence made him appear almost professorial. "*If* you set aside the obvious problem," he said at last, "she's smart, she's beautiful, she's caring—"

"And she's Hispanic," Kit interpolated dryly. "On her mother's side."

Despite the difficulties, Clayton found himself watching the others rediscover their pleasure in the compulsive exercise of gift for politics, so fundamental to their natures that they could not hold back. As if reading Clayton's thoughts, Frank gave him a fleeting smile, then sat back with his hands behind his head, speaking in a ruminative tone. "How old is she, Kit—thirty-one? We haven't had anyone that young since Jackie Kennedy . . ."

"Oh," Kit retorted, "I think Lara Costello's a little more substantive."

"Not *too* substantive, I hope."

Kit smiled. "Times change, Frank."

Listening, Clayton had a sense of irony. Perhaps the others hoped that Lara could be managed, but Clayton was already adjusting—with some wariness despite his best wishes for Kerry—to the dawning realization that the Kilcannon campaign, and his relationship to Kerry, now included someone else he must take into account. Lara Costello would have opinions of her own.

"I want you two to draft a press release," Clayton ordered, "saying that Kerry's in the race to stay. Then two more, covering their relationship—a 'his' and a 'hers,' for their approval. Feel free to be creative."

The gravity of the risk showed in Frank's gray eyes again. "I guess you—and he—know we're inviting *Newsworld* in again. Just when we've gotten a breather."

"*They* know," Clayton answered. "Very well."

Frank gave an elaborate shrug of fatalism. "Then we work with what we have."

"And lucky to have him. On any terms."

Clayton's deeper meaning seemed almost to shame him. "Oh, I know," Frank said softly. "I know."

There was silence. Pensive, Frank propped his chin on folded hands, and then looked up at Clayton. "There's still an election tomorrow," he said. "Think you can get Kerry on his feet?"

At two-thirty, ample time to make the evening news, Kit Pace appeared in the makeshift pressroom.

It was even hotter and more crowded than before. But this time Nate was in the front row, next to Lee McAlpine and Sara Sax.

"He's still in," Lee predicted. "That's what it's about."

No, Nate thought, *he's not. But only I know why.*

Looking out over the room, Kit Pace seemed to ignore him.

"I have a statement to read," she began, "from Senator Kilcannon.

" 'Before I discuss my plans, I'd like to give my heartfelt thanks for all the prayers and good wishes that have come to me this past day. I can never express how grateful I am to receive them, and to be *able* to receive them . . .' "

"He's bowing out," Sara murmured.

" 'I also want you to know,' " Kit read calmly on, " 'that I'm in this race to the end. My intention, as it always was, is to win the Democratic nomination for President of the United States . . .' "

"Jesus," Nate murmured.

It was hard, Clayton thought, to see Kerry so deeply weary, to see the tube still running from his chest.

"The reception desk is like a mortuary," Clayton told him. "There're enough floral arrangements to bury all of Vailsburg."

Kerry did not smile. "Oh, I remember," he answered softly. "From when Jamie died."

Clayton watched his face. With equal quiet, he said, "You weren't meant to die, Kerry. You were meant for other things." His voice turned businesslike. "There are hundreds of phone calls from people who are thrilled you're staying in. Including several from the chairman of the DNC—"

Kerry gave a harsh laugh, wincing at the pain of it. *"Dick's* toady. How many times has he tried to cut my throat?"

"Well, he loves you *now,*" Clayton said sardonically. " 'Kerry, we hardly knew ye . . .' And, of course, there was a call from Dick himself."

Kerry nodded. "I've been expecting that."

"He wants to talk with you. Whenever you're up to it."

Kerry turned and, for a long time, gazed out the window at a blue patch of sky. "Can you dial it for me?" he asked.

To Kerry, Dick Mason sounded numbed by the savagery of their last encounter and by the events that had intervened, so threatening to his life's ambition.

"I still won't campaign," the Vice President said. "Not until you're up and at it."

"No mercy given," Kerry answered lightly. "And none expected. Except on certain subjects." His voice slowed. "As far as I'm concerned, Dick, you should continue your campaign. It's wrong whenever something like this stops the process."

There was silence on the other end, Mason taking in the emptiness of Kerry's offer: he must know too well, as Kerry did, that to campaign now would lose him votes—assuming that the voters, focused on Kerry's recovery, noticed him at all. "About this other business," Mason finally said. "Yours and mine. I mean to stick to the agreement." He finished in a lower voice: "I'm very sorry that ever happened."

Kerry glanced at Clayton, sitting across the room. "I understand," he said to Mason.

He did, of course. Mason was preserving his place in line, hoping to secure Kerry's forbearance if, by an agency other than Nate Cutler, the affair with Lara brought Kerry down. It was, Kerry thought, the usual self-interested selflessness that goes unremarked in politics—even if Kerry had not, for the next few months, some potential need for Dick's support.

"Give my love to Jeannie," Kerry told him. "As ever."

Clayton took the telephone from his hand. "So you've 'forgiven' him."

"Of course. Just not retroactively."

Though Kerry said this with a smile, Clayton could read his eyes. Should Kerry become President, Dick Mason was finished: for what the Vice President had done to Lara, there would be no forgiveness. Clayton felt himself smiling back—his friend was still recognizably himself, and comfortably short of sainthood.

"If you really want to stick it to Dick," he observed, "Frank Wells has a suggestion."

At five-thirty, the time set in Kit Pace's hasty announcement, Kerry tried to stand up.

The pain ripped through him. He gave a short, involuntary

cry, and white flashes blurred his vision. His legs felt shaky, uncertain.

Frank O'Malley grasped one arm, Clayton the other. "You don't have to do this," the doctor told him.

Kerry steadied himself. *Politics,* Liam had said, *like rust, never sleeps.*

He wished that Lara were here. But, until tomorrow, she was staying out of sight. "I'll manage," he murmured to O'Malley.

The three men inched toward the window, the tube in Kerry's chest obscured by his robe. Behind them, a nurse carried the pole on which the tube ended with a plastic bag.

"They need to see you," Frank Wells had advised. "To know that you're able to function."

About the window itself, Kerry realized, he had been profoundly incurious. He had no idea how many floors up he was; though he was touched by the knowledge that countless strangers cared for him, even loved him in a way, the idea of hundreds keeping vigil below had seemed abstract, surreal.

"Which floor are we on?" he asked O'Malley.

"The third."

They reached the window.

There *were* hundreds of them, spread across the lawn— young and old, men and women, of all races, wearing everything from suits to jeans. Beside him, Clayton spoke so quietly that only Kerry could hear.

"They're not here for *him,* Kerry. They're here for you."

A ragged cheer rose, audible through the glass, and then some in the crowd began waving.

Kerry blinked. Suddenly this was not about Dick Mason, or even about votes.

Raising his arm, Kerry waved back.

Below, Nate Cutler watched him—a slight figure, badly injured, but clearly still himself. Nate would be less than human, he told himself, not to feel the elation around him. Or to be haunted by the profile he saw on the roof above, a Secret Service sharpshooter.

"Amazing." The admiration in Lee McAlpine's voice was close to warmth. "These people don't miss a trick."

"It's Mason who's dead," Nate answered, and knew, as soon as he said it, that this was true.

Above them, Kilcannon vanished from the window.

It was time, Nate decided, to return Jane Booth's beeper message. He drifted to the sidewalk; dialing, he took in the city traffic, the line of police cars parked in front.

"Hello," Jane answered.

"It's Nate. I'm on a cell phone."

There was a brief pause. "There's a meeting tomorrow," she told him. "In New York. I want you to catch the red-eye. Now that he's in for good, we need to decide what to do."

The Campaign

Day Seven

ONE

Election day dawned clear and bright.

By nine o'clock, Clayton arrived with the news that turnout was heavy across the state. Turning to Kerry, Lara said, "That's good for you, I think."

Kerry felt the first glow of hope. "This may really be happening, Lara."

Looking from Kerry to Lara, Clayton handed each of them copies of two press releases. Perusing his, Kerry stopped to watch Lara read one, smile, then study the second more closely. "Mine should be issued through the news division," she said to Clayton.

Clayton raised his eyebrows. "Have you told them yet?"

"Yes." Glancing at Kerry, Lara smiled again. "There was a very long silence."

Clayton shrugged. "At least today it'll be story number two. After all, this election decides the nomination."

"Timing," Lara said, "is everything."

Watching her, Kerry wondered again about the wisdom of their decision. She had been a journalist since college and now, abruptly, might take a path quite different, one she had never wanted, under a scrutiny so intense that most would find it withering. But this was no time to say so; with seeming serenity, Lara had taken a pencil from her purse and begun to make changes in the margins of the press release.

It was five o'clock in Manhattan—three hours later than in California—when the press releases arrived at the conference room.

For the last two hours, the conferees—Nate; Jane Booth; Sheila Kahn, the investigative reporter; the managing editor, Courtney Wynn; and Martin Zimmer, *Newsworld*'s owner and publisher—had parsed the facts in painstaking detail. Not even Jane had tried to be insouciant or witty. There was too much at stake—the character of *Newsworld*; the career of Kerry Kilcannon; the question of what journalism now was, and should be. Nate could not yet discern what the group would decide.

Sheila passed out the releases without comment. In the collective silence, Nate began reading.

"NBC News," the first began, "announced that reporter Lara Costello had requested and received an indefinite leave of absence.

" 'Between 1996 and 1998,' Ms. Costello said, 'I served as a Capitol Hill correspondent for the *New York Times*. During that period, I formed both a professional relationship and a personal friendship with Senator Kerry Kilcannon. I deeply valued all of that.

" 'The events of the last few days, and my response to them, have now made it very clear to me that my feelings for Kerry Kilcannon go beyond friendship. The senator has found them enlightening in a similar way. It is equally plain, therefore, that I cannot continue to report on this campaign, or otherwise perform duties which might raise questions regarding my objectivity, or that of NBC News.

" 'In future weeks, I mean to be with Senator Kilcannon as he recovers, and to sort out what seems right for me to do. I expect that process to be enlightening as well.' "

Smiling quizzically, Nate turned to the second press release.

It quoted Kerry Kilcannon's reaction. " 'If enlightenment takes getting shot,' " it said in its entirety, " 'I'm just glad it worked the first time.' "

Nate looked across at Sheila. "That's *all*?" he asked.

"That's all."

Nate reread the sentence and then began to laugh. "Too good—God, it really is *too* good."

Courtney Wynn kept staring at the releases, unsmiling. "There goes one leg of the story," he finally said. "The ethically compromised reporter. At least *in futuro*." He turned to Sheila Kahn. "How's Costello's reporting from two years ago?"

Kahn, too, looked dazed. "Bulletproof," she answered. "Just like her campaign stuff. She may have done him favors, but it doesn't show."

With the suppressed nervousness of the frustrated smoker, Jane Booth hastily finished her can of Diet Coke. "The competition's caught up with us now," she said in an agitated tone. "Tomorrow they'll be all over this, trying to ferret out what 'personal friendship' means."

"And they'll probably find what we did," Wynn replied. "A lot of detail that looks very telling but doesn't quite get us behind closed doors. And Kilcannon's ex-wife won't help *anyone*, it sounds like."

Booth gave him a pointed look. "You forgot the counselor's memo."

In the uncomfortable silence, Courtney Wynn contemplated the table. Everyone knew that his second marriage had begun as an affair with an ex-colleague, precipitating the end of his first; Wynn was too self-aware not to feel the irony, and too good a journalist not to fight it.

"They're lying about an affair," Nate told the group. "Even if we can't prove it. But, to me, this isn't about adultery—there's too much of it around, and we've got no evidence that Kilcannon's pathological. It's about whether Lara Costello aborted Kerry Kilcannon's child, and what role Kilcannon played in that. And now that they're going to be America's sweethearts, the story takes on a certain 'yuk' factor—" Cutting himself off, he gazed at Sheila Kahn across the conference table. "Do you have any sense this counselor's crazy enough to have made the whole thing up?"

"Crazy? Sure. Who else would do what she's done? But I don't think she just made it up."

With a tentative air, Martin Zimmer leaned forward: he was the rich amateur who had purchased the others' talent and, for all his success on Wall Street, they seemed to intimidate him. "Isn't this situation," he asked, "the reason you're still supposed to need *two* sources? You've shown me an affair, I'm pretty sure, and I think we know Costello was at the clinic. But did she tell anyone besides this woman—with ties to the Christian Commitment—that the baby was Kilcannon's?"

Jane Booth frowned. "The circumstances argue for authenticity," she said. "It's like confessing to a priest, or a lawyer."

"Do you want Dick Mason to be President?" Zimmer asked her bluntly. "Or whoever the Republicans finally choose?"

Jane looked genuinely irritated. "As political editor," she answered, "I don't want *anyone*."

"Well, you'd be choosing *someone*. Just not Kilcannon." Zimmer turned to Nate. "We're sure Mason planted this, right?"

Nate nodded. "The debate made that clear."

"That's what Nat Schlesinger says." Zimmer shifted in his chair, more subdued. "We had another call from him—Courtney and I. The question he asked is this: Do we torpedo Kerry Kilcannon on the basis of a single source, provided by Dick Mason?"

Nate watched Courtney Wynn; without moving, Wynn subtly seemed to disassociate himself from his publisher, so that no one would think he was carrying water for the Kilcannon campaign. But Schlesinger's question, Nate had to acknowledge, was an excellent one.

Before anyone tried to answer it, Wynn's secretary arrived with a message on a slip of paper.

Wynn went to a corner, picked up the telephone, and had a brief conversation while the others listened. Turning, he explained, "That was a friend at ABC. They've done their first exit polling: they can't release the results yet, but it looks like Kilcannon's ahead."

Across from Nate, Martin Zimmer raised his eyebrows.

"This is out there," Jane Booth said at last. "And it's like the sword of Damocles. What if the Republicans use it to take Kilcannon down? How do we justify not printing it?"

Courtney Wynn gave her a measured look. "That depends on who *else* wants to print it," he responded. "The Republicans can't do it alone, any more than Mason could. Even if they want to. So *my* question is this: Who sets our standards—*us* or somebody else? And is this the kind of story *Newsworld* wants to run—at least without more than we have now? Or have we become Matt Drudge?"

Nate gazed down at the press releases. Alone among the others, he could sense what the laconic words had cost two people, and how much more their risk might cost them yet. Then Martin Zimmer broke into his thoughts. "I don't like this story," he said simply. "Is there anyone here who does?"

Jane Booth grimaced. "This whole thing smells," she persisted. "Clayton Slade let Costello in the ambulance because *he* knows the truth. And I don't think anything that's happened—not the shooting, not this meretricious story they've ginned up—cures the ethical problem of a reporter warning a candidate about a story. Especially when *they're* the story. Jesus, what kind of journalistic standards are we tolerating here?" Facing Nate, she demanded, for Zimmer's benefit, "*You're* satisfied she went to Kilcannon, right?"

Nate nodded. "Or to his people."

"But can you prove it?" Wynn asked them both.

Jane's eyes narrowed. "No," Nate answered. "But you could pick up the vibrations."

" 'Vibrations,' " Zimmer repeated.

Jane turned to Nate again. "After I asked you to follow her," she asked, "did you see anything?"

Nate hesitated. This was her final hope, he knew, of keeping the discussion alive.

"No," he said at last. "But then who would be that dumb?"

TWO

It was almost over.

By seven o'clock, Jack Sleeper had called Kerry to say that

his numbers forecast a substantial victory. "An hour to go," Kerry reminded him—at eight o'clock, the polls would close, and speculation would be overtaken by fact.

When Kerry hung up, Lara asked, "Did you reach Kate Feeney's parents?"

He nodded. "Do you know what her mother told me? That they'd gotten out to vote for me today. I suppose it's a way of keeping her alive."

"If that's so," Lara answered, "then it meant all the more to hear from you." She wished there were more comfort she could give him: for the rest of his life, Lara knew, Kerry would be shadowed by the thought that he had abandoned John Musso and thus set Kate's death in motion.

Kerry had fallen quiet again. "I need to see Peter Lake," he said at last. "Before my mother comes."

"I'll go look for him," Lara answered.

She found Peter in the hospital cafeteria, drinking coffee by himself. Lara hesitated, but only for a moment: however adrift she felt, unsure of her new life and of what it held for her, she was discovering a relief, close to joy, in her freedom to acknowledge Kerry.

Peter looked up at her and smiled. "Big day." Briefly, he paused. "All the way around, I guess."

Lara nodded. "Kerry wants to thank you. Now I can, too." She paused, as well, and then returned Peter's smile. "I guess it's a good thing that you're the Secret Service. Still."

Peter's grin betrayed his own deep relief that Kerry had survived. "Very secret," he replied.

By ten o'clock, there were three of them sitting with Kerry—Lara, Clayton, and Mary Kilcannon.

Kerry had not wanted his mother to come until now, Lara knew; he had feared that the sight of him so badly injured would be a traumatic reminder of Jamie, and of Mary's own blessing for Liam's wish that Kerry enter politics. But Mary's gratitude that he had lived shone from her still-handsome face and, with only mild bewilderment, she seemed to accept Lara's presence as God's gift to her remaining son.

We both have Catholic mothers, Lara thought with a certain

amusement—sooner or later, it would occur to Mary that Kerry was too decent to ask Meg for an annulment, and therefore Kerry could not remarry within the Church. But that worry was a luxury which would come only when Mary could take her son's recovery for granted. On this night, all she seemed to feel was love, nurtured for a lifetime.

"Kerry was so precious to me," she murmured to Lara. "Always."

Lara nodded. "I know."

With the others, Kerry watched the returns come in.

They were sluggish—as always, it seemed, Los Angeles County was slow in reporting. To fill the time, CNN showed a tape of the attempted assassination.

Mary Kilcannon turned away; Lara gripped Kerry's hand. As did Clayton, Kerry became quite still.

On the screen, in slow motion, Kerry pushed Clayton aside and reached out to John Musso. Watching, Kerry felt his stomach churn.

"Well," Clayton said softly, "you did it again."

"Among California voters," Bill Schneider's voice intoned, *"Senator Kilcannon seems to have benefited from relief at his survival and admiration for his effort to protect those around him . . ."*

It was the last way, Kerry thought with distaste, that he had wanted to win this primary. But there was this, he supposed: out of whatever impulse he had acted, this time he had not failed.

The film clip froze on John Musso's agonized face.

Silent, Kerry remembered a damaged young boy, then another boy.

What, he suddenly wondered, had helped him rise above his own abusive father? The answer both made him grateful and added to the weight of his failings—the difference must surely be the concern of a loving mother, the quiet presence of Liam Dunn. And, perhaps, the cautionary example of his older brother, so determined to escape Michael Kilcannon that it consumed him.

Suddenly the picture changed: a newswoman spoke from Kerry's Los Angeles headquarters, surrounded by celebrants.

"CNN," she began, *"has now projected that Senator Kerry Kilcannon will win the California presidential primary over Vice President Dick Mason by a margin of sixty-two to thirty-eight percent. This means that Senator Kilcannon will likely win all of California's delegates, and gives him a virtual lock on his party's nomination . . ."*

"All *right*," Clayton said with quiet elation. "We've done it."

"The senator's press secretary, Kit Pace, is expected here shortly to read a statement from Senator Kilcannon . . ."

Lara's fingers curled tightly around Kerry's. "You're going to be President, Kerry. I can feel it."

Kerry felt too much to answer.

"We understand that the senator is resting comfortably, watching the returns with his mother, Mary Kilcannon, and a few close friends . . ."

If only Liam Dunn could be here, Kerry thought. And Jamie.

This was not false sentiment, he knew. He and Jamie would have much to share now: Kerry had come a long way since, by a tragic accident, his brother had cleared the path that Kerry was meant to follow. Now Kerry had traveled it, and they stood on equal ground.

"Senator Kilcannon's victory," the reporter continued, *"follows his acknowledgment of a relationship with NBC correspondent Lara Costello, who—until last month—had been stationed overseas . . ."*

"I was planning all along," Lara murmured, "to launder us through Bosnia. I'm just sorry that it took two years."

Turning, Kerry gave her a quiet sideways smile. *"Kit Pace,"* the reporter went on, *"has declined further comment, except to say, 'Even candidates and correspondents get to have a life.'"*

"Now that," Clayton remarked, "really *is* news."

Softly, Kerry laughed, and then became pensive.

Soon it would begin again: the travel, the speeches, the crowds, the unceasing calculation, the constant struggle to remain—as Liam had—a decent man in a complex world. He should savor this moment while he could.

Quiet, he gazed at his mother, who had given him so much; at Clayton, his closest friend; at Lara, to whom, someday, he would be closer yet. Then she smiled at him, and Kerry realized that, no matter what came, he was something James Kilcannon had never been: deeply lucky, profoundly blessed. And that their one safe place would be with each other and, in time, their children.

Tomorrow, Kerry knew, he would tell her this. For now, it was enough that she was here.

ACKNOWLEDGMENTS

The least I owe the many people who helped me is to start by separating research and imagination. This is not a roman à clef but a work of fiction, all the essential elements of which I developed in 1995, before interviewing anyone or following the recent presidential campaign. To the extent that any events in the campaign paralleled my preconceived plot, that is a coincidence. Similarly, the book was finished by the end of September 1997 and prefigures, rather than reflects, any political events thereafter.

Equally fundamental, while I have grounded my story in the context of such ongoing issues as abortion, gun control, race, campaign reform, and the role of the press in reporting on the private lives of public officials, the positions, personalities, and attitudes of my central characters are not those of contemporary political figures. To me, this is a matter not only of fairness to men and women who put up with enough in real life but also of novelistic principle; in fiction, I believe, the deepest insight combines an authentic background with realistic, but invented, people. Nor is this book intended as a partisan comment; rather, successful or not, my intention is to provoke thought.

Finally, and I hope equally obviously, the attitudes expressed by Kerry Kilcannon do not reflect—in fact, frequently contradict—those of the political leaders and advisers who helped enhance my understanding of Kerry's world. None of them "approved" the book or are in any way responsible for its contents. Rather, Kerry's views reflect my sense of where his background and psychology would take him, my assessment of the possible components of an insurgent candidacy, and, at times, some biases of my own. For the book's politics, as well as any errors, the buck stops with me.

That said, I'm very grateful to all those who provided such good advice in the midst of their own busy lives:

A number of people from the real world of politics helped with my imagined one, including Rich Bond, William Cohen, Peter Fenn, Marlin Fitzwater, Barry Gottehrer, Tom King, Peter Knight, Jim Lauer, Susan Levine, Christine Matthews, John McCain, Bill McInturff, Bob Squier, George Stephanopoulos, Joe Trippi, Donna Victoria, Nelson Warfield, and, in particular, Mandy Grunwald. And Senator Bob Dole and his campaign staff, including Steve Duchesne and Jenny Ryder, graciously allowed me to tag along.

Several journalists schooled me in the rudiments of campaign coverage and in the complex of issues surrounding whether Kerry Kilcannon's private life deserved a public airing. Special thanks to Lorraine Adams, Candy Crowley, David Finkel, Blaine Harden, Jill Zuckman, and, above all, Paul Taylor. And, in particular, the book's journalistic aspects were enriched by the late Susan Yoachum, political editor for the *San Francisco Chronicle*, whose intelligence, wit, and insight reminded me of one of the real privileges of writing— meeting people like Susan.

Others who shared their knowledge included novelist Maynard Thomson; psychiatrists Ken Gottlieb and Rodney Shapiro; psychologist Margaret Coggins; Carl Meyer and, especially, Terry Samway of the Secret Service; surgeon Dr. Bernard Alpert; Elizabeth Birch of the Human Rights Campaign; Robert Walker of Handgun Control, Inc.; Robert Allen, writer, teacher, editor of *The Black Scholar*, and a director of the Oakland Men's Project; and Susan Breall, head of the domestic violence unit of the San Francisco District Attorney's Office. As always, I could not have done without the perceptive comments of Anna Chavez, Fred Hill, and Philip Rotner, the consistent insight of my gifted assistant, Alison Thomas, and the day-by-day involvement of my wife, Laurie. And many thanks to Knopf and Ballantine—in particular, to Sonny Mehta—for their enthusiasm for, and encouragement of, a project so different from my other recent work.

California has a political and social dynamic all its own. I am grateful to prosecutor Al Giannini, campaign worker Lorrie Johnson, San Francisco Treasurer Susan Leal, advance specialist Walter McGuire, political adviser Phil Perry, and demographer Rosemary Roach for their advice and, especially, to political consultant Clint Reilly for all his help and time. Similarly, Newark is a unique place, and Kerry Kilcannon had a distinctive early life. Many thanks to Dennis Caufield, Father Pat Donohue, Tom Giblin, Denis Lenihan, William Marks, and Al Zach, all of whom helped me fill in the blanks.

Some writers inspired me without knowing it, by writing. I first read Jack Newfield's memoir of Robert Kennedy nearly thirty years ago and remain struck by its vivid portrait of a complex and contradictory man, and by its effort to discern the connection between personal psychology and political beliefs. If there is a model for my approach to Kerry Kilcannon, it resides not in any living politician but in Newfield's portrait of one we lost too young. Similarly, Hedrick Smith's *The Power Game* was instructive on the problems of public life in Washington, D.C. And by writing thoughtfully about abortion, John Leo, Ann Roiphe, Edward Tivnan, George Will, and Naomi Wolff helped me feel my way through this difficult subject—to the satisfaction of almost no one, I am sure.

Finally, there are George Bush and Ron Kaufman. A few years ago, to my surprise and delight, I received a kind note from President Bush—a man I have long admired—about *Degree of Guilt*. When I conceived of this project, I wrote him, asking if he might help me understand what it feels like to run for President. His gracious response led to a meeting, much generous advice and help, and a friendship with President and Mrs. Bush that has been one of the great pleasures of Laurie's and my recent life.

Perhaps President Bush's biggest favor was to introduce me to Ron Kaufman, the President's political director during his White House years. Ron knows as much about politics as anyone in Washington, and many hours of his advice, assistance, warm friendship, and good company have made all the work worthwhile. So that President Bush and Ron don't get blamed for *this* book, the *next* book is for them.